Far To Go

Julie Ellis

Far To Go

KENSINGTON BOOKS

KENSINGTON BOOKS are published by

Kensington Publishing Corp.
850 Third Avenue
New York, NY 10022

Library of Congress Card Catalog Number: 94-073291
ISBN 0-8217-4854-8

First Printing: March, 1995

Printed in the United States of America

For Louise Nielsen and her fellow volunteers
at the Animal Rescue Fund of the Hamptons,
who provide such dedicated and compassionate care
for the abandoned animals of the area.

ACKNOWLEDGMENTS

I would like to thank the staffs of the New York Public Library, the Lincoln Center and the Mid-Manhattan branches. My special gratitude to the staff of the Periodicals Division, Second Floor, of the Mid-Manhattan branch, who've been so gracious and helpful in filling my myriad requests for microfilm.

My special thanks, too, to the wonderful staff at the Montauk Library, who've tracked down difficult-to-find research books through their inter-library connections. And to Barbara Metzger, who has directed me to special sources that would have otherwise eluded me.

My thanks, also, to the Microfilm Division of the New York University Law Library. And, as always, my thanks to my daughter Susan for diligent research assistance and word processing services—and to my son Richard of Sentinel Copy, Inc., for so imaginatively handling my endless copying and binding, which lent order to my research material.

One

Small, dark-haired Fran Goldman—in a sapphire cashmere sweater set that reflected the astonishing blue of her eyes—stared at the scrawny eight-year-old who was reaching eagerly for a half pint of milk she extended across the serving counter. Free milk was distributed in the school lunchroom each noon to needy students. At rare intervals since she'd received her BA in journalism at the University of Georgia last May, Fran filled in for her mother as a volunteer. A dozen years ago—in 1925, a year after the Jewish Ladies' Aid Society began to give free milk to needy students in Columbus—the Jewish Sisterhood of Bellevue undertook this philanthropy.

Fran dreaded these occasions. She felt sick with guilt at seeing the pale, shabbily dressed children waiting in line for their free milk. Their parents—if they were lucky enough to have jobs—worked in the cotton mills in this one-industry town. As long as she could remember, her father had talked about the horrible conditions in the mills. *"And they won't get any better until they get smart enough to unionize."* But Dad always said that unions would never come into Georgia cotton mills.

Fran knew the nation—the world—was in the midst of a painful Depression, though this was hardly part of her daily life. Josiah and Ida Goldman and their daughter lived in a fine two-story brick Colonial in the best part of town. Her mother had Lily to cook and clean five days a week, Fran acknowledged. Daddy was proud of his late-model gray Packard—which he'd taught her to drive despite her mother's objections. Last night at dinner Daddy was railing about the report in the *Bellevue Enquirer* that with the arrival of 1937 there were strong signs the Depression was letting up.

"Tell that to the families trying to live on relief," he'd said contemptuously. "The everyday struggles get hidden away in a pretty little town like this—but the desperation is there. *We* just don't see it. We think it just happens in the big cities—not here in Bellevue."

"Jo, why do you always have to talk like that at the dinner table?" her mother scolded. "We give every week to the Salvation Army and the Milk Fund and the Men's Soup Kitchen. I refuse to feel guilty because our lifestyle hasn't changed much," Ida Goldman said defiantly.

"With the kind of store I run—appealing to the ladies with fine tastes and matching bank accounts—we hardly know there's a Depression," he acknowledged. Daddy was proud of Goldman's, Fran thought—the best ladies shop in town. "The rich cry," he said with a chuckle, "but they continue to buy."

"Fran, you tell your mother we're sorry about her laryngitis," Mrs. Meyers intruded on her reverie. "We hope she'll be feeling up to our usual Thursday bridge group."

"Yes, ma'am, I'll tell her," Fran smiled politely, pulling her gaze away from the eight-year-old with the poignant smile now drinking her milk with an air of quiet pleasure.

Fran was relieved when she could get away from the milk line. She was glad that Mrs. Kline had not been on the serving committee today. Mrs. Kline and her mother were trying so hard, she thought in distaste, to bring her and Joe Kline together. So she was twenty-one and single— why was that a disgrace? She didn't *want* to get married. She wanted to do something special with her life.

Mother married Daddy right out of high school—then waited fourteen years to have her first and only child. Why couldn't Mother understand that girls didn't rush to get married these days? This was 1937. The only reason Mother had agreed to her going off to college in Athens was because she figured it was a happy hunting ground for a husband who'd have a profession. A Jewish husband.

Daddy wanted her to become a teacher. Mother harbored romantic ideas about her becoming a concert pianist. It was hard to convince her mother—even after five years of piano lessons—that she'd never make it to the concert stage. She'd chosen a degree in journalism because she had envisioned herself digging up stories that would turn the world around. In Bellevue she couldn't even land a job on the Woman's Page of the local newspaper.

She ought to stop by the newspaper and talk to Mr. Edison again. He kept saying that an opening on the paper would come up soon. He said that because Daddy was a heavy advertiser. The only job Mr. Edison would consider giving her would be as Woman's Page reporter—and Miss Effie would probably stay on that till she was eighty-five.

Fran strolled through the brisk cool of the February day with recurrent frustration. Her life was just standing still. Daddy wouldn't even let her work as a saleslady at the store. *"You'd be taking a job away from somebody else who needs it."* Working as a reporter would be all right in his eyes, she thought indulgently. But to work in the family's store would look as though he couldn't provide for his family. What he and Mother wanted to provide right now was a big fancy wedding at the synagogue and a wedding banquet at the Harmony Club.

She walked into the offices of the *Bellevue Enquirer,* asked the receptionist—who knew her by now, she thought wryly—if she might see Mr. Edison.

"He's with somebody," the receptionist said, inspecting her expensive cashmere sweater set and matching skirt with wistful admiration. The outfit cost—retail—more than the receptionist earned in a week. "But you can wait if you like."

"I'll wait," Fran told her. It would please her mother that she'd talked to Mr. Edison again about a job.

She sat on the sofa and reached for a copy of the *Literary Digest.* Maybe she ought to talk to Mother and Daddy again about trying for a job in Atlanta. Mother would get hysterical, of course. *"All that driving every day? I'd be a nervous wreck."*

A door down the hall opened. Fran heard Mr. Edison talking heatedly with someone about the efforts to unionize the mills in Bellevue.

"Those bastards from up in New York walked right into Baker Mill Village last night and started up with how bad they were being treated. Baker security guards broke it up soon as they realized what was happening."

"They're a bunch of lousy communists," the other man denounced. "We've got three of the mill workers—who kind of liked what they heard—down in the jail. How do those rabble-rousers have the nerve to come into this town and set up an office to recruit members? Who the hell rented them space?"

Mr. Edison walked his companion to the door, then turned to Fran with a courtly smile. She managed to hide her rage over what she had overheard, smiled sweetly in return.

"You're looking beautiful, as always, Fran. Come into my office and tell me what you've been up to these days."

Fran knew he wouldn't offer her a job. He was just being nice because Daddy ran regular ads in the newspaper every week. They talked for a few minutes, then she left the newspaper office and walked without any real direction for a few minutes. She was absorbed by the discussion she had heard between the two men. Some strangers had come down from New York to try to unionize the mill workers. Daddy said it could never happen here. But maybe it could. Maybe she could help. That would be doing something special with her life.

It shouldn't be hard to find out where the union organizers had set up headquarters, she reasoned, excitement soaring in her. It would be a storefront—not on the two blocks where the rents were high but at either end. Churning with anticipation she strode in the direction of Main Street, divided by a beautifully landscaped island that offered benches for those who cared to sit.

She discovered her objective at the northern end of Main Street— where a shocking number of stores remained vacant in the terrible economy that afflicted the entire country. A rumple-haired man in his early thirties sat behind the one desk in the narrow store that had been for rent for at least three years. A collection of circulars had been attached to the wall behind him. She suspected—rightly—that he was the sole recruiter who had been assigned to Bellevue.

She walked inside and with her most charming "Southern belle" smile introduced herself. The organizer said his name was Hank Weinstein and he was from New York. Fighting self-consciousness and a rare attack of shyness, Fran explained that she was eager to be useful in his campaign to unionize mills.

"This is a tough racket." Hank Weinstein seemed simultaneously astonished, amused and touched by her offer. "It's no place for a gently reared young lady like you."

"Don't you have women working in your organization?" Fran challenged, color staining her high cheekbones.

"Not in the Deep South," he admitted. "At least, not yet."

"I heard that three mill workers were arrested last night at a demonstration at the Baker Mill," she pursued. "And that they are in jail. Just because they approved of what was being said. That's outrageous—this is a free country!"

"I don't know that you could call it a demonstration," he said, his smile rueful. "The mill owners' goons came charging in when I was talking with maybe twenty or twenty-five of the workers. But yes, they're in jail." His eyes were somber as he considered this.

"What are you going to do about it?" Fran demanded.

"I tried to bail them out this morning," he told her. "We don't have the kind of money they're asking. It's rough—but we run into this."

"I'll go over and talk to the police chief," Fran decided. "Folks here can be hostile to strangers."

"Honey, we all appreciate your consideration," he assured her, "but the police aren't going to listen to you. They—"

"They just might," Fran broke in sweetly—her sharp mind in high gear. "I'm going over there right now. I'll let you know what happens." It was *important* to get those men out of jail.

Hank Weinstein tried to dissuade her from this quixotic effort. She refused to be dissuaded.

"I'll talk to you later," she promised as she strode from the tiny union headquarters. "I've got a plan."

At the local police station Fran approached Chief Atkins with the same smile she'd used when she went there to sell Camp Fire Girl cookies in earlier years. But he gaped in shock when she explained that her objective today was to secure the release of the three mill workers arrested last night.

"I considered it my duty to come over and tell you what I'd heard," she explained politely. "A classmate of mine from journalism school is working on one of those tabloids up in New York. You *know* what they're like," she said pointedly. "Well, Claire is visiting her family in Atlanta, and she drove over to have lunch with me. She heard about some ugliness at Baker Mill Village last night—and she's all set to do some awful story about the Bellevue police and the mill owners mistreating helpless workers—"

"That's not true!" Chief Atkins exploded. "We were just—"

"I'm sure it's all a pack of lies," Fran soothed, "but Claire is determined to make it a big story. You know how those New York newspapers treat us down here in Georgia—as though we were all white trash. She went shopping at Rich's with her aunt, then she's driving down here to talk to you. If you just send those mill workers on their way, then she'll have no story to write about," Fran wound up in an aura of triumph.

"Well, yeah—" The chief was struggling to accept the situation. She could see the wheels turning in his head. The police of Bellevue had no desire to be splashed across the front page of a New York tabloid. "Thank you for tipping us off," he said gratefully. He was on his feet now. "It's all been a little misunderstanding. I'll release the men right now."

"That's smart of you, Chief Atkins," Fran said, her sapphire eyes seeming to glow in admiration. "I knew you'd handle it right. And you'll be sure to call the mill superintendent and explain it was all an awful mistake? Let's don't give them a chance to say the Bellevue police cost them their jobs."

"I'll call," he agreed grimly.

Fran left the police station and walked to the corner. On the pretense of inspecting the contents of a shoe store window, she waited to see if Atkins was, indeed, releasing the three mill workers. Within minutes the men were charging from the police station—their gait unnaturally swift. Humming under her breath, Fran headed back for the union organizer's headquarters.

Hank Weinstein glanced up from his portable typewriter as Fran walked into the store.

"Chief Atkins released the men," she reported. "The last I saw of them they were headed for the Baker Mill. He's going to phone the mill office and tell them it was all a terrible mistake. The workers will get their jobs back."

Hank leaned back in his chair and grinned at her in relief.

"I don't know what kind of magic you pulled off—but you are something special!"

Fran knew it was important not to let her parents know she was working with the union organizer from New York. It was easy to fabricate reasons for her absence from the house. There was always some party that she was supposedly attending. Bellevue social life had hardly been affected by the Depression—that is, in their financial bracket. And while Jews were not accepted as members of the country club, those with the right credentials were accepted as guests of members.

She knew how to type—a skill Hank welcomed. She covered the telephone whenever he went to nearby towns to try to arouse mill workers there. She joined him in distributing circulars in the three mill villages on the outskirts of Bellevue.

Meanwhile, in Bellevue the mill owners were livid at the efforts to bring a union into town. At Hank's instigation a crew of two men and a woman arrived from New York to join in his efforts. Tensions were reaching the boiling point, with a few mill employees determined to force a change in their working conditions.

On an evening when her parents were driving to Atlanta for a performance of the Metropolitan Opera, Fran invited the union crew to the house for coffee and conversation. She had never felt so alive, she thought as they gathered in the elegant living room of the Goldman house and talked with electrifying intensity about the sordid conditions in the cotton mills.

"I couldn't believe what was happening until I saw it myself," Sybil O'Reilly said. "I don't mean just the awful working and living conditions of the mill workers in the old established mills—which are bad enough. I'm talking about all the new mills that are being opened up down here by newcomers from other parts of the country. They're being lured here by greedy southern towns with promises of cheap 'white Anglo-Saxon labor and no unions to worry about.' "

"They come here with trucks piled high with old machines, rent some old building and start manufacturing work shirts, cotton work pants, shoes—all bent on profiting from that 'cheap white Anglo-Saxon labor,' " Hank picked up, then grinned at Fran's perplexed stare. "Oh God, Fran, you live here and you don't know?"

"I know the mills pay badly," she admitted. In the privacy of their home, she recalled, Daddy talked about this with exasperation. *"The mill owners complain that to pay more would close down the whole industry—then where would the workers be?"*

"Something new has taken root in the beautiful Deep South," Hank said caustically. "What's known as the 'learner' system. You know how desperate people are for jobs. Employers put them through a 'learner' period, promising jobs when this is over. Workers end up earning as little as a dollar for two weeks on the job. Many of them put in twelve-hour days, six days a week but are paid for only a few 'standard hours.' In other words, they claim most of the work is not up to standard—and only pay for a few hours each week. When workers question this, they're fired—and another 'learner' is brought in. Did you know?" Hank challenged, "that the town of Bellevue financed some of the buildings these small mill owners from the Northeast are using? Of course, the money is paid back—by taking out a portion of the workers' wages each week."

"I didn't know." Fran was shaken by this disclosure. "I know that the mill workers are terribly poor." She flinched as she visualized those she saw at intervals around town. They were gaunt, listless, shabby. Their eyes reflected a disturbing hopelessness. That was what upset Daddy, she interpreted—and what Mother tried not to see. "But then lots of folks are in these times," she said with momentary defensiveness.

"They have to understand that their only chance to better themselves is to unionize," Hank said earnestly, then suppressed a yawn. "We'd better get out of here. We have to be out there at the mill gates before 6 A.M." Mill operators worked from sunup to sunset. "Not you," he told Fran indulgently. "Show up at headquarters around 9 A.M. We've got more typing lined up for you."

Fran knew the union team would be in town for no longer than three weeks. She didn't want to think about their leaving. She felt so good, just being with them—feeling she was doing something *useful*.

As she had feared, they were making little headway at the Bellevue mills. The workers were scared. They remembered the strikes called two years ago by the AFL's United Textile Workers Union. There had been chaos in the mill states—wholesale arrests, the National Guard brought out in force in some areas to break the resistance of workers already fighting hunger. Mill entrances protected by barbed wire, armed guards with machine guns stationed at the main gates and on roofs. Daddy, she remembered, had been privately compassionate—but it was bad for business to express sympathy.

Fran felt a poignant sense of loss when the team moved on to another town closer to Atlanta. She fantasized about leaving home to work with the union—maybe out of their newly established Atlanta office. But she knew her parents would never agree to this. It wasn't just the long drive every day to Atlanta. They'd be embarrassed at having their only child working with union organizers—which had a taint of communism.

A week after their departure from Bellevue, Fran received a phone call from Hank.

"I know this is a crazy thing to ask you," he apologized, "but we're desperate. You were so damned effective with that police chief in Bellevue—"

"They've arrested workers where you are now?" she broke in indignantly.

"They've arrested two mill workers and Sybil," he told her. "I was hoping you might pull the same story here that you did on the Bellevue police chief."

"I'll drive over and talk to them," she said—churning in rage at the image of dedicated Sybil lingering in a Georgia jail. "I have to drive my mother to a garden club luncheon at noon, but she'll get a ride home afterward." Mother complained about her driving—except on occasions such as this.

"I'll pick you up in Bellevue," Hank told her, clearly relieved that she would help. "I'll drive you there and back."

In early afternoon Fran was confronting a police chief who was less vulnerable than Chief Atkins. He didn't know her or her family. He stared in suspicion as she sweetly delivered her argument.

"Who are you to come into this town and tell me what to do?" he demanded belligerently. "Who sent you here?"

"Nobody sent me." Fran made a courageous effort to appear hurt. "I wanted to be useful. I don't like Northerners saying awful things about us."

"How do I know you're not some smart-ass girl from New York or Chicago playing a fancy trick on me?" He inspected her with mounting suspicion.

"Do I sound like some girl from New York or Chicago?" she demanded.

"That don't mean you ain't."

"My great-great-grandfather came to Savannah with Oglethorpe—" She paused. Was her mathematics correct? Someone in the family way back came to Savannah with Oglethorpe. "My great-grandfather fought with Lee in the War Between the States." That was authentic. "My—"

"All right," he capitulated suddenly. "But you have to admit it sounded kinda funny, you coming here with that story about your classmate at college."

"At the University of Georgia in Athens." Her smile said she forgave him. "Now will you please release those people so we don't have another Yankee saying awful things about us here in the South?"

Two days later her mother confronted her about having been seen with the union organizers in the nearby town.

"Fran, what is the matter with you?" her mother demanded in agitation. "Why do you always seem to pick up with weird folks? I told Mrs. Lutz you were probably trying to track down a story to take to the newspaper."

"I was," Fran improvised with a soulful sigh. "I'm dying to see my name as a byline in the *Bellevue Enquirer*."

"The only place I want to see your name in the *Bellevue Enquirer*," her mother said bluntly, "is on the Society Page—the announcement of your engagement to a fine Jewish boy."

By the end of the week Hank Weinstein and his crew were on their way back to New York. The prospect of setting up a permanent Atlanta office had been abandoned. Fran felt a disconcerting sense of desolation. For a little while she had been involved in something important, she mourned. She had to do more than hand out free milk at the Sixth Street elementary school or sell poppies on Decoration Day.

What was she going to do with her life?

Two

The four men slouched on the floor of the empty boxcar—relishing the comfort that was denied those perilously riding the rods beneath freight cars and sleepers. Bernie Garfield—ten months out of CCNY in New York with a degree in accounting and no job prospects—listened to the oldest of their group talk with infinite wisdom about surviving as a rider of the rails.

"You never hang around Atlanta," a veteran rider emphasized as the train heaved its way out of the Atlanta freight yards. "You get caught, they throw you on the Fulton County chain gang for thirty days. And that means you, too, Your Royal Highness," he jibed good-humoredly at Bernie.

In the seven months that he had been "seeing the country," Bernie had acquired the title of "Royal Highness"—due not to royal manners but to his neat overnight case containing a change of underwear, a shirt, a spare pair of pants, and toilet articles. This overnight case gave him access to railroad station washroom facilities. It distinguished him from hobos, who traveled with bundles. Only once had someone tried to steal the case. Others had leapt to his defense.

Bernie was aware that the rail riders in the '30s were mostly of a different breed from the sometimes picaresque hobos of legend. These were desperate men and boys—and sometimes women and young girls—who fought for survival in a world that seemed to offer no space for them. They were the "wandering population."

Earlier hobos, Bernie understood, had been adventurers of a sort—seeking work but knowing it could be found before desperation set in. But those who rode the rails today—and statistics said two million Americans—over two hundred thousand between sixteen and twenty-one and thousands under fifteen—were on the road, and running with insidiously growing hopelessness. They were dependent on soup kitchens, municipal lodging houses, handouts—and each year since the beginning of the Depression some died of starvation or froze to death in northern winters.

"I like East St. Louis," the youngest of them—a lanky seventeen-year-old who had been on this trek for three years—broke into Bernie's thoughts with an air of nostalgia. "They got Salvation Army stations that take real good care of folks. Not that lousy soup—not much more than water with a few vegetables runnin' through it—that we get most places."

How much longer could they hang on to this routine? Bernie asked himself realistically. He was better off than most—he had a few bucks pinned inside his shorts for some dire emergency. But that wouldn't last him more than a few days if he tried to live a normal life back in New York. What chance did he have to find a job? It was a joke, the way some people were making claims about how the economy was improving. He was part of the "locked-out" generation—the students who came out of college with a cherished degree in some profession—but no prospects.

He'd known for years now how terrible business conditions were. He'd had to fight to survive and keep himself in college. Thank God for tuition-free CCNY. But he'd harbored an unrealistic belief that once out of college he'd find a decent job—at a time when New York department stores demanded a BA for elevator operators. Searching for a job as an accountant, he'd taken his eye off the ball too long. By the time he realized he'd have to take whatever shitty work he could find, he was out of funds.

Not until he came home from the daily search for a job—any job now—and found himself locked out of his room until he paid that week's three dollars rent did he realize the seriousness of his situation. He knew he had to go on the move. There was nothing in New York for him. Maybe there was something somewhere else. But it hadn't taken long for him to recognize the futility of this. Like millions before him, he thought grimly.

Too many communities—entire states—were determined to keep "vagrants" out of their areas. California had set up forced labor camps, then posted guards on state lines to turn away the penniless. The compassionate towns and cities were few. Cheyenne, Wyoming, was notorious for its clubbings and even shootings. Quickly those on the road learned what areas to avoid.

At odd moments he considered joining up with others who were fighting against fascism in Spain—especially after two instances of being clubbed by railroad guards. But his distaste for killing always derailed him. It was enough that he'd seen a fellow traveler in the boxcars gunned down by overzealous freight yard detectives. Even now he woke up in a sweat from nightmares revolving around that episode.

He'd hop off at the next stop beyond Atlanta, he decided. Some small town called Bellevue. It had been in towns like that he'd been able to salvage a couple of weeks of work at times. Nothing to do with his hard-won degree, he mocked himself. A late only child, he'd seen his father die of lung cancer seven years ago and his mother of the same illness four years later. At least, he thought tenderly, Mom had lived to see him in college—his parents' dream for him.

He made a pretense of participating in the conversation in the boxcar as it rolled along the tracks en route to Bellevue. The two older men—one had been a banker, the other a trucker—discussed the turmoil in Europe. The menace of Hitler in Germany, Mussolini in Italy, the Imperial Japanese army threatening China.

"How long have you been on the road?" the banker asked the trucker.

"Pushin' towards three years. Business got lousier and lousier—then I was out on my ass. My wife left me, went home to her mother. I figured another town, a change in luck." He grunted in disgust. "Every town's the same."

"Are you through with that newspaper?" the teenager asked hopefully.

"Yeah, I know," the trucker drawled and handed over the rumpled newspaper. "You're dyin' to read *Flash Gordon.*"

"Where are you headed for?" the ex-banker asked Bernie.

"I'll hop off at Bellevue," Bernie told him. "What about you?"

"I'm going to Florida. I can sleep on a chunk of sun-warmed beach instead of freezing under a pile of newspapers up north. Who knows, I might even get lucky—find myself a rich old woman dying for male companionship."

As the train slithered into the Bellevue freight yard, Bernie geared himself for the stealthy departure. He had no desire to be clobbered with a club—or his worst nightmare—shot down while running away.

The early evening provided a cover. He knew that at this hour the guards assigned to the freight yards were more concerned with sitting down to a hot meal than chasing after ticket-avoiding rail riders. Still, he uttered a grateful sigh of relief when the freight yard was behind him.

He followed road signs that led him into the center of town, asked directions to the railroad station—his overnight case lending this question some validity. At the cavernous, nearly deserted railroad station—built not long after the Civil War—he retreated to the Men's Room, empty at this hour. He washed, shaved, changed into the shirt he'd washed and dried at a hobo encampment two days ago.

He returned to the waiting room, noted that the night ticket-seller was engrossed in a detective magazine. Well beyond the man's view, he sprawled on one of the waiting-room benches and allowed himself to doze. If anybody questioned him—and he suspected this was unlikely—he'd say he'd come in on a train and was waiting to meet a friend arriving from Florida. He looked neat, clean, shaven—he couldn't be picked up as a vagrant. And he had four dollars in his coat pocket—retrieved from his shorts while he was in the waiting room. That kept him safe from a vagrancy charge. In the morning he'd find a cheap café, have a roll and cup of coffee and then see if he could latch onto a few days' work.

It was almost 6 A.M. before activity in the depot prodded Bernie into action. He hastily left and walked the brief distance to Main Street, the business area. A pretty town, he noted—typically southern, with its courthouse set in the middle of a parklike square block. Neatly painted dark green benches on four sides, a fountain in the center, wartime cannons flanking each corner—as though to remind its citizenry that the Civil War might be over but the South was proud of its efforts. His smile quixotic, he remembered that in the South it was a social error to call the Civil War anything other than the War Between the States. Most southern towns, he thought, looked the same. He wondered what they were like beneath their picture-book serenity.

He strolled along Main Street in search of a place to have a nickel cup of coffee and a roll. The local movie theater was showing *Maytime*, with Jeanette MacDonald and Nelson Eddy. When was the last time he'd seen a movie? Many people—not the "wandering population"—went once a week. But a lot of others couldn't lay out a quarter for entertainment.

He located his quarry, walked inside with a calculated show of confidence. His jacket was showing signs of age, but these days plenty of people were wearing clothes until they fell apart. He always managed not to look as though he'd just hopped off a freight—that was a matter of pride with him. That and his air of quiet diffidence landed him occasional odd jobs.

He dawdled as long as he could over his roll and coffee, considered—then dismissed—the thought of spending another nickel on a second cup of coffee. Start asking at the stores in town for any work that might be available, he ordered himself.

His first stop was the local bank—not officially open for business yet but a door was ajar and he strolled inside. He sensed curiosity in the man who halted him just within the door. He knew his appearance belied his vagrant status, yet the overnight bag indicated a stranger in town.

"Nothing here," the man said brusquely in response to his inquiry, yet Bernie sensed a covert compassion.

His next two stops offered nothing. Out on the sidewalk again, he inspected a ladies specialty store across the street. It appealed to women with healthy income, he judged from its exterior. With fresh determination he headed for the store. No price tags on merchandise in the display windows, he noted—but obviously everything was expensive.

Bernie hesitated. The store was not open for business, he guessed. Then the door swung wide. A neatly dressed man of about fifty emerged with a broom in hand. He appeared impatient at this assignment. A porter had not arrived for work, Bernie surmised, and felt a surge of hope. All right, handle this right and he might pick up a few days' work.

With a polite smile Bernie approached the other man, introduced himself, and explained his mission.

"I'd be happy for whatever work is available. I'm fresh out of college with a degree in accounting, but I'm also handy with a broom and mop."

"Garfield, you said?" his prospective employer asked, eyes appraising him. "You're not from around here."

"No, sir," Bernie acknowledged. "I'm from New York. I was on my way to Florida to look for a job," he fabricated, "and on the spur of the moment I decided to stop off here. My funds were too low to carry me all the way to Miami," he added hastily to brush aside any suspicion that he had arrived via a freight car. "And I heard this was a beautiful and friendly town."

"I could use a man for a few days—maybe two or three weeks—until Zeke, my porter, gets over the 'flu. I can't pay you any more than I pay Zeke," he warned. For a moment his eyes lingered on Bernie's overnight bag. Bernie stiffened in alarm. Mr. Goldman—the store was called Goldman's—knew he was bluffing about how he arrived in town. But he saw compassion blend with comprehension in the older man's eyes. "There's a room at the back with a cot where you can sleep if you like—and a washroom you can use when the store's closed."

"I'd appreciate it," Bernie said, relieved at his understanding. "Just let me put away my bag, and I'll take over that broom, sir."

Fran dressed leisurely, hearing her mother's usual morning conversation with Lily about what was to be made for dinner and what special task was scheduled for the day. Mother kept an immaculate house, set a fine table, everybody said—though in these times folks were not inclined to boast about that. But didn't Mother die of boredom?

Lily did all the cleaning and cooking. There was the yardman to take care of the outside. Didn't Mother get sick of bridge parties and club meetings and her volunteer work? Mother loved going to the movies and driving over to Atlanta to see the Metropolitan Opera or the road company of a Broadway play—but shouldn't there be more to life than that?

She'd stop by the store this morning, she decided, and see those new sweaters Daddy said had arrived. She was dying for a look at his new employee, Fran admitted to herself. He was from New York, which lent him a special aura in her eyes—and a recent college graduate. Daddy didn't say so in words, she analyzed, but she sensed he was impressed by this new employee.

Bernie Garfield, she recalled his name. He was Jewish, had talked with Daddy about the craziness in Germany. Daddy was letting him do more than clean the store and sweep the sidewalk. He said Bernie had caught a big mistake in his method of bookkeeping. Now Bernie was straightening out Daddy's records for the store.

Fran took a reproachful glance at her reflection in the full-length mirror on her closet door—without seeing the perfection of her oval face, the elegance of her small, slender yet provocative frame. Why couldn't she be blond and willowy like Carole Lombard?

With distinctly un-Southern haste she left her bedroom, went down to the dining room for a breakfast of buttery grits, a tall fresh-out-of-the-oven biscuit, and Lily's chicory-laced coffee. She listened absentmindedly to her mother's chatter about the Bellevue Garden Club's plan for a flower show in April.

"Fran, I don't think you've heard a word I've said," her mother reproached after a few minutes.

"Of course I did," Fran defended herself. "I think it's a marvelous idea." It was always safe to agree with Mother.

Declining a second cup of coffee, Fran left the dining room, walked with her usual compulsive swiftness—which her mother decried as being unladylike—down the hall to the front door and out into the balmy late March morning. She loved the sights and scents of spring in Bellevue.

The trees were bursting into bloom, as though impatient to greet the new season. Wordsworth's "host of golden daffodils" were on extravagant display in every garden. How sweet the air, how fragrant the flowers, she thought in a romantic surge.

But her sense of blissful serenity evaporated moments later when she saw an elderly, ragged-colored man step off the curb into the street as though fearful of a reprimand from her. Bellevue had just begun a serious drive to keep out vagrants. What were poor people supposed to do? she asked herself in familiar outrage.

Daddy said he suspected Bernie Garfield had been riding the freights. But Bernie was Jewish and an accountant—that made him different in Daddy's mind. She suspected this time Daddy was pleased that Zeke was off on another of his "sick leaves"—which usually happened whenever his wife landed a temporary cooking job.

Daddy had talked about maybe hiring Bernie on a regular basis. *"He could be useful around the store. Keeping the books in order, even filling in as a salesman when we suddenly get busy or one of the women is out sick."* Daddy hadn't made up his mind yet, but she was confident he'd hire Bernie to stay on even after Zeke came back.

She wondered wistfully what was happening with Hank Weinstein and his team. She missed them, missed the excitement, the sense of accomplishment she'd found in their company.

The salesladies in the store all greeted her with a special warmth reserved for the boss's only child. Miss Helen—who had ruled over the staff since *she* was a toddler—escorted her to a counter where the latest arrival of expensive sweaters were on display, then left to help a customer. For a few minutes she was absorbed in choosing the two her father had told her to select for herself. She adored beautiful clothes, she conceded—but they weren't enough to fill her life.

Where was Bernie Garfield? She cast furtive glances about the main floor of the store. Daddy wasn't here this morning, she reminded herself—he'd gone over to Atlanta on business. And then a slim, dark-haired young man with intense brown eyes walked up the stairs with an armful of cartons. Instantly she knew this was Bernie Garfield.

"You're Bernie," she said with no preliminaries, her smile dazzling. "I'm Fran Goldman. My father says you're from New York."

"Yes." He seemed intrigued by her, yet uncomfortable.

"I was in New York with my father four years ago. When I graduated high school, he took me with him on a buying trip. It was fun to see New York," she said, "but I'd be terrified of living there."

"Why?" he asked. His voice was deep and charming, she decided. And he was so good-looking. "It's a wonderful city."

"When we walked around Times Square, I had the weird feeling that tall buildings would come crashing down on me," she effervesced. "But I loved going to the theater and eating in the beautiful restaurants." All at once her face grew somber. "But it was awful to see the folks selling apples on street corners—and the soup kitchens and—" She paused in confusion. She shouldn't have mentioned that! Daddy said he'd probably arrived in town on a freight train.

"It all hangs out in the open in the big cities," he said gently. "Here the poor are kind of swept off into a corner."

"We had a team of union organizers from New York here a few weeks ago. They were trying to enroll the mill workers in their union. I was working with them," she said, as though expecting disbelief. She saw his surge of interest. She'd make him understand she wasn't just some southern belle running from party to party. "I helped with—"

"Bernie, will you please take those cartons over to the side there," Helen intruded into what had become an exciting moment for Fran. "Fran, did you find something you liked in that new batch of sweaters?"

Fran made a habit of dropping into the store each day—always at the same time. Bernie caught on quickly, she thought with pleasure. He was always on the main floor at the time she arrived—and she was convinced that he contrived this. Nights she lay in her pretty, canopied bed and imagined romantic encounters with him.

Why didn't he ask her to go to a movie or something? she fretted—but she knew the answer to that. He couldn't ask her to go out with him—he wouldn't dare. Daddy might fire him. But the unspoken conversation between them when their eyes met in these brief meetings—in addition to the casual talk—was heated. All right, she told herself—*she* would have to make the first move. But how?

Then all at once—lying sleepless in bed far past the normal time—she knew what to do. Anticipation spiraled in her as she plotted this. Passover began next week. The eight-day celebration of the exodus from Egypt, when the Jews escaped into freedom. She'd persuade Mother to invite him for the first seder. It was their duty, wasn't it? A *mitzvah*—she clutched at one of the few Yiddish words she knew.

"Frannie, why should we invite this boy who works at the store—temporarily," Ida Goldman emphasized, "to the first seder? We don't even have a real seder," she said with the wistfulness this often evoked. Her mother was apt to talk about seders long past, at her grandparents' house—with a dozen at the seder table.

"It's a seder," Fran insisted. "And it's an important holiday." Her face felt hot with excitement. "Daddy says you and he always had a seder even when there were just the two of you."

"Daddy looks forward to all the holidays." Her mother smiled reminiscently. "His mother—your grandmother—made sure her three children knew who they were. I wish his brother and sister were alive to share it with us. I wish my sister was here." Her mother's sister had died at fourteen.

"Daddy says this boy doesn't know anybody in town," Fran said ingenuously. Mother hadn't see Bernie yet—she didn't know how good-looking he was. She wasn't suspicious. "I suppose you could mention it at your sisterhood meeting. Some family from the synagogue would invite him for the first seder." Her smile appeared innocent of subterfuge.

"No." Her mother bridled guiltily. "We'll invite him." Daddy teased Mother, Fran remembered, about her compulsion to perform *mitzvahs*, to do "the right thing." Whenever *she* tried to wiggle out of something—like running to her room when dotty old Miss Applebaum popped up for one of her unannounced visits—Mother always said, *"Frannie, we must never shirk our obligations."*

On the eve of the first seder Fran changed her dress three times before she was satisfied with her appearance. She tried to decide just what it was about Bernie Garfield that so intrigued her. Of course, he was awfully attractive, she considered—but it was more than his looks that made her heart pound every time she saw him or even thought about him.

He was only twenty-two—Daddy had mentioned this—but he'd lived so much more than she. He'd been across-country twice and had been headed for Florida when he stopped off here. And it wasn't just because he was from New York that she thought he was so special, though that lent him a kind of sophistication.

Daddy was sure he'd been riding the rails—but was impressed by what he called "Bernie's resourcefulness." Meaning, she interpreted, that Bernie had been sharp enough to keep himself above what folks expected of boys and men who were forced to live like hobos.

Fran made a point of waiting until she heard Bernie arrive to go downstairs. Then she hurried—breathless with anticipation—to join the others in the living room. He was diffident—as though not entirely comfortable at being here, she analyzed. In the first few minutes her mother seemed stiff and formal—but now she was relaxing, Fran thought in relief as her father talked about seders he'd known as a child, at his grandparents' house. These were stories she'd heard endlessly and with some impatience, yet tonight—aware of Bernie's interest in what her father was saying—they seemed new.

She sensed with some alarm that her mother was becoming conscious of Bernie's involuntary glances in her direction. She kept her eyes on her father as he reminisced about his childhood in Atlanta. But she felt a surge of warm pleasure each time her eyes met Bernie's.

Now Mrs. Goldman ordered the others into the dining room to take their place at the candlelit seder table. The special seder plate sat before her father, who would lead the seder. On it were the traditional three pieces of *matzah* in a napkin folded over twice—the two loaves set out in the ancient temple on the festival day plus an additional *matzah* symbolizing Passover, a roasted shankbone to represent the Passover sacrifice, parsley to symbolize hope and renewal, horseradish in memory of the bitterness of the Jewish experience in Egypt, and *haroset* (a combination of chopped apples, nuts, raisins, dates or prunes, with cinnamon and wine), and roasted egg as a symbol of life.

At each place setting was a wineglass, *haroset*, salt water. The wine-filled Elijah cup—for the dramatic moment when a child of the family opens the door to welcome, per parable, the Prophet Elijah who at some time in the course of the seder visits the seder table. And tonight an extra chair was brought to the table to denote the Jews who live in lands where they are not free to celebrate Passover.

Under Mr. Goldman's leadership the first part of the seder service was both lighthearted and respectful. Now Fran joined her mother in the kitchen to serve dinner—on this night prepared not by Lily but Ida Goldman herself. Instead of the more conventional gefilte fish, there was baked salmon, followed by roast chicken, *tzimmes*, broccoli salad, and Josiah Goldman's favorite potato pudding. For dessert there were both almond cookies and almond macaroons. Everyone ate with relish. Her mother glowed, Fran noted approvingly, at Bernie's compliments for her cooking skills.

At an auspicious moment Fran insinuated herself into the table talk. She began deviously to draw Bernie out. Like herself—and his parents before him—he was an only child. His father had been born on the Lower East Side, worked his way up to owning a small menswear store in Borough Park, Brooklyn, where he met his future wife. She had planned to become a schoolteacher until she met and married Bernie's father.

"They're both gone now." Bernie was somber. He'd loved his parents very much, Fran thought sympathetically. "My father died when I was fifteen. My mother four years ago. It's nice," he said, almost shy now, "to be sitting down with a family."

At intervals Fran sent covert glances in her mother's direction. She felt her mother's ambivalence—genuine compassion for Bernie's situation and wariness that he seemed so drawn to *her*. But as he talked with reverence about his mother's efforts to raise him on her own, Fran saw her mother react with warmth.

Her father spoke about the depressing situation in Europe—Italy's invasion of Ethiopia, Germany's taking the Rhineland, the formation of the Rome-Berlin axis. But he was most anxious about Hitler's treatment of the Jews in Germany.

"We're all so troubled in this country about the bad times here," he pointed out, "that we don't see what's happening in the rest of the world."

Fran and her mother exchanged an indulgent but knowing glance. Once Daddy started talking politics, he'd go on forever. But tonight the conversation must be derailed soon to continue the after-dinner seder service.

Bernie talked somberly about the pacifist movement among college students in the past two years.

"Students know that if we get dragged into a war, they'll be the ones to fight. In the Student Strike for Peace two years ago over 150,000 participated. And after that half a million undergraduates signed a pledge not to fight even if Congress should declare war."

"Students at City College?" Mr. Goldman asked.

"At City College, at Harvard, at Johns Hopkins—schools all over the country. Columbia and Berkeley are real strongholds. We've fought against compulsory ROTC and for reform in college administrations. And always," Bernie said emphatically, "against facism."

Bernie brought up the fighting in Spain. All at once Fran was anxious. He was talking about Americans who were going to fight against fascism there.

"A lot of Americans went over to join the International Brigade. They've become the Abraham Lincoln Brigade," he said with messianic fervor. "Even now—when France has closed its border to Spain and the

U.S. has made it illegal for Americans to travel in Spain—they're going over to fight for democracy and freedom."

The atmosphere was suddenly heavy. Fran's heart pounded. Bernie wouldn't go off to fight with the Americans in Spain, would he? She didn't want to think about him fighting in a war. She knew she wanted to spend the rest of her life with Bernie Garfield. She didn't know how she was going to manage it—Mother and Daddy would carry on like she was committing hari-kari. They'd carry on because he wasn't a Southerner, because his prospects were dreadful. But she meant to marry Bernie Garfield, before he left this town.

Three

The three Goldmans accompanied Bernie to the door at the close of the evening. They lingered in conversation in the foyer. Bernie was going back to the store to sleep in that awful storeroom, Fran thought in distaste. The seder was over—he'd be just somebody who worked for Daddy if she didn't do something to keep him within their family circle.

Gloria—who had been her friend since their first year in high school—said that boys didn't like aggressive women. *"You have to play games, Frannie. You don't let them realize you're chasing after them—and you don't let them know you're just as smart as they are."*

"Oh, did you know that the Royale is bringing back *The Story of Louis Pasteur*, with Paul Muni, for a one-day return engagement?" Fran asked the others vivaciously. "I'm just dying to see it again. It's next Friday," she told her mother. "Daddy has a family pass to the Royale because he rents the store from the owner," she told Bernie. "So we see just every movie that comes there."

"Friday night Daddy and I are going to Atlanta for a play," her mother reminded. "We asked you if you wanted to go, but you said you'd be busy."

"That was for a birthday party for Eleanor Jenkins, but it's been called off. She's in the hospital after an emergency appendectomy," Fran said.

"Take one of your friends in the afternoon," her father told her. "You can use the family pass."

"Oh, it's no fun going to a special movie in the daytime," Fran reproached. "I'd like to go in the evening." Then—as though on sudden impulse—she turned to Bernie. "If you're not busy Friday night, Bernie, would you like to go with me? We have that pass."

Bernie's face lighted up, then he looked apprehensive. He turned to Mr. Goldman in silent inquiry. He didn't see her mother's startled expression, Fran thought in relief.

"Bernie, you wouldn't mind taking Fran to the Royale on Friday evening, would you?" Mr. Goldman asked indulgently.

"I'd like that very much." Bernie's smile managed to be both eager and respectful.

"All right, then it's settled," Mr. Goldman concluded. "Bernie, don't let her talk your ear off about the folks who work in the cotton mills."

On Friday evening Fran was dressed half an hour before Bernie arrived. Her parents had already left for Atlanta after an early dinner. Her mother had seemed uneasy about leaving her alone in the house when Bernie was coming over, but *she* had made a point of saying they'd have to leave the minute he arrived so as not to be late. Anyhow, her parents trusted her—she was a "good girl."

She'd dallied with the thought of suggesting Bernie have dinner with them, then dismissed this as "too pushy"—and apt to alert her mother to her real objective. It would take some doing to convince her mother that Bernie Garfield was a suitable son-in-law. Mother wouldn't be deterred by the flip reminder that she wouldn't even have to change her monogram if she became Fran Garfield. And true, there was the question of convincing Bernie to marry her. Boys were slow to take on the responsibility of a wife in these times.

She was at the door the moment she heard his footsteps on the front porch.

"Hi." Her voice was demure, her smile dazzling as she opened the door.

"The temperature's dropping," he warned shyly. His suit was shabby but freshly pressed, the sweater beneath showing signs of wear at the neck—but he looked so handsome, she thought.

"I'll wear a coat." She reached into the foyer closet for the coat she'd brought down earlier, handed it to him to hold for her. The atmosphere suddenly electric as he helped her into the coat.

Aware that the feature film would not begin for another twenty minutes, they walked leisurely to the Royale in the invigorating coolness of the early evening—both delighted at being in each other's company. Fran talked about her experience with Hank Weinstein and his group and her frustration that so little progress was being made in unionizing the cotton mills.

"It's so awful, Bernie, the way the mill workers are at the looms from sunup to sunset," she said indignantly, "and paid so little! They live without hope of anything better—and what could be worse than that?"

"Unions are making some progress," Bernie soothed. "John L. Lewis of the CIO just made a deal with U.S. Steel for recognition of the United Mine Workers. That's a real step forward."

"I want to be part of helping," Fran said earnestly. "I don't want to be one of those people who goes through life just taking." Her face was luminous. "I want to give, too."

"I know." His eyes were bright with comprehension and agreement.

"Bellevue's really two towns," she said impatiently. "One of them consists of the folks who work in the mills, and the rest of us make up the other town. Even our part is divided by social lines," she added. "Those who are invited to country club parties and the others who're not. Those who're DAR or UDC, those who're Jewish and those who're not. It's a pretty town, but I wouldn't want to spend the rest of my life here." She managed a covert glance at Bernie. He probably wished he was back in New York—he said he loved the city, she remembered. Why had she told him she'd be scared to live there? Not with him, she wouldn't be!

"Bellevue is pretty, yes," Bernie agreed. "And everybody is so polite and friendly. Nobody ever seems rushed. Yet I have the feeling that they're living just on the surface. That they push aside—try not to see— all kinds of inner conflicts." Now he laughed self-consciously. "Wow, I sound like a half-baked psychologist."

"But you're right," she said with spontaneous intensity.

Oh yes, she and Bernie Garfield clicked! They thought so much alike! She'd never met a boy who shared her beliefs and feelings as he did. Hank Weinstein, of course, she conceded—but he wasn't a boyfriend. Bernie would fit right in with Hank's group. He'd seen the ugliness in the world, and he wanted to help change it. Here at home nobody she knew understood how much she wanted to be part of making life better for people who were hurting. Daddy talked about how bad life was for the mill workers—he worried about them—but he didn't *do* anything.

In the weeks that followed Fran knew that her mother was growing increasingly anxious about the excuses she contrived to invite Bernie to the house for dinner, to have him escort her to a movie, to bring him into family conversation. With these devious moves she meant to let her parents know that they must consider Bernie as a prospective son-in-law.

She knew Bernie was as deeply in love with her as she with him. But not until they'd been seeing each other for a month did he kiss her in the protective darkness of the Royale, where she had deviously chosen a pair of seats that flanked a wall—despite the fact that on this midweek night the movie house was half empty.

"This is crazy," he whispered shakily when their mouths parted.

"It's wonderful," she corrected. "What took you so long?"

They were both upset tonight by Zeke's return to his job. Still, her father talked vaguely about finding other tasks for Bernie to do around the store during the next week or two. Though neither Daddy nor Mother would admit it outright, Fran considered, they knew she and Bernie had developed a special closeness. They were unsettled, unsure how to handle this. After all, she told herself with inner laughter, they were dying for her to "marry a nice Jewish boy"—and here was Bernie.

On the nights when Bernie took her to a movie they made a point of saying good night at the door. But tonight was different—and the awareness that Bernie might soon be out of a job hung over them. They walked with deliberate slowness in the balmy night—holding hands, pausing at furtive moments to kiss with growing fervor.

Half a block from the house Fran abandoned caution and confronted their situation.

A detaining hand on his arm, she stopped dead, lifted her eyes to his. "Bernie, are you in love with me?"

"Honey, you know I am." His voice was anguished. She knew the troubling questions that darted across his mind. How could he support a wife? Would her parents fight against their marrying? "But you—"

"And I'm in love with you," she said exultantly. "We'll get married and move to New York. Oh, it'll take some doing," she acknowledged, lifting a finger to silence him. "Mother and Daddy will be horrified at the thought of me leaving Bellevue. They'll try to make you come into the store and work for Daddy. But you leave it to me, Bernie—we can work this out."

"I've never known anybody like you," he whispered, pulling her close. They ignored the hoots of a carful of teenagers driving past them. "I want to spend the rest of my life with you."

"We'll be married the end of June," she told him with soaring confidence. "Mother wouldn't consider it legal if I didn't have a June wedding. And then we'll leave for a 'wedding trip to New York City.' And we'll stay there," she promised. "We'll both get jobs. We'll—"

"In these times?" Reality lent a harshness to his voice. "I wouldn't have been here if I'd thought I could land a job in New York."

"You'll open up an office as an accountant. I'll be your secretary. Instead of giving me a big wedding, I'll insist Mother and Daddy give us the cash. We'll have enough to live on until you're earning money as an accountant."

"Fran, that's an impossible dream." His voice was tender yet pained.

"It's going to happen," she insisted. "Conditions are *not* as bad as they were. We'll both work hard—we'll have money to live on until you start picking up clients. Daddy says you're very sharp when it comes to business. We'll rent a tiny office. If we have to, we can sleep there on folding cots. We'll go on the streets and give out circulars. We'll—"

"Frannie, you're mad! But I can never say 'no' to you." He held her so close she felt his heart pounding against her.

"It'll be a roller coaster for a while, but we'll make it, Bernie. I see it in my crystal ball!"

As both anticipated, they encountered an avalanche of counter-proposals. They could be engaged, Fran's parents conceded. Bernie was to work in the store for six months. Eventually he'd take over when his prospective father-in-law retired. But neither Bernie nor Fran meant to remain in Bellevue.

"Bernie's an accountant," Fran railed at a late-night family conference. "He has a career ahead. That's what I want for him!"

"Then let him be an accountant in Bellevue," her mother countered. "Daddy will be his first client."

"We both want to live in New York for a while," Fran insisted.

"If you go there, you'll never come back here to live," her mother wailed. "And what do we really know about Bernie? How can you go away so far with somebody we barely know?"

"If I don't marry him, he's going to go back to New York and join the Abraham Lincoln Brigade. He'll go to Spain and die in action. I'll die an old maid," she said dramatically. To her mother these should be magic words. They were.

Now that they were officially engaged and the wedding barely a month away, Fran contrived for Bernie to come for dinner on a night when she knew her parents would leave immediately afterward for a special meeting at the synagogue to plan a fund-raiser for German-Jewish refugees. She and Bernie would go to the Royale.

After dinner Fran helped her mother clear the table.

"I should have asked Lily to stay and do the dishes," Mrs. Goldman fretted as they deposited dishes in the sink. "I don't like us to be late at meetings."

"You and Daddy go on," Fran urged. "I'll take care of the dishes." A rare occasion, she admitted. "Why are you looking at me like that?" She appeared innocently bewildered, though she knew exactly what bothered her mother. In their circle even engaged couples weren't left alone in the house.

"I guess it's all right," Mrs. Goldman capitulated. "Remember to turn off the fans." But she still appeared uneasy.

Her mother even frowned upon jitterbugging, Fran remembered. She complained it was so suggestive. Chaperons always hated it because sometimes when a girl got really into jitterbugging, her underpanties just might show. The older generation had such weird ideas. Like how shocked Mother was when she finally realized that Mrs. Watkins next door was pregnant. *"She has grown children already!"* To her mother's generation that was like advertising you'd had sex. Didn't they realize times were changing?

Fran did the dishes, put them away, then joined Bernie in the living room. He rose to his feet and switched off the radio.

"I guess we'd better get moving." He seemed unfamiliarly self-conscious.

"We've got lots of time," she purred, walking toward him. "So we'll miss the newsreel."

"Frannie—" With an air of reluctance he closed his arms about her as she lifted her mouth to his. "Honey, let's get out of here," he said, his voice uneven when they broke for air.

"Bernie, why? We're going to be married."

"Come on, let's go," he ordered. "Have you got your house key?"

"Yes," she sulked and walked out into the hot, humid night, fragrant with the scent of roses and honeysuckle.

They walked in silence for a few moments. Fran made no secret that she felt rejected.

"Frannie, I wanted to," he said bluntly. "Oh, baby, did I want to!" His hand reached for hers. "But I was brought up to—to respect girls. Particularly the girl I'm going to marry. All those nice Jewish boys from the Bronx who went to City College didn't mess around the way some guys do." He tried to sound humorous. "We *knew* what was going on with the couples that hung out with the Greenwich Village crowd—the young radicals, the ones in theater and those who talked about becoming painters or writers. Maybe we were just scared—how could we go home and look our parents in the eye if we were going against what they'd taught us? My parents were both gone by then," he conceded, "but you don't forget what you grew up hearing most of your life."

Late in June Fran and Bernie were married under the traditional *chupah,* set up in a corner of their living room. Her friend Gloria was her maid of honor. Gloria's brother was Bernie's best man. Only a dozen guests were present, but dinner in the family living room was elegant, the menu lovingly planned by Mrs. Goldman after much perusing of her favorite home-oriented magazines and prepared and served by Lily and her sister.

When Fran and Bernie left for the depot—the mother-of-the-bride indignantly rejected their plans to travel by Greyhound bus and provided a compartment aboard the Seaboard Airline pullman to New York—they left with an envelope of cash designed to last them for three months if they were frugal. If Bernie was not in a position to support himself and Fran at the end of that time, they were to return to Bellevue to live. Fran had overheard her mother say—over and over again, "Bernie will get New York out of his system and the kids will come back here."

That, Fran vowed, would never happen.

In the privacy of their compartment Fran reached for Bernie with none of the reticence expected of a decorous young bride. She and Gloria had dissected in detail the happenings of the wedding night. Neither had any firsthand knowledge, but Gloria's father was a physician, and they had spent fascinated hours among his medical books when Gloria's parents were off to medical conventions. With delicious naughtiness they'd pored over novels considered salacious by the more conventional. She was ready for marriage, she thought exultantly.

"The conductor will be coming in for tickets soon," Bernie warned huskily. "Then a porter will come in to make up the berths."

"Just the lower one." Fran giggled. "And tell him to make it up soon." Mother had given her that gorgeous bridal set—a white crepe nightgown and matching peignoir but Gloria's secret gift had been a black chiffon nightie and a bottle of sexy French perfume.

"I don't usually ride in such style," Bernie teased, glancing about the tiny yet elegant compartment.

"You'll get used to it," she promised.

"We'll go into the dining car for dinner," Bernie decreed, "and I'll tell the porter to make up the lower berth while we're eating."

"A very early dinner," Fran told him. "And you'll go to the smoking car after that."

"I can do without a cigarette tonight," he teased.

"You go for a smoke while I get into my nightie," she insisted. "Give me about ten minutes. Then come back to our compartment and knock three times."

"No password?" he asked while they swayed together with a passion that threatened to destroy her plans.

"Three knocks," she whispered, considering their locking the compartment door. Could she bring herself to delay what had been delayed at Bernie's insistence rather than her own? *"Bernie, we're going to be married—why do we have to wait?"*

She was spared making the decision by a brisk knock on the door. She and Bernie hastily parted.

"Come in," he called, struggling not to appear self-conscious. Did everybody onboard know they'd just been married? Fran asked herself.

At the first call for dinner Fran and Bernie headed for the dining car.

"Another first for me," he whispered when the waiter had taken their orders and left their table. Fran had insisted they be extravagant tonight. In New York they'd count their pennies. "I once rode *under* the dining car."

"I have a first, too," she reminded effervescently.

"No bridal qualms?" he asked.

"I can't wait." Her eyes made silent love. "Don't ever expect me to be the demure type."

Bernie chuckled.

"Honey, I'll never make that mistake."

Her smile was dazzling. "We'll be a team, Bernie. When you open up your office, I'll be your secretary. Well, I can type," she reminded defensively at his start of astonishment.

"Honey, that business about opening an office was playacting," he reproached. "The money your folks gave us as a wedding present will keep us afloat until I land something. The economists all say that business conditions are showing some improvement. Government support is finally pulling the country out of the Depression. I'll find a job," he promised.

"You'll set up your own office." Her smile was ingenuous, but she suspected he knew she had plotted this all along.

"Frannie!"

"We'll give it a try," she amended. "If it doesn't work, we'll both go out and look for jobs—and try again when we've saved up money. My husband is going to be an accountant with his own office—and once that's set I'm going to be a journalist." Her confidence refused to be shaken.

Over a delicious dinner they contrived to keep their conversation casual, though—under the table—Fran kicked off one pump to reach out to caress Bernie's ankle with silk-encased toes. They made a point of not lingering over dessert and coffee.

"You go to the smoking car," Fran ordered, her eyes an amorous promise. "Have a couple of cigarettes." He rarely smoked; that was a luxury he couldn't afford.

"I remember," he murmured. "Knock three times."

When she heard Bernie's knock on their compartment door, Fran surmised he'd barely had time for one cigarette.

"One moment," she drawled. In bare feet and seductive black chiffon nightie—plus a discreet whiff of Chanel No. 5—Fran hurried to the door. "What took you so long?" She lifted her eyes to his in provocative invitation. How tall he was when she was out of her shoes!

He shut the door of their compartment, locked it.

"I've waited so long for you, Frannie—"

"Don't wait any longer—" She lifted her face to his while his hands fumbled with the straps of her nightie. "Oh, Bernie," she murmured moments later—after a long and passionate merging of their mouths and as he lifted her from the clutter of black chiffon at her feet and dropped her onto the narrow berth of their compartment. "I was so afraid you wouldn't want to marry me—"

She wasn't afraid or disgusted—or plain impatient, she told herself exultantly while Bernie made love to her. How could any girl—any woman, she corrected herself—not enjoy these new, exciting feelings that came when love soared into passion?

"You know, Frannie," Bernie said huskily when they lay quiescent—for the moment. "You could make a fortune as a high-class call girl."

"But just think," she murmured, "it all belongs to you."

From Penn Station—designed in the style of an ancient Roman temple—they went directly to the Essex House, where Josiah Goldman had reserved a room for them.

"This is where Daddy stays when he comes up twice a year on buying trips," Fran told Bernie as they emerged from their taxi and gazed up at the imposing forty-three story hotel that faced Central Park. A hotel, Fran recalled with a flurry of delight, that was favored by movie stars.

They were traveling with only two pieces of luggage. Bernie had acquired a small valise that replaced his overnight case and was large enough to accommodate his old suit. A well-tailored suit from his father-in-law's wardrobe had been taken in and lengthened to fit him. Fran's mother would send her trunk by Railway Express once they found a furnished apartment.

"Wait for me here," Bernie said. "I'll run to the corner to pick up the evening papers. And don't run away," he joshed.

Daddy had paid three nights' rent here at the hotel for them, Fran remembered while she waited for Bernie to return. This was their honeymoon. But she suspected Bernie was impatient to see the Classified ads. They wouldn't wait for the honeymoon to be over—they'd be out looking for an apartment tomorrow morning.

She was here in New York with Bernie! Daddy and Mother were sure they'd come running home—tails between their legs—at the end of three months. She'd die if that happened. She wouldn't let it happen, she vowed.

Her face was bright, confident as she waited for Bernie—charging toward her now with impatient strides. He mustn't know how scared she was at being here in New York with so little money to see them into their new life. Was Bernie right? Ought they start right away to look for jobs? But that would be a trap, she admonished herself. Sure, most people worked for somebody else—but Bernie wanted to work for himself, paddle his own canoe. And as his wife, she told herself sternly, it was her duty to help him do just that.

Four

The following morning they lingered in bed until a sybaritic hour.
"These three days here at the Essex House are our honeymoon.
Your parents' orders," Bernie reminded, reaching for her.

"You said we'd spend today looking for an apartment." But the glint
in her eyes as he tossed one leg over hers told him she was agreeable to a
delay.

"We will," he promised. "Later."

It was almost noon when they emerged from their room and went
downstairs. The day was overcast and humid. Bernie took off his jacket
and threw it over one arm as he considered their brunch destination.

"The Automat," he decided. "Then we'll go to look at apartments.
We'll pick up this morning's *Times* and mark off what's in our price
range."

They bought a copy of the day's *Times*, strolled down Broadway to
the Automat between 54th and 55th streets, went inside. Fran's one trip
to Manhattan had not included a visit to the Automat. She was intrigued
by every small detail.

"I'm married to a real tourist," Bernie joshed when they at last settled themselves at a table and prepared to eat. "Nobody comes to New
York without visiting the Automat, Macy's, and Radio City Music Hall."

"It's so crowded," Fran said, amazed that every seat was taken. But
the atmosphere was, somehow, exhilarating. Aromas appealing.

"This is the lunchtime rush hour," Bernie pointed out. A welcome
break in the working day, Fran interpreted. "And where else can you eat
so well for so little?"

In deference to the hour they had lunch rather than breakfast.
Steaming chicken pot pies, baked potatoes and what Bernie professed to

be the best coffee in New York. While they ate, he consulted the "Furnished Apartment" listings in the Classified section of the *Times*.

They finished off their meal and headed on the IRT for the West 72nd Street Station.

"Our apartment here won't be like anything you've ever known," Bernie warned Fran when they came up from the subway into the steamy sunshine of the early afternoon.

"We'll be together—that's all that counts." Her smile was dazzling. "Bernie, our first home—"

Fran tried to conceal her shock when landladies showed them furnished apartments that were hardly larger than her bedroom closet back in Bellevue. Bernie rejected the first three for a variety of reasons. Then they followed yet another landlady up one flight of stairs in another West Seventies brownstone to what she labelled with pride "a modern, maple-furnished three-room apartment."

"It even includes an Electrolux," she said triumphantly.

The living room was fair-sized, Fran told herself—using the three previous apartments as an example of what they could expect. There was a pullman kitchenette and a minuscule bedroom, crowded with a double bed and a narrow chest of drawers. The living-room rug was threadbare, the furniture shockingly shabby, but a tree in glorious bloom was on display outside the window, and Fran's face lighted.

"Can we afford it?" she whispered to Bernie. He had said they should keep their rent down to ten dollars a week. This apartment was fifty a month. She'd ask her mother to send her beautiful bedspread from home, she plotted, and her bedroom draperies would be fine for the living-room windows.

"We'll take it," Bernie told the landlady and exchanged a relieved smile with Fran. They had a place to live.

Rejoicing in success on their first day, Bernie insisted that they try to get cheap seats that evening for the Vincente Minnelli musical—*The Show Is On*—starring Beatrice Lillie and Willie and Eugene Howard.

"It's at the Winter Garden," he told Fran. "A huge theater. We'll probably be able to get one-dollar seats for tonight. And tomorrow—since we're still on our honeymoon—we'll see *Having A Wonderful Time*."

"Perfect," Fran purred.

"We'll get the fifty-five-cent seats. And if we can't get second balcony seats there," he said with a flourish, "then we'll try for"—he paused to fold back the *Times* to the theater page—"the twenty-five-cent second balcony seats at something else."

Bernie loved New York, she thought tenderly. He was almost reverent when he talked about the New York Public Library at 42nd Street and Fifth Avenue—"*I used to run there every time I had a free hour or two—it's open seven days a week!*" And all the museums, she recalled with awe—all for free.

Since their hotel room was theirs for two more nights, they elected to remain in Essex House luxury for that time—though their apartment rent started immediately. They emerged from their room only to stroll briefly in Central Park—just across from the Essex House—or to eat at the nearby Automat. And in the evening they went to the theater.

On the first evening in their apartment Fran cooked dinner.

"All I can cook is spaghetti and hamburgers," she admitted, "but I have a terrific cookbook. I'll learn."

She was astonished—slightly awed—that Bernie was more accomplished than she in the culinary arts.

"I learned to cook on a one-burner electric stove. I kept it hidden in the hall bedroom I shared with another student in those years at CCNY," he told her. "I made Irish stew in a hobo camp—in a tin can over a campfire. To me," he smiled humorously, "this is almost luxury."

Now Fran and Bernie focused on finding a tiny office, where he could set himself up as a CPA. They were horrified by the cost of office space in Manhattan.

"There's no way we can lay out that kind of rent money," Bernie said bluntly after four days of canvassing available space. "I'll have to look for a job."

"No," Fran objected. "You're going into business for yourself."

"We'll give it another week," Bernie hedged. "The economists keep saying business is getting better, but try telling that to people looking for jobs."

After a dinner of cold cuts and iced tea—because the city was in the throes of an enervating heat wave—Bernie suggested they go down to Riverside Drive to cool off.

"We'll take a blanket and stretch out on the grass," Bernie said. "We'll get a breeze from the river."

"Let's splurge and go to a movie," she coaxed, tugging at her perspiration-soaked blouse. "It'll be air-conditioned." She sighed with melodramatic bliss.

"We shouldn't spend the money—" Bernie hesitated. Ever conscious of the fragile state of their finances, Fran understood. "Tomorrow we'll go to the movies. It'll be even hotter, the papers said. Let's settle for Riverside Drive tonight."

They left their apartment, headed down the stairs and to the front door. Fran frowned as they walked out into the approaching dusk. This humid blanket that hung over the city, she thought in rebellion. They left their apartment, headed down the stairs and to the front door.

On one side of the stoop a young couple sat and debated about taking the subway out to Coney Island.

"I know it'll be nice out there—but I have to go to work tomorrow," the girl said querulously. "I'm not Barbara Hutton. I only work at a Woolworth's—I don't own them."

Fran was silent until they were a few feet beyond their brownstone.

"I'll bet I could get a job clerking in Woolworth's," she said softly. "I could lie and say I've worked in a shop in Bellevue."

"You're not going to work in Woolworth's," Bernie interrupted, his color high. "Have you any ideas of their working conditions—and the rotten salaries they're paid?"

"Do they have a union?" Fran wondered.

"No such luck." Bernie's smile was wry. "There've been threats of strikes. I read somewhere that they've been asking for a forty-hour work week and twenty-dollar salaries. They work a six-day week for ten or twelve dollars. Barbara Hutton spends what a Woolworth clerk earns in a year on one dress."

"It's not just the Southern mill workers who have a bad deal," Fran said with an air of discovery.

"Honey, that's the understatement of the year."

"I'd like to get a job in a Woolworth store," Fran said, "then try to organize the salesgirls!"

"We've got problems of our own." Bernie reached for her hand. "Let's focus on us for now."

Every bench along Riverside Drive was occupied on this sultry evening. Here and there a baby cried in reproach. Fran and Bernie walked along a path that led down to the river and finally chose a spot to spread their blanket. They were not alone in escaping a hot apartment for the meager breeze coming from the river. Clusters of West Side residents sprawled on the vast expanse of grass.

In moments Bernie had struck up a conversation with a solitary young man who'd been trying to read in the dwindling light and had finally abandoned this in disgust.

"How do you like John Marquand?" Bernie asked, staring at the new Marquand novel, *The Late George Apley,* which their neighbor had dropped on the grass beside him.

"I know it's a big best-seller," their neighbor acknowledged. "A really good book. But I'm not in the mood for Boston aristocracy." He grinned apologetically. "I'm just back home for three months—after six months with the Abraham Lincoln Brigade in Spain."

Suddenly the atmosphere was electric. Bernie bombarded him with questions. Bob Peters was eager to answer. He had worked his way through law school—living on pasta and rice, scrounging for part-time jobs. A year and a half out of school and with no real job in sight, he'd joined up with the Abraham Lincoln Brigade.

"I went over there full of ideals," he said bitterly. "I was going to fight to save the world from fascism. We didn't realize we were fighting the communist war. What I saw in the months I was in Spain made me sick. The atrocities on both sides! I couldn't sleep nights. At the first chance I pulled out. I wasn't fighting for democracy; it was communists against fascists—one was as bad as the other."

Fran sat back and listened as the two men talked. At least, Bernie would never feel that by getting married he'd deprived himself of the big adventure of fighting in Spain, she told herself. Only now did Bernie admit that he'd actually wanted to go to law school.

"No way could I have swung that," he said somberly. "I broke my back with the accounting degree from CCNY. But at least I had a profession."

"Why don't we go back to our place and have something cold to drink?" she intervened at last. "I have a pitcher of iced tea in the refrigerator."

Back in the apartment they talked until well past midnight. It was as though they'd known each other for years, Fran thought. Bob came from a farm in Iowa. *"Farmers always get hit worst."* His girlfriend worked as a typist on the WPA to support herself and her family. *"We thought we'd get married when I got out of law school—fat chance!"* Bob started to rise from his chair. "I'd better get home and try to grab a little sleep. I have to be in my office to meet a client at 8 A.M." He chuckled. "One of my two clients."

But all three were reluctant to call it a night. Conversation turned to Bob's efforts to become established as an attorney.

"It's a tough time for any business," he said somberly. "If you know somebody who needs a lawyer who works cheap, send him my way."

"If you know somebody who needs a CPA who works cheap, send him my way. Not that I have an office yet," Bernie conceded. "God, the rents they're asking—even in these rotten times."

"I have desk space in my office," Bob said, all at once alert. "I'm trying to rent it. Cheap," he emphasized. "If I can get some rent money, I can afford to pay a part-time secretary." He grinned. "My typing stinks."

"What about the barter system?" Fran asked, excitement charging through her. "I'll be your part-time typist in exchange for desk space for Bernie. I'm good," she pursued. "I was a journalism major at college—I had to learn to type. I can do sixty words a minute."

"What about shorthand?" Bob stalled, yet Fran sensed he was intrigued by her offer.

"I have my own system—as long as you won't talk too fast. Look, we can work this out," she pushed. "I typed for labor organizers back home—they thought I was terrific." She waited breathlessly while he considered this. No need to say she was an unpaid volunteer.

"You go along with this, Bernie?" Bob asked after a moment.

"I think we can help each other," Bernie told him. "Fran will be our secretary. I get a client—I'll try to sell you to him if he needs a lawyer. And vice versa."

"All right," Fran said jubilantly. "We're in business!"

While admitting they didn't know just how they'd round up business but spilling over with youthful optimism, the three explored every possible avenue. Together they worked out leaflets advertising legal and accounting services. Fran ran off copies on the often temperamental mimeograph machine that had come with Bob's office. They took turns handing out leaflets on street corners, to small neighborhood businesses, shoved them under doors. They posted circulars on telephone booths, streetlights, walls of empty stores—of which there were many in this summer of '37.

Both men acquired a handful of low-paying clients. Their finances were shaky, yet they felt they'd arrived at a turn in the road. Economists reported gains in production, a drop in the horrendous unemployment— small but hopeful indications that the Depression was on its way out. Fran talked about starting a typing service.

Bernie took pleasure in introducing Fran to the richness of the city. Together on Sundays they explored the Metropolitan Museum, the Whitney Museum, the Pierpont Morgan Library, all the glorious offerings of the city that were free. *"I can't believe I'm seeing masterpieces I've read about in art class!"* Fran repeated with awed delight.

Often Bob joined Fran and Bernie. Always they talked about the time when the country—the world—would emerge into a new era of hope and accomplishment. Bernie would go back to school to earn a law degree. Together Bernie and Bob would become involved in politics—their goal to help make the world a better place in which to live. And she, Fran dreamed extravagantly, would become a woman correspondent like Dorothy Thompson—though she'd be for FDR and not against him.

Then in August the economy took a disastrous tumble. The industrial output slumped almost overnight to below 1930 levels. The stock market plunged to alarming depths.

"We should have expected it," Bernie said in frustration. "The President slashed the WPA rolls, slowed down PWA projects—all that crap about balancing the budget."

"It might have worked," Bob said, "if most businessmen weren't scared witless about where the economy was going. They're terrified of investing in expansion."

"A lot of economists were against the cuts," Bernie reminded. "The head of the Federal Reserve Board warned the government shouldn't worry about balancing the budget when private spending drops way down. It's dangerous!"

By late autumn Bernie admitted to Fran that their funds were almost exhausted. Both he and Bob sought frenziedly for clients but with little success. What had appeared to be a breakthrough in the economy proved to be false. Bernie and Fran vowed not to go back to Bellevue—nor to tell her parents of their precarious situation. Bob gave up his three-dollar-a-week hall bedroom to sleep on a folding cot in Fran and Bernie's apartment—contributing his room rent to their apartment rent to help them hang on. The three of them spent all their waking hours together—searching their minds for ways to bring in business. Fran tracked down new recipes for pasta and rice—cheap and filling. They abandoned their once-a-week trek to the Apollo Theater in Times Square to see their cherished foreign films.

Only now did Fran and Bernie realize that Bob, too, was Jewish. He and Fran exchanged sometimes amusing, sometimes bittersweet stories about life for Jews in small American towns.

"We didn't see much overt anti-Semitism back home," Bob said thoughtfully on a cold November Thanksgiving when their big splurge was ground chuck and baked potatoes. "Not many Jews live on farms," he added with a wry smile.

"I knew it was there back home," Fran said. "But we all pretended it didn't exist. Once—I think I was in the third grade—this creepy boy called me a 'Christ-killer.' I don't think I really knew what he was talking about. But Daddy filled me in. And I remember how relieved Mother was when the private school that was supposed to open in Bellevue decided against it. My girlfriend and I were all excited about going there. Then Mother found out it was 'Christian' school. I wouldn't be accepted. Daddy said that meant Justice Frankfurter couldn't have gone there. Jesus couldn't have gone. Anyhow," she shrugged, "the school never opened. Later—in high school—I went to the country club proms—always with a Jewish boy. But I knew my folks couldn't become members because we were Jewish. Dad told me about quotas in some of the fancy colleges—and how no Jew ever rose to a high position on Wall Street or in banking."

"But the governor of New York," Bernie pointed out triumphantly, "is Herbert Lehman, a Jew."

"When I went off to college," Fran drawled, "it was the custom to pair off roommates by religion. Why?"

Inevitably conversation during leisure hours turned to the increasing threat of war in Europe though most Americans seemed to consider this a remote possibility.

"How can people look at Germany and not know war has to come?" Bernie railed. "Hitler has built up his army to six times its allowed strength. Great Britain backed down and allowed him to ignore the Versailles Treaty and beef up his air force and the navy. Last year he sent troops right up the French border—but French leaders who wanted to use force were persuaded not to do this. Nobody wants war in Europe— but Hitler will force this," he predicted. "And look at the way the world sits back and allows him to ruin the lives of German Jews!"

Fran worried that Bernie was right, that Americans would be thrown into a war with Germany. He was so bright, so far-seeing, she thought tenderly. She kept telling him he'd go back to school at night when things got better for them—get that law degree. He didn't want to practice law. He wanted the background to help him break into politics. *"That's how you get things done in this world, Frannie—you run for office."*

But with increasing frequency—listening to Bernie and Bob—she worried that Americans would have to fight Hitler. She didn't want Bernie to go to war. First she'd been scared he'd go off to fight in Spain. Now this. How would she survive if anything happened to Bernie?

Fran was shaken when her mother wrote in December that she and Fran's father would be in New York for four days early in the new year.

"Daddy's coming up for his usual buying trip, and we figured I might as well come along. That way we'll both get a chance to see you. I know you can't put us up, Frannie—we'll be at the Essex House."

Fighting panic Fran geared herself for her parents' arrival. For the four days they'd be in New York Bob would sleep in the office. Her parents mustn't know how strapped she and Bernie—and Bob—were for money. She and Bernie frenziedly cleaned both apartment and office—though there was no way to disguise the shabbiness of both.

On the evening of the Goldmans' arrival Fran and Bernie hurried to meet them in their Essex House room—per her father's arrangement. *"No need to meet us at Penn Station. I know my way around."* He'd brushed aside her plan to have them for dinner at her and Bernie's apartment. He was taking them out for dinner at Lindy's. A buyer had introduced him to Lindy's, which had acquired a national reputation via such gossip columnists as Walter Winchell and Ed Sullivan.

It was wonderful to see Mother and Daddy, Fran thought with a surge of love as they were seated in the noisy, already crowded restaurant, faintly garish in its black, red, and yellow decor. Once they had ordered, Josiah Goldman questioned his son-in-law about the state of business in New York. At intervals Fran chimed in with self-conscious optimism.

"Business is bad here, but everybody's sure we'll come out of it soon. Bernie and I are managing despite all the crying we hear around town." She contrived to exude confidence.

"I don't like that business about the Japanese deliberately bombing our gunboat, the *Panay*, last month." All at once Josiah was grim. "It wasn't bad enough they shot down an American vessel in international waters—*flying the American flag*—they machine-gunned the survivors in lifeboats. I'm astonished we didn't declare war!"

"Jo, don't talk about war," Ida Goldman admonished. Fran remembered her mother's brother had died in the World War. "I hate all this talk about the insanity in Europe. This country mustn't be dragged into another world war. You were a toddler when we entered the war," she told Fran. "I used to thank God every night that you'd come along when you did. Daddy was exempt from the draft because he was a father."

"All right," Josiah said indulgently. "No more serious talk. One night before we go back, we want to take you two to a Broadway show. What would you like to see?"

"The new Clifford Odets play. *Golden Boy,*" Fran said promptly.

"You must have the cheesecake for dessert," her father ordered in high good humor when the waiter approached at this point in their meal. "Lindy's has the best cheesecake in the world!"

"And you'll take us back to your little nest for coffee," her mother decreed gaily. But Mother was anxious about how they were living, Fran interpreted.

They took a cab for the short ride up night-lit Broadway, round Columbus Circle with its hoard of soapbox orators, and up to their West 75th Street brownstone.

Fran was conscious of her parents' dismay when they saw the tiny, seedy apartment, though they quickly masked this. Why was there never enough heat on cold nights like this? she thought.

"I don't know what's the matter with the heat tonight," she lied. "I'll turn on the oven—that'll warm up the place." Back in Bellevue most families didn't have steam heat—they had to rely on fireplaces and stoves, she thought defensively. Of course, the Goldman house had steam heat.

"Come, we'll put up coffee," her mother ordered. "Let the men talk."

While she prattled lightly about the plays she and Bernie had seen—during their earlier months in the city and from twenty-five-cent second-balcony seats, Fran was aware of her mother's perusal of the meager contents of the small refrigerator, of how she managed to inspect the sparse contents of the little cabinet space provided. Mother was going to start talking again about their moving back to Bellevue, Fran warned herself, but it wasn't going to happen. Bernie and she would manage their own lives, here in New York.

Not until her parents were stifling yawns and preparing to return to the hotel did they bring up the question of Fran and Bernie's going back to Bellevue to live.

"We love living here," Fran broke into her father's cautious attempt to derail her mother's impassioned plea. Daddy was always the calm one—Mother was so emotional. "We're doing fine," she insisted.

"Living in a hovel like this?" Ida Goldman scoffed. "You could have a beautiful house of your own, a car, a maid. You don't have to live this way!"

"The city is a wonderful place to live." Fran's face flushed despite the lack of sufficient heat in the apartment. "We have the theater and museums and wonderful department stores—and the Atlantic Ocean. The subway takes us right to the beaches."

"That would beat the Chattahoochee," her father conceded with a chuckle. He exchanged a loaded glance with her mother. Fran tensed, wary of their next approach. They'd talked alone for a few minutes while Bernie and she had washed the cups and saucers. "Your mother and I have been thinking about your situation here. Why should you wait until I die to enjoy my money? We want you and Bernie—" Daddy was always the diplomat, Fran thought. "We want the two of you to find yourselves a nice, comfortable apartment on West End or Riverside—" He put a hand up to stop Fran's objection. "We'll pay the rent for the first year—by then the country will be in better shape and you'll be able to afford the rent. We'll give you a check to buy furniture. I admit, it won't be in the range of what the President is supposed to be planning to ask Congress for a buildup of our army and navy—but it'll be large enough to provide a pretty place for you to live in."

"We couldn't possibly let you do that," Bernie began, clearly touched but also upset at his own failure to support his wife in the style she had once known.

"Why can't I see my daughter and my son-in-law enjoying my money while I'm alive? Why should I have to deny myself that pleasure? Tomorrow, you start looking for a place. Then you'll buy furniture. No if, ands, or buts," Josiah insisted and nodded vigorously. "It's a done deal."

With her parents gone Fran tried to alleviate Bernie's conviction that he was a failure as a husband.

"Bernie, these are terrible times. Most families are fighting to keep a roof over their heads and food on the table. My folks are lucky—they haven't been touched by the Depression. And Daddy's right. Why shouldn't he enjoy spending his money the way he likes?"

Later—lying sleepless after Bernie had succumbed to tiredness—Fran tried to deal with her alarm at what her father had said just before he left the apartment—that the President and Congress were about to build up the army and navy. They expected war, she realized. And she remembered what her mother had said over dinner—about how her father had not been drafted to fight in the World War because he had a wife and child.

War was hovering over their heads—but she knew how to protect Bernie if the country began to draft its fighting-age men. How long would it take her to get pregnant if they forgot to be careful?

Five

Before her parents left for Bellevue, Fran chose a sunny, one-bedroom apartment in a small building between West End and Riverside in the West Seventies. Her father signed the lease with candid satisfaction.

"The living room in the new apartment is bigger than this whole place," he said humorously. "Go out and buy furniture." He handed over the check he'd written earlier. "And if you need more, you tell us, you hear?"

"Hey, it's great to have parents who're in the money," Bob drawled while he helped Fran and Bernie move their personal belongings into the new apartment a few days later. Only part of the furniture had been delivered, but Fran was impatient to be in their new home. "I'll line up a room for myself somewhere in the neighborhood," he said now that they no longer needed his rent contribution.

"This is a one-year deal," Bernie reminded. "At the end of the year we could be out on the street."

"Not a chance." Bob was more optimistic than at any time since Fran and Bernie had known him.

Fran suspected he was relieved that his family back in Iowa was getting help from the farm co-op they'd joined. He said the aid the government had set up applied just to large farms—not to single-family farms like his parents'. The only way they could compete was to form cooperative associations.

In truth, the country had fallen into worse conditions than those of the early days of the Depression. A shocking number of people were close to starvation, digging through garbage cans for food, fighting over tossed-aside rotting vegetables. Some big cities warned that—again—

they were running out of relief funds. Chicago was about to close down all of its relief stations. Unemployment rolls—which had been shrinking—soared once again.

In March Americans were shocked—and isolationists unnerved—when Hitler's troops invaded and annexed Austria.

"Where the hell will the bastard move next?" Bernie demanded over a Saturday evening dinner in their new apartment. As usual, Bob had dinner with them on Saturday evenings. "When will he be stopped?"

"Sally says we ought to get married even if we can't live together just yet." Sally was Bob's longtime girlfriend, who wrote him twice every week. "Married men won't be drafted right away if we get into war. The single guys will go first. But I can't afford a round-trip Greyhound ticket to Iowa—and Sally has to hold on to her WPA job to support her family."

For two months Fran had been disappointed that her covert efforts to become pregnant were futile. Was something wrong with her? she asked herself in recurrent alarm. Did this mean she couldn't have a baby? But maybe this month would prove differently, she thought with determined optimism. Of course, Bernie would be upset—they'd decided not to have a family until they'd been married five years.

Everybody said there was a definite upturn in the economy. Bernie would find new clients. And she could work right up to the time the baby was born. Hadn't Bob told them how his mother had been out working in the fields until just before her four kids were born? All *she* had to do was sit at the desk and answer the phone and do a little typing for Bernie and Bob—and whatever came in for her typing service. If she got pregnant, it didn't mean she and Bernie would have to go back to Bellevue. But even if it did, she thought defiantly, Bernie would still be safe from the draft.

By the end of March Fran was convinced she was pregnant—and simultaneously euphoric and fearful. This afternoon she left the office early at Bernie's insistence. He was sure she was coming down with a cold—but that wasn't what she had in mind. She'd almost fallen asleep twice at the typewriter. The books about pregnancy that she'd read in the library said sleepiness was usual in the first two months. How was Bernie going to react when she told him she was pregnant?

The day was cold and blustery. She was impatient to be within the warmth of the subway. She didn't mind not getting a seat today. She might doze off and go past her station. They could handle having a baby, she told herself yet again. And with a baby Bernie wouldn't be called to fight if war broke out. She'd do anything to keep him safe from fighting. She'd grown up hearing her mother talk about the wasteful death of her young uncle somewhere in France.

She left the subway at her station, walked hurriedly to their apartment house. Mother and Daddy would carry on yet again about their coming back to Bellevue when they heard she was pregnant. She knew they'd do anything they could to make sure she and Bernie had everything they needed. But Bernie wanted to stay in New York. He wanted to go to law school at night. They had to live their own lives.

With a sigh of relief she opened the door into the small lobby of their building and felt a surge of pleasure at the warmth that engulfed her.

"Hi, Fran—" Midore Yamamoto, the charming young Japanese-American who lived in a studio apartment down the hall from their own was holding the elevator for her. She and Midore talked often when they met at the elevator and sometimes at the grocery or the bakery. Midore had come to New York from San Francisco a little over a year ago. She taught art in a private school on the West Side while she tried to establish herself as an artist.

"Hi." Fran joined Midore in the elevator and stifled a yawn. "Oh, I'm so sleepy. Bernie sent me home from the office—it was very slow, anyhow. He told me to take a nap before dinner."

"Are you pregnant?" Midore asked softly.

"How did you guess?" Fran gazed at her in amazement.

"The sleepiness—and you have that special look in your eyes. Like my best friend back in California—both times she's been pregnant. Congratulations."

"I hope Bernie feels that way." Fran's smile was wry.

"Come in and have a cup of coffee with me," Midore invited. "I think Bernie will be very happy." Her eyes were tenderly reassuring.

"It's going to be expensive—" The elevator pulled to a stop at their floor. The two emerged and walked to Midore's apartment. "Bernie tries so hard to pick up business, but you know—" She spread her hands in a gesture of futility. Still, she knew her parents would help them. It wasn't as though it was she and Bernie against the world. Yet in a corner of her mind she worried now that Bernie might feel so beholden to her parents he'd resent her. She hadn't thought this through. She always rushed ahead without considering the consequences.

Over steaming black coffee Fran and Midore talked about the baby.

When Fran confessed she was apprehensive about all the added expenses, Midore jumped in to advise.

"Don't worry about an obstetrician," she comforted. "The brother of a colleague of mine at the school is an intern at Crawford Hospital. It's a small but very fancy private hospital, but they have a marvelous maternity clinic. He'll arrange for you to be a clinic patient—it'll cost you almost nothing and you'll have the best of care. I'll talk to him tomorrow."

"I just didn't think ahead to the technicalities." Fran managed a chuckle. "That's me. Mother always says, 'Depend on Frannie to jump in where angels fear to tread.' " Oh, she was glad Midore had asked her in for coffee. Except for Bob, she and Bernie had no friends in New York. Midore would be a good friend.

In her own apartment now, Fran debated about starting dinner or napping for a bit. The need for sleep won out. She awoke in the night-dark living room to hear Bernie moving about the kitchen. She sniffed with unexpected hunger at the aroma of onions frying on the gas range. Bernie was making their ever popular hamburgers, she guessed.

"Bernie—" She sat up and reached to switch on a lamp. She couldn't wait to tell him she was pregnant. But her heart began to pound. Was Bernie going to be upset?

"Hi, Sleeping Beauty." He grinned at her from the kitchen. "Dinner coming up in about ten minutes."

"Did you put in the burgers yet?"

"I'm just about to do it—with oceans of gorgeous onions."

"Hold it for a few minutes." She managed a shaky smile as she pulled herself upright on the sofa. "I have something to tell you."

"You're all aglow—like you'd just won the Irish Sweepstakes." He put down the spatula in his hand and walked to her—his eyes bright with curiosity.

"Bernie, I didn't want to tell until I was pretty sure—" She paused, faintly breathless. "But I'm sure now."

"Sure of what?" He was bewildered but indulgent.

"I'm pregnant. About five or six weeks, I figure from what I read in the books at the library. It's about a half-inch long now, but in another couple of weeks it'll be an inch—and Bernie, it'll look like a real baby already!" Why was she babbling this way? Bernie looked shocked.

"You're sure?" he repeated.

"Either that, or I have cancer or some dreadful terminal disease." She took momentary refuge in flippancy. "I'm three weeks late. That never happens."

"We'll have to go back to Bellevue—I'll work for your father." He was pale but determined.

"We will not, and you will not," she rejected. "We can handle this."

"There'll be doctor bills and hospital bills. Frannie, we—"

"Sssh." She reached lovingly to place a finger on his mouth. "I've thought it all out. Midore—you know, down the hall—was telling me about a friend of hers who just had a baby." God forgive her for lying, she prayed silently, but this was important. "There's a wonderful clinic in town that costs almost nothing. The brother of a teacher at her school interns there. I'm sure she could pull strings to have me accepted. Bernie, are you mad at me?" she asked, her eyes searching his.

"I had something to do with this, too." He reached to pull her close. She felt his heart pounding against her. "But we hadn't counted on it happening for another four years at least."

"I've been plotting how to handle everything. We can manage," she insisted. "I can be at the office practically until I go into labor."

"You will not be there," he told her. "I'll get a weekend job—we'll start saving money. If Bob gets that waiter's job, maybe he'll be able to bring me in, too." Desperate for bus fare for a brief visit home, Bob was on the track of a weekend job. "I'll find a weekend job," he insisted. "The economists are predicting we'll be out of this slump by midsummer. When is the little guy due?"

"I figure around late October." Bernie wasn't going to feel trapped, was he? "And stop saying 'guy,' " she scolded. "He may be a 'gal.' "

"Oh God, can you imagine what your parents will say when they find out?" Bernie grimaced. "They'll be on our necks to come back to Bellevue. They'll have his—" he hesitated, grinned, "or her first twenty-one years all planned—including college—before you're really popping out."

"Bernie, we're not going back to Bellevue." Her eyes held his—commanding him to believe this. "We're going to live in New York with our baby. You're going to law school at night, and I'm going to be a journalist. In time," she conceded. "I'll type for you and Bob here at home. It'll be rough for you not to have a receptionist in the office, but you'll manage. And when the baby is old enough to leave with a sitter for three or four hours, we might even work to help organize those salesgirls at Woolworth's. You know they're threatening to strike. Oh Bernie, I want him—or her—to be proud of us."

Letters flew back and forth between Fran and her parents. They were enthralled by the prospect of becoming grandparents, upset that Fran and Bernie insisted on staying up in New York. They were shocked at the thought of Fran's going to a clinic. They would pay all medical costs for the baby. Fran knew Bernie was upset by this, yet wanted what was best for her. Midore's friend gave Fran the name of a prestigious obstetrician, and arrangements were made for her care.

Convinced she couldn't bring Fran and Bernie back to Bellevue, Ida Goldman sent a lavish maternity wardrobe, almost weekly sent clothes and toys for the baby. A check arrived to buy a crib and other necessities plus a studio couch for the living room. Her mother would be in New York for the final month of her pregnancy—the only time since their marriage that her parents had been separated for more than the days of her father's semiannual business trips.

As the economists predicted, business was improving by midsummer—but the threat of war hung ominously over the world. Hitler was making demands now on the government of Czechoslovakia. In September Fran and Bernie clung to the radio each night to hear the latest developments. In London soldiers were digging trenches. Troops handed out gas masks to civilians, piled sandbags around government buildings. Major underground—subway—stations had been closed.

Late in the month there were a series of meetings between Hitler, British Prime Minister Chamberlain, and Deladier of France—and then Mussolini was brought in. In order to avoid war these countries signed what was called the Munich Agreement—yielding to Hitler all important Czech military posts. Small Czechoslovakia bitterly accepted this. Europe was determined to avoid war.

While she and Bernie listened to a Kaltenborn report on the Munich Agreement, Fran felt her first labor pain. Absorbed by the news, Bernie didn't notice her sudden clutch at her mountainous stomach.

"Bernie, I think the baby's going to be a bit early," she told him while she struggled to hide her alarm. Was the baby all right?

"You're not due for four weeks." He stared solicitously.

"Mother's going to be furious." Fran strived for humor. "She was determined to be with me for my last month." Her mother was due to arrive tomorrow evening. She was aboard the Seaboard Airline pullman this very moment, Fran pinpointed.

"Maybe it's false labor—" But despite the coolness of their living room Bernie was suddenly perspiring.

"I think this little character has made up its mind." For Bernie she was determined to be casual. "But we'll wait and see. I don't want to go to the hospital twenty-four hours ahead of time."

It soon became clear that this wasn't false labor. Bernie insisted on calling the obstetrician. He ordered Bernie to take Fran to the hospital immediately.

"Am I going to lose the baby?" Fran whispered.

"Honey, no," Bernie protested. "Lots of babies come a little early. This character is fine. Just impatient—like his mother," he joshed.

Five hours later Fran gave birth to a six-pound-one-ounce daughter.

"Her name is Lynne Esther Garfield," Fran told Bernie softly while she cradled her sleepy daughter in her arms. "She's all tuckered out now."

"For my mother and your grandmother." Tears glistened in Bernie's eyes. "Your folks will spoil her rotten," he warned, but Fran knew he was grateful that she would have loving grandparents.

"Call Daddy and tell him," she ordered and giggled. "He'll know before Mother. I'm not sure she'll ever forgive me for that."

The following evening Bernie met Fran's mother at Penn Station. The next night Josiah Goldman arrived unannounced. He came directly to the hospital.

"The store can run without me for a few days. How can I not be here to see my first grandchild? All right, who's going to show me?" he demanded, his face reflecting his happiness.

"Bernie, take him out to the nursery," Ida ordered. "Just look for the best-looking baby," she told her husband. "The one with a headful of black hair."

"She is pretty, isn't she?" Fran said to her mother when they were alone.

"She's gorgeous, my darling." Her mother's eyes were tenderly nostalgic. "The image of you at that age. And thank God, you're a family now. If, God forbid, we have a war, Bernie won't be drafted."

"I know." Fran smiled. Mission accomplished.

On the morning that Bernie and her mother came to take her home with the baby, Fran sensed that Bernie had special news for her. What was it that he didn't want to say in front of Mother? she asked herself in soaring curiosity.

Not until her mother went down to shop at a neighborhood grocery store did Bernie relay his news.

"I have a job three nights a week in the restaurant where Bob is working," he told her with an air of jubilation. "I'll be there Fridays,

Saturdays, and Sundays from 5 P.M. to 11 P.M. Your folks won't have to worry about how we're managing."

"You're an accountant," Fran whispered. It *did* bother him that they'd depended so much on her parents. "And you should be starting law school at night soon."

"Our time will come," Bernie promised. "We're a family now. We must do what's right for the family."

Fran's mother went back to Bellevue when Lynne was fourteen days old. Though shocked by the wages paid New York nursemaids, she'd tried to arrange for Fran to have help with the baby for her first three months. Fran insisted this wasn't necessary.

"My goodness!" Ida said in amazement. "Back home you'd have a fine nursemaid for three dollars a week—and she'd clean the house for that, too."

Midore—who had no class that morning—came to sit with Lynne while Fran and Bernie saw her mother off at Penn Station.

"I think Mother was exhausted," Fran said and chuckled. "She's not used to a world without 'help' around the house. She went through a pregnancy, of course—but after that there was Annie Mae to get up and give me the two A.M. bottle and change my diapers, and all the rest of the deal."

"You look tired," Bernie commiserated.

"So do you." Fran squeezed his arm as they made their way through the cavernous station. "I'll bet Daddy never in his life changed a diaper or gave a bottle." She was touched that Bernie was up with her at the first sound from Lynne. He changed the diaper while she prepared the bottle.

They were going to make a fine life for themselves. They had a new incentive. They had Lynne Esther Garfield. And it wasn't the end of their dreams—only the beginning.

Six

Their days and nights were hectic, but Fran and Bernie were euphoric. Their world revolved around tiny Lynne. It didn't matter that they were constantly exhausted. Bernie was grateful for his weekend job, fighting for new clients for the office. Each day he brought home typing for Fran to do while Lynne was asleep. Because her fees were low, work was coming in to her newly established typing service, which Bernie accepted for her.

Midore was entranced with the baby and enthralled Fran and Bernie with a series of sketches of Lynne. Bob came home with Bernie a night or two each week to have dinner with them. It amazed Fran that Bob was so handy with the baby—until he pointed out that he was the oldest of six children and had been drafted to help with the younger ones. Sometimes, when he picked up Lynne and sang to her, Fran suspected he was wistfully envisioning Sally and himself with a baby.

At the end of October Bob prepared to go home for a quick visit.

"Maybe I can persuade Sally to get married and come back here with me," he told Bernie in a spurt of optimism as they were leaving the office the night before his departure. "I'm damn tired of sleeping alone. You've got it made, old boy. A beautiful wife, a kid, a fine apartment."

But Bernie knew—as Bob did—that Sally couldn't walk out on her WPA job. That was supporting her parents and her fourteen-year-old sister as well as herself. Still, the economy *was* improving. It was terrible to realize it was because of the rotten situation in Europe. But orders were pouring into American factories from the British and the French for guns and planes—all the implements of war.

The two men caught the uptown subway, emerged from the West 72nd Street station and headed for their respective destinations. Bernie's mind focused now on what Bob had told him while they clung to straps in the crowded subway car—always jammed at this hour of the evening.

Bob was starting a new night job at an aircraft factory out on Long Island when he came back from his trip home. He'd work the 4 P.M. to midnight shift—which would allow him to keep a semblance of a law practice. He was jubilant about the salary.

Hell, maybe *he* should try for the same job. Bob didn't know a thing about working on their machines—somebody would train him. Bob admitted he'd felt strange going into blue-collar work when he had broken his back to earn a law degree. But the money was terrific—more than either of them was seeing from their fine professions, Bernie thought with a flicker of humor. And the aircraft planes were turning out essential materials. He felt lousy, always taking from Fran's parents. It was fine of them to want to help—but a man ought to be able to take care of his wife and child. He always felt shitty at the first of each month when a check came from the Goldmans to cover their rent.

By the time he arrived at the house, Fran had given Lynne her 6 o'-clock bottle and put her into the crib. She'd sleep till ten, Bernie reminded himself. He was nervous now about telling Fran of his decision. He'd wait until after dinner. She wouldn't want him to jeopardize his practice, he thought uneasily. But he could handle both a defense job and his few clients.

Over dinner their conversation revolved around Lynne. As usual these evenings they had coffee in the living room—where they could listen to the radio. They had both become addicted to radio newscasts, available now twenty-four hours a day.

"The days of the newspaper 'extras' are gone," Bernie mused while they waited for the international news on this November 9th. After the news, he promised himself, he'd talk to Fran about his going after a defense job.

Then their favorite commentator was on the air. With his first words coffee was forgotten. Tense with shock as the commentator's voice filled the room, Bernie reached for Fran's hand.

"Oh, Bernie," Fran gasped while they listened to the commentator report the horror of *Kristallnacht* in Nazi Germany.

A few hours earlier—night time already in Germany—Nazi storm troopers smashed Jewish homes and shops. They burned synagogues, beat Jews. It was a pogrom on a national level.

The previous month fifteen thousand German Jews of Polish origin had been rounded up and thrown into trains, then disgorged on the Polish border. Nobody knew how the anti-Semitic Polish government would handle these refugees. One couple among them managed to mail a postcard to a teenage son in Paris. Distraught and helpless, the boy had shot the Third Secretary of the German Embassy in Paris. *Kristallnacht* was the Nazis' retaliation.

Sick with horror Bernie and Fran sat gulping cup after cup of coffee while they tried to evaluate this latest atrocity.

"Please, God, let every Jew in Germany try to get out of the country before they're all annihilated!" A vein throbbed in Bernie's forehead. "We have a madman on the loose in Europe." He paused, took a long breath, exhaled as though in pain. "Fran, don't be upset by what I'm about to say—" But he saw her tense in alarm. "It doesn't mean I'm dumping my accounting clients—but I want to look for a defense job. Maybe we'll be able to stay out of the war—but England and France won't. This country will have to supply them with arms, planes. Let me at least be part of that effort. And we can use the money," he added.

"Bernie, you can't run the office and work in a defense plant." Fran gaped at him in disbelief.

"I can," he said urgently. "Bob told me tonight that he has a job in an aircraft plant. He'll start as soon as he gets back to the city. They'll train him. Clients aren't beating a track to our doors—we'll be at the office from 8 A.M. to 2:30 P.M. Juggle appointments. See clients on Saturdays. The defense job is five days a week. Fran, I can handle this. I *want* to do it. Not just for the money—though that was my first thought. But because I have to do what I can to help arm England and France. It's a matter of time before Hitler attacks the rest of Europe."

Within ten days Bernie had replaced his weekend job with a "swing shift" job in the burgeoning defense industry. Like Bob he'd be a defense worker from 4 P.M. to midnight. He fought down guilt because he knew Fran was nervous about this move. But she understood, he told himself tenderly. She knew this was something he had to do.

"I can handle this," he told Fran with genuine optimism. "New Yorkers are working crazy hours these days. I schedule Monday to Friday office hours, put in a full day Saturdays. Clients will adapt."

Fran worried that Bernie was getting little sleep. He always seemed so tired. And they had so little time together, she fretted. How long could he keep up this crazy schedule?

"Honey, stop worrying about me," he cajoled at the end of his second week of fourteen-hour work days when she voiced her anxiety. "I'm twenty-three years old. I can handle this. Pretend I'm going to med school—my hours would be worse."

All right, this was the way their lives would be for a while, Fran told herself. For how long there was no way of knowing. Let her do whatever possible to make things easier for Bernie. On Sundays, she vowed, he'd sleep most of the day. And let the little time they spent together be special.

On Monday evening—after Lynne was sleeping for the night—Fran settled on the sofa to nap. In moments she was dozing. These last two weeks she'd forced herself to stay awake until Bernie came home, to sit with him—fighting yawns, huddled in flannel nightgown and robe— while he ate a late supper. Tonight would be different.

At exactly forty-five minutes before Bernie was due to arrive, the alarm woke her. She reached instantly to shut it off, though she knew Lynne would not be disturbed by the soft sound of the alarm—chosen for this attribute. She hurried into the bathroom to throw cold water on her face, changed into one of the frilly nightgowns and negligées from her father's shop—that Bernie loved to see her wear. The heat was down for the night, but never mind.

Hearing the ticking of the clock in the silence of the night—a stern warning that Bernie was by now on the subway—she powdered her face, applied a touch of lipstick, ran a brush over the masses of dark hair that Bernie said made her look like a movie star. Feeling the night chill in the apartment, she hurried to a closet to bring out the small electric heater used to warm Lynne's room on occasion. With a glow of triumph she carried it into the dining room, flipped the switch and cozy warmth reached out to her.

In the kitchen she put up dinner for Bernie, a pot of coffee. Now she set two places at the dining table, brought out a pair of candles. Another ten minutes, she told herself, and she'd light them. She paused now to look in on Lynne, pulled up the coverlet that her tiny daughter invariably kicked off, then left the bedroom—closing the door quietly but firmly behind her.

She brought the small Emerson radio from the kitchen into the dining room, fiddled with the dials until she found the disk jockey who favored music by Cole Porter and George Gershwin. Bernie's favorite composers. With the music muted she returned to the kitchen to cut up onions to sauté as an accompaniment for Bernie's hamburger. The potatoes would be ready to mash in a few moments. The canned peas he liked could be warmed up quickly. Let Bernie understand that his life was more than running from one job to another. *Yes*, the little time they had to spend together would be special.

Her face lighted when she heard Bernie's key in the door. He kept telling her not to wait up for him. How could she do that when he was working so hard? She hurried from the kitchen to greet him.

"Hi," she said softly, lifting her face for his kiss.

"Am I forgetting a birthday or anniversary or something?" His eyes swept over her in approval. He heard the soft strains of "Night and Day" filtering into the apartment.

"I'm on a new schedule," she flipped. "When Lynne conks out for the night, I nap. I wake up for a rendezvous with my husband. Dinner will be served in three minutes."

"Have I ever told you I love you madly?"

"A few times," she conceded. "But tell me again. After dinner," she stipulated. "Unless you prefer your hamburger burnt."

At Bernie's insistence Fran wrote her parents that they could now handle the rent on their apartment.

"Bernie's working his butt off between his office and the defense plant—not just to make money but because he feels we have a responsibility to do everything we can to fight against Hitler," she wrote, and then went into her usual full report of Lynne's progress. By spring Lynne had seven teeth, was growing out of her clothes and crawling. "Everybody just adores her. She's such a happy baby!"

Their small circle of friends—Bob, Midore, Cliff Jamison—a medical student who worked part-time at the defense plant with Bernie, and a young couple who became clients of both Bob and Bernie when they opened a small restaurant in Greenwich Village—gathered in the Garfield apartment on Saturday evenings for their once-a-week socializing. They ate Bernie's lusty hamburgers or Fran's spaghetti, drank inexpensive wine. Late in the evening one of the men went down to pick up the Sunday *New York Times*—available on Saturday evening on the Upper West Side—and divided the sections among themselves for group reading. And at somber intervals they argued about the prospect of the country becoming involved in the war.

Lynne was delightfully accommodating. She now slept from 7 P.M. to 7 A.M.—ignoring the Saturday evening medley of voices that sometimes became so noisy that Fran ordered lower tones.

Then as the new year rolled along, one crisis after another erupted in

Europe. On March 15, 1939, Hitler invaded Czechoslovakia. On March 23rd, Nazi troops took Memel—and five days later the Spanish Republic collapsed. On April 7th, Italian troops invaded Albania.

"Listen to the Gallup Poll," Fran said in soaring alarm and read the figures to Bernie. "Fifty-eight percent believe we're going to be drawn into war in Europe, 90 percent say they'll fight if this country is invaded, 10 percent say they'll fight even if we're not invaded."

"But Lindbergh keeps telling radio audiences, 'We must not be misguided by this foreign propaganda that our frontiers lie in Europe. What more could we ask than the Atlantic Ocean on the east, the Pacific on the West?' Doesn't he understand that Great Britain isn't exactly a stabilizing force in Europe—and France's military is weak compared to Germany's? And they're what stands between Hitler's ambition to take *'die ganze welt.'* The whole world."

Fran was enthralled when in June a woman was elected Lord Mayor of Dublin—the first time in history. She and Midore discussed this with relish. Then a wave of depression engulfed Fran.

"I feel so useless," she confided to Midore. "What am I doing with my life? I used to think I'd make some important contribution before I was twenty-five. And here I am twenty-three and I've accomplished nothing."

"Lynne's an accomplishment," Midore protested. "And look how you help Bernie with his office. You're making a contribution."

"Look at the women in England. They're going into military service. There's a Women's Auxiliary Air Force!"

Fran was avidly following the items in the *New York Times* about the struggle between the Southern cotton mill owners and the workers. The owners complained that the government decreed a raise to thirty cents an hour, due in October, would ruin the industry. They were already battling competition from Japan. Oh, she wished she could help the workers, she thought impatiently. Those weeks with Hank Weinstein and his team had filled her with such satisfaction.

Fran's parents wrote that a second German refugee family had arrived in Bellevue. Like Bernie they were convinced that a second World War was inevitable.

"Thank God, you and Bernie have the baby," her mother wrote. "Bernie won't be called up to fight."

Like many Americans Fran and Bernie were appalled when late in May the *New York Times* reported that the passengers aboard the S.S. *St. Louis*—which had arrived in Havana, Cuba, from Hamburg with 937 Ger-

man-Jewish refugees—had been denied the right to disembark despite
arrangements that had guaranteed permission for them to remain in Cuba
while permanent destinations could be arranged. More than half of the
passengers were women and children. Some of the men had been released
from concentration camps with the proviso that they leave Germany.

Fran and Bernie listened to news reports after Lynne had been put
to bed for the night.

"They can't send those refugees back to Germany!" Fran turned anxiously to Bernie. "Can they?"

"Another country will take them in," Bernie said comfortingly.
"Probably us."

They listened to late evening radio reports—with newspapers
around the world covering the situation. But Cuba was involved in a battle between its president and its corrupt immigration minister. Entrea-
ties, threats, negotiations were futile.

"Why can't the refugees come to this country?" Fran demanded. "My
God, Bernie, the ship is so close to Miami!"

Each day they watched the newspapers for the latest developments,
listened to every radio news bulletin. Many American newspapers
stirred enormous sympathy for the refugees, yet none urged that they
be admitted to the United States—though Jewish committees were
fighting a desperate battle in their behalf. Then after long, agonizing
days of doubt word came through from Miami. The *St. Louis* would not
be allowed to dock at any U.S. port.

"I can't believe this country is turning them away!" Fran felt sick
with rage as she and Bernie heard the final decision on a newscast.
"They'll go into concentration camps if they're taken back to Germany!"

"It's politics," Bernie said quietly. "The bloody old game."

"Then people have to fight for change. Ordinary people like us.
You're going to law school. You'll get involved in politics—and I'll be
there with you," Fran said with messianic resolve. "I know how little
time we have, but from now on we're going to do more than just go out
and vote at election time. We're going to fight for what we know is
right." With fresh impatience she thought of her mother—who gave time
willingly to her charity committees but couldn't be bothered to go out
and vote. "Not just for ourselves—but for Lynne."

Her resolve was not lessened when frenzied, last-minute negotiations
allowed the refugees to disembark in stipulated numbers at ports in England, France, Holland, and Belgium.

"But we turned them away," she mourned. "The next time we fight."

When the sultry heat of the city summer rolled in, Fran and Bernie packed a picnic lunch on Sundays and traveled by subway to Brighton Beach with Lynne. Fran alternately scolded Bernie for smoking so much—something he couldn't afford in Depression days—and encouraged him to sleep beneath the umbrella they'd rented from a beach concession. She was upset when she read in the *New York Times* that a researcher—speaking at the International Cancer Congress—had told how he had induced cancer in mice when he painted them with tobacco tar. Bernie was always so tense, she fretted—that was why he smoked so much. Mother and Daddy still couldn't understand why they wouldn't give up their harried lives to come back to Bellevue.

At intervals—more frequent than in the days before Lynne's birth—Josiah Goldman came to New York on buying trips, along with his wife. Fran knew her parents made these additional trips out of a need to reassure themselves that she and Bernie and the baby were all right—and to fuss lovingly over their only grandchild. For the few days that her parents were in New York Fran contrived to keep them unaware that Bernie was working on the swing shift at a defense plant.

"Frannie, why are you so stubborn?" Her mother sighed. "You could have such a good life in Bellevue. A nice house, a girl to take care of Lynne and to do the cleaning. Daddy will give you our car when he buys a new one any day now. Bernie can come into the store. Why do you have to live like this?" her mother reiterated during an August visit—while Bernie and his father-in-law were off in a corner talking about the war of nerves Hitler inflicted on Poland.

Yes, life was easier in the South, Fran conceded—but New York was where their dreams could be fulfilled. Only to herself would she admit that she feared her parents' efforts—warm and wonderful—could destroy Bernie's confidence in himself. And she'd always felt herself an outsider in Bellevue, she remembered defiantly. She wasn't satisfied to spend her days going to parties or serving as a volunteer on some charity committee. That was *boring.*

As always when her parents left for Bellevue, Fran felt a poignant sense of loss for a few days. Ever sensitive to her mood, Bernie plotted a group outing to Brighton Beach for one day over the weekend. Fran rejected this.

"It'll be a madhouse at Brighton over the Labor Day weekend," Fran reminded. "Let's stay home. If it gets terribly hot, we'll take Lynne down to Riverside Drive."

But on Friday morning of the Labor Day weekend Fran and Bernie awoke to the news that Nazi troops were marching into Poland. Despite the heat of the long Labor Day weekend they seldom stirred away from the radio. Before the weekend was over, England and France had declared war on Germany. Fran and Bernie heard a rising young reporter named Ed Murrow announce this from an underground studio of Broadcasting House in London. And in a "fireside" chat they heard FDR announce that the United States would remain neutral.

"For how long?" Bernie said somberly.

"Bernie, don't say that!" Fran's heart pounded.

When would the world learn to live in peace? Why was this so hard to do? Roosevelt's words on that most recent fireside chat haunted her in the days ahead: "When peace has been broken anywhere, the peace of all countries everywhere is in danger."

Defense orders from England and France poured into the United States. Employment soared. Bernie closed the office on Saturdays to work at the plant. Fran worried that he was pushing himself too hard.

"You don't get enough sleep, you drink too much coffee, and you smoke too much," she wailed recurrently.

"It won't always be like this," he soothed. "And we're putting money into the bank every month."

She was anxious about the progress of the war in Europe, though most people were sure the United States would never be invaded.

"We've got two oceans between us," Bob pointed out the often-repeated rationale for this. "The Nazis will never cross the Atlantic—and the Japanese aren't interested in us. They want China."

Still, Fran was uneasy. Maybe this country wouldn't be invaded, but when would American men have to cross the Atlantic to help England and France?

On New Year's Eve the atmosphere at the small gathering in Fran and Bernie's apartment was convivial. Midore had just seen *Gone With The Wind* and was enthralled by the epic movie. Bob and Cliff were arguing good-humoredly about the outcome of the Rose Bowl game tomorrow.

"Hey, the Tennessee eleven will make mincemeat out of Southern California tomorrow!" Bob assured the others while in the background a recording by Wee Bonnie Baker brought the bouncy music and lyrics of "Oh, Johnny! Oh!" into the room.

At intervals Fran tiptoed into the bedroom to look in on Lynne, who slept undisturbed in her crib. Such a good baby, Fran thought tenderly, lifting one tiny hand to her mouth. And even if she were awakened, she'd be in good spirits. Her zest for living was a joy, Fran told herself with pride.

At 11:30 Bernie went out to the kitchen along with Midore to prepare hamburgers and coffee for their midnight snack. Midore had brought a magnum of champagne to welcome in the new decade.

They ate with relish, watchful now for the fateful moment when the radio announcer would begin the countdown and the lighted ball on the roof of the Times Building would fall to announce the arrival of 1940. And then they listened in electric excitement at the count.

"Welcome, 1940!" the radio announcer exclaimed, and they could hear the exuberant shouting of thousands of celebrants jammed into Times Square for the occasion. The sounds of horns, boat whistles, cars honking. Somebody switched to another station and the sweet swing of Guy Lombardo filled the room.

For a little while those in the Garfield apartment were caught up in the festive atmosphere. Then Bob—who a little while ago had been all involved in the Rose Bowl game—punctured this with a derisive remark about New Year celebrations in the countries overrun by the Nazis, the Japanese, and the Soviet troops.

"Don't forget what Mussolini did to the Ethiopians," Sal—the young restaurateur who had only contempt for the fascist dictator—reminded. "He sent in armed soldiers to shoot down Ethiopians who still fought with bows and arrows."

"But most people here at home," Midore said somberly, "don't want to see us fighting this war."

"They don't want to face it," Bernie said angrily. "They figure if they close their eyes, then it'll all go away. And meanwhile everybody is benefiting from the booming economy."

Maybe it was selfish of her, Fran thought guiltily—but she prayed they wouldn't get into the war. She didn't want Bernie to have to go to Europe to fight. Even if they did get into the war, Bernie wouldn't be drafted, would he? He was a husband and father.

Maybe it was time they had a second child. . . .

Seven

Fran was conscious of overwhelming relief when she realized in mid-February that she was pregnant again. But Bernie's air of anxiety when she told him was unnerving.

"You want to go through that again?" His eyes searched hers. "When the world's in such chaos?"

"Bernie, it's our baby." For a moment she felt a strange alienation. "Of course I want it!"

"I know, honey." Contrite, he reached for her. "But I worry about what's going to happen in the world. And that you're alone so much—"

"I'll be fine." Her smile was bright. It was selfish of her, she thought in silent defiance—but she'd do anything to keep Bernie safe. All her life she'd heard about how her uncle David died in the World War when he was twenty-four. That mustn't happen to Bernie. Surely, with two children, he'd never be drafted.

When Fran's parents learned she was pregnant again, they tried to persuade her to return to Bellevue. With the familiar promises—a house of their own, a well-paying job in the store for Bernie.

"You tell me how hard Bernie works," her mother reminded. "You'll have such a comfortable life back here."

Bernie wouldn't be happy in Bellevue—nor would she, Fran told herself. In time—when the world settled down again—Bernie would go to law school at night. She'd be a crusading journalist. Both of them fighting for the kind of world they wanted.

She continued to type for Bernie and Bob—both of whom managed to maintain a limited clientele along with their defense jobs. Her mother wrote that the cotton mills in Bellevue were running around the clock, that the two midtwenties sons of their next-door neighbor had abandoned their professions to take jobs in the mills.

"They figure if we do get into this war, then they'll be in an essential industry. Daddy says the mills will just convert to making military uniforms."

In April Fran watched with soaring trepidation as the Nazis invaded Denmark and Norway. In May—as the British learned that Chamberlain was to be replaced by Winston Churchill—the Nazis swept into Belgium, Holland, and Luxembourg. In this same month the British army had to be evacuated from Dunkirk by hastily assembled yachts, barges, and a determined flotilla of small, private boats. And in May Paris fell.

"In this apartment the radio stays on all the time," Fran confided to Midore, who'd dropped in for coffee with her. "Bernie's afraid we'll miss the latest disaster in Europe. There has to be a turning point soon."

"That will come," Midore said bluntly, "when this country gets into the war."

"Don't say that!" Fran flared, then sighed. "I'm sorry, Midore. It's just that I feel as though we're sitting on a powder keg all the time."

Fran knew that Sal and Gabrielle would be upset when early in June Mussolini brought Italy into the war on Hitler's side. She talked with Gabrielle about it on the phone. It seemed, she thought restlessly, that so much of her life was spent on the phone these days.

On a humid Sunday afternoon in late June Fran and Bernie's small circle gathered at their apartment for dinner. His parents filling in for them at the restaurant, Sal and Gabrielle arrived with a roast. Bernie helped Fran prepare a mammoth salad. Midore baked a platter of the cookies her late grandmother had taught her to make. They were to have an early dinner since tomorrow would be a working day.

The men gathered around the radio to listen to the baseball game.

"I wish baseball had never been invented," Gabrielle complained to Fran and Midore. "From April to October that's all Sal listens to on the radio." Her face was suddenly somber. "That and the news."

"Oh, Lynne's awake." Fran heard the good-humored summons from the bedroom. "Mommie" was such a beautiful word, she thought tenderly. "Let's go visit with her."

Again, Gabrielle was wistful about not being pregnant.

"We've been trying practically since our honeymoon—three years ago in June," she said candidly. "It just isn't happening."

"You have plenty of time," Fran consoled her. But she suspected that

Gabrielle, too, was anxious to see Sal a father in view of the war situation.

"If I was pregnant, Sal wouldn't be so upset about Italy going into the war with Hitler," Gabrielle surmised. "His parents would stop moaning about it all the time. They'd be so excited about the baby they'd forget that crazy Mussolini."

"Gabrielle, Sal and his parents aren't responsible for what's happening in Italy. Sal was born here," Midore pointed out. "He and his parents are American citizens."

In June a senator and a representative introduced a draft bill into both houses of the Congress. On September 16, 1940 Congress passed the first peacetime military draft in the nation's history. All men between twenty and thirty-six were required to register. Nine hundred thousand would be inducted in the first year. Those chosen—by lottery—would serve for a period of one year.

Convinced that married men would be deferred, couples were rushing to acquire marriage licenses. The sale of wedding rings soared. In her last weeks of pregnancy Fran rejoiced in her conviction that Bernie would be exempt and comforted Gabrielle with Sal's status as a married man.

"I feel as though I'm hiding behind you and the baby," Bernie admitted on the late October evening after the first numbers were drawn. They sat on the living room sofa—Fran with pillows propped behind her back to alleviate the discomfort of late pregnancy.

"One and three-quarters baby," Fran said, patting the mountainous thrust of her stomach. "And not everybody who registers will be called up. You're working in a defense plant. You're doing your share."

A few days before Thanksgiving Fran went into labor. Midore was summoned to stay with Lynne while Bernie took Fran to the hospital. Seven hours later Fran gave birth to a second daughter, Deborah Anne. Her mother arrived in New York the following evening to take care of Lynne while she was in the hospital.

"My three beautiful women," Bernie told Fran, his face bright with love when he brought her and their new daughter home from the hospital. "You all look just alike!"

"Remember to make a fuss over Lynne," she whispered while her mother cooed over her newest grandchild.

"I don't love her any less for having another." Bernie laughed, but he scooped up Lynne and tossed her into the air. "Hey, you've got a real live doll now," he teased her. "You and Mommie will take care of her together."

To Fran the months seemed to fly past. In the spring she and Bernie and the children moved into another apartment in the same building when it became available. The bedrooms here were tiny, but there were two of them. It was important, she insisted to Bernie, that they have two bedrooms. Juggling shifts—the defense plant and the office—he needed uninterrupted sleep in the brief hours available for this. Like with Lynne, Debbie began to teethe early—there were nights when Fran walked the floor with her.

Fran was grateful for the arrival of summer. She was able to spend hours in the park with the children. When they napped, she typed for Bernie and Bob. One week in August Bernie took Friday and Saturday off so that he and Fran could take the children away from the sweltering heat of New York for three days. Sal and Gabrielle had been offered a relative's beach cottage at the tiny town of Wainscott, on Long Island. His father was putting the family car at their disposal for the long weekend.

It would be a joyous escape from the city, Fran thought in pleasure when they arrived at the cottage and walked a hundred yards to the beach.

"This sure beats Coney Island!" Sal chortled.

"Sand pile!" Lynne yelled joyously at her first sight of the beach. "Water!"

"Oh, I wish we could stay here forever," Fran said impetuously when—after three glorious days—they prepared to climb into the car for the return trip to the city. Then she tensed at the sight of Bernie's somber face. He thought she missed the easy lifestyle in Bellevue. Why had she said that? "Of course, I'd die of boredom after three weeks," she effervesced. "Thanks, Sal and Gabrielle, for bringing us out here with you."

Sometimes she missed Bellevue, Fran thought as they settled themselves in the car, and immediately she felt guilty. New York was where she wanted to live. Bernie wouldn't be happy anywhere else. Away from the city she'd miss the theaters and the museums, the ethnic restaurants, the wonderful department stores, the aura of excitement that was everywhere. They didn't get to the theater or the museums very often these days—but that would change once the world settled down again.

Back in their apartment after the trauma of a summer Sunday battle with traffic, Fran took the children off to bed. Bernie dropped with relief into a chair and reached to turn on the radio. There had been no radio at the cottage. For the past three days they'd heard no news. They knew only what they'd read in the newspapers. Bernie listened—troubled by the inference—to the news that President Roosevelt had signed an extension to the Selective Service bill. In time of peace, the bill decreed, no draftee would serve more than thirty months.

"Bernie, how long do they expect the war in Europe to last?" Fran gazed at him in shock when he reported this to her.

"I don't want to think about it." Bernie's smile was rueful. "You notice the nine hundred thousand man limit on the army has just been abolished, too."

On Debbie's first birthday Bernie came home with a grimness about him that alerted Fran to trouble.

"Bernie, what's wrong?" she asked while he lifted Lynne into his arms and reached to scoop Debbie from the playpen as well.

"Bob's been drafted," he said. "This morning he received that famous draft notice—'Greetings: Having submitted yourself to a local draft board blah-blah-blah.' "

Fran was cold with shock. They had known it could happen, of course—but they'd clung to the knowledge that Bob had a low draft number. They'd thought.

"When does he have to report for duty?"

"He might not be accepted," Bernie pointed out. "Though we couldn't think of any reason why he won't be."

"He'll be the first person close to us who's been drafted," Fran whispered. "But it's not as though we're sending men over to Europe to fight." Her voice trailed away.

"I want to close up the office, Fran," Bernie said gently. "I can put in a lot of hours of overtime if I want—and the money is terrific." Bernie was supervising a whole department now, with an impressive raise in salary. "We can sock away a big chunk of money every week."

"After all you've gone through to build up a client list?" Fran was shaken.

"It's not that great," he pointed out. "And now—with Bob out of the office—I'll be responsible for the rent for the whole place. I'll be working to pay the overhead—with a little left over each month." His eyes pleaded with her to agree.

Fran debated inwardly. Bernie didn't like being an accountant. He didn't like the job at the defense plant, either—but that was temporary.

If he put in the hours at the defense plant that went into the office, his salary would soar.

"All right, Bernie," she said with the glow of confidence he always cherished. "We'll put the money away to see us through while you go to law school. Full time—not just evening classes. I'll work at the typing service. I can handle that from the apartment."

"That's what I love about you," Bernie said tenderly. "You're always so damned optimistic."

Fran and Bernie were revitalized by this latest approach to their future. With amazing swiftness he gave up his accounting practice and made himself available for more overtime on the job. While Midore watched over Lynne and Debbie in the late afternoons, Fran called on her handful of typing customers, left circulars under the doors of other offices. The important effort now was to put money away to support the family when the war was over and Bernie in law school.

Bob was accepted for induction into the armed services and was now at boot camp in Virginia. Cliff was sure he would be exempt from the draft until the end of the school year. Gabrielle was still trying to become pregnant—more urgent than ever to her because she was convinced this would keep Sal out of military uniform.

On a cold bleak Sunday in early December Fran decided she and Bernie would have a small New Year's Eve party. They discussed this over a late lunch while Lynne and Debbie napped.

"The kids are wonderful about sleeping through when we have people over," she reminded Bernie. "I think they'd sleep through a bombing."

"I doubt that." Bernie was unfamiliarly terse. "I doubt the British kids are sleeping through the bombing in England." In truth, many British children had been shipped away for the duration—some as far away as Canada and the United States.

"We're bringing Lynne and Debbie up right." Fran tried for an air of levity. "I made them understand—once they hit the mattresses, they sleep."

"I'll probably conk out any minute," Bernie warned, reaching for a second slab of lox and another bagel. "All that fresh air in the park with the kids, and you're stuffing me with food."

"Hey, it's easy," she drawled. "I run up to Zabar's, I buy lox and bagels and cream cheese—and voila, Sunday brunch." This had become a Sunday tradition with them—to be eaten in lazy comfort in the living room. "I don't tell you to make a pig of yourself." But he worked so hard—he had so little sleep during the week. On Sundays he slept after lunch until she woke him for dinner.

They both started at a frenzied jabbing of their doorbell.

"I don't smell smoke—there can't be a fire," Fran flipped as she pushed back her chair and hurried to respond.

She pulled the door wide. Pale and clearly distraught, Midore hovered at the door.

"You're not listening to the radio," Midore accused and pushed past Fran. She strode from the foyer into the living room.

"What's happened?" Fear clutched at Fran's throat as she trailed after Midore.

"What's up?" Bernie asked.

"Pearl Harbor has been attacked," Midore said, reaching to switch on the radio.

"Where's Pearl Harbor?" Fran asked while the tense, overwrought voice of a newscaster invaded the room.

"It's in Hawaii," Bernie told her. His eyes clung to the radio—as though willing the newscaster to become visual.

"It was attacked by Japanese planes," Midore said in anguish while the newscaster described the scene at Hickham Field. "We're in the war now. My brother's in the army. He could soon be fighting his own cousins! My parents have family in Japan!"

In stunned silence the three listened to the newscaster, reporting on the bombing at Pearl Harbor.

"Not the strongest isolationist could expect us to stay out now," Bernie said tiredly. "But the sooner we get into the war, the sooner it will be over."

"We knew it was going to happen, but I still can't believe it," Fran whispered.

What was happening to their dreams—hers and Bernie's? Was this all life was ever to be? A matter of survival? No! There had to be more!

The war couldn't go on forever. Their time would come. Wouldn't it?

Eight

M ost Americans were confident that this country could easily win the war. *"We haven't lost a war yet!"* But this country was less than two hundred years old. The Japanese had not been defeated since 1598. And Japanese fighting men had been taught that it was the greatest honor to die for the emperor.

Often exhausted and occasionally depressed, Fran told herself that their frenzied schedule—Bernie's twelve- to fifteen-hour work days, six days a week, and her own efforts to handle her increasing typing load, along with children and apartment—was a temporary situation. How long could the war go on?

Often in this bleak December Fran summoned Midore to share dinner with her. She knew Midore was upset about the blatant resentment of some Americans toward those of Japanese descent.

On a frigid night just before Christmas Fran and Midore discussed this in the quiet of the Garfield living room. Lynne and Debbie were asleep in their bedroom. Bernie would not be home for another hour or two—or more if his job dictated this.

"I knew there'd be people—on the West Coast particularly—who'd turn nasty toward anybody who had Japanese blood in their veins," Midore said, trying to sound philosophical. "We've both heard Gabrielle and Sal talk about how some people are hostile toward them since Italy came into the war. But what my father writes from San Francisco scares me." She hesitated. "Dad just sent me a huge check—almost seven thousand dollars, Fran. He told me to put it into my savings account."

"He's just being very cautious," Fran comforted, but she, too, was disturbed by the stories that were coming through about the attitude of West Coast residents to their large Japanese-American population.

"Shiro's serving in the army," Midore reminded. "With a son in military service, why should my father be nervous? But he is." Midore's lovely face was etched with pain. "Neighbors who've always been friendly toward him cut him dead. They're stupid enough to think that my father—who's been living in San Francisco since he was two years old—is suddenly a spy for Japan!"

"People will come to their senses soon," Fran predicted with a determined air of confidence. She longed to relieve Midore's anxiety. This shouldn't be happening. "This is all so crazy."

"Dad says he smells something bad in the wind. Not just for the Issei. For the Nisei as well." Midore laughed at Fran's bewildered expression. "The Nisei are American-born of Japanese descent. Issei is the first generation to come here. But the Nisei—my generation—feel no loyalty toward Japan. We've been educated here—our culture is American. But suddenly," she flared bitterly, "we're enemy aliens."

Fran and Bernie were outraged when word filtered through that on the West Coast the FBI was pulling in for interrogation and possible detention both Issei and Nisei—in those states considered most vulnerable to a Japanese attack. The news from the Pacific was devastating. Wake Island fell on December 22nd after an heroic defense by American marines. Soon after that, the Japanese drove General MacArthur and his Philippine army out of Manila. A wave of hysteria overtook many West Coast residents, even after the FBI released most of those picked up for questioning.

"I'm scared to death of what might happen," Midore confessed at a Sunday dinner party at Fran and Bernie's apartment. She felt the sympathy that radiated from Gabrielle and Sal—like that of Fran and Bernie. Those with family ties to Italy and Germany shared her own anxieties. "I've tried to convince my mother and father to close up his business and the house and come to New York for a while. But my sister is in her last year at Berkeley, and they don't want to leave. And I just wonder," Midore added with new cynicism, "if the government would stop them if they tried."

"Midore, why?" Gabrielle was shocked.

"They might be suspected of espionage," Bernie answered for Midore.

"Why did the FBI drag in five thousand American-born Japanese for questioning? Nothing's happening to the Japanese-Americans in Hawaii," Midore said defiantly.

"It comes down to dollars and cents," Bernie said contemptuously.

"The island's big industries realize they'll be out of business without the Japanese labor force. They couldn't operate. The almighty dollar rules."

They talked now about Bob and Cliff. Just before Thanksgiving Cliff had left school and enlisted. He and Bob were both in uniform. Sal was philosophical about the prospect of being drafted.

"We're the guys who'll have to fight this war," Sal said with fatalistic calm. "Let's pray it's over soon. But this means," he added in painful anticipation, "that I could be fighting against my own first cousins." Fran remembered that Midore's brother faced the same possibility.

On a late January afternoon Fran responded to an insistent ringing of the doorbell. The message was explicit: whoever was at the door was upset. She pulled the door wide. Midore hurried inside.

"Fran, you won't believe what's happened!" Her voice was harsh with shock. "The school just fired me! They've hired a replacement for the new term!"

"Why?" Fran gasped. Midore was one of the most popular teachers at the school.

"Two sets of parents complained." All at once Midore seemed exhausted. "I'm Japanese—I might contaminate the students."

"You're American." Rage soared in Fran. "Just as much as they are! Let me put up some coffee and we'll talk."

"The kids are napping." Midore intercepted Fran's involuntary glance toward the bedroom. "Did I wake them?"

"No," Fran reassured her. "You know my kids—they'd sleep through a bombing." She hesitated. "Can the school do this? Don't you have a contract?"

"There's a clause that lets them off the hook," Midore explained. "Parents complained."

Midore followed Fran into the kitchen. They talked while Fran put up the coffee, brought down cups and saucers.

"How could this happen in New York?" Fran was bewildered.

"You've heard Sal and Gabrielle talk about the ugly reactions they've seen," Midore reminded. "Sal's parents said even the postman looks at them with daggers. Because he remembers letters from Sal's aunts and uncles in Italy. Sal's mother used to save the stamps for the postman's son."

"You don't have to worry about money," Fran consoled. There was the big check from Midore's father. "Now's the time for you to concentrate on your painting. That's what you really want to do."

"I'll sign up for some classes." Midore struggled for composure. "I won't tell my parents that I've been fired. Not just yet. Let them not worry about me. But there's Shiro in army uniform—he may be going overseas to fight soon. It's all right for him to face death for his country—but his sister can't teach third graders?"

Fran and Bernie seethed at the bigotry that hung over the nation—a plague moving with insidious intent.

"I heard a man in the street today yelling at some poor old lady," Bernie told Fran. "Because her dog was a *dachshund*. The place where I run out for a hamburger at work suddenly calls them meatburgers. And Negroes can die for their country—but they can't be part of a white company."

Both Fran and Bernie felt a frustrating helplessness in not being able to be personally involved in fighting this plague.

"Frannie, there are just so many hours in a day," Bernie tried to comfort her. "But there are groups out there fighting."

"Are they being heard?" she countered.

Then Midore came into the apartment to report on the latest letter from her brother.

"Shiro is so upset—so humiliated." Her voice shook with anger and hurt and disbelief. "He'd been bursting with pride at being promoted to corporal back in November. Now he says he's had his weapons taken away—because he's Japanese. All at once he's no longer American. He expects to be discharged from service any day now!"

Midore's parents wrote about the freezing of bank accounts of certain West Coast Japanese, of limitations of travel and a curfew. An Executive Order announced the establishment of military areas along the western halves of the Pacific Coast states. Fran and Bernie tried to convince Midore that this was momentary.

"Church groups out there are up in arms about this," Fran quoted from newspapers and magazines. "Americans won't stand for such insanity." But in a corner of her mind she remembered the agony of the refugees aboard the *St. Louis*.

In March Midore rushed to Fran and Bernie's apartment after a devastating phone call from her parents.

"They can't believe they're living in the United States," Midore said. "Nor can I!"

"Let's backtrack, Midore," Bernie said gently. "What exactly is happening?"

"All Japanese-Americans—even those born here—are being sent from coastal areas to assembly centers. From there they'll be shipped to relocation centers. Internment camps! There are posters on telephone poles ordering their evacuation from what they call restricted military areas. Dad warned me not to try to come home." Midore was hoarse from anguish. "They don't know what'll happen to my sister Claire at college." Unlike Shiro and Midore, their younger sister had been given a thoroughly American name.

"When is this supposed to happen?" Fran asked, her heart pounding.

"They have to register at their nearest Civil Control station." Midore struggled to keep her voice even. "Mother and Dad have a week to appear for internment. They can bring only hand luggage and bedrolls with them. One week!" Midore's voice soared in anger. "How is Dad going to sell his business in that time? He's one of the most respected landscape designers in California! What will they do with the house? The government is offering storage space but tells them it's at their own risk. What do they do with all the things they've collected over a lifetime?"

"Tell them to ship what they can to you," Bernie urged. "I mean, whatever can go by Railway Express. We'll keep whatever we can in our apartment until you can arrange for storage space in the city." Midore lived in a studio apartment.

"Bernie, there's no time. I have to go out there and be with them," Midore decided. "I can't let them go through this alone."

"No," Fran ordered. "They'd be desperately unhappy if you did that. Nothing is going to happen here in the East—except for fanatics like those at your school," she amended as Midore winced. "Your parents will want to know that you're not living in a detention camp."

"I'll phone and tell them to ship my mother's Waterford crystal and my father's coin collection to me. They'll make time for that," Midore said defiantly. "But Dad's business—all the years he spent building a career—will be destroyed."

"This can't last long." Fran fought for calm. "We're not living in Nazi Germany. People here won't stand for this." But the plight of over 110,-000 Japanese-Americans on the West Coast—where most lived—seemed to have little impact on the lives of New Yorkers, Fran admitted to herself. The concern in New York was the plight of General MacArthur, who with his army was making what appeared to be a hopeless defense of Bataan.

Each night Midore phoned her parents in California—and afterward joined Fran in her apartment.

"I don't know how my father and mother can be so accepting of this," Midore confessed. "They say that if the President feels this is necessary for the safety of the country, then so be it. They must prove they're loyal to this country. *But how will they live in a detention camp?*" A tic in one eyelid betrayed her anxiety. "And what about Claire? It's the middle of a school year. What will happen to her?"

"They'll write. You'll surely be able to send them packages," Bernie encouraged. "Believe me, Midore—it won't be a concentration camp."

Fran was caught up in Midore's personal anguish, striving to provide whatever comfort she could. She fumed when she realized that Midore's fellow teachers at the school were avoiding contact with her. They'd worked together side by side for over three years—but now Midore was an "enemy alien."

They learned that Midore's sister Claire had been taken into an assembly center under army jurisdiction.

"I talked to people at Berkeley," Midore told Fran. "A group of educators out there—working with a Quaker group—are trying to arrange for students' relocation at inland colleges. Dr. Sproul—he's president of Berkeley—is fighting to help them. I explained to the people I talked to that Claire won't need a scholarship. I can handle the money part—if they find a school that'll accept her."

"Midore, you said she's a straight A student. She'll have no trouble getting back into school. She may lose a term," Fran conceded, "but everything will work out."

"You're always so sure 'everything will work out,' " Midore said tenderly. "I wish I could be so optimistic."

After talking with her father and mother on the evening before they had to report for evacuation, Midore went to Fran. They sat in the night-quiet apartment while the children slept and talked over endless cups of coffee. What could she possibly do or say, Fran asked herself, to make Midore feel better in this awful—unbelievable—situation?

"There was no time for anything," Midore said in frustration. "At least, Mother's Waterford crystal and Dad's coin collection should be arriving any day. Thank Bernie for suggesting they send that on to me. But Dad's business is gone. Most of his help will be interned, too. They've arranged for friends—a couple they've known for years—to move into the house to take care of it until—" She gestured desolately. "Rent-free, of course—Dad was just anxious to have somebody there. And they've promised to ship Dad's wonderful antique desk and a curio cabinet to me for my apartment—Dad said he couldn't get that done before they had to report to the camp. He sold the car—for a pittance. He's sent the money to me."

"How're your classes?" Fran made an effort to divert Midore's thoughts. She could imagine the vultures that were preying on those who had to dispose of their belongings in a matter of days.

"I'd be in heaven if it wasn't for what's happening out on the West Coast," Midore said softly. "The classes are marvelous. I'm getting such wonderful encouragement." Her smile was wry. "They think I'm Chinese. I registered under my new name. I'm Marilyn Lee at the school." Fran remembered what Bernie had told her last night—about how Chinese workers at the plant were wearing buttons reading: "I Am Chinese."

In April—while Midore was waiting impatiently for the arrival of the furniture her parents' friends were to ship her from the San Francisco house—Gabrielle called Fran to tell her Sal had enlisted.

"He couldn't take it anymore," she told Fran. "He had to show that he's a loyal American. Anyhow, he said he was sure to be called up any day—and this way he had his choice of branches of service. He's going into the Marines. His mother and dad are so upset. You know, they have family in Rome. And I have to keep telling them that Italians won't be sent to camps like the Japanese have been. After all, there are a lot of Italians in this country—they've got plenty of clout."

Midore was shocked when she realized that mail from her parents— now in a camp "in the middle of nowhere"—was being censored.

"It's as though they were enemy aliens," she said contemptuously. "They're pleased that I received the Waterford crystal and Dad's coin collection, but they can't understand why the desk and the curio cabinet haven't arrived."

"Phone the people out there and see who's the carrier," Fran told her. "It may be lost somewhere along the road. They're valuable. You should track them down."

"I'll call," Midore said with fresh determination and rose to her feet.

"Call from here," Fran encouraged.

"I'll pay you back when the phone bill arrives," Midore said gratefully. She reached for the phone and dialed. She listened for a moment, turned to Fran. "It's disconnected. I don't understand!"

"Midore, they couldn't sell the house without your father's permission, could they?" Alarm encased Fran.

"The house is in my name," Midore explained. "My father and mother were born in Japan—they weren't allowed to become American citizens, couldn't own land. I was born here, so they could buy the house in my name—even though I was just a few months old. I have to go out there," she said agitatedly. "Find out what's happening. There're things that must be done. The taxes have to be paid when they come due. We could lose the house for nonpayment of taxes!"

"If you're in California, you'll be picked up and sent off to one of the camps," Fran rejected, her mind charging ahead. Bernie would go along with what she was about to suggest. He wouldn't want Midore and her family to lose their beautiful house. "If you'll look after the kids, I'll go out to San Francisco and find out what's happened to the house." In a corner of her mind she was shocked that she could consider leaving Lynne and Debbie even for a night. "I'll check on the tax situation for you. I can do that in a couple of days. But you can't go back, Midore!"

"You'd do that for me?" All at once Midore's eyes glistened with tears.

"Of course I will." Fran reached for Midore's hand. How could she *not* do this? "You watch over Lynne and Debbie—I'll go to San Francisco. I'll fly out there," she decided. "We can't afford to waste time."

Late that evening as she served dinner to Bernie, Fran worried that she had not consulted him about rushing out to San Francisco. Would he be upset that she was leaving the children for several days?

"Bernie, I have to talk to you about something," she said haltingly while she brought two cups of coffee to the table. "Before you fall asleep in your chair." She tried for a flippant note.

"That's a real hazard these days," he admitted with a chuckle. But his eyes were curious.

Guilty now that she had taken this upon herself, she explained Midore's plight.

"We can't let her go out there," she wound up, faintly breathless. "Considering the mood in California she'd be picked up and sent to a camp."

"*I* should go," Bernie said, yet he seemed ambivalent. "We're short-handed at the plant. Half the place is out with colds."

"We can't afford for you to take time out, even if you could get it," Fran said firmly. He wasn't angry. He knew they had to do this. "And Midore will be fine with the kids. They adore her. Besides," she strived for humor, "how can I ignore a chance to fly?"

Fran battled against doubts as she explained to Lynne and Debbie that she had to go away for a few days. Her mother would be shocked that she was leaving the kids.

"Midore will be with you all day until Daddy comes home at night. And I'll bring you presents," she promised. "You be good and do what Midore tells you."

"Can we have cookies?" Lynne probed. "The chocolate one?" she asked hopefully.

"One chocolate cookie each day I'm away," Fran said. "I'll tell Midore."

Fran knew that Bernie was terrified that she was flying across the country, though he made a pretense of nonchalance. She herself was fascinated at the prospect of flying, though her mission remained in the forefront of her thoughts. Aboard the plane she toyed with the possibility of writing an article about this experience. In a journalism class she'd written about an imaginary trip aboard the Orient Express.

But on her arrival in San Francisco, she focused totally on the assignment ahead of her. At Midore's instructions she checked into a modest little hotel—ever conscious of what this venture was costing Midore.

Early the following morning she was in a taxi en route to her destination.

Fran admired the lovely houses with their spacious grounds as the taxi driver followed the winding road that led to Midore's home. But Midore's parents and sister had been uprooted from this quiet, beautiful neighborhood and placed in an armed camp.

The taxi driver slowed down, pulled to a stop before a low, sprawling, multiwindowed house that reflected the architecture of Frank Lloyd Wright. But all at once Fran was attacked by a premonition of disaster. Her heart was pounding as she paid the driver and left the taxi. Midore's father was a fine landscape designer. His own home had been featured in national magazines. Why was the grass growing wild here? Everywhere an aura of neglect. Weeds desecrated the otherwise exquisite rock garden.

Had the couple who were taking care of the house been caught up in some family crisis? Fran asked herself while she hurried up the neglected path to the entrance. Faintly breathless from the steep ascent to the house, she reached into her purse for the key—knowing even before she tried the doorbell that no one would respond.

She unlocked the door and walked into the large foyer. Midore had talked about the magnificent chandelier that her father recently installed in the foyer. *"I'll see it when I go home during summer vacation.*

Mother says it's exquisite." But no chandelier hung in the house. The foyer was bare of furniture. No rug lay on the floor.

Cold with shock Fran walked through the empty rooms of the large house. Every piece of furniture, all the rugs, even the kitchen appliances had been removed. No draperies hung at the windows. The house had been stripped as though by an invading army, Fran thought in dizzying dismay. And this must be happening to other Japanese-American families who'd been swept away from their normal lives as though hardened criminals.

Her mind in chaos she sat on the lower steps of the elegant, circular stairway. Midore said her father had put everything into his house. It was the symbol of his success, his security for the family. How could she tell Midore what she'd found here? How could Midore tell her parents?

Then Fran forced herself to be realistic. Her sharp mind moved into high gear. She had to find a broker to handle the rental of the house. Then she must check on the tax schedule so that Midore could be sure the taxes were paid on time. Salvage what could be salvaged. But again she asked herself, how could she tell Midore what she'd found here?

In forty-eight hours Fran was on a plane en route to New York—still unnerved by what she had discovered. Thank God, she told herself, she'd found a broker to handle the rental of the house for Midore—a broker who seemed almost compassionate. But how many of the millions of people in this country understood what was happening? This wasn't Nazi Germany—but right in this country a whole group of people were being imprisoned because of their race.

Why didn't people write to the President and demand this be stopped? Why didn't they write letters to the newspapers? Bernie— whose vast knowledge astounded her—said that the hard-driving, courageous Japanese on the West Coast had taken wastelands and marshes and turned them into fertile fields. Whole families worked those fields. They were law-abiding, frugal people, devoted to family. How could this be happening?

Bernie was doing his share for the war effort, but she was contributing nothing. With the children she couldn't work in a war plant. She couldn't even be an air raid warden. But in whatever way possible she would be helpful to Midore's family. That would be her small contribution.

Nine

Though train reservations became difficult to acquire in the coming months, Fran's parents came up to New York for a brief visit—her father's buying needs for the store their ostensible motivation. Only now did Josiah and Ida Goldman learn that Bernie had given up his practice as an accountant.

"Since he isn't in service—and I know it's wrong of me to pray he stays out of uniform—he decided he must go into a defense job." They hadn't known he had managed to work at both jobs since early December of '38, Fran acknowledged inwardly.

"But once the war is over," she added with an air of buoyant secrecy, "Bernie's going to law school. That's what he's always wanted to do."

"How can he manage that?" her father asked after a startled exchange of glances with her mother.

"We're saving money every week. Bernie'll get lots of overtime. And while Bernie is in school, I'll be able to keep up my typing service." They knew about this. She suspected her father was proud of her efforts, her mother ambivalent. Well brought up southern girls—in her mother's eyes—didn't go out to work. But the war was fast changing that conception, she reminded herself. "Bernie's always wanted to be a lawyer," she pointed out again. "He managed a degree in accounting. He couldn't have handled the additional years at law school."

"We'll help you when the time comes," Ida Goldman said, after exchanging a swift glance with her husband. "Tell Bernie."

"Mother, we'll be able to manage," Fran said. Bernie was never comfortable when they were taking from her parents.

"Frannie, don't deprive your mother and me of the pleasure of helping our only child," her father reproved. "When the time comes, we'll help."

"Dad and I had talked about giving you and Bernie our car when we bought a new one," her mother confided unhappily, "but then in January the ban went through on retail sales of new passenger cars."

"Having a car in Manhattan can be a problem," Fran consoled. "And the subways are fine."

Fran's parents were too polite—after their initial shock—not to mask their astonishment that her closest friend in New York was of Japanese descent. Fran was pleased that they clearly liked Midore. They were enthralled when they saw the sketches Midore had done of Lynne and Debbie. Immediately they commissioned similar sketches for themselves and were touched when Midore refused payment.

"Such a sweet girl," her mother confided to Fran while the three waited for the Georgia-bound train at crowded Penn Station—colorful with military uniforms of every branch of service. Midore was staying with Lynne and Debbie while Fran saw her parents off. "It can't be easy for her—with the war and all."

"Most New Yorkers don't think about that," Fran said quietly. "There are some," she conceded, noticing her father's raised eyebrows. "It's always the noisy few that people hear."

"What about your friends in the service?" her mother asked. She'd told them about Bob and Cliff and Sal, and her mother had told her about boys with whom she'd gone to school who were now in uniform. She'd been shaken when she learned that the president of her high school senior class had died at Wake Island.

"Bob expects to be shipped out any day. Cliff is in the Air Force— he's praying he makes it as a pilot. Sal is in North Carolina. And wouldn't you know it—Gabrielle's two months pregnant. She—"

"Our train's being posted," her father interrupted. "Let's head for the gate."

By midsummer most of the West Coast Japanese had been transferred from assembly centers to relocation centers—some as far away as the Arizona desert and remote areas of Idaho. Midore searched tirelessly among the national magazines for articles about the internment camps—which she brought to Fran and Bernie, who shared her anxieties.

Midore was upset that her parents' letters were censored. Fran reminded her of the determined efforts of the Society of Friends—Quakers—and other church groups to improve the conditions in the camps.

Fran was distraught when she learned from an indignant Quaker worker about the sordid accommodations that were provided in the relocation centers. Midore, too, was given a graphic picture of this by another Quaker.

"Fran, I can't envision my dignified father, my elegant mother living like that," Midore told Fran while the two women sat down to dinner after Lynne and Debbie had been put to bed for the night. "They're in a *prison camp*, with guard towers and armed sentries surrounding them. Several people—strangers—share one small room. Only because a Quaker group—bless them—fought for this were there dividers put up between the camp toilets and showers. My mother—the most modest of women—has to shower in the presence of male guards." Midore's voice dropped to a pained whisper. "For Claire in her camp it's no better."

"There'll be changes," Fran comforted, recoiling from the images Midore evoked. "People are working hard to see to that. And you'll keep sending packages, the way you've been doing. They'll manage. But most of all," she said softly, "I feel sorry for the children. They can't understand what's happening to their world."

"I expect this in Nazi Germany—not in the United States!" Midore flared. "Why do most people just sit back and ignore what's happening?"

"Bernie says it's because they're all tuned in to their personal anxieties. They have sons or husbands or brothers in uniform, going off to fight a war. Nobody knows how many will die. Most people aren't thinking beyond what touches them personally."

"My parents must live like animals," Midore said bitterly, "while German diplomatic prisoners are honored in a fancy resort like the Greenbriar—which only the rich can afford."

Then Claire wrote that in the fall she hoped to be allowed to study at a college in an approved area.

"She says she won't be able to come to New York to study," Midore reported. At Fran's urging—and with soaring hope—she had written to a group working to relocate Japanese-American students that she would pay for Claire's expenses as a student at New York University. "All colleges along the Eastern Seaboard are out of bounds. But a college in Utah is willing to accept her if she can get the proper clearance."

A few days later Claire wrote that she had been rejected by state colleges in Iowa and Arizona because hastily passed legislation banned enrollment of Japanese.

"I just have to be cleared by the FBI and some other government agency. Then I can enroll at the college in Utah."

The American government strived to lift morale at home, despite the grim news from the Pacific. The Bataan "Death March" in April—when the Japanese forced military and civilian prisoners to march eighty-five miles in six days on one meal of rice—cost the lives of 5,200 Americans and many more Filipinos. In early May Americans defeated the Japanese at the Coral Sea, but General Wainwright had to surrender Corregidor to the Japanese.

There was much talk about a "second front"—but nobody knew just where this would be. In Europe bitter fighting continued between the Germans and the Russians. Back in April the RAF had begun huge raids on German cities, and now American forces were arriving in England in large numbers.

At home Americans were learning to deal with rationing of sugar and—in seventeen eastern states—gasoline, with many more items under consideration. There was a general price freeze. Rents were frozen at the level of March 1942. Yet for millions of Americans—after the deprivations of the Depression—the war was a golden opportunity. Others—like Fran and Bernie—were plagued by guilt because they lived in comfort and security when so much of the world was suffering.

Fran knew that Bernie worried that she was becoming obsessed by what was happening to Midore's family. In a way, she thought with fresh insight, she was obsessed by intolerance—and what Burns had indelibly labeled "man's inhumanity to man." Hysteria had placed Midore's parents in what was a prison camp—though the government preferred to call it a "resettlement community" and even a "haven of refuge."

Then in late July the government arranged for "work furloughs" for the Nisei—because the sugar beet crops of Utah, Idaho, Montana, and Wyoming were in danger of being lost for lack of workers. Only the American-born Nisei were allowed the opportunity to volunteer to work in these fields. Thousands reported—young college students and professionals, women as well as men. Claire wrote that she had volunteered and had been accepted.

"I'll just work until college registration."

Claire convinced Midore not to come out to Montana to see her.

"We have no barbed wire surrounding us, no armed guards—but we're still in military custody. You could be pulled in and put to work here. *Stay in New York,*" Claire wrote. Fran and Bernie concurred with this advice.

In the fall Claire was enrolled in the small college in Nevada that had accepted her. But not all of her classmates approved of her being there. There were some who either ignored or vilified her.

"Claire says she never leaves the campus now," Midore told Fran and Bernie on a chilly Sunday evening in late October. "Some shopkeepers refuse to wait on the handful of Japanese students who come into town. Some restaurants won't serve them. Rather than face that, she says she stays close to her dorm."

"How awful!" Fran blazed. "Can't the government do something about that?"

"Hold on, Frannie," Bernie said gently. "Think about the South. If Lily went into a 'white' restaurant in Bellevue, what would happen?" He turned to Midore. "Lily is my mother-in-law's colored housekeeper. If Lily tried to order dinner at The Oasis, she'd be thrown out. And the government would do nothing about it."

"That's wrong, too," Fran said after a pensive moment. "I didn't realize how wrong it was until I came to New York and saw how people live up here."

"After the war," Bernie said, "we'll see serious changes. We can't send colored soldiers off to die in a war—then tell them their kids can't go to school alongside white kids, that they can't eat in 'white' restaurants nor live in 'white' neighborhoods."

"Will there ever be a time," Fran asked, "when people will learn to live side by side in peace and tolerance?"

In December Fran and Bernie received a card with Bob's APO number. They knew that meant he was overseas. He'd written that he expected to be shipped out at any time. Two weeks later they received their first V-Mail from him. He had been part of the invasion of North Africa—the new "second front." Cliff was somewhere in the Pacific. At intervals he wrote hastily scrawled V-Mails—which usually arrived with cut-out segments, indicating censorship. Gabrielle was worried that Sal, too—now a Marine lieutenant—would be shipped out momentarily.

Early in the new year, word seeped through that the government was beginning an effort to relocate Japanese evacuees in middle western and eastern cities, where they might settle themselves in new lives. Most of them would emerge from this experience with nothing.

"The government is anxious to cut expenses," Bernie interpreted. "Can you imagine what it costs to keep the camps going? Plus, with so many people running from their regular jobs into the high-paying defense plants, workers are urgently needed in other fields."

Immediately Fran and Midore explored this new situation. They were determined to come up with a way out of the camp for Midore's parents. The primary problem was housing, in a time of few vacancies.

"What about buying a tiny farm for them?" Bernie suggested to Midore. "Land is cheap out in New Jersey. You have the money to handle that." And her parents would have the income from the rental of their California house, Fran pinpointed mentally.

"Bernie, what a wonderful thought!" Midore glowed. "Daddy would be happy if he had a piece of land where he could grow things. In time he'll get back into his own field. Not now," she conceded wryly. "But when the world is normal again."

The three of them searched the real estate section of the *New York Times*—focusing on New Jersey farms for sale. Midore wrote her parents about what was happening.

"They're nervous about leaving the camp," Midore reported in astonishment. "They're terrified of what they'll encounter on the outside."

"Make them understand that the situation is different here in the East," Fran urged, then paused as Midore flinched. "I know," she continued, her face suffused with compassion. "That doesn't apply to your school and a few other places. But most Easterners aren't like that. Your parents can live comfortably here."

"Write to them," Bernie cajoled. "Why should they stay in a prison camp when they can be free?"

"There'll be procedures," Fran warned. "Once they have a security clearance, we have to prove that there is a home waiting for them."

"It might be wise for Fran or me to look for a farm, feel out the area first," Bernie cautioned. "We have to be sure it's an area that will be receptive."

Bernie didn't want to expose Midore to ugliness, Fran interpreted. Claire had written about the experiences encountered by Nisei who had gone out on "work furloughs." With alarming frequency—when they left the farms where they worked to venture into town—they had been spat upon, denied service in cafés and stores, beaten up. *That mustn't happen to Midore's parents.*

"Will they be allowed to settle in the East?" Midore questioned. "Remember, college students can't transfer to any school on the East Coast."

"Fran, ask questions," Bernie said. "Didn't you say something about a relocation office right here in the city?"

"I'll track it down tomorrow," Fran promised and turned to Midore. "You'll stay with the kids?"

"Of course." Her expressive face radiated gratitude for Fran and Bernie's efforts.

Fran found the relocation office, explored the possibilities for relocation of Midore's parents. She talked eloquently about the loyalty of Midore's family, her father's recognized talents as a landscape designer, about her brother now serving as an army interpreter. In addition to Japanese, Shiro was also fluent in French and Italian. She left the office in jubilation, impatient to relay what she had learned to Midore.

"The man at the relocation office told me that it's mainly a matter of their passing a demanding security clearance. We'll write to the Quaker group out near the camp—they'll know how to work for this."

"There are people in San Francisco who might help," Midore said. "I'll get names and addresses."

"The man did tell me that it's easier to relocate families in an urban area," Fran began, her eyes questioning.

"My parents would hate living in New York," Midore said instantly. "Especially after what they've been through. A small farm where my father can be outdoors and cultivating a garden would be good. But close to New York so that I can see them often."

Not waiting for the security clearance, Fran and Midore began their search for a home for the senior Yamamotos. This was the first requirement—after security clearance—for "relocation privileges." The country was approaching a serious housing shortage. Each Sunday they pored over the real estate pages in the *New York Times*, cut out ads that appeared promising, called brokers. Midore had funds to handle a modest house with several acres.

Then word came through. Midore's parents had received clearance. Now they were eager to leave the camp. On a cold, blustery Sunday Fran and Bernie prepared to drive out to New Jersey in the car he had been about to borrow from a fellow worker for an exorbitant fee.

"I paid the jerk a fortune for this week's allotment of gas, too." Three gallons a week was allowed under rationing. "That plus what was left from last week should get us out to Jersey and back," Bernie told Fran as they climbed into the 1933 Dodge.

"I hope the heater works." Fran pulled her coat closely about her slender frame. The sharp winds seeped through every crevice of the car.

"It doesn't," Bernie said a few minutes later. "That's why he told me there were lap robes on the back seat."

Bernie pulled up at the curb, maneuvered to reach the robes, and tucked one solicitously about Fran.

"We'll stop somewhere along the road for coffee," he promised. "Once we're through the Lincoln Tunnel and have made a little headway."

Fran was faintly intimidated by the barren stretches of farmland they soon encountered.

"How desolate," she said, frowning as her eyes swept over the fields. "Do you think Midore's parents are going to like living here after all the years in California?"

"After almost a year in that camp, they'll love it," Bernie predicted. "You know how marvelous Japanese farmers are with land. Midore's father will transform whatever land he has into something special. And they'll be free."

Fran remembered Bob's bitter denunciation of farm life. After surviving the devastating years of the Depression, he said, he never wanted to set foot on a farm again except as a visitor. *"The farmer always gets hit first and hardest. If my father knew anything else, he'd be out of there."*

With Fran watching the road map they arrived at the broker's office on the town's Main Street in commendable time. Traffic this March of 1943 was light. Drivers hoarded their gasoline for special occasions, Bernie had pointed out. Elated that at last they were on the road to bringing Midore's parents out of their infamous camp, Fran smiled brilliantly as they left the car and crossed to the neat, white shingled structure that was the broker's office.

The broker greeted them warmly and pulled out a scrapbook containing photographs of available housing.

"You're lucky to be able to find a place with as little as five acres," he told them. "In this case the owner's selling the house and five acres and holding on to the other fifty-five acres to give to his son. I don't suppose you plan on serious farming?"

"Oh, no." Fran exuded ingratiating Southern charm. "Actually, we're looking for property for a friend." The broker's smile faded a bit. "She wasn't able to come out today, but she's anxious to find something this close to the city. Her father is a retired landscape designer, and he just wants enough land to keep his hand in."

"Well, then, the place I told you about on the phone is just the ticket," he said, more confident now. "And we just might get the owner to shave the price a bit."

"I don't suppose it'll matter that our friend is Japanese?" Fran strived to be casual.

"You're looking to bring somebody from one of those internment camps into this town?" All at once he was wary.

"They're fine people," Bernie said. "He's a well-known landscape designer. He's been cleared by the government. There should—"

"I'll have to make a phone call," the broker interrupted.

Fran and Bernie sat with strained politeness while he phoned the owner of the property under discussion.

"Silas, I have some people here who're interested in the house and five acres. But there's a problem." He cleared his throat, stared at Fran and Bernie for a moment. "The buyer is a landscape designer who just wants enough land to play around with a bit. But—uh—they're Japanese." He was listening now, nodded as the other man talked. "Sure, I understand. But they're here and they wanted to see the place." Clearly he was anxious to make a sale. Another pause. "Silas, you don't have to say any more. I understand." He put down the receiver and turned to Fran and Bernie. "He said he wouldn't sell to Japs if his life depended on it. His son's a Marine, somewhere out in the Pacific."

In grim silence Fran and Bernie returned to the car.

"What is the matter with people?" Fran challenged in frustration— her heart pounding at this rejection while her mind acknowledged she should have not been totally surprised.

"That's one seller." Bernie refused to be ruffled. "One village. Let's go call on another broker. You've got three lined up," he reminded.

"All right." Fran opened her purse, brought out a notebook. "I told this next one we *might* be out. Should we look for a phone booth and call?"

"It's close enough," Bernie decided after a moment's consultation with the map. "Just another three or four miles out. Let's drive over."

They arrived at the second broker's office to find a note on the door: "Out with client. Be back by 1 P.M."

"Let's find a place to have lunch," Fran said. "By then he'll be back."

The small local café was lively, every table occupied by an after-church group. Restlessly they waited until a table was available. Their waitress was friendly. When the food arrived, it was good. Fran began to relax. As usual, Bernie was right—that had been just one seller who was rotten.

An hour later they were in the office of the second broker, a gregarious older man who instantly launched into a description of an available property that seemed perfect. It was a two-bedroom house with six cleared acres. The price was right, the taxes low.

"Let me get the key—" The broker reached to a board on the wall, from which dangled a collection of labeled key rings. "The house isn't occupied. It belonged to a widow who died just a few weeks ago. The son grows corn on an adjoining hundred acres. He's the owner now."

Fran and Bernie exchanged a swift glance.

"Will it matter to him that he'd have Japanese neighbors if my friend buys?"

"Honey, the Mahoneys aren't going to worry if their neighbors are white, yellow, black or green—so long as they're law-abiding and reasonably quiet." He pushed back his chair and rose to his feet. "Now let me show you the place."

While the house was tiny and unpretentious, it showed the loving care of its earlier resident. For a few moments the sun broke through the cluster of clouds and Fran whimsically decided this was a harbinger of good luck. Of course, this wasn't in the class of the estate she'd seen in San Francisco, she admitted to herself—but Midore's parents would make the house and the grounds beautiful. Certainly an improvement on internment camp living.

"I won't be able to bring our friend out till next Sunday," Fran began and Bernie broke in.

"Make it Tuesday," he told her. "I'll get somebody to change shifts with me." He grinned. "Everybody wants Sundays off."

"We'll have to come out by bus or train," Fran apologized to the broker—her eyes questioning.

"You let me know when you're coming. I'll pick you up," he assured her. "Tuesday's a slow day this time of year. Shouldn't be any problem at all."

Jubilant about locating a house that seemed right, Fran and Bernie settled in the car again.

"It's so cold," Fran complained a few minutes later as she huddled beneath the car robe.

Bernie stared up at the overcast sky. "I hope we get home before the snow starts." A few moments later he took a hand from the wheel to pat her robe-covered knee. "Let's go back to the café and warm up with some coffee before we go on. And pay a visit to their rest rooms," he added with a chuckle.

"Coffee would be wonderful!"

The wide window of the café was invitingly steamed over. Fran and Bernie walked into the cozy warmth with mutual pleasure and settled at a table for two that flanked a radiator. Now only a pair of tables were occupied. Several men straddled stools at the counter.

"There's the creep we saw earlier," Fran whispered and then was silent as a waitress approached them.

To justify their taking up table space they ordered apple pie to accompany their coffee.

"You want it hot?" the waitress asked good-humoredly.

"Oh, we'd love it hot," Fran effervesced.

"Hey, Gussie, give me my check." The broker had risen from his stool at the counter and turned toward the waitress. For an instant his eyes clashed with Fran's. He turned away, pretending not to recognize her. "I have to get moving," he added imperiously.

"Where's the fire?" Gussie demanded, but she was writing out the check as she crossed to the counter.

Fran tensed when she intercepted a whispered exchange between the broker and Gussie. He was telling her about how a Japanese family had tried to buy property through him, Fran surmised. Well, their waitress was shrugging this aside.

Gussie returned to their table with generous slabs of steaming hot apple pie and large cups of coffee. She lingered to chat a moment about the threat of snow.

"Hope you folks got chains for your car," she said. "The radio says this is going to be a heavy snow once it starts fallin'."

On Tuesday morning Bernie stayed home with the children. Fran and Midore took a bus to the New Jersey town where the second real estate broker was to meet them. Fran was grateful that the grayness of the last two days had given way to brilliant sunlight. Snow fast disappearing from city streets. She was touched by Midore's happiness, her gratitude.

"Fran, I can't wait to see the house," Midore said as the bus neared their destination. "None of this would be happening except for you and Bernie." Her eyes glistened with joyous tears.

The broker was waiting for them. He knew he had a sale, Fran thought. Such a nice man. She was glad he'd be making the commission. This wasn't an ideal piece of property. Most people looking for farms expected a large tract of land. He was pleased to have a prospective buyer.

They drove directly to the property. Snow was still in evidence on the ground, but the roads were cleared. Midore walked through the small house in an aura of deep relief. Her parents' nightmare was almost over.

"How quickly can we close?" Midore asked the broker.

"Let's go to the office and see what I can work out," he said briskly. "I can't see any serious holdups to a fast closing."

Fran and Midore sat in the office while the broker made phone calls. Finally he turned to them with an encouraging smile.

"We'll make record time on this one," he promised. "No financing problems since you're paying cash up front. The seller's set to roll. All we need now is for you to hire a lawyer. I'd suggest somebody in the area if you want to push the deal through fast."

"Fran, what do we do?" Midore seemed bewildered.

"Could you recommend a local lawyer?" Fran asked the broker.

"Oh sure." He paused a moment in thought. "Let me try Pete Jackson. His office is in the next town—just a few minutes' drive from here. Okay?" He turned from Fran to Midore.

"Okay," Midore agreed.

Fran and Midore waited while the broker talked with Jackson's secretary. Now he put down the phone.

"She expects him back shortly. I'll take you over there. His secretary will drive you to your bus once your meeting is over."

In mutual high spirits the three drove to Jackson's office, in the town Fran and Bernie had first visited on Sunday. The attorney wasn't there.

"He's been tied up at a closing," his secretary apologized. "But he'll be here within thirty or forty minutes. I know it's a long wait—"

"Isn't there a café nearby?" Fran asked, recalling the place where she and Bernie had lunched on Sunday.

"On the next block," Jackson's secretary said. "The Country Kitchen."

"Then we'll have an early lunch there," Fran told Midore, "then come back."

"I'll take you young ladies to lunch," their happy broker offered gallantly. "It'll—"

"There's no need to do that," Fran said with a warm smile. "We'll be fine."

"If you're sure," he said, turning to Midore—who nodded in agreement. Fran sensed he was relieved. His was a one-man office, with no secretary on duty. "I'll be in touch with Pete. Together we'll set up a closing as fast as possible."

Fran and Midore walked in the crisp sunlight past a block of one-storied businesses—typical, Fran guessed, of rural towns. Arriving at the café she noted the sparsely occupied tables.

"Are we too early for lunch?" Midore asked tentatively as they walked inside.

"I don't think they watch the clock," Fran joshed. "It's not the Russian Tea Room."

Aromas of fresh coffee, bacon sizzling on the griddle beside hamburgers whetted their appetites. Several men in working clothes sat on stools at the counter and zestfully discussed the charms of Betty Grable. Fran spied the waitress who had served Bernie and her on Sunday and waved in greeting.

"You miss that snowstorm Sunday night?" Gussie asked, handing menus to Fran and Midore.

"By hours," Fran told her. "And by last night most of it was gone in New York."

"We got plenty left around here, but not enough to cause any real problems," Gussie said good-humoredly. "Some outdoor workers took off to go huntin'—but they were lookin' for an excuse."

For a few moments Fran and Midore focused on the menu, then chose the day's "special."

"How can I turn down pot roast," Fran drawled, "when my ration stamps are so low?"

The door opened, letting in an unexpected burst of cold wind. A burly man cradling a rifle in his arms strode inside.

"Hey, Chuck, shut the door!" one of those at the counter ordered.

"You takin' off from work again?" another challenged. "Servin' venison at your house tonight?"

"All I bagged was a couple of 'possums," the new arrival complained. "I left 'em where they lay. My old lady won't even cook 'em. I was hopin' for a wild turkey—that's got enough meat on it to be worth roastin'." His eyes swung about the table area, deserted except for Fran and Midore. Fran tensed as his gaze lingered on her for a moment in bawdy approval, then moved to Midore. "Hey, Gussie," he bellowed, his face all at once hostile. "Didn't you tell them two over there we don't allow foreigners in here?"

"Chuck, shut up!" Gussie ordered uncomfortably.

"I heard somebody was tryin' to move Japs in here." His voice was loud as he stared menacingly toward the table where Fran and Midore sat frozen in alarm. "Tryin' to buy Silas Johnson's house and a few of his acres. We don't want no Japs around here."

"Bernie and I were here on Sunday," Fran told Midore, pretending to ignore their harasser. "Their coffee's awfully good." She pointedly gazed past their heckler. "Gussie, could we have our coffee now?"

The man they'd called Chuck was stalking toward them. Suddenly the atmosphere in the small restaurant was electric.

"Hey, Chuck, get your tail over here and sit down." The short-order cook abandoned the hamburger he'd been watching and moved from behind the counter.

"That white bitch, she's the one who's been askin' around about property for them Japs." He circled around behind Fran and focused now on Midore. "How many you plan on bringin' here with you? Let me tell you—you'll all be dead Japs real fast."

"Calm down or get out of here!" The short-order cook strode across the room. "Chuck, we don't want trouble." He put a hand firmly on Chuck's arm.

"Don't tell me what to do!" Chuck yelled, flailing at the other man with his left arm.

All at once the shotgun went off. Fran's eyes widened in shock for a moment. She was aware of an agonizing pain in her back. In a corner of her mind she knew she had been shot. Then—vaguely aware that the others were rushing toward her—she collapsed into unconsciousness.

Ten

"Midore, she's going to be all right?" Bernie clutched the phone with fierce intensity. His world was collapsing around him, threatening to suffocate him.

"She's in surgery now," Midore explained, sounding drained of all strength. "The doctors won't tell me anything—"

"What hospital? Where?" Bernie's voice was harsh. His eyes fastened on Lynne, sprawled on the floor and engrossed in a coloring book. He'd just put Debbie down for a nap. "I'll take a bus out with the kids." His mind tried to deal with the horror that had descended on them. "I'll wake Debbie and—"

"Bernie, call Gabrielle. Ask her to come and stay with the kids. I'll give you the address—"

"Gabrielle will be working!" Bernie interrupted impatiently. *Fran shot.* The words ricocheted in his brain. *How could that have happened?*

"Her in-laws made her stop working as soon as she knew she was pregnant. Call Gabrielle, then as soon as she arrives, take the bus out here. Write down the address, Bernie." She was talking to him as though he was Lynne or Debbie, he thought.

"Midore, why did that idiot shoot her?" His voice rose precariously.

"Bernie, that doesn't matter now." She was straining for calm. "Just come out to the hospital. Fran will want to see you when she comes out of the anesthesia."

Bernie felt a surge of relief when Gabrielle's voice came to him over the phone.

"Gabrielle, you won't believe what happened!" Feeling himself in a nightmare, he explained the situation.

"I'll come and stay with the kids," Gabrielle said before he even asked. "Give me thirty minutes."

He called Greyhound for the bus schedules, swearing that he'd just missed a bus to his destination—and he'd miss the next if Gabrielle didn't hurry. He called the hospital patient information line and was told only that Fran was in surgery.

Incessantly Bernie's eyes swung to the living-room clock. He struggled to conceal his anguish when Lynne consulted him about her coloring. He mustn't let Lynne and Debbie understand how upset he was. Kids caught on so fast.

Only now did he allow his mind to focus on how the shooting had happened. Some lunatic out in that godforsaken town had shot Fran because he thought she was bringing Japanese into his area.

Why did Fran have to get mixed up in this? he asked himself in soaring frustration. But immediately he rebuked himself. How else would Fran react to such barbarism? How would he live if Fran didn't survive? The children needed her. He needed her.

Now he phoned Fran's father at the store. Her mother would get hysterical, he warned himself. He waited impatiently while one of the saleswomen called his father-in-law to the phone. Needing to share the tragic news, he stammered out the words that sounded unreal to his own ears.

"Oh my God," Josiah Goldman gasped. "She—she'll be all right?"

"She's in surgery. I'm going out to the hospital as soon as a friend arrives to stay with the kids," he explained, then stopped. "I hear the elevator—that must be Gabrielle now!"

"What hospital?" Fran's father demanded tersely. "Her mother and I will fly up on the first plane we can get."

Bernie told him, put down the phone and hurried to the door.

"Daddy?" Lynne came back into the living room after a trip to the bathroom. Bernie heard apprehension in her voice. Kids intuitively knew when something was wrong, he thought.

"It's okay, baby," he soothed while he pulled open the door just as Gabrielle arrived there.

"Bernie, she's going to be all right," Gabrielle said without preliminaries. "You get out there. I'll stay with the kids. How's my best girl?" she crooned, reaching to hug Lynne. Hiding her own fears. "Do you know what I've brought you?"

Lynne's face brightened. "Cookies?" Fran doled out cookies and candy sparingly in deference to the children's teeth.

To Bernie the trip by bus seemed endless. At the station in New Jersey he was grateful to find a cab. It had been hours, he tormented himself. Was Fran out of surgery? Was she all right?

At the hospital he was directed to the surgical floor. Emerging from the elevator he spied Midore, staring out a window.

"Midore!"

She swung around to face him and held her arms out to him. "She's still in surgery," Midore told him. "All we can do is wait. It's all my fault," she whispered, clinging to Bernie. "I did this."

"Sssh," Bernie comforted. "Don't say that. The man was a nut case."

They sat on one of the wicker sofas in the reception area—not knowing how long a wait lay ahead of them before there'd be word of Fran's condition. Feeling himself in a nightmare Bernie insisted Midore tell him everything she could remember about the encounter in the café. He was struggling to understand how something so bizarre could have happened. He'd heard some weird stories about small-town hoodlums who went out "lookin' for some Japs to beat up," of Japanese being turned away from church services by ministers, of Japanese out on "work furloughs" being ostracized, cheated of their wages—but this was attempted murder.

"Fran's mother and father are flying up," he told Midore. "They're both scared to death of flying—and I'm not even sure they'll be able to get reservations. But one way or another they'll be here for her." They were probably terrified—as he was.

At last a doctor emerged from the operating area.

"That's the doctor," Midore stammered and leapt to her feet.

The doctor approached them. His head pounding, Bernie searched the doctor's face, trying to interpret what he saw there.

"She'll live," the doctor said encouragingly, yet the seriousness of his eyes alerted Bernie to trouble. "She had a very lucky escape. But there's neurological damage. She'll have some paralysis on the left side, I'm afraid."

Bernie was suddenly ashen.

"She's twenty-six years old! We have two small children!"

"Except for the paralysis on the left side—she'll be able to walk with crutches after extensive physical therapy—she'll be able to live a fairly normal life," the doctor encouraged. "Her youth is in her favor."

"Can we see her?" Midore asked, white with shock.

"She's in the recovery room now. A nurse will call you when you can go to her. But don't expect her to be fully out of the anesthesia," he cautioned. "Why don't you go up to the sixth-floor cafeteria and have some coffee," he said compassionately. "It'll be a while."

"Let's do that, Bernie," Midore urged. "We'll just be gone ten minutes."

In the cafeteria—almost deserted at this hour—Bernie and Midore went to the coffee station and carried their cups to a table at the far side of the room.

"Fran on crutches," Bernie said through gritted teeth. "Can you visualize that?" Fran who never walked, always ran.

"Knowing Fran, I don't doubt for a minute that she'll handle it," Midore told him. Her eyes willing him to believe this. "We'll both be there for her."

"Let's go back down," Bernie said after sipping briefly at his coffee. "I want to be near her."

After what seemed an endless wait a pretty, young nurse came to tell them that they could see Fran.

"I'll wait here," Midore said, meaning to be diplomatic.

"You come with me," Bernie said gently, reaching for her hand.

His throat tight with anguish Bernie walked into the narrow room— Midore at his side. Fran lay with eyes closed, her lush dark hair fanned across the pillow. He walked to the bed and leaned over to kiss her on one cheek.

"Hmm," she murmured, her next few words incoherent.

"She's not out of the anesthetic." The nurse repeated the doctor's words. "It'll be a while."

"Can I just stay here with her?" Bernie asked.

"It'll be better if you come back later," the sympathetic nurse told them.

With reluctance Bernie allowed Midore to prod him from Fran's bedside. He reeled with the knowledge that Fran would be forever paralyzed on the left side. A few ugly moments in that café—and their lives were in chaos.

"You'll stay here, of course," Midore told Bernie. "I'll go to the apartment and relieve Gabrielle. I'll stay with the kids until you get home. You're not to rush, Bernie," she exhorted. "I'll make Lynne and Debbie understand that Mommie has to be away for a while—but that you and I will be there for them." Midore's voice broke. "This wouldn't have happened except for me."

"You're not to blame yourself." Bernie fought for composure. "But I hope they put that bastard away for a hundred years!"

Each minute seemed an agonizing hour to Bernie before he was at last summoned to Fran's bedside. She was still in the recovery room.

"We'll be moving her into her own room shortly," a nurse told Bernie. "We've kept her here so we could watch her. But she's doing fine," the nurse added hastily as Bernie tensed in alarm. "She'll be able to talk with you."

"Does she know—" Bernie couldn't bring himself to give words to her physical debilitation.

"The doctor told her. She understands." The nurse's eyes told him that—though she'd probably held this conversation many times before—she was still able to feel compassion.

Bernie opened the door and walked inside. Subconsciously he was aware that the nurse was leaving them alone. He heard the door close behind as he crossed to Fran's bed. The other bed in the room was unoccupied. Fran's eyes managed a poignant welcome.

"Oh, baby," he whispered, reaching for her hand. She looked so small and fragile, lying there, with the sides of the bed raised in protective custody. "I was so scared." He kissed her gently on one cheek, as though she were a delicate, priceless porcelain figurine.

"It's going to be all right," she said, her voice weak but determined. Her eyes held his, ordering him to believe her. "Isn't it lucky it's my left side?"

"Well, if you had to get shot—" He struggled to match her air of flippancy.

"I asked when I could go home," Fran said and sighed with impatience. "They won't tell me."

"You'll come home when they say you're ready," Bernie told her, bringing her hand to his mouth.

"Midore's with the kids?"

"She will be. Gabrielle came over to stay with them until she got home. Frannie, you're not to worry. Lynne and Debbie will be fine. They love Midore."

"Tell Midore to go ahead with the closing," Fran said with sudden urgency. "She mustn't let that lunatic stop her from buying the house."

"I'll tell her," Bernie promised, clinging to her hand as though to reassure himself that she was alive. Even now she worried about Midore's parents. In a corner of his mind anxiety about the cost of Fran's hospitalization took root. The nurse had told him he must stop by the business office before he left, he reminded himself.

"There are some nice people in that area," Fran said. "She mustn't think they're all bad." But one nut pumped a bullet into her back.

Bernie stayed by her bedside even after Fran drifted off to sleep. A nurse came in to explain that she would sleep for a while. She'd been given an injection.

"Go to the cafeteria and have something to eat," she coaxed. Why did people always want you to eat when you were sick inside with anxiety? he thought. "Come back in an hour."

He left Fran's room. Scrounging for change, he sought for a phone booth and called the apartment. Midore had just arrived. Gabrielle would stay for a while, too, to divert the children from any anxiety. He would remain at the hospital until visiting hours were over, he vowed. He had vacation time coming, he remembered. He'd call up the plant and explain he'd take it now. He had to be here with Fran every day—until he could take her home.

Lynne and Debbie were asleep when he arrived home. Midore assured him they were fine. She had coffee waiting for him, and they sat down—both exhausted—to ponder over the day's happenings.

"It's all my fault," Midore said again as she prepared to leave.

"No," Bernie insisted. "You're not to blame yourself. Fran was doing what she wanted to do. And this is not the end of the world," he said defiantly. "Fran is going to have a full life. Together we'll see to that." But he was haunted by the image of her on crutches—and that after considerable physical therapy.

While he sat listening—fighting to stay awake—to a late news broadcast about the fighting in North Africa, the phone rang. With a new trepidation, he picked up the receiver.

"Hello—"

"Bernie, we've just checked into the hotel here in New York," his father-in-law's agitated voice came to him. "I called the hospital, but the patient information office was closed."

"She came through the surgery fine," Bernie assured him, then geared himself for what must be said.

"Ida, wait," he heard Josiah order sharply as he spoke in faltering tones. "Let Bernie talk to me."

"Fran wants to be moved to a New York hospital as soon as this is possible." Bernie punctured the stunned silence at the other end that followed his report of Fran's condition. "I'm not sure how to do this," Bernie admitted awkwardly.

"I'll take care of that," Josiah told him. "Ida, I'll tell you in a minute," he told his wife with unfamiliar impatience. Bernie felt his father-in-law's anguish and his dread at what he must tell Ida. "I assume we can't see Frannie until tomorrow morning. You'll be going out, too?"

"I'll pick you up at your hotel at eight o'clock," Bernie said. "Since you're from out-of-town, you won't have to wait for the regular visiting hours. We'll take the bus out together."

"Good, Bernie." Bernie sensed his relief. "I know my way around New York—but New Jersey is like a foreign country."

Fran lay awake, listening to all the morning hospital sounds. She'd been in the hospital twice, but a maternity floor was so different. It was—usually—a joyous place to be. Her poor babies, she thought in a surge of pain. How could they understand what was happening?

The doctor said that in time she'd be able to walk with the aid of crutches. She could manage once she was on her feet, she told herself defiantly. Lynne and Debbie weren't tiny babies, thank God. She'd have to give up the typing service, with her left hand of little use at this point. But she could raise her children. That was all that mattered. She'd need help for a little while—but she would *manage*.

A nurse came in with a bouquet of flowers, already placed in a vase.

"These just came for you," she told Fran. "Aren't they beautiful?"

"Yes." Fran's eyes were questioning. Who had sent her flowers?

"Shall I open the envelope for you?"

"Please." All at once conscious of the arm that lay flaccid on the bedspread, Fran extended her right hand as the nurse withdrew the card from the small envelope.

In astonishment she read the brief message: "Please get well soon. The crew at The Country Kitchen."

Tears filled her eyes as she remembered the short-order cook at The Country Kitchen. He'd tried to save her from that bigoted lunatic. Then she tensed in astonishment at the sound of familiar voices in the hall. Mother was here! And Daddy!

"Frannie, my baby—" Her mother dashed across the room to her bedside and reached down to kiss her. "Don't believe what that doctor told you! Daddy and I will bring in the best specialists! You're going to be fine again."

"How did you get here so fast?" She laughed shakily as her father pushed her mother aside to kiss her.

"We flew," he told her. "Only for you would we do that. But you know, Fran, it was wonderful."

"Maybe it was worth my getting shot for you to find that out." Fran tried for a humorous note. They looked so frightened.

Now Bernie leaned over to kiss her.

"The kids are fine." He read her mind. "They miss you, but they're handling it."

"Jo, you call Dr. Dalton back in Bellevue," Ida ordered. "He knows a lot of important doctors up here in New York. He'll help us find a good specialist."

"Fran's getting great care here," Bernie said, glancing nervously toward the door.

"Everybody's been so nice." Fran forced a smile. Why was she so tired?

A nurse came in and banished them from the room.

"You can come back again in a few minutes," she told them. "But don't stay long. The doctor wants her to rest."

For most of the day she drifted in and out of sleep. She wished her mother and father didn't look so scared, she thought in wakeful moments. And Bernie looked exhausted. He never got enough sleep—and he was forever smoking.

On her second morning in the hospital she awoke to the sound of her doctor's voice.

"It's remarkable the way she's bouncing back," he said cheerfully. "The young have such resilience. She'll probably have full use of her left arm again—after therapy."

Fran forced herself to open her eyes and managed a wisp of a smile for the two beside her bed. She glanced at the clock on her night table— brought yesterday by Bernie. He always teased her about her obsession for knowing the time.

"It's barely seven A.M.!" she said in astonishment. "Do your hours begin at sunrise?"

"I start making rounds at seven sharp." He grinned. "Doctors live double lives. Half the time at the hospital, half at the office. My wife complains that I should be triplets. She'd like to see me at home sometimes."

"When can I get out of here?" Fran asked. Except that her left leg refused to cooperate—and she was so tired, she didn't feel sick.

"Hey, you have some healing to do first," he joshed. "And I hear there's a movement underfoot to transfer you to a New York hospital."

"So my husband won't go crazy trying to get out to see me," she explained, lest he think she underrated her treatment here. "And my parents—"

"We'll see how fast we can arrange that." He patted her shoulder comfortingly. "Since you're such a good patient."

Shortly after 10 A.M. Bernie arrived with her parents. Each kissed her in turn and inspected her with touching anxiety. But she wouldn't succumb to self-pity, she vowed. That would accomplish nothing.

"They told us not to be here before ten o'clock—even if we are from down in Georgia," her mother began in irritation, then managed an aura of cheerfulness. "Darling, I went to Altman's and bought you some pretty nighties." Ida took the box Bernie had been carrying and began to open it up. "You've always adored pretty nightwear."

"I stopped by the office before we came up," Bernie told her while her mother held up a beautiful white satin, lace-trimmed nightgown—more for bride than hospital patient.

"It's gorgeous, Mother," Fran said dutifully while her eyes prodded Bernie to continue.

"In another three or four days they'll move you by ambulance to one of two New York hospitals," Bernie began. "They'll let us know as soon as word comes through."

"Is that wise?" Ida turned to Josiah with an air of alarm. "To move her so soon after surgery?"

"Mother, I want to be moved to a hospital in the city," Fran said urgently. "Bernie can't come running out here to New Jersey every day in the week and hold his job."

"Frannie, you're always so impulsive," her mother scolded. "Let Daddy talk to—"

"The doctors here won't allow her to be moved until they're sure it's safe." Bernie was struggling to appear calm, but Fran knew he felt he was being pushed aside.

"Frannie never thinks clearly—she just jumps. Like this crazy move to New York." She and Bernie had been living in New York for almost five years. There was nothing crazy about it, Fran thought angrily. "I knew it would turn out bad. Didn't I say so a thousand times?" Ida appealed to her husband.

"Ida, you're upsetting Fran," her husband said uneasily.

"I was right, wasn't I? If Fran hadn't come up to New York to live—if she'd stayed in Bellevue where she belonged—this horrible thing wouldn't have happened."

"Mother, it was just one of those freakish things." Fran's eyes clung to Bernie. He looked stricken, she thought. He mustn't blame himself for this. "When the doctors say it's all right, I'll be moved to a hospital in New York," she forced herself to continue. "They've told me I'll need a lot of physical therapy to—to get back to a normal life again." She saw her mother wince—knew that Bernie had noticed this.

"As soon as you're able to travel," her mother pursued, "you'll come back home, where I can take care of you and the children. My poor sweet baby—" Her voice broke.

"Mother, we're not moving back to Bellevue." Fran tried to keep her voice steady. "Bernie and I will manage. Midore has offered to help with the children until I can take over. And—"

"Bernie, talk to her," her mother said agitatedly. "Make her understand that coming back to Bellevue is the only way to handle the situation. My poor little Lynne and Debbie—they'll need me now."

"We're not leaving New York." Bernie was pale but determined. "Fran wants to stay here."

"You're being as ridiculous as she!" Ida said impatiently. "Jo, make them understand!"

"They're adults, Ida," her husband said gently. "We can't tell them how to run their lives."

"But they're not looking ahead. They don't—"

"Ida, enough already," Josiah told her. "We're upsetting Fran." He turned to his daughter, his eyes apologetic. "You do what the doctors tell you. Make sure she does, Bernie." He hesitated now. "I'll have to fly back to Bellevue this afternoon. I can be away from the shop just so long."

"I know, Daddy. And thank you and Mother for coming."

"Daddy's going home. I'll stay as long as you need me," her mother said quickly. "I have to be here for Lynne and Debbie, poor babies."

"Mother, you don't have to stay," Fran began. She was assaulted by visions of her mother with the children—her mother bemoaning her fate, upsetting them. *Your poor mother! What she's going through!* Lynne and Debbie were too young to understand. "Bernie and Midore will be able to cope just fine."

"You don't want me here," her mother gasped.

"You belong at home with Daddy." Fran's eyes pleaded with her mother to understand. "He *needs* you. Bernie will manage, and Midore is wonderful with the kids."

"All right." Her mother was close to tears. "I know when I'm not wanted. Your father and I will fly home to Bellevue on the first flight available. We'll phone once a week to see how you're doing."

"Mother, it's not like that at all," Fran protested. "You know I—"

But her mother was rushing from the room. Fran stared at the door in consternation.

"She loves you very much, Frannie," her father said as he bent to kiss her goodbye. "Be well." He turned to Bernie. "Whatever you need, just let me know."

"I didn't mean to upset her that way," Fran whispered, tears flooding her eyes. "Why can't she understand I'm not a little girl anymore?"

Eleven

O n schedule Fran was moved to a Manhattan hospital. She was shaken when—at her insistence—Bernie told her what her care in the New Jersey hospital had cost.

"Bernie, how awful!" she whispered.

"We could handle it," he told her quickly—but she knew that their savings account had been drained. All the money that was to go toward seeing them through Bernie's law degree. "You just concentrate on getting well."

Ever conscious of her needs, Bernie cajoled the hospital into giving her a room on a low floor. Every afternoon Midore brought Lynne and Debbie to the sidewalk below, where she could see and wave to them. Poor babies, they must be so upset, she thought. Thank God for the telephone. At least, she could talk to them every day on the phone. But always they asked, "Mommie, when are you coming home?"

Each day was an obstacle course. She must hide her moods of desperation, of anger. Why did this have to happen to *her?* Could she handle what lay ahead through the years, the way she kept insisting to Bernie? She would be such a burden to him—when she'd wanted only to help.

She knew how Bernie hated taking from her parents, yet they had no recourse once their savings were exhausted. How could hospitalization cost so much? Bernie tried to keep the figures from her, but she'd called down to the business office and asked about her bill. She'd read that in England some important man was promoting a law to provide free health insurance to everybody in the country. Why couldn't that happen here?

She fretted, too, at the painful—endless—sessions with the physical therapists. Yet she doggedly persisted in all that was asked of her. The foremost thought in her mind: When will the doctors let me go home?

At last she was to be released from the hospital—though scheduled for intensive physical therapy as an outpatient. Her heart was pounding when Bernie arrived at the hospital to take her home. She had left all those weeks ago on her own two feet. She was returning in a wheelchair, though she was able to take some tentative steps on crutches. Would Lynne and Debbie be upset when they saw her this way?

Bernie had been able to borrow a car for the trip from hospital to apartment. He seemed so nervous, she thought tenderly, as though she was a fragile doll that might break into bits if he made one misstep.

"Do the kids know I'm coming home?" she asked when he had her settled in the car and was seated beside her.

"Do they ever!" He chuckled in recall. "Lynne made me go out and buy daffodils before I came for you. She remembered how much you love them."

"Bernie, I'm going to be able to manage," she told him. "Little as they are, the kids will help me."

"I know you are, baby. But don't you push too hard. Midore will be there for you, too." He took a hand from the wheel to press hers encouragingly. Yet she sensed his anxiety.

She gazed out the window of the car as Bernie drove through the morning traffic—drinking in the sights denied her all these weeks. Winter was gone. Spring was here.

"What's the latest word on Midore's parents?" she asked, yearning to see him relax.

His face brightened. "She told me just last night. They'll be closing on the farm in two weeks. They'll move right in. Everything's gone through."

Conscientiously Bernie told her that her father was coming through with funds to pay for her medical care now that their own savings had been drained—a fact which she had taken for granted.

"Bernie, what do people do who have no savings and no family to help?" Fran asked, overwhelmed by the vision of such circumstances.

"They suffer," Bernie said grimly.

He felt humiliated that he couldn't handle her medical expenses on his own, she told herself. But how many families could cope with the bills for her care?

She churned with impatience while Bernie sought a parking spot, found one, left the car to bring out her wheelchair from the trunk. Now he gently lifted her from the car and carried her to the wheelchair. He brought her crutches from the rear seat and placed them across her lap.

Was everybody staring at her? she asked herself in a tidal wave of self-consciousness. Would the kids be upset when they saw her like this? Thank God, she was able to use her left arm again. The leg was the horrendous problem.

While they waited for the elevator at the apartment house Bernie talked about Lynne and Debbie's love affair with a young puppy newly arrived on their floor.

"They're absolutely out of their minds over this scruffy little pup," he said humorously. But *they* wouldn't be able to have a dog, Fran taunted herself—not until they were old enough to walk him on their own. "His name is Harry, and he may be the most spoiled little guy in this city— between his owner and the kids."

Her throat was tight as Bernie pushed the wheelchair toward their door. She could do that much for herself, she thought in momentary petulance. Then the door flew open. Midore smiled down at her in joyous welcome.

"Mommie, Mommie!" Lynne and Debbie flung themselves upon her, holding their small, beautiful faces up to her to be kissed.

"You're gonna stay home now?" Lynne asked, her blue eyes—so like her mother's—wide with hope.

"Darling, yes!"

"Midore made cookies." Debbie glowed in anticipation. "We're having a lunch party."

Fran was determined to take on much of the care of the children and the apartment. Midore would shop for her, take the children to the park each day. But from the time the children were back in the apartment until dinner—which Midore would prepare—she'd be self-sufficient. Now Midore could resume her afternoon classes, her painting.

Everybody must understand she wasn't helpless just because one leg was partially paralyzed, Fran told herself. Soon—very soon—she'd be preparing dinner every night. With Lynne's help she'd be able to handle lunch now.

Bernie arranged his work schedule so that one morning a week he was available to take Fran to the hospital for her physical therapy sessions. Each night when he came home, she had the children in bed. Most nights he came home in time to read them a story. Then Bernie brought dinner—waiting on the range—to the table for them.

She provided humorous little anecdotes each evening about her efforts that day. She pretended amusement at the minor accidents—the dishes she broke in her impatience not to depend on Lynne—or even tiny Debbie—as she made lunch for the three of them. The substitutions she made because neither Lynne nor Debbie could reach a high shelf. She was conscientious about using her crutches each day for the time specified by the therapist, but was learning to zoom about the apartment in her wheelchair with efficiency.

"Look, don't make me have to write out speeding tickets for you," Bernie joshed regularly.

Yet at frustrated moments she was inundated with depression. Each time she forced herself to thrust this aside. For Bernie's sake and the children's she must do this. She was *alive.* Eventually, she'd be out of the wheelchair and on crutches most of the time. Her life wasn't over.

Religiously her father phoned from Bellevue every Sunday evening, then put her mother on for a few moments. Her mother was obsessed by the trial of the man who had shot her, resentful that his sentence was not heavier. She would be berating the judicial system ten years from now, Fran thought.

Her mother was still hurt at that emotional encounter in her hospital room, she realized. It hung over them like a dark, reproachful cloud. She was eager for the Sunday night phone calls, yet felt defeated when she couldn't break down the wall between her mother and herself.

Midore's parents were pleased with their new home. Midore went out to spend each weekend with them and reported on their progress. It was wonderful the way Midore and Gabrielle had rallied around to help, Fran thought with recurrent affection.

When she progressed from wheelchair to crutches on a regular basis, Bernie brought home a bottle of champagne to celebrate. The hot August night she triumphantly prepared dinner herself—"with Lynne and Debbie's help," she told Bernie tenderly—she saw his eyes fill with tears of relief and pleasure.

"That's my girl!"

But she wasn't his girl anymore, Fran taunted herself. She was this strange shadow of herself who shared his bed and nothing else.

Though grateful to be on her feet at last—with the aid of crutches— she was haunted by a deepening conviction that Bernie no longer felt passion for her. How could he? she tormented herself. This wasn't the woman he married. She was the mother of his children—but she wasn't a wife anymore.

Yet the doctors had been explicit—they said that Bernie and she could enjoy a normal married life again. When? she asked herself. Or was Bernie repelled by the sight of her?

Night after night she lay sleepless, deriding herself for feeling the familiar need to be loved by her husband. Where once they'd fallen asleep in each other's arms, he clung to his side of the bed now. Was this all there was to be for them in the years ahead? *It wasn't enough.*

The first week in September Lynne was to enter kindergarten. Fran struggled to hide her disappointment that she wouldn't be taking her older daughter to school on this very important day. Bernie asked for time off to perform that special assignment. Midore had offered. Bernie insisted he would take Lynne. After this Midore would walk Lynne to her kindergarten class and pick her up. Midore would take Debbie to the park each morning to play.

Fran stood at a living-room window with Debbie at her side and watched while Lynne and Bernie—her hand in his—walked in the direction of the school. It was such a special occasion, she thought, flooded with love. Lynne looked so adorable—in one of the new dresses her grandmother had sent last week—with her lush dark hair falling about her shoulders.

When she was more adept with the crutches, Fran promised herself, she would be more involved in the children's outside lives. People would grow accustomed to seeing her on crutches—they would accept this. She wasn't the only mother on crutches in this world.

She made a special fuss over Debbie today—her baby, who felt somewhat left out. Bernie kept telling her the children wouldn't suffer because of her limitations. *He* was suffering, she tormented herself again. He'd always been so passionate. But he hadn't touched her since before the shooting.

Tonight much of the conversation revolved around Lynne's first day at kindergarten. Lynne was euphoric about this new experience. Fran was grateful that Bernie had been able to come home in time to see the children before they went to sleep—despite the fact that he'd taken two hours off this morning. He'd been so attentive to Lynne's repetitious account of her adventurous day.

"Sit down and I'll make us coffee," Bernie said when the children were at last asleep and they headed for the living room.

"Your program's on in four minutes," Fran warned. Bernie was addicted to radio newscasts.

"I'll put up the coffee, then come back," he promised.

Together they listened absorbedly to the report that the Allies had invaded the Italian mainland.

"Thank God, Sal's not in Italy," Bernie said. "Can you imagine how rough it must be for Americans of Italian descent—not knowing if they're fighting members of their own family?"

Now a first lieutenant in the Marine Corps, Sal was somewhere in the Pacific. Bob and Cliff wrote from time to time. Gabrielle kept Fran and Bernie up to date on Sal's activities.

Bernie went out to the kitchen during the commercial and brought back steaming cups of black coffee. He'd never stop feeling guilty that he wasn't in uniform, Fran thought wistfully. He was always so tense, so tired. He used to say that making love washed away all his tension and tiredness.

Despite the black coffee Bernie's eyes began to close. She knew he'd drift off, Fran thought tenderly. With his work schedule, he dozed almost every time he sat down. In a sudden need for closeness, she dropped her head on his shoulder and allowed her right hand to rest on his thigh. What could she do to win back her husband? For her nothing had changed.

She lifted her head from Bernie's shoulder and brought her face to rest against his. Why was he shutting her out? She'd never made a pretense of passion, the way some women did. For her that was an important part of their marriage. She kicked off a shoe and allowed her foot to caress his ankle.

On long, empty nights she'd thought about making the first overture. Bernie had been so pleased when she did that—in earlier days. But she wasn't his outgoing young bride anymore. Each glance in the mirror reaffirmed this.

Her hand tensed at his thigh as she remembered how it used to be for them. Her left leg might not be working properly, but the rest of her hadn't changed.

"Oh, Bernie—" she whispered in anguish.

"Hmm?" he mumbled and she hastily withdrew her hand, moved her face from his. She shouldn't have awakened him. "Honey?" All at once he was awake. Alert.

"You drifted off." She managed a smile. "Maybe we'd better call it a night."

"I was dreaming," he said huskily, an unexpected arousal in his eyes. "I was back in that narrow berth of the pullman car on our wedding night—"

"I wish we were back there right now—" she whispered.

"Frannie?" The question in his eyes brought a rapturous smile to her face.

"Oh, Bernie, yes! What took you so long?"

"I was afraid," he confessed. "I wasn't sure you were ready."

"Let's don't waste another moment," she exhorted.

Bernie lifted her in his arms, contrived to switch off the radio, then carried her into their bedroom.

"Oh, Bernie," she murmured later, cradled in his arms, "now 'all's right with the world.' Well, almost," she conceded. "But we shouldn't be greedy."

She could handle living, she told herself with fresh conviction. Bernie made her a whole person again.

Fran was disappointed that her mother didn't come up to New York with her father on his next buying trip. She yearned to heal the rift between her mother and herself. How was she to do that? She knew her mother's tendency to cling to slights endlessly.

"I was lucky to be able to get a plane ticket." Her father tried to cover for her mother's absence. "You know how it is these days. Two tickets would have been impossible."

Bernie continued to put in much overtime each week. He'd had two promotions, was now in a responsible executive position. At last, money was going into their savings account again.

"I wrote Bob I'd try to start law school the minute this lousy war is over," he told Fran. The fighting in Italy continued to be fierce, but now Italian troops were fighting with the Allies. In the Pacific the Allies were island-hopping, determined to drive back the Japanese. Hopes for an early peace began to flare. "Even if it's night classes in the beginning, I'll be in law school. Remember how we used to talk about starting up a practice together? Bob will have to wait a while for me," he conceded humorously, "but we'll make it."

Bernie and Bob had talked so much about practicing law together—about becoming involved in politics. *"Together, we'll make good things happen."* Bernie's words were etched on her brain. She meant to be a part of "making good things happen."

Midore's parents were fearful of coming into New York City, but regularly they sent gifts of hothouse fruits and vegetables for Fran and Bernie—with poignant notes expressing their gratitude for what the two had done for them. Fran and Bernie's bedroom walls were lined with delicate paintings of the children by Midore.

The second anniversary of Pearl Harbor came and passed, with Americans yearning for an end to the war. Production continued at high speed on the home front. The economy was booming. The unions, Fran thought impatiently, were not using their heads. Of course, people were upset when the United Mine Workers demanded more money. Didn't they—and the Musicians Union—understand that it was obscene to ask for higher wages when so many American boys were dying in the war? Yet she remembered the mill workers in the South and sympathized.

Early in April a letter arrived with a return address from a Mrs. Hammond in an unfamiliar town in Pennsylvania. Curiously Fran opened it and read the brief message:

"I'm Bob's oldest sister. He told me if anything happened to him to write and tell you, his best friends in New York. My mother received a telegram from the War Department. Bob was killed in battle in Italy. We'll miss him desperately."

Fran sat frozen in shock. They had known, of course, that this could happen—but she and Bernie had blocked this from their minds. *Bob dead?* For a little while she was too stunned to cry. They'd been through so much together, shared such dreams—and now Bob was gone.

Later—still crying inside—she told Midore, then Gabrielle. She'd tell Bernie tonight. It was as though part of their lives was gone, too.

Fran waited until after dinner to tell Bernie. He gazed at her for long moments in dizzy disbelief.

"I had a letter from him yesterday. Just a short V-mail, but he said he'd write a real letter at the next chance he got. Why did we wrap ourselves so smugly in the belief that those close to us would come home?" he railed in anguish. "Oh, God, Frannie—we'll never see Bob again."

"I hurt, too," she said, eyes blurred by tears as she held her arms out to Bernie.

"I'll have to be double the lawyer I planned to be," Bernie said later when they had retired for the night—knowing sleep would elude them. "Bob will always be there beside me."

Their magic circle had been broken, Fran thought as Bernie reached to switch off the lamp. They'd been so close—and now one of them was gone forever.

Twelve

As always Fran fretted that Bernie worked too hard, got too little sleep, and smoked too much. But she was conscious of a new conviction that her life was back on course. Once the awful war was over and Bernie could pursue his dream to become a lawyer, all would be well with their lives—except that her mother still played the wounded martyr.

She continued her physical therapy with a zealous determination to recover as much as humanly possible. She was becoming less uneasy on crutches in public, more confident that she was in control. She vowed to keep herself in tip-top condition—to ignore her limitations. She reminded herself of all the war vets who had come home with physical disabilities. They were going on with their lives. So would she.

At intervals Gabrielle came over with tiny Sal, Jr., for dinner—always a happy occasion for Lynne and Debbie, who adored the baby. At other times she and Bernie would go to dinner at the restaurant, with Midore baby-sitting the two little girls. Gabrielle now lived with her in-laws. She and her father-in-law ran the restaurant while Sal's mother took care of the baby.

"I can't believe Sal's never seen his son," Gabrielle said with recurrent astonishment. "But I keep the Kodak people in business with all the snapshots I send."

With the arrival of 1944 the Allies continued their bloody fight to push the Nazis out of Italy. It was a slow, agonizing process. In the Pacific the Allies were pushing back the Japanese, took over the Marshall Islands, then moved into the Marianas—but the cost was shockingly high.

In 1944, FDR was running for an unprecedented fourth term. Like most Americans, Fran and Bernie could see no other choice. The feeling in the country was that it was just a matter of time before Germany and Japan would be defeated. On a personal level Fran felt that she and Bernie were in a holding pattern.

Her periods of deep depression about her physical limitations were becoming less frequent. She drove herself—to a point of exhilaration—with the exercises prescribed by the therapists. Except that she needed someone to do the shopping, to take Lynne to school and bring her home again, she felt growing independence. Their social life was limited because of Bernie's extremely heavy work schedule—not because of her physical disability, she told herself. But these days socializing was on hold for many people.

On June 6, 1944—under the leadership of General Eisenhower—the Allies began an assault on the Normandy coast with forces that would consist of almost three million Americans, British, and Canadians. The Allies had five thousand ships, four thousand landing craft, and more than eleven thousand planes.

Americans first became aware of this mammoth invasion around noon on the following day. On CBS radio an announcer broke into the broadcast of *The Romance of Helen Trent,* and Edward R. Murrow gave a brief report of the dramatic happenings.

That evening—like millions of Americans—Fran and Bernie clung to the radio.

"They'll zero in on Paris," Bernie said, his face luminous. "And once Paris is liberated, it'll be the beginning of the end."

"They won't reach Paris in a day or a week or even a month," Fran said realistically. "But yes, God willing, it'll soon be the beginning of the end." She hesitated. "Bernie—"

"Yeah?" He raised an eyebrow inquiringly.

"Don't you have to take exams to get into law school?"

"Sure." He seemed puzzled.

"Start studying for them now. You be ready the next time the law exams are given."

"Isn't that jumping a bit?" he protested. But she saw the eagerness in his eyes.

"Take them," she insisted. "The next time around." Everybody was sure Columbia had a quota on Jewish students—but with the war enrollment was way down, Fran reasoned. Bernie had a good chance of being accepted. It was important to have a degree from a top school.

When on June 22nd FDR signed the Servicemen's Readjustment Act—quickly dubbed the "GI Bill of Rights"—she was more determined than ever that Bernie be prepared to sign up for law school at the earliest possible moment. The "GI Bill" promised returning servicemen a college education. The college campuses would be loaded.

Fran felt a continuing frustration because of the wall between herself and her mother. Her mother showered Lynne and Debbie with gifts, pleaded for a constant flow of snapshots—but when her father came up on buying trips, he came alone.

She'd hoped that when he arrived in July he'd be accompanied by her mother. He called in high spirits from his hotel room.

"I'm here," he said blithely. Not "we're here" she noted. "Expect me for dinner around seven." He hesitated. "Why don't I stop off at the Stage and bring up deli?"

"That'll be great," Fran agreed, hiding her disappointment that her mother wasn't with him. "But tomorrow I cook dinner." It was understood that his days would be focused on buying. Each evening he would be at the house. "Lynne and Debbie have been painting up a storm. All for you. They're so excited that they're going to see you."

"Why didn't Mother come with you?" she demanded of her father after they'd had dinner and the children had finally been put to bed— long past their normal bedtime.

"You know how awful New York summers are," he hedged.

"I know how awful summers are in Bellevue," she shot back.

"Give her time, Frannie." He, too, was unhappy at this situation. "You know she loves you—"

"How long do you think it'll be before the war is over?" Bernie intervened, trying to change the subject. "It's great to hear about the advances in France. Everybody says it's a matter of weeks before Paris is liberated."

"That won't mean the end of the war," Josiah predicted gloomily.

The Allied forces pushed doggedly into France—with casualties lighter than they had feared. By August 6th General Patton's Third Army had stormed to the south and cut off the Brittany Peninsula. Canadian and American forces trapped one hundred thousand German troops. On August 15th American and French forces made an amphibious landing close to Cannes. Ten days later Paris was liberated.

With the approach of September Lynne was enthralled at the prospect of starting first grade.

"That's *real* school," she crowed.

Again, watching Bernie set off with Lynne for the first day of school, Fran felt rebellious at her own inability to accompany her small daughter on such a momentous occasion. A fresh determination took root in her. She had felt triumphant at progressing from wheelchair to crutches, though for much of the time she utilized the wheelchair for expediency. But to be able to walk without the crutches—with braces and a cane, perhaps—would make her far more mobile.

Saying nothing to Bernie lest he be disappointed, she questioned the doctor who supervised her continuing—though less frequent—physical therapy.

"Look at President Roosevelt," she said earnestly. "He walks with braces now."

"It took years for him to arrive at that point," the doctor pointed out, his eyes compassionate. "And much of the time—though I doubt the general public is aware of this—he uses his wheelchair."

"I want to be able to walk—at times—with braces," Fran said, her color high. "And perhaps with a cane," she conceded. "I don't care how hard I have to work at it."

Tears filled Bernie's eyes when she told him what she meant to undertake.

"You are the most stubborn woman alive," he said, his voice husky. "And I love you for it."

"It'll cost money," she admitted. "But let Daddy and Mother do this for us," she pleaded. "It'll be important to them. And it might just break down that wall between Mother and me. Please, Bernie?"

"All right." He reached to pull her close. "But promise me you'll remember that the doctors say it *may* work. There's no guarantee."

Fran spent long, painful hours at new exercises, gritted her teeth to bear the pain of the braces. But as long as there was a chance she could throw away the crutches—part of the time, at least—she meant to pursue this. As the months sped by, she saw only slight progress. Still, she vowed to see this through.

On April 12th of the new year she felt a special anguish at the sudden death of President Roosevelt.

"His dying had nothing to do with his legs," she told Bernie, fighting tears as they listened to the radio broadcast that reported on the progress of the train bearing the body of the late President from Warm Springs, Georgia, to its ultimate resting place at Hyde Park. "He worked himself to death for this country."

"How sad," Bernie mourned—no doubt, with millions of others, "that he couldn't have lived to see that the war is all but over in Europe."

American armies in the west were barely forty miles from Berlin. In the east Soviet forces were just thirty miles away. The fighting—accompanied by heavy bombardment from the air—was furious. The world waited for word that the fighting in Europe was over.

On April 20th a report was released by the Associated Press, asserting that the Germans had agreed to an unconditional surrender. All over the country people ran from their homes, offices, stores and into the streets in joyous celebration. Then only hours later the disappointing word came through. The report was false.

On May 1st the German government announced that Hitler had died in the defense of Berlin. A day later Berlin fell. On Monday, May 7th, Germany accepted unconditional surrender. The papers were signed shortly before midnight. At 9 A.M. on May 8th Americans heard President Harry S. Truman announce on the radio that there would be no more fighting in Europe.

Minutes later Bernie was on the phone with Fran.

"Baby, the war in Europe is over! I don't think we'll be working today! I'll get home as soon as I can!"

Fran clung to the radio. People were pouring into Times Square, a newscaster reported, filling the streets. Ticker tape was flying out of windows along Wall Street.

"The city's going wild with joy," the excited newscaster said ebulliently. "Soon American GIs will be homeward bound. But let's not forget," he added in sudden sobriety, "that we're still fighting a war in the Pacific."

Now—with most people convinced the war would be over in a few short months—Fran prodded Bernie into applying for admission to law school in the fall.

"Fran, you're rushing too fast," he scolded. "We're not ready yet."

"Once the war is over, servicemen will be rushing home and onto college campuses," she predicted. "Let's make sure you'll have a place."

"I'm not quitting my job," he warned. "Maybe I'll try for evening classes."

"Sign up now," she insisted. "For *day* classes. If the war isn't over and you're still at the plant, then you'll get a tuition refund."

"I'm not sure we can afford for me to stop working," he said cautiously.

"If we budget the way we should, we can handle your first year at

Columbia. You remember what Bob said." Her face softened in recall. Even now it was difficult to believe Bob wasn't coming home. *"Let me tell you, kids—that first year of law school is a bitch."*

"We'll have no cushion if an emergency arises," he pointed out.

"Bernie, we have my parents. Daddy wants to see you get a law degree. You know—'my son-in-law, the attorney.' He was the one who said you should try to get into Columbia, even though tuition is so high."

"Once I'm in practice, I'll pay back every cent he's laid out for us," Bernie vowed.

"Just concentrate on law school. And please God, let you start in the fall."

"From your mouth to God's ear. Let the war be over."

In the Pacific—on Easter Sunday, April 1st—U.S. Army and Marine troops had invaded Okinawa. In the following two and a half months the Japanese air force launched an estimated 6,000 kamikazes—suicide planes. By the time the Japanese in Okinawa finally surrendered on June 21, these planes had sunk 36 ships and damaged another 332. In the fighting the Allies suffered 60,000 casualties, the Japanese over 109,000. But Americans rejoiced that troop ships were already bringing servicemen home from Europe—though they knew these vets would be heading for the Pacific after a brief furlough.

On the night of July 5th Midore sat with Fran and Bernie while they listened to the reports that General MacArthur declared the Philippine Islands liberated.

"How much longer can this go on?" Midore asked in pain. "Until the war is over, no Japanese-American walks without fear. My parents are happy at being on their own small farm," she said quickly, "but they leave the property only to shop for essential items. They're afraid. My mother insists on leaving lights on in the house all night. She jumps at every unexpected sound."

"Midore, you know there're people around them who're sympathetic," Fran reminded earnestly, yet she understood.

"It's the handful of fanatics out there that terrify them." Midore flinched in recall. "Like that lunatic that shot you, Fran."

"We can feel the breath of peace on our necks." Bernie's smile was encouraging. "The Japanese can't take much more of what we're handing out."

But it wasn't until after two atomic bombs were dropped—the first on Hiroshima on August 6th and the second on Nagasaki on August 9th—that Japan agreed to unconditional surrender. On the eve of August 14th—when many Americans were homeward bound after the day's work or already gathering at the dinner table—President Truman made this announcement to the American public on radio.

Bernie brought the news to Fran, who had fed the children and prepared them for bed. She was in the midst of reading them their nightly story while a fan whirred atop a nearby dresser, when he burst into the apartment and charged into the girls' bedroom.

"Fran, it's over!" he told her. "The war is over! The Japanese have surrendered."

"How do you know?" She teetered between exhilaration and disbelief—remembering the fake report of the end of the war in Europe.

"President Truman made an announcement on the radio," he said. "Let's go listen!"

"Daddy! Daddy!" Lynne and Debbie darted from their beds to clutch at their father.

"All right, you can stay up a little longer," he agreed. "Tonight is very special." His eyes met Fran's above their heads. "Finally we know there'll be a peaceful world for them." It sounded, Fran thought, like a benediction.

"Bernie, go turn on the radio," she ordered, and followed him and the girls into the living room in her wheelchair. It was a family understanding that nobody pushed her wheelchair without this being requested.

The uncomfortable heat of the night forgotten, they settled before the living-room radio and listened to the jubilant newscaster.

"All across the country as the word is spreading, people are celebrating," he reported. "President Truman has declared the next two days a national holiday."

Now Bernie began to explain to his daughters the tremendous joy that engulfed the world tonight. And while he did this, the radio elaborated on the reactions across the country. Yet Fran knew that for many of those celebrating—like themselves—joy was tinged with fresh grief for those who would not be on homecoming troop ships and flights.

Moments later Midore arrived—her incandescent face telling Fran she'd heard the news.

"Thank God, it's over." She reached to embrace Fran, then Bernie. "Now Cliff and Sal can come home."

"You'll have dinner with us," Fran said. "We'll—"

"I'm going to try to get out to my parents' house," Midore interrupted. "I'm hoping the buses are running in all this pandemonium." She laughed shakily.

"Try to call the bus terminal," Bernie suggested and he, too, laughed. "If the operators haven't left their stations." This, in fact, had happened on V-E Day.

"My parents need me," Midore said, reaching for the phone. "They're Americans in every way, but it's only natural that they grieve for their old homeland." Where atomic bombs had left such devastation, Fran interpreted in sympathy.

The buses were running, Midore reported in relief.

"Maybe now my father and mother will be able to breathe freely. I know they want to go back to California." But Fran saw the anxiety in Midore's eyes. While the war was over, would there be a welcome on the West Coast for those they'd sent into exile?

Midore left. Bernie insisted he'd heat up dinner and bring it to the table. Fighting yawns but determined to be part of tonight's celebration, Lynne and Debbie—in the pretty seersucker pajamas sent by their grandmother—settled themselves at the table.

"All right," Fran agreed, reading their minds. "You can each have a cookie and a glass of milk. Then you go to bed."

After dinner—with the girls now fast asleep, Fran and Bernie sat listening to the newscast. They cherished the reiteration that the war was over. A terrible part of their lives was finally behind them. They listened, Fran thought, to reassure themselves that this wasn't a mirage, that the war was truly over. Tonight Bernie remained fully awake—no dozing off in his familiar pattern.

The phone rang. Fran reached over quickly to pick up the receiver from the table at her right, lest the girls be awakened.

"Hello—"

"Fran, I know it's late—but I had to call." It was Gabrielle, her voice oddly husky. "I received a telegram this morning from the War Department. V-J Day came too late for Sal. I knew you'd want to know. He died on Guam—fighting for his country."

Thirteen

N ow that the war was over, many Americans worried that the country would fall back into the Depression. *"The war kept us going,"* some warned. *"Where will all those vets coming home from Europe and the Pacific find jobs?"* Magazines and newspapers were filled with articles predicting that starving veterans would roam the streets in angry packs, that there would be ugly labor-baiting, riots on the streets. Dying H.G. Wells warned that the human race was doomed to expire.

Despite the undercurrent of dire predictions about the economy, Fran had not expected Bernie to hedge on quitting his job and entering law school. She gazed at him in shocked astonishment when he expressed doubts about this.

"You've registered! It's all set!"

"The plant has cut shifts, but it's still running," he said, avoiding her eyes. "They'd be sorry to lose me."

"You want to be a lawyer. Bernie, we can handle this." And when their money ran out, she reminded herself—and Bernie *knew* this—her father would come to their aid.

"Right now our bank account—and our war bonds—make us seem healthy financially. For a while," he amended this. "But once price controls go off, I'll take any bet that inflation goes up like a cut-loose balloon. The dollar will drop in half—or less."

"Truman and Congress won't let inflation get out of control," she rejected impatiently. "You're going to law school. That's what you want and that's what I want. Bernie, it's important to the four of us!" Her eyes dared him to refute this.

"You're a very special lady, you know," he said after a heated moment.

"I'm looking after my best interests." She felt a surge of relief. "Mine and the kids. We don't want a husband and father who hates his job. I know you loathed that job at the plant, but it was temporary—" She paused to chuckle as he managed a whimsical smile. "All right, it was long-time temporary, but now it's over. We can begin to live again."

"I'll work part-time and during the summers," he said seriously. "That'll help."

"My mother will brag about her son-in-law, the attorney. And my father will be so excited when you move into politics. I don't think you'll ever be president," she joshed. "This country isn't ready for a Jewish president. But you'll push for important things, and I'll be so proud of you."

On a morning in late September Fran was joyous when she picked up the phone to hear Cliff's voice at the other end.

"Cliff! Where are you?"

"I'm in New York—out of uniform, and getting set to intern again at Bellevue," he told her. "I raised hell. I told the big brass I had to get back quick to my internship or I'd be out in the cold."

"When can we see you?" Fran asked, and in a corner of her mind remembered that he hadn't seen her since the accident. But she had written him. He was a doctor. He knew what to expect.

"Grab me fast before I get sucked into those crazy hospital hours. I'm at your service for the next two days."

"Come to dinner tonight?" she asked eagerly. He didn't know yet about Bob and Sal, she realized—but this was not the moment to tell him. "I can't wait to see you. Bernie, too!"

"Tonight's great. What time?"

"Around six?" she asked. "Then you'll get to see the kids. They'll still be awake."

"Oh, God, they were so little when I enlisted. I probably won't recognize them." His voice softened. "It was great to get your letters—and the snapshots of Lynne and Debbie. I passed them around along with the snaps of my sisters' kids. Mail was like reaching out to home."

"Are you still mad about spaghetti?" she asked, mentally searching her food supplies. Sal used to tease him, saying the way he loved spaghetti he had to be Italian.

"Just pile it high!" he ordered. "After C-rations and Spam, I'll be in ecstasy."

Fran was impatient for Bernie to be home from the Columbia campus, to tell him Cliff was out of uniform. His schedule today allowed him to pick up Lynne from school. Midore would bring Debbie home from kindergarten. Oh, he'd be so happy to see Cliff! But there'd be sadness, too—because they'd be more conscious than ever that Bob and Sal would not be coming home.

The apartment ricocheted with the pleasurable sounds of reunion when Cliff arrived. Later Midore would join them, Fran explained. She was teaching an evening art class now. They tossed questions at one another in joyous abandon—faces glowing, voices elated. Then Cliff asked about Bob and Sal. All at once the room was ominously quiet.

"They didn't make it, Cliff," Bernie told him.

"Oh, God!" Cliff stared first at Bernie, then at Fran, as though pleading for a rejection of these words. "I just took it for granted they were okay," he said after a moment. "You hadn't written anything—"

For a while they were caught up in painful reminiscence, then— mindful of the children's somber faces, Fran made a point of bringing them into the conversation.

"Cliff, did I tell you that Lynne is in the second grade already and Debbie is in kindergarten?"

"Wow, I can't believe that!" Cliff was properly impressed.

Now he began to ply the two little girls with questions about their school. Lynne and Debbie were delighted by his affectionate inquiries.

Their social lives were too limited, Fran scolded herself. Only Midore and Gabrielle came to the apartment these last years. For Bernie and the children she should make an effort to enlarge their circle of friends. She was working hard at the new exercises the therapist had given her. Soon, she vowed, she'd ask to try to make the switch from crutches to canes. Then she'd be able to get around more easily outside of the apartment.

Over heaping plates of Fran's tantalizingly sauced spaghetti, the three adults talked about current conditions in the country—the two little girls not understanding much of what was said but enjoying Cliff's presence.

"You know, it's crazy the way some people are making such pessimistic predictions about the future," Bernie said earnestly. "Now that the war is over, they're sure we're going to turn right back into the Depression. They're wailing about 'where will the returning GIs get jobs?'"

"With all the women quitting work to think about raising families, they'll *find* jobs," Cliff guessed. "My two sisters are back at home already. My mother told them it was time to take care of their kids themselves," he said humorously. "And I gather they're not crying about that."

"Plenty of guys will be signing up for the Fifty-two-Twenty Club," Bernie predicted, "which gives vets twenty bucks a week for a year— and a load will be heading for college under the GI Bill. I don't see heavy unemployment in the cards."

"In the Depression nobody had money," Fran pointed out. "But most people here at home have been saving for years now. Salaries kept going up, but there wasn't that much to buy—"

"My father's got himself on the list for a new car," Cliff told them, "but he knows it'll be a long wait. Yeah, he has money now," he added reflectively. "And think of all the money Americans socked away in war bonds."

"Good times are ahead," Fran said with conviction. Despite her physical problems, she thought, the future looked fine.

In the coming weeks it seemed to Fran that she had never been so happy. Bernie spent endless hours studying, so absorbed in this that she felt a new richness had entered their lives. She'd forced him to abandon his plan to work part-time. His sole concern, she reiterated, was to focus on earning his law degree.

She made a point of serving dinner early, so the four of them could sit down at the table together. After dinner she took the children off to bed so Bernie could focus on schoolwork. She relished sitting quietly in a corner with a novel while he poured over textbooks. She read *A Bell for Adano* and *Blackboy*, and Kathleen Windsor's *Forever Amber*. As always she and Bernie were avid newspaper readers.

When Bernie took a break from the books, Fran made coffee for them. At the winter break between semesters Fran felt as though she and Bernie were on a second honeymoon. Each weekday morning he took Lynne and Debbie off to school, then returned to the apartment for a leisurely breakfast with her. In extravagant moments he'd stop at Zabar's for bagels and lox. And with a frequency she relished they made love.

There was something deliciously decadent about making love in mid-morning, she told herself. A rare occurrence in their lives since the children were born. And this was a cherished reassurance that Bernie still found her desirable.

Late in January—with the college intercession almost over—Bernie insisted on taking a part-time job with an accounting firm in the neighborhood.

"Honey, it's a snap for me. This is the busy time of year for accountants, and the money is terrific. It's just for three months." He tried to coax a smile from her. "And with the wild inflation we're seeing, I'll feel better."

"Why did Congress dump wage and price controls?" Fran shook her head in disapproval. "Truman wanted to phase controls out gradually."

"Too many special-interest groups lobbied against it," Bernie said. "Government control was too much like communism in their eyes— meaning they couldn't go berserk and jack up prices."

Despite the unexpected crises that arose in the country in the months ahead—shortages, galloping inflation, strikes, riots because the government was so slow in bringing servicemen home—Fran was supremely happy. Bernie continued to work for the accounting firm on Saturdays, but he insisted it wasn't interfering with his studies. They lived a very insular existence, Fran told herself—but for now that was good, she concluded.

Midore's parents planned to return to their home in San Francisco when the current lease expired. Her father was making contacts with former clients and indications were that he could resume his career with little effort. Midore was acquiring assignments with increasing frequency.

In August Cliff told them he was switching his internship to a hospital in St. Louis in order to be near his family.

"My father has a heart condition," he explained. "He and my mother need me out there. And when I finish my internship," he told them quietly, "I want to settle in some very small town near Saint Louis. Some place where I can fill a real need. I'm not interested in a fancy society practice, like some guys I know. I want to be useful. That's all I ask of life. Doing what I like to do for people who need me."

Debbie was euphoric at entering first grade in September. Fran felt a new freedom with the girls in school until three o'clock. She was devoting much of these hours to the exercises the new doctor—recommended by Cliff—had devised to help her discard the crutches and walk with the leg brace and canes. *One* cane, she vowed. Even Bernie didn't realize how close she was to achieving that status—if all went well. Six months, she promised herself.

Her father continued to come up twice a year on buying trips. Her mother had not come up since the encounter in the hospital after the accident. She talked once a week with Fran and each time asked that Lynne and Debbie be put on to talk with her. She sent extravagant gifts for the children, and regularly a box of clothes came up for Fran. Her mother was polite, friendly—and Fran knew her mother loved her—but the wall remained between the two women.

"You wouldn't recognize Atlanta these days," Ida rattled on the Sunday evening after Thanksgiving. "The traffic is just unbelievable! Everybody seems to be driving. And there's so much building going on! It's spilling over into Bellevue. Some gorgeous houses are being built on the outskirts now. More and more people are talking about moving away from the downtown area, but it's so convenient for Daddy to be able to walk to the store that I don't see us becoming suburbanites. Can you imagine, Bellevue having its own suburbs?"

Fran knew that Midore was relieved that her parents were resettled in their home in San Francisco, though she was afraid they would never fully recover from the traumatic experience of their year in the internment camp. There had been an emotional dinner party at the Yamamoto farmhouse when Fran and Bernie and the children met Midore's parents for the first time. Shiro, too, had come from his teaching post in Massachusetts for the occasion and would join his parents in San Francisco at the end of the school year.

Instinct told Fran that Midore yearned to go back to San Francisco, too, but felt obligated to remain in New York because of *her*. Bernie took the children to school in the morning before heading for the Columbia campus, and Midore brought them both home after school. But that shouldn't keep Midore in New York, Fran told herself guiltily. Midore never stopped feeling that the accident—as they preferred to call the shooting—was her fault.

Early in the new year Fran made her first efforts—known only to the new doctor and herself—to walk with the leg brace and one cane. *She could do it.*

"You must take it slowly," the compassionate doctor cautioned. "Increase the distance you can do in easy stages. You know it'll be very tiring at first."

"I'll be careful," Fran promised but she was light-headed with pleasure. All the pain, the hard work was paying off.

Bernie knew that she could maneuver with the leg brace and a pair of canes—for a short distance, though she never ventured beyond the apartment in this fashion. Now she was determined to prove she could go out on the street with just the one cane. On her first try she was perspiring despite the coolness of the day—terrified that she might fall. But she made it. She was exhausted but triumphant. Each day she would travel a little further. Not even Bernie knew yet of this new small triumph.

She was joyous when she went into a store and shopped for small items that fit into her oversized shoulder bag. And in a few days she would go to the school and wait—like other mothers—for her two daughters to emerge. She would talk with them about Lynne and Debbie, and they'd talk to her about their kids.

The evening before she plotted this small adventure, she waited impatiently for Bernie to sprawl on the living-room sofa with his books. Then—her heart pounding—she walked from their bedroom into the living room with leg brace in place and using only one cane. She stood in the doorway and waited for him to realize she was there. While he watched in rapturous astonishment, she slowly walked toward him.

"Fran!" He reached to help her sit beside him, his face incandescent. "When did this happen?"

"I've been working with that new doctor Cliff recommended," she reminded. "Tomorrow I'm going to the school to pick up Lynne and Debbie and walk them home."

"Go with Midore," he urged, his eyes anxious. "The first time."

"Midore can go with me—the first time," she said with a dazzling smile. "I didn't tell you before because I wanted to be sure I could do it."

"Honey, there's practically nothing you can't do," he said tenderly.

"I just want to be there for you and the kids," she whispered. "Always."

That would be her dream, she told herself sternly. It would be enough.

As Fran had anticipated, Midore returned to San Francisco once she was convinced she was not truly needed.

"Oh, I'm going to miss you all!" Midore's eyes were bright with tears as she sat with Fran and Bernie on her last night in New York—Lynne and Debbie at last asleep after poignant farewells. "Promise me that you'll come out to visit."

"We'll come." Fran managed a smile. Cliff was out in a small town near St. Louis. Midore was going home to San Francisco. They saw little of Gabrielle these days—she was going steady with a teacher who'd been in the Marines, like Sal. "Once Bernie's out of law school, and we have some time."

"I can't believe he's in his second year already." Midore's eyes turned affectionately to Bernie. "But you ought to take care of that cough," she admonished as he broke into a spasm of coughing.

"I keep telling him," Fran said. "No matter how bad the weather is, he runs off to school. He goes from one bad cough to another. Never gives himself a chance to clear one up."

"It's this crazy New York winter." Bernie shrugged.

"He keeps saying he's going to stop smoking," Fran reminded Midore, "but he never does."

Awakened later in the evening by Bernie's wracking cough, Fran promised herself she'd insist he see a doctor. The medication he picked up at the drugstore wasn't helping at all. He was run down, she thought—all the years of the crazy hours at the plant, then the law school rat race without a break. That was why he couldn't shake the cough.

Bernie stalled on going to a doctor. He was in the midst of exams, he pointed out. They took precedent over everything. He'd go at end of the semester, he promised.

Upset at these delays—and with Bernie's cough lingering—Fran decided to phone Cliff and enlist his help. After four tries, she got through to him. He, too, kept torturous hours.

"I'll call Bernie tonight," Cliff promised. "He's nuts to ignore a cough that's gone on for months. It's probably nothing serious," he soothed, yet Fran sensed anxiety in his voice. "I'll send him to a specialist I know from medical school. A great guy and he won't hit you with a big fee. What's a good time to reach Bernie?"

Somberly Bernie listened to Cliff's exhortations when he called late in the evening—when the children were asleep. He shook his head in reproach that Fran had enlisted Cliff's support.

"All right," Bernie agreed at last. "I'll call and make an appointment." He frowned, listening to Cliff with obvious impatience. "Of course I think about Fran and the kids. I told you—I'll call this guy."

Three days later Bernie took the girls to school, then headed across town to the specialist Cliff had recommended. Fran waited impatiently for Bernie to come home from the doctor. Despite Cliff's reassurances he'd worried that a specialist would charge high fees. This wasn't the time for them to encounter unexpected expenses, he railed. But whatever the doctor told him to do, he must do, Fran told herself.

Searching Bernie's face as he came into the apartment she felt her heart begin to pound.

"The doctor wants me to check into the hospital tomorrow morning for tests," Bernie told her. He was pale, visibly shaken. "He's bringing in a lung specialist."

"Then you'll do that," she said with supernatural calm after a leaden pause. "Whatever it is, at your age the doctors will handle it."

She was remembering—as Bernie was at this moment—that his mother and father had both died of lung cancer. Both heavy smokers—as he was. Both dead at an early age.

Fourteen

F ran fought not to fall apart when the medical tests indicated that Bernie was suffering from lung cancer. The specialist recommended surgery as soon as possible.

"His age is on his side," the doctor comforted Fran on the morning Bernie was being prepared for surgery. Bernie was thirty-two years old—his father was forty-one when he was diagnosed as having lung cancer, Fran reminded herself, clinging to this.

She waited with soaring anxiety for Bernie to emerge from surgery. This was how Bernie had felt when she was in surgery after the shooting, she thought. But she had come out of it. She had a life that was normal now. Almost normal. Please, God, let Bernie be all right, she prayed. She wouldn't want to live without him.

After an agonizing period of time, Fran was told that Bernie was out of surgery and had responded well.

"The damage was far more extensive than we suspected," the doctor said gravely. "But the other lung appears untouched." He paused. "Was your husband's father also a heavy smoker?"

"Both his father and his mother," Fran told him.

"I suspect that affected him as a child." The doctor was contemplative. "I wouldn't be surprised if someday researchers will tell us that being exposed to cigarette smoke as a child is a factor in contracting lung cancer."

Forever, Fran thought painfully, she would worry about the girls. But they wouldn't smoke, she vowed. No matter that women were smoking openly these days. She remembered how back in high school those girls who were considered "fast" would sneak a smoke in the gym. She'd tried it once and decided it was disgusting. No matter that some of the girls thought it was so sophisticated.

For the first three weeks after his surgery Fran and Bernie were euphoric. The doctor pronounced him on the road to recovery. After a brief period of convalescence, Bernie could resume his life. Then they faced reality. The financial drain of his hospitalization was shattering.

"We'll be all right," Fran insisted. "I'll write Daddy and explain what we've been through." She'd said nothing to her parents about their travail. She'd been determined to spare them anxiety and to salvage what she could of their own feeling of independence.

"The economy is great," Bernie said with fabricated high spirits. "I'm a CPA. I'll bet I can go out and latch onto a decent job in a week."

"You're going to earn your law degree. Nothing's going to stand in your way!" She was shocked that he would consider leaving school.

"Fran, your father's going to balk at all this extra money." His eyes were apprehensive. "And I won't blame him."

"He won't balk." Fran was convinced of this. "You're my husband and the father of his only grandchildren. Even if it was hard for him—and it isn't," she emphasized, "he'd want to do this for us."

When her father received the letter about Bernie's surgery and their straitened financial situation, he phoned them.

"Frannie, why didn't you tell us?" he scolded, clearly unnerved. "Why should you go through that alone? Your mother and I would have flown up to be with you."

"I didn't want to worry you," she confessed. "And it all happened so fast. Bernie went into the hospital for tests, and right away he was scheduled for surgery. But he's all right now," she reassured him. "It's just that we're squeezed for money. We've paid part of the doctor bill, but he's expecting the rest by—"

"I'm sending you a check," her father interrupted, then he hesitated. "The doctor feels Bernie's all clear now?"

"Oh, yes. We were lucky to catch it so early." But in a corner of her mind she remembered that the damage had been more extensive than they'd expected. "And the doctor feels that Bernie's being so young was all in his favor. He has to go in for a checkup in two months, then after that it'll be every four months for three years. But they're sure they removed the malignant area."

"If you think at any time he should see another specialist, make sure he goes. I want him to be around for your golden wedding anniversary,"

Josiah said with an effort at humor. "Now let me talk to Bernie for a minute."

Dad and Mother were so shaken, Fran thought tenderly. They cared for Bernie. But when would her mother come up to New York with Daddy? They hadn't seen each other for four years!

Fran knew Bernie was upset that her father would have to help them survive until he was out of law school and in a job.

"I'll take the first job that comes along," he vowed. "None of that old nonsense about trying to set myself up on my own. That'll come later," he said with a show of bravado. "Tell your father we'll start paying him back as soon as I'm drawing a paycheck again."

Fran's father arrived in New York on his usual buying trip. As usual he came laden with gifts. As usual her mother hadn't accompanied him.

"She's all involved in some charity drive," her father alibied her absence. "She couldn't get away."

Fran was touched by her father's obvious concern for Bernie's health. He waited until Bernie retired to their bedroom to study to discuss this with her.

"Frannie, we're your parents," he scolded. "When you have problems, we want to share them with you. Don't you know our lives revolve around you and Bernie and the children?" But her mother still kept that wall between them, Fran thought in silent despair.

On his second day in New York Josiah Goldman insisted on taking Fran with him to a favorite buying office.

"I need your advice," he improvised. "This 'New Look' craziness is sending me up the wall. This man Dior is giving buyers for women's specialty shops nervous breakdowns. Of course," he said expansively, "in England they don't have this problem. There they're still rationing materials. Skirts are short and narrow—with not an inch of unnecessary material. The women are stuck with low heels—nothing higher than two inches." All at once he was self-conscious. Fran, too, must wear low heels.

"In England I'd be right in style," she said effervescently. "But, Daddy, you know what to buy. You don't need me."

"I need you," he insisted. "I'm buying expensive dresses—they have to please my fancy customers. Tell me what you like—and I'll have an idea. And while we're there, we'll pick up a few dresses for you."

Fran was enthralled by the Dior-inspired dresses she and her father saw in the showroom. After the years of austerity—no ruffles, short and narrow skirts, stripped-down suits, no belts wider than two inches—

most American women greeted the new fashions with delight. Seeing her pleasure in the new designs Fran's father insisted on buying extravagantly for her.

"Remember, I buy at wholesale prices," he said in high spirits. Though he loved Mother, Fran thought, he enjoyed these brief trips on his own.

Back in the apartment Fran tried on the new dresses for her father. The long full skirts, the narrow waists were flattering to her slender figure—and the long skirts hid much of her unattractive leg brace, she noted happily. But she knew that Bernie would feel yet another twinge of guilt that her father was buying her clothes.

Today, she vowed, she'd allow nothing to dampen her spirits. Bernie was all right. The children were fine. And tonight Daddy was taking the four of them out to dinner at Lindy's—his favorite New York restaurant. Lynne and Debbie were so excited at being taken to a restaurant for dinner, she thought tenderly. They felt incredibly grown-up. She loved their zest for living. Their exuberant warmth.

In deference to the children they made a point of being very early diners. Later the popular restaurant—its bright red, yellow, and black decor awesomely dramatic to Lynne and Debbie—would be crowded and noisy. Both little girls were blissfully conscious of their beautiful new dresses, sent up by their grandmother.

"Mommie, can we have the cheesecake?" Lynne whispered while they focused on their main course. "Grandpa says it's terrific."

"We'll have the cheesecake," she promised.

Bernie and his father-in-law were in avid conversation about the rash of new household innovations flooding the stores. Electric clothes dryers, automatic dishwashers, garbage disposal units, frozen orange juice.

"It's a real revolution," her father was saying with infinite respect. "You should have heard Lily when we put in the dishwasher last month." He chuckled reminiscently.

"Mom must have been so glad Lily stayed during the war years." Fran remembered how domestic help—so prevalent in southern households—had all but disappeared as the war plants offered high wages.

"We're good to Lily, and she appreciates that," her father said. "She's like family."

Privately Bernie had pointed out to Fran that there would be no return to the old routine of houseworkers who came in for long hours at three dollars a week. Now, she recalled, there were rumors coming out of Washington that Truman meant to integrate the armed forces.

Before her father left for home, he presented Fran and Bernie with a batch of theater tickets. Startled and touched, she pulled the tickets from one of the half-dozen envelopes he'd handed her. Not the cheap second balcony seats they occasionally allowed themselves—choice orchestra seats.

"Hire a baby-sitter and go to the theater once a month," he ordered. "I don't know what the going rate is up in New York, but it can't be that much higher than in Bellevue. Your mother tells me teenagers sit for twenty-five cents an hour."

Fran exchanged a glance with Bernie. "We've never left the kids with a sitter." Both she and Bernie loved the theater. "Just with Midore."

"Then it's time," her father said calmly, but his eyes were somber. "Life shouldn't be all work and struggle. Enjoy yourselves a little."

He knew they'd had more than the normal share of heartache in the years of their marriage. But the bad was all behind them, Fran told herself. Good years lay ahead.

In September Bernie took on a backbreaking schedule, despite Fran's objections. In the months ahead she worried. Bernie was always so tired. He was losing weight. He was plagued by colds that developed into coughs. His course load was insanely heavy, she thought in frustration. But he was reaching out with painful intensity for his law degree, already cramming for the New York bar exams.

Even before completing requirements for graduation, Bernie talked himself into a job in a prestigious law firm. He and Fran were jubilant— no doubts in their minds about his passing the bar exams. At long last his dream was about to become a reality.

The Saturday before his final classes Bernie was scheduled for another checkup. When he casually suggested rescheduling the appointment for a later date, Fran was adamant.

"You were two weeks late for your last checkup," she stormed. "You'll keep this one." Always she was a nervous wreck for at least ten days before he saw the doctor. It was routine—yet she was always so anxious. It was uncanny, she thought, how Debbie always knew when she was upset—no matter how hard she tried to conceal it. She was much better at hiding this from Lynne.

When Bernie left for his doctor's appointment, Fran saw him off with a confident smile. He was doing fine, she tried to convince herself. Masking her anxiety she took Lynne and Debbie with her to the bakery on Broadway. They'd buy cookies to celebrate Bernie's passing another hurdle. It was normal for her to feel this way, she told herself. It happened each time Bernie went to his doctor.

In the bakery Fran managed a convivial air as she debated with the girls about which cookies to choose. Then—all three exhilarated by this small accomplishment—they headed home.

"No cookies before lunch," she warned. "And since it's so cold you can have hot chocolate, too." She rarely doled out sweets to Lynne and Debbie, so this was a special treat. "*After* you've eaten."

She was grateful that Lynne and Debbie immediately settled down to listen to their favorite Saturday morning radio show. She hadn't told them yet, but Dad insisted he was buying the family a television set on his next trip to New York. "*Frannie, the kids will love it. People are lining up to buy TV sets these days.*"

Much of the time at home she removed the cumbersome leg brace and utilized either wheelchair or a pair of canes to navigate about the apartment. Today she wore the leg brace and used the single cane. She'd put up hamburgers the minute Bernie arrived. Potatoes were already baking in the oven. The tiny green peas Bernie liked so much could be heated up in minutes. Now she set the table and put up a percolator of coffee. The first thing Bernie would want would be a cup of hot coffee. She returned to the living room, where Lynne and Debbie were enraptured by their radio show.

She tried to read the *Times* she'd picked up on the way home, but discarded it in moments. She was too anxious to focus on the newspaper. The aroma of perking coffee filled the apartment—oddly reassuring.

Her pulse began to race when she heard a key in the door. Contriving a confident smile she hurried to greet Bernie.

"Coffee's ready," she said, her eyes searching his.

"Daddy!" Lynne deserted the radio to run to him. "We're having cookies and hot chocolate with lunch!"

"Hey, that's great!"

For a few moments he concentrated on his small daughters while Fran churned with frustration. Couldn't he just give her a signal that all went well? Didn't he understand how worried she'd been?

"Coffee?" She interrupted the girls' exuberant report about their radio program to ask Bernie.

"You bet." He smiled warmly. "I walked all the way home."

"Let's go out to the kitchen. Bernie?" Her voice was an anxious whisper. "What did the doctor say?"

Bernie cleared his throat in a way that forewarned her. It was a nervous, uneasy sound.

"We have a problem," he admitted. "I have to go in for tests again."

"What exactly did he say?" Her voice was unintentionally sharp.

"Something bothered him about the other lung," Bernie said after a minute. "He says it's important to catch it early."

"Surgery?" She was cold with fear.

"He's not sure," Bernie soothed. "But he wants me to go in for tests. It'll just be for a couple of days." His air of apology was painful to her.

"Maybe you ought to see another specialist," she began and he cut her off.

"Doctor Roberts is considered tops in his field," Bernie rejected. "Let's go along with him. He knows I have to be out of the hospital in time to start on the new job." He paused. "I suppose I can ask to start a couple of weeks later if it's necessary."

Again they were living a nightmare, Fran thought—knowing every hour of every day until the test results came through would seem endless. She fought to keep up an optimistic front and tried to prepare the girls for their father's absence from the apartment for the two or three days he must be in the hospital for tests. *Dear God, let the tests show nothing was wrong.*

The children were not allowed to see their father in the hospital, of course. Fran arranged for a teenager in the building to stay with them when she went to visit on his first evening there. She was grateful that his roommate was well enough to entertain his visitors in the reception area. She and Bernie had the room to themselves.

"It's not good," he said quietly. "I'm scheduled for surgery day after tomorrow."

"So soon?"

"It's always best to act fast," he reminded her. "I don't dare think about the bills." He closed his eyes for a moment, as though to brush away a fearful image. "My poor baby—I've ruined your life."

"Don't you dare say such a thing!" she blazed. "You're the most wonderful thing that ever happened to me. You'll come out of this fine. Like Doctor Roberts said, your age is on your side." Later they'd worry about the bills.

On the night before Bernie's surgery she sat alone in the living room and tried to deal with what lay ahead. He shouldn't have taken on such a heavy schedule after the last surgery, she berated herself. He needed rest—and he didn't have it. But this time would be different, she vowed. If he lost that job with the law firm, so be it.

Now she reached for the phone to call her parents. They'd always stood by her. They would do it again. She didn't want them to come up, she reasoned—she just wanted to talk with them, to hear their reassurances that Bernie would be all right. And again, she thought with pain, they'd need financial help.

What kind of a world did they live in, she railed, when they had to be terrified of being sick—to worry as much about the cost as the physical traumas? Recurrently she thought about the effort in England to provide their population with help in medical emergencies. Would that ever happen here? Here only the very rich could feel truly safe.

She could hear the alarm in her father's voice when she told him that Bernie was to undergo surgery again. Her mother was shrill with fear when they talked.

"What hospital will he be in?" her mother asked. "We'll call there—you'll be with him, not at home."

Fran told her, explained that he was scheduled for surgery in mid-morning.

"Don't call before noon," she told her mother. "He'll be in surgery until then." She remembered the agony of waiting during his earlier surgery. Why were their lives so involved with hospitals? she asked herself in sudden rebellion. Why did these things happen to *them?*

In the morning—after a sleepless night—Fran took the children to school as usual, then found a cab to take her to the hospital. She managed to see Bernie for a few moments before he was wheeled into surgery.

"I love you," he whispered. He seemed to be fighting off sleep. He'd probably been given a sedative, she thought. "You and the kids—my precious jewels."

"I love you—" She managed a bright smile before she was told to return to the reception area.

She knew the wait would be long. As though acting under their own power, her eyes swung with relentless frequency to the wall clock. Each minute seemed endless.

She sat at the edge of a chair, rose to pace, sat again. Why must it take so long? There was a problem now with the lung they'd thought was *all right.* God gave us two arms, two legs, two lungs, she thought—fighting against hysteria. We could live without two arms or two legs—not without a lung.

She was relieved that she was alone in the reception area except for the two middle-aged daughters whose mother was also in surgery. They were Catholic, clinging to their rosary beads as they huddled on the sofa—seemingly oblivious to her presence. She tensed at every small sound that punctured the silence.

She started as the elevator stopped with a raucous sound. The door slid open, noiselessly, and her father and mother hurried toward her. She struggled to her feet, clutching the cane—realizing her mother had never seen her with brace and cane. Had not seen her since that day in the New Jersey hospital. She was conscious of a torrent of relief as they embraced. Always, she thought—her throat tight—Daddy and Mother were here for her. As though she was still a little girl.

"Where are Lynne and Debbie?" her mother asked.

"In school." Fran's voice was unsteady. "I don't have to pick them up until three o'clock."

"We took the first flight out of Atlanta this morning," her mother said, her eyes searching Fran's face. "Bernie's going to be fine. He may have to take it easy for a little while, but he's going to be all right."

Bernie always teased her about being the eternal optimist, she thought while tears flooded her eyes. She was like Mother in that. The realization was simultaneously startling and comforting. Sometimes she'd been sure she was entirely her father's child, inheriting nothing from her mother. She needed to feel a tie.

"It's so good to see you, Mother," she whispered and saw tears well in her mother's eyes. "I should have known you'd come."

"Did you have breakfast?" Ida demanded and without waiting for a reply turned to her husband. "Jo, find out where the cafeteria is and bring us all coffee and Danish." She turned again to Fran. "I know you never eat when you're upset. And in a way that's good," she rattled on, as though expecting to provide comfort with conversation. "Some people just gorge like pigs when they're nervous. But you don't have to be nervous," she added quickly. "Bernie is going to be fine."

Fran allowed her mother to draw her down to one of the chintz-covered sofas while her father headed for the elevator to seek out the cafeteria.

"You must have been up with the sunrise," Fran said with a wry smile, "to be here at this hour."

"We couldn't wait to be with you," her mother said, her effort at effervescence evaporating. "Neither of us could sleep all night."

"Bernie's just passed his thirty-third birthday . . . How could this be happening?" She voiced the rebellious question that never seemed to leave her mind. What had she and Bernie done in their lifetimes to bring such chaos upon themselves? She searched her mind for some reason for their devastating punishment. In silence she railed at God for forsaking them—destroying them.

"We can't ask questions, Frannie." Her mother's voice was troubled. She wasn't a religious woman, yet Fran knew her mother was neither atheist nor agnostic—she believed with the faith of those who might attend church or synagogue or mosque only occasionally but carried their house of worship within them. "I'm not smart enough to have the answers. I don't think anybody on this earth can answer that. But we accept and move on," she said resolutely.

Most of the time her mother lived on the surface, Fran thought— these were rare moments. Did her mother have secret dreams that were never realized? She knew, of course, how her mother and father had waited agonizingly long years before she was conceived. But what ambitions had her parents laid to rest in the passing years? All at once she wished with painful intensity that she could read into their minds.

Her father returned from the cafeteria with paper containers of coffee and a selection of Danish. To please him and her mother she forced herself to eat. Why was the surgery taking so long? she agonized. When would Dr. Roberts come out and tell them Bernie was going to be all right?

Trying to distract Fran from unspoken fears, Ida Goldman talked with atypical swiftness—her words tumbling over one another—about the newly opened air terminal in Atlanta.

"During the war years the army expanded their airport facilities, of course. But once the war was over, the original acres were deeded back to the city and the air force facilities moved to Marietta. Now everybody's bragging that it's one of the most modern passenger terminals in the country." She hesitated. "Now that it's so easy to travel between New York and Atlanta, you and Bernie and the children must come down to visit for a couple of weeks. I know Lynne and Debbie would be so excited at flying."

Fran managed to make the necessary comments as her mother continued what was basically a monologue. Her father smiled at regular intervals, but his eyes were somber. The three of them were ever conscious that Bernie was in surgery just beyond the pair of doors they faced.

Fran's heart began to pound when at last the doors opened. Dr. Roberts stood there in deep discussion with another doctor. Fran reached for her cane and pulled herself to her feet. *Why didn't he stop talking and come to them?*

Fran stood motionless, conscious of her father's arm closing in about her shoulders as Dr. Roberts approached them. She tried to read his face—a futile task. Except for rare moments of compassion his face was always inscrutable.

"I'm sorry to have kept you waiting so long," he apologized to Fran. His eyes rested on her parents now. "Your family?"

"My parents." She stammered introductions.

"I'm sorry, Fran," Dr. Roberts said gently. "Bernie survived the surgery, but he suffered a massive heart attack immediately afterward. We couldn't save him."

Fran stared at him in disbelief, vaguely conscious of her mother's strident *"Oh, my God!"*

"But how?" she demanded, her voice a high thin outcry. "There was nothing wrong with his heart! You said that," she pinpointed in a burst of rage. "How could he have had a heart attack?" *Bernie gone?* She'd known almost from the minute she saw Bernie that she must spend the rest of her days with him or her life would be empty. How could he be *gone?*

"I'm so sorry, Fran," Dr. Roberts said gravely. "A heart can appear normal at an examination, and ten minutes later the patient suffers an attack. There was nothing we could do."

In a daze Fran allowed her parents to lead her to the sofa. She was conscious of Dr. Roberts hovering above her. How could Bernie be gone? She needed him. Bernie was always there for her. He'd made her feel whole again after the shooting. *What was she to do with the rest of her life?*

She was conscious of a needle pricking her arm, of her parents leading her—as though she was a small child—from the hospital floor to the elevator. Not entirely understanding she listened to her father's voice.

"I'll take care of everything, Frannie. You're going to be all right."

Back in the apartment she experienced a few lucid moments of agony until her mother pushed a glass of water in one hand and a pill in another.

"Doctor Roberts said you must take this," Ida ordered and Fran obeyed.

She was faintly conscious of the small, worried faces of her daughters. How could she tell them their father—whom they adored—

wouldn't be coming home again? But drowsiness overcame her, and she succumbed to sleep.

She went through the next days in a haze, aware that her parents were moving about the apartment, caring for Lynne and Debbie. Obediently she did as her parents instructed, going with them to the services at the funeral home, riding with them in the limousine to the cemetery. She knew that Gabrielle and her parents were with them. A pair of neighbors from the apartment house, several students from the law school. Gabrielle held her close—fighting tears, murmuring words of comfort. Feeling herself removed from her surroundings, she heard the rabbi's voice as they gathered about the graveside. Lynne and Debbie looked so scared. Little girls like that shouldn't be so frightened.

At last alone in the apartment with her parents and the girls, Fran struggled for a grasp on reality.

"Bernie wouldn't expect you to sit *shivah*," her father said gently. She would sit *shivah* for the rest of her life, she thought in a corner of her mind. "We'll all leave for Bellevue tomorrow. I'll make arrangements about the apartment and the furniture. Mother will help you pack what you want to take with you."

All she wanted to take with her was Bernie, she thought, on the edge of hysteria. And then her gaze settled on the faces of Lynne and Debbie, who clung anxiously to her now. She couldn't let go of her sanity, she admonished herself in a sudden burst of clarity. She must take care of Lynne and Debbie—that was what Bernie would want of her. Now she must be mother and father to them. She couldn't allow herself to fall apart.

Their daughters were her inheritance from Bernie. For them she must be strong. Yet fear invaded her and turned her cold. How would she manage? How would she make them understand their father would *never* come home again?

Fifteen

In the weeks ahead Fran watched the children anxiously, gearing herself for problems. Not only had they lost their father, they had to adjust to a strange environment, a new school—to make new friends. They had been awed by the prospect of flying to Atlanta. Aboard the flight they badgered their grandfather with questions. He, of course, flew regularly now. They had never been aboard a plane before. But then the flight was over, and reality had set in.

Lynne seemed to adjust more easily. It wasn't just that she was two years older than Debbie, Fran reasoned. Lynne was like Bernie had been in accepting changed situations. Debbie had a soaring imagination, which was both a gift and a curse. Each new encounter was suspect. Lynne was more outgoing—Debbie clung to her, yet Fran sensed she was eager to move out into this strange new world. But she mustn't push Debbie, Fran cautioned herself. Let her move at her own speed.

Fran struggled to fit into this new lifestyle decreed by her mother, though she chafed at such idleness. Couldn't Mother understand that she'd managed a household, cared for two children on her own? She wasn't accustomed anymore to having domestic help. She loved Lily, of course—but the constant solicitude of Lily and her mother was, somehow, an affront. She wasn't *helpless*. And she was frustrated by her mother's inability to understand the importance of her daily exercise schedule. *"Frannie, why do you wear yourself out with all this exercising?"*

Since stairs were difficult for her, what was once the family's formal dining room had been transformed with amazing speed into a beautiful first-floor bedroom. The smaller, casual dining room off the kitchen was refurnished with the elegant furniture from the formal dining room. Lily now served breakfast in a designated corner of the large, sprawling kitchen.

Lynne and Debbie were enthralled at having individual bedrooms. Fran acknowledged that her mother was wonderful in diverting them from somber contemplation. She involved them in the selection of new drapes and comforters for what had once been her bedroom and the guest bedroom. She fussed along with them over new color schemes, the choosing of wallpaper and paint.

At wayward moments Fran felt herself drowning in grief. Relentlessly her mind taunted her—how was she to survive without Bernie? For almost eleven years Bernie had been there for her. He'd made her feel whole again after the shooting. But now he was gone. What was she to do with the rest of her life?

Each morning she dragged herself out of bed to begin a new tortuous day without Bernie. She fretted that the stairs to the girls' bedroom were too difficult to manipulate. Once school opened, it was Lily who cheerfully went up to their rooms each morning to make sure they were awake.

"They's awake," Lily would call to her and remained until she was sure Lynne and Debbie were out of bed.

For the first few days Fran stood at the foot of the stairs and conferred with them about what they should wear to school—a small chore they all relished. Then Fran's mother intervened.

"Sugar, you'll wear yourself out with all that yelling," she admonished. "I'll go in and see that they're properly dressed. I did it for you. I can do it for my granddaughters."

Fran sat down to breakfast with the girls and her father. After seeing that Lynne and Debbie were dressed, their grandmother retired to her own bedroom. Lily would take her coffee, and she'd appear downstairs a couple of hours later. Her mother probably thought that she, too, went back to bed, Fran surmised. This was an unfamiliar world to her now.

She tried to pass the morning away with reading. Newspapers, magazines, the endless inane novels her mother brought home from the library. When her mother came downstairs—before her round of phone calls about her club activities, the two of them sat down for coffee. Why did Mother keep fussing over her this way? Fran asked herself restlessly. She wasn't sick—she was widowed.

She was grateful that her mother didn't try to involve her in her own socializing—but then her mother conceded she needed time to become accustomed to her widowhood. Remembering lively debates with Bernie and Fran about politics, her father struggled to involve her in current happenings around the world. Each evening after dinner—while his wife and granddaughters listened to their favorite radio programs—Josiah Goldman talked to Fran about the subjects commanding national and world attention. He was deeply concerned that Stalin had seized Czechoslovakia, equally anxious about the way the Soviet Union was now blockading West Berlin from the outside world.

"If we let the Soviets get away with it, we're giving them the idea that they can get whatever they want through a show of force. But if we try to stop the blockade with military force, we might find ourselves in World War Three," he worried. "There's a lot of sharp heads up in Washington, D.C., and by God we're going to need them."

Each night—with initial reluctance—Fran let herself be drawn into discussion with her father. He was proud of the way the United States had replaced Great Britain as the world leader, yet was conscious, too, of the responsibilities this leadership mandated. He was recurrently furious that the Republican party—in the '46 election—had carried both houses of Congress for the first time since '28. It was a slap at the man he deeply admired.

"Damn it, Fran, how can some people say Truman ought to resign? Even Senator Fullbright—a Democrat!"

"Must you talk so loud, Jo?" Ida scolded from across the room. "We can't hear our program."

"Have you done your homework?" Fran asked her daughters.

"You know I wouldn't let them listen to the radio if they hadn't," her mother said good-humoredly and turned to the little girls, their faces only inches away from the radio. "When this is over, let's go out in the kitchen for milk and cookies."

"Mother, they're only to have cookies on Sunday evenings," Fran said, all at once tense.

"Frannie, you always had cookies and milk before you went to sleep." Her mother was reproachful.

"Sugar is bad for their teeth." Why did Mother put her in this position? Fran asked herself tiredly. *She* was Lynne and Debbie's mother—they must realize she made the decisions. "They've never had a cavity."

"All right," Ida said, her smile cajolingly. "We'll just do it this night and not again until Sunday."

Fran churned with impatience. When would her mother stop treating her like an invalid? And Lynne and Debbie mustn't be allowed to manipulate their grandmother. Mother adored them, of course—and they loved her. But she mustn't spoil them. Fran brushed aside a surge of guilt. She wasn't trying to hurt her mother. She just didn't want the kids to be spoiled rotten.

With the Democratic convention only two months away Fran sympathized with her father's anxiety about the "dump Truman" movement.

"I like that Harry Truman," he said with relish on a hot May evening, fragrant with the first blossoms on their towering magnolia. "The man comes out and says what he thinks." He chuckled reminiscently. "Like calling this Congress the worst in history. And lambasting all this craziness about finding a communist in every closet."

"Do you think he'll be reelected?" Fran asked.

"He damn well better be," Josiah said. "This country needs him. We're in for a lot of changes, and he's got the gumption to see them through. I don't have to tell you about the galloping inflation. You wouldn't believe what I was offered for this house just last month. Of course, I never intend to sell it," he added quietly. "One day it'll be yours, Frannie." He smiled with satisfaction. "You'll always own your own home."

His words evoked a startled realization in her. To Dad, her life was over. She would sit out the rest of her days. No, she told herself in unexpected rebellion. She was thirty-two years old. She wouldn't vegetate for the rest of her life. The young dreams must be relinquished—she would never be a crusading journalist. But there had to be more than this.

Now—knowing Bernie would want it—she focused again on the exercises devised for her by her New York doctor. She contacted him, asked him to refer her to an Atlanta doctor who would guide her along the same path as he. She fretted that it would be necessary for her father to drive her to Atlanta for her appointments with the new doctor. She longed to be independent, to be able to fend for herself.

She could hear Bernie's voice—*"Fran, you can do anything you want to do."* He'd want her to be a whole person—not just for herself but for Lynne and Debbie. Fighting to pull herself out of her grief, she felt a poignant closeness to Bernie.

Her father was delighted when she told her parents of her determination to continue treatment in Atlanta. Her mother was ambivalent.

"Frannie, do you think you should put yourself through this?" Ida asked uneasily.

"I have to do it." It was time to take charge of her life. "I need to build more strength in my left arm. I—"

"But you use it now," her mother pointed out. "The doctor said it was a small miracle that you could."

"I want to regain full strength in it," Fran told her. "I want to develop strength in my left thigh. That's important!"

"I don't want to see you disappointed," her mother whispered. Meaning, Fran thought defiantly, that she should accept the fact that her left leg was partially paralyzed.

"You'll work with the doctor," her father said firmly. Fran intercepted the warning glance he shot at her mother. Her mother was not to reject her efforts. "Work out the schedule. I'll drive you to your therapy sessions."

At first meeting Fran liked the new doctor. He was young, brusque sometimes, frank in cautioning her that what they were trying was experimental. But she welcomed Dr. Bennett's keen interest, his encouragement at any minute progress. Still, she felt a growing restlessness at the idle hours of each day.

She was startled when her father suggested that she go with him on his July buying trip to New York.

"You've got a sharp eye for fashion," he said. "Come along and advise me."

"But the girls," she hedged, though the prospect of flying to New York for three days was unexpectedly appealing. All her married life had been spent there. The happiest years of her life.

"Lynne and Debbie will stay with their grandmother. And Lily'll love the opportunity to spoil them to death while you're away. They're not little kids anymore. They can handle it."

"If Mother agrees, all right," she told him. She'd pick up some fashion magazines, look for trends, she told herself. Dad was serious about her helping out with his buying. She felt less of a parasite.

There were traumatic moments when she and her father left the airport for the long drive into Manhattan. Memories of Bernie caught at her unawares. Her loss all at once fresh and painful. Fascinated by flying, Bernie had never been in a plane. He'd had so much to give, she thought in anguish—and so little time on this earth. It had been a mistake to come to New York, she admonished herself.

The three days in Manhattan rushed past. As though to protect her from familiar sights, her father chose another hotel on this trip. There was no visit to Lindy's for dinner. They spent one evening at a Broadway movie—no theater performances.

Fran found time to have lunch with Gabrielle, who was remarrying in

the fall—but most of her hours were spent with her father in buying offices. She vacillated between suspicion that her father had brought her
along to provide her with diversion and a sense that she was, truly, being
helpful.

On their first night back in Bellevue, her father came home from the
shop with news that Laura—his favorite saleswoman who had been with
him for a dozen years—was leaving.

"I couldn't believe it when she told me she was pregnant. Her husband insists she stop working as soon as I can replace her."

"Laura must be thirty-five if she's a day." Ida was startled. "She's
been married thirteen years!" Her mother forgot that *she* had been married thirteen years before giving birth, Fran thought.

"Is she excited about the baby?" Fran asked her father.

"Out of her mind," Josiah said. "She was sure it was never going to
happen. It's going to be hard to replace her. So many women are back
into the home these days."

"Dad, what about focusing on a cashier instead of a saleswoman?"
Fran's mind rushed into high gear. Her heart began to pound. "That
would free your sales staff to concentrate on selling. And it'll be easier to
find a cashier," she said with bravado. "Me."

"Frannie!" Her mother was startled.

"Why not?" Her face grew flushed as she contemplated this. "All I'd
have to do would be to sit there behind the counter at the cash register—
and wrap, of course," she added. "I'm tired of just sitting around doing
nothing. Dad, let me come into the shop."

"But how would that look to people?" her mother sputtered. "They'd
think—"

"Mother, women go out to business now," Fran interrupted. "It
doesn't mean I'm destitute. This is 1948!"

"Maybe part-time?" her father said seriously. "If you're sure you
want to do it."

"Full-time." She hesitated. "Except for my appointments with Doctor Bennett."

"We can handle that." Now her father smiled reassuringly. "Ida, stop
looking so disturbed. It'll be good for Frannie to get out of the house.
You'll start the first of the week," he told her. "And no quibbling about
salary," he teased. "Prove you're good, and you'll get a raise."

Fran was relieved to be away from the house much of the day. She had too much time to remember what she had lost—what she would never have again. She needed to fill every waking hour, she told herself. The way she tried to make sure Lynne and Debbie's waking hours were filled—because she knew how their father's death had hurt them.

She plotted to become an active parent at the girls' school. But this highlighted another problem: she needed to drive again. She mustn't depend on her father to chauffeur her everywhere. It was important to be independent if she was to be a whole person.

"I haven't driven in years, of course," she confided to Dr. Bennett— striving to sound casual—"but do you think I could apply for a driver's license?"

"Why not?" he asked calmly, yet she sensed heart was battling head in him. His mind rationalized—his heart feared for her. "You control accelerator and brakes with your right foot. You have fairly normal control in your left hand. Why shouldn't you drive? If there're any questions, I'll handle them."

Her mother was close to hysteria when she suggested driving again.

"It's too dangerous," she wailed. "You could kill yourself. Lynne and Debbie need you! I won't be around forever!"

"Doctor Bennett says there's no reason I shouldn't drive," Fran said, conscious that, despite his show of approval, her father, too, was uneasy. Couldn't they understand how important it was for her to drive? "It's just a matter of whether I can get a license." It was only eleven years ago that it became necessary in Bellevue to have a driver's license, she remembered with a touch of humor. "Doctor Bennett will give me a letter if it's necessary." Her eyes moved anxiously from her mother to her father.

"We'll buy a second car," her father said after a moment of hesitation and turned to Ida with a teasing smile. "Maybe you'll decide to learn to drive, too." Knowing, Fran thought, that this would never happen.

She'd suspected it wouldn't be easy to settle down in Bellevue. She remembered a sympathetic high school teacher who had told her that she "marched to a different drummer." An old cliché—but so true. Now she felt herself an alien in the town where she was born. She told herself she didn't have time to pick up old social contacts. In truth, she knew she'd moved worlds away from everyone she'd known in Bellevue. Now that she was working in the shop, her mother abandoned trying to bring her into her own round of volunteer and synagogue groups—for which she was grateful.

The town had changed amazingly in the years she'd been in New York. People were moving away from downtown into a pretty new suburban area. The places where they'd gathered on hot nights for a "dope"—the Georgian title for a Coke—or an ice-cream soda had disappeared. These days everyone seemed to drive away from downtown for a soda fountain or a restaurant. Television sets were popping up in houses all over Bellevue.

She knew her parents were disturbed—like many of the old families in Bellevue—over the feeling of change that permeated the town in this election year. It was more than just that people were moving away from downtown to live in their new suburbia, she analyzed. It was a fearful sense that change in their whole society was about to descend on them.

Dad said, she remembered, that if Truman won the election—and he wasn't sure this would happen—the South would see a civil rights plank that would cause much controversy.

"I've never been one to vote Republican," he said candidly a few nights after the Democratic convention—while Ida gestured for silence because Lily was coming in from the kitchen with dessert, "but you'll be seeing some switch-overs in the South this election. You won't see any civil rights plank in the Republican platform."

"I'm reading *Intruder in the Dusk*—that new novel by William Faulkner," Fran told him. Still a victim of insomnia she read late into each night. "Faulkner claims Southerners need more time to adjust to changes like throwing out the poll tax—" She was somber. There was a lot more than that to consider in this postwar year. Negro soldiers had seen a whole different world outside their country—and they liked what they saw.

"We're seeing a split in the Democratic party," Josiah reminded. "Those damn Dixiecrats are going to cause trouble for Truman."

"I like how that mayor from Minneapolis—what's his name?" Fran frowned in thought. "Hubert Humphrey—he's running for the Senate now. I like the way he's campaigning for civil rights, along with Paul Douglas and Adlai Stevenson. It was after his convention speech that a bunch of Southern delegates stomped out and formed the Dixiecrat Party."

"I liked that speech, too," her father said.

"You won't like it so much," Ida whispered, her face grim, "when the coloreds get so uppity they don't want to take in washing or be domestics. And all this talk is not good for the children," she scolded.

Lynne and Debbie were avidly drinking in everything that was being said, Fran realized. But then, why wouldn't they? Since they were old enough to understand, they'd listened to Bernie and her discuss what was happening in the world. Young as they were, let them know what was right and what was wrong in government.

Bernie had been within a fingertip of winning his dream, she thought with recurrent anguish. His law degree—framed now—hung in her bedroom. And her own dream was just that—never to be a reality. But Lynne and Debbie would make a difference in this world, she vowed. Always the realist—and so bright, Lynne would be a lawyer. Never mind that it was so hard for a girl to get into law school. Lynne would make it. And imaginative, romantic Debbie would be a journalist. Her dream and Bernie's would come alive in their children.

Fran acquired some satisfaction in the knowledge that she was helpful in running the shop. Approaching sixty-eight, her father admitted he felt a need to slow down. When he prepared to go on his January buying trip, he took it for granted that Fran would go with him. And he left most of the buying to her.

"Hell, you read all those fancy fashion magazines like *Vogue* and *Harper's Bazaar*. You know what women like these days. I'm tired of trying to read their minds."

Fran settled in a pattern now. Six days a week she was in the shop. The evenings and Sundays were devoted to Lynne and Debbie. She wasn't depriving them of anything by working, she reassured herself at intervals. They were at school until three o'clock. Their grandmother took them to their dancing classes twice a week and to piano lessons once a week. If there was a birthday party to attend—and parties seemed endless—*she* left the shop to drive them. Recurrently she was grateful for driving again.

Involved now in the fashion world because it was important for the business to know what was chic and attractive, she spent more thought on her appearance than she had in years. Now she adopted what was to become a kind of uniform for her—expensive, exquisitely tailored slacks and beautiful blouses or sweaters. Never mind that most women adored full skirts, the ultra-feminine look. The slacks hid the brace, which she loathed.

"It's just not womanly to wear pants all the time," her mother fretted uneasily.

"It's practical." Fran refused to be ruffled. "And I like them," she admitted. She liked the concealment of her brace, she liked the comfort of wearing slacks—and she came to like the image she was building for herself. An independent woman, confident despite a physical handicap. On a buying trip to New York she sought out a shop that specialized in British walking sticks. She bought herself a cane that was a conversation piece. The image was now complete.

She was amazed at the way the months seemed to race past. She battled with her mother when both girls pleaded to go to summer camp the following year.

"Frannie, you never know what happens there," her mother railed. "I'll be worried every minute."

"I used to die every summer when my friends went off to camp and I didn't," she said gently. "It's only for four weeks. You and Dad and I will drive out every Sunday to see them." She knew her mother never felt comfortable with her at the wheel—as though her bad leg would cause her to have an accident—but Dad was glad now to be relieved of some of the driving. Or was it because she was a woman? Mother couldn't understand how women had moved ahead in these last few years.

After Margaret Mitchell was tragically killed by a speeding car in Atlanta in August 1949 Fran knew her mother worried every time she drove into Atlanta. Mother didn't worry about Dad driving, Fran fumed. Why about her? And yet—reluctantly—she was beginning to understand her mother's concern. When Lynne and Debbie went out in a car driven by a friend's mother, she, too, was anxious. They were so very precious. But why did she feel more anxious when there was a woman behind the wheel? That was nutty.

Early in 1950 her father announced he'd bought a summer house for the family on Pine Mountain—near Atlanta.

"Your mother and the girls will go out for the summer," he decreed. "You and I will go out Friday nights after we close the shop and drive back on Monday mornings. We'll appoint Alice as Saturday manager," he said with relish.

It was on those summer drives with her father—to and from the Pine Mountain cottage—that she truly came to know him. Always drawn into world happenings, he talked unhappily about the invasion of South Korea by the North Koreans, about the hate-mongering of Senator Joseph McCarthy. But also on those nights in the car he talked about his early years. She was astonished to learn that he'd run away from his home in Atlanta when he was sixteen—just short of high school graduation.

"It was a terrible thing to do to my parents," he acknowledged with a rueful smile. "I was the youngest—the one that would go to college, they planned. But I ran off to join this road company that had been appearing in Atlanta at the New Lyceum Theater. I loved theater with a passion. I still do," he admitted. She'd always thought it was her mother who was forever arranging for them to go to see the road companies that came to Atlanta regularly. "But it wasn't meant to be. I wrote home regularly from the road. Papa and my older brother tracked me down, came and brought me home."

"They took away your dream," she said softly, tears filling her eyes.

"We all start off with dreams," he told her, his smile whimsical. "But we learn that the big dreams come to reality for the very few. We learn that we have to compromise."

"You had a small dream for me," she remembered. "You wanted me to be a teacher." It was her mother who longed to have her become a concert pianist.

"By the time you came along I'd learned to be practical. Teaching seemed a nice, safe way of life. And all that vacation time," he joshed. "I thought you'd like that. Even when you were a little girl, I knew you'd never be satisfied with club meetings and playing bridge and going to parties."

Fran knew her father was concerned about the tensions developing in Atlanta between Negroes and whites—and which spilled over into Bellevue. There were strong protests in Atlanta when 376 new Negro housing units were scheduled to be built near a white residential area. On a smaller scale this was happening, also, in Bellevue.

President Truman's civil rights package ordered the elimination of segregated seating on interstate trains and buses. Governor Herman Talmadge—running for a second term in 1950—vowed to retain segregation on trains and buses, in schools, playgrounds, parks, restaurants, theaters. In fact, to retain it everywhere.

Fran tried endlessly to make her mother understand the need for integration. She talked about this yet again on the chilly election eve while they waited for radio reports of the gubernatorial election. Along with her father, Fran feared that Governor Talmadge would be reelected. Talmadge was exploiting the Federal Court ruling in New Orleans four years ago, declaring white primaries illegal. He ignited alarm in many white Georgians—who could know what would happen with the polls open to Negroes? He vowed to keep the FEPC—the Fair Employment Practices Commission—from operating in Georgia.

"We all know Talmadge is going to cause trouble. We know segregation is wrong," Fran said in frustration while her mother—from habit—gestured for silence. "Lily has gone home," she pointed out impatiently. "And do you think it's wrong for Lily to want to sit anywhere she likes on the bus or in a restaurant or movie theater?"

"You've lived too long in New York." Ida's voice was shrill. "You just don't understand the Southern way anymore. You've lost touch with your own people. I'm going up to my room and read. I don't see any point in sitting around all evening, just listening to election returns." Ida walked from the room with unfamiliar briskness. The embodiment, Fran thought involuntarily, of outraged Southern womanhood.

"Don't be too hard on your mother," Josiah said after a moment, his eyes pleading for compassion. "She was brought up with certain beliefs. She—"

"But it's wrong," Fran interrupted. She didn't want Lynne and Debbie to grow up believing segregation was right. "How can ordinary people not understand what President Truman is saying? That the South has to change."

"We know. Most of us nurture a guilty conscience, though we manage to keep it under wraps," he said wryly. "We all feel guilty. But we can't change over a 150 years of thinking in weeks or months—it's going to take a lot of years. They tell themselves they have a good world. Why change it?"

"It's good for whites!" Fran said passionately.

"Frannie, I'm first-generation Southern. Your grandparents on my side both came over from Germany as children. Right after the War Between the States. They settled in Atlanta, where I was born." Fran nodded. She'd heard this many times. "I feel Southern—this life is all I've ever known. Think of people like your mother, whose family has been in the South for five generations. They don't see the bad parts of our lifestyle."

"Because it's good for them," Fran pinpointed, impatient with her father's logic.

"You didn't worry about these things when you were growing up," he reminded. "You took them for granted."

"Bernie showed me the other side of the coin," she said softly. "He made me understand about how the South must change. Particularly after the war—"

"We've hidden behind awful guilt for generations." Her father seemed suddenly tired. "Every time I read about a lynching, I die a little."

She had hardly known her father through the years, she thought again with poignant regret. She'd lived in the same house with him so many years—but only now was she learning to know the real man.

He was fearful of the years ahead, she realized. Bernie had felt that way, too. When would she be able to think of Bernie without this awful sense of loss?

Sixteen

A t intervals Fran exchanged letters with Midore, Gabrielle, and Cliff. Midore had found a niche for herself in commercial art and was also teaching. Cliff had completed his residency and was in practice in a small town close enough to St. Louis to see his family frequently. Gabrielle was pregnant again, involved in suburban life.

Like most sisters, Lynne and Debbie seemed at times to be mortal enemies—yet Fran was pleased at the closeness she felt in them. Ever anxious to do whatever Lynne wanted, Debbie abandoned her beloved Dale Evans cowgirl outfit when Lynne—enthralled with the prospect of being a teenager within a few months—pleaded with her grandmother for one of the new felt skirts with poodle appliqués. She was euphoric at skipping a grade and thus being only one year behind Lynne.

Fran tried to convince herself she'd devised a full life for herself. She had Lynne and Debbie, her work at the shop—with her father handing increasing responsibility over to her. Yet at unwary moments she was restless. She remembered the twenty-one-year-old Fran, who had gone out to battle on behalf of the mill workers. That had been such a short period in her life, but she had felt so *alive*, she remembered.

The mill workers were doing far better these days—in most cases. The textile industry was booming. Wages rising steadily. But the undercurrents in small southern towns such as Bellevue—as well as in booming cities like Atlanta—were worrisome. She felt dark clouds gathering and longed to speak her mind.

Business would prevent this, she knew. She couldn't afford to antagonize their clientele. The ladies who came to shop at Goldman's—and spent much money—were charming, soft-spoken, devoted to good causes. They were also strong-willed and opinionated. Any individual who spoke unkindly of the world as they had always known it would be considered a mortal enemy. If she were to voice what her conscience directed her to say, Goldman's customers would desert en masse.

These were difficult years to be a white Southerner, Fran thought uneasily—and they would become worse.

On this eve of Lynne's fourteenth birthday, Debbie—at their grandmother's orders—invaded her sister's room just before dinner. She was to stall Lynne from going downstairs until the surprise birthday party guests had arrived and were seated at the dinner table.

"Who'll we watch tonight?" Debbie asked, settling herself at the foot of Lynne's bed while Lynne—whom she had labeled "Miss Neatness"—stacked schoolbooks in an orderly pile on her desk. "'I Love Lucy'?" Both girls had done their homework this afternoon so they could watch TV after dinner.

Lynne shrugged. "Grandma will choose. She always does."

"Did you do all your homework?" Debbie pursued.

"I did it," Lynne said impatiently. Debbie knew she was disappointed that the family seemed so casual about her birthday. "What kind of cake do you think Lily is making for my birthday? It had better be all chocolate."

"We'll find out at dinner," Debbie flipped, enjoying her role this evening. "Did you like the Eddie Fisher record I gave you?" she asked quickly because Lynne was sliding on her saddle shoes. *Lynne wasn't supposed to go downstairs for another five minutes.* "You said you just die every time you hear him sing 'Any Time.'"

"Sure, it's cool." They'd presented Lynne with her gifts at breakfast, pretending that she always complained about having to wait until after dinner. "Okay, let's go downstairs. I'm starving."

"Lynne—" Debbie searched her mind frantically for a stalling tactic. "Do you think I should cut my hair? Maybe have a poodle cut?"

"Are you nuts? You're too little," Lynne dismissed this.

"I'm tired of my page boy." Debbie inspected her lovely reflection in the mirror with an air of distaste. "Anita Collins has a poodle cut."

"Anita's sixteen. Besides, if you have a poodle cut, you have to have a Toni or put it up in a million pin curls every night. I could get away with a poodle cut—" Lynne joined Debbie at the mirror. "I look more than fourteen."

"Mom won't let you," Debbie guessed. "And Grandma would have a fit."

"Let's go down to dinner. Mom and Grandpa must be home by now."

"Are you going down to dinner in jeans?" Debbie clucked in disgust. "On your birthday?"

"We're not going out to dinner at a restaurant." Her tone was faintly reproachful. Lynne adored going to a restaurant for dinner on special occasions. "You look so silly in that long skirt—just to eat dinner and sit around on the floor to watch 'I Love Lucy.'" She giggled at Debbie's raised eyebrows. "It's my birthday," she said complacently. "Grandma will let me choose tonight."

Sauntering downstairs they argued good-humoredly about who was the cutest—Tony Curtis or Rock Hudson. Not a sound from the dining room, Debbie noted with pleasure. Then the two girls walked into the dining room—where a small table had been added to accommodate the guests—and suddenly giggling, girlish voices were screeching.

"Surprise! Surprise!"

The party had been a huge success, Fran thought with pleasure when the last guest had left and she and her mother were clearing away the table. Lily had prepared and served dinner, then gone home as usual. Since tomorrow was a school day, a curfew had been set. It was protested but respected.

"Thank God for dishwashers." Ida eyed the pile of china with distaste. "Smartest thing your father ever did was to buy one the minute they came on the market."

"We'll have two loads," Fran pointed out, stacking with one hand and supporting herself on her cane with the other. "You managed to save a piece of cake for Dad, didn't you?"

"She'd better!" Her father sauntered good-humoredly into the kitchen. "The birthday girl happy?" He'd been banished from the all-female party.

"Jo, she was truly surprised." Ida glowed. "Debbie was wonderful."

"I'll have a cup of coffee with my cake," Josiah told the two women. "Meanwhile, let me watch the news. I want to hear what craziness Joe McCarthy has come up with now."

Fran, too, was eager to be out of the kitchen and to listen to the news. Like her father she loathed Senator Joe McCarthy. He was a plague that threatened everything decent in the country, she thought. And it troubled her that once again the nation was at war. Yet few people reacted as they had in World War II—and that troubled her. It was a nonwar, she complained to her father—except that every day more American fighting men and women were dying.

Fran brought her father his coffee—her mother trailing her with a generous wedge of birthday cake. Now she joined him on the sofa that faced the 14-inch TV set of which he was so proud. Ida settled herself in her favorite club chair and began to skim the pages of the latest issue of the *Ladies' Home Journal*. The ceiling fan whirred softly in the night stillness. Indian summer brought a sultry heat even at this hour.

Instead of a report on McCarthy's latest activities or the fighting in Korea, the newscaster was discussing the coming presidential election.

"It'll be sad if we don't elect Adlai Stevenson," Josiah said, yet Fran understood the hint of defeat in his voice. Was it possible that anyone could defeat General Eisenhower?

"I have such respect for Stevenson," Josiah said. "He's brilliant, compassionate, and such a great speaker. It amazes me, Frannie," he mused, "that one man could win the backing of both the intellectuals and labor. But instinct tells me—and a lot of other people—that twenty years of Democratic control is about to come to an end."

"Would you like more coffee, Dad?" Fran asked, reaching for her cane. The commercial had interrupted the newscast—the signal for such activity.

"You sit, sugar," he said tenderly. "I'll bring it in for us." He turned to Ida. "More coffee for you?"

"Jo, you know I never drink coffee after five o'clock. I can't get to sleep if I do." She focused again on her magazine.

Josiah returned with two cups of coffee and settled himself at one end of the sofa again. He moved about restlessly until the end of the newscast. Usually he sat almost motionless, totally absorbed by what was being said.

"Dad, are you all right?" Fran asked.

"I don't think that roast beef I had at the restaurant agreed with me. Would you get me some bicarbonate of soda?"

"Sure." He never really enjoyed eating out in restaurants, she remembered guiltily. But her mother had pointed out that Lynne's birthday dinner was a "hen party."

Fran went out to the kitchen and brought down the bicarbonate of soda. While she poured water into a glass, she heard her mother talking again about Lynne's birthday party. Dad had turned off the TV, she noted. They'd all go to bed in a few minutes.

She returned to the living room. Her mother was still talking about the birthday party—all the while scanning pages of the magazine. But her father wasn't listening. He sat slumped in his chair. His eyes closed.

"Dad?" Suddenly galvanized in alarm, she stared at him, the glass of bicarbonate and water in a perilous grasp now. "Dad!"

"Frannie, what's the matter?" Conscious of the anxiety in Fran's voice, Ida dropped her magazine and jumped to her feet.

"I don't think Dad's feeling well," Fran said unsteadily, hurrying to her father's side.

"Oh, my God!" Ida's voice was a high, thin wail. "I'll call Doctor Bernstein."

"No," Fran ordered sharply. "Call for an ambulance. Do it!"

She reached for her father's wrist and tried to find a pulse. Unable to do this, she leaned over him. *Was he breathing?*

"Dad?" she tried again, but there was no response.

Her mother was at the phone.

"Please hurry!" Ida screamed into the phone. "He's unconscious."

"Mom?" Debbie's scared voice drifted from upstairs. "Is something wrong?"

"Go back to sleep, Debbie," Fran called up, knowing this was illogical.

"What's the matter?" Lynne had come out into the upstairs hall, too.

"Grandpa's awfully sick!" Ida was close to hysteria. "We called for an ambulance!"

"Mother, sit down," Fran ordered. She heard the sound of feet hurrying down the stairs. Lynne and Debbie must be terrified. "The ambulance will be here in a few minutes."

"Why doesn't he respond?" White and trembling, Ida hovered over her husband. "Jo! Jo, don't leave me. We need you! Jo!"

Why was the ambulance so slow in coming? Fran took refuge in rage. Then the night quiet was shattered by the frantic shriek of an ambulance siren. Fran rushed into the foyer and reached to open the door—subconsciously aware of the lights switched on next door. The neighbors had heard the siren—they were worried.

The ambulance crew rushed inside. The intern leaned over Josiah. It was all happening again, Fran thought. Fate turning their lives upside down in a matter of minutes. Knowing even before the intern—still obviously inexperienced in such situations—spoke to them. Hating what he had to tell them.

"I'm sorry." His eyes were compassionate as they swung guiltily from Ida to Fran. "He suffered a massive heart attack. He's dead."

Fran knew instantly that she must not give way to grief. It would be her task to handle all the painful details of laying her father to rest. Despite the hour, she phoned the shop's employees, explained that the store would be closed for the next three days. She forced herself to drive through the night-deserted streets to post a notice on the entrance to the shop.

For the next forty-eight hours friends and neighbors streamed in and out of the house. Dr. Bernstein saw to it that Ida was under constant sedation. Lily slept in, cooking endlessly—her eyes red and swollen from crying.

Lynne and Debbie clung to each other, never allowing their mother out of their sight except for her brief, necessary trips from the house. Only now did Fran fully understand the affection her father had earned in this town. But coming home from the cemetery she knew she must take charge of their lives—hers, the girls', and her mother's.

Ida was horrified when—on the fourth morning after her father's death—Fran prepared to go to the shop. Lynne and Debbie were back in school—but that was acceptable.

"How can you go to the shop?" Ida stared at her in disbelief. "We must sit *shivah.*" The traditional period of mourning in the Jewish faith, where the immediate family remained within the home for this period. "Eight days, Fran—not three! Have you no respect for your father?" Her mother only called her Fran when she was furious.

"Dad would want me to take care of the shop," Fran said gently. "He'd say 'life must go on.' Mother, we need the income—" But her mother continued to stare at her with no sign of comprehension.

"How can we run the shop without your father? I'll have to sell it." Ida's voice faltered. "I'll talk to Aaron about finding a buyer." Aaron was the family's longtime attorney.

"I'll run the shop," Fran told her—struggling for calm. "For the past year Dad let me handle almost everything."

"The buying! He let you handle the buying." Terror drained Ida's face of color. "But how much will I get from the sale? How long can we live on that?"

"You won't sell," Fran insisted. "Dad trained me well. I can run the shop!"

All at once Ida's eyes were loving, compassionate. "Frannie, how can you do that?" Her gaze settled—involuntarily, Fran thought in a corner of her mind—on her daughter's paralyzed leg.

"I don't run the shop with my legs," Fran shot back, stung by the inference. "Dad said it often enough, didn't he?" she challenged. " 'Frannie was born to run the business.' I don't run it with my legs—but with my mind and my heart."

"I didn't mean that," Ida stammered.

"Mother, listen to me!" Fran's eyes held her mother's and commanded her attention. "I'll run the shop. We'll have a good income. You won't have to worry about money."

"Jo did everything. He paid all the bills. I never even wrote a check." Ida shook her head, as though unable to comprehend a future without her husband. "The one time I tried to balance our checkbook, he took it away and told me not to worry my head about such things. I never had to worry about a thing because he was always there. And now he's gone—"

"We're going to be all right," Fran told her with shaky conviction. "We'll hurt," she conceded. "For a long time. But I can manage the shop. I'll do what needs to be done. I'll handle the household accounts, pay the bills. You run the house," she said, striving to be diplomatic. "And together we'll raise the girls. That's the way Dad would want it."

"I'm so scared, Frannie," Ida whispered. "Your father took care of everything." She spread her hands in a gesture of bewilderment.

"I'll stand in for him." Fran remembered how her parents had rushed to her side when Bernie died. "Dad would expect that."

When Bernie died, she'd fallen apart. She couldn't afford that luxury now, Fran warned herself. Somehow, she must find the strength to manage the shop, raise her daughters, and care for her mother. Bernie used to tease her—with such affection—of wanting to care for the whole world. Not the world now, she conceded—her family.

Seventeen

F or the first time in twenty-four years a Republican president was in the White House. They were there, Fran pointed out to Lynne and Debbie, because of conservative southern Democrats. She was ever anxious to remind her daughters that they *opposed* segregation. She remembered their shock when they realized colored children were not allowed to attend the so-called white schools.

"You mean here in Bellevue Sally couldn't go to school with me?" Debbie had demanded indignantly. Sally had been her "best friend" in New York.

With the same fierce determination she had utilized to improve her physical condition after the shooting, Fran worked to convince her mother she could manage Goldman's on her own. It was not enough to keep up the profitability the shop had always enjoyed. She was determined to expand. She became an omnivorous reader of fashion and business magazines. She studied trends. She began to plot her next move.

At the same time she was obsessed by the need to be a "good mother." She worried that Lynne and Debbie would spend too many hours a week in watching television. She was concerned by studies that reported the typical American family was sitting before a TV set for four or five hours a day. She fought constant guilt that she was not spending more time with Lynne and Debbie.

Ten months after her father's death—with the war in Korea at last over—Fran shocked her mother with the announcement that she meant to open a branch of Goldman's at the new shopping center under construction in the growing suburban area.

"We'll go broke!" Her mother was terrified. "How can you think of that?"

"Shopping centers are the wave of the future. With the town growing the way it is, it's a nightmare to try to find parking space in town. People will go where there's easy parking. They'll—"

"I think you've lost your mind!" her mother shrieked. "I won't permit it!"

"We'll talk about it later," Fran soothed. "When the shopping center is near completion, and you see everybody's reaction." Her mother didn't realize that a year before his death, her father had given her full power of attorney. She had already signed a lease at the new Bellevue Center. It was best, she told herself, that her mother believed the major business decisions were hers.

"Why do you always have to be different from everybody else?" Ida wailed. "You've been lucky so far with the shop. Don't rock the boat."

In September Debbie was enthralled at starting junior high school, to be able to take the bus to school with Lynne. She gloated at being only one year behind, though she was two years younger. At the same time Lynne abandoned her avowed wish to become another Dinah Shore—a fortunate decision, Fran confided in a letter to Midore, because Lynne couldn't carry a tune.

On Lynne's fifteenth birthday she came downstairs to her mother's room after the others were asleep to make a confession.

"I know what I want to do with my life, Mom." Wrapped in her favorite red and gray plaid bathrobe, Lynne curled up at the foot of her mother's bed. Her face was touchingly serious.

"What darling?" Fran asked.

"I want to be a lawyer. Like Daddy." Her eyes told Fran that Lynne—always the calm, practical one—had grieved deeply for her father. "I want to be able to help innocent people who're thrown into jail."

"I think that's wonderful, Lynne." Fran felt tears well in her eyes. The girls knew how their father had struggled for his law degree. They knew how important it had been to him. "It won't be easy for a woman to break into the legal field," she warned, "but I'll be there right behind you every minute."

"Why can't a woman be a good lawyer?" Lynne sighed. "Marilyn said women lawyers and women doctors have a terrible time." Marilyn was her close friend since the first day of high school. "But I'm going to be a lawyer, and Marilyn's going to be a doctor."

"Daddy would have been so pleased." Fran felt a surge of happiness. She and Bernie couldn't reach out for their dreams. Their daughters would do this for them. Already, Debbie was emotionally involved in the latent battle for integration. She could never forget that Sally—whom she'd liked so much in New York—would not be able to go to school with her here in Bellevue.

Her mother was appalled when Fran told her she'd arranged for a fashion show on the opening day of the branch shop. Local society debs would serve as models and 20 percent of the day's proceeds would go to charity.

"How can you give away 20 percent of the profits?" Ida shrieked. "Look at what it cost us to open up that shop!" In truth, her mother never looked at the figures.

"Mother, we're ahead of the game," Fran assured her confidently. "And the publicity is invaluable."

Fran approached the opening day of the new Goldman's with an air of total confidence. No one guessed the anxiety that held her prisoner. Had her mother been right? Was she taking an alarming gamble?

But by noon of opening day Fran knew the elegant new shop would be a success. Her father would have been so proud, she told herself as she stood near the flower-drenched entrance in one of her signature pants ensembles and personally welcomed each new arrival.

The afternoon fashion show was covered by the local press and with an on-the-spot radio commentator.

Her mother was enthralled by the turnout.

"Frannie, every important woman in town is here today," Ida whispered. "And I heard several people say that you look just like a movie star!"

In May the Supreme Court handed down a decision on Brown vs. Board of Education—a decision that outlawed segregation in public schools. Though the ruling had long been expected, it was greeted with ferocious resistance in the Deep South. Fran watched with horror in the long, hot summer that followed as rage erupted in many white quarters. Governor Talmadge swore to fight the court decision. There was talk of passing a constitutional amendment to turn Georgia's public schools into private schools. At the end of the school term many young teachers left the South. Older teachers—with pension payments in place and families to support—were compelled to remain.

Fran was agonized by the need to keep silent about her own beliefs. Debbie was upset at the callous remarks of a classmate—*"Do they really expect us to have colored kids in our classes? I'd rather die!"* Debbie and

Lynne's early years in New York schools had not prepared them for this.

For Fran to speak out in favor of integration was to face a boycott on the part of some of the shop's best customers. The shop provided security for her mother, her daughters, and herself. The memory of the Depression days—even though her own family suffered not at all from this—was etched on her brain. She knew she must be silent. She mustn't do anything that would endanger the girls' security.

During the past year she had forced herself to become involved in local social events. It was important for the business, she had decided. She had built herself into a personality in Bellevue. Women admired her sense of style, her exquisite clothes. They didn't feel threatened, she thought wryly—she was a woman with a disability.

At a local charity dinner Fran was seated next to a newcomer in town. Her mother was at a table close by. A widower about her own age, Craig Hendricks had opened an architectural office in Bellevue a few months earlier. In a corner of her mind Fran recalled hearing her mother talk about him. His wife had died of cancer several years ago. They'd had no children. *"He should join the synagogue, get to meet people,"* her mother had said. But perhaps he didn't want to meet people, Fran thought sympathetically.

"Where are you from?" she asked after they'd introduced themselves. It was clear he wasn't southern-bred.

"New York." His smile was almost apologetic. "Then I decided I didn't want to be the busiest architect in the country. I had a hankering for a much slower pace. Most of the time it's heavenly to be away from that rat race."

"I lived there for years. There are times when I miss it," she confessed and saw his eyes light in comprehension. "But I get up to New York three or four times a year on buying trips. I enjoy being back for little swatches of time."

"You're the one who runs Goldman's," he pinpointed. "When I wanted to buy a birthday present for one of my nieces, a neighbor told me that was the place for beautiful sweaters. Carol's in her freshman year at Barnard. I can't believe I have a niece old enough for college." His chuckle was warm and contagious. "Where do the years go?"

"They run." Fran laughed. "I can't believe I have a daughter who'll be heading for college in two years."

"You?" His eyebrows shot upward. "I don't believe that. Unless you're referring to a stepdaughter."

"Lynne's my daughter." Fran was amused by his comic amazement.

"She'll be having a 'Sweet Sixteen' birthday party next week. Debbie will be fourteen in November." She intercepted his covert glance at her left hand. She was here alone—he was wondering if she was unattached. He didn't know about her leg, she thought, all at once self-conscious. She'd been seated when he came to the table.

It was absurd, she rebuked herself, to feel so flattered by his obvious interest. *He didn't know about her leg.* But for a little while—in the course of the evening—she felt herself being pursued by an attractive, intelligent man. She was conscious of covert interest in men from time to time—and then they'd become aware that she walked with the aid of a cane and a leg brace. Not that she was interested in any man, she reminded herself at such moments. That part of her life had died with Bernie. He'd been with her for eleven wonderful years—that was enough for a lifetime.

"Frannie, we're going over to Edna's for coffee," her mother called at the end of the evening. "I'll meet you at the car."

"Right." Fran nodded vigorously, lest her voice be drowned out by the cacophony of sounds around them.

She hesitated as Craig Hendricks rose from his seat. This was ridiculous, she chastised herself. So Craig would see that she was physically disabled. With a self-conscious smile she pulled herself to her feet and brought her cane from where it had been resting—out of sight.

"I'm glad we had a chance to meet," he said. She saw his eyes rest fleetingly on her cane. "It was fun talking with you." They had shamefully ignored the others at the table, she realized now. But yes, it had been fun.

"We'll probably meet again." She strived to sound casual. "In a town of this size it's inevitable."

"Craig, I was looking all over for you." A breathless, feminine voice was cloyingly reproachful. "I knew you were coming, of course. I sold you your ticket. Oh, hi there, Fran."

"Hi, Geraldine." Fran smiled, resenting the other woman's patronizing attitude.

Geraldine Roland had been two years ahead of her in high school, voted "prettiest girl" in the senior class—but the passing years had been unkind to her. No boy had seemed good enough for her, Fran gathered—until suddenly she was thirty-five and the choices narrowed. At forty, she zeroed in on any presentable, unattached man, rumors said. It didn't even matter, Fran thought, that Craig Hendricks was Jewish and she was fashionably Episcopalian.

"See you, Fran," Geraldine cooed, linking an arm through Craig's and prodding him away from the table.

"Good night," Craig said and exchanged a smile of wry amusement with Fran.

The following day Fran glanced up from her desk at the rear of the shop to see Craig Hendricks hovering at the entrance to her office.

"I'm seeking your advice," he said ingratiatingly. "I want to choose a sweater for my niece at Barnard. I hear it's going to be a cold winter up there. Would you help me?"

"With pleasure."

Still fighting self-consciousness in Craig's presence, she drew herself to her feet and with her ever-present cane walked with him from her office to the sweater department of the elegant shop. She understood this was a ruse to see her again. She was simultaneously flattered and unnerved. She had never expected to find herself reacting to any man the way she was reacting now. She was elated by his obvious interest in her, and aroused as she had never expected to be aroused again.

In the years since Bernie had died she had not become immune to passion. In the solitude of her bed she was conscious of needs. She remembered—in vivid recall—the exquisite pleasure of their lovemaking. It was Bernie's legacy to her, to be forever cherished.

"Describe Carol to me," she told Craig as she stood behind the counter and surveyed the shelves of fine wool and cashmere sweaters that were offered for the wealthy of Bellevue.

"She's quite lovely," he began, squinting in thought. "Masses of dark hair, gorgeous blue eyes like yours—"

Her heart traitorously pounding she brought down sweaters from the shelves. Why was she behaving like a wide-eyed sixteen-year-old? she rebuked herself.

"These colors would be flattering to her," Fran said, striving to sound casual. "And cashmere is always smart."

Craig allowed her to make the final choice, and she turned over the sale to a waiting saleswoman.

"I wonder," he began when the saleswoman left them, "if—as a fellow ex-New Yorker—you'd take pity on a lonely old man and have dinner with me one night?"

Fran laughed.

"Fellow New Yorker, yes," she conceded. "Lonely old man? Hardly," she jibed. She hesitated—exhilarated by the invitation, yet uneasy. "Yes," she said after a moment of doubt, "I'd like that very much."

"Tomorrow night?" he asked, his smile radiant. "I hear there's a great new restaurant about five miles out of town."

"Tomorrow night," she agreed.

Fran dressed with infinite care for her dinner date with Craig Hendricks. She considered one of the few dresses in her closet, discarded this. No, slacks concealed the leg brace. Slacks were classic these days, and this evening was unseasonably cool. Well-cut black crepe slacks, she decided, with a white linen blouse and a Chanel-style black jacket.

How wonderful, she thought, that legendary Coco Chanel had come back onto the fashion scene at seventy-one, after being away since 1939. And her spring collection had been so well accepted! Was it time, she asked herself, for Goldman's to send a representative to the Paris couture shows? She might even buy two or three items and arrange to have them copied by a Seventh Avenue house. It would be great for business.

Bellevue might be a small town—though in truth it was growing rapidly—but its nearness to Atlanta gave it a cosmopolitan air. Her face softened as she remembered how her father always boasted that Atlanta was the New York of the South, and that some of its cosmopolitan air rubbed off on Bellevue.

"Mom!" Debbie stormed into her room in a flurry of indignation. "Will you tell Lynne that I can, too, hang a picture of James Dean in my bedroom!"

"Darling, Lynne is just teasing you," she consoled. "Of course, you can hang James Dean's picture in your bedroom." Debbie was prone to extravagant displays of affection—Lynne more inclined to casual friendships.

"Grandma says you won't be here for dinner." Debbie inspected her curiously. "Where are you going?"

"Oh, this is just a business meeting," Fran fabricated. Usually when she went out in the evening, she was accompanied by her mother. "Don't you stay up late watching television," she warned.

Why had she lied to Debbie? she asked herself guiltily. There was nothing wrong about her going out for dinner with a friend. Now and then she took the saleswomen at both shops out for dinner. This was nothing important in her life—just a pleasant evening with an ex-New Yorker. But in her mind she relived the encounter with her mother:

"You're going out to dinner with *who?*" her mother asked in astonishment.

"Craig Hendricks," she repeated. "He misses New York. He's dying to talk to someone who'd lived there for years. I gather he's kind of lonely." She saw astonishment suddenly become hope.

"I hear he's awfully nice." Her mother glowed now. "He's been widowed for years."

"Mother, this isn't a romance," she said bluntly. "We're just having dinner at this new restaurant about five miles out of town." Where nobody was likely to see them. "To talk about old times in the city."

"I saw Geraldine Roland dragging him off at the dinner the other night." Ida's smile was smug. "Now wouldn't she just die if she knew you two were having dinner together?"

"That's all we're having," Fran told her mother. She hesitated. "Don't say anything to the girls."

"Frannie, their father has been dead over six years," Ida said. "You have a right to go out with another man."

"Don't say anything to them," Fran repeated. "I'll probably never go out with him again," she said, laughing. "No need for them to get crazy ideas in their heads."

She was relieved that the two girls were upstairs in Debbie's room when Craig arrived.

"You're looking beautiful," he said softly as they left the house and headed for the car.

"Thank you." Could he really believe that? she asked herself. Ever seeing herself as imperfect. "It's a lovely night, isn't it? Usually it's still hot and sticky this time of year."

"I ordered it especially for us," he joshed, helping her into the car. "I hope the restaurant lives up to its press."

On the drive to the restaurant they talked somberly about the desegregation situation in the South.

"We're doing well here in Bellevue—and the same holds for Atlanta. We're going to avoid the violent confrontations that are popping up in other cities. It's a matter of moving slowly."

"Our housekeeper Lily is one of the sweetest, mildest women in the world," Fran said softly, "but she told me she figures all this talk about 'taking it slow and easy' means it'll probably never happen. Lily would never have said that to my mother." A hint of laughter crept into her voice. "But in Lily's eyes I'm not truly a Southerner anymore. I lived too long in New York for that. But what brought you down here?" Belatedly she remembered asking him this at their last meeting.

"I had a longing to get away from New York pressures, into a more leisurely way of life. Atlanta was my first thought. With so much building going on there, I figured I could tie up all the work I care to handle. Then I saw Bellevue—and I knew it was for me. I do some work in Atlanta," he acknowledged, "but more and more it's here in Bellevue."

The restaurant was charming, spacious, and softly lighted. In the course of a delicious dinner Fran grew relaxed. Occasional glances about the tables assured her there was no one here whom she knew. It was ridiculous to be concerned about that, she chided herself, yet she was relieved.

Craig admitted to being lonely in town.

"Not that I don't receive a stream of invitations. It seems there's always a dinner party that requires an extra man. But I suppose I'm too choosy." He chuckled reminiscently. "I can't bear being tied down at a table between two women who can talk about nothing except bridge, club meetings, and television." His smile was warm. "Right off the bat I knew you'd be different. Almost the first thing we talked about was the horror that Joe McCarthy brought to this country."

Gradually their conversation moved into a more personal vein. Fran talked about Bernie. Craig talked about his late wife, Rhoda. Each had enjoyed a fine marriage, aborted tragically early. Fran sensed that she would be seeing much of Craig in the future. It was an awesome miracle to her that he found her attractive. He didn't see the leg brace and cane—he saw Fran, the woman.

On Saturday evenings the girls were involved in their own socializing—often away from their house. Ida played bridge at the Wildwood Club—the Jewish version of the country club. On Saturday evenings Fran usually stayed late at the shop in town to go over weekly records. On Sunday mornings she drove out to the shopping center to check the records there.

Now Fran had Saturday dinner with Craig—at one of the charming restaurants he'd found outside of Bellevue. Sunday mornings they had a late breakfast together. They had a tacit pact to try to keep their meetings secret, though Ida knew that Fran was seeing Craig regularly and approved.

"Why all this chasing around where nobody can see you?" Ida challenged Fran when they were en route to a Hanukkah party at the Wildwood Club—where Craig would be in attendance, too. Were people beginning to notice how he attached himself to her at those times? Or did they just think that their New York backgrounds brought them together on these occasions? "Why do you have to hide?"

"You know how people talk," Fran hedged. They'd be astonished, she taunted herself, that a bright handsome man like Craig was involved with a woman who was disabled.

"So what's wrong with that? You're both unattached." Unexpectedly Ida chuckled. "If you came right out and said you're going steady, then—"

"We're not going steady," Fran countered.

"You're going steady," Ida said bluntly. "You see each other at least two or three times a week. And the way he looks at you when you two meet at parties is a dead giveaway."

"He's just lonely—and we enjoy talking to each other." Fran felt her face grow hot. "He—he makes me laugh."

"I hope you've gotten beyond that." Ida's eyes were bright with questions.

"A friendly good-night kiss," Fran said after a moment. "And don't try to make something out of that." She sensed that Craig was afraid of rushing her. Why was she so afraid? It wasn't being unfaithful to Bernie. She'd never love anybody the way she loved him. But there were moments when she wished that Craig would take her in his arms and make love to her. She remembered the wonderful peace that enveloped her after she and Bernie had made love. No matter how traumatic the day had been, they had the beautiful oasis of the night, where they were alone in a special world that allowed only euphoria.

Could she have that again?

Eighteen

T he country was experiencing a fresh burst of prosperity. The building industry was booming. Fran was proud of Craig's soaring success. He was enthusiastic—as were most architects—over the
introduction of dramatic new materials such as aluminum and plastics
into construction. And at last there was an easing in the Cold War.

On a January buying trip Fran was enthralled to meet with Midore,
in New York on an art assignment. Together they visited the Museum of
Modern Art exhibit of modern American artists—and Fran predicted
that one day Midore's paintings would be shown here. They had dinner
at Fran's favorite restaurant, the Russian Tea Room. It was a cherished
reunion for both women.

Fran knew her mother was always anxious when she left Bellevue—
as though her leg brace and cane placed her in jeopardy. It was a never-
ceasing miracle to her the way Craig ignored her handicap. Yet at
intervals she asked herself if he would truly be able to ignore this in intimate moments. It could be so awkward, she told herself with brutal
honesty, if they made love. But it had not been awkward with Bernie—

Early in the spring Craig took her to a performance of the Atlanta
Symphony Orchestra. Caught up in the beauty of the music, Craig
reached for her hand and held it tightly in his. It wasn't the first such
occasion, but tonight Fran felt a new urgency in him.

"It was a marvelous concert," Fran said as they settled in the car
again. "I'm so glad you thought of it."

"It was painful for me," he said, and she turned to him in bewilderment. "Because I could only sit there next to you when I wanted so much
to hold you in my arms."

"That was then," Fran whispered in the darkness of the car—feeling herself wonderfully young and adventurous. "What stops you now?"

She lifted her face to his while he pulled her into his arms. His mouth tender at first, then demanding. His arms folding her so close she felt the pounding of his heart against her. Then—with a reluctance that matched her own—he withdrew his mouth from hers.

"I want to love you completely," he whispered. "We have no other commitments. What's to stop us?"

"Where?" For an instant she was uncertain. Not at her house, of course—nor at his apartment.

"That new motel just down the road," he told her and chuckled. "I'll register as Frank L. Wright."

"And I?" Fran was caught up in the magic of the moment—unreal but beautiful.

"You won't need to register. It'll be very discreet." He was gently teasing. "Oh, Fran, I've waited so long for you."

"Then let's not wait any longer," she ordered, a lilt in her voice. This wasn't Fran Garfield—this was an audacious stranger.

The motel room was neatly furnished, the illumination soft.

"Craig, turn off the lights," Fran whispered, all at once tense. Passion blending with self-consciousness in her.

"Stay right there," he told her and crossed to switch off the bedside lamps.

She waited, clinging to her cane, assaulted by misgivings. Why was she here? *This was insane!* Then in the darkness Craig came to her and pulled her close while her cane fell to the floor with a faint, reproachful clatter.

"I have you, Fran," he reassured her, his arms protective. "Just relax. It's going to be marvelous for us."

"My leg," she stammered. "Craig, I don't know—"

"I'm not in love with your leg," he scolded, swaying with her, his face against hers. "It's beautiful, fascinating you."

While he held her close with one arm, a hand found its way beneath her coat-style blouse and fumbled for the hooks of her bra. She caught her breath in the exquisite darkness while he fondled her breasts. Her hands tightened at his shoulders.

It was going to be all right. To Craig she was a *whole* woman.

———

Despite her joyous reaction to their new relationship, she was reluctant to be open about it. She was terrified that Lynne and Debbie would be upset, that they would feel she was depriving them of part of herself. But how wonderful, she told herself, that Craig understood. They saw each other over the weekends, as before—and both contrived to meet at local social gatherings, where each made a game of concealing their closeness.

"When you go up to New York in July on your buying trip," Craig confided on an already sultry Saturday evening when they dined at a new lakeside restaurant, "I'll just happen to be up there for an architectural event."

"Do we dare?" Her smile—belying her words—was dazzling.

"We dare." He reached across the table for her hand. "Stay a week this time. We owe it to ourselves. I wish it was Paris," he said exuberantly. "I haven't seen Paris since the war." Fran knew he'd been part of its liberation.

"Could you get away for ten days in Paris?" she asked, her mind charging ahead on a revolutionary path that had invaded her thoughts for the past three weeks.

"I'll make time!" His eyes were bright with a blend of astonishment and anticipation.

"You know I've been planning on opening a third shop—in Atlanta." As with the second shop, her mother was alarmed by the expenditure this would entail—yet at the same time fascinated by what she called her daughter's *chutzpah*. "I'll need a major promotion to attract attention. I've been debating about flying to Paris to the couture shows, buying one or two Paris originals, then having them copied in New York." From her Seventh Avenue contacts she knew how to handle this. "I could wrap up a lot of publicity both here and in Atlanta on that kind of a deal."

"It sounds great." He nodded in approval. "But what about the time schedule? Have you settled on a site yet in Atlanta?"

"We're quibbling over the rent," she said and Craig began to chuckle.

"I wouldn't want to have to bargain with you."

"The July show in Paris is for fall and winter dresses. If I buy, I'll have copies made for an early October opening in Atlanta," she plotted. "I'll go over as a trade buyer." As usual she had researched every angle. "That means in order to get into a show I have to put up money to cover the purchase of at least one model. But that's no problem," she dismissed this.

"What about your New York buying?"

"I'll wrap that up in two days, then plan to fly on to Paris. Craig, can we have ten days in Paris?" The prospect was awesome.

"We'll do it! Apply right away for a passport. And I think we'll need vaccinations. Oh God, Fran, it'll be wonderful!"

Right away Fran moved into action. For a harried moment she feared the whole plan was about to go awry. As always, her mother was anxious about her venturing away from Bellevue alone.

"You're going all the way to Paris?" Her mother gaped at her in consternation. "I'll go with you," she said determinedly, "though I'll be terrified at flying over the ocean!"

"Mother, there's no need," Fran soothed. "I can manage. And how can we both go away and leave the girls? I wouldn't have a moment's peace if you weren't here with them."

In the privacy of their motel room on Saturday evening Fran told Craig about her mother's offer.

"That proves she loves me," Fran said with gentle laughter. "Mother's always been frightened to death of flying to Europe. *Over water.*" Two of her friends had futilely tried to persuade her to fly with them to Puerto Rico last month.

"Does she know I'll be with you?" Craig asked.

"No. She may be suspicious," Fran admitted, "but I haven't told her. But we have Mother's blessing," she drawled. It was unbelievable, she thought in amusement, that her tradition-bound mother accepted her having an affair.

"I'm not pushing you," he cautioned, "but wouldn't your mother be delighted if we came back from Paris formally engaged? Maybe with a November wedding? I know—you'll be busy in October," he joshed. "You have that new store to open."

"Let's talk after Paris," she hedged, her heart pounding. Here it was—what she'd been trying to block out of her mind all these months. Fearful of having to make a decision. Could marriage fit into her life again? she wondered. "We'll talk after Paris," she reiterated. Torn between elation and alarm.

Fran was caught up in the excitement of the imminent trip to Paris—both on a professional and a personal level. And only three weeks before their scheduled departure Craig persuaded her that they make London their first stop.

"How can we go to Paris and not see London?" he chided in high good humor. "Just for three days. You'll love London," he predicted.

"But can we get reservations this late?" she hedged, yet already she was exhilarated by the prospect.

"Let me work on it," he coaxed. "We'll spend three nights in London, then fly to Paris. It'll be great. We'll do this in high style!"

The days raced past with astonishing speed. Each day Craig reported on his progress.

"We'd never have been able to get into a top hotel in Paris this month," he told her. "Or into any hotel. There hasn't been an empty bed available. But the *Grand Saison* will be over when we arrive."

"What about London?" She'd never been out of this country—and now she'd be seeing London and Paris if all went well.

"I'm waiting for confirmation. It looks as though we'll actually have a room at the Claridge."

"Craig, it'll be so expensive!" But she was smiling. After much argument he'd capitulated and allowed her to assume half the cost of their trip.

"We never would have gotten a reservation if this old army buddy hadn't arranged it. He's a big wheel in the diplomatic corps now, living in Geneva. God, London will be a whole different city than what I saw a dozen years ago!"

As planned Craig closed his office for three weeks in July. He flew to New York a day prior to Fran's scheduled early morning departure. On arrival Fran was astonished to find him waiting for her at the airport. She'd expected to join him at the Carlyle—chosen by Craig because of its continental elegance and because it was in a quiet residential neighborhood.

"Craig, how sweet of you," she murmured, lifting her mouth for a kiss.

"I know you'll be busy tomorrow and the next day on your buying spree," he said, guiding her through the summer vacation crowds to collect her luggage. "So today has to be special. A late lunch at the Russian Tea Room, then a rest before dinner and the theater."

"What are we seeing?" she asked. For a poignant moment she remembered how she and Bernie had waited for the cheapest seats for the occasional plays they could afford. No question in her mind that tonight she and Craig would sit in choice seats.

"*Silk Stockings,*" he said. "I remember that you love Cole Porter and how you adored *Ninotchka.*" The Garbo film that became the basis for the new Broadway musical. "Nothing serious these two weeks," he said with mock sternness. "I mean to hear you laugh."

They took a cab to the huge Carlyle, which occupies almost a city block, yet—Craig told her—managed to be warm and inviting. She was grateful that he'd chosen a hotel new to both of them. The lobby was exquisite, she thought—fresh flowers everywhere, fine tapestries, Aubusson rugs.

They left Fran's bags in their room and headed for the Russian Tea Room, ate blini with caviar amidst the splendor of green walls, red booths, and pink tablecloths, then lingered over tea with a rare sense of freedom.

They made love in the afternoon, then hastily dressed to have a pre-theater dinner in the Carlyle dining room. Conscious of the passing time they kept conversation to a minimum over dinner, then hurried by cab to the theater.

In the morning Fran dashed off after breakfast in their room to call on her manufacturers. She knew she must be swift in her buying. She and Craig were flying to London tomorrow evening.

Fran slept little on the flight to London. This was a glorious adventure—made more glorious because it was shared with Craig. They saw dawn light up the sky over the Atlantic and watched impatiently for the approach of land. Fran was enchanted at the prospect of being on foreign soil. She had never been out of the United States in her life—not even to Canada or Mexico. And London was one of the great cities of the world!

English history—which went back to the arrival of Julius Caesar in 55 B.C.—had always fascinated her. Their own country, she thought in a burst of romanticism, was a brave offshoot of England. And now they'd walk on the same ground as Edward the Confessor, Henry VIII, Elizabeth I. The land of Shakespeare, Dickens, the Brontes, George Bernard Shaw. And for Craig, she thought tenderly, London was an architect's dream.

At last their plane came down at Heathrow Airport. In a delicious haze of awe that she was truly here, Fran moved with Craig through the customs routine. Fighting sleepiness they found a taxi and headed for the Claridge. On the drive into London, Fran's eyes clung avidly to the passing scenery. At intervals she emitted a faint squeal of delight as a billboard for an American product appeared on the horizon.

"Don't expect the Claridge to be impressive from the outside," Craig warned, "though it's one of the top hotels in the world."

Moments later their taxi pulled up before an unpretentious—almost drab—red brick building. A tiny canopy announced that this was the Claridge. But from the moment the smartly uniformed doorman led them across the marble foyer until they were alone in their exquisitely furnished suite, Fran was enthralled with the elegance the hotel offered.

Their brief time in London sped past. She was rhapsodic at visiting Westminister Abbey, stood enthralled at the "Poets' Corner"—before the graves of Tennyson, Wordsworth, Coleridge, and Burns. They spent a delightful morning at the Tower of London, bypassed seeing the Crown Jewels—in deference to their tight schedule.

"We must spend a whole chunk of time in London someday," Fran said wistfully while she and Craig waited to board their flight to Orly. "There's so much more I want to see."

"We'll do that," he promised, his eyes tender. "With air travel so marvelous these days, people fly to London the way New Yorkers used to run up to Boston or down to Washington by train."

"The world's changing so fast it scares me sometimes," Fran admitted. Just the way her personal world changed since Craig came into her life. It was astonishing and marvelous—and sometimes unnerving.

Nineteen

C raig had extravagantly arranged for a suite for them at the Ritz. July was an off-season month for the hotel, Craig told Fran—though it was high season for American tourists.

"I promised myself when I was here during the war that one day I'd come back to Paris and I'd stay at the Ritz," he told her as they began the eleven-mile drive from Orly into the city. The traffic told them that—as usual—Paris was being overrun by visitors.

"I can't believe I'm really here." Fran gazed at the passing sites with towering excitement. "It's a fairy tale, Craig."

"I understand there are not any great plays here this season," Craig said and chuckled. "That's courtesy of the *New Yorker*. But in Paris eating is an art. I have a list of restaurants we mustn't miss."

"American cars," Fran chortled and pointed to a pair of long, sleek Cadillacs alongside them. "Rich American women are here for the couture shows. With their cars."

"I've worked out a schedule so we can cram in as many of the highlights as possible. I know you're here on business," he conceded good-humoredly, "but let's keep that to a minimum."

"Oh, I promise." Fran's smile was dazzling. "We have to see the Louvre, Notre Dame, the Eiffel Tower, the Left Bank—"

"You'll see them. We'll stroll down the Champs-Élysées, shop on the Rue du Faubourg Saint-Honoré, explore the Left Bank. Paris is supposed to be especially fond of its trees," Craig told her. "The last count I heard was that there are eighty-five thousand here, more than in any city in the world. Plane trees, chestnuts, poplars, maples, elms, scyamores. Most streets are green from spring through November—and that was planned."

"What a beautiful idea." Fran remembered the broad, tree-lined avenues in Bellevue, that lent the town such charm.

"But I hear—and we'll soon see," he warned, "that the magnificent chestnuts at the Place de l'Alma were cut down so that a new tunnel could be built, and that the Avenue de l'Opéra's sidewalks are being shortened in order to give the cars more roadway. And there's talk of huge new underground garages being built around town. Even under the Tuileries gardens."

Fran winced. "Oh, Craig, that sounds almost sacrilegious."

She was astonished that at first sight the Ritz—from its frontage on the elegant and beautiful Place Vêndome—seemed small for one of the most famous hotels in the world. But its guest list included kings and queens, heads of state, the world's wealthiest and most famous.

As an architect, Craig was fascinated by the Ritz's architecture.

"It's really three buildings," Craig explained after he had registered for them and they were following the bellman with their luggage across the unpretentious lobby to the elevators.

"We'll have to visit the bar," Fran said, her eyes bright despite little sleep. "All the legends we've heard through the years are racing around in my mind. All the people who've lived in the hotel, frequented the bar."

Alone with Craig in their suite, Fran gazed about in candid admiration—the walls upholstered in exquisite brocades, the tall French windows framed by rich draperies, fine boiserie in lush display.

"Craig, have you ever seen such high ceilings? They must be twenty feet high! And look at the call buttons. Four," she counted, puzzled by this array.

"Three are usual in Europe," Craig explained. "Waiter, maid, valet. Red, yellow, and green. The blue is for your own private servant."

"Do you suppose," Fran pondered whimsically, "that Coco Chanel, once lived in this suite? Or F. Scott Fitzgerald or Ernest Hemingway?"

"Let's unpack," Craig said with an air of heady anticipation. "Then let me show you Paris."

The next three days passed in an ecstatic haze for Fran. This was her cherished introduction to Paris—before she ventured into the business aspect. With Craig as tour guide they explored the beloved tourist sites. They lunched at the Hotel Plaza Athénée's superb dining room.

"This is where Christian Dior often comes for lunch," Craig told her after a conversation with their waiter in French too swift for her to follow. "Though he spends little time over lunch."

"I wonder what he orders—" Her smile was whimsical.

"The *poularde grillee Plaza Athénée*," Craig told her and chuckled. "I figured you'd wonder about that. I asked."

"We're having lunch in the restaurant favored by the best-loved Paris couturier," she murmured. "It's a long way from Bellevue, Georgia."

They had dinner in the three-star Maxim's—as much impressed by the grand paneling, the elegant mirrors, the dramatic display of red roses as by the superb cuisine.

"Being here is like living in the Belle Epoque," Fran said softly.

"And guess what famous English couple eats here when they're in Paris?" Craig drawled.

"Who?" Fran prodded.

"Sir Laurence Olivier and Vivien Leigh. He likes the *sole Albert*. She orders *frivolites de Langoustines*."

"Oh, how are we going to settle for homestyle food after this?"

"Tomorrow we'll go to Les Halles," Craig told her. "The central markets of Paris. We'll have lunch there at one of the bistros. And the following day you have your Paris collection to attend."

"Even if I just *show* a haute couture original in the shops, it'll be worth what I'm spending on it," Fran said with conviction. "But I'm fairly certain this contractor in New York can provide me with excellent copies."

"You have the original made up in your size," Craig said. "*You* wear it and sell the copies."

"Do I dare?" Fran was taken aback. She had meant only to display it—first in one shop, then in another.

"Why not?" he countered. "You have a beautiful figure. And you know you'd love it."

"I'd love it," she confessed. Craig thought she had a beautiful figure—despite her handicap. She felt bathed in pleasure. "We'll be here just long enough for the fittings, I think. I'll have to ask." She was giddy with anticipation. She'd order an evening dress—probably more expensive than the daytime dress she had planned—but a long dress concealed her leg brace. And she could demand extravagant prices for the copies.

As scheduled Fran and Craig spent the next morning at the colorful, chaotic Les Halles.

"The greatest markets in the world," Craig proclaimed with satisfaction as they moved among the throngs of Parisians and tourists from every corner of the world. "How do you feel about lunch at one of the bistros here?"

"I'm ready whenever you are," Fran said, a lilt in her voice.

"Let me check to see whom we'll honor with our presence." Craig reached into his jacket pocket for his notebook, consulted his listing. "We're on Rue de la Reale. Chez Monteil is just ahead."

They located the modest but charming bistro—open only for lunch—and walked inside.

"Let's eat lightly," Craig cautioned as they consulted the menu. "We're having dinner at Le Grand Véfour, at the end of the Palais Royal gardens. One of the best restaurants in Europe. I knew about these great places when I was here during the war, but they were way beyond my means." He chuckled reminiscently. "I promised myself that one day I'd come back and dine sumptuously in all of them. Well, as many as we can manage."

Chez Monteil had just opened. Fran and Craig were seated at a table in a private corner but with a perfect view of the entrance. They quickly realized this was a favorite luncheon rendezvous. People were arriving in such numbers the small room would soon be crowded, Fran surmised. Then a man with an engaging smile strolled into the bistro and was instantly welcomed by *Le Patron* himself.

"Craig," Fran whispered, clutching at his arm. "Isn't that Jean Gabin?"

"I think so," Craig said, his eyes following hers. "Yes, it is!"

Fran's mind darted back through the years to the cherished trips she and Bernie made to the Apollo Theater on West 42nd Street in Manhattan, to see each new Jean Gabin film that was offered. All at once she felt a surge of guilt that she was here in this delightful French bistro—seeing their favorite French film star. She was here—but not with Bernie.

"I haven't seen him in a film in years," Craig confessed, "but it gives me a kind of thrill to see him in person."

Fran was aware of a somber undercurrent in Craig now. Had he watched Gabin movies with his late wife? The past was never truly put to bed, she thought somberly. It popped up when least expected.

The following morning Craig escorted Fran to the haute couture showing where she would spend most of the morning. She would buy an original and arrange for her fittings. The dress must go back with her to New York to the contractor who would make up the copies—just six for each of the shops.

"If all goes well, I'll be tied up on the business end for hours," Fran guessed. "I'll grab a taxi back to the hotel."

Caught up in an air of unreality Fran became part of the enthusiastic crowd gathered for the prestigious showing of a major fashion collection. The moment she saw the gray satin evening gown that elicited enormous applause she knew this was the one she would buy—despite its astronomical price. Six copies for each of the shops—guaranteeing exclusivity for the buyers. But she would own the original. *She* would wear it.

Fran returned to the hotel in a haze of euphoria. Craig ordered a light lunch sent up from the Ritz dining room.

"This seems slightly decadent," Fran said as she settled herself at the table to consume the Ritz's gourmet fare. "To be at the Ritz and eat in your suite!"

"We'll play the tourist bit this afternoon. Be thoroughly normal," Craig promised with a grin. "We'll walk over to the Tuileries gardens. It'll be a beautiful, leisurely time. Then we'll come back to the hotel and dress for dinner." Fran lifted an eyebrow in astonishment. "Darling, Le Grand Véfour deserves this. But finish your lunch and let's go be tourists."

Although the Tuileries gardens—sixty acres that remained, Craig told Fran, much as when they were originally designed in the late 17th century—were formal in layout, with elegant flower beds and wide avenues of lime and chestnut trees, they radiated a casual charm. Because of the children playing along the paths, Fran mused—riding on the merry-go-round, sailing boats in the pond.

"At moments like this I wish I could paint." Craig's face grew tender as he watched a pair of pretty two-year-olds reaching eagerly for the ices bought by their nannies at a nearby stand.

"The dark-haired little girl reminds me of Debbie," Fran said and remembered belatedly that Craig was pressing to meet her daughters. Why was she shying away from that? she asked herself. Lynne and Debbie knew that she had long been faithful to their father's memory. It wasn't wrong for her to be seeing another man. "Shall we have an ice, too?" No serious thoughts this afternoon, she rebuked herself.

In their suite at the Ritz again, Fran was faintly uneasy when Craig became amorous. She took refuge in the dark. In the protective covering of the night she could feel young and beautiful and perfect.

"Do you suppose we would have time before dinner for me to shop at one of those fascinating little boutiques on the Rue du Faubourg Saint-Honoré? I'd like to find some special little gift for the girls and my mother."

"We'll make time." His smile was gentle. Fran felt color flood her face. He understood her reticence.

As usual Fran and Craig were among the first arrivals for dinner. Le Grand Véfour lived up to its name—its walls adorned with exquisitely carved and painted paneling, the furnishings 18th-century Directoire. Fran was drawn to the delicate beauty of the sweet peas that graced every table.

"You know," she reminisced, "I never remember seeing sweet peas in New York. When I was growing up, they were my favorite flowers."

"Are Lynne and Debbie much like you?" Craig asked. "I mean, in appearance."

"People usually say the three of us are very much alike." He was so eager to meet the girls, Fran thought. He was hungry for family. They were a houseful of women. Could Craig fit into their lives?

Over dinner Craig told her some of the history of Le Grand Véfour.

"As a young general, Napoleon dined here often. He met Josephine at the coffee house next door."

"Sitting here I feel as though we've moved back in time." Her eyes moved about the elegant room—a favorite, Craig had read, of Alec Guinness, whose latest movie was *To Paris With Love*. "Can you imagine the people who must have dined here through the centuries? Voltaire, Emile Zola, George Sand, Proust."

"Speaking of time, you said you have to be at the couturier for a fitting tomorrow," he recalled. "What time? So I can plan our itinerary around that."

There were not enough hours in the day, Fran thought—though they managed to squeeze an incredible amount of sightseeing into the waking hours. Her Paris gown would be completed with rare speed, for which she was grateful.

"I lied a little," she confessed to Craig. "I said I had to leave Paris in four days."

She was conscious of a covert impatience in Craig to formalize their relationship. And she was shaken when he paused in their stroll through the Luxembourg Gardens to gaze tenderly at an infant in a carriage by the beautiful de Medici fountain—a replica of an Italian grotto.

"What can be more beautiful than to bring a child into the world?" he said in a surge of sentimentality. "To watch that little part of yourself grow through the years." He dropped an arm about her waist. "Our child, Fran—"

"We're past the stage for that," she said wryly.

"Are we?" he countered. "My mother was thirty-nine when I was born, forty-one when my sister was born. If we had a child, it would be like starting a whole new life, Fran. A second chance."

"Craig, you're moving too fast for me," she hedged, striving for a lightness. "Tell me more about the Luxembourg Gardens." Being in Paris with Craig was almost like a honeymoon, she thought carelessly—then retreated from this comparison.

Each day they played the tourist scene, and each night they made passionate love. It amazed her—and filled her with joy—that Craig found her attractive and desirable. He was so sweet, so compassionate—traits she had loved in Bernie. And so anxious, she forced herself to admit, to have a family of his own.

Tenderness stirred in her as she remembered her two pregnancies, her joy when each of the girls was born. She'd never considered having another child. After the shooting she had been convinced that part of her life was over. *Was it?*

Walking into the Ritz lobby with the precious couturier box—which had attracted envious eyes as she hurried back to the hotel, Fran told herself it was absurd to feel so euphoric at owning a Paris original. In a corner of her mind she knew this was an escape because for a little while she could divest herself of decision-making.

She wasn't being unfaithful to Bernie to feel as she did about Craig. The girls would—in time—accept him in the family. Other women with children remarried. It didn't become a crisis situation. Craig and she couldn't go on forever in this never-never land they'd created for themselves.

Craig glanced up with a welcoming smile as she came into their suite. Sprawled on the sofa, he was reading the day's *International Herald-Tribune.* His eyes settled on the elaborate box Fran carried. "So that's the masterpiece."

"This is it," Fran said gaily, then lifted an eyebrow in curiosity when the phone rang. "I'll get it." She picked up the phone. "Hello."

"I know it's seven hours later in Paris, so I figured I wouldn't be waking you up." Ida's voice jolted Fran into anxiety.

"Mother, is something wrong?" Her mother thought twice before making a long-distance call a hundred miles away.

"Not really," Ida said with an air of hesitation—prompted, Fran guessed, by Lynne, whose voice filtered in from the sidelines. "Lynne didn't want me to tell you, but she fell and broke her arm last week."

"Let me talk to Mom," Lynne insisted, her voice coming in strongly now. "You don't have to worry, Mom. It was a nutty accident. I was talking to somebody on the stairs above me and didn't look where I was going. I fell on my left arm and fractured it. I'll be fine."

"Tell her about the surgery." Ida's voice was shrill.

"What surgery?" Fear wrapped Fran in ice. Her mind hurtled back to her own surgery after a bullet lodged in her back. "Lynne, let me talk to your grandmother!"

"It's not serious," Ida said. "But you're her mother—you should know," she added defiantly.

"Why does she need surgery for a broken arm?" Fran was assaulted by a montage of alarming images.

"Grandma, you're scaring her!" Fran heard Lynne say. Then Lynne was talking into the phone. "It's just some minor surgery to make sure the fracture is set properly—or something like that. I told Grandma not to tell you. I go into the hospital tonight—the doctor does the surgery tomorrow morning—and he says I'll be home in three days. It's *nothing*."

"I'm flying home right away." Fran couldn't control her trembling. Subconsciously she saw Craig rise from the sofa and walk to her. "I've finished my business. I want to be with you, Lynne."

"Mom, you've got three more days in Paris," Lynne said. "Stay there. I'll be okay."

"I'm coming home." Fran was firm. "If my daughter is having surgery, I belong there with her."

She put down the phone—knowing it was absurd to be so upset, yet the memory of her own travail was suddenly vivid in recall. *There must be no permanent damage to Lynne's arm.*

"Fran, sit down." Craig drew her down to a chair.

"I can't believe it. Lynne broke her arm—and now she had to go back for surgery. What the devil was wrong with the doctor?" She sought refuge in anger.

"Tell me exactly what she said," Craig pleaded.

Haltingly Fran repeated the brief conversation, her mind in chaos.

"Lynne doesn't want you to lose three days in Paris," Craig scolded. "This isn't serious surgery."

"I have to fly back as soon as I can get a reservation," she said shakily. "I'll call the airlines—"

"I'll call and change our reservations," Craig soothed.

"You stay here. I'll fly back alone. No, don't come with me," she said as he began to protest. "I've come down to earth at last. These last months we've been living a fantasy. It won't work for us, Craig. It's too late for us!"

"You're all shaken up, and that's natural," he said gently. "But you don't have to throw away what we've found with each other. Lynne's almost seventeen—she'll be going off to college in another year. We—"

"There can be no 'we' for us," Fran told him. She saw him flinch and knew the agony she was inflicting. He wanted a wife and a child—a new life for himself. She couldn't provide *that*. "It's not enough for me to love you, Craig. For me the girls will always come first. It would be unfair to let you think otherwise. I have the children and the business—that's my life. There's no room for more."

"Fran, this is crazy! Lynne and Debbie are not small children that demand your attention. You don't have to—"

"I'm obsessed," Fran broke in. She didn't want to do this to Craig, but she couldn't divide herself into two women. "Until the day I die Lynne and Debbie will come first with me. My loyalties will always be for them. It's too late for me to begin another life, another family."

"We'll talk about this later—when you're not upset," he tried, striving for calm. "We can work things out."

"I have to go back to my girls, Craig. That's where I belong. My life is set. It's too late to draw new lines." *This was reality.* "We'll meet back in Bellevue—and we'll be friends." What she was doing was right for both Craig and herself. She would hurt for a while—but she would heal.

"I don't know that I can be just a friend," Craig admitted.

"Let's work at it," she pleaded. Yet she knew that each encounter would be painful. She would avoid them, she acknowledged silently. "You'll always be very special to me, Craig. But Lynne and Debbie are my life."

Twenty

F ran returned from Paris with a determination to fill every waking
moment with demanding activity. Her mother was baffled and
upset that she had cut Craig out of her life.

"Frannie, why?" she asked repeatedly. "He's such a fine man."

"It wouldn't work." Each time Fran gave the same response. "Craig
needs more from me than I can give. It wouldn't have been fair to him to
try when I know my priorities. My life revolves around Lynne and Debbie
and the business. I couldn't be the wife he needs."

At times Fran was assaulted by doubts. Had she made a dreadful
mistake in breaking off with Craig? With him she'd felt reborn, given a
miraculous second chance at life. With Craig she felt young and adventurous. She'd learned to laugh again.

Each time she forced herself to face reality. She wasn't prepared to
dismantle the safe, secure life she'd built for herself and the girls—and
her mother. No matter how strong her feelings were for Craig, she knew
Lynne and Debbie's needs would always take precedence. And Craig
yearned for a family of his own. Even if she could have another child, she
thought, her basket was full. There was no room in her life for that.

On schedule she opened the new Atlanta shop—with much fanfare.
At the Atlanta opening she wore the "Paris original" evening gown—
being copied for her three shops. It was an off-the-shoulder gray satin
gown with a Japanese *obi* sash that tied just below the bosom, with one
end tossed over a shoulder as though part of a stole. She carried a pearl-
handled cane that some thought was part of the costume.

The Atlanta shop proved an exhilarating success. The lavish promotion of the Paris copy brought in heavy traffic—resulting in commendable sales figures. Perhaps she should make this a yearly event, she

considered. Yet the prospect of going to Paris each year without Craig elicited painful images. But life was made up of compromises, she reminded herself. She had made the right choice.

It continued to disturb Fran that she couldn't become involved in the local group dedicated to integrating the local school system. She ached to be part of bringing about the necessary changes, as decreed by the Supreme Court but running into much opposition. While she had been in Paris, Fran learned, the state's Board of Education had voted to revoke the license of any teacher who supported school integration. It was a subject not to be discussed with her mother or with customers at the shops. Only with Craig could she have talked about this.

Fran made a point of avoiding as much as possible those social events where she suspected Craig would be present. Total avoidance was impossible, of course, in a town as small as Bellevue. When they did meet, she pretended not to see the questions in his eyes. The reproaches. But they were outwardly cordial, revealing none of their earlier closeness. Each time Fran was haunted by doubts—remembering the cherished times they'd spent together. But that wasn't meant to be.

In the spring of the new year Fran was caught up with Lynne in the selection of a college for the coming fall. It was Lynne's choice to make, she told herself while she dreaded the possibility of Lynne's attending a school far from Bellevue. She greeted with relief Lynne's decision to attend the University of Georgia in Athens—close enough to come home for frequent weekends. And she reveled in Lynne's decision to go on to law school after college. How proud Bernie would be to have his daughter follow in his footsteps!

While Lynne talked incessantly about the college year ahead, Debbie was ecstatic about soon becoming a high school senior. She would follow Lynne to the University of Georgia—as a journalism major. This choice of career, too, was a delight to Fran. Debbie would accomplish all the things *she* had yearned to do. Debbie would become a crusading journalist, intent on saving the world. Their children, she thought with joy, would fulfill her dreams and Bernie's.

Like Atlanta, Bellevue was exploding in population. The usual southern accents were now mixed with those of every part of the nation. Fran knew from gossip that Craig had become Bellevue's most popular architect. Late in the summer her mother reported—with an undercurrent of reproach—that he was seeing a new young teacher at the elementary school. A New Yorker, like himself.

"She's barely out of her twenties," Ida reported disdainfully, on the eve of Lynne's high school graduation. "And Craig must be pushing fifty."

"He's forty-one," Fran corrected, fighting off a sense of loss. But this was *right*. Craig deserved a life for himself—a family of his own. "I hope it works out for him."

In September Fran saw Lynne off for college. In another year Debbie would join her, she thought in a surge of loneliness. There would be just her mother and herself in the house. Thank God, she thought, her mother had her close circle of friends. And *she* had the shops. Perhaps, she considered, it was time to think of a suburban Atlanta shop. There was talk of a fifteen-million-dollar shopping center—to be built on a seventy-acre tract at Peachtree and Lenox Road. She must follow the developments on that. She would never be lonely, she promised herself defiantly. She would be far too busy.

In November Eisenhower was reelected by a landslide. For the first time in twenty-five years Republicans won the most Negro votes.

"I can't believe it," Ida said plaintively as she sat before the TV set with her daughter and granddaughters, "that southern cities are voting Republican. They're against everything the South stands for."

"You're talking about the Old South," Fran told her. "We're living in the New South now."

"I read that this is the first time since McKinley was reelected in 1900," Fran gloomily remarked at dinner the following night, "that a Republican president has won a second term."

"But the Democrats control both houses of Congress," Debbie pointed out. "I'm doing an article about it for the school newspaper."

"It's a strange world we live in," Ida said with a martyred smile, "when a sixteen-year-old turns down a 'sweet-sixteen' birthday party to go with some political group for a weekend in Washington. And I think it's awful, Debbie," she pursued, "that you dropped out of your ballet class after all these years."

"I don't have time for ballet. Not with being editor-in-chief of the newspaper and working with my political group." Debbie avoided discussion of her "political group"—for which Fran was grateful.

Georgians were dismayed by the Supreme Court ruling just a few days ago that segregation in railroad depots, bus stations, airports, and other places involving interstate travel was illegal. Already the word charging about Bellevue was that the "Colored" signs in waiting rooms would come down. Debbie was euphoric that Bellevue understood this ruling could not be fought.

At a Hanukkah party at the synagogue in December Fran learned that Craig and Joyce Miller would be married on New Year's day at her parents' home in Westchester County, New York. Fran had an odd feeling of relief. It was over. She could no longer ask herself if she'd made a mistake in breaking off with Craig.

The house reverberated with excitement when Lynne came home from Athens for the Christmas break. Debbie plied her with endless questions. The two girls' friends were in and out of the house in noisy high spirits. Ida admitted it was a relief when the school "break" was over, and both Lynne and Debbie were back in school.

"I'm getting too old for all this partying," Ida said frankly. "All the record-playing—and such crazy music! The television going all the time! At seventy I appreciate a little quiet." But Fran knew her mother wove romantic fantasies about the girls going off to college and "meeting the right man." She herself was not concerned about their marrying early. First let them be set in careers. Let them be self-sufficient.

She was forty—with forty-one breathing down her neck. What had she accomplished in her life except for running the shops? she asked herself. And then she felt a flood of tenderness. She'd raised her two daughters—wasn't that some accomplishment? Yet she remembered herself at twenty-one—when she'd met Bernie. She'd thought that together they could change the world.

She contributed to a flood of charities; she gave money anonymously to the group fighting to integrate the Bellevue school system. Her mother, she remembered, was upset that Debbie had joined a small group of teenagers working with the group.

"People outside the South don't understand our problems," Ida wailed at regular intervals. "We're not bigots. Most of us hate the Ku Klux Klan. But the government is just pushing us too fast."

Time seemed to be rushing past with the speed of a crack subway train, Fran thought. Right after the first of the year—when Lynne had returned to college—Debbie began excited preparations for her own exodus the following year. Fran was plotting to join the roster of shopowners at the Lenox Square shopping center when it would at last be ready to receive the public.

Late in May Fran attended Debbie's high school graduation—the auditorium hot and humid, drenched with the scent of the bouquets of summer flowers the girl graduates carried in their arms. Debbie looked so beautiful, she thought tenderly, exuded the intense optimism that she, too, had felt at high school graduation.

In September she saw both girls off to college. Already she was conscious of an aching loneliness. Ida loved the new quiet but lamented the absence of her two granddaughters—though Fran and she knew they would be home for frequent weekends. Business was booming. Fran planned to open another two stores in the months ahead. She'd be too busy to be lonely, she promised herself.

She was troubled by the increasing violence in the civil rights arena. At the end of last month South Carolina Senator Strom Thurmand had set a new filibuster record—twenty-four hours and twenty-seven minutes of talking against civil rights. On September 24th President Eisenhower sent one thousand Army paratroopers to Central High School in Little Rock, Arkansas, so that nine Negro students could enter the heretofore all-white school. Fran chafed under the self-imposed restraints that kept her from speaking her mind. But she couldn't afford to antagonize her customers.

Just before Thanksgiving Fran learned from her mother that Craig's wife was pregnant. Despite the difference in age, she gathered, the marriage was working out. Some of the guilt she'd harbored about severing her relationship with Craig evaporated. Still, when they met at a local charity affair, she sensed that—like herself—he would always carry the memory of their times together in sweet recall. In April Craig's wife gave birth to a son—Joshua Paul Hendricks. *She* might have given Craig a child if she'd married him, she thought wistfully.

In the summer of 1958—with her chain of shops growing—Fran went again to Paris. This time Lynne and Debbie accompanied her—both girls enthralled by the magic of Paris. With stern discipline Fran chased away the ghosts of two years earlier. That was a poignantly beautiful memory, to be brought out at intervals and enjoyed in retrospect.

Yet at unwary moments—walking with Lynne and Debbie on the Place Vendôme while they gazed in awe at the Ritz, lunching with them at a bistro in Les Halles, strolling with them in the Tuileries gardens— she felt Craig's presence beside her. But she had recognized the path her life must take. She had loved—and been loved in turn—by two special men. That was enough for one lifetime.

In the summer of 1959 Fran took Lynne and Debbie with her to New York. Lynne would enter her senior year at the University of Georgia in September, but was ambivalent about where to go to law school. Her grades were excellent; however, she was worried that being female would be a strike against her at many law schools.

On one humid afternoon Fran took Lynne and Debbie to see the sprawling Columbia campus. She remembered Bernie's pride—his joy—at being accepted here. And she felt again the anguish that arrived simultaneously with his graduation from law school.

"Do you suppose I could get accepted at Columbia Law?" Lynne's face was luminous. "Wouldn't Daddy be pleased if I could go on to his law school?"

Tears flooded Fran's eyes. "He'd be thrilled."

"But it's so far away," Debbie protested. "You could never come home for weekends."

"And so expensive," Lynne conceded.

"Darling, if you want to go to Columbia, we can afford it," Fran told her.

She made a point of not stressing the family's very healthy financial situation, she acknowledged to herself. They remained in the old house, drove unpretentious cars. She was extravagant on wardrobe for the four women in the household because she considered this not only a pleasure but good business. On business travel she made a point of staying in the finest hotels, dining in the best restaurants. Her mother understood and quietly enjoyed their growing affluence. But Fran vowed to build her chain of shops into lifetime security for her daughters. She saw this as her obligation.

When Lynne applied for admission to Columbia Law School—and was accepted—Fran felt a sense of personal accomplishment. This was *her* small contribution to the world—to have brought a daughter to this point. Lynne talked avidly about the amount of *pro bono* work she hoped to do, about how she meant to become involved in politics. *To do good.* As Bernie had vowed to do, Fran remembered with bittersweet nostalgia.

In July Fran went with Lynne to New York—to search for a small apartment near the Columbia campus in addition to her usual buying jaunt. Both were shocked at the difficulty in finding a vacant Manhattan apartment, appalled by the soaring rents.

"Think what I'll save in hotel bills," Fran said when they considered an apartment that Lynne liked but which was far more expensive than they had expected. "I can stay here on buying trips. You're sure you like it, Lynne?"

"I love it," Lynne said rapturously. "That gorgeous view of the river! Can you imagine the sunsets?"

Fran was delighted that Lynne was going to Columbia Law, that she had a small but charming furnished apartment. Yet, on the rainy August morning when she drove Lynne to the airport for her flight to New York, she was conscious of a sense of foreboding.

She wasn't losing her daughter, she derided herself. Lynne was going to law school in New York, but her law practice would be in Bellevue. Hadn't she talked endlessly about how—once she had her law degree— she would become involved in local politics, fight for what was important for the town?

But Bernie had come into town all those years ago—and she had fled joyously with him to New York.

Twenty-One

L ynne reveled in the independence of having her own apartment, in the cornucopia of entertainment provided by Manhattan. The theater, ballet, fabulous museums, exciting restaurants, fascinating ethnic enclaves. But she was always practical; she quickly understood that law school studies allowed little time for diversion. By the end of the second week of classes she was remembering wistfully that there would be no weekends home until the long Thanksgiving weekend.

Early in the third week of classes she acquired a friend among the few women in the law school. Charlotte Delaney was a tall, pretty redhead with green eyes and strong opinions. She'd graduated from Queens College and lived with her family in Greenwich Village.

"Living at home I can get by with just a Saturday job," she told Lynne over hamburgers at the West End Bar, across from the Columbia campus. "My folks are springing for my tuition—which is a real shocker after Queens College," she said humorously. "A lot of parents say 'We paid for your BA—*you* handle the graduate school.' "

"Wouldn't you think that by now there'd be more women in law classes?" Lynne felt a sudden self-consciousness. She'd always taken it for granted that Mom would provide funds for graduate studies. "Even in 1960 too many women think law is a man's job."

"If you're from out of the city," Charlotte reminded, "you'll have to register to vote. Our first presidential election," she said with satisfaction.

"I know. It's kind of exciting. I can't understand how my grandmother never bothers to go out and vote." Lynne sighed. "After all the battles of the suffragettes so we can vote."

"My mother never votes, either." For a moment Charlotte was grim. "She always insists she will—but she doesn't."

"Are you interested in politics?" Lynne was curious.

"Honey, why else am I in law school?" Charlotte's smile indicated a zest for living that matched Lynne's own. "Okay. That and the money," she acknowledged. "And once John F. Kennedy is in the White House, we'll—"

"If he gets in," Lynne interrupted. Like her mother, she was disappointed that Adlai Stevenson had not won the Democratic nomination. Some of the talk about the Kennedy steamroller at the Democratic convention still disturbed her.

"He'll get in. All that Kennedy money behind him!" Charlotte whistled in candid respect. She glanced at her watch. "What are you doing tonight?"

"Studying." Lynne lifted an eyebrow in reproach.

"On a Friday night? Shame on you. Let's grab a cheap dinner down in the Village and make the Eighth Street scene. Maybe go over to one of the coffee shops in the East Village." Charlotte giggled. "I know this sharp colored guy from Harlem who got himself some African duds, rented a hole in the wall, and runs this coffeehouse with poetry readings and readings from new plays on weekend nights. Got himself a new name, too."

"Okay." Lynne capitulated. She was eager for companionship. There had been furtive pitches from a couple of male students, but she had not been drawn to either of them. "Sounds great."

They arranged to meet at the 116th Street subway station at seven—after Charlotte's last class.

"We'll eat Italian," Charlotte said. "Italian and Chinese are always cheap. It's Italian in the Village and Chinese everywhere else. After dinner we'll stroll around Washington Square, head up to Eighth Street to the bookshops, then swing east for the New Morocco. That's the coffeehouse."

Lynne was at the subway entrance at seven sharp. She waited in the coolness of the early evening—welcome after a sultry day—for almost fifteen minutes before she spied Charlotte's slender figure rushing toward her.

"I'm sorry to be late," Charlotte apologized. "I always mean to be on time—but somehow I never make it."

"I'll remember." Lynne smiled, her impatience evaporating. "My sister's like that. I make the mental adjustments."

Lynne was pleased that they had missed the subway rush hour—one aspect of New York life that dismayed her. Their train pulled into the station. They found seats and settled down to discuss classes.

"Everybody warned me that the first year at law school is a bitch," Charlotte bubbled, "but this is the pits. Still, money's to be made, and that's my goal."

"Just the money roped you in?" Lynne joshed. She remembered how her father had talked about practicing law—as though it was a special mission in life. She could close her eyes and hear her grandfather talking with such heat about the need for great defense lawyers to save the innocent. He'd been so against capital punishment—*"it's easy to take a life, but only God can give it."* To the day he died, he'd insisted that Leo Frank—convicted of murder in the Georgia courts—had been innocent.

"I have a hankering for the good life," Charlotte conceded after a moment. "If it wasn't for that, I'd be out there chasing down a singing job. But look, how many girls make it to the top as vocalists? For every Peggy Lee or Rosemary Clooney there're thousands who end up clerking in Macy's or slinging hash at a Child's. With a law degree I stand a chance to buy my clothes at Bergdorf's and to drive a late model Cadillac."

They left the subway at the Eighth Street station and pushed their way through the Friday evening crowds toward the small Italian restaurant that Charlotte labeled "tried and trusted." Already most of the candlelit tables were taken. By the time they were seated, they saw latecomers waiting in a growing line. The atmosphere was convivial, the crowd mostly young. When it arrived, the food was good. Lynne was glad Charlotte had suggested their coming down here for dinner.

They left the restaurant and strolled toward Washington Square, crowded with Manhattanites and visitors from other boroughs enjoying the Friday evening crawl. This was the Manhattan that Mom talked about, Lynne thought tenderly. And she herself had vague memories of Washington Square on pleasant weekend afternoons when they'd lived in the city.

Lynne and Charlotte walked up to 8th Street again, browsed in the bookshops, then headed east—their destination the New Morocco. At 8th Street and the Bowery Charlotte stopped dead and called out exuberantly. "Arnie! Arnie, over here!"

Lynne saw a slim, dark-haired man about their own age come toward them with an embracing smile. He wasn't movie-star handsome, but there was something commanding about his appearance. An aura, she analyzed, that said here was somebody special.

"Charlotte! I haven't seen you since graduation. What are you doing these days?"

"Law school," Charlotte told him while they hugged enthusiastically. "What a grind! Oh, this is Lynne Garfield. Arnold Alexander. We were at Queens College together," she told Lynne. "Both of us were in an Off-Broadway choral group down in the Village."

Lynne liked Arnie on sight. It was clear he shared this feeling. He was so charismatic, she thought, grasping at a word acquiring popularity these days. Together they sauntered in mutual high spirits toward the New Morocco—a former Laundromat that had been converted into a gawdy, low-budget illusion of a corner of the casbah. They settled themselves at a tiny table in the overcrowded, dimly lit room and consulted the menu to choose from the exotic list of coffees. After cheerful debate they gave their orders to a Negro waiter with a Bronx accent and in African attire.

"We're hearing excerpts from *Don Juan in Hell*," their waiter told them impressively. "I think it's from a play by a guy named Shaw."

"What's with the singing?" Arnie asked Charlotte when their waiter had pranced away.

"It's history," she told him. "I told you, once out of college I had to get down to serious business."

"I'm working on a new song." Arnie's magnetic blue eyes swept from Charlotte to Lynne—appraising for a moment—then returned to Charlotte. "When I finish it and hang on to enough cash to handle the studio costs, will you do a demo for me?"

"Sure," Charlotte agreed while Lynne listened avidly. "But it has to tie in with my school schedule."

While the other two discussed Arnie's latest effort, Lynne dwelt on the discovery that Arnie was an aspiring songwriter, though he worked for an accounting firm. He had earned a degree in accounting, he'd mentioned earlier—"to take care of eating and rent money"—but his heart was in the music business.

"What about you?" Arnie turned to Lynne with an ingratiating smile. "What's your secret vice?"

"I just want to be a lawyer," she admitted. "No ulterior motives. I know it's rough for a woman, but I figure I'm stubborn enough to beat the odds."

"She's smart, too," Charlotte said. "You don't make it into Columbia Law without some brainpower."

"Brainpower helps in school," Arnie said flatly. "In the outside world you need a lot more."

"I know," Charlotte drawled. "Talent, *chutzpah*, and a shitload of luck."

"You're not from New York," Arnie told Lynne. "I can't place the accent."

"I was born in New York but moved to Georgia when I was ten. The accent is a hybrid," Lynne explained.

"I can pick up tickets for an Off-Broadway play opening tomorrow. I saw part of a dress rehearsal, and it looks good. You two interested?" He gazed from Lynne to Charlotte. "The producer is hungry for warm bodies in the audience."

"I've got a ten-hour shift as a restaurant hostess on Saturdays, from noon to ten P.M.," Charlotte said. "But you're not working, Lynne—"

"No," Lynne conceded expectantly.

"Why don't you and I have dinner, then go on to the playhouse? If you're not busy—" Arnie's eyes were a wistful plea.

"I'm not busy." This wasn't really a date, Lynne reasoned.

"Do you like Chinese?" he asked.

"Love it." He was on a budget, Lynne interpreted.

Her mind hurtled back through the years. Daddy had taken the family out to a Chinese restaurant on special occasions. He'd made a convivial production of eating with chopsticks, which she and Debbie had tried—unsuccessfully—to follow. Daddy would have liked Arnie.

Lynne listened while Arnie and Charlotte exchanged bittersweet stories about the music business. Now she understood what they'd meant when they talked about a "demo"—a recording of a song, with vocalist and background music. Charlotte had indicated that Arnie was a pianist of some skill. He'd accompany her on the "demo."

"I feel so positive about this new song." Arnie's face radiated a mesmerizing excitement. "It's the closest I've come to something that's really commercial. Of course, try selling it to a publisher. I spend my lunch hours in the Brill building—but so far, no luck." The Brill building, Lynne gathered, was the home of many music publishers.

"It's like you said all through school," Charlotte recalled. "Without luck on your side, forget it."

They ordered another round of coffee—at exorbitant prices—because all three were loathe to puncture the spell of the moment. They listened to four would-be actors read a scene from *Don Juan in Hell*. They applauded politely, eschewing the noisy—unwarranted—applause that came from other tables.

"Shaw would turn over in his grave," Charlotte whispered. "But at least they're trying."

One of the actors showed genuine promise, Lynne thought. The others were awful. Without knowing, she was convinced that Arnie had talent as a songwriter. And he had drive. Mom would respect that, she thought, and felt her face grow hot. She wasn't dating Arnie—they were just going to an Off-Broadway playhouse because he happened to have passes.

Fran waited impatiently at the busy Atlanta airport for Lynne's flight to arrive. Lynne had never been away from home so long. She'd written that she loved her classes—though she admitted she'd never worked so hard. But Lynne wasn't happy unless she earned top grades, Fran thought tenderly.

Lynne enjoyed being in New York, she gathered. How lovely that she'd found friends right away. In her letters—and their regular Sunday night phone calls—she talked about Charlotte, another first-year law student, and about a young man named Arnie. It seemed the three of them traveled around together. Despite the heavy school schedule, Lynne was seeing some theater—usually Off-Broadway, Fran noted.

Then Lynne's flight arrived. Fran was caught up in the joy of seeing her, relaying messages from friends who knew she was coming home for the Thanksgiving weekend. Lynne would be dashing around like mad, she thought wistfully—but they'd see a lot of her.

"Is Debbie home yet?" Lynne asked, depositing her suitcase in the back of her mother's new Chrysler.

"She'll be there by the time we get to the house. Is the apartment all right? Is there anything you need to make it more comfortable?"

"It's great, Mom. I gave a small dinner party last night—to celebrate the holidays. I'm even learning to cook. Not that I'll ever be competition for Lily," she confided with a chuckle.

Fran relished Lynne's obvious pleasure at being home. "What did you make for your dinner party?" she asked.

"We had three cooks for eight people," Lynne confessed. "I made the roast. How wrong could I go on that? And Charlotte baked a chocolate bourbon pecan pie. Wow, it was fabulous! She said it was Ernest Hemingway's favorite pie. And Arnie—" She giggled reminiscently. "Arnie brought a big salad and threw Idahos into the oven. He even brought a chef's hat to wear in the kitchen."

"You've mentioned Arnie several times," Fran said, deliberately casual. "Is he a law student, too?"

"No, he went to Queens College with Charlotte. He's an accountant." She hesitated. "But he really wants to be a songwriter. You know, do the music and lyrics for a Broadway musical someday. Some of his songs are beautiful."

From the faint undercurrent in Lynne's voice, Fran suspected that Arnie was special to her. Why did she feel so unnerved about this? Because Lynne was interested in a young man *she* didn't even know?

"Is Debbie still carrying on because she couldn't vote in the elections?" Lynne asked.

"You know how emotional Debbie gets because she can't vote yet. And of course, she's been upset—as I have—about Dr. Martin Luther King Jr. and those fifty students from Atlanta University who were arrested for the sit-in at Rich's lunch counter."

"The New York papers have been full of it." Lynne was serious now.

"But it's all being worked out," Fran said with a show of optimism. Let it be true, she entreated. "The students are all back in school, and it appears that on a designated date the stores will desegregate their lunch counters and restaurants."

They arrived at the house moments after Debbie. Lily had stayed late and was holding dinner for them.

"Y'all set yourselves down at the table," Lily commanded after a joyous round of greetings. "That pot roast is just aching to be served."

"What are you doing here so late, Lily?" Lynne reached to hug her.

"I wasn't gonna leave without seeing you," Lily scolded. "I won't be here tomorrow. I think maybe New York agrees with you. Both my babies are looking so pretty." She gazed from Lynne to Debbie. "Now y'all go to the table and let me get dinner served."

As always, Thanksgiving dinner was scheduled for early afternoon. Last night and this morning the phone had rung incessantly, Lynne thought as she dawdled over breakfast with Debbie. Her mother and grandmother were fussing with turkey stuffing in the kitchen.

"I don't know why Lily couldn't have come in for three or four hours,"

Ida fretted. "Just long enough to put the turkey in the oven and get the pumpkin pie ready."

"Mother, she wants to be with her family today," Fran said calmly. "We can handle Thanksgiving dinner between us."

The phone rang, shrill in the morning quiet.

"One of you girls answer it," Ida called. "It's sure to be for one of you."

"I'll get it." Lynne leapt to her feet and hurried toward the living room.

"What's wrong with the kitchen extension?" her grandmother demanded. "Or are you expecting a call from some boy up in New York?"

"Grandma, stop trying to marry us off," Debbie scolded. "Anyhow, she's got almost three years of law school ahead of her."

"I don't know what's the matter with girls today," Ida grumbled. "I hear these stories at my bridge club—about married daughters and daughters-in-law. It's not enough anymore to have a husband and a beautiful house and a couple of kids. They're bored," she drawled contemptuously.

Lynne listened to the conversation in the kitchen while one of her friends from the fifth grade on through college recited a list of complaints about her not keeping in touch.

"Anita, I know it's awful of me not to write," she finally interrupted, "but I'm so busy with school."

"I want you to be one of my bridesmaids at the wedding," Anita bubbled. "You'll be home by then."

"I won't be here for the summer," Lynne said, her voice apologetic. "I'm staying up in New York to work in a law office." Arnie had persuaded her that this would help her career-wise. *"I can't bear the thought of you being away all summer."* He was sure she'd have no trouble lining up a job. It was hard to believe she had known him less than two months!

"Oh, Lynne, how can you do this to me?" Anita wailed. "I counted on you. First, Marilyn begs off because she's going on a cruise before she starts medical school—now you."

"I'm sorry, Anita. But thanks for asking me." She was impatient to be off the phone, to leave it clear in case Arnie tried to call.

"But you won't stay up there all summer," Anita pounced. "The wedding is in June. Won't you come home between school closing and starting your job?"

"I can't be sure." But she'd have to come home for Debbie's graduation. Debbie would never forgive her if she didn't.

"You're becoming another of those girls who think they'll just die if they don't have a career!" Anita's voice deepened with distaste. "I don't know what's the matter with y'all."

"Will you be at Ronnie's party tomorrow night?" Lynne asked.

"Of course."

"Great, I'll see you there." In relief Lynne put down the phone.

Throughout the morning friends called—for Lynne or Debbie or Ida. Shortly before they sat down to dinner, a box of long-stemmed red roses arrived for Fran.

"Who are they from?" her mother asked avidly while Fran reached for the accompanying card. "Frannie, what have you been keeping from us?"

"Nothing." Fran was firm. "They're from Robin Sanders. He's thanking me for helping him with the fashion show/luncheon he ran for that foundation of his."

"Who's Robin Sanders?" Lynne asked.

"He's a sweet young fellow who moved here from Atlanta a few months ago. He heads a charitable foundation his father set up in Atlanta just before he died two years ago. The Robert and Ethel Sanders Foundation. Lynne, will you help me in the kitchen? It's time to take the turkey out of the oven."

The four women were caught up in the convivial task of transferring turkey, homemade cranberry sauce, yams, and a salad to the dining-room table. The pumpkin pie was to remain in the oven.

"I'll set the timer. For how long, Mom?" Lynne asked.

"Twenty minutes," Fran told her. "Then we'll check."

"The roses are gorgeous." Debbie brought the vase of roses to the table. "Who is this guy?"

"I told you," her mother said. "He's head of a foundation. I helped with one of his fund-raisers."

"What kind of a foundation?" Lynne probed. "Here in Bellevue?"

"The foundation itself is situated in Atlanta," her mother explained. "I understand it provides grants for young people in the arts. I don't actually know much about it. Robin Sanders is the administrator."

"You mean for artists and writers and musicians?" Wouldn't it be wonderful if Arnie could get a grant, Lynne thought in sudden excitement. He got up at five in the morning to write music before going in to work. He was dying to tie up with a librettist to concentrate on an Off-Broadway musical. With a grant he could afford to do that. "Songwriters?" she pinpointed.

"I imagine so," her mother said. "They're part of the arts."

"What does someone have to do to apply?" Lynne pressed.

"I'll ask. You know of someone who might be interested?"

"Arnie," Lynne told her. "If you can get me the application form—or whatever—I'll give it to him."

"I'll call Robin tomorrow. But you know, Lynne." Her mother hesitated a moment. "I can't pull any strings. It's all on merit."

"I know, Mom."

She couldn't wait to get back to New York to talk to Arnie, she thought in towering anticipation. Oh, wouldn't it be wonderful if he could get a grant!

Twenty-Two

At Lynne's urging, Fran called Robin Sanders on Friday morning before leaving for her office, located in what was now regarded as Shop Number One. It was just 8 A.M., but she knew Robin was an early riser.

"I'm sorry, Miz Garfield. He's away for the weekend," his housekeeper told her.

"I'll call him Monday," Fran promised Lynne, and was touched by her disappointment. This Arnie *was* somebody special, she told herself again. Normally, on a holiday Lynne slept till noon. She couldn't have known him long—just since the beginning of the school term at the most. But it was absurd to be anxious, Fran reproached herself. It was natural for Lynne to be interested in young men. That didn't mean she was abandoning career plans.

Lynne sighed. "I just know he'll be so excited about applying."

"He'll apply a few days later. These things probably take months to be decided," Fran warned. "And there must be other grants he can apply for—"

"Not many foundations are interested in the creative arts." Lynne was somber. "But thanks, Mom."

The holiday weekend rushed by with poignant speed. Each time the girls took off for school, she felt an odd sense of loss for a few days. Then she was swept up in work and local socializing—important for business.

On Monday she phoned Robin and explained Lynne's request.

"Give me her address," Robin said. "I'll have my secretary send the application form right out." He hesitated a moment. "I was wondering if you'll be free the first Saturday in December. I have tickets for that theater benefit in Atlanta. Please say you are," he said ingratiatingly before she could reply. "And save me from the predatory little girls who're in pursuit here in town. Not that they find me so charming—but I'm still young enough to be regarded as a 'great catch.'" He was in his late twenties, Fran gathered—and wealthy. And yes, local girls were in pursuit.

"I'd love to go," Fran said and laughed. "I think."

"I'm not putting you down," he said apologetically. "It's just that I like company at these bashes, but not some nubile young girl who has marriage in mind. Nobody believes me when I say I'll never get married. I like living alone."

"I believe you," Fran said gently. He had just confirmed her vague supposition. There was nothing overt about his sexual leanings, she told herself—and whatever, this was none of her concern. "I'll protect you from the thundering herd."

"I loathe this nutty business about pairing off couples at dinner parties. Why is it a calamity if there's an extra woman at the table—or an extra man? When I go to a dinner party, I like to feel that—at least on one side of me—there's a bright intelligent being to whom I can talk. If we team up, we can beat the odds. You're not just beautiful, Fran—you're bright. And you wear such gorgeous clothes."

"I'll suggest you as my escort when I'm invited somewhere," she agreed. "And vice versa." This could be fine for business. Her social circle would widen even further. Robin Sanders was a sought-after guest. And charming.

Her mother was startled when she mentioned she was going to the Atlanta theater benefit with Robin.

"He's so young." Ida was dubious about this.

"This isn't a romance. It's a convenience for both of us. I've been stuck with some horribly dull dinner partners—and so has he. We're very simpatico." Her mother continued to appear dubious. "We both love theater and the ballet. I would love to know more about art, and he's promised to teach me." Robin painted a little, but not well enough to please himself. He wrote poetry, but never considered this a profession. *"If it were not for my job as head of the Sanders Foundation, I'd be a dilettante,"* he'd told her.

"Folks are going to talk," her mother warned. "A forty-four-year-old woman going out with a boy in his twenties. Even if strangers think you're thirty."

"What can they say?" Fran shrugged this aside. "That we're having an affair? We won't be," she assured her mother. That part of her life was over—except for memories. But in the darkness of her bedroom she relived moments of perfect passion. "But if people want to believe it, nei-ther Robin nor I could care less."

With the winter "break" almost upon them, Lynne and Arnie were spending every possible moment together. The anticipation of the coming month-long separation was painful. How had they come to mean so much to each other so fast? Lynne asked herself repeatedly.

Arnie had filled out the application forms and sent them to the foundation, along with the samples of his work that had been requested. Why was it taking so long to hear from them? Yet she knew in her heart it wasn't long at all.

On the evening before flying home, Lynne was to have dinner with Arnie at their favorite Italian restaurant in the Village. She knew he was hoping she'd come to his apartment after dinner. He lived in a tiny basement studio on Gay Street. Up till now she'd avoided going there alone with him. She wouldn't tonight, either, she told herself with fresh determination.

She remembered the late-night exchange of confidences with Debbie her last night home during the Thanksgiving weekend. She'd told Debbie about Arnie, with instructions not to elaborate to their mother or grandmother. Not just yet. She remembered especially what Debbie had said about sleeping with a man before marriage:

"I haven't really met anybody that made me all that excited. Anyhow, I don't think I'd want to do it. I know—a lot of girls do. Nice girls. Maybe if I was wild about a guy. But I don't know."

Arnie thought she was being silly to draw lines—though at small parties in one apartment or another, with the lights low, they'd come close. What Arnie called "everything but." They could wait, she told herself defensively.

She'd pack before she left to meet Arnie, she decided. That would make it easy in the morning—she had an early flight. She packed swiftly with an eye on the clock and debated about what to wear. It was awfully cold out, she remembered—it was supposed to snow later.

She settled on warm gray slacks and a brilliant red cashmere turtleneck, then reached into the closet for her gray leather coat. Mom kept sending her such smart clothes. Charlotte—with what she called Paris tastes and S. Klein's pocketbook—said Yves Saint Laurent had decreed turtlenecks and leather coats for this winter. Leave it to Mom to know.

She'd never been conscious of what she wore until she met Arnie,

Lynne mused as she left her apartment. She yearned to look her best for him—because she knew how attractive he was to other girls. Charlotte said it had been like that all through college, and admitted she'd had a brief fling with Arnie. But Charlotte said, too, that what *she* and Arnie shared was different. *"You two are something!"*

She waited almost twenty minutes in the tiny lobby of the restaurant before Arnie arrived, breathless from rushing.

"I got stuck at the damn office," he apologized. "Why didn't you take a table?"

"They were getting busy. I didn't think it was fair until you arrived." She glowed at the love for her she saw in his eyes. They knew this was forever. They didn't have to put it into words. But they both had roads to travel before they could make commitments.

Once seated, they lingered long over dinner. Lynne ignored the question in Arnie's eyes.

"It's going to be hellish not to see you for almost a month." His hand reached across the table for hers. "I'll probably go out to my folks in Hempstead over the holidays." She knew he wouldn't enjoy that. His parents couldn't understand his wanting to be a songwriter. They kept reminding him of the sacrifices they'd made to support him while he earned his degree in accounting at a school with no tuition fees. "I'll be thinking about you every minute."

"I'll phone you once a week," she promised. "On Sunday nights?"

Arnie nodded in approval. "I'll be waiting by the phone." Now he frowned and shifted in his chair with an air of restlessness. "When the hell will I hear about that grant?"

"Mom says she understands it takes three or four months, at least," Lynne reminded. It was awful to have to wait so long for something so important. "There's a committee and all kinds of red tape."

"I sent them everything they asked for. Right after the first of the year I'll go into a recording studio—a cheap one," he said with a grin. With all the firing going on, he was nervous about his job. He wanted to keep some savings on hand. He'd been the last hired—he'd be the first to go. "Charlotte will do a 'demo' for me. I'll send that down to the committee, too."

"Charlotte loves the new song." Would he be upset if she offered to help with money? No, better not try that, she decided uneasily. She glanced at her watch. "I ought to get home soon." Her smile was apologetic. "I have an early flight tomorrow."

"I'll take you home." Again, a question in his eyes.

"Charlotte's staying at my place while I'm away. She's moving in to-night." Lynne heard his faint sigh. "We'll send her out for Danish when we get there," she cajoled. Charlotte would understand.

On the night before her return to New York, Lynne sat with her mother in the living room. Her grandmother was playing bridge at a friend's house. Debbie was back at school. It was nice being alone with Mom this way, she thought. A cozy blaze in the fireplace, coffee cups within reach.

The TV was silent now that they'd heard the news. The world seemed in such tumult, she thought—a civil war raged in Laos, there was fighting in the Congo, Russia made ugly threats, and now hostility in Cuba. And Mom was troubled by the rising unemployment here at home.

"More coffee?" her mother asked, already reaching for her cane.

"Let me get it, Mom." Lynne rose to her feet.

"I wish I could have spent more time with you while you were here." Her mother's eyes were wistful. "But everything seemed to be happening this month. I hadn't expected to be dashing off to the Alabama shops so much."

"Mom, I know you have business commitments." Lynne smiled tenderly, reached for cups and saucers, and hurried off to the kitchen.

It forever amazed her that Mom was such a dynamo despite her handicap. But Mom had always been there for Debbie and her, she acknowledged conscientiously. When they were sick—when they clamored for her to be at school events. Yet she sensed that her mother was forever worried that she was cheating them by being a working mother. *Not at all.* They were proud of Mom.

Lynne returned to the living room with refilled coffee cups, deposited one on the end table beside her mother's chair and took the other to the coffee table before the sofa.

"You're sure you want to work this summer?" her mother asked. "You'll be exhausted by the end of the school year."

"I'll be home in the spring and probably for a couple of weeks before I start on the job. I'll make that playtime." She hesitated. "Mom, why does it take so long for grants to go through?"

"I told you, Lynne." Gentle reproof in her mother's voice. "They have certain procedures to follow. And remember, they received hundreds of applications for each grant."

"I know," Lynne said wryly. "It's just that Arnie's so anxious."

"I gather Arnie's someone special." Her mother's smile was casual, but Lynne knew she was eager to hear more.

"We see a lot of each other." Why couldn't she come out and tell Mom she was in love with him?

"What's his last name?"

"Arnold Alexander." Lynne sighed indulgently, interpreting her mother's uneasy frown. "Mom, he's Jewish. His father had their name changed from Berlfein when Arnie was a baby."

"Has he ever been in this part of the country?"

"No," Lynne said, her heart all at once pounding. Mom got the message. "I don't think so."

"When you come home for the spring break, why don't you bring him along with you? It's so beautiful down here that time of year."

"I don't know if he can get away," she hedged, but the prospect was appealing. "I'll ask him." Could he take his vacation week then? Would he want to?

She felt oddly better now that Mom understood there was a special man in her life. Mom understood, too, that they'd made no commitments and respected this. But her mind bluntly told her that *she* had made a commitment. Would Arnie be afraid to come down here with her? Would he look on that as a commitment?

On a bitterly cold January 20th John F. Kennedy was sworn in as President of the United States. Fran drove home from her office in time to watch the inaugural ceremonies. A new generation was in power, she thought sentimentally. Her generation. John Kennedy was a young man among ageing giants—Nehru was 71, Khrushchev 66, de Gaulle 70, Adenauer 84.

Unemployment was on the rise—up to almost 8 percent, Fran recalled. People said business would improve with Kennedy in office. As a Democrat he'd be inclined toward government spending, which many economists said would stimulate the economy. In truth, she was not affected by the downturn in the economy. Her customers, she thought wryly, were the last to feel the pinch.

As always, in the weeks ahead, Fran filled every waking moment with activity. She looked forward to Debbie's graduation from college this year. She and Debbie would fly to London and Paris in late July— business for her, a well-earned vacation for Debbie before she began to look for a job. Enthusiastic as ever about becoming a journalist, now Debbie was anxious about her qualifications, her lack of experience.

"Mom, I haven't done anything," she wailed over a Sunday breakfast with her mother and grandmother during a March weekend at home. "Just the school newspaper and that column they let me do last summer at the newpaper in town—and now that's gone."

"Debbie, stop fretting," her grandmother scolded. "You can always go into one of our shops."

"I don't want to go into one of the shops." Debbie stared at her grandmother in shock.

"Calm down, Debbie," Fran ordered. "You'll find a job on a newspaper in town or in Atlanta." Her mind hurtled back through the years, to her own futile efforts to land a job on the *Bellevue Enquirer*. But that was in the midst of the Depression.

"And I'll brag about my granddaughter, the newspaper reporter." Ida beamed as she envisioned this. "And in another two years, my granddaughter the lawyer."

"I can't figure out why Lynne didn't come home this week, the way she'd planned." Debbie squinted in thought. "What did she say exactly?"

"She figured she needed the time to study," Fran said. Was it because Arnie couldn't—or wouldn't—come down with her? She wished with an unexpected passion that she could read into Lynne's thoughts.

"Maybe she's got a boyfriend hidden away up there that she isn't talking about," Ida said good-humoredly, but Fran knew her mother was unaware of Arnie's existence. Ida turned to Debbie. "How long do I have to wait for you two to make me a great-gran?"

Lynne left the law library at a few minutes past five and hurried back to her apartment. The campus—the surrounding area—was quiet this week when Columbia students were out of their classes. The day was unseasonably warm, rife with the promise of spring.

Lynne paused at a brownstone to gaze at the first crocus, on display in a patch of earth behind a wrought-iron fence. For a moment she felt a sudden yearning to be back to Bellevue—where spring was already bursting into being. She hadn't even suggested to Arnie that he take a week off from work to go to Bellevue with her. She realized now that this was the heaviest season of the year for accounting firms.

He'd promised he'd leave the office promptly at six today. He'd been working fourteen-hour days all week, ate lunch at his desk—which deprived him of the chance to pop into a music publishing or record company office, as was his lunchtime habit. He'd warned her he'd have to go in to work tomorrow, but then he'd been working Saturdays for the last three weeks, she remembered grimly.

At the apartment she put away her notes, changed into warmer slacks because the temperature was supposed to drop, and reached into her bedroom closet for her camel hair polo coat. Arnie liked her in slacks and turtlenecks, and beige and cinnamon was his favorite color combination for her.

She hurried from the apartment and over to Broadway to the subway station. She missed not going home, she thought as she waited for her train—but she'd got a lot of work done this week. She'd been studying reports on prisoners who'd had their sentences overturned because of bad representation in court. It was ever exciting to think that she might one day go into court and clear the wrongly imprisoned. As Dad had yearned to do.

Out of the subway she walked swiftly because already a sharp chill had driven away the balmy warmth of the afternoon. She wouldn't wait outside for Arnie today, she thought, drawing the collar of her coat about her throat. Arnie wasn't at the entrance. She went inside and was seated at the corner table they always tried to snag for themselves. It was early—only a sprinkling of prospective diners had arrived thus far.

She slid out of her coat, draped it across the back of her chair, and settled in the cozy warmth of the restaurant with a sigh of pleasure. This was the first night she'd be seeing Arnie since Tuesday, she realized. They talked on the phone, but that wasn't like seeing him.

A smile lit her face as she saw him stride into the room—not tall and conventionally handsome but with a commanding presence that brought admiring glances from women. She was aware of a sense of pride that he was hers. They didn't talk about marriage in so many words—but they knew it was in the cards for them, she thought with a surge of sentiment.

"Sorry to be late, baby." He leaned forward to kiss her, then shed his rumpled suede jacket and sat across from her. She frowned when she saw the faint tic in his right eyelid. That meant he was upset about something. "I made a pit stop at the apartment." His voice was all at once bitter, matching his eyes. "To pick up the mail."

"Arnie, what's wrong?" Her heart began to pound.

"The bastards turned me down," he said. "The grant," he explained because for a moment she stared blankly at him. "A polite, short note. They admire my work, but it doesn't quite fit their requirements. Meaning, they're looking for another Beethoven or Shubert. I'm just a would-be commercial songwriter."

"Arnie, you knew that was a long shot." Lynne struggled to appear casual.

"It would have made life so much easier. I'm so damn sick of this job. I don't have time to write." He slammed a fist on the table in frustration. Lynne reached in alarm to steady the candle in its small red-glass bowl.

"You'll have time after April Fifteenth," she comforted. Every accountant was harried this time of year, she realized now.

"Maybe I ought to quit, look for a job at one of the 'temps.' Then I could salvage some—" He paused as their waiter approached and consulted the menu with a sigh that evoked pain in Lynne. Arnie had so much talent, she mourned. Why had the foundation turned him down?

They ordered their dinner. As usual Lynne avoided the extravagant items, and was surprised when Arnie told the waiter to bring them a bottle of red wine. On festive occasions they would order a glass for each—never a bottle. Arnie was conscientious about keeping "a small nest egg" in the event he was fired. This was his small rebellion at being denied the grant.

"Have you talked to that librettist you thought was so good?" Lynne asked. Arnie was dying to do the music and lyrics for an Off-Broadway musical.

"Ron finally caught up with me late last night. He's giving up on the Off-Broadway scene. He says it's getting to cost a bundle to do a musical even downtown. The one possible backer he knew got cold feet. Ron's heading for California next week. So the idea of our collaborating on a musical is right down the drain." He ran one hand through his hair in the impatient gesture that telegraphed his depression. "Maybe he's got the right idea. Maybe I should head out there, too."

"Arnie, no," she protested. How would she survive with him out there? "The record business is here. That's what you always tell me." The big deal was to land a hit record. That or a Broadway—or even Off-Broadway—musical.

"You could transfer to a school out there," he said tentatively.

"No." Not that there weren't good law schools in California, she conceded—but she was not going out to California to live with Arnie.

"Then I don't go out." His smile was wry.

Their waiter arrived with their dinner. Arnie made a production of pouring the wine.

"One of these days," he vowed, "we'll be drinking champagne. Dom

Pérignon," he predicted. "I'll have a musical running at the Winter Garden, and you'll be high up in the Attorney General's office."

"And we'll live in a penthouse on Central Park South with a gorgeous view of the park," she said, and suddenly stopped dead.

"We'll be married at the Hampshire House," he continued the convivial mood, and her heart pounded in anticipation. He meant for them to be married. Not just living together. "Unless your family insists we get married down in Bellevue."

"They probably will." Lynne's face was luminous.

"There'll be a wait," he reminded. "You with your law school to finish and me still waiting for that first break."

"In five years you'll have a record on the Top Forty stations." She felt giddy with the knowledge that Arnie had brought up the subject of marriage. *It was going to happen.* They'd just have to wait a while. "When we walk into Lindy's, everybody will recognize you."

Arnie poured a refill for them. He said it wasn't very good wine, Lynne thought tenderly—but to them at this moment it could have been Dom Pérignon.

"I've got this mad urge to write something different from what I've been doing," he confided, mellowing as he drank in gulps. "It can be incorporated into musicals—" To Lynne it seemed Arnie was trying to convince himself. "But I'm becoming fascinated by folk music. You know, Lynne—music that tells a story."

"You mean, like the Kingston Trio and Peter, Paul and Mary, and Joan Baez?"

"Yeah. I know it's not typical Broadway music, but it reached out to me." Lynne saw the messianic glow in his eyes. "I think it's going to be big."

"It's big already with the college crowds," Lynne pointed out. "And look how popular Mitch Miller's folk album has become."

"It's the way to go, Lynne." His hand reached across the table for hers. "It's going to be important."

When their coffee arrived, Lynne noted the line of patrons waiting to be seated.

"I think we'd better go," she said softly, interrupting Arnie's intense discussion of the music he meant to write. "So many people are waiting for a table."

"Let's pick up hamantaschen at that bakery around the corner and go back to my place—" His eyes were an eloquent plea. "It's getting damned cold out. That's the trouble with spring—you never know what to expect. Baby, why not?" Under the table, one foot reached to caress her leg. "We know we're going to spend the rest of our lives together. Why do we have to wait for a license to say it's legal?"

"Let's stop at the bakery and then go home," Lynne whispered, her smile dazzling. "Wherever you are, Arnie, is home."

They walked swiftly, hand in hand, through the now unspringlike night. They paused to take their places at the counter of the bakery, spilling over with tantalizing aromas, and ordered more hamantaschen than they could possibly consume this evening. It was a show of their love and their happiness, Lynne thought whimsically as she accepted the box from the clerk—to have ordered so bountifully.

At the door to Arnie's tiny apartment, Lynne clung to his arm as he reached for his key. This was the first time she'd been to Arnie's apartment when there was no one else here except themselves. Charlotte said she was mentally living in another era. Girls their age weren't in a rush to get married these days—but that didn't mean they didn't need to make love. She remembered Charlotte's blunt remarks just a few nights ago—when they'd taken time out from shared studying to have coffee:

"Look, a lot of girls our age hop in and out of bed with their boyfriends—and they don't stop with just one guy." Charlotte had paused to giggle. *"Just one guy at a time,"* she'd emphasized, *"unless you've got some weird ideas."*

Arnie unlocked the door and pulled her inside. With one foot he kicked the door shut, reached—in the darkness of the small studio—to draw her close.

"Arnie, let me put down the cake," she protested gently, but already she was aroused.

She deposited the hamantaschen on an end table and untied the belt of her polo coat. Arnie was quick to help her remove it—his face close to hers.

"I've waited so long for this," he murmured, his hands moving beneath her sweater, roaming about her back until he found her bra hook and released it.

After a momentary shock at the coldness of his hands, she murmured soft approval as they caressed her breasts. Her own hands closed about his shoulders. This was as far as they had ever gone before—along with passionate kisses. Oh, she'd been so silly, she told herself defiantly.

She laughed softly while he swore at the difficulty of pulling her turtleneck over her head.

"Wait here," he whispered when the turtleneck had been tossed aside into the darkness. "Don't move."

While Arnie stripped in the shadows, she did the same. Nothing would be between them tonight, she told herself with heady excitement—eager to touch him and to be touched. No limitations tonight. What Arnie humorously called "the whole *megillah*."

Nobody but themselves knew—but this was their wedding night. . . .

Twenty-Three

F ran was delighted that Lynne had come home to be with the family for Debbie's graduation, though tomorrow she'd be flying back to New York. She'd acquired a job for the summer in a prestigious law firm. *"It'll be a great experience, Mom!"*

She'd hoped that Lynne would talk about Arnie, the young would-be songwriter who'd applied for a grant from Robin's foundation. How serious was she about Arnie? But perhaps it was all over, she decided. Lynne never mentioned him now. In the spring her conversation had been dotted with references to Arnie and Charlotte. Now she only talked of Charlotte.

"I'm sorry, Fran," Robin had apologized when she'd—ever so casually—asked if Arnie had received a grant. *"The committee didn't feel his talents fitted in with the stipulations my parents had set up. They're very demanding,"* he acknowledged. *"Leaning more to the classical style than popular music."*

Tonight the family was having dinner at a charming new restaurant in town so that Lily could attend a niece's high school graduation.

"Lily's so excited," Fran told the others when the waiter had taken their orders and left the table. "Alice is going to college in September. She's the first one in the family to finish high school—and now she's going off to college."

"Mom, do you think we're really going to see school integration in Atlanta this fall?" Debbie asked. Hopeful but dubious.

"It's about time, isn't it?" Lynne said before Fran could reply.

"I expect we will," Fran said seriously. "It'll be that, or Atlanta will lose its public schools. Nobody wants to see that happen."

"We'll be back from Europe before school opens." Debbie's face was luminous. "If I have a job on a newspaper, maybe I'll be covering the integration of the Atlanta schools."

"It'll just be a few token kids in three or four schools at first," Lynne pointed out. "It won't be real integration overnight."

"Bellevue will be right behind," Debbie predicted. "You know how we follow Atlanta in almost everything."

"Except their traffic problems, their fancy new skyscrapers, and all that hustle." Ida's voice was slightly acerbic. "Sometimes I think Atlanta just forgets it's part of the South."

"Are you excited about going to London and Paris again?" Lynne asked her mother.

"Next to Bellevue, I love London," Fran admitted. "And Paris has all the excitement of New York. And, of course, I can't wait to see the couture shows again."

It would be a great promotion deal to offer another Paris original at the shops in the fall, she thought with anticipation. Yet she knew this trip would be fraught with bittersweet memories of that first trip to London and Paris with Craig. She had been right, she told herself. The girls and the business were her life. Compromise was part of living. You had to make choices. She was happy that Craig had married, had two darling sons.

In the morning Fran drove Lynne to the airport. She made a strong effort to hide her disappointment that Lynne wouldn't be home for the summer. Several times she was on the verge of asking about "your friend Arnie"—yet each time she stopped herself. She mustn't be a nosy mother.

"Debbie and I will see you in New York in late July," she reminded Lynne as they waited for her flight to be ready for boarding. "I'll do my rush shopping before we head for London."

Fran waited until Lynne's flight was airborne, then walked back to the parking area. Lynne had a whole year of law school behind her, she thought with satisfaction. How proud Bernie would be if he knew she was going to be a lawyer.

Arriving at her apartment Lynne was startled to discover Arnie sprawled on the floor before her door.

"You made great time," he said, grinning as he rose to his feet and reached to kiss her.

"I picked up my suitcase and walked right into a taxi," she said, her eyes searching his. Why wasn't he at work?

"I called in sick." He'd read her mind. "I couldn't wait until tonight to see you." He flashed the charismatic smile that mowed down women from twenty to seventy, she thought with proprietary pleasure. "How was the trip?"

"Okay," she told him, relinquishing her suitcase. "But it's so hot in the city."

"Like me," he drawled—nuzzling her, one hand at her curvaceous rump as she found her keys and unlocked the doors.

Inside the apartment Arnie flipped on a switch. Without pausing they walked hand in hand into the bedroom. Not speaking except for their eyes—content to be together. Thank God for air-conditioning, Lynne told herself. One of the great inventions of all time.

"Honey, I thought this week would never end," he whispered in her ear while they swayed together in the darkness.

"Arnie, what's bothering you?" She felt an inner restlessness in him that was beyond the norm. "Besides the usual," she said with a pretense at laughter.

"Later." His mouth reached for hers.

At last they lay supine on the bed, exhausted yet relaxed. Her head on his shoulder, his left leg thrust across hers.

"This has been such an insane week," he told her. "Especially these last two days."

"What's been happening?" Already she felt herself growing tense. He was so unhappy about not getting the grant.

"You know Ron's out in California." Ron Bernstein, the librettist, she interpreted. "He's phoned me five times in the last forty-eight hours. From California. He woke me at two A.M.—you know the time difference out there."

"What did he want?" All at once her heart was pounding.

"He wants me to fly out. Pronto. He latched on to this weird millionaire on the plane. The guy wants to do a musical with a showy part in it for his wife. He figures on trying it out in Los Angeles. You know what a great promoter Ron is. He talked to this character about a book idea we have, and he loved it! Ron told him about me—how well we worked together. Lynne, fly out there with me."

"Arnie, you know I can't do that." She was startled that he would ask it.

"Honey, we'll get married first." He chuckled reproachfully.

"But I have a summer job coming up in a law office. I—"

"They have law offices in California. You'll get a job there." His face glowed. "They have law schools in California. Lynne, this is my big chance!"

"But how can we do this so fast?" she stammered. Oh yes, she wanted to marry Arnie. But she needed time to explain this to Mom.

"Three days. We get our blood tests, our marriage license—and in three days we can be buying our plane tickets to California. I've got enough cash to handle that."

"But what about our parents?" Her mind was in chaos. Mom and Grandma hadn't even met Arnie. How did she make them understand she hadn't lost her mind?

"We'll get married at City Hall and tell them about it afterward. My folks will carry on that we're too young to get married. And they'll have a shit fit because I'm giving up a 'steady job,'" he mimicked contemptuously.

"Maybe we could fly home. To Bellevue, I mean. I have some money, too," she comforted. "My mother will—"

"No time for that," Arnie dismissed this. "We have to strike while the iron is hot! This guy—he's made a fortune in real estate—married some singer half his age, and he's dying to see her on Broadway. Ron says he'll put up a small advance to get us moving—"

"Arnie, my mother and grandmother will be so upset." Why hadn't Arnie gone home with her in the spring? Then Mom would have at least met him. "They've been so good to me—" Her eyes pleaded with him to understand.

"Then I'll have to go alone." He turned away from her—his face set in determination. "I can't turn down the one chance that may ever come my way."

"No," Lynne whispered. How could she let Arnie go off without her? Her mind was assaulted by a devastating image of the beautiful girls that flooded Hollywood every year. She'd lose Arnie. "We'll get married at City Hall, but I'm sure Mom and my grandmother will fly up to be with us."

"Tell them after we're married." Arnie swung back to face her and pulled her into his arms again. "I'm scared of what they'll try to do. You just explain about the rush. This could be the most important moment in our lives. Let's don't screw it up."

Mom would be so hurt, she thought in anguish. And Grandma. Debbie would make a crack about being deprived of being maid of honor. But she'd make it up to them, she vowed. "All right! Let's get this show on the road!" Her smile was dazzling, but inside she was a shambles.

Every waking hour now was filled with last-minute assignments. Later she'd arrange for the transfer to a Los Angeles area law school, she promised herself. Arnie quit his job, amid recriminations at his not giving notice. Charlotte and another classmate decided to take over Lynne's apartment. They'd ship her personal belongings out to California. For now, she explained, they'd stay in Ron's apartment.

"I don't think it'll take long to find a place for ourselves," Lynne told Charlotte.

She was faintly concerned about funds. She couldn't expect Mom to continue her allowance once she was married. Tuition, yes, she decided— Mom would want to take care of that. She withdrew what remained in her bank account. Along with what Arnie had, it should see them through for a while, she consoled herself. The advance Arnie and Ron were to receive from their backer might take a while to come through.

In a sentimental moment she allowed Charlotte to persuade her to buy a new dress for the City Hall wedding. She chose a blue-and-white-checked cotton coatdress with a wide skirt, white pique cuffs at the sleeves, and a scooped neckline.

"It's a copy of Brigitte Bardot's wedding dress," the saleswoman confided, startling Lynne. She'd said nothing about getting married. "Very pretty *and* very sexy."

"Hey, that's a good omen," Charlotte whispered.

Four mornings later—with their luggage packed and waiting at her apartment and plane tickets stashed away in his jacket pocket—Lynne and Arnie were married in the usual brief ceremony at City Hall. Charlotte and a law school friend were their witnesses. They left City Hall in high spirits for a wedding luncheon at Arnie's favorite Village restaurant.

Lynne managed a festive smile, at furtive intervals inspecting her simple wedding band. But her joy at becoming Arnie's wife was tempered by her sharp guilt at the absence of her family at their wedding.

"Look, we've got to break up this bash," Arnie said finally. "Lynne and I have a plane to catch."

And she and Arnie had phone calls to make, Lynne told herself grimly. Back in her apartment Arnie called his mother—at this hour his father was at work. He explained that he'd quit his job and was heading for California. With a grimace he held the receiver away indicating to Lynne that his mother was delivering a tirade. Now he told his mother that he'd just been married, and tried to explain that this wasn't because he was drunk, out of his mind, or stupid. With a grunt of disgust he abandoned the effort to explain.

"I'm sorry you feel that way, Mom," he said in a surge of impatience. "I have to go now. I'll call you from California."

Arnie went out to the kitchen to put up a pot of coffee. He labeled coffee his "great antidepressant." Her heart pounding, Lynne went to the phone. Ever since they'd left City Hall, she'd been trying to frame the words to tell her mother.

Her mother was not in her Bellevue office. Lynne caught up with her at the Buckhead shop. Trembling, her voice unsteady, she babbled her news in a rush.

"I didn't want it to be this way," she apologized. "Later, Arnie and I will come home for a religious ceremony. But right now it's so important for us to get out to California. This could be Arnie's big break. Mom, I'm sorry you didn't have a chance to meet Arnie before we were married— but I know you'll love him. He's very special."

"And he has a very special wife." Her mother was almost successful in her effort to sound happy about this unexpected announcement. "Darling, where do I reach you out there? Has this friend of Arnie's found an apartment for you?"

"We'll stay with him while we look for a place," Lynne began.

"Darling, no," Fran protested. "This is your honeymoon. I want you to spend your first two weeks at some lovely hotel. It'll be my wedding present. Check in at some charming, romantic place, and I'll take care of the bill."

Mom was trying so hard, Lynne thought tenderly, not to let on that she was upset. But she knew this was a bad moment for her mother. And Grandma would throw a fit. Grandma had all those plans in her mind for a big splashy wedding for her and for Debbie.

"We had this tiny little wedding for your mother—but it's going to be different for you girls. A gorgeous wedding gown, bridesmaids, ushers, a ring-bearer. At the synagogue, of course. And a sit-down dinner afterward."

Fran sat motionless at the desk in her tiny office at the rear of the Buckhead shop. She'd realized that Arnie was important in Lynne's life. Why hadn't she realized *how* important? She was Lynne's mother—she should have known.

What was Arnie like? She knew nothing about him except that he had a degree in accounting and he wanted to write music. But if Lynne loved him, she told herself defensively, then he must be warm and compassionate and bright. Lynne would demand this in the man she loved.

Yet she couldn't shake off an aura of unreality, of dismay. Lynne was so young—and then she remembered that she had been a year younger when she'd married Bernie. But things were different today, she tormented herself. Girls didn't rush into marriage. They were interested in careers before they settled down. She relished their air of independence.

What about law school? she asked herself with fresh alarm. Lynne said she'd enroll in a Los Angeles law school in the fall. Lynne was usually so practical, she forced herself to acknowledge. Yet she'd recognized a hint of uncertainty in Lynne's voice when she talked about transferring to another school—as though doubtful that her mother would come through with financial support now that she was married. How could Lynne doubt that? This was her daughter. Her precious child.

She'd thought sentimentally about how she would talk to her daughters about marriage when each arrived at this stage. She'd meant to tell them how beautiful her own marriage had been, though so tragically short. In a traitorous corner of her mind she thought how beautiful marriage to Craig could have been.

Lynne would go on to finish law school, wouldn't she? The possibility that she might not was unnerving. Lynne as an attorney would fulfill the dreams denied Bernie. Their children making a contribution to the world—to make up for what their parents hadn't given back.

It was stupid, of course, for parents to try to be the architects of their children's lives. They must make their own decisions, plot their own course. But oh, she wished she'd met Arnie, had got to know him! Had Lynne met his family? What were they like? Were they upset, too, about this sudden marriage?

In a sudden determination to find an answer to some of the questions hammering away at her brain, Fran reached for the phone and dialed Robin's office. He was in a meeting. His secretary said he'd be free shortly.

"Would you ask him to call me, please? I'm at my Buckhead office." Fran gave Robin's secretary her phone number, though she was sure he knew it. They saw each other at least twice a week—except for that one week in every six or seven when he took off for New York. *"I refuel on new plays, whatever's happening at Carnegie Hall, the ballet. Then I can handle Bellevue and Atlanta again."*

Five minutes later Robin called.

"Could we meet for an early dinner tonight?" Fran asked. This was her mother's bridge night. Debbie had some high school reunion deal. "I need to talk."

"Shall I pick you up at the shop?" Robin asked. "We can eat in Buckhead."

There seemed to be no end of charming restaurants opening up in the Atlanta area, Fran thought as she and Robin were seated at a corner table that afforded much privacy.

"I'd heard this was a great place," Robin said when the waiter had taken their order and left them.

"It's lovely," she agreed, glancing about at the low-keyed decor, the delicate floral arrangements. "It'd be lovely in New York."

"Haven't you learned yet?" he joshed. "This is the New York of the South." His eyes probed hers now. "What's bothering you, Fran?"

"I had a phone call from Lynne. My mother and Debbie don't know yet." She took a deep breath. "Lynne was married at City Hall in New York this morning. All of a sudden her boyfriend had to move out to California—some rush business deal. I don't understand these things—" Her smile was rueful. "Of course, I understand. She's obviously mad about him, and she was scared to put three thousand miles between them. Robin, I need to know more about him. He applied for a grant from the foundation. He was rejected. But you must have a file on him—"

"We turn down hundreds of people every year." He was apologetic. "My father was specific about qualifications. I have nothing to do with the selections—a committee takes care of that."

"Oh, Robin, I know that. But I'd just like to find out a little more about his background—"

"After dinner I'll take you over to my office. You'll know as much as we do."

Now Robin set about—in the fashion she found so endearing—to lighten her mood. He'd just seen Jean Kerr's new play, *Mary, Mary,* and repeated with relish a parade of choice Kerr lines.

Choking with laughter Fran reached for her glass of water.

"Robin, you missed your calling. You should be in the theater."

"I'd never be first rate. I couldn't settle for less."

"How do you know that?" she challenged. "You're so young—you should take a fling at acting." He'd never have to worry about money. He could afford to gamble.

"I know," he said with a sardonic smile, "because my parents told me that endlessly. They said the same about my efforts at painting. As for writing poetry," he drawled, "that was enough for my mother to reach for her bottle of Valium. Dad sold his business for an astronomical sum and then established the foundation on the assumption that I couldn't piss away the money and I'd always have a job."

"They had no right to do that to you." Fran winced as she visualized the sensitive, creative child he must have been.

"I enjoy my life. I've adapted." His eyes were defiant. "God knows, you've had adapting to do. All of it successful."

After dinner Robin drove Fran to his office, which was deserted at this hour. He searched in the files, brought out a folder labeled "Arnold Alexander," and gave it to her. Fighting off a cloud of guilt, she opened the folder and began to read.

"There's not much here, actually," she conceded after a few minutes. "He went to Queens College—which I knew. He was active in music groups in high school and college. He sang in a chorus at some Greenwich Village playhouse. And the consensus is that he displays some talent but not sufficient to warrant the committee's approving a grant."

"Don't write him off," Robin said gently. "The committee's looking for major talents. He might be a huge success as a composer of popular music."

"He pointed out that he writes both music and lyrics and that he hopes to do a Broadway musical one day." A major ambition.

"With a lot of drive and a chunk of luck he may do it. Some people go a long way with a little talent and a lot of luck—and drive," he reiterated. "But don't go out and finance a Broadway show for him."

"Robin, I'm not in that bracket," she scolded.

"The way you're expanding your shops, you're getting there. When the hell are you going to take a break and build yourself a smashing house?"

"I've never thought about it," she admitted. "I've been too busy with the shops." Would her mother be upset? They could afford a more luxurious house—and it'd be great for entertaining.

"Talk to Craig Hendricks," Robin suggested. Fran shot him a startled stare. Did he know about Craig and her? "He did a sensational job on my house."

Robin didn't know, she told herself in relief. They'd been supercautious.

"I'll think about building," she promised. "But right now I've got to break the news to my mother and Debbie that Lynne is married."

Lynne had her feet on the ground, Fran told herself. But she was so young. And anxiety tugged at her because Lynne was leaving Columbia Law. Would she transfer to a California law school? A law degree had been Lynne's dream for such a long time. Would she abandon it now that she was married?

Twenty-Four

F ran parked in the driveway and hurried into the house. She'd garage the car later, she told herself. She was impatient to read the letter Lily said had arrived from California in today's mail. Lynne had been married two months today, she remembered. It was difficult for her to accept the fact that Lynne was married and living on the other side of the country. Was she going back to law school? This question plagued her constantly. Lynne said nothing about registering at a Los Angeles law school.

"Fran?" Her mother called from the living room while she paused in the foyer to collect her mail from the console table. "There's a letter from Lynne."

"Lily told me when I phoned earlier." She smiled cajolingly as she walked into the living room. It had unnerved her mother that Lynne had married a man they'd never even seen except in snapshots Lynne had sent them. She felt uncomfortable in telling her tradition-bound friends about her granddaughter's unconventional marriage. "We'll read it together."

Fran settled herself on the sofa beside her mother and slit the envelope and withdrew the sheet of tightly scrawled notepaper. With an air of conviviality designed to set her mother's mind at rest, she began to read. Lynne was pleased with the furnished apartment they'd rented— *"it's tiny but charming"*—and loved living in Los Angeles. *"The weather is wonderful."*

"She says Arnie has learned to surf and is trying to convince her to give it a whirl," Fran reported. Lynne said nothing about returning to school.

"I don't understand this business about Arnie trying to write a musical." Ida grunted in disapproval. "He'd be better off with a regular job. He's an accountant, isn't he?"

"He hates accounting." Like Bernie, Fran remembered. "He wants to write music."

"So he'll write music until Lynne gets pregnant." Ida's tone was philosophical now. "Then he'll get himself a job. Lynne's not going to let him sponge on us," Ida predicted.

"She's a kid yet," Fran protested, recoiling from the prospect of Lynne's being pregnant. She had two years of law school ahead of her. "Girls today don't rush to have a family."

"They don't rush," Ida drawled, "but it happens." Her eyes held a sentimental glow. "I wouldn't mind being a great-gran."

They heard a car pull up into the driveway.

"That's Debbie," Fran guessed. Debbie had a job on a new Atlanta weekly but wasn't happy with the minor assignments that came her way. "I'll tell Lily she can serve dinner."

Over dinner Fran and Ida listened to Debbie's wry report of her day as a very junior newspaperwoman.

"I know, I can't expect any important assignments yet," Debbie admitted, "but I hate reporting on the social scene." She sighed. "I'm covering some charity ball tonight. Isn't that the pits?"

"Darling, you've been working there only three weeks," Fran chided, but she understood Debbie's impatience. Still, Debbie had a job on a newspaper—that was more than *she* had ever been able to do. "It was damn nice of them to let you work two weeks, then take off for our trip to Europe."

"Mom, there's so much happening in the world! All the trouble in South America, our problems with Cuba, the Cold War, the pressure the Soviets are putting on West Berlin. And my most important assignment to date is to cover this charity ball tonight." Debbie grunted dejectedly.

Don't let her grow discouraged with this job, Fran thought in fresh alarm. Don't let her go chasing off after a job in another city. Already there were moments when the house felt desolate because Lynne was gone. It would be devastating if both girls settled in other cities.

Now she understood how her mother had felt when she married Bernie and took off for New York. In those days she was the rare one. Children married and settled in their hometowns, raised their families there. Today was so different. Families were scattered. They came together once or twice a year. That was sad.

After dinner Debbie hurried up to her room to dress for the charity ball. She was exempt tonight from clearing the dinner table. Fran and her mother undertook this chore.

"Twenty-five years ago I never thought I'd be doing housework when I was seventy-six," Ida grumbled. "The old days were better. Frannie, when is that Milk Fund dinner being held? It just slipped my mind—"

"Not till next month. And I've made our reservations," Fran said.

"I just don't know what's the matter with my memory these days." Ida frowned. "Do you think I'm getting senile?"

"No, Mother. Everybody forgets things sometimes. Debbie was going crazy last night trying to remember the name of a foreign correspondent who gave a lecture in the spring at the university. Three hours later it finally came to her." Ida had been so conscious of age since her friend Clara went into a nursing home last month.

"My memory's still sharp enough for me to do my volunteer work." Ida was faintly defiant.

"I've been thinking, Mother." Fran braced herself for a battle. "We ought to let Lily off at three instead of staying until she's served dinner—and hire somebody to come in to prepare dinner, serve it, and clean up afterward."

"Frannie, at the wages they're asking?" Ida's eyebrows shot upward. "We don't hire a girl for three dollars a week anymore!"

"We can afford it," Fran pointed out. Her eyes dared her mother to deny this. "Lily deserves lighter hours."

"You know how I feel about Lily." Her mother was defensive. "But giving her shorter hours is going to cause trouble. You know how the word gets around. The other girls will be asking for shorter hours. I can imagine what my friends will say." She winced. *"You're spoiling it for the rest of us."*

"The whole world is changing." Fran's voice was gentle. "We have to accept that. And while we're talking about changes, I've been thinking about the house. It's beginning to show its age." Her mother bristled, but she ignored this. "Every few weeks there's a plumbing problem or a leak in the roof—or something else. I sat down and looked at the repair figures. I think it's time we built ourselves a new house. Out in the suburbs. All on one floor, so you don't have all those steps." Her mother's arthritis was mild, but why not make life a bit easier for her?

Her mother was contemplative.

"We can afford this?"

Fran chuckled. "We can afford it."

"All right." Her mother startled her with this swift capitulation. "Let's do it." Her eyes were twinkling. "Wait till the girls hear about this. Millie will eat her heart out. She never stops bragging about the new house her son and daughter-in-law built last year."

She'd hire Craig as architect, Fran decided, fighting self-consciousness. It was the natural thing to do—he was the most popular architect in Bellevue. And she anticipated with pleasure the prospect of living in a house he had designed.

He had his life, and she had hers, she reasoned. She no longer avoided being in his presence. Much of their social life revolved around the same people. It might be awkward just at first—but people they knew well would expect her to call in Craig to build her house. And she suspected that he would be pleased.

In her delightfully feminine bedroom Debbie inspected her reflection in the mirror. She was annoyed that she was under orders to wear an evening gown. She was on an assignment, such as it was—not a guest. "Mingle with the crowd," her boss had ordered. "If they forget you're a reporter, they'll talk openly. You might pick up something we can use." He'd said that, she pinpointed, to make her think she was doing something more important than society reporting. She'd been making noises about doing a feature article on school integration in Atlanta. Everybody was so anxious about what would happen when nine black students would apply for admission to four previously all-white schools at the end of the month. Mayor Hartsfield was vowing it would be a peaceful integration despite that new black Muslim extremist group operating in the city.

Debbie ran a brush over her lush near-black hair and charged from her room and down the stairs with her usual breakneck speed.

"Mom?" Debbie paused at the living room entrance. Her mother was on the sofa—studying figures on a sheaf of papers, no doubt dealing with store business, she assumed. "Do I look all right?"

"You look beautiful," her mother assured her. "That dress is perfect."

"It should be, considering what you paid for it." The gown was an Yves Saint Laurent.

"It was a business purchase," Fran said, her eyes lit with laughter. "Didn't you model it as an original in every one of the shops?"

"I felt like a dumb debutante," Debbie said with mock reproach. In truth, she shared her mother's fondness for beautiful clothes. But Lynne, she thought with a blend of indulgence and impatience, would live in jeans and beat-up sweaters if Mom didn't get after her. "And now, here I am parading around in this expensive concoction—when my salary says I should be buying my clothes in a bargain basement."

"What's the charity involved tonight?" Georgia cities and towns—including Bellevue—reveled in charity affairs.

"It's some new organization planning to build housing for the poor. They're following the pattern of a philanthropist from up in North Carolina. Her name's Richards. Margaret Richards."

"Richards Cotton Mills?" her mother asked.

"I think so. One of the national magazines did a spread recently on housing she built for her workers. She's the guest of honor tonight." Debbie uttered a melodramatic sigh. "I'm going to be bored out of my skull." She paused. A car pulled up out front. "That must be Jack—the photographer who's picking me up." Unexpectedly she giggled. "I'll bet the boss didn't order him to rent a tux. A tux would go on our expense account and our budget's weak."

Debbie hurried out to join Jack in his eight-year-old Valiant, inherited from his mother.

"No tux?" she jibed, sliding into the car beside him.

"Over my dead body." He grimaced. "I'm not a guest. But I did put on a tie and a dress shirt," he added virtuously.

As prearranged, they arrived early. The ballroom was banked with summer flowers. Vases of tea roses adorned the collection of small tables set about the perimeter.

"Smells like a funeral parlor," Jack remarked and sneezed. "I'm allergic to roses."

"Here." Debbie reached into her evening bag—large enough to contain only notebook, lipstick, and tissues. She handed him a batch of tissues. "Sneeze away."

With camera about his neck Jack positioned himself—along with photographers from other newspapers—to snap guests as they arrived. Debbie stood at his side to identify important guests. She recognized society reporters from major Atlanta newspapers. Later she'd "mingle." The orchestra was playing a medley of tunes from *Camelot*. Debbie contrived a charming smile, but her mind was in rebellion. There was so much happening in the world, and she was stuck at a charity ball.

Guests arrived in swift succession. Many of the women wore gorgeous dresses, Debbie thought admiringly. Probably all the men hated wearing tuxes—like Jack. All at once there was a round of applause from some of the guests milling about the ballroom. Several couples stopped dancing to applaud.

"That's Margaret Richards," Debbie whispered to Jack, who was already camera-active. "I saw photos of her in the newspaper's morgue."

Debbie gazed at the tall, smartly gowned woman in her fifties—almost regal in bearing. She was a power player in the cotton mill industry, Debbie recalled. The Richards mills were located in several areas in North Carolina and were family-owned. Mrs. Richards was accompanied by a young man in his early twenties—slim, dark-haired, casually handsome. He didn't like being here, she decided in sudden sympathy.

"This chick goes for young guys," Jack drawled, snapping rapidly as Mrs. Richards was being welcomed by the chairwoman of the event.

"It's her son," Debbie surmised.

She'd researched Mrs. Richards's background with the errant hope that she would latch onto something tonight that would lend substance to her report of the charity ball. Richards was a widow with two sons—one of whom was active in her cotton dynasty.

Despite her boss's orders "to mingle," Debbie discovered this was not a simple task. The guests gathered in small cliques. They smiled a lot, seemed to be having fun, Debbie conceded, but they were another generation. She chatted at intervals with several people she knew—all of whom asked if her mother was present.

"Mom's not here," she repeated each time. "She had another commitment tonight." Mom couldn't go to every charity affair. "I'm actually working." She explained about her job on the newspaper.

At last Debbie wandered over to Jack's side.

"Can't we cut out now?" he asked, reading her mind. "I'm practically out of film."

"It's time," she agreed—but her eyes roamed across the room to where Margaret Richards's son stood with an air of boredom. At least, she thought he was Richards's son. At intervals she'd been aware of his furtive glances in her direction.

"That guy's been trying to get up the nerve all evening to ask you to dance," Jack joshed.

"I'm not here to dance," Debbie reminded. "Anyhow, this isn't our kind of music." The young crowd—notably absent here—did the Twist these days. This orchestra played show tunes.

She'd danced with two middle-aged acquaintances of her mother. Mom had insisted she and Lynne learn ballroom dancing in their middle teens. She suspected it was something her mother loved to do before the accident.

"I think he's coming over," Jack murmured. "Shall I take a walk?"

"No," she ordered, but she was conscious of a sudden flurry of excitement.

"Hi." Mrs. Richards's escort sauntered to Debbie's side. "I'm Scott Richards." His "friendly puppy" gaze included Jack. "You two are from one of the local newspapers, aren't you?"

"How did you guess?" But her smile told Scott his presence was welcome.

"We're a minority here," he said. "The 'under thirty' crowd." He hesitated. "I hope if your paper runs photographs, they won't include me."

"You're camera shy?" Jack lifted an eyebrow in astonishment.

"I'm starting Emory Law," Scott said, his smile wry. "I was kicked out of a North Carolina school at the end of last semester for being involved in campus demonstrations. We had our faces splashed all over the newspapers up there. I wouldn't want anybody at Emory to connect me with that deal." Jack nodded in sympathy. Debbie's face lighted. "I'd like to keep a low profile in this town."

"We'll be cool about it," Jack said, "but I can't say what the other photographers will do."

Scott sighed. "I'll have to take my chances."

"Did they throw you in the clink?" Jack asked.

"My mother pulled strings." Scott was self-conscious now. "She got us all out. But the four ringleaders—including me—were expelled from school. Of course—if there's any action down here—I could get involved again. My mother will kill me."

"I was up at the University of Georgia when there was all that nastiness about the two black students who enrolled. I hated being a Southerner when I saw what was happening!" Debbie's eyes blazed in recall.

"Ssh—" Jack glanced about nervously.

"I have to fly back up to North Carolina with my mother tonight, but could we get together for a beer or something when I come back to start school?" Scott asked.

"Sure." Debbie pulled a sheet from her notebook and scribbled her phone number. "I'm Debbie Garfield," she added, "and this character is Jack McIntyre."

———

One week later Debbie sat with Scott Richards in a cozy booth at a popular Bellevue hangout for the young. He was settled in Atlanta and had started classes at Emory Law.

"Atlanta's a great town," he said. "And real close to Bellevue." He was making no secret of his determination to see much of her in the months ahead—and Debbie was euphoric in this knowledge. This was a real hip guy. They were on the same wave length.

"My sister was up at Columbia Law last year," Debbie told him. "But it looks like she won't be going back for the new term. Not unless she can commute from California." How could Lynne be so dumb? she thought.

"They have law schools in California." Scott's eloquent brown eyes were carrying on a different conversation. He looked laid back, but he was so intense, Debbie decided—liking this.

"She got married." Was Lynne going to be one of those girls who gave up a career to stay at home and have kids? She'd been so sure nothing would stop her from being a lawyer, making a contribution.

"So?" Scott lifted his eyebrows in quizzical inquiry.

"Her husband—whom we've never met," she said with an undertone of disapproval, "wanted to go to Los Angeles to work with some guy on a musical that they *might* get produced. So Lynne's supposed to forget her own life."

"If she wants to be a lawyer, she'll go to law school out there. Getting married these days doesn't mean a girl throws career plans out the window. That's not this generation. What about you?" he pursued. "What do you want to do with your life?"

The evening sped past—both Debbie and Scott reluctant to call it a night. Their conversation jumping from one topic to another as they lingered in front of her house in his late model Cadillac. The night was hot and sticky, the air pungent with the scent of honeysuckle.

"My mother's so sharp. I can't figure out her mania for building a bomb shelter the size of a city apartment, stocked with everything from food to toothpaste!" Scott shook his head in bewilderment.

"It was probably that television speech by Kennedy—when he urged Americans to build shelters—that set her off," Debbie surmised. Half the country, it seemed, was intent on building a bomb shelter. "My mom wanted no part of it."

They'd talked about so much, she thought—feeling as though she'd known Scott forever. They thought *alike*—that was what was important.

"School nights are going to be rough," Scott said. "What about getting together Friday night?"

"That sounds like fun." No game playing, she told herself. She liked Scott. She wanted to see him again. "Call me and let's set a time."

Her grandmother was in the living room with the TV on, but she was dozing. Grandma would deny it, Debbie thought indulgently, but she was waiting up for *her* to get home. And Mom, too, she guessed. Mom had gone with Robin to some summer theater production.

"Grandma, wake up." She turned off the television set. "Grandma, I'm home."

Ida opened her eyes and smothered a yawn.

"Did you have a good time?" Her usual question.

"Yeah, I did."

"Work or pleasure?" Again Ida followed her customary routine.

"Pleasure." Debbie dropped onto a corner of the sofa.

"So?" Ida waited for further enlightenment.

"Nothing special." Wow, that was the understatement of the year! "Just a hamburger and Coke date with this law student from Emory. I met him at that charity ball last week." She anticipated her grandmother's next question. "His name is Scott Richards." She knew her grandmother didn't mean this to be an inquisition.

"He's related to that woman from North Carolina?" Ida was suddenly alert. "The one interested in housing for the poor?"

"Her son." Now Debbie was wary. Again, she read her grandmother's mind.

"He's not Jewish!"

"His father wasn't," Debbie conceded. His father had died years ago, and his mother had taken over the company. "His mother is." She knew that from research on Margaret Richards. "But she prefers to ignore it."

"Only a stupid woman ignores her faith." Ida was indignant.

"Grandma, cool it," Debbie ordered. "I'm dating Scott Richards—not marrying him."

But she'd never been attracted to anybody the way she was to Scott. They fitted together like pieces of a jigsaw puzzle. And he didn't expect a girl to give up her career when she got married.

Twenty-Five

In an exquisite sapphire silk overblouse and matching slacks Fran sat at the beautifully laid luncheon table in the popular restaurant and ordered herself to relax. She'd told herself it was cowardly to have arranged for Robin to be here with her at this first meeting with Craig to discuss the new house. Still, she was glad she had brought him along. He was carrying much of the conversation at this point, for which she was grateful.

This was the restaurant where Craig had first taken her for dinner. The awareness hammered at her brain. Craig had forgotten, she tried to rationalize—it was seven years ago this month. But he hadn't forgotten. Each time their eyes met she knew he remembered. He'd been deliberate in choosing to meet here.

The restaurant was as charming as it had been the first time she and Craig had come here. It was larger now, with another room added. The lighting was subdued and relaxing, the ambience luxurious without being ostentatious. The food was superb. Did Craig come here often? Since Paris it had been off-limits to her. Yet being here today brought back cherished memories—wonderfully sweet in recall. They could allow themselves that.

Robin didn't know that she and Craig had been lovers. Nobody knew. She joined Craig in laughter now as Robin spun another of his delicious stories. This meeting was going to be *all right*.

She and Craig had encountered each other at regular intervals during the years. It was inevitable in a town as small as Bellevue. But today was different. In a silent communication they acknowledged that they lived separate lives, yet there was a new acceptance of this that made no effort to blot out the past. *It was all right to remember,* she thought, relieved.

"How're Joyce and the boys?" Fran asked at a break in the conversation.

"They're all fine," he told her. "And Lynne and Debbie?"

Fran filled him in on her daughters' current activities.

"Lynne and Arnie—her husband—may be returning to New York soon." She gathered that Arnie and Ron were unhappy about the advances their would-be backer was providing. Lynne was working in a dress shop in Los Angeles. She'd written a glowing reference for Lynne's boss—who didn't know this was from her mother. *"I tried for a job in a law office but came up with nothing. But this is a fun shop— movie stars and would-be stars float in and out."* "It's all indefinite, of course—"

"New York is a lot closer than California." Craig's smile was gentle. He knew how much she missed Lynne.

"Now that we've praised my house to the skies," Robin picked up, "what do you have planned for Fran?" he asked Craig.

In the months ahead Fran saw much of Craig—usually with Robin tagging along. After that first luncheon she was no longer afraid these meetings might be painful. In truth, she looked forward to them and sensed that Craig shared this feeling. She suspected, too, that what he felt for his wife was not the deep, passionate love they'd shared—but life was made up of compromises. She was impressed by his comprehension of what she needed in a house, touched by his eagerness to please her.

At intervals she sent small checks to Lynne—latching on to holidays to make them appear casual gifts. Lynne's talk about their returning to New York grew more positive. Their prospective backer was having marital problems. *"If he divorces his wife, the musical's down the drain."* But Lynne nurtured great hopes for Arnie's future. It bothered Fran— though she refused to admit this even to her mother or Debbie—that Lynne was supporting herself and Arnie. For this she gave up law school?

Fran knew that Debbie was in love with Scott, though there was no talk of a formal engagement. She was sure that Scott was in love with Debbie but understood any serious plans were on hold until he finished law school. He was often underfoot on weekends. Even her mother— who had been uneasy about "Debbie's 'half-*goy*' boyfriend"—now adored Scott.

"Invite Scott for the first seder," Ida ordered Debbie at the approach of Passover—the celebration of the Jews' escape from Egypt. "For too long we've sat down to a male-less seder."

Debbie had been startled, yet pleased.

"I'll ask him. No guarantee that he'll come." She'd giggled. "That sounds awfully much like asking him to make a commitment."

"So what's wrong with that?" Ida asked with a smug smile.

"Scott has to finish law school. And I'd like to see myself reporting something more exciting than charity balls and fancy weddings before—" She hesitated.

"Before you marry Scott and give me great-grandchildren," Ida finished for her. "Sugar, I'm seventy-seven. Don't expect me to hang around forever."

Scott arrived for the seder with an armful of long-stemmed red roses. Debbie placed them in water and then led the way to the festive seder table.

"The last time I was at a seder I was eight years old," Scott said— seeming abashed, Fran thought. "It was at my grandmother's house—on my mother's side. My mother and Perry didn't come." Fran recalled that Perry was Scott's brother, eight years older than he and recently married. "The chauffeur brought me over. Kids should know where they belong," he said with sudden intensity.

"Amen," Ida said softly.

"Before Dad died, he used to go to church most Sunday mornings," Scott recalled. "Perry went with him because he knew Dad would slip him a ten dollar bill for 'being a good boy.' My mother never went to the synagogue. What I know about her faith—mine, too, my grandmother always said—was what I learned from going to my grandmother's house for holidays. But she died before my ninth birthday, and after that I didn't belong anywhere."

"Here you belong to the synagogue," Ida said gruffly. Fran saw tears in her eyes. "Tonight you'll see a real seder—even if we're all women in this house. In the Reform synagogue this is allowed."

"Scott, tell Grandma she should vote," Debbie urged.

"Debbie, elections are months away," Fran reminded. This was an uncomfortable issue between Debbie and her grandmother.

"I'll tell you the truth." All at once her mother seemed self-conscious, Fran thought, yet felt a new resolve in her. "I don't vote because I'm afraid I'll make a fool of myself when I go into the booth. I don't know what to do." She gestured in frustration, her eyes pleading for understanding. Fran was startled—she'd never considered this.

"I'll give you a run-through before the next election," Scott promised. "We'll have a few dress rehearsals—and bingo, you'll know."

There was such a warm feeling in the house tonight, Fran thought in a surge of sentimentality. This would be their last seder here. In two weeks they would move to the new house in the suburbs. She suspected that her mother, too, was aware of this. And her mind darted back to twenty-five years ago, when she'd persuaded her mother to invite Bernie to the first seder. And now Scott—whom Debbie loved—was sharing a seder with them.

Lynne was ambivalent when—early in May—her mother proposed sending plane tickets so that she could fly home for a week. Round-trip tickets, Lynne acknowledged. Mom knew California was home for now. Mom offered tickets for both her and Arnie, but Arnie was too involved with the musical to take time off now—particularly when the whole situation had become so precarious. Still, her boss at the shop preferred that she take her week's vacation now rather than in midsummer, when tourist business was heavier.

"Go," Arnie encouraged when she told him. "You need a change of scenery. I can take care of myself for a week."

"If you're sure." Her eyes searched his. She felt guilty at taking off yet welcomed the prospect of a week back home.

"I'm sure," he insisted.

Lynne relished the prospect of seeing her family, of being away from the job. She'd never admit to Arnie how she loathed working in the dress shop. She had to keep reminding herself that this was temporary. As soon as Arnie had a foothold in the music business, she'd go back to law school.

Bellevue was at its prettiest in May, Lynne thought as she drove into town with her mother. Summer was in full stride already, flowers in glorious bloom.

"Is your car holding up?" Fran asked.

"It's fine, Mom," Lynne assured her. They'd needed a car to get around in Los Angeles. Her mother had sent an "advance Hanukkah present" to pay for the secondhand Chevvie they'd bought last summer.

"I think you'll like the new house," Fran said. "Grandma adores it. I was scared she'd miss the old place."

"It's strange going to a new house." Lynne felt an unexpected rush of nostalgia. "But Debbie says it's great."

The week sped past. While she missed Arnie, Lynne conceded, she wished she could have stayed another week. But Arnie's delight at having her home filled her with an exquisite pleasure.

"How did it feel, being a spoiled lady of leisure?" he joshed while he carried her suitcase—bursting now with new clothes from her mother's shop—into their tiny apartment.

"Great, but I missed you. How did things go with you and Ron?" Arnie had phoned once but kept the call short out of respect for their phone bill. And, strangely, she had done the same—though she knew her mother wouldn't have objected to an inflated phone bill. But she was a married woman now, not a college student calling home collect. "And what about the old boy?"

"Everything came to an ugly head while you were away," Arnie said after a pregnant pause. "Ron's been tied up with his job—you know how it's been these last three months. He's pissed at the old man. He doesn't want to do any more work on the book until we see more money. I feel the same way about the music. And that's not likely to happen."

"What changes are you supposed to do now?" Arnie's songs were beautiful, she thought in frustration.

"I'm not doing them." Arnie was somber. "Let's face it, the old man's playing games with this chick. We're the bait. It's all off, baby. Ron and I decided it's useless to spend more time. But we've got a musical on our hands," he said with a show of defiance. "And we think it's good."

"It is, Arnie." Her face was tender. "But what now?"

"We'll try to get some action out here. If nothing happens in three months, we'll head back to New York." He hesitated. "I'll look for a job and in the evenings try to interest some Off-Broadway producer in the play. Oh, Ron's staying out here. He says he's making some studio connections—and he hates New York winters."

"But what about the play?" He and Ron had put in so much time and effort!

Arnie shrugged. "He's leaving it to me to handle. He says the way prices are soaring for Off-Broadway productions—particularly a musical—our chances are slim."

"You don't feel that way," Lynne protested.

"I'll make a stab at it, sure. And if we get a nibble, maybe then Ron'll head back to New York. We have to play it by ear."

Early in September Lynne and Arnie arrived in New York. They stayed at a grubby little hotel while they searched for a furnished apartment. In desperation—because housing in the city was in short supply

and expensive—they rented an unfurnished apartment in a small building set between rundown tenements on East 5th Street. They spent a
chunk of their tiny capital on a box spring and mattress plus frame and a
card table.

Arnie was triumphant when he overheard the "super" complaining
about the need to remove an abandoned studio piano from an apartment
vacated in the middle of the night. "I'll have it moved!" he promised eagerly. Later—when funds were less tight, he'd have it tuned.

"We're young—we can do this," Lynne said spiritedly. "And we're in
the middle of Off-Broadway. You can chase after a production."

At Lynne's prodding Arnie decided to look for work through one of
the "temporaries"—the life-preserver for out-of-work and would-be actors, musicians, and songwriters. He'd work three days a week, make
show business and music publisher rounds twice a week.

"I'll get a clerical job through one of the 'temps,' too," Lynne told
Arnie. "It's too late for me to go back to law school this year."

Mom would pay the tuition—that wouldn't be a problem. She was impatient to be back on the cherished law school treadmill. Arnie had made
it clear he'd go after a full-time job once she was back in school. With luck
he'd make a dent with his music by then. He was so talented, so determined. He had to have this chance.

In a matter of days Lynne and Arnie both were being sent out by a
"temp" agency. Because their funds were low, Lynne was working a full
week. Arnie spent two days a week making rounds of the music publishing houses.

"I don't know why it's so hard to get a commitment out of the lousy
publishers," he railed. "I have the demos we made out on the coast." He
and Ron had gone into a cheap recording studio. Arnie played the piano,
Ron sang. "They listen. They like the songs. So what's the holdup? It's
not like they're record companies, who have to invest a fortune. They
give a writer a small advance. Lots of times writers go along without an
advance. Sometimes the demo you bring to the publisher is the one he
uses to sell the song. Hell, the publisher invests practically nothing!"

"You said you have a date with the producer at that new Off-Broadway group," Lynne reminded, striving for optimism. "Maybe he'll give
you and Ron a production. You could get a record deal from that. You
might even land a Broadway production."

"You are great for my morale, you know?" He reached to pull her
close. "How did I survive before you came along?"

Life had been good to her, Fran told herself with the approach of Thanksgiving. She loved the new house. Craig had wrought pure magic for her. And she cherished the new openness between Craig and herself. The shops were doing so well she considered adding another. Lynne was happily married. While Debbie and Scott were not formally engaged— they considered this gauche—their behavior made it clear they would be married when Scott had obtained his law degree. At times she wondered how Scott's mother felt about this.

At intervals her mother made morbid comments about growing old. Two of her friends were now in nursing homes. *"Maybe we ought to look into that place where Millie's living,"* Mother had said just last week. That was ridiculous; Fran dismissed this. Mother was in excellent physical condition except for mild arthritis when the weather was bad. And if the time came when her mother needed care, she'd receive it right here at home, Fran vowed—no matter what the cost.

Everything was going so well with her life, she thought. So why did she feel this disconcerting unease? Then all at once she understood. She worried about Lynne.

What kind of man had Lynne married? Was she happy? It was disturbing not to know her son-in-law, not even to have met him. Only with Craig did she admit to misgivings.

All right, it was time she met Lynne's husband, she told herself in a burst of determination. She'd phone Lynne tonight, coax her—and Arnie—to come down to Bellevue for the long Thanksgiving weekend. Both worked at temporary jobs—they'd have no excuse about not getting off from work. She'd supply plane tickets and a substantial check as an "advance Hanukkah gift."

It was absurd to worry about antagonizing Arnie by offering gifts. Why shouldn't she do these little things? Lynne and Arnie knew she was doing well financially. Arnie shouldn't resent her helping out. She understood they wanted to be independent. And she realized, too, that she worried about this because Bernie had been so uncomfortable in the face of her parents' generosity.

Fran was rapturous when she finally persuaded Lynne and Arnie to come to Bellevue for Thanksgiving. Scott, too, would be with them rather than going home to North Carolina. His mother would be in the Caribbean, his brother and sister-in-law in Palm Springs.

"Frannie, it's going to be so nice," her mother said at breakfast on the day before Thanksgiving. "We'll be like a real family again. There'll be a man to carve the turkey."

"Grandma!" Debbie shook her head in mock impatience. "What's wrong with Mom carving the turkey? What's so special about men?"

"I'm tired of all this talk about independent women," her grandmother scoffed. "Wives rushing out to chase after careers."

"You want us to be Barbie dolls," Debbie accused. "That's not me."

"Debbie, you said you'd be able to pick up Lynne and Arnie at the airport," Fran reminded. She could have postponed her business meeting this morning, she recognized guiltily—but she recoiled from being introduced to her son-in-law in the impersonal surroundings of the airport. "Their flight's due in at 11:05."

"I'll be there," Debbie said.

Fran had lunch at her desk in the Buckhead shop, then drove home in rising eagerness to see Lynne and to meet her son-in-law. She told herself she was being casual when Lynne introduced her to Arnie. Casual yet warm—but her heart was pounding. She liked Arnie, she decided with relief. He was nervous about meeting Lynne's family, but that was natural enough. And she respected his ambition.

Scott arrived in time for Wednesday evening dinner. Fran was pleased that he and Arnie seemed compatible. It was like old times, she thought while she listened to Debbie scold Lynne about her lack of interest in clothes while Scott and Arnie argued about who would win the AFL championship.

"I know Mom must have sent you some gorgeous dresses. Why do you always settle for a pair of slacks and a sweater?" Debbie was on familiar ground.

"I feel comfortable." As always Lynne shrugged aside such complaints. "Arnie doesn't mind."

"When you get through law school and are out there in practice, you'd better dress well," Debbie warned.

Fran was conscious of a sudden change of mood in Lynne. The talk about law school, she thought painfully. For so long Lynne had dreamt of becoming of lawyer.

"You do plan on going back to school?" Fran asked softly.

"Sure, Mom." Lynne was defensive. "You'll know, I promise." She giggled. "The tuition isn't in our budget."

"Don't you have to register very soon for the new term?" Fran pressed.

"I can only register for law school in September." Her smile was shaky. "You forgot that, Mom—"

"I had forgotten. And there's no summer school," Fran recalled, her mind darting back through the years to those painful last months of Bernie's brief life.

"I lost a couple of years of law school, but I gained a husband." Lynne's eyes sought out Arnie, engrossed in friendly debate with Scott. "Don't worry. I'm going back to school. It'll just take a little longer than we'd planned."

The house seemed so empty, Fran thought on Sunday evening when she sat down to dinner alone with her mother. Lynne and Arnie had flown back to New York in midafternoon. Debbie and Scott were off at the last of the Thanksgiving weekend parties. Their part-time domestic, Betty Mae, came in to prepare dinner, serve, and then clear up. Her mother, too, felt this emptiness, Fran realized.

"Arnie's nice," Ida broke into her thoughts. "But wouldn't you think he'd settle down into an accounting job now that he's married?"

"They're both so young," Fran said defensively. "Let them find their way."

"I wish they'd find their way back here. They could have a good life in Bellevue. Why do young people always think the grass is greener in a big city? And if they have to have a big city, why not Atlanta?"

"We can't design their lives for them, Mother." Fran's smile was wistful. She, too, wished Lynne and Arnie would settle in Bellevue or Atlanta. In the past few years Atlanta has become the second fastest growing metropolitan area in the country. It was a major financial center, rich in cultural activities—the crown jewel of the South. But for Arnie, Lynne had explained, it was important to live in New York or Los Angeles. Here were the centers of the music business. "What's on TV tonight?" she asked with an effort at cheerfulness. Her mother loved television.

They finished dinner and settled themselves in the living room to watch television with dessert and coffee at hand. But Fran saw nothing on the television screen. She was upset by the knowledge that Lynne could not return to law school before the following September.

Becoming a lawyer had been the focal point of Lynne's life since she was fifteen. Would she allow marriage to obliterate this dream? Women today married and pursued careers. She'd lost her own dream to a bullet, Fran thought painfully. All these years she'd tried to blot that out of her mind—but part of her mourned for the career denied her. That mustn't happen to Lynne.

Twenty-Six

F ran was delighted when Lynne phoned early in December to report that she was no longer "temping."

"I've latched onto a job as a clerk in a law office," she bubbled. "It's not law school, but it's a learning experience."

"Oh, Lynne, that's terrific." She wasn't giving up on law school, Fran comforted herself. She'd be back in school in September. "And the next few months will rush by. You'll be back in school before you know it."

In January Fran flew to New York on her usual buying trip. Robin accompanied her on the flight, though he warned her he'd see no more of her until they were both back in Bellevue.

"This is my time to play," he reminded, in jovial spirits. "I'm staying at this hotel down in the Village, and I'll sop up fun and entertainment to see me through to my next escape."

"You don't have any contacts in the music business, do you?" she asked.

"Sorry, sugar," Robin apologized. "I know a few people in the art world and in the dance field. That won't help, will it?"

"Thanks, anyway." He knew she was anxious to see Arnie get a song published or to land a record deal. He still felt guilty that his foundation hadn't offered Arnie a grant, she thought compassionately.

"I don't suppose you'd stay away another three days and go with me to this new ski lodge up in Vermont? It's supposed to be sensational."

"Robin, what would I do at a ski lodge?" She patted her cane with good-humored reproach.

"The same thing I'll do." He reached for her hand. Trying, Fran recognized, to convince the elderly woman across the aisle that they were a romantic twosome. "Pay brief respects to that fresh mountain air, then collapse in a chair before a roaring fire in the lounge and drown myself in hot buttered rum. At night there's entertainment."

"When my buying's done and I've seen Lynne and Arnie, I'm rushing back to Bellevue. I run a business." But she relished Robin's company, she thought affectionately. Her dear friend.

At the airport Robin prodded her into a taxi, dropped her off at the Essex House, and headed for his Village hotel. Fran was delighted with her room, which faced Central Park. If there was snow—as the weather-casters were predicting—the park would be a winter wonderland.

Mindful of the few days she would be in the city, Fran unpacked and made phone calls to her buying offices. Tonight she would take Lynne and Arnie out to dinner. Tomorrow she would meet Lynne for lunch, then continue her buying. Tomorrow night they would have a delicatessen dinner at Lynne and Arnie's apartment.

As always, her first hours in the city were fraught with bittersweet memories of earlier years. But this would pass, she told herself. Back in her hotel room she dressed for dinner—black wool pants and jacket with a charming frilly blouse, her signature outfit.

Was she making a mistake in taking Lynne and Arnie to the Russian Tea Room for dinner? Craig had taken her there for lunch on the day she arrived in New York before their trip to London and Paris. Yet, perversely, she wanted to go there, wanted to relive in memory the exquisite pleasure of that day seven and a half years ago.

As planned, Lynne and Arnie picked her up at the Essex House. They walked together to the Russian Tea Room. The past seven and a half years seemed to vanish. For a moment—while Lynne and Arnie argued playfully about what to order—Fran closed her eyes and felt Craig sitting across the table from her. She'd made the right decision, of course. Craig had his family, and she had hers.

Fran spent the following morning in her favorite showroom on Seventh Avenue, then headed in the sharp cold for the small midtown restaurant where she was to meet Lynne for lunch. Yesterday's threat of snow had disappeared, but sharp winds belied the above-freezing temperature. With business out of the way she focused on what she meant to say to Lynne. She was grateful for this chance for mother-daughter talk.

She arrived at the restaurant shortly before noon—contriving to precede the lunch hour rush, commandeered a private table for two in a rear corner, and ordered a cup of Earl Grey while she waited. Ten minutes later she spied Lynne hurrying into the restaurant. Her face lighted with love.

"Have you been waiting long?" Lynne asked, settling into her chair.

"Just a few moments," Fran fabricated, then laughed as Lynne's eyes dwelt on her near-empty cup of tea. "I made a point of arriving before the mob—to nab a corner table."

Fran waited for an opportune moment to deliver her carefully plotted message. *She mustn't muff this,* she promised herself. Lynne talked about Arnie's efforts to break into the music business, his pursuit of an Off-Broadway production of the musical he and Ron had written.

"It's rough to make that first dent, but the rest of our lives depend on it. I figure that even when I go back to law school in September, I can work over weekends. I want Arnie to have at least two days a week to fight for a publishing contract—or—" she crossed her fingers, "a recording contract."

"I've been giving a lot of thought to your future," Fran began gently. "Yours and Arnie's," she forced herself to add. "I don't want to cause problems—but once you start school, I'd like to give you an allowance that'll match what you earn now. After taxes." Her smile blended affection with raillery.

"Mom, that's wonderful of you." Lynne was somber now. "But I don't know how Arnie will feel about it."

"Will he be upset?"

"I don't know." Lynne squinted in thought. "Let me talk to him. From my viewpoint it'll be great. If you're sure you can handle it?"

"I'm sure." Fran nodded vigorously.

"I don't want to see Arnie locked for the rest of his life in a job he loathes," Lynne confided. "His father has been selling insurance for thirty-two years—and he's hated every minute of it."

"Most people spend their lives in jobs they dislike. Jobs that pay the rent, keep food on the table, see their kids through school. They wake up each work day with a sense of resignation or rebellion. I didn't want that for your father." Oh yes, she understood Lynne's feelings.

"I remember, Mom. I remember how proud you both were that he was making it through law school. And as young as I was, I was proud, too."

"You have one year of law school behind you. Surely Arnie can accept your need to earn your degree."

"Oh, he does," Lynne leapt in with conviction, then laughed. "He's already telling me to zero in on music publishing and recording contracts."

"Make Arnie understand that I don't mean to be an interfering mother. I want to help." In a corner of her mind Fran remembered Craig's off-repeated sentiment. *"Fran, I'm so lucky to be involved in work that I love, that gives me such satisfaction."* In dark moments—in painful crises—that knowledge was to be cherished.

Over dinner that evening in Lynne and Arnie's apartment, he told Fran with halting words that he understood what she was doing for them—and he was grateful. Her mission was accomplished, she thought with relief.

In the spring Debbie vowed to try to track down a more stimulating job. On a Sunday evening after Scott had headed back for his Atlanta apartment, Fran listened sympathetically to a frustrating tirade from Debbie as they sat together in the living room.

"I carried on about all the society coverage, and what do they give me? Zoning laws and sludge! At a time when so much is happening right in Atlanta! Look at the way the Lovett School wouldn't admit Martin Luther King Jr.'s son to their kindergarten class. And the sit-ins that keep popping up in the restaurants and hotels."

"Good things are happening, too," Fran pointed out. "Archbishop Hallinan ordained two young black priests who earned their degrees in Atlanta." It was considered proper now to refer to Negroes as blacks, Fran remembered. "A black contracting firm entered the winning bid on the housing development sponsored by the Wheat Street Baptist Church. I hear Grady Hospital will announce next week that it's accepting its first black intern—"

"Mom, it's so slow," Debbie interrupted.

"Darling, good things are always slow in happening. But they *are* happening."

"Scott's upset about all the emphasis on the space program," Debbie confided. "He says how will the country have money to handle problems here on earth if it's all going up there? And he worries about American troops being in Vietnam. I didn't even know where Vietnam was till Scott showed me on the map."

In a corner of her mind Fran remembered Bernie saying—early in World War II—that most Americans had never heard of New Guinea or the New Hebrides or Iwo Jima.

"He's not army reserve, is he?" This wasn't the harbinger of another world war, was it? Why did the world always seem on the edge of disaster?

"No!" Debbie frowned. "If this country was attacked, he'd fight. But doesn't everybody understand that another war could mean total annihilation?"

"Darling, let's not be so grim," Fran scolded. She didn't want to remember the war years. She didn't want to remember that Bob and Sal had not come home. Even now—all these years later—she felt tears sting her eyes when she recalled the awful moments she'd learned that Bob and Sal had been killed in action. "What's Scott planning on doing for the summer?"

"He'll stay in Atlanta," Debbie said. "He'll be working with a group fighting to integrate Atlanta restaurants. He says it's just a matter of time before it happens."

"Let's pray there's no more trouble," Fran said softly.

In the weeks ahead it became clear that Atlanta was moving forward in its efforts to integrate the city. Its citizens were coming to understand that integration was the law of the land and must be observed.

Driving to the airport with Robin in late July, Fran was conscious of the changes that had occurred in the South.

"You're quiet," Robin drawled. "Does this mean you're going to sleep all the way to New York?" Again, Robin chose to travel with her. Sometimes Fran was sure he relished shocking Bellevue with blatant hints that the two of them were having an affair.

"Don't count on it," she tossed back. "I expect you to keep me laughing all the way to New York."

"I wish you'd go with me to Acapulco," he said, charmingly wistful. "Instead of leaving me to the mercy of all those predatory women."

"You'll be brave."

She was glad that Robin had become part of her life. He amused her. He comforted her in moments of crisis. He never said a word, but she knew he sensed a special feeling between Craig and her. He had become very dear to her. Her mother found their relationship incomprehensible. She suspected Lynne and Debbie understood.

As before, Robin found a taxi for them at the airport, drove with her to her hotel, then headed for his own destination in the Village.

"See you in two weeks," he said at her hotel entrance and kissed her goodbye.

Today Fran was pleasantly conscious that Columbia Law classes would begin in less than six weeks. At last, Lynne would be on track again. For a while she had been afraid that marriage would be the end of Lynne's dreams of becoming an attorney.

Always conscious of the need to utilize every hour on these trips into New York, Fran checked into the Essex House, mindful of her schedule. She'd head for Seventh Avenue, spend the day buying for the shops. At seven o'clock Lynne and Arnie would pick her up for dinner. Tomorrow she'd have lunch with Lynne—a cherished mother-daughter time, then in the evening go to Lynne and Arnie's apartment for dinner. The next day she'd finish up her buying and take an afternoon flight to Atlanta.

Emerging from the hotel into the late morning sunlight, she remembered with distaste that July in New York was often sultry. The city was in the grip of a heat wave. She flagged down a taxi, gave the driver her destination, and focused on the business ahead.

By 6 P.M. she was en route to the Essex House again—churning with impatience because of the stop-and-go traffic uptown. She'd been up since before 6 A.M. to make the early flight, and was exhausted from the city heat. She longed for a leisurely tub, a brief nap—but the shower would be quick, the nap nonexistent. She reveled in the knowledge that in an hour she'd be with Lynne.

She was dressed and waiting when Lynne called from downstairs.

"Darling, I'll be right down."

She hurried from her room to the elevator—her face aglow with pleasurable anticipation. Emerging from the elevator she spied Lynne and Arnie. Lynne looked lovely, she thought with tender pride.

"Mom!" Lynne darted toward her. "Oh, it's so good to see you!"

Fran and Lynne kissed with joyous warmth. Then—almost shyly—Arnie came forward to kiss his mother-in-law.

"I ordered better weather for you, but I guess I don't have much influence," Arnie joshed.

"I made reservations for us at the Russian Tea Room," Fran said. Not only was this her favorite, but the favorite she'd read somewhere, of great pianist Arthur Rubenstein—a fact that endeared it to Arnie.

Over dinner in the romantic, Old World restaurant Lynne talked ebulliently about Arnie's efforts to get a production for the musical he and Ron had written out on the coast.

"It's not set yet," Arnie broke in self-consciously. "The producer has some of the money up, but not enough for the Equity bond."

"But he's sure he'll raise it," Lynne broke in. She didn't want it to sound as though Arnie was fishing for an investment, Fran interpreted. "The real problem is whether we can convince Ron to fly out here to work on revisions once a production is definite."

"Anyhow, we're walking around with our fingers and toes crossed." Arnie seemed to alternate between optimism and anxiety.

"How's the job going?" Fran asked Lynne. Her letters were short and sketchy.

"I love it," Lynne said. "I'm learning so much." Again, Fran was conscious of an odd withdrawal on Lynne's part.

"It's like serving an internship," Arnie joshed. "You know, there was a time when people were admitted to the bar in some states without even going to law school. They just took the bar exams after working for years in a law office."

Later—lying wide awake when she'd expected to fall asleep the moment she was in bed—Fran tried to dissect the strange undercurrent she'd sensed in Lynne and Arnie. An air of exhilaration that was dampened by apprehension, she realized. But that was natural, she told herself—they'd waited so long for Arnie to see some success, and now it seemed almost at hand.

When she left the hotel in the morning, Fran was pleased to discover the heat wave had broken. She sensed an air of relief in the hordes of New Yorkers that walked with the usual rush-hour swiftness to nearby stores and offices, to the subway stations and bus stops. It was as though they'd emerged triumphant through yet another obstacle course that was part of city living.

She found a coffee shop and went in for breakfast. She tried to concentrate on the morning's activities, but at errant moments she remembered her feeling that Lynne and Arnie were holding something back from her. Still, they seemed genuinely happy. It was just that they were nervous about the possible Off-Broadway production, she comforted herself.

Should she offer to invest in a small way? In a corner of her mind she heard Robin's warning *not* to back a production for her son-in-law. But this wasn't costly Broadway—and Arnie said some of the money had been raised.

She left the coffee shop and searched for an empty taxi—not a simple matter in the morning rush hour. She was astonished when a distinguished middle-aged man made a dash for a cab she was trying to flag down, then retreated in her favor. He'd deferred to her cane, she thought in amusement—but she was aware, too, his glance had been admiring.

Her morning buying was satisfying. She always arrived at the showrooms with a knowledge of what she wished to offer in her shops—a knowledge based on advance rumors of what Paris couture would be promoting. Lynne had said apologetically that she couldn't be sure when she'd be able to get out for lunch, so they'd decided to meet at the Charleston Gardens in B. Altman's. Lynne would pick her up in the ladies lounge.

Walking into the elegant store, Fran felt a surge of nostalgia. Midore had loved to meet her for lunch at the charming restaurant—a luxury they could afford at rare intervals in those days. She was so pleased at Midore's success in the art world. The next time Midore was in New York for a gallery showing, she must arrange for a brief reunion. Midore had seen Cliff and his wife at a doctors' convention in San Francisco four years ago. The next time Cliff wrote that he'd be in New York for a convention, she'd contrive to be in the city, too. On his last newsy letter at Christmas—their annual exchange—he'd said he was hoping that Atlanta would be the site of their next convention. Atlanta had become such an important convention city.

Rather than lingering in the ladies lounge, Fran strolled about the area and viewed the merchandise on display. She heard footsteps racing down the aisle from the elevator and instantly knew Lynne was approaching.

"Have you been waiting long?" Lynne prodded her mother back toward the bank of elevators.

"Just a few minutes," Fran fabricated. "Then I heard those quick footsteps and I knew it was you. Nobody walks as fast as you and Debbie," she said, laughing.

They went up to the restaurant and joined the line at the picturesque entrance. Fran was relieved that their wait for a table was brief. The Charleston Gardens—a whimsical ode to the Old South—was huge, with endless tiny tables scattered about the enormous, high-ceiling room. Its walls were adorned with mammoth murals depicting scenes from earlier days in Charleston. The atmosphere, Fran thought, was that of a charming, private women's club.

Fran knew Lynne was nervous about taking longer for lunch than the allotted one hour. But she'd be quitting soon, anyway, to start classes at law school.

"You're looking terrific," Fran told Lynne when the waitress had taken their orders and left. "There's a special kind of glow about you—" And there was something else. A kind of anxiety?

"I'm feeling great," Lynne said, and hesitated. "Oh, I wasn't going to tell you until after lunch. I made Arnie promise not to say anything last night. Mom, I'm pregnant."

"Oh, Lynne, how wonderful!" This was her initial, spontaneous reaction. "Are you pleased?" she asked hesitantly.

"Mom, how can I not be pleased?" she reproached. "But it doesn't mean I'm giving up law. It's just another delay. You know how stubborn I am. Like you." Her smile was tender. "Grandma will be out of her mind. And you?" Her tone was teasing, yet Fran sensed her apprehension. "Do you mind becoming such a young-looking grandmother?"

"Oh, darling, I'll love the baby," she promised, but her mind was in chaos. "I'll be the most fatuous grandmother in this world!" Lynne was right, she told herself. This didn't mean Lynne wouldn't go back to law school later. Women today had careers and were mothers, too. Lynne was so young. She could handle it.

"Arnie's going to look for a full-time job in another month," Lynne said with a confident smile. That was what bothered her, Fran understood—that Arnie would be tied down to a job he disliked. "The next three or four weeks are crucial for the Off-Broadway production. But even if it comes off, we won't see money for ages. And we both know the uncertainty in the theater—and in the music business. We know Arnie has to work for a while—until he has a hit musical or a record that makes the charts. But it won't be forever. Even when he's working, he'll be writing music."

On the flight back to Atlanta Fran tried to deal with Lynne's pregnancy and its ramifications. Was it wrong for her to be disappointed that Lynne wouldn't be going to law school in the fall? It wasn't just that she wanted Lynne to fulfill her father's dream, though that was part of it. She yearned to know that her daughters could have a life outside of the home, that they would have the skills to insure their being independent women. That they could cope with whatever life dealt them—and never be tied down, as Lynne wished for Arnie, to jobs they loathed.

The world was changing so fast these days. *Values* were changing. Women were asking more of life than the "joys of being a housewife." And many husbands, women declared, weren't upset about this. How did Arnie feel about Lynne's going back to school after the baby was born? she wondered.

She had no right to interfere, Fran warned herself—but she would do anything within reason to help Lynne go back to earn her law degree. That was her responsibility as Lynne's mother.

Twenty-Seven

F ran was met at the ever-crowded Atlanta airport by Debbie and Scott.

"Grandma told Betty Mae to hold dinner until you got in," Debbie said after she'd exchanged a warm embrace with her mother.

"Pecan pie for dessert, Mom." Scott leaned forward to kiss her. "I invited myself for dinner."

"There's always room for you at the dinner table." Fran enjoyed the way Scott attached himself to the family. "And in the guest room."

Frequently since the end of school Scott slept over. Her mother had been scandalized at suspicions that he used the guest room as a formality and shared Debbie's room. She herself had been uncomfortable about this for only a brief period. Young people today were more casual about their sleeping arrangements than her own and her mother's generation. And she knew that Debbie and Scott would marry the minute he got out of law school.

At the house Ida informed them she'd checked with the airport and learned Fran's flight had arrived on schedule.

"Dinner will be on the table in five minutes." Ida brushed past preliminaries. "Did you convince Lynne that it was time she moved back to Bellevue?"

"Not yet," Fran conceded. "What's been happening around town in my absence?" Later she'd tell them Lynne's news.

Fran listened with the attentiveness her mother appreciated while Ida reported on her local socializing until Betty Mae summoned them to the dinner table. As usual, conversation jumped from topic to topic—ranging from the continuing battles in the South against segregation to the increasingly serious situation in Vietnam, where American military advisers were accompanying Vietnam soldiers into combat.

"Sitting down to dinner with this family," Ida grumbled—and Fran noted affectionately that her mother's eyes said she included Scott in this category, "is like sitting down to a news conference. We can't worry about the whole world."

"Don't try to convince your daughter and granddaughter of that," Scott teased.

"What do you hear from your mother these days?" Ida asked him. Fran knew she was consumed with curiosity about the woman she expected to be Debbie's mother-in-law.

"She's still teed off at me for not coming home to work in the mill office this summer." Fran was sure his mother was unaware that he was involved with a local group fighting to speed up integration. He'd talked vaguely about working in an Atlanta law office. "And I gather she's not exactly pleased that union organizers are in Glenwood." The mill town where Scott's family lived was thirty miles out of Raleigh, the state capital. "Not that it'll cause her any trouble." All at once he seemed defensive. "She pays higher wages than the unions are asking for. And she built housing for her workers that's way above the national average."

"With so many mills closing down in the South," Debbie said, "workers are glad to have jobs."

"I don't know much about the business," Scott confessed. "That's Perry's scene."

Fran's thoughts raced back through the years to her brief encounter with union organizers here in Bellevue. What had happened to that girl? she mocked herself. Now the shops were her major concern—was she buying well, were the staffs efficient, was she showing the maximum profit? But above all, she told herself conscientiously, she was concerned for Lynne and Debbie.

At their ages she'd expected to go out and change the world—or at least to make a real contribution. She'd felt so good—that she was accomplishing something—when she'd fought to get those union organizers out of jail. When she'd fought for the release of Midore's parents from that awful internment camp. But after that, what had she done to justify her being on this earth? For some it would be enough to survive, to be able to raise a family. For her, she told herself with brutal candor, it wasn't enough. For all her success in business she felt a failure as a human being.

After dinner Debbie and Scott dashed off to a meeting of a student group supporting sit-ins at a local restaurant—which Ida pretended to ignore. Fran settled down with her mother to watch "Hazel" on television. But at the first commercial—despite her intention to wait till Debbie was home to tell her mother and Debbie together—Fran blurted out the news that Lynne was pregnant.

"Frannie!" Her mother was ecstatic. "Wait till I tell the girls! I'll be the first great-gran among them! I knew that sooner or later Lynne would come to her senses. They won't want to raise the baby in the city," she said with conviction. "They'll come to Bellevue and Arnie will get a steady job. I could talk to Ethel about a job in her grandson's firm—"

"Mother, hold on. They're not coming home. Couples do have babies in New York—but yes, Arnie's going to find a full-time job."

"Living is so expensive in New York," Ida protested. "You said so yourself. And we have crazy inflation—"

"I don't think the inflation is all that bad," Fran said candidly. "I think people are demanding more—partly because of television. We watch TV and see lifestyles that are unrealistic for the average family. Since the end of World War Two so much that seems almost miraculous has come on the market!"

"So what's wrong with that?" Ida bridled. "It's progress."

"People see all these marvelous new things—and they want them. So many young couples put themselves into debt to buy a larger TV set, a new car, a house—"

"Frannie, you talk like we were still living in the Depression!" her mother scolded. Not that they'd suffered in the Depression, Fran thought subconsciously. "This is a whole different world. The economy's thriving. You've said so yourself. Look how well you're doing," she wound up with a triumphant smile. "This country has never had it so good. Oh, we'll talk later—'Hazel' is back."

Fran was reliving her own pregnancies with Lynne—remembering the joy of those months. Her mother shopped rapturously for baby clothes until Lynne protested that she wasn't expecting triplets. Fran contrived a business trip to New York in late October—"resort clothes are becoming a major item." Arnie was all wrapped up in Lynne's pregnancy, she noted with pleasure—he wasn't depressed because he was making no headway with his music—and he was philosophical about his accounting job.

She was wistful that Lynne and Arnie wouldn't be coming to Bellevue for Thanksgiving. It was agreed among the family that it would be unwise for Lynne to travel this late in her pregnancy. Nor would Lynne and Arnie be going to his parents for Thanksgiving. Never warm, his relationship with his parents had become—Lynne said—"as cold as the Arctic Circle" since his parents had retired to Florida. His relationship with his sisters—also in Florida now—was similar.

Fran was pleased that Lynne had seen Midore on one of her occasional trips to New York.

"We had a wonderful evening together," Lynne wrote. "She says that strange things are happening on the Berkeley campus. The *New York Times Magazine* just ran an article on campus activities, saying that students are mainly concerned with success and their own personal lives—but at Berkeley, Midore says, there are rumblings of concerns about issues—like integration and what's happening in Vietnam."

Then thoughts of Thanksgiving gave way to the horror of the JFK assassination. The whole nation spent the next four days glued to television sets. On Friday afternoon—in Dallas—the President was assassinated. At 4:34 A.M. on Saturday—a day of heavy rains and strong winds—the flag-covered casket containing the late President's body was brought into the White House, to be placed upon the catalfaque in the East Room. On Monday the body was taken to St. Matthew's Cathedral for a funeral mass and then to Arlington for internment. It was a grim interlude that would remain forever in the memory of Americans who lived through those days.

On New Year's Eve—with Debbie and Scott opting to spend the occasion with her mother and grandmother—Debbie announced that she and Scott would be married in June, after his graduation from law school.

"I knew you'd never forgive me, Grandma, if I didn't have a June wedding," Debbie joshed.

"At last a woman in this family with brains." Ida sighed with pleasure. "Fran, you have to start right away with the reception plans. And book the synagogue for—"

"Grandma, a June wedding—but not a spectacle," Debbie warned. "And no engagement announcements. Just send out wedding invitations at the latest date. If it gets too fancy, Scott might walk out on me."

Soon there would be just her mother and herself in the big new house, Fran thought at disconcerting intervals. Debbie had confided that she and Scott would live in North Carolina—"*at least for a while.*" His mother insisted on his becoming the company lawyer.

"She's offering a great salary plus we'll have our own house rent-free.

She built it for Perry and his wife," Debbie explained, "but they're happy living in the family house. I gather it's a real showplace. Perry's wife, Olivia, manages the house so Mrs. Richards is free to concentrate on the mill. And Scott is sure—with his mother's pull in town—I'll land a job on the local newspaper at the first opening—or maybe even a job on a Raleigh newspaper."

Now the two concerns in Fran's life were Lynne's pregnancy and Debbie's coming marriage. Lynne was due to deliver in late January or early February. Fran had scheduled her next New York buying trip for the end of January—and hoped that she would be in the city when Lynne went into labor. Meanwhile, her mother had avidly taken on much of the responsibility of handling Debbie's June wedding.

Fran followed her usual New York schedule. She phoned Lynne from the airport, arranged to meet her and Arnie at the hotel at dinner time—with the day's buying complete.

"Darling, you are enormous!" Fran greeted Lynne with a rush of love and tenderness that was almost painful.

"I just hope she can fit into our table at the restaurant," Arnie teased. "This may be her last night out before delivery."

"Then I'm glad we're having dinner at the Russian Tea Room," Lynne said ebulliently.

Out in the crisp cold of the night Fran and Arnie joined forces to insist they take a cab for the short trip to their destination.

"This is ridiculous," Lynne chided her mother and husband. "Having a baby is a normal act. Stop coddling me." But she capitulated.

Lynne refused to be depressed over the last-minute collapse of plans for Arnie's musical to be presented Off-Broadway. Now he was waiting for word from a fledgling music publisher who appeared interested in his latest song.

"Not that we'll be rich if Arnie sells a song to a publisher," Lynne admitted with a practicality that Fran relished. "But he'll have a foot in the door."

Before Fran left New York, she made arrangements for a baby nurse to come to stay with Lynne when she was home from the hospital. She remembered how her mother had spent two weeks with her when Lynne was born. She brushed aside incipient guilt that *she* couldn't be there for Lynne. But Lynne understood, Fran comforted herself. These were different times. Women had jobs, careers.

Lynne was fretful in these final days of her pregnancy.

"Stop complaining," Arnie scolded good-humoredly as they prepared for bed on a night that promised a snowstorm. "When the little guy's ready, he'll let you know."

"He—or she," Lynne emphasized, "should realize his lease is up. It's time to move into the outside world."

"Relax, honey." Arnie reached to hold her close—as close as was possible in her present condition. "Maybe he's waiting for me to finish the lullaby I'm writing for him."

Three hours later Lynne awoke in the night cold with a sudden realization that she was in labor. After all these months, she thought with a sense of wonder, *it* was going to happen. Her baby—hers and Arnie's—would arrive.

"Arnie," she whispered. "Arnie—" She reached to shake him into wakefulness. "It's time—"

Though they realized it would be hours before she would deliver, Lynne and Arnie prepared to head for the hospital. The middle of a snowstorm would not be the time to look for a taxi on Manhattan streets. The car they had bought in California was long gone.

"They can't throw us out of the hospital," Arnie said with an air of defiance as they left the apartment house and began the search for an empty taxi. "We'll go to the cafeteria and have coffee if they don't want to admit you yet."

"You'll have coffee. I'll watch," Lynne said flippantly. "I'm a woman in labor. No eating, no drinking."

In late afternoon—with Manhattan a winter wonderland—Lynne gave birth to a seven-pound-three-ounce daughter.

"She's the image of you," Arnie decided when the three of them were united in Lynne's private room—a luxury provided by the new grandmother. "Jessica Anne Alexander." Jessica in memory of Lynne's grandfather, Anne for her great-grandmother.

"I'll call Mom," Lynne said. "I know she's been nervous these last two weeks. They're probably sitting down to dinner now, but nobody'll mind."

"I'll dial for you." Arnie reached for the phone.

"Arnie, I just had a baby—not major surgery," she said with tender laughter, but she allowed him to dial for her.

"It's ringing," Arnie said and handed the phone to her. "I'll take Jessie." Already the diminutive was in use.

"Hello—" Her grandmother's voice came to her.

"Grandma, it's me," she effervesced. "Is Mom home yet?"

"She's going out for dinner with Robin—straight from the office," Ida said. "Are you all right?" Lynne heard a note of anxiety now.

"I'm fine." Lynne hesitated. "I wanted to tell you and Mom together—but I can't wait another minute! Grandma, Jessica Anne Alexander was born a couple of hours ago. You're a great-gran!"

Lynne exchanged an indulgent smile with Arnie as she listened—beckoning to him to eavesdrop—while her grandmother erupted into a joyous monologue. Then she waved Arnie away. Now came the familiar exchange between two women who'd experienced the pain and joy of childbirth.

"If I can stay awake late enough, I'll call Mom," Lynne promised at last and said goodbye. No doubt in her mind that—despite business obligations—her mother would be in New York within twenty-four hours to see this first grandchild.

Scott tried to conceal his tension as he waited at the Atlanta airport with Debbie for his flight to Raleigh to be announced. Since his first year at boarding school it had been tradition for him to spend Christmas and the school spring vacation at the family house.

"Scott, you can't chicken out," Debbie warned, holding his hand as though this would be a year's separation rather than a week's. "You have to tell your mother we're getting married. Grandma says she can't hold up the invitations for more than another week."

"I'll tell her," Scott soothed.

"But it'll be a bitch," Debbie surmised.

"Sort of," he conceded. He'd made no secret that he expected his mother to be upset. "She'll scream I'm too young. Perry got married at twenty-five and was divorced five weeks later. He didn't marry Olivia until he was thirty. This one seems to be taking, though Mom is annoyed that they haven't presented her with a grandson." He chuckled. "The heavens will fall if we do that before them."

"Tell her my mother will call her shortly."

"She'll hate that," Scott surmised. "Your mom is so up front—she doesn't play silly games."

Then Scott's flight was announced.

"You make sure your grandmother doesn't move the wedding from the synagogue to the football stadium," he said with mock sternness as they walked to the boarding gate. "Every time I talk to her, she tells me how the invitation list is being extended. If I didn't like her so much, I'd insist we elope."

Scott was restless every moment of the short flight to Raleigh, on the thirty-mile drive to Glenwood. He dreaded the imminent encounter with his mother. He felt a painful tightness in the back of his neck as he emerged from the taxi and headed for the stairs to the tall, white, colonnaded mansion that had been the Richards's home since Perry was two.

He rang the doorbell. Moments later Amos—the longtime houseman—arrived to admit him.

"Welcome home, Mist' Scott," Amos said with genuine warmth as Scott reached to hug him. "Your mother told me you'd be arriving sometime today."

Scott was relieved to learn that only the servants were in the house. His confrontation with his mother would be delayed. He'd wait until after dinner to tell her about his getting married, he stalled. A hundred to one Perry and Olivia would be going off somewhere for the evening. He and Mom would be alone.

Perry and his mother were probably still at the mill, he guessed. Olivia would be out socializing. She and Perry were constantly plotting to acquire friendships that would be useful when Perry entered politics. A date that his mother would choose, he thought with a touch of humor.

Perry would go into local—and then state—politics in order to protect their mother's financial interests, Scott reminded himself. *He* was to be the mill's lawyer and to be backup for Perry in politics. How did he get through to his mother that he meant to lead a life independent of the family?

He'd told Debbie they'd stay in Glenwood no longer than two years. His salary with the mill would be large, their expenses low. He meant to build up their finances to cover the period when he would be fighting to start up a private law practice in Bellevue. Early on he'd fought against going to law school—until he realized that as a lawyer he could fight for what he believed in. Mom would explode if she knew what he considered good.

At this point he was dependent on his mother. He'd been five years old when his father died—there'd been no inheritance provided in his father's will. Sure, he could go out and probably land some kind of job—but with two years of mill salary he and Debbie would have some security.

It was weird how he'd never felt that this was his home, he considered as he settled himself in the library. It was the place where he'd lived when he wasn't away at boarding school or camp or college. He thought of his grandmother on his mother's side—he'd never known his father's parents. She'd always made him feel so loved, so safe. He'd felt deserted when she died.

Mom would be upset that he was marrying young—and marrying a girl who happened to be Jewish. She'd made every effort through the years to divorce herself from her Jewish background. She had an elderly aunt whom the family hadn't seen in twenty years, distant cousins whom he had never met. And now, he thought, he was bringing Mom back to her roots. She'd hate that.

Shortly past six his mother and Perry arrived from the mill. Ten minutes later Olivia came home. As always, their meeting was casual—none of the beautiful warmth that permeated Debbie's house existed here.

As Scott had anticipated, Perry announced over dinner that he and Olivia were going to an affair at the Museum of Art and would have to forego dessert.

"I like to get to these things early," Perry said smugly. "That's when I can do business."

Dinner conversation alternated between mill activities and state politics. Margaret Richards was furious that a local black man was considering a run for the General Assembly.

"He can consider it," Olivia said coldly. "It'll never happen in this state." But wasn't North Carolina known as "The Dixie Dynamo"? It wasn't quite like the Deep South states, Scott mused.

After dinner Scott and his mother retired to the library. He knew the routine. He'd read the Raleigh newspapers and his mother would study whatever reports she'd brought home from the mill. At one point she'd suggest a half hour of television. *"I need to relax a bit."* After that he'd tell her that he was marrying Debbie.

But before his mother brought up a discussion of what TV program they should watch, Scott blurted out his news. His mother gaped at him in shock.

"You're just getting your law degree!" She found her voice—shrill and angry. "It's absurd to consider marriage now!"

"Debbie and I are marrying in June," he said, prepared to battle. "Her mother will be calling you in a couple of days."

"Who is this girl?" Her arrogance set his teeth on edge.

"Debbie Garfield." He saw his mother's brain computing this information.

"She's Jewish," Margaret Richards exploded. "You can't do that to this family!"

"I'm marrying Debbie—not the family." So his mother would throw him out. He'd find a job. He'd be coming out of law school with honors. He hesitated at his mother's silence. "Debbie's mother owns the Goldman Shops." A prestigious and lucrative chain.

"The daughter of a shopkeeper," Margaret Richards said contemptuously. As she herself had once been, Scott thought subconsciously—but his mother preferred to forget that. What was so great about being a mill owner? "What can she do for you?" Scott knew how proud she was of Olivia's family connections. "She's a nobody!"

"I'm marrying Debbie because I love her." Scott strained for calm. "I'm not concerned about what she can do for me."

"You should be!" Margaret shrieked and launched into a tirade against what she labeled a "demeaning marriage."

Scott was accustomed to his mother's rantings when she disapproved of his actions. He listened in grim silence. He'd been born out of favor. She'd never wanted a second child. She'd been fascinated by then with the business of running the mill, side by side with his father. Perry was the child she adored—the prospective heir to her mill empire.

"Debbie's mother will be calling you," he said again when Margaret Richards was at last silent—trembling with rage. "Will you come to the wedding?"

"I'll expect you to be at work at the mill by the last week in June," she told him. "I'll have the cottage painted by then."

"Will you come to the wedding?" he repeated. Why did he care? he thought miserably.

"If it fits in with my schedule." She gathered together the papers she'd been studying and slid them into a folder. "Good night, Scott."

Twenty-Eight

F ran was relieved that her mother was delighted to handle the myriad details of Debbie and Scott's wedding. She was touched that Robin took on the task of arranging for the flowers. His taste, she knew, was impeccable. It was Ida who insisted that the guest list include Craig and Joyce. *"He designed our gorgeous house—he deserves to be invited."* And in her mother's mind, Fran knew, Craig should have been Debbie's stepfather. Oh, she was happy Craig would be at Debbie's wedding. It seemed *right.*

At times she worried that she and Craig might betray their true feelings for each other. Joyce mustn't be hurt. That was their tacit agreement.

Lynne would come with their precious Jessie and remain in Bellevue for a week, Fran remembered tenderly. She was still shocked by Scott's warning that his mother might not show up, though—like Perry and Olivia, Scott's brother and sister-in-law—she had returned her RSVP card indicating attendance. Her brief conversation with Margaret Richards had been disconcerting. Scott's mother had been barely polite. Such a show of arrogance, she recalled—yet she knew of Mrs. Richards's reputation for philanthropy. Was her hostility based on her disapproval of Scott's marriage?

Each glance at a calendar was a shock to Fran. How the days and weeks were racing past! Despite Ida's grim warning that tradition required that the bride not see the groom on her wedding day before the ceremony, Debbie encouraged Scott to sleep over the previous night.

"Grandma, we're not superstitious," Scott coddled Ida. "We're too bright for that. Besides, I'm a nervous bridegroom—I have to be here for you to hold my hand. And you know you were my first choice," he teased. "I'm marrying Debbie to get into the family."

"Scott's family is weird," Debbie said somberly in a bedtime conversation with Fran and Lynne in their mother's bedroom. "But it's his family, and he loves them."

"Arnie's parents and his sisters are like strangers to us," Lynne said. "They're down there in Florida, and we might just as well not exist. They don't give a damn about Jessie. But you and Grandma make up for them," she told Fran. "And you and Scott," she turned to Debbie. "Jessie won't miss Arnie's folks."

"We'll always be there for one another," Fran promised, fighting back tears. "We're real family."

The family liked Arnie. They cherished Scott, Fran thought with candor while they prepared to go en masse to the synagogue. Betty Mae had been drafted to stay with tiny Jessie so that Lily could attend "her baby's" wedding. Debbie would have one of those rare "made in heaven" marriages, Fran told herself. How happy Bernie would have been today!

It upset Fran that Margaret Richards had wired two days ago that she would be in Chicago on business and unable to attend the wedding. On a *Sunday?* Fran asked herself in skepticism. Perry and Olivia were flying down in the small company plane for the ceremony but "would be unable to remain for the wedding reception and dinner." Again, business was cited as the reason. Their wedding gifts—Waterford crystal from Scott's mother, a silver serving tray from Perry and Olivia—had arrived.

How could she expect Debbie's in-laws to react in a normal fashion? Fran asked herself. Scott's relationship with them was often strained. Why couldn't Scott and Debbie settle in Bellevue, where they'd be so welcomed? She couldn't understand his insistence on working for his mother. Could the Richards's mill require a full-time attorney?

From early morning Sunday was hot and humid. Thank God for air-conditioning, Fran thought as the family—including Scott—climbed into the car for the drive to the synagogue. In her exquisite white chiffon wedding gown—the veil in a box in the trunk—Debbie sat up front with Scott, the other three women in the rear. Lily would be at the synagogue with one of her sisters—so proud to be there for Debbie's wedding.

How unexpected, Fran mused, that Debbie had chosen a traditional wedding. Of course, Debbie insisted this was to please her grandmother—but Fran suspected Debbie herself wished this to be a beautiful, memorable occasion.

"Wow, the place looks gorgeous," Lynne said when they paused to inspect the interior of the synagogue before heading for the "bride's room" at the rear. "Robin did a terrific job with the flowers."

"Scott, disappear before anybody knows we arrived together," Debbie hissed. "Go find Robin."

Fran was pleased that Scott had chosen Robin for his best man. There had been no thought of his brother's playing this role. Lynne was Debbie's matron of honor and only attendant. Debbie would be escorted to the *chupah*—the canopy under which the wedding service was performed in the Jewish faith—by her mother and grandmother.

While Lynne and Debbie talked about honeymoon plans—a ten-day stay at the Grand Hotel at Point Clear, Alabama—Fran tried to deal with her anxiety about Debbie's future in Glenwood. Their cottage on the Richards's estate was the equivalent of three city blocks from the family house, Scott said. Instinct told her that Debbie would do little socializing with Scott's family. But how awful for Debbie not to meet her mother-in-law until she and Scott returned from their honeymoon. Debbie had seen Margaret Richards—at a distance—the night she met Scott, at that affair in Atlanta. Fran squinted in recall. Wasn't it in honor of Margaret Richards? Something about the housing she was providing her mill workers?

Shortly before the ceremony was to begin, Olivia Richards presented herself at the "bride's room." She was tall, slender, blond, elegantly dressed. She exuded a strained politeness, Fran thought in annoyance. But Debbie, she decided, was too euphoric today to notice.

"I wouldn't trust that one any farther than I could throw her," Lynne whispered to her mother while Olivia and Debbie exchanged brief pleasantries. Then—trailing expensive perfume—Olivia left with an air of having performed a necessary, but disliked function.

With her teary-eyed mother Fran waited for the moment to escort Debbie—radiantly beautiful—to the *chupah*. Scott looked so handsome in his tux, she thought sentimentally. No two brothers could appear more different than Scott and Perry. At thirty-three Perry already displayed an air of dissipation. From wry remarks that Scott had dropped, Fran suspected his brother was a heavy drinker. In ten years, she guessed, Perry would be overweight and puffy-faced and appearing twenty years Scott's senior.

Suffused with love, Fran reached for her mother's hand when the rabbi at last pronounced Scott and Debbie husband and wife. Involuntarily she glanced about the guests—seeking Craig's eyes. For a precious moment they met and then veered on separate paths.

Even before Debbie had disappeared to change into her traveling outfit, Fran felt a poignant sense of loss. Debbie was going off on her honeymoon. Tomorrow Lynne would return to New York with darling Jessie. Already, Fran thought, she dreaded going home alone with her mother. Such a big house for two women. She was happy that both girls had found husbands they loved, she acknowledged, yet wistful that they would live in other cities. Thank God for planes, that brought cities close together.

"We'll be here for a lot of weekends," Debbie promised when she reached to kiss her mother goodbye. "You're not getting rid of me, you know."

"I've acquired more than a wife," Scott said gently, drawing Fran close. "I've acquired a family."

Lying awake long past midnight, Fran tried to dissect the apprehension that tugged at her. Why was Scott so insistent about going to work for his mother? With his record at law school, and his personal charm, surely he could have found a place for himself in Bellevue. What prompted him to work in a situation he frankly disliked?

"Mom's paying me a huge salary. We'll live rent-free. In two years we'll have a healthy bank account."

Yet there had been a strange undercurrent in his voice each time he made this same statement, Fran recalled. And her impetuous, outspoken daughter went along with this. What were they *not* telling her?

Debbie and Scott chose to honeymoon at the Grand Hotel at Point Clear, Alabama, where miles of sandy beaches are cooled in the summer by southwest winds from Mobile Bay. Scott had stayed there at fourteen with his boarding school roommate and the roommate's recently divorced mother.

"It was one of my good memories," he reminisced while he and Debbie settled themselves in their room in one of the two residential wings of the charming, low-slung building. "We happened to be there to witness a phenomenon that happens only here in the whole Western Hemisphere. For no reason we could understand—out of the blue—every kind of fish poured out of the bay and onto the beach. It lasted for several hours." Scott chuckled in recall. "Everybody had a feast of fish that night."

The sunsets were magnificent, meals a gourmet pleasure in a charming dining room that looked out on both beach and bay. An older couple who'd spent their honeymoon here forty-eight years ago and returned each year regaled Debbie and Scott with stories about the hotel.

"The first hotel was built in 1847," the recently retired judge told them. "There were two wharves in those days—one for men and one for women. Mixed bathing was not acceptable. During the War Between the States the hotel was used as a hospital to treat Confederate wounded. The present hotel was built in 1940. During World War Two it was a Marine training school for nine months. The legend is that the Marines removed their shoes before walking into the main building so as to protect the beautiful wood floors."

Debbie and Scott cherished their idyllic ten days at the Grand Hotel. She was wary of what lay ahead of them in Glenwood. With wistful reluctance she said goodbye to the hotel and the spectacular view from their room. Now it was time to put the honeymoon behind them and return to what Scott called the real world.

In Raleigh they stopped off at the car salesroom to pick up the new white Cadillac Coupe de Ville that was Fran's wedding gift.

"I'm scared—a little," Debbie confided, her head on his shoulder while they drove toward Glenwood. "I wasn't enthralled with Perry and Olivia. I'm intimidated by your mother."

Scott chuckled and reached to squeeze her hand for a moment. "Sugar, nobody intimidates you. You'll be fine."

"She'll be furious when she realizes why you're going to work at the mill," Debbie reminded for the hundredth time.

"I can't just stand by and do nothing. She made *promises*. I believed all those things she said about how she was dedicated to building terrific housing for her mill employees." Scott's face tightened, his eyes glittered. "Damn it, I should have known better! My mother has never made a move that wasn't to her personal advantage. She dragged me over to the mill village—for the first time in my life I was allowed there—because not only the Glenwood and Raleigh press but a crew from a national magazine would be there. You know, the philanthropic Margaret Richards and her two sons on display. Perry and I were props."

"I remember the shindig in Atlanta." Debbie's face was luminous. "I complained about having to cover it. If I hadn't been there, I might never have met you." But she felt Scott's pain, his anger at being used for his mother's promotional purposes.

"She showed the press the fourteen houses she'd had built—the ones photographed for the article. Conveniently built on a knoll away from the others. And she pledged to replace every one of the rickety shacks in the mill village. But I know, Debbie—not one more has been replaced. I was sick when I went back—on my own—and saw all those dilapidated two-room shacks that were home to the mill families. Five or six people crammed into each one. I mean to go into the mill and make her improve the living conditions of the workers."

"I love you for wanting to do that, but what chances have you got to sway your mother's way of running her empire?" Scott always said *she* made every decision. Not even Perry had any impact.

"I know I'll have to move slowly," Scott acknowledged, "but changes have to be made. She won't allow the unions in the mill. She's forever boasting that she pays higher wages than they're asking. But she rules their lives. She robs them of their dignity."

"We don't have to stay in Glenwood," Debbie reminded. "If it gets too rough, we'll move back to Bellevue."

"This is something I have to do." His hands tightened on the wheel of the car. "It's my responsibility to try to turn things around. My family grew rich from the pain and sweat of hundreds of mill workers. It's time they were given a fair shake."

Debbie grew tense when they approached the Richards estate. The relationship between Scott and his family was unreal, she thought. Scary. But she wouldn't be seeing much of them, she comforted herself. Working at the mill, Scott would be the one who'd have to deal with his mother and brother.

"This is all our land," Scott interrupted her introspection. "On both sides of the road."

Wooded fields lent an air of beautiful serenity to the atmosphere. The scent of summer flowers was everywhere. Then Scott was turning off the road into a long driveway flanked by towering oaks—the house not yet visible.

"Mom and Perry will be at the mill," Scott surmised. "We'll probably be expected to have dinner at the house and spend the first night there. But tomorrow we'll settle in our own cottage."

Debbie gazed with admiration at the Doric-columned Greek Revival mansion that came into view.

"It's beautiful, Scott." But the life within that house had been less than beautiful for him, Debbie remembered.

"We may see the inside of it once a month. And that'll be enough for me," Scott admitted. "When I was a little kid and Perry and I would fight, he'd tell me I was adopted. I wasn't really a Richards. But then I'd tell Grandma, and she'd kiss away all my doubts. 'You're *my* grandson,' she'd say with such pride. 'Your mother is my daughter. But what you'll be is what you make yourself.' "

They were greeted at the house by Olivia.

"Your mother is at the mill," she told Scott—which, of course, he knew. "She'll expect you both for dinner tomorrow night. Seven sharp." Debbie remembered that his mother lived on a tight schedule—like military school, Scott had once derided. "She asked me to give you the keys to the cottage." She turned to Debbie with a condescending smile. "I furnished the cottage for Perry and myself, but we've never lived there. I do hope you like it."

"I'm sure it's lovely." Debbie managed the Southern politeness the situation demanded.

"Your mother arranged for domestic help," Olivia told Scott. "Edith sleeps out, but she'll come in each day to cook and clean. It's become awfully difficult to find domestic help these days." She pantomimed her distaste for the current situation. "We have to close our eyes to so much."

Debbie and Scott left the house and returned to the car.

"A respite until tomorrow night," he said and chuckled. "Be brave, Sugar—you can handle it."

The white clapboard cottage was charming, Debbie conceded after a warm welcome by Edith, who conducted them on an impromptu tour of the six sprawling rooms.

"Dinner tonight can be ready twenty minutes after you say you want it," Edith said. No more than eighteen, Debbie guessed, Edith radiated an ingratiating warmth. "I stay until I serve and clear away and clean up. Then I goes home." She hesitated. "What time would you be wanting dinner most nights?" she asked, a hopeful glint in her eyes.

"As soon as my husband comes home from the mill," Debbie told her and turned to him. "What time will that be, Scott?"

"About six, I imagine," he said casually. "Unless there's some late meeting."

"Is there a dishwasher?" Debbie asked.

"Oh, yes, ma'am," Edith said.

"Then you can serve and leave each night," Debbie told her. "We'll clear away ourselves."

"Thank you, ma'am." Edith's smile was dazzling.

"I'm starving. What about you, Debbie?" Scott asked.

"Famished. As soon as dinner's ready, Edith, we'll sit down."

The following day Scott drove Debbie into Glenwood. He understood he was not to report to work just yet.

"Mom's giving me a break," he drawled. "We'll sightsee today."

Glenwood was a replica of most small mill towns, Debbie noted. She'd driven through several in Georgia and Alabama. Dreary little enclaves, she thought sympathetically—with one or two blocks occupied by drab stores, the requisite bank and church.

"Okay, you've seen Glenwood—except for the school," Scott teased. "Let's drive on to Raleigh. It's the state capital. A very progressive city."

Debbie admired the gently rolling terrain of Raleigh, the wide residential streets lined with towering oaks, the mixture of old and modern architecture.

"You have to see the Capitol, of course," Scott said. "There are always tourists there."

"I'm not a tourist," Debbie flipped. "We're residents."

Scott parked at Capitol Square, and they left the car to follow a group of teenagers who were clearly tourists.

"There are forty-eight different trees here," Scott told her. "The huge ones white oak and very old."

Scott pointed out the statuary of Andrew Jackson, James K. Polk, and Andrew Johnson. "North Carolina gave the country three presidents."

The State Capitol—in the center of Capitol Square—was a magnificent, granite, Greek Revival structure.

"To appreciate it," Scott said, "you have to see it floodlighted at night."

From the Capitol Scott took Debbie to see North Carolina State University, set on a wooded landscaped campus of over thirty acres. Debbie admired the War Memorial—a 116-foot tower of white granite that dominates the eastern campus. Scott led her to the Andrew Johnson house, where the seventeenth President was born.

"Scott, it's so tiny," Debbie marveled.

The two-story frame house, surrounded by a picket fence, was about twelve by eighteen feet, Debbie judged.

"There're two rooms downstairs," Scott told her, "and just one upstairs." He pointed to the dormer window under the shingled gambrel roof. "It was a long way from the White House."

Debbie was impressed to learn that education received enormous respect in North Carolina—and she remembered, too, that back in 1960 in Raleigh—as well as in other North Carolina cities—black students had staged sit-ins at the lunch counters at the local F.W. Woolworth store. Scott referred to the sit-ins as North Carolina's version of the Boston tea party.

"I'm going to try for a job on a Raleigh newspaper," Debbie said determinedly. "They won't know what rotten assignments got thrown at me back home. I'll improvise a little."

Later—driving up to the entrance to the Richards's home—Debbie ordered herself to be sweet and casual and properly deferential to Scott's mother. If Scott was to work at the mill, it was important not to create a hostile environment. And while she wished they were settling in Bellevue, she respected Scott's need to be here.

There was a new mood in the country in the last year—particularly among their generation. Their generation was concerned about *people*, Debbie thought with pride. Scott wasn't playing Don Quixote—he was recognizing that the world had problems that must be solved. She smiled, visualizing the decals they'd seen on college campuses—both in Atlanta and in Raleigh: "I Am a Human Being—Do Not Fold, Spindle, or Mutilate."

At the house Debbie and Scott were greeted by Perry. He exuded arrogance, Debbie thought in distaste. Did this family—except for Scott—think they'd cornered the market on that? Still, she forced herself to smile when Perry referred to her as "the little woman"—but then Margaret Richards was the rare woman who'd made a phenomenal success in the business world. But that was going to change, Debbie reminded herself fiercely. Women were making demands now.

"Let's be realistic," Perry drawled. "Labor unions are fading away—between 1960 and 1962 they lost a half-million members, and the last two years they've lost more. What blue-collar worker wants to take a chance on losing his job permanently when blue-collar jobs are disappearing?"

"Perry, do you have to talk business even at home?" Olivia strolled into the library in what Debbie guessed was a Paris original. Pale green silk shantung, beautifully cut and draped. The dress probably cost as much as a mill worker earned in a year. Olivia's emerald necklace and matching earrings confirmed her expensive tastes. "Hello, Scott." She turned, faintly smiling, to Debbie. "How do you like the cottage?"

"It's lovely," Debbie lied politely. Too formal, too ornate for her—but then they wouldn't be living there forever. Hopefully, for less than the two years Scott estimated. "And Edith is a treasure." She sounded like one of the new brides back home, Debbie mocked herself.

While the two women carried on superficial chatter about current books—Debbie was enthralled by Rachel Carson's *Silent Spring* and Olivia was "wading through" Mary McCarthy's *The Group*—Scott switched on the TV in search of news.

"Shouldn't there be some Wall Street report about now?" Perry asked Scott.

"I'm looking for some word about what's happening in Vietnam," Scott said grimly. "Later worry about Wall Street."

A few moments later Margaret Richards—wearing one of her expensive "little black dresses," ash blond hair drawn into a French twist—walked into the library. Debbie felt an instant tightness in her throat, a touch of panic.

"I knew Scott was here when I heard the television news," she said with an air of amused indulgence. "He can't be home for ten minutes without looking for a news program." She turned to Debbie. Her hazel eyes opaque now. "You must be Debbie."

"Yes." Debbie managed what she called her "sweet young thing" smile—uncertain about how to respond. Mrs. Richards made no effort at any physical contact. No embrace, not even a handshake.

"That's a smart frock," Mrs. Richards remarked after a swift inspection of Debbie's deceptively simple, beige crepe coatdress. "But then your mother's a shopkeeper," she recalled. "She has to know style."

Debbie was relieved when they were summoned to the handsomely paneled dining room. The table and chairs were Chippendale—the seats covered in needlepoint. Debbie guessed that the magnificent chandelier that hung over the table was Waterford crystal.

The conversation over dinner ranged between mill talk and an exchange between Mrs. Richards and Olivia about a charity event sponsored by the United Daughters of the Confederacy.

"Are the women of your family members of the UDC?" Mrs. Richards asked Debbie. The condescending glint in her eyes told Debbie she knew the answer would be negative.

"No, we're not," Debbie confessed with deceptive sweetness. "But my great-grandmother was a DAR member." Would membership in the Daughters of the American Revolution take precedence over the UDC? she asked herself irreverently.

"I'm president of our local UDC," Olivia intervened. She was aware, Debbie sensed, that their mother-in-law was startled and annoyed by her own retaliation. Did she know that there were Jewish members in the DAR? Scott was struggling to hide his amusement. "We're much involved in raising the educational standards in Glenwood."

"Are you and Perry going to Saint Simon's Island in August?" Mrs. Richards asked Olivia. "Or is he still bent on going to Monaco?" Debbie caught a hint of hostility between Perry and his mother. Scott had always said Perry could do no wrong in their mother's eyes.

"I'm writing for reservations at The Cloister on Sea Island," Olivia said, her smile reassuring her mother-in-law. What did Mrs. Richards have against Monaco? Debbie wondered. It was a popular resort among rich Americans. Debbie noted the tightness about Perry's mouth—he was annoyed at being overruled. "What does Monaco have other than its gambling casino?"

So that was the problem, Debbie pinpointed. Perry had a taste for gambling—something Scott didn't know—and their mother and Olivia meant to break him of that.

Debbie was pleased that the evening was to be cut shorter than she had dared to hope.

"Tomorrow is a work day. Perry and I have to be up at six A.M.," Mrs. Richards told Debbie and turned to Scott. "That means you, too. We strive to set an example for our employees. There was a time," she said with a bitter smile, "when the day shift was at the shuttles by six A.M.— but they've gotten spoiled through the years."

Before they left the table, a maid arrived with a pill on a small plate and a glass of water, which she handed to Margaret Richards.

"I have a minor heart problem," she told Debbie. "The doctor insists on this stupid medication."

Her mother-in-law was preparing for the day—no doubt, distant— when she would have to ease up on her sixty-hour work week, Debbie interpreted. She meant for Perry and Scott to carry on her dictates. But Scott wouldn't be here, Debbie vowed.

Tomorrow morning she'd drive Scott to the mill so that she could have the car, Debbie planned. And at a respectable hour she would present herself at a Raleigh newspaper and ask for a job. She suppressed a sudden impulse to giggle. She doubted that Margaret Richards had sent a social note to the Raleigh papers to announce Scott's marriage. In her mother-in-law's eyes she was not socially acceptable. Nor did she wish to be hired *because* she was Margaret Richards's daughter-in-law.

Twenty-Nine

I n late July Fran headed for New York on her usual buying trip. This year she was allowing herself an additional two days in the city. Cliff would be in New York to deliver a paper at a medical convention, and Midore was flying to New York to arrange for a showing of her work in the city in the fall. It would be a glorious reunion for the three of them. And, of course, she mused as the plane came in for a landing, she was always eager to see Lynne and tiny Jessica—now in a painful teething stage.

Today she went directly to Lynne and Arnie's apartment once she'd checked into the Essex House. In the afternoon she'd call on her buying offices. The day was sultry, even in midmorning. It would be a scorcher by noon, Fran thought, remembering the torpid heat that could inflict the city in the summer months.

Her face alight with anticipation, Fran hurried from the elevator to Lynne's apartment. Holding fretful Jessie in her arms, Lynne stood at the open door.

"Can it be just six weeks since I saw you?" Fran shook her head in disbelief as they exchanged a warm embrace. "It seems so long." She took Jessie into her arms and crooned affectionately while her granddaughter squirmed.

"She's having such an awful time with these new teeth," Lynne apologized. "We're up half the night with her, poor baby."

"It's hot in the apartment." Fran brushed moist tendrils of dark hair from Jessie's forehead. "The fan doesn't help much. Will the wiring here handle air conditioners?"

"I suppose—" Lynne thought a moment. "The people above us have air conditioners."

"I'll leave a check for two air conditioners," Fran said promptly. "Your advance birthday present." She used her customary excuse for a gift. "Let the three of you be comfortable in this ghastly heat."

Fran relished every hour she was able to spend with Lynne and Jessie. She listened to exasperating reports by Lynne and Arnie—each interrupting the other to add some omitted detail—about his efforts to crash the music business, his "near-misses" with prospective Off-Broadway productions. Still, Fran thought, they were sure Arnie would find success. On her third evening in New York, Fran met with Midore and Cliff for dinner in a Greenwich Village restaurant recommended to Midore by art world friends.

It was incredible, she thought with a blend of sentiment and affection, that it was so many years since they'd been able to spend time together. They'd shared such an important segment of their lives—time etched forever on their memories. She thought about Bob and Sal, who'd been part of their tight little group—and who had died in World War II. Each Memorial Day evoked fresh pain at their loss. She harbored such special memories of each.

Midore's parents had died four years ago—within three months of each other. Sitting in the charming Village restaurant while Midore talked enthusiastically about her fall show at a New York gallery, Fran remembered the poignant gratitude of Midore's parents for her efforts to rescue them from that horrendous internment camp during the war. She remembered Cliff's determination to practice medicine in a small town where he could fill a real need. *"I want to be useful. Doing what I like to do for people who need me."*

Midore and Cliff were both totally dedicated to their work. Like Craig, she thought involuntarily. No matter what happened in their lives, they had the beautiful satisfaction of knowing they were fulfilling themselves. She'd been robbed of that, she thought with a sense of loss.

Would there be a time when Lynne would go back to law school? For so long this had dominated her thinking. But there was no doubt in her mind that Debbie would follow through on her ambitions. Her impetuous, outgoing Debbie, she thought tenderly.

"How did you like London?" Midore's question to Cliff brought Fran back to the moment. "And how did you manage to take time from your practice to go there?" she teased.

"It was the first vacation Wendy and I had in six years. I figured it was a good time to see how the new associate I'd just taken in would handle the situation. You don't find many new young doctors who want to settle in such a small town. A financially depressed small town," he emphasized wryly, yet Fran recognized his satisfaction with his practice. "But you know what really excited me?" His eyes glowed now. "It was the socialized medicine setup in England. Wendy developed an abscessed tooth—and that wasn't going to wait until we got back home. The dentist there took care of her tooth," Cliff chuckled reminiscently. "Courtesy of the British government. And a woman who was staying at the same bed-and-breakfast as we were broke her wrist—and couldn't get over how all she had to pay was forty pence for a painkiller."

"I'll bet you still make house calls," Fran teased affectionately. House calls had become almost nonexistent in most places.

"You're damn right I do." Cliff was emphatic. "I don't want a mother with a kid running a high fever having to drag him from bed to my office, sitting there alongside other kids and spreading whatever he's got. I laid it on the line with my new associate. This is the way I run my practice— take it or leave it." His face softened. "And what do you know? He took it."

"I'm not entirely surprised," Midore said. "You know I've been teaching an art class at Berkeley for the last year. Kids today don't show the apathy we saw back in the fifties. They're concerned about what's happening in the world. I've become involved with a new group that's forming on campus—made up of undergraduates, graduate students, and some faculty. It's being called the FSM—the Free Speech Movement. We're all outraged at the way the university wants to silence political and civil rights demonstrations."

"They want to make it a concentration camp," Fran picked up, remembering the Japanese experience in World War II. "How sad!"

"There'll be trouble on campus when the new semester opens," Midore predicted. "But these kids are a new breed. They feel such a commitment to make the world a better place." Her gaze settled lovingly on Fran. "You know, Fran, you were born years before your time. You would fit right in with this new college generation."

But what did she do with all her commitment? Fran taunted herself. So she sent hefty checks to organizations she felt were fighting for a better world. She was an outsider, looking on—when she'd dreamt of being part of the action.

The three of them parted with candid reluctance almost three hours later and decided to manage lunch the following day. It was such a special time for them, Fran thought. They'd come a long way from those early days in New York. Midore and Cliff had stayed with their dreams.

She had not. In the eyes of the world she was a successful woman. Circumstances forced her to accept less than her dreams. Let that not happen to Lynne and Debbie.

From New York Fran took a flight to Raleigh. She'd planned on making just a few hours' stopover, but both Debbie and Scott insisted on her staying overnight. Debbie met her at the Raleigh airport.

"We're just getting settled in," Debbie told her while they walked to the car. "I have a lead on a job on a small weekly newspaper in Raleigh. And not," she said with satisfaction, "because I'm Margaret Richards's daughter-in-law. The editor asked if I was Perry's wife, and I said 'no.' Nobody seems to know that Scott's married. Anyhow, the editor is supposed to let me know in a few days."

Debbie and Scott made a pretense of being happy, Fran analyzed when the three of them sat down to dinner. They were happy with each other—not with their lifestyle. Scott admitted he detested the long hours each day at the mill.

"You know the situation, Mom." He spread his hands in a gesture of resignation. "I'm supposed to learn everything about the operation of that gigantic mill. How do people spend their whole lives working in the noise those machines generate?" He shuddered expressively. "Some of them represent three generations of a family."

"There's no sign of any more houses being built. Scott asks, but he gets no answers." Fran saw a new cynicism in Debbie's eyes. Debbie worried that Scott would become hurt and disillusioned, she suspected.

"Remember, I expect you both to come home for the long Thanksgiving weekend," Fran told them. "Lynne and Arnie will come down with Jessie."

"My mother will go to the Homestead with Perry and Olivia," Scott surmised. "Or to the Greenbrier. Thanksgiving was never a family holiday with us. When Grandma was alive, I went to stay with her. She served this huge Thanksgiving dinner to a collection of people she knew who had no place else to go for the holiday."

"We'll be four generations at the table this Thanksgiving." Fran's face was luminous. "That's beautiful."

For Fran the next months seemed to drag. The house seemed so empty, she thought, without the girls here. Robin sensed her loneliness and goaded her into heavy socializing. Her mother was always busy with her own friends and her volunteer groups.

When Robin decided to remain in Bellevue rather than to go to New York for Thanksgiving as he usually did, Fran invited him to Thanksgiving dinner. She'd realized he was unhappy, even before he confided that his long-term relationship with a young Greenwich Village artist—pursued through the past several years via his sporadic escapes to New York—had been broken off.

Lynne and Arnie flew down from New York with Jessie on Wednesday evening. Debbie and Scott arrived the following morning. The atmosphere in the house reverberated with festive spirits that Fran relished. At noon Robin arrived with an armful of chrysanthemums and a magnum of champagne. Almost immediately she sensed hostility in Arnie. Everybody else present knew Robin and liked him. Oh God, she thought, she'd forgotten Arnie's disappointment at not receiving a grant from Robin's foundation. Hadn't she made it clear to Arnie that Robin had no part in the selection process?

Ida abandoned the kitchen to Fran and the girls. She was euphoric at being able to monopolize ingratiating little Jessie. In the living room Scott and Robin were talking animatedly about the way President Johnson—newly elected with a landslide vote—was bringing a Texas aura to Washington.

"I had to go up there on business for the foundation a couple of weeks ago," Robin mused, "and you should have seen all the staid businessmen bouncing around town in cowboy boots and five-gallon hats. All of them wanting to look like John Wayne."

Checking on the turkey, Fran smiled as she listened to the voices of the two men. She glanced up when Arnie strolled into the kitchen.

"Anything I can do to help?" he asked. "I'll let Scott entertain your gay friend." His eyes showed a certain smugness that he'd deciphered Robin's sexual preference.

"Would you put out the plates and the silver?" she asked, forcing back an angry retort. How dare Arnie be so bigoted! It was his way of getting back at Robin because he'd lost out on his application for a grant, she interpreted. Still, she resented this attitude.

Fran was relieved that the lively conversation at the dinner table masked Arnie's covert contempt for Robin. She was conscious of Lynne's occasional anxious glances in Arnie's direction. How stupid of her not to have anticipated this, Fran berated herself. But how could she have not invited Robin for Thanksgiving dinner?

Late that evening—when Robin had left, Scott and Arnie were arguing good-humoredly in the living room about last month's World Series,

and Jessie slept in what was designated as "Lynne and Arnie's room"—
Lynne confided her news to her mother, sister, and grandmother.

"I'm not absolutely certain," she conceded, "but I suspect I'm pregnant again." She radiated happiness.

"Oh, a little brother for Jessie," Ida crooned, gathering Lynne into
her arms. "And another man in the family."

Though joyous that she would have a second grandchild, Fran was
conscious of a poignant sense of loss. Was it enough for Lynne to be
Arnie's wife and their children's mother? Women today demanded more
for themselves. They wanted to fulfill themselves as human beings. They
could be more than wife and mother.

Yet Fran knew she must be silent. This was a decision that Lynne
must make. But she was so young—let her use those years ahead well.
There was time for her to become a lawyer. She had to make it clear to
Lynne that the money—whatever it took, including a nursemaid for the
children—would be there for her.

Once confirmed, Lynne's second pregnancy became the focus of
Fran's life. She knew that having a baby was a normal process, yet there
was anxiety always in the back of her mind. Let nothing go wrong—let
Lynne be well and deliver a healthy baby.

She was grateful in the months ahead that Debbie and Scott managed
frequent weekends in Bellevue. Debbie liked the people with whom she
was working, yet she was restless in the newspaper's conservative philosophy.

"I know the publisher's fighting an uphill battle to stay afloat," Debbie conceded on an April weekend. "If he antagonizes advertisers, he'll
go under. But there's so much happening in the world that he and our
editor are scared to death to tackle! How can he ignore the fact that last
month more than thirty-five hundred U.S. Marines were sent to Vietnam—that in addition to the twenty-three thousand other Americans
serving as advisors to the Vietnamese? Why don't we write about the
twelve-hour all-night seminar at the University of Michigan protesting
this? And other schools are doing the same!"

"Honey, the paper's interested in local matters," Scott soothed. "And
those that are not controversial," he admitted.

"Yeah, they just loved J. Edgar Hoover's statement that there's an
overemphasis on civil rights," Debbie drawled.

"How're things at the mill?" Fran made an effort to divert the conversation.

"Lousy." Scott was grim. "There won't be any further new housing. My mother's on a soapbox now about how she's paying ten cents an hour higher to her workers than even the Textile Workers Union of America are demanding. What she doesn't tell them is that she holds a gun to their heads to make sure their production is higher than in any mill in the country. The workers have no health insurance—the mill won't even pay a part of that. The company provides no accident insurance—"

"And women," Debbie interrupted, rage in her eyes, "are all paid fifteen cents an hour less than men workers! For doing the same job!"

"My mother and Perry call me a commie for wanting to better working conditions." Scott all at once seemed exhausted. "I'm getting nowhere."

"Scott, you don't have to stay there," Fran said gently. "You can—"

"Mom, I have to stay," Scott interrupted. "I have to help make changes."

"But we have a deadline," Debbie reminded. "Two years and we're done."

June was memorable to Fran for two reasons. Early in the month Lynne gave birth to a second daughter, named Beth Isabel for Arnie's grandmother—and ten days later Debbie joyously reported in the course of a weekend in Bellevue that she was pregnant.

While Scott affectionately allowed Ida to beat him at a game of checkers, Debbie discussed this with her mother in the kitchen as they prepared a pitcher of iced tea to accompany the strawberry tarts Ida had made earlier in the day.

"We hadn't planned it," Debbie admitted, "but maybe it'll convince Scott that we ought to leave Glenwood. We haven't told his mother yet, but she won't be happy. She has the scenario all worked out. Olivia was to get pregnant and provide an heir to the Richards dynasty. *Then,* I suppose, it'd be all right for Scott and me to present her with a grandchild. What she doesn't know is that Olivia is determined not to have a baby—she's scared to death it'll wreck her clotheshorse body."

"It'll change your plans somewhat," Fran said carefully.

"Not for long, Mom," Debbie said with conviction. "I'll stay home with the baby for the first year. Then I'm going back to work. Scott agrees with this. He knows I'd go berserk just staying home and playing wife and mother. Some women can handle that. I know I can't."

"Why do you think your being pregnant will push Scott into moving out of the mill?" Fran probed.

"Because he'll remember how unhappy he was as a child. He'll want our baby to have the kind of love it'll have in this house. Mom, you don't know how much it's meant to Scott to be part of this family. He's like an alien in his mother and Perry's world."

Tonight Fran found sleep elusive. She lay restless in the darkness, sought—futilely—for a position that would be conducive to slumber. She couldn't blame the torpid heat, she told herself—the air-conditioning provided a blissful coolness. She worried about Lynne and Debbie—each with such a wonderful zest for living. Each so sure that motherhood would be only a temporary stopgap on the road to personal fulfillment.

They could be good mothers and good wives and still follow careers. Was that asking too much in this world?

Thirty

D ebbie studied her reflection in the full-length mirror of her bedroom closet and sighed. She had faced reality several days ago and had gone into Raleigh to buy her first maternity clothes. The sapphire blue velvet dress—cut fashionably above the knees—did little to conceal her blossoming pregnancy. But she couldn't go to their once-a-month dinner at Margaret Richards's house in one of Scott's old shirts hanging over a pair of slacks. If Olivia got pregnant she'd probably have a maternity wardrobe designed by Halston.

"Scott, I look fat," she wailed and turned to face him.

"Hey, don't talk that way about the mother of my child." He abandoned buttoning his shirt to pull her close. "Besides, I'm not a guy who goes for the Twiggy type."

"Your mother and Olivia will look like pages from *Vogue*—then I come in like the drab little housewife," Debbie mourned.

"That bulge is beautiful," he crooned, allowing a hand to rest on her tummy. "But let me warn you—don't bring up the subject of unions tonight." His eyes reflected a recurrent frustration. "Mom chewed me out like mad today when I suggested she might sit down and talk with the union representatives in town. 'Nobody's coming into my mill and telling me how to run it.' " He parroted her with such skill Debbie laughed.

"And of course, Perry backs her up."

"She's a little pissed at Perry lately." Scott frowned contemplatively. "I'm not sure why."

"Because Olivia isn't pregnant?" Debbie lifted an eyebrow in amusement.

"That could be part of it," he conceded. "But there's something else.

Perry is the son who could never do wrong—I'm the maverick. But she's been snapping at him."

"Maybe she knows he's into gambling?"

"What makes you think he is?" Scott appeared startled.

"Oh, you men," Debbie jibed. "Olivia has been dropping nasty hints since our first night in town." They saw Olivia once each month—at the requisite family dinner. Neither Olivia nor their mother-in-law made any effort to involve her and Scott in their social lives. Probably because both were scared to death she might drop the word that she was Jewish. "Olivia made that crack about 'what does Monaco have except a casino'— and there've been others. Your mother's sharp—she knows."

"Why would Perry gamble?" Scott was puzzled. "I'm not privy to figures but I'm sure he draws a hefty salary." Something that couldn't be said for Scott, Debbie thought grimly. He'd been led to believe his salary would be much higher. "He lives in a beautiful house, drives a late-model Jaguar. What's missing in his life?"

"Maybe he doesn't like his velvet prison." Debbie's eyes were eloquent. Margaret Richards ruled her empire like Catherine the Great, she thought—and everybody close to her knew this.

"He's impatient to move out into politics," Scott said after a moment. "I've heard them arguing about that. Mom wants him to wait until she thinks I'm able to take over some of his responsibilities at the mill."

"When are you giving her the message that we're not staying around unless you see drastic changes?" Debbie challenged.

"It's too early. I won't be able to accomplish anything with threats. She'll balk."

"Scott, we've been here thirteen months." Debbie's voice was involuntarily sharp.

"If I can just get through to her and make her understand that when workers are comfortable in their living conditions, they're in a better frame of mind. Productivity increases. In the long run it'll be financially profitable for her to build decent housing. I've been talking with the firm who built those first fourteen houses. Smart as my mother is, I know they padded the costs. I'm getting quotes from other builders—all lower by a long shot. When they're all in, I'll try again."

"Does your mother know you're talking to the builders?"

"Sugar, be real," Scott clucked. "Now let me finish dressing so we can get out of here. Thank God, we're always invited midweek. That means we can cut out early."

They drove the short distance to the Richards house. Sitting in the

car Debbie could feel the tension building up in her. She dreaded each
meeting with Scott's family. She respected Scott's obsession to make
changes in the mill, yet harbored little hope that this would happen.

Maybe her dislike was fed on the knowledge that Scott's childhood—
except for his times with his grandmother—had been so unhappy. Margaret Richards was constantly being described in magazine articles as
one of the country's most successful women—but as a mother to her second son she was a disaster.

At the house Debbie and Scott exchanged brief pleasantries with
Amos.

"Miz Margaret is in the living room," he told them. "With Mist'
Perry." He smiled warmly at Debbie. "You're looking mighty pretty, Miz
Debbie. Like always."

"Thank you, Amos." She felt a special fondness for him. Like his wife
Beulah, he'd been with the family since Scott was a baby. It was Amos
who used to drive Scott to and from his grandmother's house. Amos still
talked with deep affection—out of Margaret Richards's hearing—about
her mother's wonderful baking.

In the living room Perry and his mother were talking with matching
contempt about the efforts of the Textile Workers Union to organize in
the South. Debbie caught Scott's warning glance not to speak her mind.
She hated these games they had to play! she thought bitterly. His
mother abandoned the conversation about the union to complain about
the hot spell that had kept the area in thralldom for the past nine days.

Olivia—just back from two weeks in London—strolled into the room
with a guarded air. She was unsure of the reception her new "look"
would receive, Debbie interpreted.

Olivia had abandoned her slavish Jackie Kennedy image—the slim-
skirted, two-piece dress or suit, no collar, semifitted top, sleeves never
full-length—for Jean Shrimpton "mod." She wore a garish print that
ended inches above her knees, which skimmed her fashionably lanky figure.

"Is that what you bought in London?" Mrs. Richards lifted an eyebrow in amusement.

"It's a whole revolution," Olivia said. "The British are really taking
over fashion. They—"

"We'll go in to dinner now," Mrs. Richards interrupted as Amos appeared at the door. "I don't know what's happening in the fashion
world—" Her smile indicated both amusement and distaste.

As usual dinner conversation was led by Mrs. Richards. She drew

Perry and Scott into an in-depth discussion of the mill's direction. Olivia made no effort to conceal her boredom. Debbie managed a strained air of interest. At one point Scott tried to switch to talk of the situation in Vietnam, but his mother aborted this. She had no patience, Debbie remembered, for what she called "Scott's stupid obsession for the little people."

Debbie was relieved when—as usual—Scott's mother brought the evening to an early conclusion with the reminder that "tomorrow is a work day." In truth, she thought with a flicker of humor, this was a dismissal of Scott and herself. No doubt in her mind that there would be some catty criticism of her by her mother-in-law and sister-in-law once she was out of hearing.

"That was fairly painless," Scott teased when they were in the car. "You're off the hook for another month."

As Mom always said, Debbie reminded herself, she was married to Scott—not his family. But she clung to Scott's promise that they'd leave after two years in Glenwood—unless he saw a real opportunity to improve the mill workers' conditions. She loved Scott for his determination to do this, but—again she told herself—his chances were nil. He was just serving a self-imposed sentence.

Like many Americans of all ages, Fran worried about the situation in Vietnam. President Johnson announced late in July that the U.S. armed forces would be increased from 75,000 to 125,000. The draft would be doubled to 35,000 a month. In mid–October demonstrations against this country's participation in the war in Vietnam took place in major cities from coast to coast.

Fran was upset when—despite her advanced pregnancy—Debbie insisted on going with Scott to be part of the demonstration in Washington, D.C. Lynne wrote that she and Arnie were part of the New York demonstration. Would she have expected less of her kids? Fran asked herself. Her daughters were mirrors of herself, she thought lovingly.

Fran and her mother went up to Glenwood to spend Thanksgiving with Debbie and Scott.

"There's no way you'll make the trip home now," Fran insisted.

It was a warm, beautiful holiday that Fran treasured. But as Debbie approached her due date, Fran was anxious. Everything would be fine, of course—yet as with each of Lynne's pregnancies, she knew she'd never rest easily until Debbie gave birth.

Then the new year arrived—and Fran knew it was a matter of weeks before she'd be a grandmother for the third time. Making her routine shopping trip to New York in mid-January—with precious time spent with Lynne and her small family—she stopped off for a day's visit with Debbie and Scott. They were both deliriously happy about the baby. Debbie confided that Scott was frustrated that he could make no serious changes in the mill operations.

Home again, Fran found herself battling insomnia. This would stop, she knew, once Debbie had the baby. At this time of year morning was slow in arriving. When the insistent ringing of the phone—seeming more shrill than normal in the quietness of the house—nudged Fran into semi-wakefulness on the final day of the month, she squinted at the clock without seeing. It must be the middle of the night! She reached for the phone with one hand and the lamp switch with the other.

"Hello—" It was 6 A.M., she noted.

"Mom, it's me—" Scott's voice. Instantly she was alert. "Debbie told me to wait for a respectable hour to call you, but I couldn't. You have a third granddaughter—about fifty minutes old!"

"Oh, Scott, how wonderful! How's Debbie? And the baby?" Questions tumbled over one another as she was assaulted by joy, anxiety, and a need for reassurance.

"Mom, hold it!" Scott chuckled. "Debbie's great. The baby has all the standard equipment. She's gorgeous—like all you beauteous Garfield women. Debbie says she'll call you around eight A.M.—after you've had your morning coffee. She—"

"I may not be here," Fran interrupted blithely. "I'm calling the airport—I'll be on the first flight to Raleigh this morning."

"Call me before you board the plane and give me the arrival time. I'll pick you up."

They talked a few moments, then Fran ordered Scott off the phone. She was impatient to schedule her flight. But she didn't leave the bed immediately—she allowed herself a minute to lie back and savor this latest gift. Oh, she was rich! Three precious granddaughters. She remembered—amused and tender—her mother's insistence that Debbie carried a boy. She hesitated, bursting to pass along the news. Should she wake her mother and tell her that Diane Janice Richards—Diane for Scott's grandmother—had arrived? Her mother complained about getting one good night's sleep in three—*"It's part of growing old, Fran-nie"*—but conceded that her "catnaps" during the day were rewarding. Tell her, Fran decided. Joy like this must be shared!

"Mother—" Fran hovered over Ida's bed. "Wake up—"

Ida frowned and slowly opened her eyes.

"I just had a call from Scott," Fran began.

"Debbie had the baby!" Ida reached out for Fran's arm. "A boy?"

"A girl," Fran cajoled.

Ida hesitated an instant. "Oh well, then she can inherit all of Jessie's and Beth's clothes."

"I have to call the airport and make a reservation."

"Wake Lily and tell her. Then the three of us will sit down to coffee."

In minutes the kitchen was fragrant with the aroma of freshly brewing coffee. In her bedroom Fran dressed with feverish speed and hurried to join the other two women in the kitchen.

"So when will one of my grandchildren give me a great-grandson?" Ida demanded. "I won't be around forever, you know."

"Stop looking at the calendar," Fran ordered. "Enjoy each day as it comes along."

"Eat something," Ida said, her smile complacent. "The new grandmother needs to keep up her strength."

As arranged, Scott was at the Raleigh airport to meet Fran's flight. They clung together in the knowledge that this was a most special day in their lives. Fran was impatient to see Debbie and the baby, and hid her irritation when she learned that Margaret Richards had not yet seen her only grandchild—nor would she today.

"I called her. She sent flowers." His eyes wore that guarded look Fran recognized—it meant he was upset by his mother's actions but felt obliged to cover for her. "She's taking an afternoon flight to Boston on business."

At the hospital Scott prodded Fran to the nursery even before she saw Debbie. They stood together at the window and made fatuous sounds as a nurse held up tiny Diane.

"Didn't I tell you?" Scott crowed. "She's the image of the Garfield women. She wouldn't dare be otherwise."

Debbie looked beautiful, Fran thought sentimentally as they embraced. She was pleased that Debbie's roommate—Debbie had rejected the luxury of a private room—had just checked out with her baby.

"Scott, run down to the cafeteria and bring up lunch for Mom," Debbie told him. "She never remembers to eat when she's excited."

"I should call Lynne and tell her," Fran began.

"I phoned her an hour ago." Debbie chuckled. "She said we'd better tell Grandma she'll have to make do with granddaughters."

"How are they all doing?"

"Arnie just got fired," Debbie said and frowned guiltily. "Damn, she didn't want you to know. Didn't want you to worry."

"What happened?" Fran was solicitous.

"Arnie called in sick one day last week. He had a meeting with a music publisher who's been trying to get a record for one of his songs. He walked out of the Brill Building just as his boss walked out of Dempsey's after a business luncheon. That did it."

"He'll pick up a job fast," Fran predicted after a moment. "He's a good accountant. And there are plenty of openings out there these days." She hesitated. "Did the music deal go through?"

"No. Lynne said it was another of those 'almost' deals."

Fran felt a touch of guilt that she wondered at times about the extent of Arnie's talent. Robin always said that the greatest talent could go unrecognized for years without a most important ingredient—luck. But Arnie was young, she reasoned. Only twenty-eight. She mustn't have doubts, she admonished herself. This was Lynne's husband.

In their bedroom—fragrant with the scent of the May roses that bloomed beneath a window—Scott reached into a closet for a fresh shirt while Debbie paced with Diane in her arms. Neither she nor Scott had slept much last night. Why must a tiny baby suffer so with teething? Debbie asked herself.

"I could call Mom and say we can't make it tonight," Scott offered.

"You go to dinner," Debbie insisted and managed a shaky laugh. "All you'd get here tonight would be a hamburger or an omelet." Edith was home with a bad cold. "And not that shirt—a white one." An amenity his mother expected for dinner at the Richards house.

"Damn, I don't want to go without you," Scott grumbled. "I saw her all day long at the mill."

"Nobody rewrites your mother's script. This is the night you have dinner at the house each month."

"Did you talk to the pediatrician about the teething?" He hung away the shirt and brought out a white one.

"I have the prescription she called in to the druggist," Debbie soothed. "Honey, every baby goes through this."

"Of course, my mother will ask, 'Why couldn't she get somebody to stay with Diane?'" Scott smiled wryly.

"I wouldn't do that when she's feeling so miserable. I'm her mother—I want to be here."

"I know. But my mother wouldn't understand that." His eyes were tender as they rested on tiny Diane. "Look, let's go out to the kitchen," he said, buttoning his shirt. "I'll make you an omelet, then hold the baby while you eat."

"Do you have time?"

"I'll take the time. Let's go."

While Debbie ate, Scott sat across the table and rocked Diane in his arms.

"Scott, when are you going to tell your mother you're leaving the mill in six weeks?"

"I know I can't stall much longer," he admitted.

"We made a pact," she reminded. "You know now you'll never change things there."

"I got the lounge for them," he said, sounding defensive yet unhappy. "At least, they have a place to eat their lunch instead of floating around the grounds. Yeah, I know. I have to tell her within the week. I feel rotten at leaving now because I know there's going to be an ugly confrontation soon between her and a group of the workers who want to fight for a union."

"Scott, you can't help them!" He was just hitting his head against a stone wall, she thought with recurrent anger.

"Diane's asleep," he said in sudden relief. "Poor little kid—she's exhausted. I'll put her in the crib. You finish your omelet."

Ten minutes later Scott left the house and slid behind the wheel of the car. As he drove away, he was conscious of darkening clouds. The first storm of the summer, he thought. A clap of thunder confirmed this.

His mother would be furious when he told her he was leaving. But he had accomplished nothing in the almost two years he'd been here. Debbie was right—it would never happen. They hadn't even been able to save the kind of money they'd anticipated.

He'd hoped that when the baby was born his mother would loosen up, show real affection for her only grandchild. That she'd stop being so cold—so distant—toward Debbie. It hadn't happened for him, he taunted himself. Why should he expect it to happen for his daughter?

By the time he pulled up before the house, rain was coming down in torrents. Lightning darted in blinding flashes across the sky. Scott left the car and hurried up the stairs, across the veranda and to the entrance. Amos must have heard the car, he realized. The door swung wide before he could touch the bell.

"It's a real bad one," Amos said. "But when it comes down like this, it don't last too long." Loud voices were coming from the living room. His mother and Perry were arguing again. Amos cleared his throat nervously. "Miz Margaret said to hold dinner until she calls me."

"No problem, Amos." Scott managed a reassuring smile. He understood. His mother disliked having the servants witness family battles. They knew to keep themselves in the kitchen wing until summoned.

Walking down the hall to the living room, Scott heard his mother furiously upbraiding Perry. Debbie was right—Perry was in over his head to local gamblers.

"You swore you'd never get involved with those thugs again!" Margaret Richards's voice soared in rage. "Now they come to me and threaten your life!"

"They had no right to go to you!" Perry pretended to be indignant. "I told them I'd handle the situation!"

"We can't afford one blemish on your name," she shot back venomously. "You'll never win an election in this town—much less on the state level—if word of this gets out. You know how hard I've worked— how I've planned for you to be sitting in Congress within a dozen years. And now this scum comes to me and tells me you owe them almost a hundred thousand dollars in gambling debts!"

"I'll pay them off," Perry said, his face florid. "I'll—"

"With what?" his mother scoffed. "You and Olivia spend every dollar as fast as it comes in. You—"

"Margaret, you mustn't upset yourself this way—" Olivia had walked into the room, unnoticed by the others. "You know Doctor Bader warned you about that." Olivia's tone was conciliatory. Scott intercepted the warning glance she beamed at Perry. He felt sick at being a witness to this ugly confrontation.

"All along I told myself I must be fair to my sons." A vein pounded in her forehead. "My will divides everything equally between you and Scott," she told Perry. "But now I ask myself if this makes sense. Perhaps Scott is not the ideal person to handle my mill—but at least I can be sure he won't gamble everything away."

"Excuse me for a few moments," Scott stammered, feeling himself being cornered. "I want to call Debbie to see how the baby's feeling—" He hurried toward the library door—suspecting the other three had not even heard him. His mother was lashing out at Perry again.

In the living room Olivia tried to calm her mother-in-law while Perry stood by in impotent rage. Why did those bastards go to her? They were ruining everything!

"Olivia, shut up!" his mother commanded. "You are no better than Perry. You both think only of yourselves! To the devil with my mill. I'm telling you right now—" All at once she was silent, her face contorted in pain. Her hands clutched at her chest. She reached out for the back of a chair, and missed—then collapsed on the floor.

"Oh God, why did you try to argue with her?" Perry yelled and crossed to his mother's side. His face drained of color as he knelt and reached for her wrist, sought her pulse. "Olivia, she's dead." His eyes swung to the half-closed library door. Scott was talking with Debbie—he didn't know what had happened.

"She didn't change her will," Olivia said, darting to close the door. The tautness of her face told Perry her mind was charging ahead like a steamroller.

"I'll have to share everything with Scott!" Perry seethed, stumbling to his feet. "The mill, her stock portfolio, the real estate! Even this house."

"Maybe not," Olivia told him with a secretive smile.

"We can't change her will!"

"If Scott died first, you'd inherit everything. You'd be her sole survivor."

Perry gazed uncomprehendingly at her. "What the hell are you talking about?"

"Scott is murdered by an intruder. Your mother rushes into the library, sees him lying dead on the floor, and has a heart attack. *Scott died first. You inherit everything.*"

"You're dreaming!" But already his mind was following hers.

Olivia crossed to the drum table beside their mother-in-law's favorite lounge chair. Everyone in the household knew the drawer contained the revolver Margaret Richards had kept there ever since she had been threatened by an irate worker two years ago. Olivia withdrew the revolver and handed it to Perry.

"Olivia, they'll know—" But Perry took the revolver and gazed at it as though mesmerized.

"Do it," Olivia ordered. She reached for a throw pillow from the sofa. "Muffle the sound with this. Nobody's going to hear out in the kitchen. *Scott died first. Your mother found his body, had a heart attack. Doctor Bader will sign her death certificate. You're the sole heir.*"

Feeling time breathing down his neck Perry rushed to the library door and pulled it wide. Like Olivia said, he'd inherit everything.

"I'll get home as soon as I can," Scott said into the phone. His back to the other two—unaware of their presence. "Bye, Sugar."

"Now, Perry!" Olivia said, her voice harsh with excitement.

Startled, Scott spun around. Perry fired, saw the disbelief in his brother's eyes, and fired again, and then a third time. Olivia darted across the room, knelt beside Scott's body.

"He's dead," she confirmed. "It's all *ours* now."

Thirty-One

W orking in concert—in mutual triumph, Perry and Olivia rushed to set the stage. He brought his mother's body to the threshold of the library, placed it to indicate she had walked to the door, saw Scott's body, and collapsed. Olivia wiped the revolver clean and returned it to its usual place. Nobody would think to look for it, Perry thought complacently. Olivia picked up the throw pillow that had muffled the sound of the shots and returned it to the sofa. Perry reached for an andiron from the library fireplace and smashed one of the windows to indicate forced entry. He swung around to face Olivia. "Now," he told her—terse with excitement.

"Oh, my God!" Olivia began to scream hysterically.

Perry rushed from the library, across the living room, to the hall. "Amos! Come in here!"

Already Amos—trailed by Beulah, was running toward the living room. They'd heard Olivia's screams. Perry retraced his steps. "Olivia, call the hospital! Tell them to send an ambulance! Tell them what's happened!" He swung around to face Amos and Beulah, both gaping in horror at the sight that met their eyes. "Amos, help me get my mother onto the sofa."

"We need an ambulance," Olivia said into the phone—her voice shaken. "This is the Richards home—Mrs. Richards has had a heart attack, and her son has been shot—"

While Perry and Amos lifted Margaret Richards's body to the sofa, Olivia dropped to her knees beside Scott.

"Scott?" she said with a show of anguish. "Oh, please, hold on. The ambulance is coming—"

"Mist' Perry," Amos said after a moment. "She's gone. We've lost Miz Margaret." Behind the sofa Beulah began to wail.

"No!" Perry said, his voice strident. "I don't believe it!"

"I'll call Doctor Bader," Olivia said and rose to her feet.

"I think we best call the police." Amos looked to Perry for agreement.

"Call Doctor Bader first, then the police," Perry told him after a moment. "Tell them an intruder shot my brother. And he's responsible for my mother's death!"

Perry and Olivia clung to each other in well-staged disbelief while Amos made the phone calls.

"Make sure Sheriff Stanton comes over personally," Perry ordered Amos. "I want this monster caught!"

Dr. Bader arrived first. Minutes later the sheriff and his deputy plus ambulance attendants were on the scene. Dr. Bader had already confirmed the deaths of Margaret Richards and Scott. Sheriff Stanton and his deputy—both long beholden to the Richards family—were making the prescribed investigation of the premises.

"No doubt about it," Sheriff Stanton told Perry. "The intruder gained access through the broken French door. He—"

"Olivia and I were just about to go into dinner with my mother and brother," Perry interrupted. "Then Scott excused himself to phone his wife—their baby isn't well and she stayed home with her. We heard the sound of glass breaking in the distance, and my mother thought Scott had knocked over the lamp by the phone in the library. He's sometimes impetuous—" Perry flinched. "He *was* impetuous. My mother must have found him lying there on the floor. When she didn't return to the living room, Olivia and I were worried—we went to check." He gestured his shock.

"I'm sure sorry," Sheriff Stanton commiserated. "This town won't be the same without your mother running things."

"Sheriff, you want the photographer to come in?" his deputy asked.

"Yeah, call him," Stanton ordered and turned apologetically to Perry. "I'm sorry to do this. It's routine procedure. But we'll be out of your way as soon as possible."

"We'd like to have the—the bodies released so we can arrange for burial," Perry told the sheriff.

"The coroner will make sure that happens," Stanton promised, almost obsequious, and turned to his deputy. "I want you to close off the roads into town. Let's catch this murderer before he skips."

Perry cleared his throat. "My mother died of natural causes."

"Yes," Dr. Bader said. "That's not a matter for the coroner. I'll sign the death certificate."

"Oh my God," Olivia said and turned to Perry. "Debbie doesn't know!"

"We'll have to tell her," Perry said somberly.

"That would be your sister-in-law?" Sheriff Stanton asked and Perry nodded. "By rights I ought to talk to her. Ask if she knows of anyone who might want to kill your brother."

"Sheriff, Scott was killed by an intruder." Perry frowned in irritation.

"We have to be thorough. It's just a formality," Stanton soothed.

"Debbie's alone with the baby," Olivia reminded. "They have no sleep-in help."

Perry sighed. "I'll have to call and tell her what happened. Amos, you take my car and drive over to bring Miss Debbie here. Beulah, you go along and stay with the baby." He sighed again. "I'd better call and give her the awful news."

Debbie hovered beside Diane's crib. She was still asleep but restless. Poor darling baby. Debbie reached to take one tiny hand in hers and frowned at the shrill ring of the phone. But Diane hadn't been awakened, she thought in relief and hurried to answer the bedroom extension.

"Hello—"

"Debbie, this is Perry."

"Yes, Perry—" Instinctively she was wary.

"I don't know how to tell you this—" He hesitated and she froze in alarm. "My mother suffered a massive heart attack. She died almost immediately."

"Oh, Perry, I'm so sorry." She was cold with shock.

"She had the heart attack when she went into the library. She discovered Scott lying on the floor. He'd been shot. I'm sorry—there's no easy way to tell you. Scott's dead."

"No!" Debbie clung to the phone in denial. *Perry was wrong.* "I talked with him just a little while ago—"

"He caught an intruder in the library—right after he called you," Perry said. "The sheriff would like to ask you some questions. Routine, but he has to know if you can think of anyone who might have wanted to kill Scott. It's obvious, of course, that he walked in on an intruder."

"Not Scott," Debbie whispered. "Nobody wanted to kill him." *Scott dead?* They were going to leave here, go home to Bellevue. This wasn't real.

"Amos is driving over to bring you to the house. Beulah will stay with the baby." Perry paused at her silence. "Are you all right?"

"I'm all right," she managed. *How could she be all right if Scott was dead?*

She stood immobile beside the phone after Perry hung up. In these few moments her life had turned into a nightmare. Then she reached for the phone again, dialed home. Let Mom be there. *Please God, let Mom be there.*

In Bellevue Fran was listening to radio news about a demonstration of sixty-three thousand people at the Washington Monument—in protest of U.S. involvement in the Vietnamese War. Robin was due momentarily to take her to a benefit dinner in Atlanta. As always, she thought indulgently, Robin was running late.

The phone rang. "I'll get it," she told her mother, wrapped up in a borrowed copy of *Valley of the Dolls*—becoming a runaway bestseller. "It's probably Robin." She reached for the phone. "Hello—"

"Mom, something awful has happened." Debbie's voice broke.

"Debbie, what is it?" Fran felt herself turn to ice.

"Scott's dead—" The words were barely audible. "I just received a call. He's been murdered."

"I'll be there in hours," Fran said immediately. "Don't worry about my getting to the house. I'll arrange for a cab to be waiting. Darling, you'll see this through. For Diane you have to be strong."

"We were coming back to Bellevue in a few weeks." Debbie's voice was anguished. "Mom, why did this happen?"

"Darling, we can't ask questions." Why did Bernie die so young? She'd thought her life was over then—as Debbie must be feeling now. "Who's with you?"

"Nobody. Someone's coming to drive me over to the house. Scott's mother is dead, too. She had a heart attack when she found Scott. Mom, I can't believe it."

"I know, Debbie."

"It's my fault." Debbie's voice soared in self-accusation. "Scott didn't want to go tonight. I made him go. He'd be alive if I hadn't insisted."

"It isn't your fault. Don't ever believe that," Fran ordered. "I'll be there soon. We'll see this through together."

Caught up in a sense of unreality, Fran told her mother what had happened and shook her head in painful impatience as her mother plied her with questions.

"I don't know how it happened," she interrupted with unfamiliar sharpness. "I just know that I have to go to Debbie. I'll call the airport for the next flight out."

"There won't be anything at this hour of the night," Ida warned.

"Then I'll drive," Fran said. "Or arrange for a charter flight. I'll be there in a few hours," she reiterated.

Was there some curse on the Garfield women? First Bernie, dead so young—and now Scott. What had they done to bring this on themselves?

At just past midnight Perry sat behind the desk in the library of the Richards mansion while Olivia served coffee to him, the sheriff, Dr. Bader, and the coroner. The two bodies had been removed. At Dr. Bader's insistence Debbie had been given a sedative and driven home by Amos. Amos and Beulah had been instructed to remain with her until morning. Smart of Olivia to suggest that, Perry thought. He wanted Amos and Beulah out of the house tonight. The other servants were day workers—they'd left before Scott had arrived.

"Listen to me," Perry said with fresh authority. "This is a terrible time for Olivia and me. We don't want the situation to be prolonged. Let's face it—the bastard that broke into the library was probably just passing through town. He'll never be caught. Bert, I want you to close this case at the earliest possible moment," he told the sheriff.

"There has to be an investigation," Bert said apologetically.

"Make it brief." Perry was terse. "I don't like my personal life dragged before the public." He turned to Dr. Bader. "You'll sign my mother's death certificate, of course—she was your patient." Now his eyes swung to the coroner. "Her death is not a matter for the coroner's office." He cleared his throat. "I want it established in the official records that my brother died first. My mother saw his body and suffered a heart attack. Which, of course, is exactly what happened." Nobody could prove differently. And these jerks were too stupid to understand the significance of what he said. Perry was aware of a glint of satisfaction in Olivia's eyes. They were pulling this off with no sweat.

At just past noon the following day—while Debbie slept under sedation in the guest room because she couldn't bear to lie alone in the bed she'd shared with Scott—Fran argued with the coroner's office about an early release of Scott's body for burial. In the Jewish tradition burial was to take place within forty-eight hours of death.

"This is a murder case, ma'am," the coroner explained. "We have procedures to follow." He hesitated. "And I don't understand. The Richards family have long been members of our Baptist church."

"Scott Richards is half-Jewish." Something his mother preferred to conceal. "He would wish to be buried as a Jew—beside the body of his grandmother."

"We'll do the best we can, Mrs. Garfield. I'll be in touch."

On her arrival in Glenwood late last night she'd talked with Perry. A local doctor had signed Margaret Richards's death certificate. Her funeral would be held tomorrow. Perry had been incensed that Debbie wouldn't go along with a double funeral. Like his mother, Perry was anxious to conceal his Jewish heritage.

In the kitchen Edith—red-eyed from weeping—crooned lovingly to Diane and fed her lunch. Fran felt a fresh rush of anguish. Diane was too young to retain any recall of her father. Lynne and Debbie had been old enough to collect cherished memories.

Fran frowned at the sound of a car pulling up out front. She hoped it wasn't the sheriff again. Debbie was in no condition for more questioning. She walked to the front door and saw Robin emerge from the driver's side of an unfamiliar car. She hurried out into the noonday heat. Bless Robin for coming!

Then he was helping someone from the passenger side. Her face lighted. He'd brought Mother with him.

"Oh, God, it's so good to see you both!" She kissed her mother, then Robin.

"You knew we wouldn't let you go through this alone," Robin chided.

"How's Debbie?" Ida asked, tears filling her eyes. "I can't believe this is happening again—" Fran remembered how her parents had rushed to her side when Bernie died.

The three went into the house, talking in hushed tones lest they awaken Debbie. Edith brought Diane into the living room to be fussed over by her great-grandmother and Robin. How wonderful to have a warm family, Fran thought in recurrent gratitude. How wonderful to have a friend like Robin. Lynne arrived hours after her mother and Robin. "Arnie's taking time off from work to look after the kids," she explained.

The next three days were chaotic. Robin took over the multitude of tasks that arose. The sheriff had no lead on Scott's murder. He and his deputy were convinced someone passing through town had meant only to rob, but—cornered—had murdered Scott. And each day—when Robin supplied him with the Glenwood phone number—Craig called.

Despite her grief Debbie was outraged when she realized the sheriff was about to close the case.

"Scott was murdered!" she reminded him at a meeting called by him at the Richards mansion. "You can't just let the murderer go free without a serious investigation."

"They have no leads." Perry's tone was acidic. "It'll be a waste of taxpayers' money to prolong this."

"We're talking about your brother's murder!" Debbie lashed back. "I won't stand by and let it be washed away!"

Anger helped see her through, Fran thought when at last they stood at Scott's graveside, barely thirty feet from where his grandmother had been buried.

Many local people attended the services at the funeral home. Fran suspected they came out of respect for the Richards standing in the town. Only a few came to the cemetery. Perry and Olivia in one car plus the family servants in another. A group of mill workers who'd understood what Scott had tried to do for them. Scott had not really been part of this town since he was shipped off to boarding school at thirteen.

Fran was touched by the obvious grief of Amos and Beulah, and their tenderness toward Debbie. They had loved Scott, had been the closest thing to family—except for his grandmother—in his growing-up years. Fran suspected that Perry and Olivia seethed inwardly at being here— at Scott's Jewish funeral. But not to be here would have been unthinkable.

Yesterday morning at Margaret Richards's heavily attended funeral, Fran had overheard Olivia telling a local attorney that "Scott's wife insisted he not be buried as the Baptist he had been born." The inference was that Debbie had pulled him away from his family's faith to her own.

The morning after Scott's funeral Robin drove Lynne to the Raleigh airport in his rented car. Fran stood on the veranda with her mother and Debbie while the car pulled away.

"I'll ask Edith to make us some coffee," Ida said and went into the house. Unaware of the tragedy that had entered her life, Diane napped in the nursery.

"As soon as you feel up to leaving, Debbie, we'll fly home," Fran said gently. The house and the furnishings belonged to the estate, she remembered. Debbie would have to arrange for shipment of only her personal belongings.

"Mom, I'm staying," Debbie said, her face radiating determination. "I'm not leaving this town until the sheriff arrests Scott's murderer."

Thirty-Two

D ebbie was conscious of a devastating loneliness when she walked back into the cottage after seeing her mother, grandmother, and Robin drive off to the Raleigh airport. Mom had been so upset that she insisted on staying on here. But how could she leave? She had to be here to make sure the investigation continued. She'd never have a moment's peace until Scott's murderer was caught.

She wandered aimlessly through the rooms. Edith was loading diapers into the washing machine in the tiny laundry room off the kitchen. Diane was napping.

"Diane can't hear it when I close the door," Edith told Debbie with an apologetic smile. "She's sleeping like a little angel." Her eyes were warm with compassion. "Miss Debbie, I can sleep in if you like. As long as you need me."

"I'd like that," Debbie said gently. "Thank you, Edith." Now she forced herself back into the everyday world. "How's Henry doing with his civil rights group?" Henry was Edith's boyfriend and a junior at college. He'd been active in the sit-ins—which simultaneously elated and alarmed Edith.

"Henry says folks have to do what the law says—and he won't stop fighting until that happens." Edith hesitated. "My mama says maybe we're getting too uppity, but the law's the law."

"It'll happen," Debbie said. "It'll just take time. Remember how long it took women to get the vote."

Sounds from the nursery told them Diane was awake. Such a good baby, Debbie thought tenderly as she hurried to the nursery. Always so happy. But Diane didn't know that she would have to grow up without a father. She didn't know this was the sixth day of their "sitting *shivah*"—the traditional eight-day period of mourning in the Jewish faith.

Debbie was grateful for Edith's presence in the house. Except for her mother and grandmother—who phoned each evening—she spoke to no one. Her mind leapt between grief and anger. Sheriff Stanton couldn't be serious about closing the case. *She wouldn't let that happen.* And always she was taunted by the knowledge that if she hadn't insisted Scott go to his mother's house for dinner that night, he would be alive.

On the ninth day after Scott's death, Debbie told herself she must return to work. She must be practical. She and Scott had managed to put money away in their joint bank account each week, but that would be gone in months. By mill messenger Perry had sent over a check representing Scott's final week's salary plus one week extra. There would be nothing from Margaret Richards's estate. Scott had died before her. Perry was the sole heir. Her own earnings at the newspaper were small but would help.

She knew she shouldn't be astonished that neither Perry nor Olivia had been in contact since Scott's funeral. They wanted no part of Scott's widow and baby. And Perry rejected her determination to push Sheriff Stanton into a thorough investigation. Perry claimed it would "just create ugly notoriety." Didn't he care that Scott's murderer was on the loose?

That afternoon Debbie drove to the sheriff's office. Leaving the car and walking to the small white frame structure, she geared herself for a battle. She'd spent endless hours these past few days in an effort to reconstruct what had happened that awful night. The intruder had not been a stranger. The Richards house was off the beaten track, the sole house off an obscure road. It was incomprehensible that a stranger "passing through town" would have encountered it. *Somebody who lived in Glenwood had killed Scott.*

She sensed the sheriff's hostility the moment she walked into the office. Stony-faced and silent—not bothering to rise from his chair—he listened to her first few words, then interrupted her.

"Mrs. Richards, there ain't no use going on about this again. We haven't got one lead to go on. Nothing." He pounded a fist on his desk. "It'll be filed under 'Unsolved Cases.' I spent a lot of time thinking about it. I went over the whole thing with Perry Richards. He agrees. We've got nowhere to go on this case. We'd just be spinning our wheels if we tried."

Debbie lay sleepless far into the night—her mind searching for a way to break through this impasse. Talk to Mr. Norris, she ordered herself at last. He was a publisher—he had responsibilities to his readers, he always said. She was going back to work tomorrow. Talk to him. He'd understand that Sheriff Stanton and Perry were wrong not to continue the investigation. Even a small newspaper could put pressure on the sheriff's office.

Arriving at the office in the morning Debbie received the compassionate condolences of the small staff. Everybody had been so shocked.

"Mr. Norris, could I talk to you?" Debbie asked. The others moved away in the polite discomfort that inundates acquaintances in the face of tragedy.

"Of course, Debbie." His smile was warm. "Let's go into my office." He hesitated. "If you feel you need more time off, we'll understand."

"No, I want to get back to work," she told him. "I need to be busy. But I'm outraged at the attitude of the Glenwood sheriff."

Struggling to keep her voice even, Debbie reported on the sheriff's actions, her conviction that the intruder had been a resident of Glenwood.

"Now that's not something we can get into." Norris was all at once evasive. "It's Glenwood news, Debbie. If it's outside of Raleigh, we can just report what the sheriff's office releases to us."

"But they're letting a murderer go free!" Debbie said passionately.

"Debbie, you ought to know," he chided. "We don't go in for controversial matters. Remember last month when you wanted to go to that town near Charlotte to do an article on another sit-in? I told you then—nothing controversial. We can't jeopardize our advertising base." His eyes telegraphed a message.

All at once she understood. Mr. Norris solicited the Richards mill regularly for advertising. He remembered Perry's brief statement to the newspapers: *"I've reluctantly concluded that my brother was murdered by an intruder who happened to be passing through town. Sheriff Stanton has done everything that can be done. It's a tragic loss that was made more tragic by my mother's fatal heart attack at discovering my brother's body. But life must go on."*

Later in the evening—when Diane was asleep and Edith watching television—Debbie went out to the kitchen to phone Perry. She must make one last effort to persuade him to push the sheriff into action. But Perry was impatient at being disturbed.

"Debbie, stop being hysterical." *She wasn't being hysterical.* "I'm in the midst of a business meeting here. With my mother gone I have a lot of work to do. I have no time for this nonsense."

"Good night, Perry." Hot with anger, she hung up the phone.

Three evenings later—when Debbie still fretted about her next move to bring about a further investigation—Perry phoned.

"Debbie?"

"Yes, Perry." Had he changed his mind? She felt a surge of hope.

"I'm sorry to have to be so blunt." He paused and cleared his throat in a gesture of nervousness. "But I have to ask you to vacate the cottage sometime during the next thirty days. That should give you plenty of time. I have a tenant who'll be moving in then."

For a moment she was silent, encased in shock. "I'll be out before that time." How dare he behave this way! "Good night, Perry."

White and shaken Debbie slammed down the kitchen extension and reached to turn off the gas under the teapot. She was his brother's widow—Diane was the only niece he'd ever have. But Perry couldn't wait to get her and the baby out of his life.

She was suddenly assaulted by a tidal wave of claustrophobia. She wouldn't stay here another night! She and Diane were going home.

"Edith!" She hurried from the kitchen into the living room.

"Yes, ma'am?" Reluctantly Edith pulled her gaze away from the TV screen.

"I've decided not to stay on here." She couldn't bring herself to say "my brother-in-law is throwing me out." "I'll give you two weeks extra pay—and the best of references. I'm sure you'll have no trouble finding another job." Debbie's words tumbled over one another in her haste. "Anyone who wants to talk to me can call me at my mother's house in Bellevue. I'll—"

"Oh, Miss Debbie, I was worried about telling you I'd have to quit at the end of the summer. I'm going to college." Edith's face was radiant. "Henry was after me to try for a scholarship—and I got it. I'm sure Mr. Scott's letter helped."

She knew that Scott had encouraged Edith—so bright and ambitious—to return to school. He hadn't told her, Debbie reasoned, because he didn't want her to worry about losing Edith until the scholarship was definite.

"Edith, do you suppose you could go down to Bellevue with me in the

car?" she asked on sudden impulse. "Then you can take the train back. I'd
be afraid to drive with Diane unless there was someone to hold her."
Only now did she focus on the realities of leaving Glenwood.

"Of course I'll go with you," Edith said eagerly. "It'll be kind of an
adventure. I've never been on a train by myself."

"It's a long drive. You'll stay overnight with us, then take the train
the next day. Your mother won't be upset, will she?"

"No, ma'am. But I'm sure going to miss you and Diane."

"We're going to miss you, too," Debbie said tenderly. "Now—if it's all
right with you," she stipulated, "we'll leave early tomorrow morning."
Thank God, the car was air-conditioned. "We'll drive straight through,
just taking some rest periods along the way."

"I'll call Mama and explain," Edith said. "There won't be no problem."

At a few minutes past 7 A.M. the following morning, Debbie slid behind the wheel of the car. Edith was settled in the rear with Diane, an
assortment of toys, a thermos, and a freezer bag. Already the day was
hot and humid, the air fragrant with the scent of summer flowers.

Don't look back, Debbie ordered herself—her throat tight with anguish. Her mind was all at once a kaleidoscope of precious moments in
the cottage—their first night when they'd made sweet and passionate
love—joyous at being in their own home, the parade of hours when Scott
had talked to her with such eloquence about what he wanted to do with
his life, the Sunday morning when she'd told Scott she was almost certain she was pregnant. The snowy evening when she felt the first con-
traction and Scott had held her in his arms with such love for her and the
baby when she told him. Why must someone so sweet and warm and
wonderful have to die so young?

"Miss Debbie, are you all right?" Edith's solicitous voice brought her
back to the moment.

"I'm fine," she insisted, her gaze straight ahead. "Glenwood, here we
come."

All that remained of her marriage to Scott was packed into the trunk
of the car and in her heart, she told herself, her hands clutching the
wheel. Scott's books and records and hers. Their photo album—snapshots from their wedding, their honeymoon, all the pictures they'd taken
of Diane. That would have to do for the rest of her life.

As always in hours of crisis Fran appeared calm and sympathetic—
belying her inner chaos—while she sat in the air-conditioned living

room and listened to Debbie. Edith was putting Diane to sleep in the room designated as "the children's room"—with crib and youth bed for what Ida called "my precious jewels." Ida was with Edith and Diane.

"I didn't know what else to do, Mom—except come home." Debbie reached for her glass of lemonade. Poor baby, Fran thought painfully—driving all those hours when she was so upset.

"Of course, you came home," Fran said vigorously. "You and Diane belong here."

Her mind hurtled back through the years. She remembered her own parents bringing her back to Bellevue with Lynne and Debbie. It was all happening again, she thought sadly.

She'd emerged from her grief and built a new life for herself and the girls. So many women envied her for her success in the business world. Just last month she'd opened another shop. But what did it all mean when her daughters were unhappy? Despite Lynne's pretense that all was well, she sensed Lynne's frustration that Arnie was growing embittered at his lack of success, that Lynne was anxious about their financial state. Was there some weird covenant that with success must come pain? That her daughters must pay for her gain?

"I remember when we came down here after Daddy died," Debbie said softly and Fran was startled. She'd thought that traumatic era had long been put to rest. "I was so scared, but I knew you would always be there for us. At first I didn't want to let you out of my sight—"

"Diane doesn't know." Fran fought against tears. "And we'll give her so much love. Your grandmother and Lynne and me. We'll always be here for her."

"Mom, how did you survive when Dad died so young?"

"For you and Lynne I had to survive," Fran told her. "Your grandfather—may he rest in peace—and Grandma were there for us. Without family I don't know what would have happened."

"I'm not giving up on tracking down Scott's murderer—no matter what the sheriff and Perry say. It had to have been someone who knew the family, the house. I've gone over it in my head a thousand times." Debbie closed her eyes for a moment. "I wake up at night sometimes, and I forget for the moment. I reach out for Scott—"

"It won't be easy, darling," Fran admitted. "But you're here at home with those who love you."

"What's happening with Lynne and Arnie and the kids?" Debbie was making an effort to pull herself out of her grief, Fran thought, and yearned to help. Debbie wasn't three years old—she couldn't pick her up and hold her close in comfort. "Arnie's working again, isn't he?"

"He found himself a good job," Fran told her. Yet in her heart she knew that Arnie would be in and out of jobs in the years ahead. Success in the music world kept eluding him, but he would jeopardize jobs in his reach for recognition. He complained that musical tastes were changing too fast. *"God, I hate rock!"* He said that the quality of Broadway musicals was dropping into mediocrity at its best. "He's still writing music, of course."

"Lynne said something about taking night classes at Hunter," Debbie recalled. "Education courses."

"She's still talking about it. She said that New York teachers' salaries—and their benefits—have become so good that it could be a great deal for her." How could Lynne talk about teaching when all her life she yearned to be a lawyer? She had a year of law school behind her.

"All she'd need would be those few education courses. But I can't imagine her giving up on law school."

"She's thinking about security." Impatience and frustration crept into Fran's voice. She'd offered Lynne financial help to see her through law school. Whatever she needed—including a full-time woman to be with the kids. Why did Arnie have to be so stubborn about not being dependent on *her?* "Lynne was always the practical one."

"And I had my head in the clouds." Debbie managed a wisp of a smile. "But those days are gone forever."

In the days ahead Fran worried that Debbie never stirred beyond the house. Her eyes seemed never to stray from Diane. But that was natural, Fran encouraged herself. Debbie was struggling to come to grips with the future.

Fran was startled when—five weeks after her return to Bellevue— Debbie said that she wanted to go up to Glenwood.

"Just for a day," she said, avoiding her mother's eyes. "I have to talk to the sheriff again, do some digging. I'll get a sitter for the day and—"

"You'll do no such thing," Fran chided. "Grandma and Lily are here during the day to take care of Diane. I'll be sure to leave the office early to be here with her." She hesitated, understanding Debbie's need to see Scott's murderer brought to justice—but fearful this would become an obsession. "Maybe we ought to turn this over to a lawyer or a private investigator. I'll check around and—"

"It's something I have to do myself." Debbie's eyes reflected a ferocious determination. "Nobody has a stronger incentive than me." She paused. "I'm not sure that a lawyer or private investigator would follow through in face of the sheriff's—and Perry's—attitude."

"Debbie, what can you say to them that hasn't been said?" Fran asked gently.

"I've done a lot of thinking, Mom. There're questions that need to be answered. I've thought about other angles that ought to be explored."

"When do you want to go?" Fran asked after a moment. She'd put her scheduled trip to the out-of-town shops on hold until Debbie was back in Bellevue.

"On Monday," Debbie told her. "I'll take an early flight, be back by dinnertime. I'll try to talk again to Sheriff Stanton, and then to Perry. I know Perry has the local newspaper under his thumb—but maybe I can shame them into pushing for further investigation."

On Monday morning Debbie was on the first flight to Raleigh. Staring out the plane window without seeing, she plotted her approach to Sheriff Stanton, her first quarry. He couldn't be so stupid as not to see the logic of what she meant to tell him.

Two hours later she was confronting the obviously belligerent sheriff.

"Sheriff Stanton, can't you see that it had to be someone who knew the layout of the house? Someone who knew that at that hour the family would be sitting down to dinner—and that the dining room was across the hall from the living room, and the library beyond that. He didn't expect to be caught breaking in!"

"Only somebody passing through would be stupid enough to break in at that hour of the day," the sheriff dismissed this. "Now if you'll excuse me, I—"

"It was a local person who was sure he wouldn't be caught," Debbie pushed on desperately. "He knew that Mrs. Richards had expensive tastes. Perhaps he knew that she kept her collection of antique clocks in the library breakfront," she emphasized. "It's worth a fortune. In minutes a robber could sweep everything from the cabinet into a knapsack and tear off on a motorcycle or in a car. The robber might even have been a woman!"

"You've been reading too many mysteries," Stanton shot back. "I'm sorry, ma'am, but—"

"Remember the benefit for the day nursery program that the Glenwood Garden Club ran last month?"

"I don't," he said grimly, shuffling papers on his desk.

"It was a tour of local gardens, and as a highlight they offered a guided tour of the lower floor of the Richards house. Sheriff Stanton, get a list of those who bought tickets for the tour!"

"I'm doing no such thing! I'd be run out of town. I'd tried to be polite, Mrs. Richards—but I've had enough. Goodbye, ma'am."

When she tried to talk to Perry over the phone, he was furious.

"You're obsessed!" he shouted. "You can't run around this town insulting local citizens. You'll have a libel suit on your hands. It'll look terrible for the family."

She froze in shock when Perry slammed down the phone. But she had known she might be rebuffed by both the sheriff and Perry. Don't stop now. She left the public phone booth and walked off to the offices of the *Glenwood Observer*. At the information desk she asked for newspapers in the week of the Garden Club benefit. With a small glow of triumph she noted the name of the woman who had headed the benefit committee. Praying the local socialite would be home, Debbie left the newspaper office and phoned her.

"Miz Anderson's residence," a polite maid answered.

"I'd like to talk to her, please." Debbie's heart was pounding. "This is Deborah Richards."

Moments later Mrs. Anderson's voice came to her.

"Yes, Mrs. Richards?" She sounded wary, Debbie thought.

Stammering in her excitement Debbie explained her mission—praying this would be the important breakthrough.

"How dare you suggest such a thing!" Mrs. Anderson was outraged. "The ladies who took the tour were all fine, upstanding citizens. I don't wish to continue this conversation."

Inundated with disappointment Debbie stood motionless in the phone booth. There was nothing else she could do now. She reached for a coin and dialed the taxi number posted on the wall of the booth.

"I'd like a taxi to drive me to the Raleigh airport," she said tiredly when a voice responded.

Fran was upset at the way Debbie seemed to be retreating into isolation. For weeks after returning from her trip to Glenwood she never left the house. Her withdrawal was frightening. She could deal with Debbie's grief, Fran told herself—but not this terrifying depression.

"Debbie needs professional help," Fran told her mother as they returned from a synagogue party. "But I know it's useless to suggest it. She's my child, and she's suffering. But I don't know how to help her—"

Thirty-Three

I n her bedroom Fran inspected her Yves St. Laurent black velvet pantsuit with ambivalence. The calendar might say this was late October of 1966, but the weather was more Georgia-hot August. Still, the restaurant where she and Robin would be joining two other couples for dinner would be air-conditioned to accommodate male diners in woolen suits.

"Frannie—" Her mother's voice filtered down the hall of the bedroom wing of the house. "Robin's here."

"Coming," she called back. She hadn't wanted to go out to dinner tonight, but Robin had insisted. He'd been scolding her for cutting back on her socializing since Debbie had come home with the baby. *"It's important for your image and your expensive shops to be seen with the movers and shakers of this area."*

In the living room Robin was teasing her mother about reading *Valley of the Dolls* for the third time.

"I know, you're just a hot little number pretending to be a virtuous grandmother."

"Great-gran," Ida shot back. Only from Robin would she take such talk, Fran thought indulgently. "And don't you forget it."

Fran was relieved to discover—when she and Robin walked out into the night—that the day's heat had disappeared. There was a chill in the air that was most welcome after the daytime temperature.

"You're worried about Debbie," Robin said when they were seated in the car.

"Robin, yes." Only with Robin did she abandon her usual calm facade. Not even her mother knew the despair that filled her days and nights.

What could she do to lessen Debbie's anguish? "She's twenty-four years old, and she's convinced her life is over. How can I help her?"

"Prod her into going back to work," Robin said. "She'll have less time to brood."

"She has a baby to raise," Fran said defensively. But she, too, had realized that a return to work could be the solution.

"Career-minded women with babies work these days," Robin reminded. "And you know how determined Debbie was to become a first-rate reporter. The way you were at her age."

"I'm afraid," Fran admitted after a moment. "I'd die if she thought I was trying to push her out on her own. But I can't bear to see her so unhappy. I *know* what she's going through."

"You've been there—and you came out of it," Robin reminded. "But you've told me yourself—going into the shop was your salvation."

"Bernie died a natural death. Debbie won't—*can't*—accept the fact that Scott's killer is going unpunished. She blames herself for pushing Scott to go to his mother's house that night—and she feels she's failing him in not forcing the sheriff into a serious investigation."

"She's too young yet to accept the fact that justice doesn't always prevail." His tone was sardonic, but Fran understood he was sympathetic. "We know. But be the tough mother, Fran. Tell her she has to rejoin the human race. It's for her own good."

Fran sighed, dreading such a confrontation. But this was her precious child, who'd lost her beautiful zest for living. Somehow, it must be restored.

"I'll try," she promised. As the months dragged past, she'd prayed that Debbie would accept that Scott's killer would never be tracked down—but that wasn't happening.

The following evening Fran settled herself in the living room with a briefcase of reports from the shops that required studying, but her main agenda was to talk with Debbie about resuming her career. Debbie had put Diane to bed for the night and sat on the corner of the sofa with yet another gothic novel. At the sound of a car pulling into the driveway Ida rose from her chair and went to switch off the television set.

"That's Bessie. We're playing bridge tonight," Ida said, reaching for her purse and sweater. "See you later."

The stillness in the house seemed unbearable to Fran as she stared unseeing at the report she'd fished from her briefcase. Debbie sat motionless on her corner of the sofa. The tightness of her grasp on the novel she was reading telegraphed the tension that imprisoned her.

"Debbie—" Fran struggled for a casual air. "Did you read that article in the *Bellevue Enquirer* about the new women's group forming in town? I gather their bible is Betty Friedan's *The Feminine Mystique.*"

"I didn't notice it." Debbie managed a faint smile. A year ago, Fran thought, Debbie would have been enthralled at such a group coming into existence in town. This was a family who had long believed in equal rights for women.

"You ought to get involved in the group," Fran urged. "Most of them are young like you. You could probably get a great article out of it." Her heart pounding, she pushed ahead. "Darling, why don't you look around and see if there's an opening on a newspaper either here or in Atlanta?"

"No," Debbie said sharply. All at once her body was rigid.

"But you've always been so enthusiastic about journalism." Fran tried to sound in high spirits. "You—"

"I hated working on the paper down here and in Raleigh." Debbie grimaced. "What a drag! All those stupid benefits and women's club meetings and weddings." And now an agonizing sadness darkened her eyes. She'd met Scott at one of these affairs, Fran remembered.

"You've built up your background—you can move away from those assignments into more exciting ones." Fran tried again. "Debbie, you could—"

"Mom, I don't have what it takes to be a real reporter." Fran recoiled from the contempt in Debbie's voice. "Look how I bombed out in Glenwood. Oh sure, I wanted to be an investigative reporter," she said derisively, "but I couldn't come up with anything but stupid, weak leads to Scott's killer. I don't have what it takes to be a serious reporter." She paused, seeming to be in some inner debate. "If you think I can handle it, I'll come in to help at the shop here in town or out in Buckhead."

"Of course you can handle it." But Fran's mind was in chaos. Debbie shouldn't settle for working in the shop. But she'd be out with people— that would be a start, Fran reasoned. Yet she was shaken by this proposal. She remembered how she had emerged from her own grief to go into the store. The end of her dream came with the bullet in her back. *But it didn't have to be that way for Debbie.* "Come in part-time," Fran said, her smile strained. "Perhaps from one P.M. to five P.M. That way—even with a girl to be with Diane—you'll be there to feed her. And Grandma and Lily will be there to supervise."

But this wasn't what she wanted for Debbie, Fran told herself in frustration.

The following Tuesday Debbie came into the shop. It was arranged for her to be there from 1 P.M. to 5 P.M. Tuesday through Saturday. It was a beginning, Fran told herself. But still, Debbie refused to socialize.

The cluster of girlfriends with whom Debbie had grown up made strenuous efforts to involve her in their activities. She came up with constant excuses. Her longtime best friend, Nora Fields, dropped by regularly to report on the group of young women—including herself—who'd organized to promote women's rights in Bellevue.

"Debbie, we need you," Nora scolded. "You've always been the one to light fires under us. Everybody is brave at our meetings, but they're cowards when we're supposed to go out and make ourselves heard."

Nora talked about the new National Organization for Women—to be known as NOW—which had been formed in late October. One of the first members was Anna Roosevelt Halsted, Eleanor Roosevelt's daughter. She talked about the latest bestseller she was reading—Truman Capote's *In Cold Blood*—and stopped herself in horror with a fast apologetic glance in Fran's direction.

Shortly before New Year's Eve Nora dropped by one evening to report that the group was sending a congratulatory letter to Cesar Chavez for his work on behalf of the California grape pickers. Watching a TV documentary about the hippie scene in San Francisco, Fran shamelessly eavesdropped on the conversation between Nora and Debbie.

"Debbie, you used to be so vocal about Chavez," Nora chided. "Aren't you interested?"

"Of course, I'm interested," Debbie defended herself, all at once self-conscious. "It's just that between the baby and my job I don't have time to get involved."

"Make time," Nora said, and Fran blessed her for this. "You have to be at our next meeting. We need you. You can write it up for the *Enquirer*. We need publicity."

"I suppose I could do that," Debbie said with a self-mockery that eluded Nora but elicited a wince from Fran. Still, it was a start, Fran comforted herself.

Through the months ahead Fran watched for some indication that Debbie was relinquishing her conviction that she was responsible for

Scott's death, that she had failed him in not tracking down his killer. There were no such signs. Nora had brought Debbie into weekly attendance at the group's meetings—but where was the enthusiasm and ambition that had always been just under the surface in Debbie? Even Nora—in a private moment with Fran—admitted that the old Debbie had not emerged.

In July Fran went up to New York on her usual midyear buying trip. She was pleased to see that Lynne and Arnie seemed to be happier than she'd remembered on her last two visits. Arnie was working with a librettist on a new musical.

"We'll do it Off-Broadway, of course," Arnie said with a deprecating smile. Broadway was Arnie's real goal, Fran knew. "Tim's mother is putting up the money."

"The book needs some revisions," Lynne said quickly. She was uncomfortable, Fran thought, at the subtle inference that *she* had never offered to bankroll a musical production for Arnie. But Arnie had frowned on her helping to see Lynne through her last year of law school! "And the music and lyrics just need a little more work. We're so excited, Mom."

"These things all take time," Arnie reminded. "But we're hoping to be on the boards by next spring."

"And meanwhile it looks pretty certain that I'll have a teaching job this fall." Lynne's eyes didn't meet her mother's. Lynne guessed, Fran told herself, that she was disappointed at the switch from law to teaching. "I know private schools pay less than the public school system," Lynne conceded, "but this is a sure thing. And a woman in our building will take care of the kids along with her own little boy during school hours. It'll be incredibly inexpensive."

"I still think she ought to take the city exams," Arnie told Fran. "At least, she should get herself on the list. Don't you think so?"

"Whatever Lynne feels is best for her," Fran evaded. "But I'm so looking forward to having her and the girls in Bellevue for a month." That had taken some doing, but Fran was delighted at having pulled it off.

On the flight down to Atlanta Fran listened tenderly to the excited chatter of Jessie and Beth, both awed at being aboard a plane. But part of her mind sought to deal with her disappointment that neither of her daughters was following the paths that had seemed so important in earlier years. She remembered the words of Beverly—her longtime "second in command"—just last week. *"I'm so disappointed in my daughters.*" Did parents expect too much? Were they trying to live their own dreams through their children? That was what *she* was doing, she reproached herself. She'd wanted Lynne and Debbie to live Bernie's dream and hers.

Lynne's visit with the two little girls ended far too soon, Fran thought wistfully when she saw them off at the airport. But it had been so sweet to have her two daughters and three grandchildren under the same roof for a while. It was her own success in the business that made it all possible, she reminded herself with satisfaction.

At the end of September—with the school year launched—Lynne wrote enthusiastically about her job. Fran suspected the enthusiasm was generated by her paycheck. Three weeks later Lynne wrote that Arnie had left his job to focus on the musical. Now that she was working they could afford to take the chance.

"And Arnie will be with Jessie and Beth while I'm teaching so we'll be saving that money."

Was she wrong, Fran asked herself, in being upset that Lynne was working—deserting her own dreams of becoming a lawyer—so that Arnie could play at being a songwriter? Then guilt rushed in. Arnie wasn't playing. He was serious. His music dominated his life. Lynne felt he deserved his wife's support. She was convinced he would one day become another Cole Porter.

"*Mom, Arnie has the talent and the drive. I know one day he'll be there on top.*"

But for every success in the arts there were thousands of failures, Fran thought uneasily.

Lynne wrote with soaring optimism about the progress Arnie and Tim were making on their new musical. As prospective producer, Tim's mother was already looking at East Village playhouses that might be available in early spring. What fifteen years ago was the upper region of the Lower East Side had blossomed into the bustling East Village, home to tiny playhouses, artsy little shops, coffeehouses, and hordes of young people now being labeled "flower children."

"*Arnie says he never remembers a Broadway season as lean as this fall,*" *Lynne wrote.* "*That means if Arnie and Tim's show gets great reviews—and it should—they'll have a strong chance of moving it uptown.*"

In January Fran went to New York on her usual buying trip. This first night in town she was to go to Lynne's apartment for dinner so that she could spend some time with Jessie and Beth before their bedtime. Then a sitter was coming in so that the three adults could go to the theater. Fran was impatient for the day to pass.

At shortly before 5 P.M. she took a cab to the apartment and was greeted joyously by Lynne and the two little girls.

"I can't believe how they've grown since I've seen them!" Fran crooned, dropping to her haunches to cradle them in her arms. "Do you remember your grandma?" she asked.

"Yes!" Jessie said exuberantly. Beth hung back—shy but eager to be kissed.

"Arnie's at a rehearsal studio with Tim," Lynne reported while they settled themselves in the living room. "He'll be here about seven o'clock. That'll give us time to have dinner and get to the theater." Fran had sent a check so that Lynne could pick up tickets for *Mame*, with Angela Lansbury.

Fran relished the time with Jessie and Beth—Jessie so effervescent, Beth shy and poignantly sweet. Arnie arrived in time to take them off to bed while the two women focused on getting dinner on the table.

"Lynne, if there's a need for more financing," Fran began self-consciously. "I can help a bit."

"No, Mom." Lynne was firm. "You've done enough. Arnie and Tim have to see this through. Besides, Tim's mother is loaded—and she's having a ball playing the producer."

"Hey, when do we eat?" Arnie strode into the small kitchen. "I'm starving."

"Sit down in the dining area," Lynne ordered. "We'll eat in a couple of minutes."

"Did Lynne tell you about Jessie?" Arnie asked Fran. "She's already showing musical talent. She won't be four until next month, and already she can carry a tune. Perfect pitch!" he crowed.

"Arnie, stop it," Lynne shook her head in mock disapproval.

Lynne seemed so happy, Fran told herself several times in the course of the evening—yet she worried that the day might come when Lynne would grow bitter at having shelved her own dreams to help Arnie fulfill his own.

Early in March Lynne wrote that the musical was in rehearsal at an East Village playhouse.

"Barring unexpected problems the opening is set for April Fourteenth. Since the company is Off-Broadway Equity, we should get some reviews. Do you suppose you could fly up to be with us?"

Fran arranged to go up for the musical's opening with her mother. Debbie had just been promoted to manager of the Bellevue shop and used this as an excuse not to accompany them.

"Does the time ever come when you stop worrying about your kids?" Fran asked Beverly.

"I told my kids that once out of college they were on their own," Beverly said bluntly. "They both wanted master's degrees. I told them, 'fine, go for it. But it's your problem.' I'd done my share."

She'd never feel that way, Fran knew. She'd brought them into the world—and they'd always be her responsibility. And she'd felt a special guilt because they'd been without a father for so much of their lives.

Please, God, she thought, let this be Arnie's big break. Let Lynne have that to enjoy.

Fran relished her mother's excitement in the trip. She herself remembered—but mercifully Ida had forgotten—that her last trip to New York had been when Bernie died. They arrived the afternoon before the opening, registered at the Essex House, then cabbed to Lynne's apartment.

"Isn't it wonderful that the opening was set during school spring vacation?" Lynne bubbled when they'd exchanged loving embraces. "There's a dress rehearsal tonight, but Arnie doesn't want us to come."

"Is it a good show?" Ida asked eagerly, holding Beth on her lap while Jessie clung to Fran.

"The music is lovely." Lynne seemed guarded now, some of her effervescence evaporating. "Somebody's coming down from the *New York Post* to review it—and from *The Villager*."

"I'm gonna sing in a musical when I grow up," Jessie said, her face radiant in anticipation. "Daddy says I can take dancing lessons next year," she added with pride, then focused on the cane that lay beside Fran. "Can you dance, Grandma?"

"Not since I hurt my leg," Fran explained, startled at the question. The leg brace, her cane were part of her in the eyes of those she knew. "But I used to love to dance."

"Lynne, what's the matter?" Ida asked. "All of a sudden you don't look too happy about the show."

"Arnie's thrilled, of course, at just having the musical produced."

Lynne was serious now. "But I've sat in on a couple of rehearsals this week. The cast is uneven. Of course, with these Off–Broadway companies in very small houses this often happens. Two non–Equity members walked out just a week ago when something came up. They were good." She was blunt. "Their replacements are not. Arnie's praying the book and the music are strong enough to carry the show."

Twenty minutes after the curtain rose on the intimate musical Fran sensed that its life would be brief. But Arnie and Lynne were young— only thirty. How many people made a real dent in their professions by that age? They came out of college and expected to reach out and claim success in five years. That was so unrealistic. It wasn't that *easy*.

Fran and her mother remained in their seats during intermission. Lynne went to encourage Arnie, who hovered at the rear of the tiny playhouse—too anxious to sit in the audience.

"The music is nice," Ida said, her eyes taking inventory of the audience—most of them friends of the cast and producer.

"You and I are giving a cast party," Fran told her mother—determined to appear optimistic. The audience was responsive, she noted. It was a friendly audience, of course—except for the two reviewers present. "We're taking them to Ratner's."

On the following morning Fran and Ida went for a late breakfast with Lynne and Arnie. They would be on an afternoon flight to Atlanta. Fran was anxious about the reviews. Despite all the animated conversation over the late supper at Ratner's last night, she'd suspected the others, too, were uneasy about the two reviewers' reactions.

When she opened the door, Lynne's face told Fran the news was not good.

"Arnie's on the phone now with Tim," she said softly. "Tim's mother is closing the show. The *New York Post* panned it."

"Oh, Lynne, I'm so sorry." Fran reached to pull her close.

"Yeah, I know she was upset about the reviews," Arnie was saying belligerently, "but couldn't she have kept it running for the week? The Equity bond covers that. The reviewer liked one song. If it stayed open, I might have been able to get some record people down." The three were silent while Arnie grimaced in response to Tim's voice. "Yeah, we'll get together one of these days."

"The *Post* reviewer liked one of the songs," Lynne repeated defensively. "Arnie's hoping to get a record out of that."

"You're young," Fran told Arnie. Trite, but true, she thought. "There'll be other musicals, other opportunities."

"We're moving into a weird stage in the music business." A new bitterness colored his voice. "All of a sudden singers are writing their own songs. It's getting to where if you're not a singer, you're out in the cold! Look at the Beatles, Bob Dylan, Simon and Garfunkel—"

"Arnie, you write beautiful songs—singers will come to you," Lynne said earnestly. "Your time will come."

Fran saw the love for Arnie that radiated from Lynne. For her it was enough to help Arnie find his place in the music world. For now it was enough.

Thirty-Four

F ran worried that Lynne was upset that Arnie's musical had closed, though her letters were optimistic.

"Arnie's made contact with a small but aggressive music publisher. He was impressed by the mention in the New York Post *review about 'One Precious Moment' and he's trying to work a deal with a record company."*

"One Precious Moment" was a rather lovely song, Fran remembered—but it was more '40s music than late '60s. She suspected Arnie could write music like "Blowing in the Wind" and "Puff the Magic Dragon"—but he wasn't. He hated the messages of the songs made popular by the Beatles. He loathed acid rock. He was born out of his time, she thought compassionately.

Fran wished urgently that Arnie would focus on landing another accounting job. Despite the lunacy that had taken over a chunk of the young people in the country, Arnie and Lynne kept clear of that, she reminded herself. They weren't into the drug scene. To them New York's East Village was still the cradle of Off-Broadway—not the hotbed of crash pads and flower children for which it was becoming famous. They hadn't participated in last year's big "love-in" in Central Park's Sheep Meadow—though the age spread of those dedicated to Timothy Leary's message of "turn on, tune in, drop out" spread from teenagers to draw in thirty-year-olds. As in every decade it was the noisily rebellious who garnered all the attention.

Still, it disturbed her that Arnie seemed to forget that he had a wife and two children to support. He was obsessed by his music. Did he expect Lynne to support them forever? Robin warned her repeatedly that people in the arts often lost touch with reality. *"They're another breed, Sugar. Accept that."*

She'd worked while Bernie pushed his way through law school—but that had been for a predetermined period. These days many wives worked, she conceded. But damn it, Lynne had career goals, too. She wasn't enthralled with teaching—that was coming through loud and clear now. Lynne longed to be a crusading attorney.

Fran forced herself to be silent when Lynne came down to Bellevue with the girls for the month of July and talked about how Arnie had left his would-be publisher to pursue one with stronger credentials—ever convinced that another would work out a record deal for him. She mustn't interfere in Lynne's marriage, she exhorted herself.

Back in New York Lynne wrote that Arnie wanted to send Jessie for piano lessons in another few months—if they could afford it by then. He was sure she had a terrific future in music. Fran wrote back, warning Lynne not to push Jessie too hard. But she offered to pay for piano lessons.

Lynne and Arnie flew down with Jessie and Beth during the school break between Christmas and New Year's. Fran glowed with pride when—after their first dinner in Bellevue—Jessie sang for the family. Jessie was adorable—and Arnie was right. She had perfect pitch and a natural ability to sell a song. And such confidence, Fran marveled.

"Chip off the old block, hunh?" Arnie beamed when Jessie stopped performing.

"That was wonderful," Fran agreed and reached to pull Beth close. "Wait another year," she said gently because she felt Beth's wistful need to match her sister's performance, "and Beth, too, will be singing for us."

When Lynne came home alone with the girls, Fran analyzed, Debbie seemed comfortable—almost happy. When Arnie was here, Debbie retreated. Arnie's roughhousing with Jessie and Beth was a stark reminder that Diane would never enjoy this experience.

A few nights after Lynne and her small family returned to New York, Fran met Robin for dinner at a charming new restaurant that had just opened in Buckhead. She sensed he was in one of his recurrent moods of depression.

"Fran, I feel awful," he confessed when they were alone at a corner table bathed in soft lamplight. "I stare in the mirror, and I see the years catching up with me. I look *old.*"

"Robin, you're out of your mind," she chided. But she understood. A once ardent lover—a soap opera actor in New York—had moved on to someone else. "You look so young I suspect that people who see us together are sure I'm your mother."

"Then they're thinking incest." Robin shot her his pixie grin. "We're the scandalous couple of Bellevue."

"Why, look who else has found this darling place," a cotton-candy-sweet voice intruded.

"Hi, Valerie." Robin exuded his special brand of charm and Fran echoed his greeting. "Would you like to join us?" He half rose from his chair.

"Thanks, no. Jeff's with me—he's table hopping. It's a special night for us. We're celebrating our fifteenth wedding anniversary. I just can't believe it's so long."

"The years run past," Fran said and smiled as Jeff Maddox—a popular local surgeon—joined them.

They chatted briefly, then Valerie and Jeff were led to their own table.

"How the hell did that marriage last fifteen years?" Robin said with detached amusement when the other couple was out of hearing.

"I know there're rumors every now and then that they're splitting up," Fran recalled. "But gossip is a major industry in this town."

"I don't know how any woman can take the kind of shit Jeff dishes out." Robin flinched in eloquent distaste. Fran lifted an eyebrow inquiringly. "Every time he gets frustrated, he beats the hell out of her. She tells everybody she's accident prone."

Involuntarily Fran's eyes sought out Valerie and Jeff's table. No one here—seeing the attractive, well-dressed Valerie and Jeff Maddox would suspect their lives were anything but perfect.

"Men like that totally destroy a woman's self-confidence," Fran told him. She'd been startled by his revelation—but then she wasn't part of local daytime socializing, where gossip was as rampant as talk about clothes and diets. "They tear her to shreds mentally and emotionally. I had a lovely, sweet neighbor like that years ago in New York. She told me one time after he'd blackened her eye and fractured a wrist that it was her fault. '*I provoke him.*' And it happens in every layer of society." But Debbie had a perfect marriage—and it was destroyed in a senseless moment.

"All these picture-book couples," Robin drawled, his eyes rebellious. "Both straight and gay. Nobody knows what lies behind the surface."

"The games we play—" Fran's smile was wry.

"I've been thinking about a face-lift." All at once Robin was self-conscious. "Men do it, too, you know. Not just actors—business executives, lawyers."

"You don't need a face-lift," Fran rejected. "When you begin to sag, I promise to tell you."

"What's with Debbie?" he asked, retreating from the traumatic subject.

Fran sighed. "It's two and a half years now since Scott's death, but she still can't accept the fact that the Glenwood sheriff's office has written it off. Every time there's a murder case reported in the newspapers, she reads every word. Punishing herself when other cases are solved but Scott's killer walks free."

"Did you ever consider hiring a private investigator? You can afford it, Fran—" His voice was gently mocking, but she felt his compassion.

"Robin, I don't know." She had gone over this in her mind during a parade of sleepless nights. Debbie had rejected this. "If nothing came of it, she'd be more upset than ever."

"Don't tell her," Robin said. "It can be done without her knowing. And the guy might just come up with something."

"Not a local investigator," Fran stipulated, trying to deal with this possibility.

"I'll make inquiries in Atlanta," Robin told her. "If nothing comes of it, Debbie doesn't have to know."

Three days after returning from her buying trip, Fran met with the investigator in Atlanta. Robin had made a swift check of his credentials—he was among the tops in his field. While his office was small and unpretentious, it managed to convey the message that its owner was highly successful. As Robin had warned, his fees were high.

"I want you to be candid on every question I ask," Tyler Corman told her. "Fill me in on every little detail, no matter how insignificant it appears."

Talking with Corman, Fran was conscious of fresh hope, a feeling that this might be the breakthrough to bring Debbie back to herself. She wished that Debbie was here to talk with Tyler Corman, but that might be offering false expectations. Debbie mustn't know about this unless there was positive action to take.

Fran searched her mind to ferret out what she knew of the Richards family—all of which was public knowledge, she berated herself. She added Debbie's own conviction that the intruder who killed Scott was a local man—or woman—and explained Debbie's arriving at this.

"I'll go on what we have." Corman was noncommittal when she finished. "I'll get back to you as soon as possible."

Five days later—after a brief trip to Glenwood—Corman summoned Fran to his office. She tried to read past his impassive voice, but came up with nothing. She left her own office to rush to his.

"This won't be easy," he warned her when his secretary had ushered her in and left them. "As far as the police go, it's an open-and-shut case of some wanderer through the area trying to rob the home of the wealthiest family in town. The murdered man's brother feels the same way. So we have to try another approach." He forestalled the question forming in Fran's mind. "We work under the assumption it was a local job. Your daughter's conclusions were sharp. Did you know that Mrs. Richards had bought a famous diamond and emerald necklace shortly before she died? It had belonged to some Russian czarina."

"No." Fran's heart began to pound. She doubted that Debbie knew. "You think a jewel thief was after the necklace? And Scott was killed when he walked in on this?"

"I found an item about it in a Raleigh newspaper. It was sold by an auction house up in New York. A jewel thief could easily have traced it to Glenwood, then hooked up with a local person who knew the habits of the Richards family, the layout of the house. I tried to discuss this with the sheriff up there, but he blew me off. I gather the word came through that Perry Richards wanted no more publicity in the newspapers about the murder. And in Glenwood what Perry Richards wants he gets. Now why would a man like that be so publicity shy?"

"I gather from what Scott told me that Perry has political and social ambitions—" Fran tried to recall what Scott had said. "He wants to be a power in state politics—and to be accepted in the top Raleigh social circles. I suppose he feels there's something unsavory about having a murder in the family."

"Would Perry have anything personal to hide?" Corman probed. "That an investigation might bring out—"

"My daughter suspected he was into heavy gambling," Fran said slowly.

"Then there's a possibility," he pounced. "Way out, of course. But Perry himself could have been involved in a heist. To pay off gambling debts," he added at Fran's blank stare. "He'd be able to provide a layout of the house, the location of the jewels. But if Perry wasn't involved in stealing the jewelry, somebody on the domestic staff may have been part of it. They knew about the necklace. I should check out the domestic staff. It'll take time," he warned, his eyebrows lifted in question. And time meant money.

"Go ahead." Fran was almost terse in her excitement. "I want this murder solved." She wanted Debbie *free*.

When she met Robin for lunch ten days later, she was startled by his annoyance at Corman's activities.

"The bastard's trying to run a big bill for you," he interpreted. "All this crap about investigating the domestic staff. Why doesn't he go to the sheriff and bring out the fact this could have been an attempted jewel heist? From what you tell me, there was no mention of that before. It should have been brought out."

"He tried, Robin," Fran defended Corman. "I have to give him all the leeway he wants. I'm praying he can come up with something we can take to the authorities—above the sheriff's level—and have the case reopened. I don't care what it costs!"

"You're a good mommie," Robin said tenderly. "I hope your kids know it."

Fran waited for further word from Tyler Corman. He called from Raleigh with an interim report.

"Perry Richards has a history of ugly scrapes, starting back in elementary school. His mother has always bailed him out. I want to check out this gambling habit of his. It could be an important lead."

Fran told herself she mustn't hold out false hope—but there was a chance Corman was on to something. She teetered between optimism and despair. If Tyler Corman came up with nothing, there was little chance that Scott's murder would ever be solved.

Then a gigantic bill came from the private investigator, along with instructions to phone him. The following day Fran was in his office.

"We've gone as far as we can on this," he told Fran. "I'm sorry." His smile was sympathetic but perfunctory. From a phone conversation his secretary had been conducting in the outer office when she arrived, she'd gathered he was off on another case. "I have suspicions," he conceded. "If you'd like to hear them?"

"Yes, I would." She struggled for poise.

"Through my contacts in Raleigh, I learned that Perry was in over his head to a gambling syndicate. It's my suspicion that he hoped to get off the hook by leading the syndicate to his mother's expensive jewelry, probably kept in a safe in the library—where Scott was killed."

"Then why can't we—" Fran broke in, then paused as Corman shook his head.

"It's all conjecture," he pointed out. "We haven't one shred of proof. Perry didn't expect them to kill his brother—but he can't talk. He—"

"He could pay off the syndicate now," Fran interrupted—her head reeling. *Could Perry know who killed Scott?* "He inherited his mother's whole estate. She died after Scott. Perry was her sole heir."

"But he can't identify the killer," Corman reiterated. "He'd be involved in the robbery. He'd go to prison. He has to be silent." He paused. "I have a gut reaction this is on target. But it's all speculation."

Driving back to Bellevue, Fran reran the conversation with Tyler Corman in her mind. She felt sick at Corman's assumptions. How could warm, sweet Scott have a brother who was so loathsome? How could Perry live with himself when he was allowing Scott's killer to go free? All along she'd tried to tell herself that some local thief had been caught in the act and had shot to cover his own hide. Debbie was right, of course— it was terrible to know that a murderer was escaping punishment.

It would have been better not to know that Perry might be involved. There was no proof, Fran acknowledged, yet everything pointed in that direction. *That was why Perry insisted on no further investigation.* Corman had agreed right off with Debbie's conviction that Scott had not been murdered by "somebody passing through town." But how could she tell Debbie what Tyler Corman suspected?

Scott's murder would never be solved. Debbie would be denied that satisfaction. Fran fought against a tidal wave of helplessness. What could she do to drag Debbie out of that vacuum she'd built for herself? She must—somehow—bring about some change in Debbie's life. If she didn't, she dared not contemplate what would happen to this precious child.

Thirty-Five

It seemed to Fran in the months ahead that life was on hold. But not the world, she thought grimly. The world was writhing with unrest. The war in Vietnam continued, though recently inaugurated President Richard M. Nixon promised a withdrawal of American troops. Students demonstrated on campuses across the country because American servicemen continued to die in Vietnam. Police—even the National Guard—were brought out to quell the disturbances. And inflation raced on unchecked, evoking fears of a serious recession.

Fran watched her mother struggle with fears of aging. Her health was good, Fran kept reassuring her—but friends were failing and it frightened her. Every time she forgot something she was sure she was coming down with Alzheimer's disease.

"Everybody forgets sometimes," Fran would protest. "I forget. Debbie forgets."

Debbie continued her half life, emerging from her shell only when she was with Diane—who beguiled all who knew her. Nothing seemed to be changing in Lynne's situation other than that Jessie had begun piano lessons.

"Her teacher says it's uncanny," Lynne wrote, "the way she can play by ear. Arnie keeps warning her she has to learn to read music."

The light of their lives in Bellevue was Diane, Fran told herself regularly. If not for Diane, she thought, Debbie would fall apart. Any overtures to Debbie about seeking professional help to deal with her emotional pain elicited prickly responses—and Fran abandoned this.

In July Lynne came down with the girls again for a month's visit. Arnie was working at intervals through a "temp" agency, which allowed him time to pursue his music publishing and record contacts. Meaning,

Fran interpreted, that his earnings were minuscule. She flew up to New York with Lynne and the girls for her usual summer buying trip.

In a confidential moment with Lynne, she learned of Lynne's efforts to persuade Debbie to date again.

"Mom, she's young and beautiful. I was blunt—I told her to go out and find herself another life. She said nobody would ever match up to Scott. She'd compare other men to him—and that wasn't fair." And in a corner of her mind Fran remembered harboring similar thoughts herself—until Craig came along.

She was ever grateful for the brief encounters with Craig—at synagogue affairs, local parties, benefits—and their occasional lunches in Atlanta, often with Robin in attendance. She knew Craig was there for her in any crisis that might arise. They were depriving Joyce of nothing, she reminded herself each time.

Early in October Fran opened yet another store in her chain—this one in South Carolina. Returning from the opening day, she called her mother from the airport. The crash in Indianapolis last month, when eighty-three people had died, had made her mother nervous about her flying, Fran remembered.

"Hello—" Debbie's voice came to her.

"Tell Grandma I'm back," she said. "You know how she worries when I fly these days."

"They changed her bridge night to Thursdays," Debbie explained. "Grandma hasn't come home yet."

"Everything all right?" Her grandmother was out playing bridge, but Debbie sat at home except for the one night a week Nora dragged her off to their women's group meeting.

"Fine. Diane's asleep—" Otherwise, Fran interpreted, she'd be clamoring to speak to "Nana." She was "Nana," her mother was "Grandma"—as she was to Lynne and Debbie.

"I'll pick up my car and be home soon," Fran promised.

When she arrived at the house, she found her mother watching a TV newscast. Debbie was engrossed in a book—as usual.

"Can you believe the Department of Health, Education, and Welfare is suspected of blacklisting hundreds of famous scientists from their panels because they've come out and said they're against the Vietnamese War?" Ida said indignantly, and Fran chuckled. She'd never been able to involve her mother in politics, but Lynne and Debbie had managed that. And now she remembered that Debbie and Scott had pushed her mother into her first voting. "Isn't that outrageous?"

"Outrageous," Fran agreed. "How'd you make out tonight?"

"I lost six thousand dollars. Nice that it's all on paper." All at once her eyes had that guarded look that told Fran she was about to say something she wasn't sure should be said. "They were talking tonight about how Joyce and Craig are having marital problems."

"Mother, they're such gossips!" Fran flared.

"Joyce is bored with Bellevue, it seems. She wants Craig to join some fancy firm up in New York." Ida was suspiciously nonchalant. *Mother couldn't know how she felt about Craig. Could she, after all these years?* "Joyce says he met these people at some architectural convention, and they were terribly impressed with his ideas."

"I doubt that Craig would leave Bellevue—he's so well established here." She was shaken at the prospect of Craig's moving away. In a quiet, unobtrusive way he was part of her life. "And he wouldn't want to uproot his kids."

Fran was relieved that her mother veered away from this subject to talk about the coming Bellevue Garden Club benefit. She managed an aura of interest, though inwardly she was shaken. She didn't want Craig to leave Bellevue.

She remembered the poignant pleasure of having Craig at Debbie's wedding, the many hours they'd spent together while he was building the new house, his comforting words when they'd met for lunch not long after Scott's death. Local social events were made special because Craig was there. She would be devastated, she thought in soaring anguish, if Craig moved away from Bellevue.

Three weeks later Craig phoned on her private line at the office.

"I thought you might want to talk again about the guest house you were considering," he said with a casualness that told her this was meant for camouflage.

"Yes, I would, Craig." Her heart was pounding. Was he calling to confirm that he and Joyce had decided to move to New York?

"Lunch tomorrow?" he asked.

"I can manage that."

"Shall I ask Robin to join us?" Craig seemed hesitant.

"He's still up on Fire Island," Fran explained. "At a community called Cherry Grove. He won't be back until after Labor Day."

"Shall we meet at Robin's favorite lunch place?" Craig asked.

"That'll be fine." Did Craig want to tell her he was moving away? *Don't let it be that.* "What time?"

"I'll make a reservation for noon—before the mob descends."

"Great. See you then."

When she arrived at the restaurant the next day at noon sharp, she found Craig had already been seated at their table.

"You look beautiful," he greeted her. "As always."

"You're great for my morale." Her voice was light. Her eyes betrayed her anxiety.

"I don't know if you heard the rumors floating around town." He was tense, annoyed. "That Joyce and I might be moving to New York."

"I've heard." Her smile was shaky. "But then you know how gossip floats around this town."

"I'm not leaving, Fran. I can't give up my practice here. I wouldn't uproot the kids at their ages." He paused, then took a deep breath. "I couldn't bear not to be able to see you."

"I'm glad you're staying," she whispered.

"I've gone along with most of Joyce's whims." She was startled by this first indication of bitterness. "I've told her bluntly we're not leaving Bellevue. I'm not accepting the offer from that firm in New York. I've known for a long time that Joyce detests living in Bellevue. It was all right the first three or four years. We've had no real marriage since Josh and Zach were little. We make a pretense in public. Joyce wants to be very rich and very social. She smokes like a fiend, drinks more than she should. I think," he said wryly, "that she expected me to become wealthy and socially prominent."

"You do very well," Fran reminded. Never once in these past years had Craig admitted to problems within his marriage. She'd known, of course, that he had never stopped loving her—but she hadn't realized he was having problems with Joyce. "You're very successful."

"Not in Joyce's eyes. I was afraid you'd heard the rumors—I didn't want you to think I was leaving. The good hours in my life are those I spend with the kids and the hours we see each other."

"I was scared you'd go out of my life." Her smile was tremulous.

"That won't ever happen," he promised. "And whenever you need me, I'll be here for you."

Sitting in a comfortable armchair before the fireplace in the spacious wood-paneled den that had become the family's favorite room, Fran was sharply conscious that this New Year's Eve—which she would welcome in the company of her mother and Debbie—was the end of a decade. The last year had been chaotic, she thought, caught up in retrospect. There had been the horror of the carnage at My Lai in Vietnam, the landing of a man on the moon, rebellion on campuses across the country, Woodstock—where four hundred thousand young people gathered to listen to rock and blues, to smoke pot, drink beer, and spread the word of universal love. Why did the last hours of a decade seem so portentous? she asked herself while her mother fiddled with the TV set in search of a festive program. Birch logs blazed in the fireplace grate, lending a specious air of serenity to the occasion.

Debbie was putting Diane to bed. Fran knew that for Debbie every holiday was a traumatic occasion, fraught with memories of sharing it with Scott. She'd talked with Debbie about going with her to New York to become familiar with the buying scene for the shops. But Debbie rejected any effort to draw her more deeply into the business. She managed the Bellevue shop. She spent one evening a week with Nora's group. Beyond that she remained isolated from the world.

"I'll call Midore now," Fran told her mother, leaving her chair to cross to the phone. It had become tradition to call Midore and Cliff on New Year's Eve.

"So early?" Ida objected. "Are you forgetting the three hours' difference in time?"

"She spends New Year's Eve as a volunteer at a home for the aged," Fran explained. "She'll be leaving soon."

For a little while Fran was caught up in nostalgia as she talked with Midore. They were forever bound together by the early years they'd shared. For this small parcel of time Bernie and Bob and Sal were alive again.

She had just finished the phone conversation with Midore when Cliff called. He was to attend a medical convention in Boston—this time with his wife, who was eager to see New York.

"Can we coordinate our schedules?" Cliff demanded blithely. "It'd be great to spend an evening with you in New York."

"We'll do it," Fran said, eager for this reunion. "When do you expect to be in New York?"

"I'm staying up till midnight," Ida announced when Fran was off the phone. "I won't fall asleep like last year. Don't ply me with wine, Frannie," she scolded in high good humor. "That's what did it. And I want to be awake when you phone Lynne."

They'd call Lynne close to midnight, Fran decided. Lynne would be cheerful, full of talk about Jessie and Beth—and Arnie's music. He always seemed about to make a breakthrough in the music business—but

Lynne had taken on private tutoring to increase their income. Lynne loved Arnie, and she was convinced he would land a record deal that would make him another Cole Porter. Her own ambitions were dead. Face that, Fran ordered herself.

Fran arrived in New York on a raw, bone-chilling morning late in January. The city was gray and forbidding. Up to the last moment she'd tried to persuade Debbie to come with her, but Debbie continued to reject this.

Looking ahead—determined to be realistic—Fran plotted to prepare Debbie to take over for her should the need arise. And playing a major role in the business would guarantee Debbie financial security.

Fran checked into the Essex House, then headed for Seventh Avenue. She relished the air of excitement that permeated the city—yet she knew that she was always pleased to be back in the serenity of Bellevue after a few days of city living. She was eager to see Lynne and the kids, but Lynne was teaching and Jessie and Beth were at their respective schools. She'd be at the apartment no later than five, she promised herself—missing the afternoon rush hour scene.

She felt guilty at spending tomorrow evening with Cliff, but she'd cut her buying in midafternoon to spend some time with Lynne and the children before she was to meet him. He was coming into New York just to see her, she remembered tenderly. His wife had decided at the last moment not to accompany him to the medical convention. *"She's shy, Fran—she thinks she wants to meet all these people, then backs out."*

Fran rushed through her buying, impatient to be at Lynne's apartment. Maybe in July, she thought while her cab threaded its way through the already heavy late afternoon traffic, she'd fly to the Paris shows. She hadn't presented a Paris original at the shops in years. Perhaps the prospect of seeing Paris again would persuade Debbie to go with her.

At the apartment she was welcomed by Lynne and the girls with the affection she cherished. She was secretly pleased that Arnie didn't arrive until they were ready to sit down to dinner—Jessie and Beth allowed to stay up late in honor of her presence.

"How did it go?" Fran heard Lynne ask Arnie as he hung away his overcoat in the tiny foyer closet.

"It's too early to tell," Arnie said. "But they promised to let us know soon." Fran knew that he'd acquired a music publisher, and that the two men had met late this afternoon with a record company executive. "I've got good vibes about this one, honey."

The following evening Fran left Lynne and the girls to meet Cliff at a midtown restaurant. He was seated at their table when she arrived.

"Fran, you never change!" he scolded with mock reproach after a warm embrace. "Other people age—you don't."

"You haven't changed that much," she said, her smile radiating affection. "A few pounds here and there, a little less hair," she teased.

"Tell me about the family," he ordered, "then I'll tell you about my brood."

It was so good being here with Cliff, she thought. He was one of the few people she knew—he and Craig—who truly loved their work. And each knew he was blessed in that, she told herself. In the changing world of medicine Cliff still made house calls, still had time to talk with his patients.

She wondered at Cliff's suddenly somber expression when their desserts and coffee were served.

"Fran, something came up at the convention in Boston that I must discuss with you." He seemed to be searching for words. "I have to be honest and tell you there's some risk involved—there's always a certain element of risk in surgery. But at the convention an orthopedic surgeon from New York read a paper on a new procedure he's developed. I talked with him later. It's too complicated to go into—but by introducing a steel support into your bad leg, he could most likely make it possible for you to abandon your brace."

"He's performed this surgery?" All at once Fran felt light-headed.

"On four patients. Each time it's been successful. But we have to realize that there's no guarantee. Doctor Morse can't know exactly what he'll find until he's doing the surgery." He paused, but he was clearly excited about the potential of this new procedure. "There's a very slight possibility that the surgery could cause further damage—"

"I could end up in a wheelchair," she verbalized his thought.

"A very slight chance. I want you to think about this, Fran," Cliff urged. "I've talked with him about you already. He'll be willing to see you at any time. It's radical surgery that could create almost a miracle for the right subjects. And I think you fit into that category."

"Cliff, I can't believe it." Her voice dropped to an awed whisper. "After all these years—"

"I'll give you his card. You go home, think about it, then call him." Cliff's eyes said he was sure she'd go ahead with it.

"I've always told myself I could handle the situation," Fran said slowly. "I've refused to admit the tiredness that seems almost unbearable at the end of some days. I've prided myself on hiding the brace by always wearing slacks—making them a part of my 'look.' But suppose it doesn't work?" A coldness closed in about her. "I could be stuck in a wheelchair for the rest of my life."

"Consider the possibilities," Cliff urged. "The surgery could give you back the mobility you used to know."

"I get around all right," Fran said in sudden defiance. "I drive a car. I conduct my business."

"Of course, you'll probably cling to the cane for a few months," Cliff pushed on. "Until you gain confidence. You'll need to be in New York for six weeks. Ten days in the hospital, then daily therapy until you can get around in comfort. Without the leg brace, without the cane in time," he emphasized. "It'll be like getting your life back again."

"I'll have to think about it," Fran hedged, and he nodded in understanding. But would she get her life back? Her dream was gone. She'd replaced it with a business career. Still, the prospect of abandoning the cumbersome leg brace—perhaps even her cane—was exhilarating. "I'll talk about it with the family."

"As long as you're here in the city, let me take you up to see him," Cliff urged in sudden impatience. "No commitments, Fran. Just let him check you out and tell you his prognosis."

"Cliff, my schedule is tight," she protested, simultaneously excited and fearful.

"Tomorrow morning at nine sharp," Cliff said. "We talked about you. I made a tentative appointment. He's very interested."

"All right," Fran agreed after a moment. "But I can't believe this is happening—"

They dawdled over dessert and coffee, taking refuge now in reminiscences about the early years together. But the promises this new surgery offered dominated Fran's thoughts. What she had never thought was possible might be hers. But suppose it failed? Suppose she became wheelchair bound—or worse? Who would run the business? The business was security for the family. For her mother and Debbie and Diane, for Lynne and Jessie and Beth. Did she have the right to gamble with that?

Thirty - Six

C liff had suggested Fran meet him for breakfast at the Automat on Broadway near 55th Street. He was nostalgic about meals taken there during med school days. Walking into the busy Automat—fragrant with the aroma of what many declared the best coffee in New York— Fran felt her mind charging back through the years. Bernie had taken her for breakfast here on their honeymoon and teased her about being such an avid tourist. It was the first time she'd seen this New York City institution, and she had been enthralled.

A few minutes before 9 A.M. Fran and Cliff were in Dr. Morse's waiting room, devoid thus far of patients. But the receptionist had been briefed on their arrival.

"Doctor Morse is studying X-rays," she explained. "He'll be with you shortly."

Fran liked Dr. Morse on sight. He exuded a personal warmth, an enthusiasm for his profession. He talked away her nervousness, yet she sensed that nothing escaped his sharp eyes.

"You've exercised the leg regularly," he guessed. "You realized the importance of this."

"Yes." All those years ago the therapist had made it clear to her.

"You're a fine candidate," he said at last, and Cliff beamed. "I wouldn't want to do it five years from now—or after that. Now," he emphasized. "Within a year. I'm sure Cliff has told you that no surgery is without risk. But I feel very optimistic about your chances. I don't expect you to make an immediate decision," he anticipated her reply. "Go home, think about it. Consider what it can do for you. Then let me know."

The evening after her meeting with Cliff—and with Jessie and Beth finally asleep—Fran told Lynne and Arnie about the new medical procedure.

"Mom, it sounds great!" Lynne was enthusiastic.

"How many times has this been done?" Arnie asked, his skepticism obvious.

"I think four times," Fran said. "Of course, with surgery there's never any guarantee." She repeated Cliff's warning.

"You owe it to yourself to take the chance," Lynne persisted. "Things would be so much easier for you."

"I'll have to give it a lot of thought," Fran hedged.

"If it doesn't work, you could be in real trouble." Arnie ignored Lynne's annoyed glare. "It's like with plastic surgery. All these women going under the knife to look younger and ending up with weird results."

"Arnie, this is different," Lynne protested. "Mom's life would be so much more comfortable."

"If it works," Arnie pinpointed.

Lynne turned back to her mother. "You said the doctor who does this is in New York?"

"That's right. He's created a lot of interest in the procedure."

"So I could be there with you," Lynne pursued. "It's not as though you'd be alone in the city."

"I can't make a decision right away." Fran forced a smile. "It's major."

Her first evening back in Bellevue Fran told her mother and Debbie about the proposed surgery.

"An operation?" Ida's voice was shrill with alarm. "Frannie, didn't you go through enough of that? I'm against it," she said firmly before Fran could reply. "Crazy things happen in operating rooms."

"Grandma, Mom's friend wouldn't have recommended it if he didn't feel it was safe," Debbie chided gently.

"I don't know how I could be away from the business for six weeks," Fran admitted.

"We can manage," Debbie said with fresh confidence. "You have a great team. I'll work with Beverly, check with each store every day and call to tell you what's happening. It'll be your leg that's laid up—not your mind," she said, sounding—Fran thought with a surge of pleasure—like the old Debbie. "You'll still be running things."

"I have to think about it." Fran managed a faint smile. "It's a big step."

"I'll be a nervous wreck," Ida warned and sighed. "I wish your father was here to advise you."

"Dad would want me to take the chance," Fran said after a moment. "But I don't know. I just don't know."

She lay sleepless far into the night, awoke tired and battling doubts. At the office she took care of the usual minor crises, but this morning her mind rebelled at dealing with business. What was she to do about the operation? How could she gamble? she asked herself for the hundredth time, yet part of her was reluctant to relinquish the hope Dr. Morse offered.

On impulse she reached for the phone and dialed Craig's private line. Let him be in the office, she prayed. *She needed to talk with him.*

"Hello." Craig's voice was crisp, oddly reassuring even before they spoke.

"Craig, would you be free for lunch?" she asked. "I'd like to talk."

"Of course," he said instantly, then hesitated. She felt his sudden tension. "Is something wrong, Fran?"

"No. I just want to hear your reaction to something that came up. Twelve o'clock?"

"That'll be fine. I'll make reservations." No need to ask where. Robin's favorite restaurant had become "their restaurant."

This was Craig's private line, used by only a few people—yet he was always careful to keep their conversation casual in the event anyone should hear. Not that anything ever happened, Fran reminded herself—except in the silent communication between them.

Fran arrived early. Even if Robin was in town—and this was one of his "mad weeks in New York"—she wouldn't have discussed this with him. She knew his answer would be "to run with it." But Craig would consider every angle—he'd weigh the pros and cons.

Her face lighted when he approached their table. If anybody from Bellevue saw them here, she'd have a ready explanation, she thought defensively. She was talking with Craig about a guest house on their property. But thus far she saw no one they knew.

"How are you?" he asked, his eyes searching hers.

"Bewildered," she confessed. "I need your clear mind to help me with an answer." It was absurd that she could feel so good just to be sitting across the table from Craig. She knew it was the same for him. No one was hurt, she reiterated yet again.

Their waiter arrived, and they made a light game of ordering. All at once, it seemed to Fran, they were back in Paris all those years ago—

having lunch at Chez Monteil, when Jean Gabin strolled into the bistro. She was dismayed to feel a rush of passion. Even now she remembered the first time they'd made love—in that motel just outside of Atlanta. Craig had been so sweet, so understanding of her discomfort at being physically handicapped. It had been so wonderful. Each time they'd been together had been wonderful.

The waiter left them. As calmly as she could manage, Fran told Craig about the evening with Cliff, then the meeting the following morning with Dr. Morse.

"I'm torn, Craig—I want to have the operation, yet I'm terrified of what might happen."

"You have it," Craig ordered. "I know what you're thinking—'What if something goes wrong, and I can't carry on the business?' Fran this is your time. The odds are in your favor. Stop thinking for once about your family. Think about *yourself*." His eyes held hers—simultaneously commanding and reassuring her.

"All right," she whispered. "I'll call Doctor Morse and set a date."

"I'll invent an excuse to go up to New York to be with you," he promised. "I'll be there when you come out of surgery."

Her face was luminous. Thank God for Craig's presence in her life. Then doubt seeped into her mind. "How will I explain you to Lynne?"

"I'll tell her that I had to be in New York on business, and your mother asked me to drop in on you. You know how insistent your mother can be," he joshed. "And Lynne knows. I won't let us be cheated out of that, my darling."

Fran contacted Dr. Morse and made arrangements to be in New York in late March for the surgery. At intervals she suffered misgivings. Was she doing the right thing? Her mother was upset. Lynne and Debbie were happy that she had made this decision. Craig constantly reassured her that she could not let this chance slip by her. Robin, too, was supportive.

She clung to the knowledge that Craig would be in New York when she underwent surgery. Lynne would be there with her. She insisted her mother not come up to New York.

"You've been through it once, Mother," she told Ida. "That's enough." While her mother's health was good except for borderline high blood pressure, Fran was ever conscious that she was about to celebrate her 85th birthday.

"If you're laid up for a year," Ida demanded, "will Beverly and Debbie be able to carry on the business? Will we be able to afford it if I have to go into a nursing home?"

"Grandma, you'll never go into a nursing home," Debbie intervened. "You'll always be here with Mom and me."

"And we could afford it," Fran said, knowing her mother yearned for this assurance. "We're doing very well. But it won't ever happen."

Yet at moments Fran cringed at the prospect of being away from the business—from her mother and Debbie and Diane—for six weeks. It seemed a terrifyingly long stretch. But Lynne and Jessie and Beth would be with her, she comforted herself. And Craig would be there when she came out of surgery.

She'd arranged—through Lynne—to rent an apartment in an apartment hotel in the West Eighties.

"It's not like the house back home," Lynne warned apologetically. "But it's comfortable and clean and neat. And it's near enough to my school so that I can even run over at lunchtime."

At other moments Fran was consumed by one vision: that she would be able to walk alone without brace or cane, wear dresses without feeling self-conscious—though not the popular mini-dresses, she joshed inwardly. Not at 54. Beautiful clothes had always been her weakness, she admitted—and if the surgery went well, she could choose her wardrobe with glorious abandon. Was that a vain, silly hope?

The night before she was to leave for New York, Fran had dinner with Craig and Robin. Without a word being said Robin knew how she and Craig felt about each other, she'd realized. Tonight he was in an ebullient mood and carried most of the conversation. He'd decided to have Craig build him a studio on a wooded tract midway between Bellevue and Atlanta that he'd inherited from his parents. Without his putting this into words Fran understood the studio was to tempt the young New York artist he'd met recently to come down to Bellevue at regular intervals.

"Craig, you'll make the studio something special," he ordered. "A place where I can run away and paint when I'm in the mood."

Robin still kept up the pretense even with Craig that he was heterosexual. And everyone in Bellevue knew he possessed a small talent for painting. Was that what Arnie had, Fran asked herself involuntarily—a small talent? A generous talent was a precious gift—a meager one a curse, she thought in pain.

"I should get home early," Fran said while they lingered over second cups of coffee. "I know my mother and Debbie will be waiting up tonight." Her last night at home before surgery.

"I'll drive you home in ten minutes," Robin said. "First let me make a trip to the 'little boys' room.' "

Robin was giving her these final few minutes alone with Craig. Not even Robin knew that Craig would be at the hospital while she was in surgery.

"You're going to be fine." Craig's eyes made love to her. "I'll be there at the hospital with Lynne. Tell her I'm standing in for your mother," he reminded. "It's going to be all right," he repeated, and in the anonymity of the softly lit restaurant he reached to cover her hand with his.

"It's so unreal." Again, she fought off a wave of fear.

"It'll be real and beautiful," he promised. "And I want to be there with you."

Fran was touched that Lynne insisted on meeting her at the airport in New York.

"I'm taking off today and day after tomorrow," she explained. "I couldn't quite swing tomorrow, too."

Behind Lynne's smile she saw inchoate fear and much love. She had to be all right, she told herself—she had responsibilities to her family.

"We'll go straight to your little apartment and put away your luggage, then run down for lunch."

Lynne was trying to make it seem that she was here on vacation. She was putting them all through a traumatic experience, Fran thought. But tomorrow afternoon she was scheduled to enter the hospital. The following morning Dr. Morse would do the surgery.

She spent the day with Lynne in an atmosphere of determined gaiety. In the afternoon they went to Lynne's apartment, where Arnie was with Jessie and Beth. Everyone pretended this was a joyous occasion.

"Did Lynne tell you," Arnie asked, "that Jessie is writing songs now?"

"No! How wonderful. Let me hear one," Fran ordered. At the same time she reached to pull Beth into her lap. It wasn't that Arnie favored Jessie over Beth, she comforted herself. Jessie was two years older and displaying a talent that he relished. Beth, too, would probably be musical—and if she wasn't, Fran told herself, she would be just as special as Jessie.

Fran had not expected such a painful reaction at entering the hospital. All the horror of her hospital experience after the shooting engulfed her again. But this was different, she tried to convince herself. This was to make her life better—not to insure survival. But suppose the surgery failed?

Shortly before 8 P.M. Craig called her.

"I'm staying at the Carlyle," he said. Instantly she remembered that they had shared a lovely room there before flying to London. She sensed that Craig, too, remembered.

"Great," she said, her voice tender. They'd had lunch at the Russian Tea Room, then had gone back to the Carlyle to make love.

"I love you—" Craig told her. "I always have—I always will."

"I love you, too," she said softly. "I thank God every day that you're part of my life."

Craig rose early after a night of restless sleep. He'd shower and shave, stop in somewhere along the way for coffee, and be at the hospital by 9 A.M., when Fran was scheduled to go into surgery. He felt a trickle of self-consciousness now at encountering Lynne in the waiting room on the surgical floor. They'd met a number of times, of course—and Lynne knew he had designed their house.

He arrived at the hospital before Lynne and introduced himself as a friend of the family. He saw Lynne emerge from the elevator. She looked so scared, he thought compassionately. He walked toward her with a determined smile.

"She's going to do fine, Lynne," he reassured her. Lynne knew he'd be here. Fran had told her.

"I'll be glad when it's over." Her own smile was shaky.

"I'll go down to the cafeteria and get us coffee. It'll be a long wait."

Over containers of strong, black coffee they talked about President Nixon's stressing in his first State of the Union Address the need to control the environment—both very articulate on the subject.

"I didn't vote for him," Lynne admitted, "but I'm so glad they're saying he's going to sign that bill to ban cigarette advertising on radio and television."

"I've been trying for years to persuade Joyce to stop smoking." Craig spread his hands in a gesture of futility. "First thing in the morning she grabs for a cigarette." Sometimes he thought she did that to annoy him. She was still carrying on about his rejecting the partnership in the New York firm.

Lynne told him about Arnie's efforts to break into the music business. They both talked compulsively, he thought, because they didn't want to think about Fran lying there in the operating room.

"I promised Mom I'd call home the minute we have some word. My grandmother and sister are probably chewing their nails down to the cuticle." Lynne's eyes swung for the dozenth time to the wall clock in the waiting room.

"It'll be a while yet," Craig reminded gently.

Did Lynne have any inkling of how Fran and he felt about each other? Fran wouldn't hear of him divorcing Joyce, of course—he knew that without her putting it into words. Nor would Joyce want a divorce. She was furious with him for not providing a more luxurious life—though she lacked for nothing, he thought in a flurry of impatience—but she'd never relinquish her role of wife.

She'd never been a real wife, other than giving him two terrific sons. In the beginning she'd been so sweet, seemed so adoring—she'd made him feel he could forget Fran. It hadn't taken him long to realize that sex was something she tolerated. It was an obligation. After Zach was born she'd made excuses—and finally moved into her own room. *"I like to read in bed until late—I'd just keep you awake."*

"There's Doctor Morse—" Lynne leapt to her feet.

"He looks pleased," Craig said, rising also. In truth, Morse wore an inscrutable smile that said little, he mocked himself—his throat tightening in anxiety.

Dr. Morse walked toward Lynne and included Craig in his greeting. Assuming, Craig guessed, that he was a member of the family.

"She came through it well," Morse told them. "We won't have any real answers for three or four days—but I'm optimistic. She's being moved into the recovery room. A nurse will tell you when you can see her."

"Thank you, Doctor Morse." Lynne was radiant.

"With a few weeks of therapy she'll be walking on her own," Craig told Lynne while Dr. Morse strode away. "Your mother is a very special lady." Thank God, all had gone well. He hesitated. It wouldn't look right for him to hang around, he warned himself. He'd see Fran later today. "Don't forget to phone your grandmother."

"I'll call right now—" Lynne was reaching into her purse for coins.

Fran would understand why he hadn't stayed, Craig told himself while he walked to the elevators. He'd be back for afternoon visiting hours. Lynne would be here this evening, he remembered. The afternoon would belong to Fran and himself. He'd fill her room with red roses, he decided ebulliently. Fran's favorite flowers.

So Dr. Morse said they wouldn't have "any real answers" for three or four days. But he was optimistic. The operation had to be successful. Don't think otherwise, he told himself.

Yet he knew these next three days would be the most harried he'd ever encountered.

Thirty - Seven

F ran drifted in and out of sleep and awoke in midafternoon to find her private hospital room a bower of red roses and Craig at her bedside.

"Hi." Her smile was dazzling.

"How do you feel?" He reached for her hand.

"Strange," she said. "I gather everything went well."

"Doctor Morse was very pleased."

"But we won't know the results for a few days," she reminded. She must be realistic. No celebrations until she knew there were grounds for that.

"I wish I could be here until you're ready to go home," Craig said. "I'll have to leave late tomorrow. After visiting hours," he added with an air of triumph.

"It means so much to have you here." Without Craig she wouldn't have had the courage to go through with this. "I realize you have to get back home." She glanced about at the vases of flowers. "You sent them," she guessed, and he nodded sheepishly. "You must have bought out a florist shop!"

"A tax write-off," he joshed. "Wooing a client." But his eyes told her she was much more. "I'll phone you every morning," he promised. When she'd have no visitors, she interpreted.

The first few days she was inundated with anxiety. Each morning Dr. Morse stopped by in the course of his rounds. His comments, his enigmatic smile told her nothing. Midmorning each day Craig called from his office. With him she made no effort to conceal her fears, clung to his words of encouragement—but both faced the possibility that the surgery had accomplished nothing.

Fran was touched by Lynne's strained smile when she came each evening. Poor baby, Fran thought tenderly, she was so anxious. And every night there was a call from her mother and Debbie. Her mother seeking reassurances, Debbie determined to set her mind at ease about business. Special to Fran were the moments when Jessie and Beth in New York, and Diane in Bellevue chattered on the phone with her.

Then—after a terrifying delay—Dr. Morse announced that it was time for Fran to walk. Her heart pounding, she tossed aside the sheet, slowly swung her legs to the floor, and waited for his instructions. Clinging to his arm for support, she felt a growing desolation at her efforts.

"We've won!" Dr. Morse exuded satisfaction.

"But how?" She stared at him in confusion. She was so awkward, so shaky. "I need the brace!"

"You'll need weeks of therapy," he corrected, "but you'll walk without the brace. When you acquire confidence, you'll toss away the cane," he predicted. "The operation was a success."

With each passing day Fran was conscious of minuscule improvement—but there *was* improvement. At the end of six weeks she'd go home and walk on her own, she thought exultantly. She felt a wonderful new freedom. Incredible what medical research could accomplish!

If she could be blessed with this miracle, then a miracle could happen for Debbie, too, Fran told herself. Out of the blue one day some police officer would become interested in unsolved murder cases and would throw himself into exploring Scott's murder. Scott could never be restored to Debbie—but to know that the murderer had been discovered and punished would be a kind of freedom for her.

Fran left the hospital in the care—at Lynne's insistence—of a practical nurse.

"Mom, you can't be alone," Lynne insisted. "And I'll be fired if I try to take off any more time. But I'll be here every afternoon after school."

At the end of her first week in her apartment Fran agreed with the nurse that she could manage on her own. The therapist would continue to come daily. Her improvement was slow but steady, Fran reassured Debbie and her mother in nightly phone calls. By the end of the allotted time she would fly home. Debbie insisted she would be at the Atlanta airport to meet her.

Two mornings before she was to fly home Fran received her usual phone call from Craig.

"Guess what?" he said ebulliently. "I'm here in New York!"

"Oh, Craig!" He'd guessed how impatient she was to show him she could walk without the brace.

"I'm at the airport," he continued. "I'll check in at the Essex House—then pop up to your apartment." He paused. "If all's clear?"

"All's clear!" She felt young and in love and adventurous. "I can't wait to see you—"

"I wish I had wings so I could fly to you. But since I don't, I'll have to take the more prosaic route. I should be there in a couple of hours."

Feeling herself in a dreamworld, Fran changed from slacks and blouse into a simply cut sapphire wool—Craig's favorite color for her. With a blend of pleasure and disbelief she inspected her reflection in the mirror. The scar from the incision in her leg was concealed by her pantyhose. She wore low heels as ordered by Dr. Morse. She felt, she thought in glorious abandon, as though she'd been born again.

There are moments in our lives, she mused, that are forever etched on our memory—wonderful moments and devastating moments. Even now she remembered the moment at Bernie's bedside when his eyes clung to her face as though to memorize each feature for some other life. She remembered with recurrent pain the disbelief on Debbie's face when Scott's body was lowered into his grave—and Debbie's total happiness at their wedding when Scott lifted the veil to kiss his wife. Another she'd forever remember would be the moment when Craig walked through the apartment door and saw her standing here without brace or cane. He wouldn't love her any more or less—but she'd feel reborn.

She put up a pot of coffee, set out cookies on a plate, brought dishes and silverware to the living-room coffee table. At intervals she walked to a window that looked down on the sidewalk and watched for Craig to emerge from a taxi. Sunlight poured into the apartment. A perfect early spring day, Fran thought, that reflected her own personal joy.

In a burst of energy she searched for a dust cloth and began to dust the tiny living room. Then the stillness was shattered by the sound of the phone. The switchboard operator announced that Craig was on his way to the apartment. Her heart pounding—too eager to see him to wait for him to ring the bell—Fran opened the door and watched for the elevator door to slide open. There he was!

"Here, Craig," she called out because he was gazing in the other direction.

"The damn traffic into the city was heavy," he complained, hurrying toward her. "I swore every inch of the way." He paused for a long inspection of her. "You look beautiful—as always."

"Come inside," she ordered high-spiritedly. "Before the coffee gets cold—"

"To the devil with the coffee." He strode into the apartment and reached for her. "I just want to hold you in my arms. That's allowed, isn't it, on a momentous occasion like this?"

"Craig, yes!"

She knew even before his mouth met hers that the long waiting would be over now. They were away from Bellevue—in a world of their own. Joyce hadn't been a wife to Craig in years. Why deny themselves?

"Fran?" Craig's eyes pleaded with her when their mouths parted.

"Darling, yes," she whispered. "Oh yes, Craig!"

He swept her into his arms and carried her into the darkened bedroom—the drapes drawn tight against the noonday sun. They stood together by the side of the bed in a passionate embrace—in a mutual determination to savor every instant of this reunion.

"Remember Paris?" he teased. "You always shied away from making love in the daytime."

"Not anymore," she whispered, all at once impatient. "I feel a little decadent," she confessed, "but not enough to stop."

She reached for the zipper at the back of her dress. Craig quickly relieved her of this activity. This wasn't wrong, she told herself, and chuckled at Craig's muted swearing when the zipper resisted his efforts.

"Let me," she murmured and coaxed the zipper the length of its track.

Craig pushed the dress from her shoulders and prodded it to the floor. She closed her eyes in exquisite pleasure as his hands reached to release her bra, then captured her breasts with a sensuous tenderness.

"It's been so long," she whispered while they moved together in passionate impatience.

She knew that her life would never be the same after today. A whole new era lay ahead for Craig and her. They would be discreet, she vowed—but they would not deny themselves.

Fran was grateful that both her business and Craig's allowed them flexibility to see each other at will. They planned this new way of life with calculated precision. They permitted themselves one afternoon a week together—never the same day of the week in succession so as not to establish a pattern. Always in the blessed anonymity of Atlanta. One day a week they lunched with Robin—when he was in town—to discuss, if anyone should inquire, the studio-cottage Craig was building for Robin.

She would have been incredibly happy, Fran thought, if life was going as well for Lynne and Debbie as for herself. Lynne and Arnie were jubilant that a new record company had scheduled one of his songs for a coming record session. Then—two days before the session—the head of the company was killed in a small plane crash and the whole deal was scuttled.

"It's unbelievable," Lynne wrote. "Everybody in the company was excited about this session. They'd found a new young singer they were sure would hit the charts once they found the right music for him—and what Arnie writes is great for him. Now they've dumped the singer and Arnie's out in the cold again."

Fran worried that Debbie was creating a disturbing image in Diane's mind about Scott. Diane was at the age where she was asking questions about her father. She understood that her friends had fathers but she didn't. Must that poor baby try to cope with the knowledge that her father had been murdered?

Fran felt a recurrent helplessness in knowing that every time a murder was reported in the Bellevue or Atlanta newspapers, Debbie followed the details with fanatical intensity. Blaming herself for not seeing Scott's murderer brought to justice, Fran knew, when each case was solved.

"The police are wrong in not keeping on with investigations," Debbie chastised each time an investigation was stopped for lack of evidence. Would there ever be a time, Fran asked herself as months rolled past, when things would be *right* on all fronts?

At long last Robin's cottage was finished. His friend Jamie came down from New York and settled in to paint. Robin was ecstatic. There were no more trips to the city. He was content to remain in Bellevue. But in less than a year Jamie announced he was returning to New York. He was breaking off the relationship with Robin.

"He says there's no future down here for him," Robin confided to Fran. "He wants to go back to New York. And he doesn't want to see me anymore. Damn it, Fran, he used me! He doesn't need me anymore. I feel like burning down the fucking cottage!"

"Just close it up for a while," Fran said gently.

"You use it," Robin told her and reached into his pocket for the keys. "For me it has nothing but ugly memories. For you and Craig it can be beautiful. Let it serve you well—my two best friends."

For Fran and Craig the cottage in the woods became their secret home. Occasionally Fran was anxious that this would become public knowledge—but, as Craig pointed out, they were both supercautious. They knew that Joyce would be vindictive if she discovered Craig was having an affair.

"I just don't want the kids to find out," Craig told Fran. "Though by now they know their parents don't share the perfect marriage." He sighed. "I wish I could spare them that, but Joyce won't allow it."

Fran knew that neighbors gossiped about Joyce's temper tantrums—heard at regular intervals. Joyce was not forgiving Craig for turning down the offer from the New York firm of architects. When they appeared socially, she continued to play the adoring wife—but the spell had been broken.

Life had fallen into a pattern, Fran thought—and the years were rolling by with unnerving speed.

On New Year's Day, 1974—after the family's usual quiet welcoming of the new year on the previous evening, Fran went into her mother's bedroom with the customary wake-up cup of coffee. Both Lily and Betty Mae were with their own families today.

"Happy 1974," Fran said brightly. Last night her mother had been annoyed with herself for having fallen asleep and having to be awakened to watch the traditional Times Square scene in New York. "Mother?"

She put the coffee on the night table and reached out to her mother's shoulder. All at once she was immobile. Her hand at her mother's shoulder told her that sometime during the night her mother had died—in her sleep, as she had wished to go.

She'd been so sure her mother was indestructible. *"Mother, you'll be around to celebrate your one-hundredth birthday."*

For a little while she stood beside her mother in solitary grief. Mother had been a woman who had grown through the years, Fran thought with pride. Everybody in Bellevue liked Ida Goldman. Oh, she would miss her, Fran thought. For a while they had been four generations in this house—and that brought her mother such pleasure.

Reluctantly she left the bedroom to summon Debbie. They must explain to Diane that "Grandma" had "gone to heaven." She must call Lynne and tell her that her grandmother was gone. Later—in a private moment—she'd call Craig. Now there were arrangements to be made. They must lay her mother to rest beside her father. Long ago the plot had been bought.

Enveloped in a sense of loss but too stunned as yet to cry, she left the bedroom to go to Debbie. She felt an overwhelming awareness of her own mortality. In truth, she had been the mother in this household for years—mother to her own mother as well as to her children. But now she was conscious that she wanted to do so much for her children and grandchildren before she left this earth. *How could you know how much time you had left?*

Fran was touched by the huge turnout for her mother's funeral. Lynne flew down from New York. Arnie had remained home to watch over the girls. He'd insisted that they mustn't miss several days of school to attend their great-grandmother's funeral.

At the cemetery Fran stood at the graveside flanked by Lynne and Debbie, with Diane clinging to her mother. So solemn, Fran thought, and managed a reassuring smile for her granddaughter. Robin—as close family friend—stood with them. Craig, too, was here.

Involuntarily Fran's eyes sought Craig's. Her mother had so liked him. Tears filled her eyes as she remembered her mother's eagerness to have her go out with Craig—in those days before he married Joyce. She would have so welcomed him as her son-in-law.

She was of a generation that was uncomfortable with what was labeled an adulterous relationship, Fran admitted to herself. Yet she knew she was incapable of cutting Craig out of her life.

Thirty - Eight

Lynne was exhausted from the traumatic days in Bellevue. Arriving at LaGuardia, she hesitated, then decided to splurge on a taxi into the city. With Grandma gone, she thought as she settled herself in the taxi, it was though part of her life was over.

She'd talked with Arnie and the girls each night she was in Bellevue. He hadn't said so in words, but she suspected Arnie believed that she and Debbie would be remembered in Grandma's will. She hadn't told him that everything went to Mom. But that was as it should be, she thought defensively. Grandpa had left a good business, but Mom had built it up into a chain that far eclipsed anything he had anticipated. And they knew that in a crisis Mom would always be there for them.

She cringed mentally when she paid the fare in front of their apartment building. Arnie hadn't worked in months—he'd been so tied up with a new record deal that he was sure would put him into big money. He'd slaved to adapt his style to fit the singer being promoted as a young Bob Dylan. But the record had never got off the ground. And each year, Arnie pointed out, it was harder to sell a song.

"I'm a naked songwriter. Today you have to be a performer. Like Billy Joel and Neil Diamond. I don't have a singing voice. That's two strikes against me. Why should it be like that?"

Arnie kept saying they needed a larger apartment, but how could they take on a higher rent? Rents in the city kept going up—and vacancies were hard to come by. And already the dentist was talking about a probable need for orthodontia for Jessie. She knew Mom would come through with the money, but Arnie so resented their having to take from her.

At the apartment she was greeted ecstatically by Jessie and Beth, though both retreated into sobriety at the reminder that their great-grandmother had died. Arnie's eyes told her how glad he was that she was home.

"I've dinner ready to go on the table, honey. You look bushed," he commiserated. She read the questions in his eyes now, which wouldn't be answered until after Jessie and Beth were in bed.

"I'm bushed and starving," Lynne admitted. "What are we eating?"

"My repertoire is limited," Arnie reminded. "Spaghetti and eye round roast. Tonight we're living high. Eye round."

Over dinner Jessie and Beth were eager to report on their school activities. Jessie attended the neighborhood public school. Beth was a student at the school where Lynne taught—on a scholarship arrangement. This division had been contrived by Lynne because she was conscious of the strong sibling rivalry between the two. Sometimes she worried that Arnie made so much fuss over Jessie's musical talents. She saw the wistfulness in Beth's eyes each time this happened. Beth adored singing, and waited avidly for words of approval from her father.

"I wrote another song," Jessie said triumphantly. "Daddy says it's good."

"I don't think you're about to get a record," Arnie teased. "But yeah, it shows a lot of promise."

After dinner Lynne shooed the two girls into their bedroom to do homework.

"And close the door to your room," Arnie ordered. "Your mother and I may want to watch television."

Lynne knew that Arnie would be upset to learn that her grandmother had left everything to her mother. She hadn't expected the outburst that followed her report.

"She left nothing to you and Debbie?" His voice soared in rage. "What kind of deal is that?"

"Arnie, don't let the kids hear you," she ordered, her eyes moving anxiously to the door to their bedroom. "She left Debbie and me her jewelry. Everything should go to Mom."

"Bullshit," he hissed. "The old lady was forever throwing around that crap about how important family was—but she leaves you and Debbie out in the cold! Forever bragging about how four generations sat down to dinner in that shitty house. Hell, she could have afforded a showplace."

"Craig designed a beautiful house. Grandma and Mom both love it!" She was conscious of a surge of impatience. Arnie had developed such grandiose ideas through the years. He only respected Hollywood mansions. "It's one of the finest houses in Bellevue."

"Your mother loves living in that creepy little town," he taunted. "She loves being a big fish in a small pond."

"I don't want the kids to hear you talking this way." She strode to the television set, flipped the switch—not caring about the program that filtered into the living room. Let it just drown out Arnie's tirade.

Later, lying sleepless beside Arnie, Lynne tried to figure out what was going wrong with her marriage. It was Arnie's lack of success with his music, she finally concluded—the constant near-breaks that never materialized. He needed a whipping post, she thought grimly—and at this point that was Mom.

The early June night air was humid, seeming to drape Bellevue in a sinister, all-enveloping tent. Tonight even ceiling fans were inadequate. Thank God for air-conditioning, Fran thought, glancing at the ormolu clock that sat atop the living room mantel. It was time for her usual Sunday evening call to Lynne. Late enough so that dinner was out of the way but early enough so she could talk with Jessie and Beth, too.

She crossed to the phone and settled herself in a comfortable chair. She saw Lynne and the kids three times a year. These calls bridged the time between visits.

"Hello—" The lilt in Lynne's voice said she'd been waiting for the call.

"How are you, darling?" These were treasured minutes each week.

"Bedraggled a bit this late in the school year," Lynne said wryly. "I can't wait for school to be over and to be preparing for the trip home." Fran heard Jessie's voice—faintly imperious as she demanded to be allowed to talk with her grandmother. "Mom, the kids want to talk to you—"

Fran talked first with Jessie and then with Beth without quite understanding their excitement about a coming musical event.

"Lynne, what's this about singing dates?" Fran asked when Lynne was on the line again. "Are the kids going to summer school?"

"No, Mom. It's something Arnie's cooked up." Fran heard stress in Lynne's voice. "It's all so ridiculous. He's worked up a singing act for Jessie and Beth—with him at the piano. He's trying to book them for summer engagements at two-bit clubs within a commuting area."

"Jessie's ten years old and Beth eight. They're too young for that sort of thing." Fran was involuntarily sharp. What was the matter with

Arnie? she wondered. "Isn't it illegal for such young kids to perform in clubs?"

"These are not regular nightclubs," Lynne explained, but her hostility to the plan was clear. "They're part of family-type bungalow colonies. They'll probably earn just enough to pay for the car rental and gas—but you know Arnie when he gets his mind set on something. And the kids are out of their mind with excitement." She cleared her throat in a familiar nervous gesture. "I told him I'm going home for a month as usual. He'll be stuck with the kids on his own—I'm not giving up my vacation time." But Fran sensed that she was distressed that Jessie and Beth would not be going to Bellevue with her.

"He may change his mind by then," Fran comforted. "The kids may decide they won't want to do it. You know how Jessie flip-flops on things." Of course, Beth always fell in line with Jessie's wishes.

"I don't like it." Lynne was grim. "Nobody believes Jessie is only ten. Right now she's taller than me—and developing breasts already. It's absurd, but Mom, you haven't seen her in a few months. She's the sexiest ten-year-old you ever saw!"

"When Jessie opens her mouth, everybody knows she's ten years old," Fran said. How unlike Beth and Diane, she thought subconsciously. "Maybe they won't get any bookings. This could all blow over before you're ready to come down here."

Off the phone, Fran sat in somber thought. From the family room in the west wing of the house came the reassuring laughter of Diane and her "best friend," Louise Winston. Two sweet, uncomplicated children, she thought tenderly. Like Beth. Lynne always worried about Jessie, she remembered. Except for her looks Jessie was all Arnie's child. He was leading her into music, even though he knew the terrible odds against success in the field. All his hard work through the years and what had he accomplished? Was that what he wanted for Jessie?

Debbie sat in her favorite lounge chair in the family living room and tried to focus on the latest paperback mystery she'd picked up at the bookshop. Mom sounded tense, she thought sympathetically while her mother talked with Lynne on the phone. The conversation centered about Lynne's dislike of the new principal who'd just come into the school. Lynne had never really liked teaching, but how could she avoid it when Arnie worked so irregularly?

"Lynne's miserable since this new principal took over." Fran put down the phone. "School's only been open three weeks, and already the new man is creating hostility among the staff."

"Lynne could handle it if she wasn't upset about things at home," Debbie said with unfamiliar bluntness. "I don't know why she doesn't sit down with Arnie and tell him to get real." Mom didn't know that this summer she'd lent Lynne money so he could buy a secondhand car. *"We'll never pay back Mom if she lends it to us—and I know she would. But Arnie knows that if we borrow from you, Debbie, we have to pay it back."*

"Arnie—and Jessie—can manipulate Lynne any way they want." Fran sighed. "I wish he'd let Jessie and Beth be kids and stop shoving them into singing."

"What's happening with Jessie's piano lessons? Are she and Arnie still arguing about that?"

"She wants to play the guitar now," Fran said. "Maybe I'll give her one for her birthday. I missed not having Jessie and Beth here for a month in the summer." Her smile was wistful.

"You'll see them in January," Debbie comforted. "And before you know it'll be next summer. Lynne will insist they come down with her. She told me she wouldn't let them go out on these singing dates again. It was crazy."

"I think I'll call it a night." Fran rose from her chair. "I'll get into bed and go over the reports from the shops that I didn't have time to look at all week."

"Good night, Mom. I'll turn out the lights in another half hour and go to bed, too."

Alone in the night stillness of the living room Debbie laid aside her mystery novel—only one chapter unread—and thought about her mother. She was so driven, always fighting to make the business expand—as though money could solve all their problems. It couldn't make up for Diane's growing up without her father. But Diane knew he'd been a wonderful person—she knew she could be proud of him.

Her father and Lynne's had died tragically young—but she and Lynne had memories. Warm, wonderful memories. For a while she and Lynne had Grandpa, too. But Diane had no memories of father or grandfather. She was growing up in a house of women.

Debbie settled down to finish her novel—where the murder was always solved. *Scott's* murder was still unsolved, she tormented herself for the thousandth time, because Perry had made sure the investigation was abandoned. She leaned back in her chair, closed her eyes and began a mental dissection of the plot of the novel she'd just finished reading. A familiar routine now. *Somewhere along the line she'd read a mystery that would point her in the right direction to solve Scott's murder.*

Fran was pleased when Nora persuaded Debbie to go—along with Diane—to her family's cottage on Pine Mountain for the last week in August and the Labor Day weekend. The recent heat wave had been devastating.

"You just go up there and rest," Fran ordered Debbie as they clung together in a farewell embrace on the front deck of the house—luggage stashed in Nora's car. "Lie around and read and relax."

"Mommie, Nora's waiting for us," Diane said anxiously, though Nora sat behind the wheel of her car with no sign of impatience.

"You be good, darling." Fran bent to kiss Diane. "And have a great time."

She stood at the door while Debbie and Diane hurried to the car and settled themselves inside. She waved a gay farewell, and then watched the three drive down the long circular driveway to the road. She'd left the office early today to see them off. She was conscious of an odd, guilty sense of freedom.

Debbie and Diane would be away ten days. Earlier Lily and Betty Mae had chosen the last two weeks in August for their vacation. She was totally alone in the house. And for the first time since Paris—years ago—she and Craig would be able to spend a night together.

Joyce was at Sea Island with her sister for the month of August. Josh and Zach were at a camp in Spain for the month. When the boys returned from camp, Craig would take them to spend the Labor Day weekend on Sea Island. This had been a special time for Craig and her, Fran thought tenderly. And now they'd be able to spend a night—possibly two—together in Robin's cottage. She'd be afraid to remain away from the house longer than that. Neighbors might become curious.

She walked into the house now—her mind focusing on business calls that must be made. But after that she'd have a long, leisurely bath and dress for dinner with Craig. No need to pack for her overnight, she thought lightly. She kept clothes and cosmetics at the cottage.

People—even his domestic help—thought Robin stayed there at intervals. He sent his housekeeper, Peggy, over there once a week to clean and straighten up. She'd known about Jamie and the breakup. She assumed, Robin said, that he used the cottage for short-term flings. *"Peg adores me—whatever I do is fine with her."* His easel was always set up by the window, as though he meant to resume work at any time. Bless Robin for making this precious little world possible.

Early—to avoid the dinner crowd—Fran met Craig at a new restaurant on the outskirts of Atlanta. Only a handful of diners were scattered about the charming, spacious, softly lit room. Tonight she and Craig exuded a special aura of conviviality, she thought while they concentrated on the lavish menu. They were a man and woman long in love and relishing a rare sense of freedom. Tonight she wasn't just Debbie and Lynne's mother, the girls' grandmother, the head of the Goldman shops—she was *Fran*. Craig had shed all the accoutrements of his everyday life—he was *Craig*.

"I didn't get much work done today," he said with mock reproach. "I just kept thinking about tonight."

"You work too hard," she scolded. "You never take a real vacation." Nor did she take a formal one. She labeled the two trips to New York each year her vacations. Her mother had complained that work had become her obsession.

"My vacation," Craig said with sudden bitterness, "is when I'm away from Joyce."

"Things aren't getting better?" Did she honestly believe they would?

"The kids notice." He shrugged in a gesture of frustration. "I'd hoped they'd never guess. Zach got so angry at her just before he and Josh left for camp that he said, 'Why don't you divorce her?' That threw me."

"Still the old bit about your refusing to leave Bellevue?"

"That's part of it. She's so damn dissatisfied. She's jealous of every rich woman in Bellevue. Our house isn't big enough. We don't move in the right circles. We don't entertain like New York millionaires. She's even jealous of you."

"Oh, Craig!" Fran's face drained of color.

"She doesn't know about us," he added hastily. "But you're very successful and beautiful. You're a threat to her."

"Would you care to order now?" Their smiling waiter approached their table, and private conversation was abandoned.

Craig waited until they were alone again to continue their conversation.

"I've always avoided talk of a divorce because of the kids," Craig picked up. "But Josh is sixteen, Zach thirteen—and they know Joyce and I have a rotten marriage. Maybe now I can—"

"Craig, no," Fran objected in an anguished whisper. *She couldn't be part of breaking up his family.*

"What's the point in keeping up this charade?" he challenged. "I'll give her whatever she wants. I don't think she'll ask for custody of the kids—she's in constant battle with them. She—"

"Craig, you know she won't give you a divorce. She *likes* being the wife of a prominent architect." Fran was fighting panic. Of course it was illogical, she told herself—but if Craig and Joyce were divorced, she'd feel responsible. She couldn't live with that. "Joyce would hate being a divorced woman in a small town!"

"Don't I have any say?"

"If you divorce Joyce, I'll never see you again," she whispered. "Please, Craig. Don't do that to us."

"You know I couldn't do anything that would make me lose you," he said after a moment. "I cherish every minute we have together."

In a silent pact they tried to pretend the last conversation had not taken place. Tonight was a very special occasion for them, Fran thought defiantly. Joyce mustn't spoil it.

"Let's pretend this is Paris." Craig reached across the table for her hand. "Just the two of us, and the night is all ours."

But later in the cottage—after making love—Fran lay wide awake long after Craig had fallen asleep, one leg thrown across hers, an arm about her waist. She was troubled by Joyce's hostility toward Craig—so obvious even her sons were upset. Yet the prospect that Craig and Joyce might divorce was unnerving.

Thirty-Nine

In the months ahead Fran was conscious of a new urgency in her relationship with Craig. She was agonized by his unhappiness, yet saw no way to alleviate it except for those times when they met at Robin's cottage and pretended the outside world didn't exist. It was no secret in their Bellevue circle that Joyce resented living in Bellevue. She had become addicted to extravagant shopping sprees, was antagonizing the women with whom she played bridge and did volunteer work.

Craig was afraid to talk about his problems with Joyce, Fran realized, lest he jeopardize what they shared. He talked about everything else with her—problems with his work, what was happening with Josh and Zach, his concern about the hostility between the boys and their mother.

She had been alarmed on several occasions by snide remarks from Joyce when they met socially. But Debbie's friend Nora had mentioned Joyce's growing propensity toward sarcasm. It wasn't because she was suspicious of Craig and herself, Fran realized. It was the act of an angry, unhappy woman.

As always Fran was glad when spring arrived. Bellevue became a wonderland of flowering shrubs and trees, clumps of glorious daffodils, tulips, and hyacinths bursting upon the scene in fast succession. On this Friday she left her office at 5:30 P.M. sharp. She'd pick up Chinese from the new restaurant in town, then head for the cottage. Craig had been in Atlanta today—he was presumably having dinner with a client there.

Diane had gone home with Sandra after school and was sleeping over tonight. Debbie was going to a special dinner meeting of her women's group to prepare for a protest about the discrimination in pay and promotion among women with advanced degrees. Fran was grateful that

Nora kept Debbie involved with the group. *"Debbie, we need you to handle our publicity. Nobody else in the group can do it."*

Fran stopped off in town for take-out Chinese, then drove to the cottage. She knew Craig wouldn't leave Bellevue, yet there was ever this vein of anxiety in her that it might happen. She'd told him she'd never see him again if there was a divorce—irrational as that might be—and he knew she meant it. But the prospect of a life that didn't include these intimate hours with Craig was unnerving.

Turning into the long, private road to the cottage, she saw Craig's car parked at one side. He was here. Her face grew luminous. Just knowing she'd have a few hours alone with him brought her a sense of joyous anticipation. It was absurd, she thought, to feel this way at their ages—yet she knew Craig shared this with her. The young believed that love was their province—they didn't understand that love and passion could thrive until the grave.

The cottage door opened as she maneuvered into the small, open area at one side.

"Hi!" Business jacket and tie discarded, Craig stood there with a welcoming smile. "I hope you brought a lot of food. I'm starving."

Because there was a chill in the air, Craig had started a fire in the grate. He'd set up the small table they used for dining before the fireplace. The aroma of coffee perking filtered in from the kitchen. Their precious oasis, Fran thought as she moved into his arms for a moment.

Fran opened up the containers while Craig went into the small kitchen to bring in the coffee. She felt so young alone with Craig. Devoid of responsibilities and worry.

"What do you hear from Lynne?" Craig asked, returning from the kitchen.

"Nothing much has changed," she admitted. "Lynne's still teaching, and Arnie's still sure that success is just around the corner."

"It could happen that way," he chided gently.

"I know—but after all these years of Lynne supporting the family I'm skeptical. Arnie's talking again about doing 'summer gigs.'" Resentment deepened her voice. That meant Jessie and Beth wouldn't be coming down this summer. For all her ranting against the "summer gigs," Lynne wouldn't stand up to him. "What's the latest on Josh and college?" In September Josh would be a high school senior. He was already studying college catalogs. She knew that Joyce was determined Josh go to an Ivy League college.

Craig sighed. An eloquent sigh, Fran thought.

"Josh has finally made her understand that there are a limited number of openings in each freshman class of the Ivy League schools—and if he doesn't make it into one of them, his life isn't over." He paused. A nerve quivered in one eyelid. "She's got another bug in her bonnet now. She's decided that once Josh is in college I should retire. We're to ship Zach off to boarding school and settle down on an island in the Caribbean."

"That's ridiculous." She felt a surge of panic.

"I'm not about to retire. I love my work. Maybe some people can't wait to leave their jobs and settle down to play golf or tennis—but that's not me. Anyhow, with the cost of college soaring the way it is, I'd better stay on the job." He tried for a touch of humor. "Also, she'd had a touch of bronchitis twice this winter—and she's convinced a Caribbean island is just what she needs."

"What she needs," Fran said bluntly, "is to give up chain-smoking."

"Let's put aside the outside world," Craig said, his smile whimsical. "Do you suppose Chinese food makes everybody passionate?"

Again Lynne came down to Bellevue alone, while Jessie and Beth went out on low-paying, insignificant singing engagements with their father. In August Arnie was euphoric when he landed a deal with a small music publisher who then convinced an even smaller record company to include one of his songs in their next recording session.

"Arnie says this girl is going to be big—and she can't write her own material. This is a terrific opportunity for him," Lynne wrote. *"He'll ride right along on her coattails."*

How could Lynne be so confident after all these years? Fran asked herself—yet she knew how long many creative artists waited for recognition. For Lynne's sake she hoped Arnie's record would become a huge success. It didn't matter that the advance was minuscule, Lynne wrote. If the record was a hit, Arnie would make a lot of money.

"Tell Lynne not to start spending it," Robin warned when Fran told him about the imminent recording session. Robin had much knowledge about the record business and theater because two lovers had been in these fields. "Before Arnie sees another cent of royalties, the recording company takes back the cost of the session. Even with fair distribution, he could end up with nothing more than his advance."

In early autumn Debbie's group voted on sending representatives to a three-day conference on feminism in Raleigh. Nora and Debbie were chosen to attend. Fran was anxious when Debbie announced that she'd like to go. To Raleigh, with all its bitter memories? she thought grimly.

"They're insisting I go with Nora," Debbie said. "To write up a report. And I have vacation time coming at the shop. Diane said she won't mind if I go. It's all right with you, isn't it?"

"You know it is," Fran said. "I'll make sure I'm home early those evenings—and Lily and Betty Mae will be at the house to keep an eye on her. If you're sure you want to go." Her eyes were troubled.

"We'll stay at the same hotel where the conference is being held." Debbie understood her mother's anxiety. Nora, too—remembering about Scott—had thought going to Raleigh might be too traumatic. "We'll have our meals there. We'll just be away two nights. We'll fly back Wednesday afternoon."

"If you get to a record store, look for the album with Arnie's song," Fran told her. "Lynne said they were pressing records already. As soon as the album covers come through, they'll be shipping."

"I'll look," Debbie promised.

The evening before Debbie was scheduled to leave for Raleigh, she found herself battling insomnia. As soon as the question of the conference arose, she'd known what she must do. There'd been no doubt in her mind that she would be asked to go with Nora. Diane was asking so many questions about her father—about why the person who murdered him hadn't been caught. She had to make one more attempt to come up with leads.

She mustn't say a word to Mom, she reiterated for the dozenth time. Mom would be so upset. But she could afford to hire a private investigator, she told herself—most of her salary went into the bank each week. Mom wouldn't let her give a cent to the upkeep of the house. She'd made several phone calls to Raleigh as soon as she knew about the conference. She had an appointment with a private investigator there. Please, God, let him come up with a lead, she prayed.

She and Nora were on an early morning flight to Raleigh. On the plane she made a point of complaining about a sore throat. Tomorrow morning she'd tell Nora she'd stay in bed late, then come to the conference. The office of the private investigator was no more than ten minutes by cab from their hotel.

She'd convinced herself she could handle going to Raleigh again, yet she felt a sense of near-suffocation as the plane prepared for a landing. All the horror of Scott's death swept over her with an agonizing freshness. But she was coming here with a purpose. She had to see this through.

"Are you all right?" Nora asked, all at once solicitous.

"Sure." Debbie forced a smile.

They went directly to their hotel, unpacked, and went downstairs to the conference quarters to register. At lunch Debbie made a point of ordering tea and lemon.

"What a ridiculous time to have a sore throat—in the midst of Indian summer," she told Nora—feeling guilty at this subterfuge. "But it'll probably clear up overnight."

She and Nora attended the late afternoon meeting and had dinner in the hotel dining room. It was unreal, she thought, that she was here in Raleigh. En route to their room again, she stopped to pick up a copy of a Raleigh newspaper. Her heart pounding, she scanned the first page. Nothing about Perry or the mill here.

She was relieved that Nora was talking nonstop about the afternoon meeting. Little was required of her other than positive nods of agreement. Already she was bracing herself for the encounter tomorrow morning with the private investigator. How could she know if she'd chosen well? she asked herself with last-minute reservations. She'd chosen from the Raleigh telephone classified. He'd *sounded* efficient.

In their room she scanned every page of the Raleigh newspaper. She sensed Nora's concern. Nora understood what being in Raleigh was doing to her.

"My sister-in-law is on her usual committees," Debbie said and read an item that testified to this. "Though I doubt that Olivia considers me a sister-in-law any longer."

"You won't be bothering to call on them." Nora was flip, but her eyes telegraphed sympathy. "Why don't we watch a little TV and then hit the sack? Breakfast is at seven and opening meeting at eight," she reminded. "I know they're trying to squeeze in an awful lot tomorrow, but we're supposed to be bright-eyed and bushy-tailed by eight A.M.?"

Debbie wasn't surprised that she slept little during the night. At 6:15 Nora's alarm clock went off.

"Nobody can say we're not dedicated to the cause," Nora grumbled and reached to shut off the clock. She slowly tossed aside the light blanket and swung her legs to the floor. "Debbie—"

"Yeah, I'm awake," Debbie confirmed.

"How're you feeling?"

"The throat's raw," Debbie said. "Maybe I ought to skip breakfast, just order some tea sent up from room service." She paused, self-conscious at lying to Nora. "Would it be awful if I stayed in bed until ten or ten-thirty and then slipped into the meeting?"

"You do that." Nora was firm. "I'll take notes until you come down."

Debbie called room service for a pot of tea while Nora hurried to shower and dress. By ten minutes to seven Nora had left for breakfast and Debbie was finishing up her tea. Her appointment with Frank Kelly wasn't until 9 A.M. She'd dress, then sit down and go over all her notes again. The private investigator had been cautious about what he could accomplish, yet he agreed from what she'd said over the phone that the investigation had been aborted far too early.

At 8:40 Debbie left the hotel and took a taxi to Kelly's office. His receptionist was there when she arrived. He was expected momentarily. Struggling to hide her anxiety to talk with him, Debbie sat down and idly flipped through the pages of a magazine.

The door to the office opened. Debbie looked up expectantly.

"Ms. Richards?" A pleasant-faced man in his forties smiled down at her.

"Yes—"

"I'll be with you in a couple of minutes," he said and turned to confer with his receptionist. She gave him his early morning calls. He glanced over them quickly, reached for the door to his private office, and beckoned to Debbie to join him.

Almost breathless in her rush, Debbie gave him all the details she'd stored through the years about Scott's murder. She told him how convinced she was that he was killed by someone who lived in Glenwood—not an intruder. Now he shot question after question at her.

"You realize this is expensive business," he told her. "And there's no guarantee we'll come up with a real lead."

"I've told you how far I can go." She had a tenuous hold on composure. It was an awful lot of money, but there had to be a lead out there somewhere.

"Where can I contact you if I need to talk?" he asked, reaching for a pen.

"I don't want to upset my mother about this. Please leave messages for me with a friend at this number." She'd tell Nora now about Frank Kelly. No point in upsetting Mom. And Nora wouldn't say a word to anyone.

Two days after she and Nora returned to Bellevue, Debbie received a call from Nora.

"I just got off the phone with the P.I.," Nora said. "He wants to talk to you. He'll be at his office until seven."

"I'll drop by your house on my way home. Okay?" Nora understood she wouldn't want to call from the office or home.

"Sure. I'll be there by a quarter of six. I'll tell Lisa to close up." Lisa was Nora's salesclerk at the bookshop.

Debbie churned with impatience the remainder of the afternoon. Nora was at the house when she arrived.

"Get on the phone," Nora ordered. "I'll bring you coffee."

On the phone with Kelly's office, Debbie waited for him to be off another line. Nora came in and slid a mug of coffee beside the phone and raised crossed fingers.

"Hello—"

"I was told you wanted to talk to me, Mr. Kelly."

"Right." His voice was crisp and confident. "I've been to Glenwood and researched the *Glenwood Observer*'s old files. I think you're dead right in believing it wasn't an intruder who killed your husband. A simple little thing told me that. I saw photographs taken only hours after the murder taken by a police photographer," he emphasized. "They zero in on the French doors that was the murderer's entrance into the library. A pane was shattered to allow the door to be unlocked."

Debbie sighed impatiently. "We know that, Mr. Kelly!"

"But the glass from that broken pane doesn't appear on the floor *inside* the library. The glass fell *outside* the door," he pointed out. "That means that someone inside the house broke that pane of glass."

"You mean one of the staff killed my husband?" Debbie's voice was harsh with shock. "Who would want to do that? They all loved Scott."

"The Richards are one of the wealthiest families in the state," Kelly reminded. "The house probably has a large staff."

"Five," Debbie recalled shakily. "Is this enough to demand the case be reopened?"

"It all depends upon the local sheriff," Kelly conceded. "If he wants to be nasty, he can claim the crime scene was cleaned up before the photos were taken. If you like, I can contact the Glenwood sheriff on your behalf—"

"Please do." Debbie was dizzy with excitement. "Let's hope that Sheriff Stanton is gone. I gather he was put into office with Perry Richards's help—and Perry vowed there would be no further investigation. He was nasty to me when I tried to talk to him."

"I'll call you as soon as I have something to report," Kelly promised.

Two evenings later Debbie was talking again with Kelly.

"Sheriff Stanton is still in office. He told me in very rough language to stay out of his town. It'll take time," he warned, "but I can try to track down the staff members. See what that dredges up. If you're willing to pursue this." Meaning, Debbie interpreted, that he'd want more money than she'd budgeted for this.

"Go ahead with it," she said recklessly. "I want my husband's murderer caught and tried."

She debated about confiding in her mother at this point, and decided against it. Mom would be upset. Not about the money, she conceded conscientiously, but because she still wasn't willing to accept that Scott's killer would never be caught and brought to trial. She would *never* accept that.

Debbie waited with fevered impatience for more word from Frank Kelly—ever conscious of what each day of investigation was costing her. Sheriff Stanton must have gone to Perry by now and told him about Kelly's investigation. And Perry was furious, she guessed.

It was almost two weeks later when Frank Kelly contacted her again. She phoned him from Nora's house.

"I've exhausted every possible lead on the servants at the Richards's house. They all left within months of your husband's death," he explained. "No forwarding addresses. Nobody seems to know where any of them live now—only that they're 'out of the state.' It's a rotten scene, but we have nowhere to go. I—"

"What about the business about the broken glass?" Debbie interrupted. "Can't we go over the sheriff's head and—"

"No dice." His voice was sympathetic but firm. "Stanton claims the glass on the library floor was cleaned up by a maid. Perry Richards will back him up. There's a lousy cover-up here, but these things happen."

"It's wrong! Damn it, it's wrong!"

"Unless some unexpected lead pops up, this will remain in the sheriff's 'unsolved file.' He'll do nothing to change that status." Kelly paused for a moment. "Did you tell me your mother-in-law died of a heart attack right after your husband was killed?"

"Yes."

"Pity. If she had died first, Scott would have inherited half the estate, I imagine. You'd be a very rich woman today."

Off the phone with Kelly, Debbie sat motionless by the phone. Was he inferring that Margaret Richards had died first—but Perry had connived to conceal that so he would inherit the entire estate? Was that the reason for his insistence on stopping the investigation? *Could Perry be that evil?*

Forty

F ran extended her January visit to New York by two days. For two
years in a row now Lynne had come down to Bellevue for a month's
stay without bringing Jessie and Beth with her. She saw so little of them,
Fran mourned. Debbie and Diane hadn't seen them for two years.

Tonight—her last night in town—Fran had taken Lynne and the girls
out to dinner. Arnie hadn't come with them. It was ridiculous, Fran
thought with recurrent rage, that Lynne came home from a day of teaching and had to worry about cooking dinner when Arnie wandered around
doing practically nothing all day. After dinner Lynne corrected papers
or worked on lesson plans—Arnie collapsed in front of the TV.

Arnie was off on another wild-goose chase, Fran gathered. Not until
they were back in the apartment and Jessie and Beth shipped off to their
room to study did Lynne elaborate on Arnie's latest venture.

"He's got this wild notion that he'll write material for the girls and
promote a record with them," Lynne said tiredly. "In his mind he's practically signed them up at Professional Children's School. He's talking
about making TV rounds with them. Mom, I want the kids to have a normal childhood. This is so nutty."

"You have to take a stand, Lynne. You're their mother. Tell Arnie
you don't want them exposed to that kind of life," Fran urged. She
sensed, too, that the tension between Lynne and Arnie extended beyond
this new business about the girls.

"We're in the season when any kind of accountant can pile up hours at
good money." Lynne's voice was sharp. "Arnie's 'temp' agencies call
practically every day, and he brushes them off. And the first thing he
says when I come home from school and grocery shopping is 'what's for
dinner?' "

In the past Lynne had tried to hide her disagreements with Arnie. Every couple had arguments, of course—but Fran knew instinctively that Lynne and Arnie had crossed beyond that.

"Are the kids still gung-ho about this singing *schtick?*" Fran asked, disconcerted by Lynne's disclosures. "Jessie, of course, adores having an audience—but Beth is so shy."

"Oh, Jessie is as bad as Arnie," Lynne said impatiently. "Beth, poor baby, won't admit she's scared to death each time they go out to sing—but I know. And they're not making any real money. I just wish Arnie would be realistic and take some 'temp' work. We have to start the kids' orthodontia soon."

"Lynne, don't worry about the orthodontia," Fran said quickly—on safe ground here. "I'll help with that."

"For all he balks at taking from you," Lynne said bitterly, "Arnie knows he can goof off because you'll come through when it's necessary."

Fran was aboard an early morning flight for Atlanta the following morning. She'd brought along the *New York Times*—eager to read the latest news about Jimmy Carter's race for the Democratic presidential nomination. Carter and his wife were fine people, as well as being Georgians—she hoped he'd make it to the White House. But this morning her mind refused to focus on politics.

Seeing the discord between Lynne and Arnie, she remembered Craig's too frequent battles with Joyce. He was so upset about the boys' reaction to this. *"Josh said he can't wait to get away to college—to get out of the house. Zach just runs out of the room when Joyce starts up a fight with me. I tell myself I should just keep quiet—but I get drawn in despite that."*

She didn't believe Lynne and Arnie would split up. For all the fighting, in some perverse way they needed each other. But it upset her to see Lynne put in that position. No, Fran reassured herself—Lynne and Arnie wouldn't even think about divorce. They wouldn't do that to the kids. But was a bad marriage of any value to children? The question was disconcerting. Yet so many unhappy husbands and wives stayed together "for the sake of the children."

Nobody was benefiting from Craig and Joyce's marriage, she admitted with a candor she'd avoided until this moment. The boys were miserable. They made no secret of that. Joyce was embarrassing some of her more staid acquaintances with her ugly remarks about marriage. And Craig—so sweet and patient—was desperately unhappy. If not for her, Fran realized, Craig would be talking with Joyce about a divorce. Joyce could name her own settlement—Craig just wanted out. Did *she* have the right to keep Craig in a marriage that was bringing him such unhappiness?

She'd tell Craig that she'd been wrong in saying she wouldn't see him again if he and Joyce were divorced. They wouldn't make plans for themselves after the divorce—provided that Joyce could be pushed into agreeing to it—but *she* mustn't stand in the way. Craig and Joyce's splitting up wouldn't change how she felt toward Lynne and Debbie and the girls. They were her *family*. Nothing could ever change that.

Fran felt suddenly young and adventurous, aware of a new zest for living. She was eager to see Craig's face when she told him she wouldn't stop seeing him if he were divorced. She would be lifting an onerous load from his shoulders—one she'd had no right to place there. Afterward they could plan *their* lives.

Now each minute of the flight seemed brutally long. She'd phone Craig from the Atlanta airport. Perhaps they could have lunch together. He'd be so happy when she told him. She was offering him a release from his prison. He would never try for a divorce as long as her threat hung over his head.

At the Atlanta airport she called Craig on his private line. She let the phone ring a dozen times, then reluctantly hung up. Craig wasn't there, she realized with childlike disappointment. Long ago his office staff had been instructed never to pick up his private line. He was out on a construction site or with a client, she surmised. She'd talk with him later in the day.

She debated about calling Debbie to pick her up and decided instead to grab a taxi for the long haul to Bellevue. She went directly to the house, left her luggage in her bedroom, and tried again to reach Craig. Still there was no reply on his private line.

Now she headed for her office. With the chain expanding the way it was, she ought to look for larger quarters, she thought. Maybe build, she plotted in sudden exhilaration. Another assignment for Craig, that would provide them with legitimate time together. Bellevue property was a solid investment. Once Craig made a deal with Joyce—and surely by now she, too, saw the absurdity of their remaining together—there would still be a long interval before the divorce was final. Another business deal between Craig and herself provided good cover for their seeing each other.

When Fran arrived, Debbie was having lunch at her desk while she went through the morning's correspondence.

"Mom, why didn't you call me to pick you up?" Debbie scolded, rising to embrace her.

"I knew you were busy this time of month." Fran dropped into a chair beside Debbie's desk. "How's Diane? Did Sandra's birthday party go off well?" It was a surprise party planned by Sandra's mother and Diane.

They talked for a few minutes about Diane's activities during Fran's absence from Bellevue. Then Fran told Debbie what was happening with Lynne and Arnie and the girls in New York—without revealing marital problems.

"Any earth-shattering news here in town?" Fran asked, smiling, and glanced at her watch. She'd call Craig again in half an hour.

"Robin came back yesterday. He forgot you were away and phoned you last night."

"Did he seem in good spirits?" Fran was solicitous. Robin was a creature of highs and lows, she thought affectionately. More lows than highs lately.

"He sounded concerned about Craig," Debbie told her and Fran tensed. "He has no love for Joyce, but with her so sick he worries about Craig."

"What's this about Joyce being sick?" Fran's heart began to pound. More anguish for Craig?

"She's been bothered by bronchitis on and off, Robin said—but a couple of nights ago she was so bad Doctor Otis put her into the hospital."

"Craig must be upset." Fran strived for calm.

"She's probably giving him one hell of a time," Debbie guessed.

"I suppose we ought to send flowers." Fran was uncomfortable. This was hypocritical, she mocked herself.

"Wait and see if Doctor Otis keeps her there," Debbie suggested. "Nobody really likes Joyce, but they'll send flowers for Craig's sake if she stays a few days longer."

It was close to 4 P.M. before Craig responded on his private line. This was not the time to tell him about her decision.

"How was your trip?" he asked, his voice tender.

"Business-wise it was fine. I worry about Lynne as usual." She hesitated. "Debbie tells me Joyce is in the hospital."

"Since night before last. She had a bad bronchial attack. Otis wants to do a series of tests." He paused. "He's worried about her lungs. You know she's smoked like a chimney for years." *Like Bernie.*

"Oh, Craig!" Fran remembered that his first wife had died of cancer.

It had been a heart-wrenching experience for him. "He's just being supercareful," she comforted.

Her timing was abysmal, Fran taunted herself in the weeks ahead. Joyce was diagnosed as suffering from lung cancer. Surgery was scheduled. The prognosis was good, Craig reported to Fran four days after surgery, but there would be months of chemotherapy.

"She's driving the hospital staff up the wall," he confided over a hasty dinner with Fran—before he was to go to the hospital for evening visiting hours. "Josh and Zach are distraught. They feel guilty because they were fighting so much with her before she went into the hospital. I'm trying to make them understand they have no reason to feel guilty. God, half the misery in this world is caused by unnecessary guilt feelings."

Fran and Craig settled down into an existence of numb desperation. They salvaged what time they could manage together—telling themselves they would *not* feel guilty about this. Joyce's convalescence was slow. Her mood was vitriolic. In the months ahead one practical nurse after another left the job.

Craig arranged for Joyce to spend the summer with her sister in a cottage on Saint Simon's Island. By midsummer, Craig reported, Joyce's sister was threatening to go home.

"I'll have to fly out for a week and referee," he told Fran.

In September—with Joyce settled in the house again—Craig began to work on the building to be the Goldman Shops's office and warehouse space.

"It's a blessed excuse for us to have lunch together regularly," Craig told Fran as they waited to be served in a popular Bellevue restaurant. And no need to hide away. They were talking shop. "You give me a hold on my sanity. How would I have survived these last months without you? Joyce has no sense of time—she expects me to run whenever she calls."

"How does Josh like Columbia?" Fran tried to divert him.

"You know what the first weeks of freshman year are like." His smile mixed warmth and indulgence. "He's in love with New York. He still hasn't the faintest clue about what he wants to do with his life. Joyce is still talking about his going to med school after college, but nobody is telling Josh what to do."

"Plans never work out," Fran said ruefully.

"We can't make decisions for them," Craig scolded. *"That* never works out."

"I wasn't making decisions." She sounded defensive, Fran thought.

But she'd never pushed Lynne or Debbie in any direction. Had she? Circumstances made their decisions.

"I wish Joyce wouldn't light into the boys each time they come home." Craig was somber. "I know she's not really well—even though Otis says the operation was successful."

"She's using Josh and Zach as whipping posts," Fran said. "But Josh won't be home often, and Zach is off with his friends on the weekends he's home from boarding school." At the onset of his mother's illness he'd been enrolled in an Atlanta boarding school—at his own request.

"All I can do is take one day at a time," Craig said after a moment. "Thank God, you're here for me."

Acquaintances stopped at their table and talked enthusiastically about Craig's new project for Fran. Then they went on to their own table, and Fran and Craig made a point of discussing the coming presidential election—loudly enough to be heard by those at nearby tables.

Fran was surprised but elated when Lynne told her on a Sunday night phone call in early December that she was coming down to Bellevue during the school holidays between Christmas and New Year's. Lynne was unhappy, though, that Jessie was refusing to come with her and Beth.

"Jessie's getting to the crazy teens." Lynne sighed. "I can't tell her anything. And Arnie always backs her up."

"Come down, darling. The change will do you good. And Diane and Beth haven't seen each other in ages. They're first cousins!" She'd always cherished a wish that her three granddaughters would be close.

Fran enjoyed having Lynne and Beth in Bellevue. She made a point of avoiding late hours at the office to be with the family. Craig, too, was tied up with family at this period, with Josh home from Columbia and Zach from boarding school. Still, she and Craig contrived an afternoon together at Robin's cottage.

"Something to see me through," Craig told her tenderly when they left the cottage and headed for their respective cars. "Both boys are trying very hard to keep the peace in the house. And sometime in February—when they can get reservations—Joyce and her sister are going to The Breakers down in Palm Beach for a week."

Fran knew that Dr. Otis was pleased with Joyce's physical health, but her mental state was not good.

"She's terrified of a relapse," Craig confided. "I guess that's understandable. But it makes her constantly miserable. People are sympathetic, but after a while they lose patience with her."

Fran had a TV set brought to the office so the office and sales staffs could watch the inauguration of Jimmy Carter. Georgians—wildly proud of having given the nation its newest President—had been pouring into Washington for the occasion. At noon yesterday the 18-car Peanut Special pulled out of Plains, Georgia—Jimmy Carter's hometown—with 350 passengers, bound for Washington. The *Atlanta Constitution* said that at least 8,000 Georgians would be in Washington.

"I hear a lot of people from Georgia are going up there with thermal underwear in their luggage," Debbie said in rare high spirits. "Washington is having its coldest January in years."

"Those poor gals in evening gowns," Beverly drawled. "They'll have warm bottoms but freezing backs."

"Robin told me that every shop in Atlanta that rents tuxes is sold out," Fran mused. "And I love the way Jimmy Carter said, 'Y'all come, you hear?' "

"I read somewhere that four hundred thousand personal invitations went out—printed in brown ink and on paper that had been recycled," the Goldman Shops bookkeeper contributed.

"Hear, hear!" Debbie chortled.

Debbie ought to be in Washington, reporting on the inauguration for some local paper, Fran thought, suddenly wistful.

The cluster gathered about the TV set—*nobody* was shopping this morning—watched while the Carters emerged from the Baptist church after morning services. Now they went to the White House to pick up the Fords, the outgoing President and the incoming President traveling together to the Capitol.

At the East Front of the Capitol an estimated 150,000 were gathered to watch the swearing-in ceremonies.

"Everybody looks so cold," Debbie said sympathetically. "But at least the reviewing stand is solar heated—and if that's not enough there're electric heaters there, too."

Earlier, Fran recalled, about 100,000 people were at the outdoor prayer service—the first ever on such an occasion—held near the Lincoln Memorial. Carter's evangelist sister, Ruth Stapleton, read the Scripture. Martin Luther King Sr. spoke briefly—at the very spot where thirteen years earlier his son had given his "I have a dream" speech.

The crowd seemed amazingly patient as they waited for the swearing-in ceremony to begin, Fran thought. And then all at once it was happening. Chief Justice Warren Burger was administering the thirty-five-word oath that would make Jimmy Carter—wearing a business suit rather than the formal attire of his predecessors—the thirty-ninth President of the United States. Rosalynn Carter held the family Bible.

Fran watched entranced—caught up in the drama of the occasion. She noted that both Rosalynn Carter and Joan Mondale wore cloth coats. Like so many others she was delighted when—after his inaugural speech—the President brushed aside his bulletproof limousine to march the mile and a half from Capitol Hill to the White House. It seemed to Fran that in a town where presidential security called for such intensive precautions, it was reassuring to see the President and the First Lady—with their youngest child between them—strolling down Pennsylvania Avenue. There was a gentleness about this inauguration that was a harbinger of the future, she thought for a sentimental moment.

When Carter held a two-hour radio news conference on March 5th, over nine and a half million people tried to call him, though only forty-two would be able to ask him a question directly. Later in the month Carter held his first "meet the people" town meeting in Clinton, Massachusetts, and spent the night with a local family. Most Americans were confident that the new President meant to carry out his campaign promises.

Much national attention was focused on the soaring population and increasing influence of the Sun Belt. People were talking about the population movement in general. More Americans were moving to the rural areas of the country, at the same time that suburbanites were returning to the major cities.

In New York Lynne was upset when she discovered Jessie was regularly cutting classes to go with a pair of classmates to Times Square movie houses. Arnie battled with her over her new infatuation for punk rock, the new hot music in this country. Both were outraged when she emerged from her bedroom—on an April night when Beth was sleeping over at a girlfriend's house—to display a spiky punk haircut.

"You're out of your mind!" Arnie yelled as she spun around in triumph. "How are you going out to sing when you look like that?"

"For the shitty lodge dates we get, who cares?" Jessie shrugged her disdain. "By summer it'll be grown out again. If we're going out to the bungalow colonies again," she added, her eyes in defiant challenge.

"I'm not sure we'll be going out to the country this summer," Arnie shot back. An odd triumphant look in his smile. Jessie and Arnie spoke a silent language she didn't understand, Lynne thought.

"Why not?" Jessie seemed taken aback. She liked getting out on those tiny stages or a segment of floor designated "the stage" and singing for those people, Lynne recognized. Arnie called her "a Class A ham"—with a mixture of pride and annoyance. "What do you expect to be doing?"

"There's a real chance I'm going to have a record out again. With a major company," he emphasized. His previous record had died from a lack of promotion. *"How could they expect it to sell with no 'air plays'?"*

"I didn't want to talk about it until it's a set deal."

"What song?" Jessie demanded.

"A new one," Arnie told her, and again Lynne watched the silent by-play between them.

"Why didn't you give it to me to learn?" Jessie's eyes blazed in reproach.

"It's sexy. I couldn't give it to you to sing."

"I can sing sexy songs." Lynne sensed an unnerving wildness in her. "Nobody thinks I'm just thirteen," Jessie pursued. "I can pass for seventeen."

"You're not singing this song," Arnie said flatly. "Anyhow, we won't be doing it when we go out to the shows. It's for the recording session."

"Nobody knows I'm thirteen. I could have done a 'demo' for you."

"This chick I run into at the Brill Building all the time did a 'demo' for me. She's hoping to ride along with the song."

"Will she?" Jessie was seething now.

"No," he told her. All at once Lynne understood. Jessie wanted to do the "demo" as an audition for herself. "They want the song for somebody in their own stable. Even I don't know who it is. But with one of their 'hot singers' doing the session, it'll get plenty of 'air plays.' "

On her Sunday evening phone call from her mother—with Jessie and Beth both grounded in their room doing homework—Lynne told Fran about the raging ambition she sensed in Jessie.

"She's a baby, Mom—but all she thinks about is going out and making it as a pop singer. Even Arnie tries to make her understand she's not ready for a singing career."

"You must make her realize that she has to finish school," her mother said. "Make Arnie back you up. Once she's out of high school and college, then she can consider a singing career."

"It'll be a miracle if we can get her to go to college," Lynne said grimly. She'd wanted the girls to have a profession—something they could depend upon to support themselves. "I just want to see her earn her high school diploma."

"What's with Arnie's recording session?" Fran asked.

"It looks good, but you never know until you walk into the studio and everything's in place."

Lynne watched with a fatalistic calm while Arnie went through the "on" and "off" phases of the proposed recording session. Mainly because of Jessie's insistence he made the rounds of two-bit agents and picked up some low-paying weekend singing dates for the girls in July and August. The midweek days were off-limits because of the possible recording session. Still, his excitement was contagious when the recording date was finally scheduled for mid–June. After all, this was a major record company.

Jessie dawdled over breakfast. Could she cut school today and get away with it? Why wouldn't Daddy take her with him to the session? He could make up some excuse for bringing her along.

"Jessie, finish your breakfast." Her mother's voice was sharp. Her father was still asleep. He didn't get up until the other three were out of the apartment. *"With one bathroom I'm just in the way."*

"I don't know why Daddy can't take me to the session," Jessie tried once more.

"Because it's unprofessional," her mother said sharply. "Come on, finish up your breakfast and let's get on our way." Beth had gone to their room to get her books.

"I don't want any more." Jessie's voice was sullen. Mom wasn't going to leave without her, she interpreted. "Let's go."

She wasn't going to her morning classes, Jessie decided when she emerged into the unseasonably hot morning with her mother and Beth. The other two headed north for their school. She swung south, presumably en route to her junior high.

She'd walk down to Lincoln Center, pick up a Coke or Pepsi in a deli, then sit out front until the library at Lincoln Center opened up, she plotted. Then she'd go inside and read the latest *Billboard, Cashbox,* and *Variety*.

At the first red light, she pulled out lipstick and eyeliner and created her usual magic. Mom would kill her if she knew, Jessie thought. Lipstick and eyeliner made her look at least sixteen. With a deftness learned from practice, she reached at her back and released her bra through the sheer fabric of her dress. A moment later—when the light had changed to green—she saw the hungry gaze of a twenty-year-old as his eyes rested on the unrestrained bounce of her Marilyn Monroe breasts.

Despite the heat she walked with her usual compulsive swiftness. Perspiration trickled down her throat and caused the back of her summer cotton to cling to skin. Daddy should have let her make that "demo" for him. He should have included one of her songs, too. He always said how proud he was that she could write songs. So why was he always trying to stand in her way?

Forty-One

F ran was rushing to meet Craig for lunch. Presumably they were to discuss the windows for the Goldman Building. Joyce had returned from her summer at Saint Simon's with her sister and—restless and unhappy—was making unexpected demands on Craig's time.

Fran saw Craig's car when she pulled into the parking area beside the restaurant, at the edge of town. As always she felt a lift in spirits as she hurried inside to meet him. They always chose a time that was a little early or a little late, when the luncheon crowd was light and they felt less of a need to be on guard. Yet at their ages, she mused, who would think they were carrying on a clandestine affair? It was incredible to realize she and Craig were both sixty-one. Where did the years go?

"Hi." Craig's face lighted as she approached their table.

"We're here before the mob descends." She smiled in satisfaction and slid into the comfortable, cushioned captain's chair across from him. She noted the attaché case on the floor beside his chair. "Did the boys get off to school?"

"Josh flew out this morning. Zach leaves tomorrow. I'll miss them." His smile was rueful. "But these last days have been harried. Anyhow, I'll be seeing Zach on most weekends. How did your sales meeting go last night?"

"Good." Despite all the talk of another recession—along with a threat of inflation—Seventh Avenue reported that orders for fall and winter were coming in heavy.

"If we believe the economists, we're in for a worldwide recession— what with the high trade deficit and the falling dollar. Still, we're not feeling it yet." Craig's smile was whimsical. "Neither your customers nor mine are affected by the seven percent unemployment figures."

"Lynne expected a raise this year, but it's not coming through," Fran reported. "She said the owners of the school are scared to death that Carter's going to be heavy on social programs and demand higher taxes, so they're tightening their belts."

Their waiter arrived with menus. They focused now on ordering—the waiter suggesting the day's specials. He beamed when they accepted his choice, and he sauntered off.

"What's with Arnie's record? You said it was due out about now." Craig's face reflected a special serenity that Fran recognized and shared. This was a cherished oasis in the midst of a chaotic day.

"Lynne and Arnie are both out of their minds. The first pressings were shipped last week, and Lynne wrote that the promotion will be heavy. That means 'air time,' I gather." She wasn't familiar with the inner workings of the record business—only what Robin explained to her.

"I hope he has a good contract." Craig's eyes were questioning.

"Arnie was in no position to bargain. He's riding on Cloud Nine now, just to know that his song was recorded by an up-and-coming singer—and it's the 'A' side of the album's first single." Fran hesitated. "I hope they keep their feet on the ground. Robin says Arnie can end up with very little money unless he has a solid contract."

"But it could be the jumping-off point for his career," Craig encouraged.

"I keep asking myself if there'll ever be a time when I don't worry about the children. Or does worrying go with the job?"

"Did you read that item last week—I think it was in the *Constitution*—about how violence has declined in TV programming?" Fran nodded in approval. "You said a few times how you worry about kids being exposed to so much violence on television."

"I think the English have an interesting approach," Fran mused. "When Diane's friend Sandra went to London with her mother last summer and they tried to buy tickets for a hit play that was a murder mystery, they were turned down. Children are allowed to see performances with sexual overtones—but no violence."

"One is natural, one isn't," Craig interpreted. *"Viva la nature,"* he joshed.

"I worry about Jessie," Fran confided. "The way you worry about Zach." But not for the same reason, she conceded inwardly. Lynne had told her—and she'd seen this herself when she was in New York in July—that Jessie had become an outrageous flirt. Young as she was, she knew her effect on men. Craig's problem with Zach was that every other day Zach was zeroing in on a new career.

"We love them, but we worry. I guess love carries price tags. Zach's a great kid. One of these days he'll decide what he wants to do with his life. But he's always so intense."

"Like Diane," Fran said tenderly. "The way Debbie was at her age." The way *she* was, she recalled in a crevice of her mind.

The November afternoon was bone-chilling raw, but Arnie was barely conscious of this as he walked in and out of record stores between Times Square and West 57th Street. He was on a rare high. On sale for six weeks now, Bonnie Lane's album was on display everywhere. *His* side—the lead-off single that introduced the album—was rolling up heavy air play. Royalty statements were due in a few weeks. The prospect was exhilarating.

Lynne was making noises about his picking up some "temp" work for now. That was a joke—considering the royalties he was piling up. Okay, so the album wouldn't go gold—it was selling a hell of a lot of copies and the advance had been peanuts. He'd see a bundle.

It had been months since he'd gone out as a "temp." God, he loathed sitting in an office! But maybe he'd drop in on Ted Lucas—he was right down in the Palace Theater building. Ted's clients were mostly in the music and entertainment field. Ted would give him a rough idea of how much he could expect on this first royalty statement.

He left the Colony Record Shop and headed for Ted's office. This wasn't the rush season yet—and Ted loved to schmooze. At one point he'd worked part-time for Ted.

"Hey, how's the new king of Tin Pan Alley?" Ted glanced up in welcome as Arnie strolled into his small, cluttered office.

"Waiting for royalty statement time," Arnie said, grinning. Ted knew all about the Bonnie Lane album. He wasn't exactly setting the world on fire, but he did have a hit song on the air waves. "You know this racket, Ted. I want you to clue me in on what I can expect in the way of a check. Who knows?" he said with a chuckle. "One day you might be my accountant."

"You got figures, Arnie?" Ted approved but he refused to be genuinely impressed. Okay, so he wasn't Irving Berlin or Cole Porter yet, Arnie conceded.

"I've got ballpark figures." Arnie dropped into the chair that flanked

Ted's much-worn desk and reached into his jacket pocket for a sheaf of notebook pages. "Here—"

He leaned back expectantly while Ted juggled figures.

"We have to remember the packaging deduction, the free goods allowance—and to deduct thirty percent for reserves against returns," Ted said, making swift notations.

"What do you mean, thirty percent against returns?" All at once Arnie was defensive.

"Arnie, you've been around the music business long enough to know that," Ted reproached. "Later—if there're few returns—you get it back."

"Yeah—" In all his years around the business he *didn't* know about the reserve for returns. "But what does it break down to in dollars and cents?"

"Look, you gave me just ballpark figures—but I'd say you'll rake in close to nine thousand bucks."

Arnie stared at him in disbelief.

"Ted, it's got to be more than that!"

"Let me show you the breakdown." Ted was patient. "You know how many times I've been through this. Now just listen to me—"

His teeth clenched in rage Arnie listened and double-checked Ted's figures.

"Son of a bitch!" He slammed a fist on a corner of the desk. "I've been batting my brains out for twenty years. I finally come up with a hit. And all I'll see is nine thousand bucks?"

"Arnie, the money has to be split in a dozen directions. A songwriter isn't buying a beach house on Fire Island and a new Porsche on one hit song. Even if it had gone gold."

"It should be going gold," Arnie said in frustration. "The lousy company stinted on promotion."

"Look, Arnie, be sensible. You can't make big money as a songwriter these days. You have to be a singer/songwriter—or a record producer yourself. It's getting harder and harder to sell a song. So few singers are looking for them—they're writing their own. The whole business has changed. How many Steve Lawrence and Eydie Gormés are around now?"

"The only way is to write a musical." Arnie was grim. "Even if you have to share with the person who writes the book, you still own fifty percent of the action. I knew that twenty years ago! Why the hell didn't I stay with it?"

"On the other hand, this is just one song." Ted was thoughtful. "Nine thousand isn't big bucks, but it's a nice piece of change. How long did it take you to write the song?" Ted spread his hands in an eloquent gesture of respect. "You'll write more. You broke the ice, kid."

Arnie left Ted's office and headed uptown. Now he clung to what Ted had said about breaking the ice. He'd given Bonnie the strongest song on the album—she *needed* him. He had two new songs to show her, but she was dashing around on promotion gimmicks. If she'd just pop into town long enough to listen to the new ones, he'd feel better. And that nine thousand—stinkingly low that it was—would be welcome. It was time they bought a car instead of having to rent. Not that he and the kids would be going out on those one-night gigs after this.

Despite his earlier rage, Arnie was whistling as he let himself into the apartment. From the girls' bedroom came the sound of Jessie's surprisingly powerful voice and the plaintive sound of guitar music. A chip off the old block, he told himself in satisfaction. He envisioned himself giving interviews, talking about his two daughters who were aspiring singers. Someday they'd be out there singing his songs.

The singing and the guitar-playing in the bedroom stopped. Jessie hurled herself in the hallway with her usual electric intensity.

"Daddy, is that you?"

"Yeah, Jessie." Arnie hung up his topcoat and strolled into the living room.

"I just wrote a terrific new song," Jessie announced in triumph. "I want you to hear it!"

Exasperated that he couldn't reach Bonnie and give her the new songs, Arnie decided to call her newly acquired manager—the signal of her soaring success. It took three tries before Arnie reached him.

"Yeah. Well—uh—Bonnie should be in town sometime tomorrow afternoon." He sounded strangely evasive, Arnie thought. "Try her at her apartment. Though she and the boyfriend may be over at his pad. I think you should call her, Arnie." He was more decisive now. "Do it tomorrow. They're running down to Key West later in the week for a little vacation."

"I'll call her tomorrow," Arnie said. He wanted her to have the new songs before she took off again.

Arnie phoned Bonnie at four the next afternoon. She wasn't at her apartment. He called three more times before he caught up with her.

"Arnie, honey, how are you?" she trilled.

"I'm great," he said automatically. "Thrilled by the way the album's doing. How are you?"

"Oh, just exhausted. But I'm taking off for a little vacation day after tomorrow." Arnie detected a false gaiety in her voice.

"I've got two numbers finished for you. Let's get together sometime tomorrow so I can give them to you."

"I've been meaning to talk to you about that." She hesitated. "I think I'm going to be traveling in another direction."

"What do you mean?" He was startled. The album was selling because of his "A" side. *Everybody knew that.*

"If I'm really going to move up on the charts, I need something different for the next album. My boyfriend's got some terrific ideas, and we—"

"What about me?" Arnie was cold with fury. *The boyfriend was a songwriter?* "What about loyalty? The side I wrote for you is what's getting the plays!"

"I need something hot for the next album," she repeated coldly. "Something young. My boyfriend's my age. He's hip. Sorry, Arnie, this is where we part company."

Jessie deliberately cracked her bedroom door to listen to the conversation in the living room. Beth was baby-sitting tonight—she'd holed up and done her homework in the afternoon. For now the bedroom was all hers—a situation Jessie relished.

In the living room her father was blasting about how Bonnie Lane had shafted him. Didn't Daddy understand? He belonged to another generation. Bonnie wanted the new funky music.

She waited until her mother went into the master bedroom to work on lesson plans before joining her father in the living room. She'd been working hard to revise the new song. Daddy was nuts to complain about the contents, but he'd been right about the technical mistakes. She'd fixed them now.

"Daddy," she began with the sultry sweetness that worked not only with heavy-breathing teenage boys but with fathers. "I've got the kinks out of the new song, the way you told me to do."

"Good," he approved, but she knew he was only partly with her. He was still stewing about losing Bonnie Lane. "Now do something about the lyrics. Stop trying to be Miss Sex Queen of 1977. You're thirteen years old."

"I'll be fourteen soon," she said coolly. She understood he didn't feel comfortable that she could write the way she did about sex. But then he didn't know she'd been screwing around with guys since she was twelve. Nobody knew except the guys—who all thought she was three or four years older than she was. "And that's the way kids talk today."

"I don't like it." He sounded belligerent. Part of it was due, she understood, to his being uptight about Bonnie Lane.

"Daddy, you know what I was thinking," she said with a devious smile. "Now that I've ironed out all the bad things in the new song—my best to date," she emphasized, "why can't I make a 'demo' and get it around to the record companies?"

"Are you nuts?" He stared at her as though she'd lost her marbles, she thought. "You're a little kid—who's going to listen to you?"

"Who has to know that?" she challenged. "I can pass for seventeen any day." With her looks and plenty of eye makeup—which she put on out of the house.

"You're not ready to go out as songwriter or singer," Arnie blustered.

"Songwriter/singer," she said, pretending to ignore his shock at her pinpointing this. "That's the easiest way these days. You're always complaining about how singers are all trying to write their own songs."

"You're a little kid!" he yelled again. But she was a *better* songwriter than he was—and she could *sing.* "In five years maybe we'll do a 'demo' for you. And you don't do a 'demo' with one song. You have to do at least three—you haven't got that many at a professional level." So he considered this one professional, she thought in triumph. From Daddy that was a *big* admission.

"I'll work on two more," she pursued. "It won't cost much to do a 'demo.' I'll sing, you'll be my accompanist. We can go into one of those two-bit recording studios. I can pay for it with my baby-sitting money."

"Cork it," he said brusquely. "This isn't a business for babies."

Rage welled in her. If he was going to be rotten, then he'd pay for it. He liked her refusing to go down to Bellevue at Christmas vacation time. He got a real charge out of that because he knew Grandma was disappointed when she didn't come down with Mom and Beth. This year she wasn't going to refuse.

"When we're down in Bellevue during Christmas vacation and Grandma asks what I want for my birthday, I'm going to tell her I want a tape recorder." She contrived to appear wide-eyed and innocent, but she felt giddy with triumph. Daddy was not going to keep her sitting around another five years before she tried for a record deal.

"You're going to Bellevue with Mom and Beth?" His gaze was skeptical.

"Sure thing. Beth says Grandma always asks her at Christmas what she wants for her birthday present—and I want a tape recorder real bad. You know Grandma," Jessie drawled. "She always buys the best. I can play my guitar and sing—and zingo, there's a 'demo.' "

"All right, play with a tape recorder. But it's not going anywhere, you understand? I'll tell you when you're ready to play the professional."

Fran sat with Lynne before the living room fireplace and already felt a sense of loss because Lynne and the girls would be going back to New York in the morning—to be there in time for the reopening of school. It had been a wonderful ten days, she thought—and yet a disturbing time for her. She worried about the state of Lynne's marriage.

"Shall I put up some hot chocolate to have ready when Debbie returns with the kids?" Lynne's voice punctured her introspection. Debbie had driven to the movie theater at the mall to pick up the three girls. They'd gone to see *The Turning Point*. "It's that kind of night."

"Wait till they get here," Fran said. "Lynne, I wish you'd learn to relax," she said gently. Everybody had always considered Debbie the intense one, Lynne the calm one. Now they seemed to have reversed themselves.

Lynne sighed. Her eyes were stormy. "Around Arnie and Jessie that's impossible."

"Arnie must be pleased about the record," Fran said. They hadn't had much time alone since Lynne arrived, she considered; but even so she sensed that the situation between Lynne and Arnie bordered on the hostile.

"He thought he'd make a hundred thousand dollars. He'll be lucky to see ten. But you know Arnie—always with the grandiose ideas." Lynne was making no pretense this trip that she and Arnie were on perfect terms. That in itself was unnerving, Fran thought. She was watching Lynne's marriage unravel. "The minute his royalty comes through, he says, he's buying a car. Not one of the inexpensive models," Lynne drawled contemptuously. "Not my husband. He's talking about a Cadillac. Never mind putting a chunk of the money aside for emergencies."

"There they are—" Fran heard a car pulling up in the driveway. "Now put up the hot chocolate."

Fran's face brightened at the sound of lively young voices. She so enjoyed having them all here in the house together. Yet she was aware that Jessie kept herself somewhat aloof from Beth and Diane. There wasn't that much difference in ages, but Jessie seemed so much older than the other two.

"Why shouldn't women have careers?" Diane was saying earnestly as the three girls charged into the living room. "This is almost 1978!" Diane was caught up in feminism, Fran thought indulgently. She cherished every word Debbie brought home from her feminist meetings.

"Oh, Di, you're such a pipsqueak," Jessie drawled. "What do you know about careers?"

"I know I'm going to have a career," Diane said, her smile dazzling. "I'm going to be a journalist."

Fran was conscious of a dizzying sense of déjà vu. She remembered Debbie saying that, all those years ago. She remembered her own ambitions, killed off by a single bullet. And at the same time she felt a rush of joy. Diane would do what neither she nor Debbie had been able to accomplish. In a corner of her mind she remembered Craig's admonishment about trying to live through children or grandchildren. But it could happen, she thought tenderly—and it would be beautiful.

"I'm going to be a singer." Beth's sweet, soft voice intruded. "Jessie and I go out singing with Daddy now. At lodges and summer bungalow colonies."

"Oh, Beth, that's such garbage." Jessie dismissed this, but Fran remembered she had asked for a tape recorder for her birthday in February.

Were Lynne's two girls genuinely intent on careers in music? Knowing Arnie's travails, Fran was anxious for their futures. "Diane, go out into the kitchen and help your mother bring in the hot chocolate," Fran said lovingly. "And tell her Lily made a coffee cake this afternoon. It's in the bread box."

Jessie was the first to leave the small group before the fireplace.

"I want to pack tonight so I don't have to bother with it in the morning," she said with an air of boredom. "Beth, you coming?"

"Yeah." Beth rose to her feet, yet Fran sensed this middle granddaughter was reluctant to leave. Did Beth always allow Jessie to lead?

"Lynne, you said you wanted to see the material Nora brought back from the convention in Houston," Debbie reminded. Last month the largest feminist meeting since that at Seneca Falls in 1844 was held in Houston. The first National Women's Conference had been attended by 1,442 delegates. There was much talk about consciousness-raising and the elimination of obstacles to equality. Nora had spoken scathingly of the opponents of ERA and abortion rights, who held a "pro-family" rally several miles away.

"Let's do it now." Lynne was eager to see what had been circulated at the convention.

Now that the others had left the room, Diane came over to sit beside her grandmother. She gazed toward the entrance as though to assure herself that they were alone.

"You know, Grandma, you always tell us that we should love one another—I mean, all of us in the family." Diane's expression was troubled. "But I don't *like* Jessie. I love Beth and I *like* her," she analyzed, endearingly serious. "And I think I'm a little scared of Uncle Arnie. I guess I don't really know him. But I don't like Jessie," she repeated, almost defiant. "She acts like Beth and I are dumb. She thinks she's special because she lives up in New York, and we live down here in Bellevue. Why does she behave that way, Grandma?"

"Darling, don't worry about Jessie," Fran soothed. "I suppose it's part of being a teenager."

"I won't be like that when I'm a teenager," Diane promised.

"I'm sure you won't." Fran leaned forward to kiss this granddaughter closest to her.

It disturbed her to see friction between Jessie and Diane. She yearned to see the grandchildren close—to see a warm, loving family that encompassed all three generations. She'd longed to grow old surrounded by daughters, son-in-laws, grandchildren, and someday grandson-in-laws and great-grandchildren. But Scott was cruelly absent from their lives. And Lynne and Arnie seemed enmeshed in an unhappy marriage.

Her mind shot back through the years. Lynne and Arnie had been so wildly in love. What had gone wrong? It wasn't Lynne, she thought defensively. *Arnie* had changed. She doubted that Lynne would divorce him. She'd want to keep the family together for the sake of the children. *Was it better for the children? How did you know?*

Forty-Two

With the approach of Arnie's fortieth birthday in April Lynne debated about planning a surprise party. In truth, they had no mutual close friends. Arnie's parents—like strangers to them—were in Florida. They hadn't seen his sisters in years.

Lynne had her friends from school. He had friends—more acquaintances, she acknowledged—among the music world fringe, all of them strangers to her. The few times she'd invited couples she knew for dinner, Arnie had been bored. All right, she decided. They'd have a birthday dinner at home and then go out to a Broadway musical.

"Oh, Christ, I don't even want to be reminded about my birthday!" Arnie exploded when she presented her plans. "Forty years and what do I have to show for it?"

"You've got a hit song." Lynne tried for an upbeat mood. "A brand new Cadillac." He was insane about that car, she thought tiredly. "You've got two beautiful daughters."

"The trouble with you, Lynne—you're so damn penny-ante. You've got no ambition—" The vitriolic complaints she'd heard hundreds of times beat a relentless tattoo onto her brain.

She clenched her teeth to keep back the words that would only goad Arnie into further reproach. He was angry and depressed—and of course, in his mind, it was all her fault. In weird ways he used her as his whipping post. Where was the Arnie she used to know? she mourned.

"What do you want to do?" she asked tiredly when at last he paused. She would be forty in September—she wasn't acting as though the world was coming to an end. "Forget about seeing *Chorus Line?*"

"Forget the whole fucking birthday scene," he grunted.

"We'll have a nice dinner and a cake," she decreed. "The girls have been saving up to buy you a joint birthday gift. You can't deny them a small celebration."

He and Jessie were getting into a lot of arguments these days, Lynne thought uneasily. Perhaps because they were so much alike—and a different generation. He couldn't stand the music she liked—what she called funky and he called fucky. And she knew, too, that he worried—as she did—about Jessie's baby-doll sexiness. Jessie was beginning to understand the effect she had on boys. She saw it as a kind of power.

Every parent with teenagers worried, Lynne admonished herself. It went with the territory. Mom must have worried about them—though she'd never let on. But that was a different world then. No drugs, no openly sleeping around, no Pill.

Arnie never should have started taking the girls on those singing gigs. Time enough for that when they were older. But why push them into a field he knew was great for only a few? She hoped they'd settle on practical careers that wouldn't tear them apart the way songwriting did Arnie.

Already Jessie spent most of her spare time writing songs and recording them on that tape recorder Mom gave her. Jessie showed the kind of intensity toward music that she had felt for law. Even now—when she read about some spectacular trial that was hitting the front pages of the newspaper—she was conscious of the old stirrings.

"You said we were going to see *Chorus Line,*" Jessie accused when she learned the musical had been scraped from their plans.

"Daddy figured we ought to save the money," Lynne lied. "We spent so much on the car," she reminded. Both girls were excited at having a Cadillac. It had cost over $12,000—they'd had to take out a loan above what his royalties brought. *She* had to take out the loan. Arnie had no real job. The only time Arnie seemed happy was when he was behind the wheel of the car.

Fran was looking forward to Lynne and Beth's arrival for their usual summer vacation in Bellevue. Jessie was not coming down with them. She was going to be a mother's helper at Fire Island this summer. Arnie was working on a musical again. He was doing the music and lyrics, and a young writer he'd met in the East Village was writing the book, from a novel in public domain. They hoped for an Off-Broadway production. Fran understood Arnie had abandoned all thoughts of working as an accountant—even on a "temp" basis.

Lynne looked so tired, Fran thought when she and Beth arrived. She was a working wife, but Arnie had never accepted the current theory that husbands shared household duties when wives worked. His big deal, Fran seethed, was to go down to Zabár's on Sunday mornings for bagels and lox. But in the course of the month in Bellevue, Fran noted with relief, Lynne did seem to relax.

Fran relished Beth and Diane's pleasure in the new swimming pool, installed under Craig's directions. She made a point of dubbing Craig the family's official architect—which covered the times when people saw them together. The pool served as a constant meeting place for Diane and her friends, all of whom welcomed Beth with ingratiating southern warmth.

In a way, Fran told herself, it was just as well that Jessie hadn't come down. She hadn't mixed well with Diane's friends—and instinctively Fran guessed that sweet, shy Beth had few occasions to move from beneath Jessie's shadow. This summer had been good for her middle granddaughter, but she suspected that Lynne worried about Jessie's summer activities.

On Fire Island—on a phone call to her mother in mid–August—Jessie complained about her job as a mother's helper.

"Mom, I'm bored out of my skull."

"Jessie, you're committed to staying for the summer!" her mother reminded.

"Mom, people are waiting in line to use the phone," Jessie said quickly when the operator broke in to ask for additional coins. "I have to go now. I'll call you next week."

It was so dumb the way Mom insisted she phone once a week to check in, Jessie thought as she relinquished the phone and headed back for the beachfront cottage. Angela and Bill Raines had made it clear to Mom that they understood they were expected to provide parental-style supervision. Why did Mom worry?

A secretive smile lit her face now. This weekend Angela was out in California for her college roommate's wedding—and she was alone with the kids and Bill.

Walking into the cottage Jessie heard Bill reading a story to the four-year-old twins. They'd fall asleep before he was half finished, she surmised. All that sun and ocean air guaranteed that. But tonight she didn't mean to settle for summer reruns on television.

She hadn't had a chance to run around evenings. Angela was so conscientious about that. No Fire Island parties for the "mother's helper." She was supposed to hit the sack by ten because the twins were up by 6 A.M. every morning. But tonight would be different.

She'd seen the way Bill looked at her when Angela wasn't around. He was dying to hop into bed with her. He wasn't bad for thirty-four, though Angela kept warning him he'd have a martini belly before he was forty if he didn't stop the drinking. He was in advertising and devoted to the four-martini lunch.

She went to her closet-size bedroom and changed her blouse for the red tank top she'd secretly bought with baby-sitting money. Mom would flip out if she saw her looking like this, Jessie thought complacently, inspecting her reflection in the mirror. The tank top barely covered her lush breasts. The nipples were pressed in sensuous bas-relief.

She waited until she heard Bill emerge from the twins' bedroom and head for the kitchen. He'd be fixing a shaker of cocktails, she surmised. All right, go out and give him the message.

"Hi," she drawled, pausing in the kitchen doorway to provide the full effect—her eyes inviting.

"You after a glass of milk or a soda?" She saw his heated reaction.

"Milk and soda are for kids," she reproached. "I moved out of that league when I was fourteen." He and Angela thought she was sixteen, she reminded herself smugly.

"Do you know what you're doing?" he asked uneasily—their eyes in blatant communication.

"Are the kids asleep?" Her gaze settled on his crotch.

"They're asleep."

"Then I know what I'm doing. Let's fuck."

Debbie was relieved that Nora's expansion of the bookstore was doing so well. When the shop next door had closed in September, Nora had jumped right in—at *her* impulsive suggestion—to take over the space and focus on a mystery novel section. She'd felt guilty until Nora reported shortly after Thanksgiving that increased sales warranted the additional rent.

"I've been thinking all day about something to focus interest on the shop," Nora confided to Debbie over coffee at her house after a little theater performance of Ibsen's *Hedda Gabler*. "What do you think about a series of wine and cheese parties—one evening a month—with an interesting guest speaker from the mystery field?"

"Sounds terrific," Debbie approved.

"Actually, my sister out in Texas suggested something like that almost a year ago." Nora grimaced in recall. "She thought it was a way for me to meet men. I can't make her understand that the older I get the more finicky I am. I mean, my life is full the way it is. Unless somebody really great comes along—and the odds of that are not good—I'd rather stay single. I just wish my sisters could accept that."

"Mom gave up on me, thank God," Debbie told her. "Grandma used to nag."

"I'll have the first party right after New Year's," Nora plotted. "You'll be co-hostess with me."

"You don't need me." Debbie was startled.

"Yes, I do," Nora insisted. "For moral support. You come over so calm and sophisticated. I get nervous."

"Me calm and sophisticated?" Debbie broke into laughter. "Nobody's ever accused me of that." She paused. She was thinking of the old Debbie. Is that the way she appeared to people today? Calm and sophisticated?

"You'll be co-hostess," Nora reiterated. "Otherwise, I'll be a nervous wreck."

The evening of the first wine and cheese party, Debbie went directly from the office to Nora's shop to help with the preparations. Nora rushed to the door to meet her.

"Debbie, you won't believe what's happened!" Nora was pale and distraught. "You know my big deal about 'Atlanta Mystery Writer to speak at Nora's Bookshop'? He was taken to the hospital two hours ago for an emergency appendectomy. What am I going to do?"

"Postpone it," Debbie said after a moment's hesitation. "This wasn't something you could control."

"How can I reach people? They'll be here in less than two hours! I know a few customers who said they're coming, but what about others?"

"We have to try for a fast replacement." Debbie struggled to appear calm.

"In two hours?"

"It doesn't have to be a writer—just someone familiar with mystery writing. What about somebody from the faculty at Columbus College— you know Marilyn Satlof over there—or one of the colleges in Atlanta? Think, Nora," she exhorted, managing to conceal her own alarm. The

Bellevue Enquirer had run a large article, and Nora had spent money on an ad. "There has to be someone—"

"Eric James," Nora said with an aura of hope. "I told you about him. He came down from New York to teach at—"

"Call him," Debbie interrupted. "This minute!"

Prodded by Debbie, Nora darted to the phone, dialed Information— too anxious to search in the phone book for Eric James's number.

"He lives right here in Bellevue," Nora said while she waited for the operator to check. "He's Miss Freeman's grandnephew—he has his own little apartment in her house."

Nora paused when the operator returned to the line, made a note, then dialed—holding up a pair of crossed fingers while she waited for him to answer. Then her face brightened.

"Hi, Eric?" She nodded to Debbie as he replied. "This is Nora Fields. We met a couple of weeks ago at that—" She nodded hopefully to Debbie while he responded. "I know it's awful to ask you at the last moment this way, but I have a crisis on my hands."

She explained the situation to Eric. Her face reflected her relief. "Oh, Eric, that would be marvelous! I'm sure everybody will be pleased."

Off the phone, Nora explained that Eric James was a mystery buff as well as a creative writing teacher at Emory.

"He said he'd use his notes from a lecture he gave at a summer workshop, on mystery novelists. Oh, God, Debbie, am I relieved!"

Now Nora and Debbie occupied themselves with setting up an attractive offering of cheeses, crackers, plus wine bottles and plastic glasses.

"I know, plastic glasses are tacky," Nora said, sighing, "but they'll have to do. Oh, where did I put the napkins?" She glanced around in a flurry of nervousness.

"They're right over here," Debbie soothed.

Thirty-five minutes before the shop was to open for the evening party, Eric James arrived. Nora rushed to welcome him. Debbie hadn't expected him to be so young—about thirty, she guessed—nor so handsome. He was slim, probably three or four inches taller than she, and with dark hair and eyes, well-chiseled features, a sensitive mouth that was unexpectedly sensuous. His female students must give him a hard time, she thought with sudden sympathy. She sensed a certain shyness in him—an eagerness to please. Almost a lack of self-confidence. Why, she wondered, when he was so obviously charming?

"Eric, this is my friend Debbie Richards," Nora introduced. "Eric James."

"Hi." Eric's eyes were admiring. "I saw you at the library book sale last month. You were leaving just as I was arriving."

"I did leave early," Debbie remembered, self-conscious at his scrutiny. "Diane—my daughter—was home with a bad cold, and I was anxious to see how she was feeling."

Eric turned to Nora.

"I hope my talk won't seem too academic," he said with an air of apology. "I know your guests will be disappointed at not having a mystery writer here."

"They'll be happy to hear you talk about mystery writers," Nora soothed. "And if you won't mind taking questions?"

"Questions are great." His smile was warm. "If you think I'm going on too long, just give me a sign." He chuckled. "Take off one earring, then put it back on."

Guests arrived in a bunch, all in high spirits, most concealing their disappointment that the Georgia mystery writer was unable to attend. Eric was doing well, Debbie thought as he finished his talk—with no signal from Nora to cut it short—and began to accept questions.

Despite the cluster of guests who surrounded him after the question session, he seemed eager to talk with her, Debbie noted in astonishment. His eyes kept seeking her out. Probably because Nora had told him the extent of her own reading in the mystery field. But wouldn't he be amazed, she asked herself with sardonic humor, if he knew the basis of her omnivorous reading? In that special corner of her mind that was ever alert, she stored away bits of detective lore that might one day tell her how Scott's murderer managed to escape detection. Even Mom believed she constantly read mystery novels for diversion.

When the last guest had left and she and Debbie were disposing of the debris, Nora teased Debbie about Eric's obvious interest in her.

"Nora, don't be ridiculous." Debbie felt her face grow warm. "He's a kid. Hardly thirty," she guessed. "And you know I wouldn't be interested even if he was older."

"He's having a few people over—mystery buffs like us—for a buffet supper Sunday evening. I accepted for us. Now how could I say 'no' after he saved my neck tonight?" she challenged when Debbie grew wide-eyed with reproach. "Besides, it'll be good for you. You live in such a male-less world."

"I like my world!" Debbie said defiantly.

"I'm not telling you to get married again," Nora pointed out. "But it's fun to play a little."

Debbie was startled to realize that she was looking forward to the buffet supper at Eric James's apartment. The wine and cheese party had been fun, she conceded. For the past dozen years—ever since Scott's murder—she'd avoided socializing as much as possible. Nora had dragged her into the feminist group and she liked that. Mom insisted on her attending occasional synagogue parties and local benefit dinners, but she always contrived to leave early. She couldn't leave Nora's wine and cheese party early—she'd been co-hostess. She hadn't wanted to leave.

Nora drove by Sunday evening to pick her up. Debbie knew her mother was surprised but pleased that she was going to a buffet supper at Eric James's apartment.

"He's Miss Betsy Freeman's great-nephew," Nora explained to Fran while Debbie conferred with Diane about homework.

"Oh, Miss Betsy was my mother's friend." Fran's smile was warm. "Such a sweet lady."

"She's been nervous about being alone in that big old house," Nora said. "You know, since those five women were killed right here in Bellevue—"

"But the murderer was caught," Debbie pointed out. "He's serving time now."

"She's still nervous." Nora exchanged a sympathetic smile with Fran. "So when Eric wrote that he was leaving New York to teach in Atlanta, she insisted on fixing up a little apartment for him."

"We'd better leave, Nora," Debbie said, checking her watch. "I hate being the last to arrive."

"Usually people say, 'I hate to be the first to arrive,' " Nora chuckled. "But yeah, let's move."

Several guests were there already, the conversation animated. Eric introduced them to the others, then dashed off at a summons from the kitchen. His apartment was small but charming, Debbie thought, approving the preponderance of bookcases in the living room. While Nora allowed herself to be involved in an argument between two other guests about the place of women in the mystery field, she began to inspect the titles of the books.

"Nora tells me you were born in New York." Eric's voice intruded. She glanced up with a smile.

"Yes, but we moved to Bellevue when I was eight. My sister Lynne lives up there. She went to law school in New York—at Columbia."

"She's a lawyer?"

"No, she left at the end of her first year to get married. Later she went back for some education courses. She teaches now, at a private school on the Upper West Side."

"Does she like teaching?" Eric appeared genuinely interested, Debbie thought.

"I don't think she's mad about it. But it's a job with some perks." Did anybody end up doing what they'd planned for their lives? "What about you?" Debbie was curious.

"I love teaching. Oh, there're pros and cons in every job." He shrugged this aside. "But the pros outweigh the cons."

"My father was a lawyer. At least, he'd just graduated law school when he died. He'd had the determination to go back to school when he was almost thirty because he wanted so much to be a lawyer."

"My parents expected me to go to law school. They were furious when I settled for teaching. But then I rarely do anything that meets with their approval." He managed a sardonic smile. "You loved your father very much."

"Oh yes. He was a wonderful man. My mother's a wonderful woman. Our family has always been close."

"You're so lucky," he said gently. Scott's reaction to their family, Debbie realized with a start. "I envy you."

"Eric, have you finished reading the new Stanley Ellin?" somebody called from across the room. "May I borrow it?"

Debbie was startled to find herself drawn into the small group that came together often in Eric's apartment. He made a habit now of inviting several friends for Sunday evening buffet suppers.

"It's so easy. My aunt has her cook do everything. All I have to do is pour the wine."

It was an eclectic group—some university people, Debbie and Nora, a new doctor in town, a woman from the *Bellevue Enquirer*. The conversation ranged from mystery novels to politics to religion. There was much talk now about the possibility of a woman—Margaret Thatcher—becoming Britain's first prime minister. Debbie and Nora avidly followed the developments.

"You have to know that Eric is mad about you," Nora told Debbie on a magnificent April evening when they were driving away from one of his Sunday buffet suppers.

"Nora, stop being such a romantic!" All at once she was upset. She didn't want to lose Eric's friendship. It had become important to her. "There's no room in my life for anything like that."

"Make room." Nora was brusque.

"What about all that fine talk of yours?" Debbie challenged. " 'A woman can have a full life without a man. This is 1979!' "

"Eric is special," Nora said softly. "You could have something great with him."

"You make him understand I don't want anything but friendship from him. He's fun. I like being with him. As a friend," she emphasized. *"Nothing more."*

Fran was pleased to see Debbie's social life expanding. She wasn't dating anyone, Fran acknowledged—but she was emerging from that male-less world of hers that consisted of her feminist group meetings, movies and dinners with Nora, and the women she met at the office during business hours.

Now Fran contemplated reviving the "Paris original" promotion that she had done in earlier years. Craig encouraged her to go to Paris. It would always be special for them. And the timing was right, he told her. The doctors had decided that more surgery was indicated for Joyce.

"Go to Paris," he urged her. "That's about when Joyce will be into the hospital. I'll be tied down to her every minute." And he'd be exhausted from Joyce's petty demands, her constant recriminations, Fran knew. "We'll have no time to be together. And you need some relaxation."

Fran launched a plan to take Lynne and the three girls with her for a week in Paris and another week in London. Debbie insisted she must remain with the business. *"Mom, we can't both go flying off."* But Jessie refused to go.

"Mom, it's a wonderful gift for us. I can't understand Jessie—I never understand her," Lynne confessed in a phone call. "But that won't keep me home. Jessie will stay with her father—I'm going with you."

"Did she say why she wanted to stay?" Fran was puzzled. "Is she going out to Fire Island as a mother's helper again?"

"I think she's hoping Arnie will work out some deal to go out with her to play small club dates. All she talks about is her singing. My God, Mom, she's only fifteen years old! She's a baby."

On schedule Fran and Diane left Atlanta on a nearly morning flight. With an active thirteen-year-old curiosity Diane pelted her grandmother with questions to which she already knew the answers but enjoyed hearing them again. If she had accomplished nothing else in her life, Fran told herself, she'd been able to provide her daughters and granddaughters with security and some luxuries.

"I can't believe I'm going to see New York and London and Paris!" Diane bubbled. "Jessie's nuts not to go with us!" But Diane was not disappointed that Jessie wasn't going, Fran suspected.

From LaGuardia Airport in New York Fran and Diane headed by taxi for the Essex House. *"Where you always stay, Grandma!"* Without bothering to unpack they hurried downstairs when Lynne called to say she was in the lobby. There was much to be crowded into today and tomorrow. Tomorrow night they'd be on a flight to London.

Jessie stopped in at her father's favorite Chinese take-out to pick up dinner. Mom and the others were en route to JFK for their night flight to Heathrow. Daddy gave her money when he'd left this morning to buy Chinese. He said it was too damn hot to cook—not that he ever did. When Mom was away, they ate Chinese or deli.

He hadn't come home to see them off, she recalled with amusement. He'd thrown some crap about an important backers' meeting. Didn't he know that his music was twenty years behind the times? So he had one song that was almost a hit—that didn't make a career.

She was glad she and Daddy would be alone tonight. She'd waited three days for this chance to talk with him without Mom butting in. She wanted him to go into a studio with her to record her newest song. She felt a rush of excitement as she visualized the clipping from *Billboard* tucked away in her purse: GOODRICH, LANE, AND CARMINE SEEK NEW YOUNG SINGER.

That was the hotshot ad agency that was packaging a new TV variety show to debut this fall. Mom would have a fit if she even talked about trying out for it. Mom and her narrow little mind, she mocked scornfully. All that mattered to her was that they paid their bills on time and that she could go down to Bellevue twice a year.

Daddy lived back in the Sixties. When was he going to admit that the kind of music he wrote was long dead? Nobody sang folk rock anymore. Nobody cared about "issues." They wanted to hear music they could dance to! Mom was a nut not to make him go back to being an accountant. Then they wouldn't have to live in their crappy apartment. If Daddy was working, they could move. She and Beth wouldn't have to share a room. Beth was so square.

She heard her father at the piano while she slid the key into their apartment lock. He was still fussing around with that dumb musical, still sure he'd get an Off-Broadway production.

"Hi, babe—" He glanced up from the piano. "I'm starving. Pull a couple of sodas out of the fridge and let's eat."

Jessie waited until they'd finished eating and she'd put away the remains of the Chinese for a later *nosh.* Her father sprawled on the couch with a copy of *Cash Box.*

"Daddy, I need to talk to you," she said with devious sweetness and settled herself on the hassock before the club chair.

"Did you see the way Bonnie Lane's new single is climbing up the charts?" Arnie asked, his eyes belligerent. "I broke the ice for the little bitch, and what did she do to me?"

"Did you read this week's *Billboard?*"

"How could I?" he drawled. "You've had it stashed in your room."

"Goodrich, Lane, and Carmine are packaging a new TV variety show for a client. They're looking for a new girl singer. An unknown," Jessie emphasized. "Go into a studio with me and let me do a 'demo.' That's what they want before interviews." She ignored his incredulous stare. "I need a 'demo' to submit to the agency."

"Are you off your rocker? You're a fifteen-year-old kid! You—"

"They don't say anything about age," she pointed out impatiently. "Anyhow, I can pass for eighteen. It doesn't have to be a big studio. One of the cheapos. I can pay for it with my baby-sitting money." Her smile was expectant, pleading.

"Honey, you'll be wasting your money. You know how many singers—with lots of experience—who'll be sending in 'demos'?"

"I want to do it, Daddy." She abandoned the diplomatic approach for defiance. "I have the money."

"I'm busy right now," he hedged.

"We go into a studio and do it in half an hour. So you'll watch a half hour less of television," she challenged.

"It's nutty—" He paused. She waited, anticipating capitulation. "Maybe you could do three of my numbers from the new musical. You have to do at least three to—"

"Daddy, I don't want to do your songs." She geared for battle. He figured she'd never make it, but he'd have a showcase for his songs. "Three of *my* songs." Including the new one he'd never heard. He'd blow his stack, of course, when he heard the sexy lyrics.

"Are you out of your mind?" His voice was harsh, blending anger with shock. "If you have a chance at all, it'll be with my songs. Look what I did for Bonnie Lane. I—"

"That was a fluke," she dismissed it. "Bonnie's doing New Wave now. That's what's pushing her up the charts."

"She's doing punk—and punk is shit!" he shouted.

"It sells records," she shot back. "And it's not punk."

"Punkers are no-talent jerks—they have no musical training." Arnie ignored the fact that punk had given way to New Wave—which was far more commercial. "They write so simple, just a few chords and a lot of noise!"

"I'm talking about Patti Smith, the Ramones, the Talking Heads! Look at Blondie! Their new album is a smash hit!" Maybe she ought to go blond, Jessie thought in a corner of her mind. "Daddy, New Wave is where the action is!"

"If you do a 'demo,' it's with numbers I approve." He was on his feet now. His face flushed, his eyes blazing. "None of that New Wave shit you've been playing with. That's final!"

"You don't know what's going on in the music world!" she shrieked and stalked from the room.

She wasn't giving up on making the "demo," she vowed, flinging herself across her bed. Then all at once she knew how to do this. *She didn't need Daddy.* She could accompany herself on the guitar. It would have been nice to have him play for her—but maybe it would be even better if she sang her own numbers with a guitar background.

Daddy knew a lot of people, she fumed in fresh frustration. He could help her if he wanted to. He always said, "It's not just your talent that counts—it's who you know in the business."

She knew somebody. She felt a dizzy surge of triumph. Bill Raines. He was in advertising. He didn't know it yet—but he was going to open doors for her!

Forty-Three

Jessie told herself she had to get cracking before her mother and Beth came home. Mom—with all her questions, all her rules—could screw things up. Yet instinct told her she must do everything just right. She dismissed her father's reminder that hundreds of girl vocalists—with real experience—would be making tapes to submit to the TV Director at Goodrich, Lane, and Carmine. She was hot. Her songs were hot.

She plotted her course. The first deal was to make her tape. It was okay to go into a cheap studio without fancy equipment, she comforted herself. You didn't need that for punk or New Wave. Still, she wanted to work on the songs. Now—once her father was out of the house—she focused on revising the three numbers she'd chosen to tape. Nobody could say she was scared to work hard, she thought defiantly. And Daddy wouldn't have a chance to censor her lyrics.

Five days after her confrontation with her father—who pretended to ignore her rejection of his music—Jessie prepared for the taping. She wouldn't just go up to that dingy studio with her guitar and sing. She had to dress the part, too. She had to *feel* the music.

From a classmate who was grounded for daring to go to a disco on the last day of school, she borrowed a red vinyl miniskirt—despite the summer heat—and spike heel shoes. With it she'd wear black patterned stockings.

Before she'd finished the first number, she knew she was on the right track. The guy at the controls was so hot he was almost popping out of his pants. It wasn't just the way she looked, she decided in triumph—it was what she sang and how she sang it.

With her tape hidden away in her lingerie drawer, Jessie dug out the Raines's phone number from her address book. With any luck at all he'd be in the city. He only went out to their Fire Island cottage on week-ends—except when his wife was away, she remembered. They hadn't called her to go out with them this summer. She suspected Bill made sure that didn't happen. He'd got real nervous after their nights of partying.

She exhaled in relief when her father phoned to tell her to run down to buy cold cuts at the deli for dinner.

"I have to see these people down in the East Village about a possible playhouse for rent." Now Daddy had this great brainstorm about doing a production Off-Off-Broadway. Even that took backing. Where did he expect to raise it? "If we can work out a low budget, my partner might get the money from his in-laws." Oh, sure—she'd heard that before.

"What about franks and beans?" she asked.

"Sure thing," Arnie approved. "I'll eat when I get home."

Jessie hung up, then dialed the Raines's number. She was just about to concede that he wasn't home when Bill Raines picked up.

"Hello."

"Hi," she drawled. "This is Jessie Alexander." She heard his sharp intake of breath. "Remember me?"

"Sure, Jess," he said quickly. "We didn't take on a mother's helper this summer. My kid sister-in-law came out to stay with us." She heard the constraint in his voice.

"I wasn't free anyway," she said. "What I'm calling about is for some advice. I know you're in advertising, and there's this deal at Goodrich, Lane, and Carmine—"

"That's my agency," he said, sounding startled. Wow, what luck! All at once she was churning with excitement. "What kind of deal?" She could sense his wariness now.

"There's this search for an unknown vocalist. I read about it in *Bill-board.* I—"

"That's the TV department," he broke in. "I don't have anything to do with that."

"I'm good, Bill. I don't expect you to know that. I just want you to make sure my tape is heard by—" She paused, reached for the article from *Billboard.* "By Tom Henderson."

"Oh. Sure, I can do that."

"I'll want a letter from Mr. Henderson to make sure you haven't forgotten to give it to him," she said pointedly. Not trusting Bill. "He doesn't have to know I'm only fifteen. Last summer—when we partied—I was fourteen. You wouldn't want anybody to know about that, would you?" Because she was what Daddy called "jailbait." Bill got the message.

"Hey, kid, who'd believe you?" But he was unnerved.

"Do you want to find out?" she challenged. She held her breath for a loaded moment. Let him bite.

"Leave the tape with the receptionist at the agency," he said tersely. "Addressed to me. I'll get it to Henderson. It may take a while before he writes—but I'll see that he does." *He was pissed—but scared.*

"You do that," she said sweetly. Triumph made her giddy.

He was scared shitless. Even if he didn't get sent up for rape, he'd see his career go down the drain. He figured she was wild enough to go through with that threat. No doubt in her mind that the tape would win her an audition, she was already planning what she would wear.

In the drive home from the airport, Fran allowed her thoughts to roam. How was Craig holding up under this latest siege? She was constantly with Lynne and the girls. There hadn't been a moment when she could call him—but he'd expected that.

On the front seat with her mother, Diane was talking with her usual jet speed—impatient to report every delicious detail of her first trip to New York, London, and Paris.

"I'm almost sure we saw Martha Gelhorn in London! I mean, I've seen lots of pictures of her—" Diane's voice was reverent. She was fascinated by the exploits of the famous American journalist.

"I remember when your mother was fascinated by Martha Gelhorn—" Fran felt a warm glow of recall. "I remember when *I* was enthralled with her. Back when she was in Spain, covering the Spanish Civil War for *Collier's*. Nobody wrote as excitingly about the fight between communism and fascism. I think I would have sold my soul to the Devil to be there." But she'd been only a journalism student—and once out of college she'd married Bernie.

"She was at the D-Day invasion," Debbie recalled. Before her time, Fran thought tenderly, but Debbie had researched Gelhorn at the college library. "She was there at the liberation of Dachau—"

"And she was in Vietnam!" Diane swung around in her seat to face her grandmother. "Remember all the work I did for that school paper last term?"

"Of course I do."

At the house Debbie helped her mother and Diane with their luggage, then headed back to the office. Lily and Betty Mae rushed out to welcome Fran and Diane. The atmosphere was warm and convivial.

In the privacy of her bedroom Fran called Craig on his private line and waited eagerly for him to pick up.

"Hello—" A faint urgency in his voice told her he'd been waiting to hear from her.

"We're back," Fran effervesced. "I loved London and Paris, but it's good to be home."

"I missed you, Fran—"

"I couldn't call," she apologized, though she knew he understood. "Either Lynne or one of the girls was always around." She hesitated. "How did things go?"

"The doctors are pleased with the surgery. Joyce responded well. Of course, she made life hell for the hospital staff," Craig admitted. "Especially when she discovered the head nurse on her floor was black. A fine woman and a dedicated nurse—but Joyce is such a racist."

"You're not responsible for that, Craig." But she understood how he felt. He was always striving to make sure Josh and Zach didn't pick up their mother's racism.

"She's coming home tomorrow. There'll be practical nurses around the clock for three or four weeks. If they'll stay with her," he added wryly.

"I'm going into the office this afternoon," Fran told him.

"And you call me a workaholic?" he jibed.

"Could we have a late lunch? I'm not entirely a workaholic." Unexpectedly she chuckled. "I'm spreading the word around that I'm considering an investment in real estate. I need to discuss this with my architect."

"Tell me when and where," he said. "I need your special brand of resuscitation."

Driving to the restaurant to meet Craig, Fran thought about the two days she'd spent in New York—on her usual summer buying trek—after the two glorious weeks in London and Paris. Arnie appeared to have simmered down. Probably because he missed Lynne, she decided—or was it that he missed having his meals prepared, his house cleaned, his clothes laundered?

Her face softened as she remembered Beth's delight when she offered—"as your birthday present this year"—to pay for singing lessons. Beth was serious about her music. She was already talking about studying at Juilliard in the future. Lynne tried to alibi Jessie's arrogance, but it was difficult to like her oldest granddaughter. She loved Jessie, of course—but she didn't like her. But then Lynne was probably right when she said Jessie was going through the pains of early adolescence.

As always Fran was glad when the oppressive Georgia summer segued into autumn. Now she was giving genuine thought to expanding into real estate. Her father had always said that real estate was a good investment. And it provided legitimate reasons for her to spend time with Craig.

It was Robin who told her he'd seen Debbie with Nora and a young man at a favorite local restaurant twice in the past few weeks.

"I don't think Debbie saw me," Robin said archly. "She seemed all wrapped up in that young guy."

"I know she'd gone out for dinner with Nora," Fran acknowledged. "He must be involved in Nora's wine and cheese parties for mystery buffs. I think she mentioned someone from Emory who was being very helpful." At times she worried about Debbie's obsession for mystery novels. Diane, too, was becoming an avid mystery buff. In some tortuous way, she suspected, Debbie was drawn to murder cases that were solved. She'd never stopped blaming herself for not tracking down Scott's killer.

True, she was eager for Debbie to go out again—yet fearful that she might be hurt. Debbie was so vulnerable. Sometimes, Fran thought, she was convinced there was some curse on herself and her daughters when it came to the men in their lives.

Jessie waited with a blend of excitement, alarm, and defiance for her imminent audition for Tom Henderson. Twice he'd been called out of town and auditions were canceled. But he'd liked her "demo"—he'd agreed to an audition, she stoked her now shaky confidence. She'd had to race home from school every day at lunchtime for weeks to catch the mail before her mother or father saw the letters. Saturdays—when both were home—had been a bitch.

Now she pretended to study for a French exam while Beth sprawled across the other bed and focused on algebra. The letter from Tom Henderson was a form letter, she forced herself to acknowledge. But he thought she was good enough to see and hear her in person. That meant something. The new audition was scheduled for tomorrow at 11 A.M.

She'd cut classes, carry her audition clothes in her book bag and change in the ladies' room at Altman's. She'd take her guitar—but Mom would think it was for some after-school activity. She'd been rehearsing like a maniac on the audition material—and the "look." This was her big chance. She mustn't screw it up!

When Altman's opened the next morning, Jessie was waiting at the Fifth Avenue entrance. Carrying her guitar case, she walked into the store looking a fifteen-year-old schoolgirl, complete with schoolbag in tow. Thirty-five minutes later she walked out of the Madison Avenue entrance—convenient to the ad agency offices—appearing a voluptuous young sexpot.

Her parents would never allow her to wear the jeans that hugged her curvaceous rump so tightly the coveted designer label—so important to this era's teenagers—appeared engraved on her rear. They would have paled at the sight of her in the white angora sweater minus bra, the turtle neckline demure but the net results blatantly sexy. Her denim jacket hung loose.

She strode out into the autumn sunlight with an insouciant smile meant to disguise her incipient stage fright. This wasn't like singing for some small lodge group or a summer bungalow colony audience. *This was network TV.*

She walked out of the elevator into the sprawling reception room of Goodrich, Lane, and Carmine and froze for a moment at the sight of the girls seated on the array of smoky blue sofa and chairs that fanned out against the wall on either side of the receptionist's desk. All of them much older than herself, wearing smart suits and much jewelry. Jessie assumed the briefcases and totes contained their music.

Almost immediately her sharp mind told her this was good. She'd stand out in this bunch. They'd stressed they wanted a *new* young singer. These chicks were carbon copies of one another. Confidence surged in her as she approached the receptionist's desk and gave her name.

"Mr. Henderson's running behind schedule," the receptionist said, checking the names on a notepad. "You'll be called in your turn."

"Thank you." Jessie smiled and went to a chair.

She slid out of her jacket and draped it across her knees. She was conscious of covert inspection by the others. They figured she was no competition. This was TV, not some disco audition where at her age she'd be barred. She even sensed an arrogance, scorn. Not one of them was hip, she thought with retaliatory arrogance. The item in *Billboard* had said the projected package was "looking toward the new decade." Disco was hot—and TV picked up what was hot.

Jessie was surprised by the swiftness with which girls were being taken into Henderson's inner sanctum and then ushered out. New candidates were arriving. She hadn't expected so many to be auditioned. She was the only one lugging a guitar. Again, her confidence lagged.

An hour and five minutes after she'd strolled out of the elevator, she was summoned by the miniskirted blonde delegated to escort girls to the audition room. Jessie rose, picked up her guitar—leaving her jacket on the chair—and followed the blonde down a maze of halls.

"In here, please," the blonde ordered crisply.

With a rehearsed smile that was both demure and sexy Jessie walked into the room, set up as a studio. A pianist sat before a small piano in one corner. Three Brooks Brothers-suited men and an expensively dressed woman in her thirties sat behind a table. She paused, waiting for direction.

"Jessica Alexander?" the woman asked.

"Yes," Jessie said.

"Tell us a little about yourself," the man whom she guessed was Tom Henderson instructed.

"I'm a high school senior," she began. "I've been singing for four years at lodges and small clubs in Brooklyn and Queens," she fabricated. "I'm definitely a new singer," she added flippantly. "I write my own material—and I accompany myself on the guitar." She sounded breathy but sexy, she decided. And she felt an aura of interest in the four sitting at the table.

"All right," the man she assumed was Henderson ordered. "Show us what you do in person."

She knew before she'd finished singing that something important was happening in this room. She felt the electricity her performance had elicited.

"Okay, we want to see how you appear on the TV screen," the woman said after some murmured conversation at the table. "Come with me and I'll set up a test date for you."

Jessie was confident even before her TV test the following afternoon that she was a leading contender. After the test she was taken back to Tom Henderson's office for more conversation.

"We like you," he said casually. "But for TV you'll have to clean up your material. Not the performance," he emphasized, his eyes telling her they wanted her to exude sex. "We want to hear you with new material that won't get us blasted off the air. How soon can you have it?"

She thought for an instant—her heart pounding. "In a week." She enjoyed their air of surprise. They didn't know how fast she could work when it was important. Another date was set up. Jessie prepared to leave.

"Oh, by the way," Henderson asked casually. "Do you have an agent?"

"Yes," she said immediately. The names of several agents her father had mentioned in the past darted across her brain. But not one of them, she rejected. His favorite word—penny-ante—popped up. "Charles Mazur," she lied. Charles Mazur was big time. He handled important TV personalities. "I didn't mention my audition with you. I figured it was too early for that."

"Okay," Henderson said. "We'll be in touch with him when the time to talk contract arrives."

Dizzy with excitement, Jessie left the office. This was just so much playacting. *She* was their new young singer. Okay, chase over to Mazur's office and tell him he had a new client. He wasn't going to turn her down when he knew she was up for a big deal like this. She wouldn't be turned aside by some kooky receptionist. She'd get through to Charles Mazur.

For the next few days Jessie cut classes with regularity. She got through to her supposed agent. Mazur had been skeptical until he talked with Tom Henderson. Then he knew she could become a hot property. He was talking terms with the agency, working with her on her material.

"Okay," he told her briskly at a late afternoon meeting. "They're talking more money. It's still small potatoes, but you'll have a foot in the door. They know we can't afford to turn it down." In her mind what they'd originally offered had seemed big bucks. He eyed her curiously. "How old are you?"

She sighed. She'd known this was coming.

"Fifteen," she admitted. "But I always tell everybody I'm eighteen and a high school senior."

Charles broke into laughter. "That's a switch. I've got a twenty-eight-year-old singer—already in the big time—who swears she's nineteen." Now he was serious. "You'll have to have a parent sign your contracts since you're underage. I need to talk with one of them."

"Sure. I'll set it up." Jessie was nonchalant.

"You may be the sexiest fifteen-year-old on record." Charles was in high good humor. "Baby, that'll buy us a lot of publicity."

———

Jessie sat cross-legged on the living-room hassock and tried to explain to her parents what had been happening.

"Are you sure she isn't running a fever, Lynne?" Arnie asked without moving his eyes from Jessie. She saw shock, disbelief, and something almost like rage in his eyes.

"She wouldn't lie about something like this." Yet her mother seemed shaken.

"You're really going to sing on television?" Beth was euphoric. "Wow, wait'll I tell the kids at school!"

"Daddy, you have to sign my contract." Jessie was the wide-eyed, demure daughter now. "Because I'm a minor. Charles Mazur said that—"

"Charles Mazur?" Arnie interrupted, his voice harsh in amazement. "You got Charles Mazur to represent you?"

"He wasn't about to turn down a good commission." Ever the chameleon Jessie was realistic now. "And he sees lots more coming in. Daddy, I'm going to be a major star." Her self-assurance seemed to shatter him.

"Jessie, you have to finish school," Lynne insisted.

"I'll finish high school," Jessie soothed. At least, Mom wasn't falling apart like Daddy. "Charles is lining up some professional children's school deal." He winced at her using the agent's first name. "But forget about college. Who needs it?"

"I thought you wanted to go to Juilliard." Beth was reproachful. "I mean, if you could get in."

"Beth, don't be a kook! I don't need that now—I'm getting a contract to sing on a new network program."

"First I have to approve the contract," Arnie reminded. "I'll call Charles Mazur and set up an appointment."

"Daddy, you'll approve," Jessie drawled. "After all, remember your commission as my personal manager."

He wasn't happy about her landing a contract, she thought. *He was jealous.*

Forty-Four

F ran was astonished, proud, yet uneasy about Jessie's sudden success. A spot on a network TV show was impressive. Jessie's aggressiveness in landing it was something Fran would normally admire. But she harbored inchoate fears about how Jessie would handle her sudden celebrity.

First planned to premiere late in the year, the initial program was scheduled to be seen in early February. Lynne sent a rash of clippings from trade newspapers that dealt with "Charles Mazur's rising young star." *"Jess Alexander, Riveting Young Singer Destined for Stardom,"* read the description beneath her photograph in a national magazine. There was talk now of a recording contract. The TV appearances would be major in this.

Lynne wrote that Arnie—after some initial opposition—had thrown himself into handling Jessie's career.

"He's pushed aside everything else. He's lined up a great publicist to handle her. Even though she has a terrific agent, he went over her contract word for word, insisted on some important changes. And he's set up a bank to be in charge of her earnings." That, Fran realized, was necessary by law. "This whole scene is absolutely incredible."

On a rainy Friday evening late in February Fran rushed home from a dinner with a group of her store managers, in town for a conference. She was determined to reach the house before 9 P.M., when the new variety series in which Jessie had a featured spot was to premiere. Jessie wouldn't appear until midway, but she was eager to see the credits at the beginning of the program. Millions of people would be watching *her* granddaughter.

With moments to spare, Fran pulled into the driveway and hurried into the house without bothering to put the car in the garage.

"Grandma, I was scared you wouldn't get here in time!" Bright-eyed with excitement Diane hovered at the living-room entrance. "The program starts in a minute!"

"We're all so thrilled." Nora smiled up at Fran. "I think most of the town is watching tonight. This is Lynne's daughter—that makes her our celebrity."

"Where's Debbie?" Fran glanced about the room.

"Right here, Mom—" Debbie walked into the living room with a tray. "Lily made a chocolate mousse cake. She'll be here with coffee in a moment."

"Sssh!" Diane ordered. "It's on!"

Lynne hadn't told her, Fran thought—not wanting to upset her, but she'd told Debbie that she was furious over the image the publicist for the program and Jessie's personal publicist were building around her. Arnie kept saying it was "commercial"—they had to go along with it.

"Look, the kid's on her way to building a terrific trust fund," Robin had comforted when she discussed this with him. But at the same time, Fran remembered, he'd warned that one thirteen-week series didn't mean Jessie was on the road to stardom.

"When will Jessie be on?" Diane demanded impatiently.

"Not until the middle of the program," Fran soothed.

How was Beth taking all this? Fran asked herself anxiously. Arnie had always made such a fuss over Jessie—and now he was managing her career. He was probably carrying on about Jessie's singing every minute he was home. Did Beth feel left out?

There were only fifteen months between Jessie and Beth, yet they might have been years apart. Beth was still a sweet little girl—like Diane. Jessie's sudden success didn't bother Diane, Fran thought with relief—she didn't feel threatened. But Beth, too, yearned for a career in singing. If Jessie continued on this upward spiral how would it affect Beth?

In New York Beth sat close to the television set—ignoring her mother's frequent plea not to "sit right on top of the TV." Mom had wanted her to go with them to watch the program with the agency people. There would be a big party afterward. She'd hate being there with all those strangers and then at the party.

Everybody from school must be watching tonight, she thought with a mixture of pride and wistfulness. She never told anybody that she didn't like Jessie's kind of music. She loved show tunes, like the songs from *My Fair Lady* and *Sound of Music*.

Jessie said if she got a record contract, she could do the kind of songs she couldn't get away with on television. *"Record people won't care if I write wild lyrics. They don't worry about censorship."* Jessie loved to shock people. She spent half her time dreaming up kooky stunts—and Daddy backed her up.

She frowned in thought—ignoring the early portion of the program. She'd felt sick last night when Jessie and Daddy started screaming at each other because he wanted her to take some of his songs to the director of the program and she said "no." Mom had got all upset, too. Didn't he understand Jessie would never do that?

All at once she sat at attention. Jessie was coming on.

Fran rose from her chair and switched off the TV. The program was over. From what Lynne had said, they knew Jessie wouldn't come on again. But Diane had insisted they watch to the very end. No doubt about it, Fran thought—Jessie's performance had been dynamic, the best portion of the program.

"You know," Diane intruded on Fran's musing, "I think Jessie's missing a lot of fun. I mean, she's going to that school for professional kids and worrying about things kids shouldn't have to worry about—like did the show get a good rating, and will it be renewed? I don't think I'd want to grow up that fast."

"You won't have to," Debbie said. "I'd never push you, Sugar."

"Lynne didn't push Jessie," Fran said defensively. "She engineered this whole deal all on her own."

Late in the evening Lynne called. "What a crazy night. It's all so unreal. Already Arnie's pushing Jessie's agent to get a recording contract."

"It all sounds so exciting. Everything's happening so fast." Lynne was right. It was unreal.

"Arnie had this crazy idea about personal appearances at Studio Fifty-four or another of the fancy discos, but I reminded him she wouldn't be allowed there at her age. Now Arnie and Jessie are talking about our moving into some fancy apartment on Central Park South. Mom, they're so unrealistic. This whole thing could collapse into nothing at the end of the series!" Lynne, thank God, had her feet on the ground.

Fran awoke the following morning with an instant sense of tension. Her sleep last night had been haunted by images of Jessie cavorting about the TV screen.

Fran lingered for another few minutes in the cozy warmth of her bedroom. She considered the day that lay ahead. This morning Joyce was flying to Palm Beach, she remembered. With a hired companion. Her sister had refused to accompany her on this trip. Craig said his sister-in-law told him never to ask her again.

"I can't blame her," Craig admitted. "Why should she put up with Joyce's moods? Even Josh and Zach avoid coming home." Josh was a senior at Columbia, Zach a freshman at Emory.

Fran's face softened as she recalled Craig's pleasure in Zach's sudden decision to go on to architectural school.

"What was he going to do with a philosophy major?" Craig had been admittedly anxious. "As an architect he has a profession."

Times were changing, Fran mused as she stalled on arising. She and Craig had grown up in the Depression—they would never lose their memories of the deprivation suffered by so much of the country—by so much of the world. To them security was vital. Today everybody seemed to be living for the present. Thank God that Jessie's earnings would be monitored by the courts. Arnie could not go completely crazy.

Tonight she'd be having dinner with Craig and Robin—and later Craig and she would go to the cottage. She wished they dared to stay overnight, but that was too dangerous. Still, she'd spend precious hours alone with Craig. Happiness came in sweet, small parcels, she thought. It was greedy to expect more.

Fran remained at the office until close to seven o'clock—involved in phone conferences with two branch managers. Debbie had left an hour earlier. They made a point that at least one of them would sit down to dinner with Diane each night. Let Diane know she had a family.

Fran closed up the office and drove to the restaurant. Craig was there already. Robin was notorious for being late, but neither she nor Craig was upset by this.

"You're looking relaxed," Fran approved when she was seated across the table from Craig.

"It's my vacation, too." His voice was tender. "How does the grandmother of the new television vocalist feel today?"

"Concerned," Fran admitted. "I know young success is supposed to be marvelous, but I worry about her. Jessie's—difficult to understand. Lynne's going to have her hands full."

"You're not to spend a moment of tonight worrying about family," Craig ordered. "Let's be selfish and think just of ourselves. There's an important architectural conference in New York in July. Plan your buying trip then." His eyes were bright with anticipation.

"Craig, that'll be wonderful!" Even with her buying schedule they'd manage time together.

"I talked to Zach already. He'll manage to be home that week. As long as one of us is there, Joyce can't complain."

Robin arrived in high good humor. He'd just returned from five weeks in New York.

"The foundation can run itself without me," he drawled. "So why shouldn't I run off to enjoy myself?" From his effervescent air Fran gathered his new love affair was joyful. Each time, he hoped, this one would be for the rest of his life. "Now fill me in on what's been happening with Bellevue Estates."

They talked absorbedly about the small housing colony Fran was investing in and which Craig was designing.

While they lingered over coffee, Robin grew playful.

"I'll bet you don't know what's happening right under your eyes, Fran." His smile was impish.

"Robin, don't tease me," she ordered.

"I saw Debbie with that gorgeous young man again last night. And Nora wasn't with them."

"You mean Eric James?" Last night Debbie had not been home for dinner. She'd said something about helping Nora with the next wine and cheese party at the shop.

"That's right." Robin nodded in approval. "If I didn't know he was straight, I'd make a play for him myself." But he wouldn't, of course, Fran realized. Robin kept his personal life totally removed from Bellevue. "They looked all wrapped up in each other."

"Robin, you're in love with love," Fran jibed. "Debbie and Eric are all wrapped up in the latest mystery novel they've read." Nora must have had a last-minute change in plan, she surmised. Why shouldn't Debbie and Eric have had dinner without her?

"All right, let's break this up," Robin said a few minutes later. "I want to make a phone call to somebody special up in New York."

The three left in their separate cars. Fran followed Craig to their hideaway cottage. Debbie knew she saw a lot of Craig. Did she ever suspect there was more than business between them? Even now Fran felt a faint discomfort at this possibility.

Inevitably, the whole family became involved in Jessie's soaring career in the months ahead. She acquired a recording contract. She was to sing at an outdoor summer concert. In the fall she was signed to do a new TV series, "The Jess Alexander Show." Arnie had gone to court to pry more money loose from Jessie's burgeoning income.

"Arnie's yelling that Jessie has to live in circumstances becoming her position," Lynne reported tiredly when Fran was in New York in July—with Craig happily installed in a room at the Essex House across the hall from her own. "We're moving to seven rooms on Central Park South. I used to walk to school. Now I'll have to take a bus. Arnie's buying his clothes at Brooks Brothers. After all," she said scathingly, "he's Jess Alexander's personal manager. And Jessie is doing badly at school. She doesn't care, and Arnie doesn't care. Hopefully she'll graduate by the time she's eighteen. If not, she'll drop out."

"She has to finish high school!" Fran was shocked—already disturbed that Jessie rejected college.

"Nobody tells Jessie anything anymore. I try," Lynne admitted. "Like the ghastly clothes she buys. I tell her she can't wear a blouse cut down to her belly button, but she goes right ahead and wears it. I can't physically tie her down, Mom," she said in frustration. "She looks at me with that condescending look and says, 'Oh, Mom, you're so square.' "

When Jessie's new show premiered in late September, Fran decided to give a small dinner party. She was torn between pride in Jessie's celebrity and anxiety about Jessie's flamboyant behavior. Pride won. Robin and Nora were invited, along with several of the people from the office. At Nora's urging Debbie added Eric to the invitation list.

"Eric's been so helpful with the shop that Nora would like him to come," Debbie said, faintly self-conscious.

"By all means, let's have him," Fran agreed.

Robin had mentioned Eric to her a couple of times, Fran recalled; but he was given to outrageous exaggeration. She remembered his triumphant claims about how Debbie and Eric had seemed "all wrapped up in each other." Within minutes after Eric's arrival—with Nora—at their small dinner party, Fran knew that Eric was in love with Debbie. What a charming young man, she thought. Strikingly handsome, diffident, intelligent—and, somehow, vulnerable. She sensed, too, that he had been put on warning—that this was a friendship with Debbie and nothing more.

From Nora she learned that Eric was thirty-four. So Debbie was six years older, she thought with shaky optimism—that meant nothing these days. Yet she warned herself not to romanticize. Debbie still lived in Scott's shadow.

The table conversation was lively. Fran was pleased that Robin—always charming and witty—seemed to bring Eric out of what she'd sensed was an innate shyness. Though a Californian, Eric had gone to college and graduate school in New York and had taught there briefly at college level. The two men talked with affection about New York theater.

What a beautiful evening this would have been if Craig could have been here, Fran thought. But with Joyce's health still fragile she and Craig didn't socialize. On occasion Craig attended local benefits or synagogue affairs—explaining to Joyce that business demanded this. Joyce had become a bitter, angry recluse.

Watching the program after dinner, Fran recognized the excitement Jessie generated. She exuded sex without being blatantly overt, Fran analyzed. She poured forth the kind of energy exhibited by both Lynne and Debbie in earlier days. Her future seemed dazzlingly bright.

Fran waited for Lynne to phone her after the premiere. Lynne had warned they were going to a party given by the sponsor, so her call would be late. It was past midnight when the private line in her bedroom rang. Diane and Debbie were already asleep.

"Mom, am I calling too late?" Lynne asked anxiously.

"Darling, it's never too late for you to call. We had a small dinner party here and watched the program together. Jessie was spectacular. Were the sponsor and agency pleased?"

"Oh, ecstatic." Lynne suppressed a yawn. "They threw this huge bash afterwards at '21'. I even persuaded Beth to come—and you know how she hates big parties."

"How's my precious Beth?" Fran asked tenderly.

"Plugging away at her singing." Fran heard an uneasy undertone in Lynne's voice. "All this hooplah over Jessie is eating away at her self-confidence—"

"Beth wouldn't want to do Jessie's kind of singing." Fran tried for a casual note. "But yes, I imagine it is a trying time for her." She hesitated. "What can we do to make it easier?"

"Mom, you're always trying to make things right for all of us. We have to take the rough with the good."

"How's the new apartment?" Fran asked.

"We have a gorgeous view of Central Park. Jessie and Arnie chose all the furniture. After all, Jessie's money is paying for it." Her air of good humor was tinged with cynicism. "I know it's a beautiful apartment, but I feel like a stranger living here." Lynne's voice had dropped to a whisper. "I don't feel as though we're a family anymore. Beth and I are onlookers. Mom, do you understand what I'm saying?"

"I understand," Fran said, yearning to find words of comfort. "But that's because your lives have changed so drastically and so fast. Things will settle down, darling."

Fran worried constantly about Lynne's unhappiness. Jessie seemed determined to create shock waves—and Arnie fostered this, Lynne confided. For her seventeenth birthday party in February Arnie rented a private room at the Plaza rejecting her demands for a party at Studio 54. Except for Jessie and Beth the guests were all adults. Jessie had brushed off her few friends. And Arnie made sure the press was there to report the festivities.

"Arnie says it's worth spending all that money for the publicity," Lynne reported afterward. "But to me it seemed such a waste. And Arnie's going to have to explain that to the bank—"

"How's Jessie doing in school?"

"That's a joke, Mom," Lynne said impatiently. "I battled with her and Arnie. They finally agreed that she should have private tutoring. But I know she'll never go beyond high school. What'll happen when her career peters out? The way she's going, the bubble's got to burst. What will she do with the rest of her life?"

"When it does burst, she'll have a terrific bank account." Fran tried to be philosophical. "Jessie's bright. She'll manage her life." Right now, Fran thought, she was more concerned about Lynne's life. She'd been shocked to discover when she'd been in New York last month that Lynne and Arnie no longer shared a room.

Her real joy now, Fran acknowledged, was Diane's determination to earn a degree in journalism. In her youngest grandchild she saw the same ambition that had burned in her and later in Debbie. She found no genuine pleasure in Jessie's meteoric success. Beth seemed to be regaining her self-confidence, talked about going into the musical theater— "after Juilliard, if I get in."

She was astonished when—early in June—Robin withdrew from plans to accompany her to New York on her coming buying trip.

"Robin, you turning down a trip to New York?" she chided over a lunch at the Phipps Plaza Mall in Buckhead. "Are you all right?" she asked in sudden alarm. "You're not keeping something from me?"

"I'm trying to keep from *getting* something," he said grimly.

"Robin, what are you talking about?"

"I think I mentioned to you how I keep up with happenings in New York—I mean, in my special circle." Fran understood he meant his gay circle.

"Yes?" She waited for him to continue.

"Well, this gay newspaper—the *New York Native*—just ran an article by some doctor who says that the disease rumors in the gay community are unfounded, but I worry that—"

"What disease rumors?" she demanded, all at once cold with shock.

"That a lot of gays in New York are dying from some weird disease. Anyhow, I figure—even though there's no proof of some wild disease killing off gays, I should play it safe and stay out of New York—or San Francisco or Boston or Washington, D.C." Where there were large gay communities, Fran understood. "Why go looking for trouble?"

"You're smart, Robin. Stay away from that scene until this situation is cleared up."

"I'm trying to persuade Dennis to spend July with me in Bermuda. I'll pay," he said hopefully. Dennis was the young dancer he adored.

It was unnerving to believe that some germ or virus could be attacking one specific group of people. It was unnerving to think that Robin's life could be in danger. He was like the brother she'd never had. No matter that there were long-held suspicions in Bellevue that she and Robin were lovers.

Robin was a blessed cover for her relationship with Craig. Would there ever be a time when she was not obsessed by guilt over that? It wasn't wrong. Craig and Joyce shared nothing but a roof. What she and Craig shared was a marriage.

Forty-Five

B ringing dinner from the kitchen into the dining room, Lynne flinched at the sound of Jessie and Arnie's voices raised in argument.

"Daddy, Charles is great for television, but I need somebody else to handle record contracts and personal appearances. You have to tell him he's history except for TV!" Her eyes were defiant.

"How can I tell him you're dumping him?" Arnie was unnerved.

"You do it, or I will. And I'm not dumping him. He's okay for television. But look how he wanted me to go along with that contract with Cosmo Records the way it was drawn up. I would have had to pay for the session!" Not unknown in the record business, Lynne had heard Arnie say many times.

"But he persuaded them to do *mucho* publicity on the single even though it wasn't part of an album," Arnie said defensively. "And you know Cosmo never does that."

"*I* persuaded them," Jessie corrected. She'd thrown a series of temper tantrums, Lynne remembered—made threats. Still, she was sharp. She knew how to protect her interests. "And now the single is on the Top Ten!"

"Will you two please eat?" Lynne had discovered that survival these days meant not losing her cool when Jessie and Arnie battled. "When I take time on a school night to make lobster bisque I expect you to have it while it's hot." Actually, she'd made lobster bisque because Beth adored it. Beth sat at the table and ignored the battling. She was nibbling appreciatively at a warm chunk of French bread. But Lynne worried that often Beth felt left out. Talk in this household seemed to revolve around Jessie.

"Tell Charles, Daddy," Jessie repeated, soup spoon poised in midair. "I need somebody strong for my next record contract—and to book personal appearances. They're important."

"You're too young to work in clubs or discos." Arnie was sullen, Lynne noted—because more and more Jessie was calling the shots on her career.

"I won't be in five months," Jessie pointed out, her smile dazzling. "Look, I'm doing dance music. I need to be out in the discos. We have to start looking for dates."

"I'll try to make him understand," Arnie mumbled. His earlier euphoria at being Jessie's manager was evaporating, Lynne had observed. "I'll look around for somebody with the right contacts."

"Jessie," Beth broke in, "is it true that you're dating Michael Jackson?"

"That's crap the publicist tried to get into the columns." Jessie shrugged this off, then giggled. "If you know about it, I guess it did make the columns."

Lynne saw the covert glance Jessie shot in her father's direction. Arnie watched over her in that area, Lynne conceded. He was as stern as any Victorian father had been. But there were times when she wondered if Arnie was any match for Jessie.

Fran picked up Robin at his house for the drive to the construction site of Bellevue Estates. He was interested in seeing the layout of the second model house. He'd been depressed these weeks since he'd come back from Bermuda. She hoped to cheer him up. She'd suggested that the two of them have lunch with Craig after visiting the construction site.

"Isn't it a gorgeous day," Fran said while he joined her on the front seat of her new white Mercedes. Autumn was at its most lush, with the colors reminiscent of a Corot painting.

"I've picked up this damn cold," Robin complained. "It doesn't want to go away."

"Maybe you need an antibiotic." He did look tired, she thought sympathetically. "Why don't you go to the doctor?" But he'd probably go to that quack in Atlanta who kept prodding him to take vitamin supplements.

"I might." He sighed. "I don't know where the years are going. I gaze into the mirror, and I look so old, Fran."

"Robin, stop it," she scolded. "You never change." That's what Craig always said about Robin and her.

"I look at myself beside Dennis, and I *see*. I always thought of myself as Peter Pan—but it ain't so, my sweet." His effort at humor was shaky. Now his voice dropped to a whisper. "I'm forty-nine years old. Dennis is thirty-one."

"I'm sixty-five," Fran began.

"And you look a beautiful and elegant fifty," he told her. "Like Audrey Hepburn or Leslie Caron."

"You know, I was furious when I was reading this morning's paper and an article referred to some woman of sixty-five as being elderly." Amusement lit Fran's eyes. "Maybe seventy-five years ago, but not today. Oh, I know sixty-five is considered the age of retirement—but why waste those years after sixty-five?"

"Craig's a year older than you, isn't he?" Robin said, and Fran nodded. "And he gets more distinguished looking every year."

"I don't want to hear a word from you about getting old," Fran told Robin. "Because then you'll make me feel ancient." But she didn't, she thought. It ever astonished her that she had a daughter who was forty-three and another who was forty-one. The years didn't count, she analyzed. It was how you felt, how you used the years.

"Oh, God, I wish I could dump this cold," Robin said and reached for a tissue. "I'm never sick." But hypochondriacal tendencies sent him to Dr. Jackson at regular intervals. "I think I will go see Doctor Jackson."

"I wish you'd see some normal doctor," Fran said, but she knew he wouldn't.

Three days later Robin phoned to say that Dr. Jackson had put him on a special diet that included "gallons of yogurt."

"He says I just have an allergy problem," Robin reported, clearly in high spirits. "He gave me this diet and told me to stick to it."

"Then you do it," Fran said affectionately.

Robin chuckled. "I made the mistake of telling Peggy about it—I'll have no choice except to stick to it. Of course, I may cheat a little outside."

When his "allergy problem" hadn't cleared up by the first of the year, Robin allowed Fran to persuade him to see an allergist. He stalled on making an actual appointment with Dr. Bartell for a month. Dr. Bartell put him through weeks of tests, all of which proved negative. Dr. Bartell concluded that he was probably suffering from chronic bronchitis but ordered X-rays.

"I'm scared to death of lung cancer," Robin confessed to Fran over a hastily arranged lunch—meant to allay his nervousness. He was waiting to learn the results of his X-rays. "Remember, they thought Joyce had bronchitis at first."

"You don't smoke," Fran reminded. "You don't have lung cancer."

A few days later Dr. Bartell confirmed her conclusions.

"There's no lung abnormality. It's chronic bronchitis. I'll give you a prescription," Dr. Bartell told Robin.

Lynne sat listening numbly, enveloped in frustration, while Arnie and Jessie engaged in another of their shouting matches. In a corner of her mind she was relieved that Beth was sleeping over at a girlfriend's apartment tonight.

"What do you mean, you're moving into your own apartment?" Arnie yelled. "You're a kid!"

"I'm over eighteen! I can do what I want!" The triumph in Jessie's voice shot chills through Lynne. "I found this apartment over in the East Seventies that's real cool." She paused while Arnie gaped, openmouthed, at her. A wariness that crept into her eyes elicited anxiety in Lynne. "And from now on I'm taking over my finances." She stared at Arnie— daring him to contradict this. "You take out your commission from my checks, and then give me the balance."

"You think you can handle that kind of money?" he challenged. "I'm an accountant," he reminded. Belatedly, he remembered this, Lynne thought. "You need me to protect your interests!"

"I earn it," Jessie shot back. "I'll decide how to spend it. You handle your twenty percent, I'll handle my share."

"I pay ten percent of my commission to Mazur," he began.

"That's on the TV stuff," she cut him short.

"What about the others?" Arnie demanded. "They get their pieces, too!"

Lynne tuned out of the raucous argument between Jessie and Arnie. The prospect of Jessie's living alone unnerved her. It was bad enough that Jessie dismissed any talk of college. They were supposed to be grateful that she stayed with the tutoring and would have a high school diploma in a few weeks.

She was having serious problems accepting the insane hours that Jessie was keeping since her eighteenth birthday—when she became legally old enough to go to the discos. She was upset by Jessie's much publicized dating—all set up, Arnie insisted, by the publicity people. *"It's great for her career, Lynne—keeps her name out there before the public."* Now this.

Their lives were upside down these days. She lay awake so many nights—waiting for the sound of Jessie's key in the door. And three hours later *she* had to go off to school. The four of them saw one another at dinnertime—and not always then.

It would be different if Jessie was going off to college to live in a dorm. But, of course, that whole scene had changed, too, Lynne forced herself to admit. These talks of coed dorms were creating headaches for plenty of parents. All right, she and Arnie had slept together before they were married—but they *knew* they were going to get married. And she'd been older than Jessie.

Was Jessie sleeping around? She'd known since Jessie was ten or eleven that she exuded sex—had known by the time she was fourteen that Jessie reveled in this. Sitting here at the dinner table while their coffee grew cold—shutting out the recriminations Arnie was hurling at Jessie, Lynne remembered what she'd overheard Jessie telling Beth several nights ago when she was dressing to go out.

"Beth, you don't know how exciting it is when you walk into a disco! All that music and noise and the lights! You keep bumping into one another on the dance floor because it's so crowded. You just keep on dancing until your legs are cramped and your head feels ready to fly off. It's better than John Travolta in *Saturday Night Fever*. It's like having an orgasm all by yourself."

Did sweet little Beth even know what an orgasm was? Was there anything kids today didn't know?

"I've signed the lease on the apartment." The finality of Jessie's voice punctured her introspection. "I'll be moving in the first of the month."

"What am I supposed to do with this place? You know how much the rent is!" Lynne heard the panic in Arnie's voice.

"You said you love this apartment." Jessie was in her "sweet young innocent" mode now. "I'm sure you'll figure out a way to handle it."

Aghast, Fran listened to Lynne's news that Jessie was moving into her own apartment.

"We can't put her under lock and key. She's eighteen. And now we have to sublet this apartment. Arnie and I can't afford it." Anger crept into Lynne's voice. "You know how rough it is to find an apartment in

New York at a decent rent these days? The old apartment was like a trust fund."

"Maybe it's time you and Arnie bought a coop or a condo," Fran said. "I don't mean a big, fancy place—just—"

"Mom, no," Lynne broke in.

"I'll advance you what you'll need for a down payment," Fran said, striving for diplomacy. Arnie would be seeing regular commissions from Jessie's earnings, she pinpointed. Along with Lynne's salary they could manage the maintenance on a nice coop or condo.

"I don't want to have anything that Arnie can use as collateral for a loan." Lynne was blunt. "We've just paid off the car loan. I hate having loans over my head."

Lynne's marriage was rocky, Fran warned herself, yet again. She and Arnie no longer shared a room. She didn't trust him to handle their finances. But Lynne shared her own feelings about the importance of family. She'd stay with Arnie to keep their small family together—though it was clear Jessie was already breaking away.

Lynne was caught in a marriage that had gone bad, and Debbie lost Scott to murder after a heartbreakingly short time. She was the fortunate one. She'd had Bernie for eleven years and Craig for even longer. Theirs wasn't a formal marriage, she conceded—but both she and Craig were so grateful for what they had.

As always, she talked at least once a week with Lynne. Despite the shortage of apartments in New York, Lynne reported they were having problems subletting. *"The rent's so damn high."* Lynne was relieved when they found a tenant acceptable to management in late August. Now began the frantic race to find an apartment for themselves. They had to be out of the current apartment by October 1.

Lynne complained that Arnie was leaving everything on her shoulders.

"He spends every moment chasing around for Jessie. He's found an agent who's setting up dates for her to play a bunch of fairs this summer, then Vegas in the fall. She's fighting over the debut album because she doesn't like the producer that Cosmo Records scheduled for it. And, Mom, my head reels from the stories circulating about her love life."

"You know it's mostly publicity," Fran consoled. *Was it?* "Do you see her often?"

"She pops in for an hour or two every couple of weeks. Arnie, of course, sees her regularly." Lynne sighed. "Arnie tries to talk to her about handling her money—but when did Jessie ever listen to us?"

Then just a week before they had to vacate the apartment Lynne found another apartment in the West Eighties.

"It's about what we had before, but the rent's two hundred a month higher. Still, it's a relief to know we have somewhere to go. And Beth and I can walk to school." Lynne hesitated. "What's with Debbie and Eric?" Lynne had met Eric during a trip to Bellevue. "Still the platonic duo?"

"That's what Debbie insists," Fran told her. "He's charming. Diane adores him. You know, Debbie's got her hooked on mystery novels, too— and you should hear the three of them dissecting a book. And Diane was enthralled when he praised an article she did for her school newspaper."

"When did Diane meet him?" Lynne sounded astonished.

"Oh, I've persuaded Debbie to have him and Nora over for dinner every now and then." Fran chuckled. "I know I can't push her into anything, but I still try. I always say, 'ask Nora and Eric to dinner—' "

Late on a steamy September evening Robin called Fran and said he was having difficulty breathing. Fran sensed his panic.

"Do you think I should go to the emergency room?"

"Call Doctor Bartell," she ordered. He was one of those rare doctors who still made house calls.

"Doctor Bartell is on Sea Island for a week—"

"See who's covering for him. Ask him to meet you at his office." The doctor just might want to do some tests. "Call me back and I'll drive you there," Fran ordered. Even over the phone she was conscious of his breathing problems. It could be a panic attack, she thought—but it was best to check.

Five hours later Robin was admitted to the hospital. He was suffering from pneumonia. After an interlude of examinations and tests he was able to talk with Fran in his private room.

"It's not the regular pneumonia," he said, his eyes reflecting an unexpected terror. "It's that crazy kind of pneumonia—Pneumocystis." He took a deep breath. "It's the kind that *The Native* says has been hitting New York City gays." Fran knew that *The Native* was a New York-based gay newspaper. *"They're dying from it."*

"Robin, you haven't been in New York in many months," she reminded. "You couldn't have picked up pneumonia up there."

"The doctor says this kind of pneumonia is bizarre. He's been hearing about it. I guess with the CDC right in Atlanta, local docs are more conscious of these strange deals." The CDC, Fran interpreted, was the Center for Disease Control. "I mean, it happens," he conceded, "but it doesn't usually hit young, healthy people." He paused. "Not fairly young people."

"But they know how to treat it." Fran was determined to appear optimistic.

"It's not just this crazy pneumonia that's hitting gays," he said grimly. "There's this Kaposi's sarcoma deal—it's being diagnosed every week—among gay men. There's some connection between them. It's an epidemic, but nobody wants to admit it!" His voice was shrill. "It's called an immunosuppression disease. Why is it hitting guys like me? And I'm not sure they do know how to treat it—"

"You're going to be all right, Robin." Fran managed a reassuring smile. "You weren't put into the Intensive Care Unit. If it was serious, you'd be there."

"Fran, pick up my mail for me. I want to see what *The Native* is saying in the new issue about all this crap. *Why isn't it being written up in the other newspapers?*"

In two weeks Robin was discharged from the hospital. He seemed infinitely less depressed, Fran decided when she arrived to drive him home. All right, so it had been that weird pneumonia. He had pulled through it. Case closed, she told herself.

"We just tell people I had a bout of pneumonia," Robin reminded Fran as they drove away from the hospital grounds. "That could happen to anybody, couldn't it?"

Forty - Six

F ran greeted 1983 with emotional weariness. She remembered a phrase Diane used in moments of frustration: *"Life sucks."* In periods such as this, how true! But blessedly for Diane these were brief, Fran thought tenderly. Most of the time Diane radiated a love of life.

Two days before the end of the year Midore's brother had phoned from San Francisco to report that she had suffered a fatal heart attack.

"At her request her body was cremated and the ashes scattered over our parents' graves," he told Fran. "There's to be no memorial service. She didn't want to disrupt the lives of those she loved. Two of her last paintings are willed to you. She loved you dearly. She never forgot how wonderful you were to our parents."

She and Midore saw each other seldom, talked once or twice a year on the phone, exchanged New Year's cards—but with Midore's death she felt as though part of her life was over. She called Cliff in Missouri, and they talked poignantly about those early years in New York.

There were times—and this was one of them, Fran thought as months rolled on—when her life seemed one of the TV soap operas that her mother had loved so much. She felt so helpless when Lynne was clearly hurting. She watched Debbie with Eric and yearned to make Debbie recognize that she had found something special with him. And she worried much about Robin. Now at last the newspapers and magazines were flooded with horror stories about AIDS. The epidemic had acquired a name.

Robin lived in constant fear that Bellevue would learn that he had AIDS, though to the local citizenry AIDS seemed to be a disease that afflicted those in places like New York City and San Francisco and Boston. They knew what was happening—but it didn't seem to affect towns like their own, they told themselves.

By spring major fund-raising events to help AIDS victims were being arranged. The deaths reported each day sounded like heavy war casualty lists—but nobody knew who the enemy actually was.

"What's the matter with the researchers?" Robin ranted in moments of towering desperation. "What about the government? The pharmaceutical houses? Why aren't they coming up with something? It's like we're living back in the Dark Ages!"

If Robin sneezed, he was terrified of another attack of the weird pneumonia. If he saw one pimple on his body, he was convinced he'd fallen victim to Kaposi's sarcoma.

"If I get sick again, we'll tell everybody I have cancer," Robin told Fran.

"Robin, your friends won't turn away from you," Fran reproached. And he had so many friends in this town. They thought he was a dilettante—but charming and witty. The few who guessed his sexual orientation kept this to themselves. "They'll stand by you."

"You want to bet?" he said in a rare flip moment. But his eyes were somber. "I suppose we could say I had blood transfusions in the hospital, and I was given tainted blood."

"Robin, you're fine now." Fran was determined to sound optimistic. "You can be that way for years. Enjoy those years."

"I know," he drawled, his voice sardonic. "Enjoy each day at a time. But how do I know the next day may not be my last?"

"It doesn't happen that way," Fran said urgently. She dreaded what lay ahead. Newspaper and magazine stories had been painfully graphic. "And tomorrow some researcher could come up with a vaccine."

"I feel as though I'm living in exile," Robin said. "I don't dare go to New York. That's been home for me, Fran—you know that. And I'm scared to bring Dennis down here to stay with me. He seems to be all right—and I want him to stay that way." He closed his eyes in anguish. "Every time I talk to him on the phone, he tells me about somebody else we know who's died."

Despite the depression that threatened her so often in the course of each day, Fran found pleasure in the events of early summer. In May Diane was graduated from high school. In September she would enroll as a freshman at the University of Georgia—still "gung-ho to be a journalist." In New York Beth graduated high school but had abandoned all thoughts of a musical career.

"I'd like to say I'm sorry," Lynne confided somberly in a Sunday evening phone conversation with Fran, "but I'm not. I'm relieved. Beth has a sweet, lovely voice but I know she hasn't the temperament to deal with the entertainment world. And she'd always fear comparison with Jessie."

"I'm glad she's been accepted at Barnard," Fran said. The soaring tuition there was something Lynne and Arnie couldn't afford, but she was happy to provide it.

"Barnard is the sister college to Columbia," Lynne said softly. "Daddy would have been so pleased."

"Oh, he would," Fran agreed.

At first she'd been surprised when Beth chose to enroll as a day student rather than to live in a Barnard dorm—and then comprehension shot across her mind. Beth felt her family being torn apart. She wanted to be with her mother.

"Has she decided what she wants to do with her life?" Fran was afraid to ask Beth—fearful of seeming a pushy grandmother.

"Just the other night she came out with the answer," Lynne's voice revealed her relief. "She wants to go into social work. It'll mean a master's after her BA—but this seems what she wants to do. You're never in New York long enough, Mom, to see the awful homelessness that's hit the city. I think—"

"Lynne, I've seen," Fran broke in compassionately. "It's happening even in Atlanta. I can understand Beth's leaning toward social work." She felt a surge of love for this middle granddaughter. "I think it's in the genes." She hesitated. "What's with Jessie?"

"She's booked in clubs in London and Paris in the fall. And if we can believe the gossip columns—and she hasn't denied it—she's having a mad affair with this divorced thirty-year-old Wall Street Boy Wonder. Steve Westcott." This was the era of Boy Wonders, Fran thought—everybody so impatient to be ultra-rich. What happened to the '60s idealism? "She says he's going with her for the London and Paris engagements. I think she enjoys unnerving me—" Lynne's chuckle was shaky.

"More publicity," Fran tried to dismiss this.

"This is more," Lynne said with fatalistic calm. "Just talking with Jessie—on those quick trips of hers to the apartment—I know this is serious, though she's flip about everything. I worry about the whole scene, Mom—" Fran sensed her anguish. "All these crazy parties, the discos, the drinking, the drugs. It scares the hell out of me."

"You've done everything you can, Lynne. You are not to blame yourself for whatever she does with her life."

"I can't believe the money she's earning! Even Arnie is impressed. Now she's taking dancing lessons and acting lessons. She works hard," Lynne conceded. "And she plays hard. And I'm scared for her future."

Craig, too, was all involved with the college scene, Fran thought tenderly. He and Joyce were flying to New York for Josh's graduation at Columbia Law. Then they'd rush back for Zach's graduation at Emory. In the fall he was entering the Harvard School of Design—though he made it clear he didn't plan to join his father's firm at graduation.

"He wants to be independent." Craig had shrugged this off, but Fran knew he was disappointed. Still, he was pleased that Zach was following in his footsteps. "But Joyce is going to be really pissed when she discovers Josh means to settle in his own apartment when he comes back home to set up practice—and that he's not going into practice with Williams, Frank, and McArdle." Fran knew that Joyce had urged Josh to accept this offer because it was the most prestigious law firm in Bellevue. "I'm sure Josh has his reasons."

Fran had known she and Debbie would find the house poignantly empty without Diane's lively presence. Now she persuaded Debbie to invite Eric and Nora for dinner at frequent intervals. Just before Thanksgiving she suggested Debbie ask him to join the family for the holidays. Nora always spent the holiday with her oldest sister and her husband and three sons.

Fran knew Eric had little communication with his own family—other than his great-aunt.

"He'll probably spend Thanksgiving with Miss Betsy," Debbie pointed out. Fran sensed that she was disconcerted at the prospect of bringing Eric here on such a personal occasion.

"Let's invite her, too," Fran said. "And I'm sure Eric will enjoy meeting Robin."

"How's Robin's health these days?" Debbie asked solicitously. "I know he had pneumonia twice in the last year—and he's looking fragile."

"He's slowly getting back some of that weight he lost," Fran said, wary lest she betray him. Nobody except his doctor knew that he was being treated for AIDS. There must be other cases in Bellevue, she thought tiredly—why must they all be kept under wraps? It wasn't a disease just affecting homosexuals. Drug users were coming down with

AIDS as a result of infected needles. Young children—people of all ages, hemophiliacs—who'd received tainted blood in transfusions. Why this secrecy?

Debbie invited Eric for Thanksgiving dinner. He explained that his great-aunt always spent this holiday with several elderly ladies whom she had known since elementary school. But he looked forward to the occasion, he told her with obvious pleasure.

"His family probably spends the day water-skiing," Debbie told her mother in candid disgust. "He never goes home for any holiday. I'm glad you decided to invite him, Mom. He would have been all alone."

Fran was pleased that Eric joined them for Thanksgiving dinner. He and Robin were kindred in several ways, she thought. Both loved the theater and had a wide knowledge of playwrights and actors. Both had a fondness for Fire Island summers—though they'd stayed in different communities. Both found New York an exciting, vibrant city, yet preferred to live in a smaller town on a full-time basis. And Robin had great respect for Eric because he was occasionally published—academic articles about the history of the mystery novel, now and then a short story in *Ellery Queen* or *Alfred Hitchcock.*

Fran knew that many local friends and acquaintances would be shocked to learn that Robin was affected by AIDS—but how much longer could he hide that? she asked herself anxiously. And they would be more shocked, she conceded, to know that someone with AIDS sat at her dinner table. Couldn't people understand that infection was not possible on a superficial basis?

"How're you enjoying your classes at college?" Eric asked Diane at a pause in the lively table conversation.

"Okay," she said. "Only I'm dying to move into something that's more relevant to journalism." She adored Eric, Fran thought yet again.

"Everything is relevant to journalism," he told her. "You need that liberal arts background. I know," he teased. "You can't wait to get out there and be working on a newspaper."

"Don't expect to be Martha Gelhorn or Marguerite Higgins in the first year," Fran joshed. She saw a sudden flicker of pain in Debbie's eyes. Debbie had been working for a newspaper—on an assignment—when she met Scott. Debbie had yearned to follow in the footsteps of Martha Gelhorn or Marguerite Higgins, as *she* had a generation earlier. Three generations with one hoped-for destination.

"Grandma, I can wait." Diane's smile was dazzling. "I don't expect to get great assignments my first year out there." Yet she felt a resolution in Diane that belied that avowal of patience.

With the arrival of 1984 Fran realigned the hierarchy in the management of the Goldman Shops so that she was no longer responsible for buying. She'd long tried to persuade Debbie—who had exquisite taste—to take this over, but Debbie recoiled from what had become four buying trips a year to Manhattan. Beverly was being trained to take over this niche.

Only to Craig did Fran admit that her visits to New York were now tortuous because she came face to face with the hostility between Lynne and Arnie. It was better that Lynne came to Bellevue for visits. Even in her presence, Fran thought with fresh rage, Arnie talked to Lynne as though she was a stupid, unknowledgeable woman. He used her as his whipping post.

Arnie boasted to everyone about Jessie's soaring success, Fran told Craig—but he was consumed with anger that success had passed *him* by. He derided Beth's growing commitment to social work. To him the homeless that roamed about the Upper West Side—as well as much of Manhattan—were vermin. *"Why do we have to look at that scum every day? Why don't they stay down on the Bowery where they belong?"*

Atlanta, too, was facing the problem of homelessness. It was arising in London and Paris and Rome—around the world. Both Fran and Craig became both financially and emotionally involved. And again, Fran thought with gratitude, they acquired another motive for being in each other's company.

"Zach is trying to tell me tactfully that he doesn't want to do the kind of architecture I've been doing all these years," Craig told Fran with wry humor on this rare occasion when they could escape to the cottage for more than an hour or two. Tonight Craig was free from twilight to close to 11 P.M. because Joyce had gone to a bridal shower. They'd brought dinner from a favorite restaurant, ate in high spirits, then had gone into the bedroom to make love. "Still, I'm pleased he's going into my field. I think he'll find real satisfaction there."

"I wish I could be sure Beth will be happy in social work." Fran sighed. "She was so certain that she would be a singer. She was serious about it—until Jessie became such a sensation. She's afraid she'd never match Jessie's success—and that's humiliating."

"Fran, you always worry," Craig scolded. "Put that behind you for now."

"I'm sorry, darling," she apologized, her head on his shoulder while they lay together in the bed, reluctant to relinquish this special time. Though the April evening was only chilly, Craig had laid and lit a fire in the grate because he knew how much she enjoyed the glow of burning logs in a fireplace. The only illumination in the room.

In the early years they'd sworn to put everything behind them when they were together this way—but their lives, she thought with defiant pleasure, had become a real marriage where they shared every thought. Sometimes she was convinced her hold on sanity depended upon being with Craig at intervals this way.

"You always think that you can—that you *must*—provide happiness for the children and grandchildren. Don't you know by now," he joshed gently, "that we're not made for long-term happiness on this earth? We live for the good moments."

"I've always promised myself I'd provide security and the small luxuries, and they would be happy. I've succeeded far beyond my dreams when I took over the business," she conceded. "But I can't buy them what they want from life."

"Stop trying to make everything perfect for them. You can't play God—that's not for us mere mortals." Craig's eyes glowed with love. "You've been a good mother in every way. And stop feeling guilty about us," he ordered. "We're doing nothing wrong. We're hurting no one."

How many times had he told her that? How many times had she said it to herself? But there was never a time in all these years when she came to the cottage that she wasn't afraid someone had seen them—had somehow made the connection.

These precious interludes with Craig were what held her together in those moments when she felt such despair about Lynne's marriage. Lynne had abandoned her own career because she had such belief in Arnie's talents—and what did she have to show for that sacrifice?

Fran sighed in fresh frustration. She was worried sick about Jessie's lifestyle. She worried because Beth was so lacking in self-confidence and comforted herself with clandestine forays into the refrigerator. Lynne reported that Beth was losing her lovely, sylphlike figure.

Always she worried about Debbie, who had achieved a patina of serenity that Fran found suspect. Scott had been a warm and wonderful husband and father—but Debbie mustn't spend the rest of her life feeling she had failed him because his killer walked free. Yet what could *she* do to change the situation? Was it abnormal for a mother to want to see her children happy? Had it become an obsession with her?

Forty-Seven

F ran was impatient for the end of the school year in New York to arrive. That weekend Lynne would come down to Bellevue for four weeks. Beth was already in summer school at Barnard. She was determined to graduate college in three years and go on to graduate school for her master's in social work. Diane was home for the summer and ecstatic at being an intern on the *Bellevue Enquirer*.

Craig was pleased that Zachary was home for the summer and working in his office.

"I was anxious at first about how he and Joyce would handle living under the same roof again on a full-time basis," he confided to Fran at a late lunch in Atlanta. "But Joyce's health is better now, and Zach works hard at avoiding confrontations. And thank God, she's socializing again. She has something beside her health to think about."

"How's Josh doing with his law practice these days?" Fran asked indulgently. On occasion she encountered Joshua and Zachary. This was inevitable in their social circles. She was fond of both. "And is he happy in his new apartment?" Briefly Joshua had shared with a friend from law school, but after four months his apartment-sharer had moved in with a girlfriend. Joshua had sublet that apartment and rented a smaller one. Craig suspected he would soon have a new roommate—female. What a change in moral attitudes in the past twenty-five years, Fran marveled subconsciously.

"Joyce is still deriding Josh's determination to make it alone." Craig sighed. "But Josh lets it just ride off his shoulders. He doesn't want to be part of a huge firm more interested in the bottom line than what kind of cases it handles. He's running against the tide," Craig conceded. "Most young people today don't see beyond the bottom line. They all want to be millionaires before they're thirty." Like the young Wall Street entrepreneur Jessie was involved with, Fran thought. Lynne complained that she'd never even met him, though she was sure they were sleeping together.

"I'll be able to send some small business Josh's way," Fran told him and Craig nodded in appreciation. "More later." She was becoming disenchanted with her current law firm. Their billing hours were unconscionable.

It was absurd, she told herself—but she felt a special closeness to Josh and Zach. How would they feel toward her if they knew that for many years she'd been having an affair with their father?

At the end of June Lynne's school closed for vacation. The following day she was to fly to Atlanta. Preparing for bed, Fran was enveloped in pleasurable anticipation. She was too wired to sleep, she thought, and reached for a magazine. Moments later the phone rang. It was Robin.

"Am I calling too late?" he asked in poignant apology.

"Robin, it's never too late for you," she soothed, knowing he must be upset about something.

"I've got the sniffles," he said. "Just a little cold—but I'm scared."

"You've had a slight cold before—it meant nothing at all," she reminded. Yet she, too, was anxious.

"Fran, if I have pneumonia again, it's the *end* for me!"

"You don't have pneumonia." Of course, he was unnerved, she told herself. His immune system was so fragile—and each day he read more terrible statistics about AIDS victims. "I'll drop by for a few minutes on my way to the airport tomorrow to pick up Lynne. Debbie asked me to give you the latest paperback mystery she's read." In his urgent search for diversion Robin had become an avid mystery fan. "She and Eric were both fascinated by this one."

"When's Eric going to stop playing humble suitor and propose?" Robin asked. "He and Debbie are perfect for each other. Everybody in town has been saying that for ages."

"They're a bunch of gossips," Fran said in annoyance. "You know Debbie—Eric's afraid he'll lose what he has with her if he starts playing that tune."

"I'm going to take a pill and try to sleep," Robin said. "You'll stop by tomorrow?"

"I promise."

After lunching at her desk the next day, Fran left the office to drive to the airport to meet Lynne—allowing time to stop off to see Robin. The air was hot and humid. Not a leaf, not a blade of grass was stirring. The area had been imprisoned in a record-breaking heat wave for three days.

Of course, Robin was depressed, Fran thought. He didn't dare stir from his air-conditioned house in this weather. If he sneezed twice, he'd be sure it was a cold. And with constant air-conditioning he was apt to sneeze, she recalled. Poor Robin—he constantly lived one step away from hysteria.

When she drove up before the elegant house, Fran heard Robin's stereo blasting away. Jessie's latest record—Number One on the charts—greeted her. It ever surprised Fran that Robin was a Jess Alexander fan. As she left the car and headed for the stairs, Robin charged out of the house.

"Did you hear the news, Fran?" he called in high excitement.

"What news?" Robin was feeling better, she thought subconsciously—his cold forgotten.

"About Jessie! I heard a bulletin on the radio about ten minutes ago. I called, but you'd left the office already."

"Robin, what about Jessie?" Fran's heart was pounding.

"She got married last night! In Vegas. To that Boy Wonder from Wall Street! Steve Westcott."

"Oh, God!" Fran closed her eyes for a moment in protest. *Did Lynne know?* "I'm on my way to the airport to pick up Lynne."

"Do you want me to come with you?" Robin was immediately aware of the impact of what he'd said. Lynne had been aboard a plane for the past two hours. *Had she heard?*

"I'm all right, Robin." She was touched by his solicitude. "But let me get on my way. You know me," she said, chuckling. "I always have to be early."

Pacing about at the airport as she waited for Lynne's flight to arrive, Fran tried to deal with the knowledge that Jessie was married. Lynne would be upset, of course. *She* was upset. How long would this marriage last? Jessie wasn't ready for the responsibilities of marriage. Her husband already had one divorce behind him. Everything was happening too fast for Jessie!

Then Lynne arrived, and Fran was caught up in the pleasure of seeing her again. She looked so tired, Fran fretted. But then she lived on a constant battleground.

On the drive home Lynne talked about Beth's involvement with one of the myriad groups springing up to fight for aid for the homeless. Fran told her about Diane's internship on the *Bellevue Enquirer*. Lynne didn't know that Jessie had been married this morning, Fran realized in torment.

Turning into their driveway, Fran ordered herself to tell Lynne. It had happened. Jessie had married Steve Westcott.

"I have to tell you something, darling," Fran began and felt Lynne tense in alarm.

"What's happened, Mom?" Lynne's voice was faintly shrill.

"Nobody's hurt or sick." Fran managed a reassuring smile. "But Robin told me he just heard the news on some radio program." She took a deep breath. "Jessie was married last night in Las Vegas."

"To Steve Westcott?" Lynne asked, pushing past her initial shock.

"That's right."

"Not a word to Arnie or me." Lynne was pale. "Couldn't she have called us? But then Arnie and I did the same to you," she added painfully. "I wanted to go home to be married, but Arnie was so insistent, so anxious about that crazy deal in California. I was so afraid I'd lose him—" Irony crept into her voice.

"Lynne, you're not Jessie. I understood what was happening with you. I knew you were in love with him—and anxious about his career."

"I have to call Arnie—" Lynne reached with compulsive haste for the door on her side of the car. "He said he'd be home today."

Fran stood by while Lynne called Arnie. Lynne held the phone from her ear because Arnie was shouting. He knew, she guessed, and listened to Lynne's brief replies.

"Arnie, let me get off the phone," Lynne said. "This is prime-time calling rates. I'll talk to you tonight."

"Arnie heard from her?" Fran asked.

"She phoned this morning—seven A.M. Las Vegas time. They were married by some judge, then partied all night. They were just going back to their hotel. She was flippant as usual. She's finishing her engagement out there tomorrow night. Then she and Steve are flying to Rio for the skiing. I hope she's careful—Jessie's never skied." She paused, fighting for calm. "She has to be back in New York in three weeks for a recording session. Arnie, of course, is furious that she was so cavalier."

"You know Jessie," Fran said gently. "She makes up her own mind—and then she acts."

"I have to learn to accept Jessie as she is," Lynne said after a moment. "But it won't be easy."

What Robin had tried to tell himself was a slight cold developed into a third case of pneumonia. This time he contrived to have himself admitted to a small private hospital on the outskirts of Bellevue. For Fran the summer became a depressing nightmare. She commuted between her business and the hospital, often in Craig's company.

Robin was shaken when he discovered that certain staff nurses refused to care for him. There were only four AIDS patients in the tiny hospital, but Robin reported bitterly that they were all pariahs.

"You tell people in Bellevue that I've gone to New York for cancer treatment," he ordered Fran and Craig when they arrived on the eve of his birthday with a sumptuously decorated cake. "Tell them I'm up at Sloan-Kettering for chemotherapy!" Except for Fran and Craig, only Peggy knew the truth—and she, too, was a steady visitor.

Some days Robin felt better than others. Fran brought sketchpads and charcoal pencils so that he could draw on the good days. Then the doctors decided to allow him to go home. Peggy and a practical nurse would care for him.

"No visitors, Fran," he insisted. "Except for you and Craig. I look just awful."

For a little while he seemed to be better. He spent hours each day sketching. Then in the autumn he began to have trouble with his arms. Sketching was out. Now he spent endless hours watching TV or videos. Though he never mentioned it, Fran knew he was in constant pain. She saw the prescriptions that lined the night table beside his bed.

"Why don't we order a hospital bed for you and bring it into the living room where you can look out on the garden?" Fran coaxed. Robin loved the magnificent array of flowers that sprawled across the huge front lawn.

"All right," Robin agreed, almost listless now.

Fran was shocked at the way he was losing weight. By Thanksgiving he was desperately thin, despite the efforts of Peggy and the practical nurse to see him gain a few pounds. His legs became affected. He was unable to leave the bed. Another nurse was brought in to cover the night hours. The doctor played the game Robin demanded.

"It'll be a matter of time before a vaccine comes through that'll restore your immune system," the doctor said at each visit.

"Tell the bastards to hurry up," Robin ordered the compassionate doctor, who acceded to his wish to remain at home. No hospital, he insisted. No hospice.

"They're working hard, Robin," the doctor told him. But now a respirator was added to the house equipment.

Dennis phoned constantly and wanted to come down to help take care of Robin.

"I won't let Dennis see me this way. I won't expose him to this scourge!" Robin told Fran. He was fearful of contaminating the few who came in contact with him. Now he was insisting that Fran and Craig wear rubber gloves when they were with him.

By the beginning of the new year round-the-clock registered nurses were in attendance. Robin looked emaciated, Fran thought in pain and made sure mirrors were banned from his presence. But despite his suffering there were moments when the familiar charm and wit shone through. Fran was grateful for the devotion of his three nurses and Peggy—at a time when so many AIDS patients were being shunned.

"Look, I've had a better run than most," he said with an air of defiance on a February night swathed in snow, while Fran sat beside his bed and talked about Jessie's very public fights with her husband. Jessie was ever a subject that fascinated him. "Look at all those poor guys in their twenties and thirties who're kicking off. The little kids. I did a lot of living in my time."

"That you did, Robin," she said softly.

"I'm ready to go," he said after a moment. "I'll welcome it."

At 6 A.M. the following morning Fran was awakened by a call from Peggy. Through her sobs she told Fran that Robin had died in his sleep.

"He didn't know what was happening," Peggy said brokenly. "Now he's at peace."

Fran awoke on the morning of Robin's funeral with an instant awareness that this was one of those February days in Bellevue when the observing knew that spring was not far ahead—in such contrast to Robin's last night on earth. Glorious sunlight filtered between her bedroom draperies. The air was fragrant. The kind of day that Robin loved. He'd be pleased, she thought, even while she dreaded facing a world without him.

Arriving at the funeral home with Debbie, Fran was approached by a slender young man whom she guessed instantly was Dennis. Craig had taken on the task—months ago assigned him by Robin—of notifying Dennis of Robin's death.

"I had to be with him once more," Dennis said, pale but composed. "It won't be long before we'll be together again." He smiled at Fran's an-guished gasp. "Unless," he amended, his smile wry, "the research people come up fast with a cure."

Dennis had never told Robin that he, too, had AIDS.

Fran was astonished by the huge turnout at the services. Now, she thought bitterly, people in this town considered it safe to come to Robin's side. Of course, they'd known he had AIDS—she'd realized that months ago. Tradespeople who made deliveries to the house had surely guessed. Word spread fast in a place like Bellevue. Robin hadn't wanted anybody to call—but they should have made the effort, she told herself in anger.

The group that went to the cemetery—where, at Robin's instruc-tions, he was to be buried beside his mother and father—was small. Fran and Diane, Debbie with Eric, Craig, Peggy, and a pair of officers from the foundation. Exhausted and forlorn, Fran placed a single red rose—what Robin called his passion flower—on the simple casket. Again, it seemed that part of her life was being chipped away. *Oh, she would miss Robin.*

One of the pains of growing older was losing dear friends, she thought. But Robin should have had years ahead of him. The researchers had discovered weapons against smallpox, tuberculosis, polio. When would they come up with a cure for this epidemic that was as devastating as war?

Forty-Eight

For Robin's sake Fran was happy that his agony was over, but she knew it would be a long time before she could accept his death as a reality. His house and furnishings were to go to the foundation, as preordained by his mother's will. His car and the funds in his checking account were willed to Peggy. The cottage—whose presence was known only to the tax collectors, Craig, and Fran—was willed to Fran.

"It was the only thing other than his car that he owned outright," Fran said tenderly as she and Craig walked through the latest section of Bellevue Estates. "And he left it to me."

"He told me once that he found vicarious pleasure in knowing we put the cottage to fine use," Craig recalled. "He didn't want it to fall into anybody else's hands."

"You decide what it would bring if it was sold," Fran said after a moment. "I'll donate that much to AIDS research."

"I'll match it," Craig promised. "Our personal memorial to Robin."

"I used to tease him and say he was our guardian angel," Fran remembered, tears blurring her vision. "And now he's gone."

"I'm sure if he's in a position to continue the role, he'll play it to the hilt," Craig said, striving for lightness.

"Craig, are you sure Joyce knows nothing about us?" Fran's eyes searched his. For a long time she'd convinced herself—along with Robin—that nobody in Bellevue knew that he had AIDS. And then the truth pierced her consciousness. Of course they knew. Did Joyce know about Craig and her? Did others in Bellevue know?

"Joyce is too self-absorbed even to consider such a thing." Craig was quietly reassuring.

"Nobody else knows?" Fran persisted with childlike stubbornness.

"They know that we're friends and involved in business transactions. Nothing more," he soothed. "Though Joyce has never stopped being envious of you, I've heard her boasting about how I'm the only architect in the area that you trust." He chuckled. "Joyce worships success. My being 'your architect' makes her feel important." He paused, his eyes compassionate. "When are you going to dump this obsessive guilt about us?"

"Probably never." Fran managed a smile. "But I won't let anything stand between us. Not ever. I promise."

Lynne ordered herself to be casual with Jessie on her occasional—brief—visits to the apartment. So she and Arnie hadn't met Steve Westcott yet. That would come in time. But it was so crazy, Lynne tormented herself, not to have even met her daughter's husband. Jessie rushed in for dinner when she was in town, always explaining that Steve was tied up in some big Wall Street deal.

Jessie and Steve were living in a huge penthouse apartment in the East Seventies—which Lynne and Arnie had not seen yet, Beth pointed out pithily at intervals—but Jessie kept her own apartment on Central Park South. A safety valve? Lynne asked herself—and then was ashamed of her skepticism.

Lynne had dutifully admired Jessie's flashy wedding band and belated engagement ring—that Beth said could light up Yankee Stadium at night. She listened to Jessie's colorful reports on her personal appearances. Arnie's major role in Jessie's career these days was to make sure royalty statements and checks arrived on schedule and to deduct commissions and deposit the balances into the bank accounts Jessie designated. But Arnie clung to his title as Jess Alexander's personal manager.

As the end of the school year approached, Beth was preparing to register once again for the summer sessions. She looked tired, strained, Lynne thought as they sat down to breakfast on the final day of classes at Barnard. Why couldn't she allow herself one summer off?

"Mom, I'm thinking of skipping summer school this year," Beth said, and Lynne stopped buttering her toasted bagel to gaze at Beth in astonishment. It was as though Beth had been reading her mind.

"Darling, you need some time off." Lynne nodded in approval.

"I want to work this summer and get ahead on cash." Beth seemed caught in some inner anguish. "Traveling on the subway is getting rough." She was struggling to be casual. "I thought that with some money saved I could afford to share an apartment with Caroline." Since their first week at Barnard she and Caroline had been close friends. "Her roommate just moved in with a boyfriend, and she's desperate for somebody to share the rent."

"I've told you from the beginning that if you wanted to live on campus, Daddy and I will handle that," Lynne said slowly. "Grandma takes care of your tuition. We can handle the living expenses." Beth was moving out to escape the battles between Arnie and herself, Lynne thought with anguish.

"Are you sure?" Beth was eager to be convinced.

"Sure." Beth would be happier away from the battlefield that was their home these days.

"I'll tell Caroline not to put up any notices at school about the apartment." Beth's eyes searched her mother's. "Mom, you're not upset about this?"

"Of course I'm not upset," Lynne lied. Arnie and she were *driving* Beth away from home. "In a few days you'll be twenty. You're old enough to be leaving the nest." She tried for a humorous tone. "But you'll be home for your birthday dinner?"

"I wouldn't miss that." Beth's laugh held a note of relief that this situation wasn't making waves, Lynne thought. "I get to choose the menu." She paused for a moment. "Will Jessie be here?" The three of them had seen Jessie's husband only once—when he'd taken them out for an expensive dinner at Lutece. She and Arnie and Beth had been totally ill-at-ease. Jessie and her husband were almost frantic to prove their marital happiness.

"I don't think Jessie can make it." Lynne fought to be casual. "She's doing a personal appearance in Boston."

"Okay." Beth shrugged. She was pleased that Jessie wouldn't be here, Lynne realized sorrowfully.

Late in June Jessie called to say she was in town and would be over for dinner the following night.

"Friday we're flying out to the Hamptons for a week. Steve wants to buy a house out there. Something right on the beach, where we can entertain his business associates. East Hampton," she emphasized. "He says Southampton is too stuffy."

"Will Steve be with you?" Lynne asked.

"Don't count on him. If he figures he can make it, I'll give you a buzz. And, Mom, tell Dad to go after my check from the Vegas club. Steve says why should they sit on my money? Why should I lose the interest?"

Lynne was upset when Beth—in the midst of moving into Caroline's apartment—said she wouldn't be home tomorrow evening.

"Jessie's coming," Lynne protested, but she remembered Beth had been pleased that Jessie wasn't here for her birthday dinner.

"I have a party up on campus," Beth said. Lynne suspected she was improvising. She didn't want to be here. "Tell Jessie. She'll understand." The touch of irony in her voice did not escape Lynne.

The next evening Arnie came home early—in honor of Jessie's presence, Lynne assumed. These days he saw little of her. Most of their encounters were on the phone, and this he resented.

Today was ungodly hot, Lynne thought. The kitchen—beyond the reach of the living room-dining area air-conditioner—was a cauldron. She ought to pick up a small fan for the kitchen, she told herself. There never seemed time between school and cooking and cleaning to take care of the little things.

Women had more rights these days, she thought dryly, but the price was high. Too many men—like Arnie—accepted their women working. They considered it a wife's *obligation* to bring home money. But they expected the old-style home life to continue. Wives came home from jobs to cook and clean and do the laundry. Husbands came home from their jobs to fall into a chair to read the newspapers, or to watch the evening news or football or basketball or whatever sports turned them on, on TV.

"Is the Boy Wonder coming tonight?" Arnie asked, flipping on a TV news channel.

"I doubt it. Jessie said she'd call if he was coming. She didn't call."

Jessie arrived thirty-five minutes late. Right away Arnie wanted to discuss business.

"Later," Jessie bubbled. "I'm starving."

At the dinner table Jessie kept up a running conversation about Steve and his exploits. It was as though he was a trophy, Lynne thought in distaste—to be shown off with pride of ownership. She'd married the super-rich Wonder Boy, and she was on the road to becoming the music world's Wonder Girl.

But after dinner—with Jessie shooting covert glances at her watch—Lynne understood that Jessie was building up to a confrontation with Arnie.

"Daddy, we have to talk," she said briskly while Lynne cleared the table. "My career's moving but not fast enough. Steve has some marvelous ideas. He—"

"What does Steve Westcott know about the music business?" Arnie interrupted ominously. "He knows Wall Street—that's a whole different ball game."

"He knows business." Jessie was belligerent where once she would have been defensive, Lynne thought. "I have to run my career like a business. I have to make changes. I'm firing Charles Mazur."

"He's one of the best!" Arnie shouted. She'd said, "I'm firing Charles Mazur," Lynne noted in a corner of her mind. Once she'd insisted that Arnie do that.

"He's not moving with the times. He thinks too small. He hasn't the faintest idea of how much money I can demand. Steve's talking with this Hollywood clique about my doing movies—with a percentage of the gross, not the net," she said in triumph. "Daddy, I need a personal manager who can keep pace with me. I've become a major package deal. Steve understands these things." She paused. "Steve and I had a serious talk. He's taking over as my personal manager."

"You're dumping me?" Arnie stared at Jessie in shock. "After all I've done for you? I don't believe this!"

"You've done shit for me," Jessie said calmly. "Believe it, Daddy. As of this day, Steve is my personal manager. Announcements have gone out. There'll be an item in next week's *Billboard* and the other papers."

"You little bitch!" Arnie shrieked. "You ungrateful little *bitch!*"

For three days Arnie didn't leave the apartment. He didn't sleep. He didn't eat. Fighting insomnia herself, Lynne heard him pacing about in his room each night. On the fourth morning she rose to prepare for the final day of the school year. She'd heard Arnie slam out of the apartment ten minutes earlier.

She arrived home after school, instantly aware that Arnie was home. Sliding the key into the lock, she heard the stereo blaring out a Cole Porter medley—a sure indication that he was in a foul mood.

"Hi," she called out warily, then froze as she saw the luggage stacked in one corner of the living room.

"I'm getting out of here," Arnie said, striding into view. "My own daughter stabs me in the back after I *made* her! I've had enough of this town!"

"Where are you going?" All at once Lynne was ashen, trembling. Next Tuesday would be their twenty-fourth wedding anniversary. She doubted that Arnie remembered. "What are you talking about?"

"It's time to think about my own career," he said viciously. "All these years shot to hell because I was concerned about Jessie. In the music business there are three places to be, New York, Los Angeles, or Nashville. I've bombed out in New York. I'm not the country music type. I'm going to Los Angeles. I've got an early evening flight scheduled." He inspected her as though she was a stranger, Lynne thought—suddenly cold. "Divorce me whenever you like. I won't contest it."

"Just like that?" She was giddy with shock.

"All you care about is your bloody teaching," he told her. "You never cared about me and my music. You're okay financially—your job's a trust fund. Oh, don't try to write any checks," he warned. "I cleaned out our checking and savings accounts this morning. I need a stake till I get moving."

"Aren't you going to say goodbye to Beth?" This wasn't real, she told herself. Twenty-four years of marriage didn't end like this.

"I'll drop her a line from California." He stared about the room with distaste. "I'm still young enough to make something out of my life. I can't do it here."

He wasn't asking her to go with him, Lynne reminded herself. He wanted to be free. She was going to be a forty-seven-year-old divorcée and on her own in New York. That wasn't what she'd expected of life.

She stood wordless, her mind in chaos, while Arnie cursed as he struggled to cart the three large suitcases to the door and out into the hall. Her fine, expensive luggage that had been Mom's birthday gift three years ago. Subconsciously she thought that he was going to pay a fortune in overweight for the flight to Los Angeles.

She heard him swearing as he made his way to the elevator. She heard the elevator slide to a stop outside, heard the door open, then close. Arnie—her husband for twenty-four years—had walked out of her life.

She sat in a corner of the living-room sofa—eyes closed as though shutting off the rest of the world—and replayed in her mind those early years of her marriage. She had been so in love with Arnie, so convinced of his talents, so eager to see him fulfill his dreams. And in the years that followed he had slowly and insidiously killed that love. A man could do nothing worse to a woman than to kill the love they once shared.

At last she was conscious that darkness had settled over the living room. She rose to her feet, sought for a lamp switch, bathed the room in deceptively cheerful light. Tomorrow she'd call Beth and tell her that Arnie had gone out of their lives. Instinct told her that Beth would not be unhappy.

In three days she was flying to Bellevue for a month. She wouldn't tell Mom on the phone. She'd tell her when she was down in Bellevue. Meanwhile, she must come to grips with what was happening in her life.

She wasn't the first woman whose husband had walked out after twenty-four years of marriage. For years it had been a rotten one. Maybe this would be a kind of rebirth. All at once her heart was pounding. Did she dare pick up where she'd left off twenty-four years ago? Did she dare try for acceptance in law school evening classes? Was it too *late?*

Forty-Nine

D riving Lynne home from the airport, Fran was conscious of an exhilarating sense of well-being. This was such a special time of year—when both daughters were here, and Diane home from college. Of course, she was disappointed that Beth had chosen to remain in New York—but summer school had been a wise decision. Beth needed self-confidence, and having a profession should do that. She would stop feeling herself in competition with Jessie.

"How did we survive before air-conditioning?" Lynne broke into her thoughts. "It's so deliciously cool." Outside the area lay imprisoned by a record-breaking heat wave.

"It wasn't easy," Fran recalled. "The big escape when you and Debbie were little was to rush to an air-conditioned movie." She paused for a moment. "What's the latest on Jessie?"

She listened while Lynne reported on Jessie's activities. It was as though Lynne was reading articles from *Billboard* and *Variety*, Fran thought and winced.

"What about her marriage?" Fran asked when Lynne was silent.

"You know as much as I do, Mom. She talks a lot about herself and Steve without really saying anything. And I've learned not to believe what I read in the gossip columns. Which I never used to read," she admitted with wry humor.

"Did you tell Beth that Diane's working with the local group that's fighting for aid to the homeless?" Fran asked. It pleased her that Beth and Diane were so much alike in their compassion for those who were hurting. A family trait that Jessie had not inherited.

"Beth's a volunteer with a group up near Columbia," Lynne said. She cleared her throat in a familiar telltale fashion. Fran tensed and geared herself for an unpleasant disclosure. "Mom, we've had a little more insanity than usual the last few days. Jessie fired Arnie as her personal manager. Her husband is taking on that job."

"You told me Jessie and Arnie were always fighting," Fran reminded cautiously. "Maybe it's best this way." But it must have been devastating to Arnie, she guessed.

"He's packed up his bags and gone out to California." Lynne stared straight ahead.

"You're going to California?" Fran was unnerved. She remembered Lynne in California—all those years ago.

"Arnie went to California. *I'm* staying in New York." Lynne took a deep breath. "He told me to file for divorce. It's way past due."

"Lynne, I can't believe it." Fran was shaken. Yet she knew Lynne was right. Her marriage was long dead.

"I'm thinking about going back to law school—at night," she added quickly. "I have a year to my credit—"

"You'll quit teaching and go to law school full-time," Fran said without hesitation. "You'll pick up where you left off." Her face was suffused with love. "You and Beth will be at Columbia together."

"I'm not sure my year at Columbia will be accepted after all this time," Lynne warned, but Fran felt her relief that this plan was not being discouraged.

"You'll work it out." Fran refused to be perturbed. "Perhaps you'll have to take another course or two, but that's no real problem. At last you'll be back in law school where you belong." In her mind she already visualized Lynne with her law degree, setting up practice in Bellevue—but time would tell about that.

"You're not upset that Arnie and I will be divorced?" Lynne asked, her eyes pleading for reassurance.

"I won't say I'm happy about it," Fran conceded. "It's always sad when a husband and wife break up. But I'm not unhappy, either," she pursued defiantly. "When a marriage is dead, then divorce is the only solution." But in her heart she would grieve a little. She had grown up believing that marriage should be forever.

Except for the divorce that was hanging over Lynne's head, this would have been a beautiful summer, Fran thought. Always a realist, Lynne had immediately concluded divorce was urgent.

"I don't want to be responsible for any debts Arnie runs up out there."

There had been a minimal exchange of correspondence between Arnie and Lynne—just what was required to expedite a New York divorce. He had written one maudlin letter to Beth and nothing more. Fran suspected that Lynne was relieved at the lack of communication between herself and Arnie. *"He's like a stranger, Mom. I don't know him anymore."*

The summer had been good, Fran reiterated inwardly as it drew to a close. Beth had come down to Bellevue for a week before the new school year began. Lynne had stayed for the whole summer except for a brief trip back to New York to fight—successfully—for readmission to Columbia Law. And this summer Diane and Zach had become close friends via their volunteer group to aid the homeless. Along with two other of the volunteers, Zach was in and out of the house—and this Fran relished. They were young and caring and determined to make their segment of the world a better place.

"They're kindred souls," Craig said gently on an early September evening when he and Fran made an escape to the cottage. He knew, she guessed lovingly, how empty the house seemed now with just Debbie and herself there. And tonight Debbie was at Eric's apartment with the small group that met there once a month to discuss the latest mystery novels. "Of course, Zach's five years older than Diane."

"Do you think there's something serious going on there?" The possibility that there could be more than friendship between Diane and Zach was poignantly sweet, yet at the same time unnerving to Fran. How would they feel if they knew about Craig and her?

"It would be special to me," Craig said quietly. "Your granddaughter and my son." He didn't see the implications, Fran thought. "But I suspect they're just caught up in the work they're trying to do. They're both so intense about it." He chuckled reminiscently. "Zach's been proselytizing. He thinks I should give up designing beautiful houses and shops and focus on low-cost housing. I'd better stay with my practice so I can help support him when he finishes Harvard."

Three weeks later the doctors ordered Joyce back into the hospital for additional surgery. She'd been complaining of pain for weeks, but Joyce was a chronic complainer. Not until she went through another battery of tests did the doctors realize her condition had deteriorated.

"After all she's been through, she keeps on smoking," Craig told Fran. "The doctors tell her. I tell her. Nobody gets through. This is an addiction that is as bad in the long run as cocaine or heroin." He shook his head in exasperation.

Joyce went through surgery early in October. Briefly she appeared to be better. By the time Josh and Zach came home from school for the winter intercession, she was in serious pain again and under heavy medication.

"The boys are on a guilt trip," Craig confided to Fran over a purported business luncheon. "You know how they've avoided being around Joyce any more than absolutely necessary—and now they realize how serious her condition is. They know she's in constant pain."

"They're not responsible." But Fran understood their feelings.

"The horrible part is that what she's suffering is unnecessary. If she had never smoked, she wouldn't be going through this. How do we make smokers understand what they may be doing to themselves?" Without waiting for a reply, Craig continued. "How's Lynne doing at school?"

"She admits it's rough after all these years, but she's determined to see it through. And she's vowing to come through with top grades." Fran's face reflected her love.

"She's your daughter. How could she feel otherwise?" In the softly illuminated restaurant his eyes dared to make love to her.

"Diane said something this morning about a dinner with the volunteer group," Fran remembered. "I gather she and the others are as determined as ever to make a dent in the homelessness here. Of course, what happens here is so little compared to what's happening in the cities."

On New Year's Day, 1986, Fran prepared to receive guests at her "open house." Lily and Betty Mae were providing a buffet that Diane declared could feed a whole regiment from Fort Benning. Lily still refused to retire, though her sisters and nieces and nephews were urging this.

"Miss Fran, you and me don't look at the calendar and say, 'okay, we're getting on—it's time to quit.' What would I do if I wasn't working? Sit in front of the TV all day?"

Inspecting herself in the mirror—in a beautifully cut sapphire velvet that reflected the astonishing blue of her eyes—Fran found it difficult to accept that in a few weeks she would be seventy. Lily was right. Life didn't change with the calendar. She inspected herself in the mirror and she didn't see a sign that said, "You're getting on in years, Fran." She made love with Craig and she felt twenty again. Why did so many people believe that part of life died an early death? But enough of this, she reproached herself. Their guests would be arriving soon.

In minutes, it seemed to Fran, the living room and adjoining den exuded an air of festivity. Beverly and two of the women from the office were in one corner and admiring the paintings by Midore that hung in a prominent position. Nora and Debbie were in high-spirited argument with Eric about a new mystery novel that each had recently read.

"I keep telling Eric he ought to settle down to write a mystery," Nora told Fran as she joined their group. "He comes up with these wonderful plots."

"I might take a stab at it if Debbie would collaborate with me," Eric said teasingly, but Fran was startled by the intensity that shone from his eyes.

"Grandma, you look gorgeous." Diane came charging toward her. "Doesn't she, Zach?"

"Always," he said with a gallant bow. How much he resembled Craig, Fran thought.

"You two are great for my morale." Fran glanced from one to the other. She sensed something new in their relationship today. Again, she was ambivalent about this possibility.

"Josh and my father said they'd be dropping by later," Zach told her. "They've heard about Lily's sweet potato pie."

"Nobody can match Lily's baking." All at once Fran's heart was pounding. Except for the period when he was building the house, Craig had never been here. There had been a few times during the years when he and Joyce had been invited along with a number of other couples for her occasional dinner parties, but Joyce had always managed to have a conflicting engagement. "But Lily's sweet potato pie is a Georgia masterpiece."

"Here they are now," Diane said as Josh and Craig strolled from the foyer into the living room. She beckoned to the two men to join them.

"How's the lawyer?" Diane drawled. "Still fighting those big corporations?"

"They woo me," Josh said, grinning, "but I'm a Sixties guy."

Fran sensed that for Craig, too, this was a special occasion. They were together in her house and surrounded by her daughter, granddaughter, and his sons.

"What about some *pro bono* work for us?" Diane prodded.

"Yeah, Josh," Zach followed up.

Fran glanced up as Betty Mae came charging from the den with un-characteristic speed.

"Miss Fran, there's a call for Mr. Hendricks," she said breathlessly.

"Which Mr. Hendricks?" Diane asked, giggling. "We have three of them here."

"I don't know—" Betty Mae was bewildered. "She just said it was urgent."

Craig exchanged anxious glances with his sons. "I'll take it—"

"In the den, Craig," Fran told him.

"It must be my mother." Josh's voice was taut. "I told her we were coming here."

Moments later Craig emerged from the den. He was pale and tense.

"It was the housekeeper," he told Fran. "Joyce has taken a turn for the worse."

Fran was ashamed that she had suspected that Joyce's turn for the worse was a bid for attention. For the next few months Joyce was in and out of the hospital with painful regularity. Craig was in constant attend-ance, though he refused Joyce's demand that Zach be brought home from Harvard. *"How can I ask Zach to sacrifice a year of school? If he's home, he's constantly trying to avoid fights with her. It's good for neither of them. Half the time Josh comes to see her, she sends him away."*

Fran felt helpless, yearning to alleviate Craig's suffering. For the second time he had to stand by and watch a wife die of cancer. The doc-tors had made it clear there would be no further reprieve. And medica-tion was providing less and less relief.

At intervals Fran and Craig met at the cottage, but now these hours were tainted with the knowledge that Joyce lay wracked with pain, that she might be trying to summon Craig to her side—which could occur any moment of the day or night. She wanted Craig to witness her pain, Fran thought in moments of involuntary resentment. A wife in love would seek to spare him—as Bernie had tried to spare her.

Then late in May—as the school year was drawing to a close—Fran was shaken by the latest news items about Jessie's highly publicized life. Lynne called to report that the columnists were right. Jessie was about to sue Steve for divorce.

"Mom, it's going to be so ugly," Lynne warned. "Jessie and Steve are making such awful allegations against each other. It'll be all over those tabloids at the checkout counters in the supermarkets. Beth called to say it was on the Channel Four six P.M. news. Why can't they manage a quiet divorce, away from the headlines? Beth says the gossip vultures may even dig up my divorcing Arnie. And Arnie won't mind a bit," Lynne said bitterly. "He'll love having his name dragged out before the gossip-hungry American public."

"Darling, none of us expected this marriage to last," Fran said gently. "Let's be grateful it's over this fast."

"There'll be an awful court battle." Fran winced at the anguish she heard in Lynne's voice. "When Jessie called to tell me, she vowed she'd walk off with half his fortune. Mom, sometimes I ask myself, how did I give birth to two daughters who're so totally different?"

"How long will Jessie and Steve stay in the headlines?" Fran tried for a realistic approach. "There's another ugly divorce in the tabloids—and on the news—every other week. This week it's Jess Alexander and Steve Westcott. Two weeks from now it'll be another celebrity couple. And Lynne, be glad they're breaking up before they had children. Children get the worst of these divorces."

Fifty

Fran was elated that all of the family except for Jessie were under one roof for much of the summer. She was pleased, too, that Eric and Zach were in and out of the house—and on occasion now Josh and Craig joined gatherings about the pool and impromptu barbecues. But Craig and his sons were ever aware of Joyce's precarious health.

Fran resented the way Jessie colored all their lives. It was Jessie's flamboyant success that had ultimately destroyed Lynne and Arnie's marriage. Beth's self-esteem—always shaky—had plummeted to its lowest depths. Debbie vocally resented Jessie's cavalier treatment of her mother.

"Diane calls Jessie 'my cousin the creep,' " Debbie confided to Fran late in August when Lynne and Beth were preparing to return to New York and school. "And I agree with her. Lynne hasn't heard from her in six weeks. Jessie knows her mother worries about her—but she's only concerned about how big a settlement she can get out of her divorce and how high on the charts her newest album will go."

"I can't believe that in another year," Fran said softly, "Lynne will have her law degree." Already she was tied up in knots at the prospect of taking her bar exams. But she was moving ahead with her life, Fran thought with pride. Jessie hadn't stopped that.

"Lynne's going to be all right. But I worry about Beth," Debbie confessed. "She's never gotten out from under Jessie's shadow."

"She loves her classes. The only reason she didn't go to summer school was that she wanted to be with Lynne—because of Arnie's walking out that way. Of course, it was the best thing that could have happened." Yet she worried about Lynne's future. Right now Lynne was absorbed in law school. She admitted it was rough going back after all these years. But once the battle was over and she was out in practice, how would Lynne handle being on her own after twenty-four years of marriage?

Then Lynne and Beth returned to New York for the new school year, and Diane left for Athens in the maroon Dodge that had been her grandmother's twentieth birthday present. Again Fran felt a desolate emptiness in the house with only Debbie and herself in residence. She was grateful that Debbie made a point of inviting Eric and Nora for dinner frequently. Debbie and Nora were encouraging Eric to focus on writing a mystery novel. It was important for his academic career.

"Eric, you've got these fascinating plots, but you don't do anything with them," Nora chided when the four of them sat down to dinner on a gusty early November Sunday evening. "It's time you did something besides those articles about 'the mystery novel and its place in literature,' " she scolded.

"I might if Debbie would collaborate with me," he said gently.

"Eric, don't start that again." Debbie's eyes settled on her plate. Why was she so upset? Fran asked herself. "I'm not a writer." But journalism was a form of writing, Fran thought—and Debbie had displayed real talent in that area.

"I'm too much of an academic." Eric shot a rueful smile at Fran and Nora, then turned again to Debbie. "You've got this great ear for dialogue. And don't deny it," he ordered because she was about to protest. "You pointed out what was wrong with those three short stories I finally sold. The characters weren't talking like real people. I don't think you picked that up in journalism classes—it's a gift."

"You write the novel, and Nora and I will play the critics," she promised. Why was Debbie so tense? Was she remembering her own lost dreams? Not lost, Fran retracted. *Abandoned.*

Eric knew about Scott's death, Fran remembered. She'd heard him talking with Debbie and Diane about similar cases—none of them subjects for mystery novels, where murders must always be solved. It was wonderful that Diane had grown up with such love for the father she'd never known, Fran conceded—but at times she'd worried that Diane would be happier in not knowing her father's killer had never been brought to justice. That was heavy baggage for a sensitive young daughter.

At the end of the year Fran received a call from Lynne to report that Beth had a brief letter from her father.

"He still sounds bitter and angry," Lynne said, "but he's picking up work doing jingles for local radio commercials, and now he's sold a song for some video. It's 'work for hire'—Beth says that means he was paid a flat fee and will never see royalties."

Fran knew it was illogical for her to be impatient that it was taking so long for Lynne's divorce to be final. Lynne would never go back to Arnie—the marriage was dead. After Jessie's lawyers and Steve's lawyers had worked out a settlement, Jessie had gotten a "quickie" divorce and was off on another tabloid-heralded affair.

Acquaintances were so impressed that Jessie was her granddaughter, Debbie's niece, Diane's first cousin. In truth, Fran thought painfully, Jessie had written them out of her life. She could handle that, Fran told herself—but it was hard on Lynne. But worst of all, it was rough for Beth to be always aware that Jessie was making such a splash in the field where she herself had hoped to shine. The dream too fragile to survive.

Diane stashed her luggage in the trunk of her Dodge and hurried behind the wheel of the car. She was impatient to be home again. Zach had arrived last night from Cambridge for his spring break. They hadn't seen each other since New Year's Day. It seemed so long. They'd promised themselves they'd make no plans for their lives before they were both out of school—but they knew they wanted to spend the rest of their lives together.

Spring was her favorite of all seasons, Diane thought with pleasure as she drove away from the campus and headed south. The trees on every side were bursting into bloom, spring flowers on riotous display. Late afternoon sunlight lent a golden glow to the earth below. She reached for the car radio and fiddled until she found the station that played show tunes.

In the privacy of the car she allowed herself to sing along with a song from *Chorus Line.* Now she broke into tender laughter. Zach loved to tease her about her lack of singing ability. *"Are you sure you're Jess Alexander's first cousin? What happened to the genes when they trickled down to you?"*

She hadn't seen Jessie in years. She had no desire to see her—not even in that movie she'd just finished. It was weird the way folks in Bellevue considered her *their* celebrity because Lynne had grown up here. The mayor was talking about naming the new road going out to Bellevue Estates "Jess Alexander Road." That was so silly.

She fumed at the heavy traffic as she neared Atlanta. She should have left earlier—there was always this insanity in the late afternoon. In sudden impatience she swung off the highway and sought out the vaguely remembered back roads that would take her into Bellevue without this stop-and-go traffic.

In minutes, it seemed, the sunshine went into hiding and grayness crept across the sky. Was it going to rain? she wondered, and reached to close the window on the driver's side. It would probably be just one of those quick spring showers—and afterward everything would be gloriously green. Then all at once torrents of rain came down and hammered on the roof of the car. Driving on unfamiliar back roads, she slowed down, watching for signs. There was a turn somewhere along here that would take her right into Bellevue.

Straining to see ahead as the thunder shower continued, she saw a car pull out of a side road. Was that Grandma's white Mercedes? There weren't many Mercedes in Bellevue. She squinted, trying futilely to read the license plate. Now another car came out of the side road and took its position between her and the white Mercedes.

All at once she recognized the gray Chrysler. It was Zach's father's car. Startling images popped into her head. Every now and then somebody made a crack about how Grandma and Craig Hendricks always seemed to be involved in the same business deal. She'd been furious at the innuendos. Grandma was into real estate, and Zach's father was a prominent architect. They were business associates who'd become close friends.

Despite a sense of guilt she made an effort to catch up with the other two cars. She wasn't sure the white Mercedes was Grandma's car—the Chrysler had cut in too fast for her to see in the dwindling daylight. But the Mercedes and Chrysler had picked up speed, leaving her behind. The other two drivers knew this road far better than she.

Suppose it had been Grandma and Zach's father, Diane reasoned. Maybe they'd been checking on another real estate deal. Don't make this into some soap opera situation. Yet she felt herself entrapped in disconcerting doubts.

Fran drove through the torrential rain as though pursued by devils. Then with startling suddenness the rain stopped. Moments later—in springtime fashion—the sun broke through again. Her heart was still pounding when she swung into the driveway of the house and of necessity eased up on the gas pedal. Had Diane seen her turning onto the road there? Craig came out directly behind her. That, she tormented herself, was the frightening prospect.

Diane knew Craig's car. Zach often borrowed it when he was home from school. Though she hadn't driven for at least two years now—and considering her health it was unlikely she would ever drive again—Joyce refused to allow Zachary or Josh to drive her Cadillac. Craig was under orders to drive it briefly once a week to keep it in running order.

Don't panic, she ordered herself, striving for calm. If Diane brought it up, she'd explain that Craig had taken her to see a piece of property he felt might interest her. Diane knew she was into real estate. But what she had feared for so long might have happened. Someone—*her own granddaughter*—might know that she and Craig were emotionally involved. At a time when his wife was terminally ill.

In a corner of her mind she knew that Joyce was the most disliked person in Bellevue, that Craig was one of the most liked. Would anyone—even Diane—begrudge the two of them the joy they found together? This was 1987—the rules were different from those with which she grew up. Yet those rules remained etched on her soul.

The young were so casual. Debbie hadn't been shocked at all when Diane said her college roommate wasn't going home for the spring break—she was running off with her boyfriend to that place in Florida that was so popular with students. Why must *she* feel so guilty, so tormented? Because, she told herself ruthlessly, she was sleeping with a man whose wife was dying of cancer.

Forcing these recriminations into the back of her mind, she went out to the kitchen to confer with Betty Mae about dinner. She knew that Lily would have told Betty Mae to make Country Captain for dinner—because that was Diane's all-time favorite chicken dish.

"And sweet potato pie," Betty Mae reported ebulliently. "She sure loves that. I always make it when she comes home from school."

Fran heard a car pull into the driveway. That would be Diane. She geared herself to go out and provide the usual warm homecoming welcome.

"I couldn't believe the way the rain suddenly came down," Diane bubbled after they'd kissed and exchanged their customary affectionate greeting. Her luggage deposited in the foyer for now. "At one point I could hardly see ten feet ahead."

"I was caught in it, too." Fran was conscious of fresh tension. Had she seen a questioning glint in Diane's eyes? "But that's the way it is this time of year." She took a deep breath, then plunged ahead—instinct urging this. "I was out at the far edge of town to look at a piece of property. Off Edgewood Road. Craig called and said he thought I ought to see it. It's being offered at a giveaway price." She was talking too fast, she reproached herself. She did that when she was nervous.

"Then I wasn't dreaming." Diane's smile was dazzling. "I thought I saw your car, then it disappeared. You were driving too fast for me to catch up."

Fran heard relief in Diane's voice. She'd known the second car was Craig's.

"I understand Zach came home last night," Fran said casually while they headed arm in arm for the kitchen so that Diane could be welcomed by Lily and Betty Mae. On Diane's arrivals from school, Lily supervised dinner preparations.

"He called me at the dorm before he left Cambridge," Diane said. "He's terribly worried about his mother. He says she's in constant pain—and there's nothing the doctors can do at this point to relieve her."

"I know." Fran's voice was compassionate. "Craig's just a wreck. He says it's so awful to watch and be unable to help her."

"How's Mom?" Diane asked, her eyes tender. "Are she and Nora still trying to push Eric into writing a mystery?"

"The three of them are being very mysterious—" Fran chuckled at her choice of words. "You know Nora—she says the bookstore is her family. And the mystery section is her favorite child."

"Oh, my beautiful baby is home!" Lily emerged from the kitchen to pull Diane into her arms while Betty Mae awaited her turn. "Your mama and grandma have been counting the hours till you got here!"

As always when Diane came home from school, dinner was a joyous occasion. The only serious note—other than another brief discussion about Joyce's illness—concerned local activities regarding the homeless. This was a subject close to both Diane and Zach.

Immediately after dinner Diane charged off to her room to call Zach. Fran saw the glow of anticipation that lighted her face. They *were* serious about each other. Thank God, she'd covered her tracks earlier, Fran thought—yet anxiety hammered within her. *Nothing must go wrong for Diane and Zach,* she vowed.

Fran lay sleepless far into the night—her mind a kaleidoscope of possible misadventures. It was so beautiful that Diane and Zach had found each other this way. Yes, they were in love, Fran told herself. But her relationship with Craig had the power to destroy that. The Garfield women had suffered such misfortune with the men in their lives. That mustn't happen to Diane.

She'd found a cherished happiness through the years with Craig. In some perverse way were Lynne and Debbie paying for that happiness? Could what she and Craig shared come between Diane and Zach?

She knew what she must do, Fran told herself with brutal intensity. Tomorrow she'd talk with Craig. He must understand they were never to meet again at the cottage. *Never to meet alone.* That part of their lives was forever over.

Fifty-One

F ran and Craig sat at a white-damask-covered table in the softly illuminated restaurant, situated midway between Bellevue and Atlanta. Only three other tables in the spacious dining room were occupied
at this hour, though Fran knew the luncheon crowd would soon be filing
into the popular new rendezvous. She had chosen The Magnolias because
she and Craig had never been here before.

She knew that Craig would not allow himself to betray his real emo-
tions in a public place—and that at this hour they would have some privacy. She geared herself for his shock at what she had just told him, yet
she was cold and trembling as he stared at her in pain and disbelief.

"Fran, you can't mean it! How can we not see each other again? I
know you're upset—" He was striving to control his voice. His eyes
swept apprehensively about the room. The nearest diners sat twenty
feet away. "But we're always so careful. We—"

"We can't be careful enough," she interrupted, her eyes pleading
with him to understand. "Craig, we've been so lucky all through the
years, but yesterday Diane was there right behind us. We can't protect
ourselves against the unexpected. And we *will* see each other. Just—not
alone."

"Oh, God, Fran, I can't conceive of a life where we'll have no private
time together." He shook his head as though to dispel dreadful images.

"Yesterday was a warning. I covered for us—I think. We can't endanger what Diane and Zach have found together. I've been so happy
about that," she whispered, fighting back tears. "We can't take a chance
on destroying their future together."

"What about us?" Craig challenged. "Don't we have a right to happiness, too?"

"Perhaps there'll be a time for us one day." Fran managed a wistful smile. "I pray that there will be. But we have obligations, Craig—and we've had many precious times together. We mustn't deprive Diane and Zach of theirs."

"You're all unnerved because of yesterday. You're overreacting. There's one chance in a million that it'll happen again," Craig said earnestly. "Fran, we'll be so careful," he tried again.

"We can't take the chance, my darling." Her eyes begged him to accept this decision. "But nothing can ever stop my loving you. And we'll see each other. Often," she said with an attempt at lightness. "How can we not in a town as small as Bellevue?"

Fran knew the coming weeks would be desolate, but she had not guessed the depths of that desolation. For so many years not a day passed that she didn't see Craig or talk with him on the phone. And at each encounter she felt his need for her, that matched her need for him. And always she asked herself if others knew about their relationship and remained silent out of compassion. She remembered the quotation from the Bible: "To everything there is a season." This was not the season for Craig and her.

Debbie left the office twenty minutes earlier than usual so that she'd have time to stop by the fabulous new bakery in town to pick up dessert for dinner at Nora's house. There would be just Nora and Eric and herself—and Nora had given instructions that dessert must be consumed at dinner. *"You know I'll stuff myself like a pig and gain five pounds if you leave half of some luscious cake with me."*

Nora watched her weight zealously, Debbie thought affectionately. Mom said she wished Beth had Nora's discipline. Nora was such a good friend—to Eric as well as herself. Eric would never have written the first few chapters of his novel except for Nora—but why did they both try to involve her in this?

Nora had prodded her into helping Eric rewrite some of the dialogue. With her he'd shifted the plot into a more suspenseful form. Tonight Eric would read the rewrite to Nora and her, and she and Eric would work out the outline for the next few chapters.

She knew why this involvement in Eric's novel was so uncomfortable for her, Debbie thought in a rare moment of inner candor. The young wife whose husband had just been murdered was so like herself at that age. That murder, too, seemed senseless—the act possibly of some vagrant passing through town. Eric admitted he was borrowing from Scott's murder. But in Eric's novel the murder would be *solved.*

At the bakery Debbie forced herself to focus on what to bring for the evening's dessert. Napoleons, she decided. Eric loved puff pastry with a custard filling. He said he's been a fat little boy and adolescent because in those days cake and candy represented love.

Once in college—away from a family where he seemed an unwelcome changeling—he'd taken himself in hand. He'd become a hiker, a runner, found pleasure in his own choice of athletics and gained a self-respect that prodded him into acquiring a healthy slimness. Sometimes his eagerness to share in her own family's activities brought tears to her eyes. Scott, too, had felt that way. Having a warm, loving family was a richness she sometimes forgot.

As always when Nora cooked, dinner was superb. Then the three of them settled themselves in Nora's living room—with more coffee close at hand. Still self-conscious at his efforts, Eric pulled out the revised chapters of his novel from an envelope and began to read. He wasn't writing about Scott and her, Debbie reminded herself—yet her mind darted back through the years to that awful evening when Scott had gone to his mother's house for dinner and was murdered.

"You were right, Debbie," Eric's voice disrupted her introspection. "That business about there being no broken glass inside the room made it clear the murder was not committed by an intruder." Eric knew about her secretly hiring the detective in Raleigh and his conviction that the murderer was an insider because of the position of the broken glass.

"Have you settled on who did commit the murder?" Nora asked.

"I suppose I should have known before I sat down to write," Eric said ruefully, "but this way seems to work better for me. Because of the position of the broken glass I have to set it as a member of the family or the staff."

"Which gives you a lot of leeway." Nora nodded in approval. "Debbie, who do you think would be the murderer?"

"Who would have the motive?" Debbie tried to thrust aside the surge of anguish that threatened to inundate her. How many times had she asked herself that about Scott's murder? All those years without answers. "What *is* the motive?" How many hundreds of mystery novels had she read through the years? How many motives, in truth, existed? "Greed, jealousy, revenge?" Why couldn't she have ever pinned down a motive for Scott's death?

Recurrently through the years she'd probed the words of the detective in Raleigh: *"I've exhausted every possible lead on the servants at the Richards's house. They all left within months of your husband's death. No forwarding addresses."* Why had they all left? And she'd remembered his odd inference about the timing of her mother-in-law's death and Scott's death: *"Pity. If she had died first, Scott would have inherited half the estate, I imagine. You'd be a very rich woman today."*

"Maybe the motive was greed—" Eric pulled Debbie out of her introspection. "And the murderer was a member of the family."

Eric's words hit Debbie with the impact of an icy tidal wave. Had *Perry* killed Scott? All at once bits of knowledge were jogging into place in her mind. Perry was in heavily to gamblers. He was desperate for money. His whole political future was in jeopardy. "The brother killed him." She forced herself to follow up on Eric's plotting. "The motive was greed. His mother had a fatal heart attack. He knew that if his brother died before their mother, then he inherited everything. So he killed his brother, then pretended their mother had a heart attack when she found him!" That was why Perry had been so determined to see the case closed, Debbie realized frantically.

"Debbie, that's terrific!" Eric was flushed with excitement. "That's always been a strong theme in fiction—the Cain and Abel *schtick*."

"I don't want to talk about it." Debbie struggled to her feet. Her mind in chaos. "Nora, you'll forgive me if I leave now. Suddenly I have this terrible headache."

On this sticky mid–May morning Fran emerged from her bedroom and headed for the sunlit, multiglassed area off the kitchen where she and Debbie had breakfast before going to the office. In her mind she cataloged her day's crowded schedule.

"Mom!" Debbie was charging toward her. "I just had a call from Diane. She's driving home after her last class today—"

"Is she all right?" Fran interrupted in alarm.

"It's Joyce," Debbie said, faintly breathless. "Diane just had a call from Zach up in Cambridge. He said his mother died in her sleep—the nurse went in with medication an hour ago, and she was gone—"

"It's a blessing," Fran said after a shaken moment. "She's escaped awful, constant pain. And Craig and the boys can begin to live again."

Fran's first instinct was to hurry to the Hendricks's home to be with Craig—but of course she couldn't do that, her mind cautioned. She brushed away the realization that at long last Craig was free.

"Zach's flying home," Debbie told her. "He said his mother will be buried tomorrow."

"We'll go to the funeral, of course. We'll both take the day off from the office. Did Diane say when she'd be home?"

"She'll be here in time for dinner." Debbie hesitated. "Since she and Zach are so close, shouldn't we ask if there's anything we can do to help?"

"You call and talk to Josh," Fran said after a moment.

Flanked by Debbie and Diane, Fran attended the services at the funeral home. The three women exchanged a few words with Craig and his sons, along with a large turnout of friends and acquaintances. For a moment Diane and Zach clung together, and involuntarily Fran turned to Craig. His eyes were on her. He mustn't look at her that way, she thought in alarm. Even now no one must know about them.

After the services at the funeral home Fran walked with Debbie and Diane to her white Mercedes, and they joined the funeral cortege. At the cemetery Diane hesitated a moment, then whispered to her mother and grandmother.

"I should be with Zach," she said apologetically and hurried off to his side. It was a public acknowledgment, Fran thought tenderly, that Diane and Zach meant to spend their lives together.

Because of friendship for Craig rather than any affection for Joyce, Fran understood, many local residents had joined the procession to the cemetery. At intervals during the graveside service Fran's eyes met Craig's. For the second time Craig was burying a wife. It would be obscene for them to think of themselves at a time like this, but months would pass and they would be free.

Fran was startled by the glint of anger in Diane's eyes when—after the services—she hurried to her mother and grandmother.

"I told Zach I'd drive to the house with him. That's all right, isn't it?"

"Darling, of course it is," Fran told her. She and Debbie, too, were going to the Hendricks's house—as would be expected. "By why do you seem so angry?"

"Some of these women!" Diane hissed. "I can't believe it! I heard Lita Franken sidle up to Zach's father and invite him to dinner at her house. His wife isn't cold in her grave and already the divorcées and widows are chasing him!"

All at once life was making frenzied demands on Fran's time. In two days she must fly up to New York for Beth's graduation from Barnard and Lynne's graduation from Columbia Law School. The three women would rush back home to be with Diane at her graduation at the University of Georgia.

Though Fran knew that she and Craig must observe a distance from each other for a while, even avoiding phone conversation, she learned from Diane that he would be in Cambridge for Zach's graduation from Harvard's School of Design—as she had assumed.

"Zach's decided to serve his apprenticeship in his father's office," Diane reported in a call from Athens. "Then he'll go out on his own. We can't go public yet, Grandma," Diane said, trying to suppress a burst of exuberance, "but I'm sure you've figured it out by now. Zach and I plan on getting married before too long." She hesitated. "I'd be wildly happy except that I worry about Mom. She's seemed so uptight these last weeks."

"I worry, too," Fran said gently. She worried about both daughters. Debbie still obsessed by Scott's death—and Lynne out on her own after a bitter divorce. "But some things we don't have the power to change."

The next few days rushed past in a whirlwind of euphoria and nostalgia. How proud Bernie would have been of Lynne and her law degree, Fran thought as she watched the graduation ceremonies with Debbie and Beth. And then—along with Debbie and Lynne—she was present at Beth's graduation from Barnard. In the fall Beth would enroll at the Columbia School of Social Work—to work for her master's. Jessie joined them for none of these activities—she was doing a film in Mexico. They were out of touch with her. And all the while Fran thought of Craig, up in Cambridge for Zach's graduation.

It was as though they were all about to embark on a new segment of their lives, Fran mused. But she was upset that Lynne insisted on living alone in New York. Lynne would work as a clerk in a prestigious law office until she passed her bar exams, and then she'd join the firm.

Debbie seemed caught up in some fresh nightmare. Diane, too, was aware of this. It was useless to suggest that Debbie go for therapy. In truth, Fran admitted to herself, she was even afraid to suggest this.

Then the four women flew home from New York, to drive to Athens the following day for Diane's graduation. Lynne would remain in Bellevue for only two weeks this summer—she had to report to her law firm job at the end of that time. Beth would return to New York with her mother. She was to be a volunteer for the summer with a group working to help the homeless.

"Grandma, I have to do this," Beth said earnestly. "How can I lie by the swimming pool all summer when so many people are hurting?"

She should have been in a wonderful mood, Fran rebuked herself when they all sat down to dinner together after returning from Diane's graduation. Three of them had acquired degrees in the past few days. While there was no formal announcement, Diane and Zach were engaged. But this was all overshadowed by the anguish she felt in Debbie.

Why couldn't Debbie put the past behind her and settle down to a full life with Eric? No one could make her believe Debbie didn't love Eric—and the whole town knew Eric worshipped her. Would there ever be a time, Fran asked herself, when she would feel her daughters were safely anchored for life?

At the end of two weeks in Bellevue Lynne and Beth flew back to New York. Diane would begin to work at a new Atlanta weekly early in July. Zach would go into his father's office at the same time. Why did *she* feel as though she was sitting atop a mountain of dynamite?

On impulse Fran decided to invite a few people in for dinner. To liven up the house, she told Debbie and Diane while they sat at breakfast this Sunday morning.

"Just a few close friends," she emphasized. "Not a party. We'll ask Nora and Eric—" She paused, startled by Debbie's air of dismay. What was happening between Debbie and Eric? "And Zach, of course," she forced herself to continue. "And Josh and his father," she concluded, trying to deny to herself that this party was meant to bring Craig into the house. Oh, how she'd missed him these last months, she thought dejectedly.

"When are you planning this?" Debbie was clearly unhappy.

"What about this coming Saturday night?" Fran gazed first at Debbie—who nodded weakly, then at Diane. "Any conflicts?"

"No."

Diane, too, had observed her mother's discomfort, Fran thought—and her unease increased. "I'll tell Zach, and he'll tell Josh and his father."

Immediately Nora and Eric accepted Fran's dinner invitation. Zach and Josh would come, Diane reported.

"I convinced them it wasn't a party—" She meant this wasn't defying their mourning period for their mother, Fran understood. "But Zach says his father won't be able to make it. He has another commitment."

"Oh—" Startled, Fran forced a smile. "Another time, then. We're almost family now."

But two days later local gossip reached Fran. Craig couldn't come to dinner at her house on Saturday because he was having dinner with Lita Franken. The word around town was that the ebullient, still attractive divorcée of fifty-six was out to land Craig Hendricks—considerably her senior—as her ex-husband's replacement. And Fran remembered Diane's rage when they were leaving the cemetery after Joyce's burial: *"Some of these women! I heard Lita Franken sidle up to Zach's father and invite him to dinner at her house. His wife isn't cold in her grave and already the widows and divorcées are chasing him!"*

And Craig was receptive to this, Fran tormented herself. He couldn't come to her house for dinner Saturday evening because he was having dinner with Lita Franken.

Fifty-Two

F ran rearranged the flowers on the dinner table for the third time. This wasn't a party, she reminded herself yet again. It would be unthinkable for Zach and Josh to be here if it were. They were a few very close friends—like family, she thought defensively. But Craig was having dinner tonight with Lita Franken.

Each time she remembered this—and the realization was a constant intrusion—she was attacked with fresh anguish. How could this be happening to Craig and her? Now when they were free to be together. After so many years of precious closeness, how could a few months of separation have destroyed that?

"Miz Fran, I made a batch of the chocolate chip cookies Mist' Eric likes." Lily—who always insisted on sharing the cooking with Betty Mae when there was a party in the house—glowed with affection. Like herself Lily yearned to see Debbie and Eric married. "Y'all make sure he takes them home with him. That man sure has a sweet tooth."

"I'll make sure," Fran promised.

Lily brightened at the sound of a car pulling up before the house. "I'll answer the door."

In minutes the living room was lively with conversation. Only Debbie seemed tense and taciturn. *Why wasn't Craig here?* Fran masked her disappointment—her towering hurt—behind a brilliant smile. If this was what Craig wanted, so be it.

Then Lily appeared to say she and Betty Mae were prepared to serve dinner.

"When Lily and Betty Mae cook, we don't keep them waiting," Fran said lightly—masking a tightness in her throat, a sense of desolation.

"Where would you like us to sit?" Josh asked Fran with the ingratiating charm he'd inherited from his father.

"Anywhere you like—we're not formal in this family," Fran told him. And her smile said that in her mind, he and Zach were already part of the family. What a wonderful evening this could have been, she thought in private torment, if Craig were here, too.

As expected, Fran observed, Eric had rushed to sit beside Debbie. Despite his convivial air, she sensed he worried about Debbie's obvious depression. Still, the table conversation was lively.

"Will you be teaching in summer school?" Fran asked Eric. Most years he did this.

"I'm taking this summer off," he said shyly. "To work on a mystery novel." His eyes strayed to Debbie. "It may be presumptuous of me." His eyes were questioning.

"You've got to do it," Nora said firmly. "You're good, Eric."

"I'd feel better with a collaborator," he said, and Fran sensed a private—silent—conversation among him and Nora and Debbie. "I'm inclined to be too pedantic."

"Your short stories are delightful," Fran told him. "Why not a novel now?"

All at once she understood. Eric was trying to bring Debbie closer through their mutual love of mystery novels. Debbie had studied journalism—she'd worked on newspapers. She had writing skills. But he was forgetting, she thought anxiously, that for all these years since Scott's death she'd shut herself off from her ambitions to be a journalist. It was Eric—meaning well but bungling—who was pushing Debbie into a frightening depression.

On Monday morning—with sunlight sneaking brilliantly between her bedroom draperies—Diane heard the insistent ringing of the phone on her night table. She sighed and groped for the receiver. It was a few minutes past nine, she noted as she struggled into a half-sitting position and brought the receiver to her ear. Zach couldn't be up this early—not when they'd vowed to sleep until noon for the next four weeks.

"Hello—" Her voice was foggy with sleep.

"I hope I'm not calling too early." Eric was apologetic.

"Of course not," Diane lied. "I've been awake for ages."

"I waited until I knew your mother would have left for the office." He paused. "Could we meet somewhere, Diane? I need to talk with you about your mother."

"Lunch today?" she suggested. Her own unease about her mother soared. "Any time that fits into your schedule."

At noon Diane and Eric sat in a cozy booth at a small restaurant at the edge of town.

"I'm afraid that in trying to coax your mother to work with me on the novel I pushed her too far," he said somberly. "We both know how obsessed she is about solving your father's murder." He hesitated. "Did you know that several years after he was killed she hired a private investigator to try to solve the case?"

"No," Diane whispered. "She talked so much about how he died, but she never told me about that."

"The investigator was convinced the murder was committed by someone inside the house—not a would-be burglar. But the servants had all moved away and left no forwarding addresses. And the same sheriff—under Perry Richards's thumb—was on the job. There was no chance of reopening the case. Your mother faced another dead end." He inhaled sharply. "Three or four weeks ago we—your mother and I, with Nora sitting in on the discussion—were trying to settle on who the murderer would be in my novel. We talked about motive. She suggested greed, jealousy, or revenge. We sat pondering for a moment, and then I said, 'Maybe the motive was greed—and the murderer was a member of the family.' Your mother stared at me as though dazed by a terrible revelation. She said, 'His brother killed him. The mother had just suffered a fatal heart attack, and he wanted to inherit the entire estate instead of just half.' Then she jumped up from her chair and left the house. She's been avoiding me ever since."

"She suspects my uncle?" Diane felt encased in ice.

"She's convinced of it," Eric said gently. "That's more horrible than anything she'd imagined. And little pieces she's gathered through the years point in that direction. They all came together in her mind when I made that careless remark."

"If Perry Richards killed my father, I want him to pay for it!" Diane reeled from this suspicion.

"Your mother'll never come out of that prison she's built around herself until your father's murderer is brought to justice." His face was troubled. "The local sheriff rejected the theory that it was an inside job because your uncle wanted the murder swept under the rug. Presumably to avoid notoriety because of his political ambitions. But there's strong evidence that there was no intruder. Perry was in debt to a gambling syndicate. And if your father died before his mother, then Perry would inherit the entire estate. It's not much to go on," he conceded, "but for the first time there's a suspect to check out."

"I'm going to Glenwood," Diane said after a moment. Her face etched with determination. "I'll ask Zach to go with me. Somehow, we have to track down the servants who worked at the house. We'll ask questions."

"From what I gather they've all scattered," Eric warned.

"We'll find them," Diane vowed. "The investigator spent a few days—we'll search all summer if that's necessary. Why would they all leave?" she challenged. "Mom talked so lovingly about Amos and Beulah. They'd been with the Richards since my father was a baby. Were they *paid* to disappear?"

"I'll go with you and Zach," Eric resolved. "I have no classes this summer. Maybe together we can come up with answers."

Diane knew her mother wasn't happy that tomorrow morning she was dashing off alone with Zach. Mom could be so conventional, she thought tenderly—even though she'd been part of the free-and-easy '60s generation. But she felt compelled to tell her grandmother her real destination.

Mom wouldn't be back from that "special event" at Nora's bookshop for another hour, she guessed, glancing at her watch. When this program was over, she'd switch off the TV and tell Grandma.

Haltingly Debbie told Fran the real purpose of the plotted "driving vacation."

"I know the odds are against us." She tried to sound realistic—but, as always, her intensity belied her acceptance of this. "Still, we just might make a breakthrough since we're focusing on one suspect. It's so urgent for Mom that we do this."

"When you were very little, I hired a detective to look into the case, too," Fran admitted, startling Diane. "Nobody ever knew except Robin. We came up with nothing concrete—just a suspicion that Perry knew more than he was saying—that he knew who killed your father. But your mother mustn't know that you're looking into the case again," she exhorted. "I don't think she could handle another disappointment."

"Our chances are slim," Diane reiterated. "But little pieces point in Perry's direction. Not to a judge and jury. Not at this point. But I trust

Mom's instincts. For the first time there's a real suspect. We must follow
through on that."

"Keep in close touch with me," Fran urged. "If there's anything I can
do—if you come up with something but need a team of investigators to
follow through, let me know. I'll hire them. It would seem a miracle, my
darling—but these things happen—"

"We have to make it happen," Diane said urgently.

"I'll say a little prayer every night," Fran promised.

The following morning Diane picked up Zach in her car, and they
headed for Eric's apartment. Eric had decided to follow them in his own
car. *"Two cars are better than one. In case we need to go in different directions."*

At Eric's suggestion they spent the first night in a motel near Raleigh. In the morning they separated to visit the local newspaper offices
and read up on Perry Richards's activities during the past twenty years.
A long, tedious assignment—but necessary. Diane was startled to discover this a traumatic experience. She was reading about her father's
only brother—his only living relative except for distant cousins. Her
only uncle. Were they wrong about Perry? she pondered. It seemed so
awful for a brother to kill brother.

Sitting with Zach in a newspaper office and reading back issues,
Diane was encased in an aura of unreality. Mom had walked these
streets, shopped in these stores, worked for a newspaper in this town.
Her great-grandmother—whom Mom said Daddy had adored—was buried in a cemetery here in Raleigh. Daddy was buried beside her. She was
reaching out to touch a part of her family that had always been in the
shadows until now.

As prearranged, Diane and Zach met with Eric for a late lunch to discuss what they'd learned thus far. Perry Richards had never become involved in politics, it was clear—though Eric pointed out that he and his
wife were very active in Raleigh's social life.

"Olivia spends more time in Europe than in Glenwood," Diane said.
"Right now she's in Paris for the fashion shows. It's obvious that she and
Perry don't have a close marriage."

"They've had some recent labor problems at the mills," Eric reported. "Which I gather has been a recurrent situation through the
years."

"Mom said my father wanted so much to make conditions better for
the mill workers," Diane remembered. Like Grandma before she was

married. "But his mother and Perry wanted no part of that. They got real nasty about it."

"We'll finish up with the newspapers this afternoon," Eric plotted. "Tomorrow we go to Glenwood. We look for some word about the five domestics who lived in the house. That's urgent."

"It'll be rough after all these years." Zach was somber.

"There must be some trace of at least one or two of them," Eric insisted. "We need to ask questions. I can't believe they all left Glenwood without strong urging. I suspect Perry wanted them out of town—but *why?*"

"They must have seen or heard something that could implicate him. Why didn't anybody bring this out years ago?" Diane demanded plaintively.

"Because the case was hushed up so fast," Zach pointed out. "Perry was a power in Glenwood. The sheriff was on his side. He wanted the case closed—so it was closed. He'd paid off the servants. He felt safe. Of course, we're working on the premise that Perry Richards is the killer. We could be wrong—"

"I don't believe that!" Diane's eyes glowed with conviction. "Nor do you," she challenged Eric, "or you wouldn't be here."

"Diane, I'd follow any lead that would put your mother's mind at rest," Eric said gently. "But yes, I think we're on the right track."

For the next five days the three of them circulated about Glenwood in a fevered effort to pinpoint the whereabouts of the five domestics on staff at the Richards mansion at the time of Scott's murder. *"We're trying to reach them regarding a small bequest left them by an Atlanta resident."* Diane and Zach traveled as a pair, Eric on his own. They made a point of not mentioning the Richards's name. Perry must not be aware of this search.

"We're doing lousy," Zach commented on their fifth evening in town. They were sitting over dinner in a roadside diner close to their motel. "We've covered every house in the black area."

"Tomorrow we move into a wider circle," Eric said. "Some black families have moved into white sections. We use the same line."

Tonight, Diane thought axiously, Eric seemed less confident. Were they—to use one of Zach's favorite phrases—just spinning their wheels? They'd been here only a few days, she reminded herself doggedly. They weren't giving up.

Exhausted by the heat wave that imprisoned much of North Carolina, Diane and Zach walked away from the small white frame house in a newly integrated development in Glenwood.

"They've only been living in the area for two years," Diane said despondently. "How could we expect them to help us?"

"Let's go down to that block of little stores just beyond and find a place to get a cold drink. I'm dying of thirst." Zach reached for her hand. "If you're a good kid, I'll buy you a chocolate ice-cream soda."

Diane mustered a lopsided smile. "Grandma would say, 'You don't have an ice-cream soda this close to dinner.' But what the hell—let's live dangerously."

The soda fountain was a replica of one of earlier days, Diane thought as she and Zach strolled into the meager comfort of a pair of ceiling fans. Four bistro tables were each flanked by a pair of wrought-iron chairs. A mirrored wall behind the marble-topped counter listed the offerings in large sprawling script. The white-aproned man behind the counter was in avid conversation with an elderly black man—the only other customer at the moment—about the current heat wave.

"I been livin' in and around Glenwood for close to sixty-five years, and I tell you, I neveh saw a hotter summer than this one," the older man said with a flourish.

All at once Diane froze. Her mind replayed his words. Zach gazed questioningly at her as he lowered himself into a chair at a bistro table. She moved toward the elderly black man with an ingratiating smile.

"Excuse me, sir—but I heard you say you've been living around here for almost sixty-five years. I wonder if you might know where I could find Amos Ferguson. When my father was a little boy, Amos Ferguson taught him to fish—" That much was true, Diane thought conscientiously.

"Amos Ferguson? Now it's strange you ask about him. He was away from these parts for about twenty years, then five months ago he came home. Said he wanted to die where he was born. Old Amos ain't doin' too well."

"Where could I find him?" Diane's heart was pounding.

"Drive down this road here till Mulberry Lane, then make a right. About a hundred yards ahead you'll see some houses. Amos lives in one of them. I hope he's all right. I haven't seen him in about ten days. Like I said, he ain't doin' too well."

Fifty-Three

T he day was hot and sticky—even by Georgia standards, Fran thought as she strolled into the house. Debbie had gone straight from the office to pick up Nora, she remembered. They were going out to dinner and then to a performance at the new summer theater midway between Bellevue and Atlanta. What a battle she'd had with Debbie to convince her not to cancel their reservations! *"Debbie, you spoke with Diane last night. Don't think you have to be here in case she calls again tonight. I'll be here."*

Diane—with the impatience of the young—was anxious that they were making no headway in Glenwood, she thought uneasily. They all knew this was a long shot—but their hopes had soared.

She told Betty Mae to serve dinner on a tray in the den, where she could watch McNeil/Lehrer on TV. She had just swigged down the last of her iced coffee and switched off the TV when the phone rang. Hopefully she reached for the receiver.

"Hello—"

"Don't be angry with me for calling," Craig pleaded, and her throat was suddenly tight. "I know we must wait a respectable time to pick up our lives again. But with Diane and Zach off together and making no se-cret of this, people must realize we're almost in-laws."

"That's true." She struggled to sound casual. What did he mean—*"we must wait to pick up our lives again?"* What about Lita Franken?

"I need protection from predatory women," he joshed. "You wouldn't believe the women who're in urgent need of my architectural services— that have to be discussed over dinner."

"We found that a convenient ploy." Had Lita cornered him and he hadn't known how to extricate himself? He was so gentle and courteous.

Was that all it was? "We could be meeting to discuss Diane and Zach's wedding," Fran plotted lightly—suffused with joy. How could she have believed Craig was serious about Lita Franken? How could she have doubted him?

"Tonight?" Craig was hopeful. "I saw Debbie and Nora driving away from town. Diane's off with Zach—"

"Hurry," she ordered, feeling twenty again. "Oh, Craig, hurry!"

Diane and Zach walked toward the tiny, shabby house where Amos Ferguson lived. The whir of a fan was the only sound that emerged.

"I'm scared, Zach," Diane whispered and reached for his hand as they mounted the rickety steps to the porch.

"Now?" he scoffed tenderly.

They approached the door. Zach knocked. They heard shuffling sounds inside. Then a white-haired man, slightly stooped with age, appeared behind the screen door.

"Are you Amos Ferguson?" Diane's smile was warm.

"Yes, ma'am, I'm Amos." He was polite but curious.

"Could we talk to you for a few minutes?" Zach asked, managing to sound casual.

"You sure can," Amos said and walked out onto the porch. "It's cooler out here than in the house, even with the fan on," he said with an air of apology and pointed to the porch glider. "Won't y'all sit down?"

"Thank you." Zach prodded Diane toward the glider, its pillows faded but immaculate.

"You knew my father," Diane told Amos. "Scott Richards—"

For a moment he seemed stricken speechless. "You be Diane? Mist' Scott's baby?"

"I haven't been a baby for quite a while." Diane's laugh was shaky. "But yes, I'm his baby."

"Your mama—Miz Debbie—how is she?" He searched her face. "You look just like her! When you was a baby, you looked just like her!"

"Mom's fine. She remembers you with such affection." Diane was light-headed with excitement. "No, she's not fine," she corrected herself. "She's always had to fight against depression because my father's killer was never brought to justice. And now it's worse. Amos, we worry about her." Diane's eyes searched his. "We think that Perry Richards killed my father—and he managed to hush it up all these years. And that's *wrong*."

"Nobody wants to cross Mist' Perry." Amos's hands were trembling. He suddenly seemed very old. "He's a bad man—"

"Did he kill my father?" Diane's eyes demanded the truth.

Amos stood before them in silent anguish. "I knowed we was doin' wrong not to tell the police what we seen," he said at last. "But we was scared. Beulah and me—we talked about it right up until the day she died. We loved Mist' Scott."

"Who beside you and Beulah knew that Perry killed Scott?" Zach asked, exchanging a swift glance with Diane.

"Just me and Beulah," Amos said. "It plagued us every day of our lives. Mist' Scott was such a fine young man. It didn't seem right that nobody paid for killin' him—but we was scared. Before Beulah died she signed a letter my grandnephew wrote for us—saying we knowed Mist' Perry killed his brother. I signed it, too. When we is both dead, I told my grandnephew—the one who's goin' to school to be a lawyer—to look through my things and take this envelope with the letter to the po-lice. Mist' Perry can't do us no harm then."

"Give it to the police now," Diane pleaded. "For my mother's sake, let the truth come out!"

"Amos, Perry Richards can't hurt you," Zach said gently.

"He gave me and Beulah money," Amos said. "We was to go to another state and never come back to Glenwood. Then last year Beulah died—and I knew my time was gettin' short. I wanted to die at home. I don't have no money to give back to Mist' Perry—"

"You won't have to do that," Diane told him. "And if there's any question of your obstructing justice—by not coming forth with evidence," she explained, "I'm sure the courts will understand."

"If it comes to that, my brother will be your lawyer," Zach promised. "He'll make the court realize why you didn't come forward."

"And my grandmother—who loved my father very much—will see that you live well for the rest of your life. For my father's memory, won't you name his killer?" Diane pleaded.

"You'll give me a nice funeral?" Amos's face lighted.

"The best," Diane promised. "My father would want that for you."

Perry scowled at the knock on his library door. Damn it, they all knew not to disturb him when he was holed up in the den. He wanted to study the specifications for the new mill.

"What do you want?" he yelled.

The door opened. Everett, the latest in a string of housemen, walked in.

"I'm sorry, sir. Mr. Roland is on the phone. He says it's urgent." Everett was deferential but uneasy.

"All right, I'll take it in here—" Perry dismissed him with the wave of one hand and rose to go to the phone. Ever since George became deputy sheriff, he was all stuffed up with importance. "What's the matter, George?" he demanded impatiently.

"Mr. Richards, something crazy is going on here. I got a white couple and some black guy who're claiming they have evidence to reopen your brother's murder." He hesitated. "They got a witness who claims you killed him."

"What the hell?" Perry reeled from shock. "Who're these people?"

"Diane Richards—she says she's your niece. The guy with her is her boyfriend, I figure. They've got this old black guy with them—he says his name is Amos Ferguson. He says he was a witness."

"Old Amos?" Perry blustered. "Hell, he's eighty years old and senile! Throw them out, George!"

"I can't do that." George was apologetic. "The old man's sittin' outside right now, waiting for his statement to be typed up. He says he and his late wife saw you shoot your brother while your mother lay dead on the floor. Mr. Richards, you'd better get your lawyer down here pronto."

Caught up in a blend of exhilaration and uncertainty, Eric sat in the club chair in Diane and Zach's motel unit while Zach spoke with Josh on the phone. They had the proof Debbie had sought so long—but that didn't guarantee a conviction, he warned himself. Perry Richards's high-powered lawyers would fight to invalidate Amos's claims.

"Josh will be here before nine A.M. tomorrow morning!" Zach said jubilantly, putting down the phone. "I told him not to say anything to the family just yet." His eyes were in silent communication with Diane's.

Diane's face was luminous. "Let Eric tell Mom."

"It's too early," Eric protested. "The grand jury may refuse to indict him."

"Tell Mom," Diane insisted. "She should know. And it's your right to tell her—"

"Would she be home yet?" Eric was ambivalent. Would Debbie be more upset that they'd come up with proof, only to have it thrown out of court? Perry Richards was such a power in North Carolina.

"She's home by now. Call her, Eric!"

His throat tight with anxiety, Eric dialed. The knuckles of the hand that held the phone were white from the intensity of his grip. He heard the ringing at the other end. Then the ringing stopped.

"I've got it, Betty Mae—" Debbie's voice filtered to him. "Hello—"

"Debbie, I want you to be calm," he said gently. "I have something very important to tell you—"

As Fran had suspected, the next few months were excruciatingly tense. With his power in the community—and his battery of high-priced attorneys—Perry was not held in jail during the pretrial period. Fran had arranged for round-the-clock bodyguards for Amos, along with quality medical care.

Josh brought out that when Perry was convicted—and he refused to believe the justice system could do otherwise—half of the estate inherited from his mother would be declared the property of Scott's widow and daughter. Debbie and Diane would be among the wealthiest women in the South. Yet Fran was anxious. Let this not be one of those awful times when justice ran amuck. She prayed for Perry Richards's conviction.

With her long-dormant impetuosity—at a Sunday afternoon dinner at the family house—Debbie had turned to Eric and said, "Don't you think it's time we got married?" One week later they were married in a flower-bedecked corner of Fran's living room. Eric's parents and sisters wired their regrets at not being able to attend. His great-aunt Betsy was a joyful guest—and delighted that for now Debbie and Eric would live in his small apartment in her house.

Early in November Perry Richards was brought to trial. Though Amos's statement implicated Olivia, she was now a fugitive, hiding away somewhere in France. The evening before the first day of the trial, Fran brought those closest to her together for dinner. Her real wealth she thought as she gazed about the table. Her daughters, two of her granddaughters, her son-in-law, and her prospective grandson-in-law. Craig and Josh and Nora.

Lily and Betty Mae—always delighted when dinner was served in the elegant formal dining room—brought platters of food to the table. Craig was opening the magnum of champagne he'd brought for the occasion. The house would seem so empty when Diane and Zach were married—a year after his mother's death—Fran thought. But a week later

Craig and she would be married. His own house was already up for sale. *"We saw such unhappiness there."* With advice from his father, Zach was designing a house for Diane and himself.

"I don't suppose you'll change your mind, Lynne, and move back here?" Fran said wistfully.

"Mom, I love my life." Lynne was radiant. She paused for a moment and turned to Beth with an endearing smile. "Darling, you know I love you—and I'm so happy we're just living a few blocks apart in New York—but I'm having a wonderful time living on my own." She turned again to Fran. "I feel so utterly spoiled. I do what I want, when I want. No compromising. And I love my job. I feel reborn."

The next few days, Fran cautioned herself, would be crucial. Tomorrow morning everyone at the table would fly to Glenwood by chartered plane to be present for the first day of the trial. She would stay in Glenwood with Debbie and Diane for the duration. How would Debbie react if the jury brought in a "not guilty" verdict for Perry? She was so convinced that he would be convicted—that Scott's murder would be avenged. What would happen to her if Perry's team of sharp lawyers managed to clear him? Fran knew that Eric, too, was anxious.

Perry's attorneys dragged out the trial. It was already in its eleventh day. Fran knew it was agony for Debbie to sit in the same room with Perry—sullen, angry, looking years older than his age. But at last each side had presented its case. The jury was about to retire.

"Should we stay here to see if the jury comes back with a verdict today?" Diane asked, rising from her seat along with her mother and grandmother. "Maybe they'll reach a verdict quickly."

"Darling, it's late afternoon," Fran told her. "Nothing's going to happen today." She paused. "But we'll call Zach and his father. If it's at all possible, I know they'll be here with us."

The three women went out to the parking area and settled themselves in the rented car. With Diane at the wheel they returned to their hotel in Raleigh. Fran immediately called Craig's office and reported that the jury was out.

"Zach and I will be there first thing tomorrow morning." Craig's voice betrayed his own anxiety. "I don't see how the jury can be out long. Not with the evidence the prosecution presented."

"I'll say a prayer," Fran said softly. "Let this not be one of those times when the guilty goes free."

At a few minutes before 8 A.M. the following morning the phone beside Fran's bed rang. She'd been awake since before 6 A.M.—after a night of broken sleep.

"Hello—"

"Zach and I are in the coffee shop downstairs," Craig said ebulliently. "Come down as soon as you can."

"In a few minutes." Thank God, he and Zach would hear the verdict with them. She needed their presence. "I hear Debbie and Diane in the sitting room now. They were being quiet, thinking I might be asleep."

"It's going to be all right," Craig insisted. "I read it in my crystal ball. But don't be upset if the jury takes some time."

They had a quick breakfast and headed for the courthouse. Only three reporters and a pair of photographers were present. When by 11 A.M. there was no indication that the jury was about to come out, Zach went to pick up coffee. In a whimsical gesture he also brought coffee for the waiting reporters and photographers.

The jury remained out. The atmosphere was tense. A handful of workers from the swing shift at the mill appeared before reporting to work. One fiftyish woman shyly approached Debbie.

"You're Scott Richards's widow, aren't you?" she asked. "I remember him showing us a snapshot of you. You haven't changed a bit—and that's more than twenty-one years ago. He was such a fine man."

"Thank you." Debbie reached a hand out to Diane. "This is our daughter, Diane."

"That Mr. Perry—he's an evil man," the woman said with sudden intensity. "Mr. Scott cared about the workers—he didn't."

"If he's convicted, the mill comes to me," Debbie told her. "There'll be no more quibbling about the union," she promised. "And there'll be new, comfortable housing. That was what Scott wanted so much."

"The jury's coming in," Zach interrupted and reached for Diane's hand.

A few minutes later the foreman of the jury rose to read the verdict: "We the jury find the defendant guilty of murder in the first degree."

Her eyes filling with tears Debbie embraced first her mother, then Diane. Zach and Craig glowed with a blend of relief and triumph.

"I have to call Eric," Debbie whispered.

"The long nightmare is over." Fran's face was luminous. "It was a long haul, but we've made it."

Her hand in Craig's, Fran followed the other three to the parking area. This was the beginning of a new era in her life, she thought exultantly. Her daughters were—at long last—settled in their lives. Diane and Beth knew where they were headed. She had long banished a feeling of responsibility for Jessie. She was a *free* woman.

Now was *her* time. Hers and Craig's. Each day would be a cherished gift.